PUSHKIN PRESS

"This is a big, compelling family drama that's also a mystery, and also a treatise on art and artmaking and friendship and getting older, and it will suck you in and refuse to let go"

LitHub

"A richly evocative work from a major new talent"

Kirkus Reviews

"A sweeping and complex drama of family, art and sacrifice... Readers will be captivated"

Publishers Weekly

"[A] warm, engaging and funny novel about the inebriation of youth and the sobriety of middle age... a thoroughly enjoyable book"

Ayşegül Savaş, author of *White on White*

"The hottest debut of the year! If Klas Östergren and Donna Tartt had a love child, who grew up in Gothenburg and became an author, well, there you have Lydia Sandgren"

Akademibokhandeln (Sweden)

"A masterpiece... Tender, and terribly convincing"

Expressen (Sweden)

"A doorstopper of narrative joy, cultivation and linguistic delight"

Borås Tidning (Sweden)

"A book that celebrates the very height of what fiction is"

El País (Spain)

LYDIA SANDGREN is the eldest of seven siblings brought up in the west of Sweden. She has studied music and philosophy, and today is a practising psychologist living in Gothenburg. *Collected Works* is her debut novel; it won the prestigious August Prize in 2020 and has sold over 100,000 copies.

AGNES BROOMÉ is a literary translator and academic in Scandinavian Studies at Harvard University. With a PhD in Translation Studies, her translations include August Prize winners *The Expedition* by Bea Uusma and *The Gospel of Eels* by Patrik Svensson.

COLLECTED WORKS:
A NOVEL
LYDIA SANDGREN
TRANSLATED FROM THE SWEDISH BY AGNES BROOMÉ

PUSHKIN PRESS

Pushkin Press
Somerset House, Strand
London WC2R 1LA

First published as *Samlade Verk* by Albert Bonniers Förlag, Stockholm, Sweden
Published in the English language by arrangement
with Bonnier Rights, Stockholm, Sweden

First published by Pushkin Press in 2023

1 3 5 7 9 8 6 4 2

Hardback ISBN 13: 978-1-78227-798-9
Export Paperback ISBN 13: 978-1-78227-994-5

The cost of this translation was supported by a subsidy from
the Swedish Arts Council, gratefully acknowledged.

SWEDISH
ARTSCOUNCIL

Designed and typeset by Tetragon, London
Printed and bound by CPI Group (UK) Ltd, Croydon CR0 4YY

www.pushkinpress.com

COLLECTED WORKS

MARTIN BERG was on his back on the living room floor, hands folded over his stomach. Stacks of paper all around him. Next to his head, a half-finished novel; by his feet, twenty-five years' worth of napkin notes in big piles. His right elbow touching an anthology of promising writers born in the sixties, the only book he'd ever been published in. Next to his left elbow, several smaller stacks, each tied with ribbon and labelled PARIS in red marker. And scattered between his head and his elbows, and his elbows and his feet, papers, papers and more papers: written in ink or pencil or typed on a typewriter with notes scribbled in the margins, double-spaced computer printouts, crumpled and cof-fee-stained, smooth and shiny, some stapled, some held together with paper clips, others loose. The beginnings of short stories, essays, novel synopses, several attempts at plays, notebooks with covers worn after a lifetime in the inside pocket of his jacket, piles of letters.

He'd pushed the coffee table aside to make room.

It was a summer afternoon in the year he was turning fifty. A quiver-ing heat enveloped the city. The windows overlooking the street were open and he could hear laughing children, ringing bicycle bells, the distant bass line of a song he didn't recognise, a tram clattering down Karl Johansgatan. People were sunning themselves in the park outside, motionless like beached white seals. Earlier, Martin had been seized by an urge to shout at them through the window, but all sound had seemed to stick in his throat. His skin was crawling and there was a sucking sensation in the pit of his stomach, a sinkhole, and his hands were clammy and shaking from too much coffee.

This was a lull in his story. Dead time between two momentous events. The stuff you cut for the sake of pacing. Nothing to do but wait. For the children to come home. For the funeral. For news. It was enough to make a person want to reach for a red marker and draw thick lines across the entire page. Cross it all out. Raymond Carver's editor took the axe to large parts of *What We Talk About When We Talk About Love*, deleted entire endings – the happy ones – and that turned out great.

Maybe he should have tried to uphold normalcy. Seen people, eaten, done a few hours of work. After all, he was still a publisher, and Publisher Berg always had things that needed doing. But instead he'd opted for organising his papers. He'd spent a long time in the attic storage space, which was crammed full of children's winter coats, a bicycle in need of a new chain, Elis's old skateboard, Rakel's ball gown from graduation prosaically wrapped in plastic, sleeping bags, a tent, posters he had to unroll to have a look at, Cecilia's tattered running shoes. How many pairs of shoes had she worn out, and why hadn't she just binned them? Martin had kept at it, sweat trickling down his back and thighs because the attic was sweltering. In the end, he'd pulled out a box marked *Martin, Writing* in what was unmistakeably his own hand.

Martin wasn't sure how much time he'd spent trying to trace a path from his current position back to some kind of origin. There must have been a crossroads at some point, but for far too long he seemed to have been simply plodding along without a thought to checking his compass. And when had all this time passed? Because it clearly had. His children had grown up. For the first time in decades, he was no one's guardian. Elis, little Elis, who was travelling around Europe – chaperoned by his older sister, thankfully – was unlikely to move out any time soon. But he'd turned his eyes towards the horizon and sooner or later Martin would have to watch his son pack his waistcoats into boxes and relocate to a commune on Hisingen, where he would listen to Jacques Brel with half-closed eyes, no longer hiding the fact that he was smoking. And then the flat would be completely empty. End scene.

Rationally speaking, Martin thought as he lay on the rug, because he sensed rationality was all he had left at this point, rationally speaking, he understood this was part of the process. That children grow up is one of the inevitabilities of life. Thirty years ago, he'd done the same thing himself, but with a more dubious haircut. It was how it went. He just hadn't been prepared for it happening so soon. He hadn't pictured the emptiness, hadn't realised loneliness would spread through the rooms and take over the entire flat while his hair turned grey, his legs got thinner, his hearing failed and the years vanished without leaving anything in exchange.

And one day it would all be over. *Leaving behind nothing but stacks of paper.*

Martin closed his eyes and pictured Gustav Becker, even though it was important not to think too much about Gustav. Especially not Gustav laughing, his thin fingers closing around a cigarette, his eyes holding Martin's until Martin looked away.

Martin looked to his right (papers), to his left (papers), and then turned his attention back to the ceiling again. So white and untouched, so unwritten!

PART I
THE GREAT LIBRARY OF ALEXANDRIA

1

HIS ALARM JERKED HIM AWAKE. It was March and still pitch-black outside. Martin heaved himself up, turning his bedside lamp on and the alarm off. A text from his son, sent at 3.51 a.m., lit up the screen of his phone. **Coming home. NB I decline to be celebrated.**

Martin sighed. Elis had marked the eve of his birthday at the House of Jazz – which apparently was no longer a place for middle-aged couples looking to take a turn on the dance floor – and somewhere between the bar and home he'd evidently felt it necessary to remind his dad not to sing to him in the morning.

On his way to the bathroom, he knocked on his son's door and was rewarded with a muffled grunt.

"Happy birthday," Martin said.

He turned on the coffee machine. He fetched the newspapers from the hallway floor. He made toast and boiled an egg. Just as he was about to start on the arts section, his youngest appeared, walking straight over to the sink, filling a glass with water from the tap and downing it.

Elis had grown at least a foot in the past few years and it was becoming increasingly obvious he had his mother's lanky, blonde physiognomy. Martin's primary contribution to Elis's genome was brown eyes and, according to Gustav, a tendency to sulk while pretending not to.

"Fun night?"

Elis nodded and downed another glass of water.

"Do you want your presents now or later?"

His son pondered that for a few moments, then his ribcage convulsed as he held back violent gagging. "Later," he groaned and dashed off towards the bathroom.

Martin finished his coffee and went to get dressed. He studiously avoided the mirror on the wardrobe door. He was well aware how he looked. The hair on his chest was turning grey. His calves were scrawny, his knees knobbly. The fact that he worked out three times a week at Gothenburg's most expensive gym seemed to make no difference. It was a futile attempt to keep the inevitable at bay. His body had betrayed him, pretending to carry on as usual when in reality it had given itself over to ageing. Little by little, while he wasn't looking. In the olden days, he could start drinking at lunchtime, smoke incessantly, and then wake up the next morning to realise it was the day of the Gothenburg Race, which he'd only signed up to run for a laugh in the first place, find his running shoes and cross the finish line in under two hours. It had lulled him into thinking that was how the human body works. And then it had been taken away from him, bit by bit, without him noticing.

Black trousers, black jacket. Martin Berg dressed like a person receiving absolution for his sins.

*

As usual, he was the first to arrive at the offices of the publishing company. He liked the way the lights flickered to life, the way the day woke up and unfolded before him.

Stuck smack in the middle of his computer screen was a Post-it note. VENUE 25th ANNIVERSARY – IS FRILAGRET OK??? Written, judging by the neat, rounded letters, by Patricia, their intern. A memory of an email he hadn't replied to stirred at the back of his mind. He moved the note to the edge of the screen, already home to an array of other notes reminding him about things he wouldn't get to until they were urgent and completely unavoidable. It didn't seem to matter how hard he worked: the number of things that had to get done *now* remained constant. Their twenty-fifth anniversary party was still three months away.

Martin leaned his forehead against his fingertips and listened to the humming of the hard drive booting up. Elis had a French test today.

He'd probably done his studying while queueing to get into the House of Jazz.

His son's grades were concerning in that they were neither outstanding nor awful. If they'd been awful, that would have at least been a fact neither one of them could deny. But Elis's grades hovered around the meridian of mediocrity, because at some point Elis always got tired of whatever he was supposed to be doing. He put his pen down and proceeded to gaze out of the window instead of going over his answers one last time. Whenever he was asked to try a bit harder, he sighed and adopted a put-upon air – as though you were asking him to pull down the moon or tame a polar bear – and said: Yes, fine, I *will*. And Martin could hear his own voice climbing in pitch as he talked about the job market and getting a university degree, and god only knew what would happen to Komvux now that Björklund had been given free reign with his senseless ideas, and how important it was that Elis realised that this was important. The kind of thing he'd never had to badger Rakel about. Rakel had always had top grades across the board.

The front door slammed shut and brisk footsteps approached.

"Good morning!" Per hollered. He always sounded like he meant it. Martin must have failed to show enough enthusiasm, because a few minutes later his partner entered his office with two cups of coffee. Per Andrén was dressed in a maroon jacket, a pale-pink shirt, and a polka-dot tie, and he was an incorrigible morning person.

"Why so glum, friend? Look what arrived yesterday," he said, handing over a book. "Doesn't it look terrific?"

On a whim, they'd decided to publish a new edition of Ludwig Wittgenstein's diaries. The latest edition was far from sold out, but another publishing company had a big Swedish-language Wittgenstein biography coming out before the end of the year, which they hoped might generate a burst of interest in the Austrian philosopher. They'd hired a historian from Södertörn University to write a new introduction.

"Lovely," Martin said. The hardback was heavy and handsome, with silk ribbon bookmarks and generous margins. He opened it and stroked the wood-free, slightly yellow paper, but avoided reading any part of the text, just as he had avoided giving it a final once-over before it was sent to print.

Per was beaming. "Amir did a great job with the old text block. You should tell him that."

"I suspect you already have."

"He wants to hear it from you."

Martin let out a surprised chuckle. "You think?"

"The young people prefer to hear it from you. Anyway, get that coffee down you so you're awake when the rest of the gang arrives."

Once upon a time, Martin would have been concerned to learn that thirty years down the line he'd be spending more time with Per Andrén than with any other adult. They'd got to know each other in the bloom of their youth, when they made up the weaker half of a rock band. Martin had been convinced he was a skilled guitarist, and that conviction had for a long time obscured the fact that he did not have much in the way of musical talent. Per had had no such conviction to lean on. Bent so low over his bass only his hopelessly non-punk hairdo showed, he'd sweated, fumbled and floundered, sometimes looking up with an expression of deep bewilderment on his full-moon face. The skin on the fingers of his right hand had refused to develop any calluses and he'd been forever plagued by blisters. But he'd read every issue of culture magazine *Kris* several times from cover to cover, knew everything about new Swedish literature and came from three generations of entrepreneurs. The publishing company had been his idea. Left to his own devices, the thought would probably never have occurred to Martin.

Per and his wife frequently invited Martin over for dinner, in the past few years even more frequently than before. They passed off these dinners as informal, spontaneous get-togethers ("Want to come over for a bite on Saturday?"), but it was always a three-course affair with several guests, flickering candles, vaguely intellectual conversation, 25-year-old port from some tiny farm outside Porto to which the Andréns had dragged their surprisingly obliging children the summer before. Martin had long since caught on to the fact that they always made sure to invite a woman who was single and of a socially accept-able age. Martin preferred the term *unmarried*; he'd always felt *single* had a pathetic ring to it. It was a word that tried to cover desperation with forced cheerfulness. It was a status communicated between the lines: "My ex-husband and I used to…", "It was back when I lived on Brännö with my ex-husband."

He always called Cecilia Cecilia. What other choice did he have?

And Per always shot him a resigned look across the table.

The rest of the company's employees arrived. First on the scene was Patricia, the intern, who started every day by wiping the dust off her computer screen and whose desk was so tidy it made you wonder if she ever did any work. But she had a knack for layout and proofing, never missed an inadvertent line break or incorrect punctuation mark, and whenever she ran into a problem, she tackled it with an Excel sheet. Martin had found her hard to figure out until she confessed that *Wuthering Heights* was one of the formative reading experiences of her life. Patricia, he mused, was definitely not a Cathy, and she would surely never go for a Heathcliff in real life. But something in her neat and tidy soul yearned for disaster, madness and the longing that suf-fused Brontë's novel.

Sanna came sweeping in next. She'd been their editor since back when they ran the company out of an old factory building, had lan-dlines and smoked indoors. Now, she shouted hello to everyone and no one in particular, tossed her yoga mat into a corner, kicked off her boots to don slippers and went to the kitchen to pour herself a bowl of cereal that she ate standing up in three minutes flat.

Martin came in for more coffee just as Sanna shoved the dishwasher closed with her foot.

"I read Karin's manuscript," she said. "It's *very* long."

"I've talked to her about making some cuts."

"What does 'some' mean? I was thinking, like, twenty-five per cent. Would that offend her, do you think?"

Martin pondered that. "It might. Why don't we have a look at it together later?"

Sanna sighed and poured coffee into the biggest mug she could find.

Back in his room, Martin spent some time searching for their first edition of Wittgenstein's diaries. These days, Berg & Andrén published about twenty titles a year, and he was running out of room on his shelves. Balancing on one of the Lamino chairs, he found what he was looking for on the top shelf, dusty and slightly faded. Other than that, the book was in remarkably good shape, considering that it had been printed on a shoestring budget in 1988. The back was glued and the paper cheap, but, even so, it possessed a kind of austere elegance. The cover was a deep shade of chestnut, with the title and author's name in black. The blurb on the back ended with a line about the translation having been done by Cecilia Berg (b. 1963), PhD Candidate in Intellectual History at Gothenburg University. The new edition just said: *Translation: Cecilia Berg.*

"Amir!" Martin hollered when he spotted the young man passing his door on his way to the kitchen. Amir stopped dead. His shirt was buttoned all the way up, but his hair was dishevelled. If Martin knew their production manager, he'd commuted to work in a sleepy daze from which he had yet to fully emerge.

"Great work on the Wittgenstein book," he said.

The other man visibly relaxed and a smile spread across his face. "Really?" He was a few years older than Rakel, closer to thirty than twenty-five. He'd joined the company as an intern, kicking off his career with genuine horror at their website ("When did you last update this? You're joking?"). Then he'd sorted it out the way he sorted out everything: sequestered behind headphones that didn't leak a note of whatever it was he was listening to, his eyes glued to the screen, a constant tapping from the keyboard. By the time Amir's internship was coming to an end, Per had been convinced the company would fall apart without him, so he hired him and bought him a ridiculously expensive computer.

Martin nodded. Amir said thank you and continued towards the kitchen.

The day passed as most days did: a string of emails and phone calls, cups of coffee, meetings and decisions. After lunch, Martin met with an author to discuss her still virtually unwritten novel. Her debut had received widespread praise and several awards, and now the anxious creature was paralysed by expectations. Martin considered telling her it wasn't all *that* important – her first book had sold well, but they still had several boxes of the paperback edition left downstairs – but that could easily have the opposite effect. In Martin's experience, the carrot and stick method worked as well on writers as it did on children, but you had to say the right thing at the right time. Lisa Ekman was sitting on the edge of the sofa with her jacket still on, fiddling nervously with a box of snus while she outlined her new project.

"So, it's about a girl going off to university," she said, her eyes on Gustav's big Paris painting. "She kind of moved there on a whim, and she meets a guy and a girl. It turns into this super dramatic love triangle, but I'm not sure about the ending. Well, I have a few ideas. I was thinking I'll write it this summer."

"Sounds great," Martin said, using his kind voice. "Why don't you send it to me when you're a bit further along and we'll talk more then."

Then he paced around Per's office, discussing a book about the Swedish art scene in the 1980s. They'd planned on using Nils Dardel's *The Dying Dandy* for the cover, but apparently Natur & Kultur were publishing a Dardel biography and had their eye on the same painting. Per suggested one of Gustav's paintings, since Gustav had had his breakthrough during the eighties art bubble. Which was a good idea, on the face of it. But they ran the risk of Gustav having a problem with being "commodified", though he would obviously never just come right out and say it. He would say yes because it was Martin asking. Then he'd be grumpy and difficult and stop talking. Martin would want to grab him by the shoulders and shake him and say come off it, it's just a bloody book, if you don't want your sodding painting on the cover, just say so.

"And he might be offended if we *don't* ask him, as well." Martin heaved a sigh. "To be continued. I have to swing by the butcher. It's Elis's birthday and he's requested lamb chops."

"I thought he was a vegetarian now?" Per said. "I guess he has a special opt-out clause for lamb."

It was still light out. Martin couldn't remember the last time he'd left work before sunset.

As he gathered up his things, his eyes fell on a pile of books he'd brought back from the London Book Fair. He was going to have a look at the English and French titles himself, but there was a German novel in there he'd have to outsource. He immediately thought of his daughter. She could certainly take on a reader's report.

Martin found the book at the bottom of the pile. It was called *Ein Jahr der Liebe*, which was decipherable even to someone with his shaky German. *A Year of Love*. Not a great title. But he'd known its German publisher Ulrike Ackermann for years and she'd sounded unusually adamant when she handed him the book. "It's a beautiful novel," she'd said. "I really think it would be a good fit for you." That remained to be seen. It was just shy of two hundred pages. Rakel should be able to get a report done in a few weeks.

Even though he didn't understand a word, Martin read a few lines, and, in his mind, he heard Cecilia's voice.

2

A din of voices rose towards the domed ceiling of the market hall. Coats were unbuttoned, scarfs unwrapped and gloves held in one hand as customers leaned across counters to talk to clerks. Martin was waiting for his lamb chops to be cut and wrapped when he caught a glimpse of a woman out of the corner of his eye. She was the right height, and her hair was cut in a curly bob, and for a second he felt like he was falling through the floor. *Is that—*

No, Martin told himself. It never was. He shook his legs one at a time to regain control over them. As soon as the woman turned around, any similarity would be gone. Look, now she's moving…

And her face was a stranger's, as he'd known it would be. She had sharp eyes and determined creases between her nose and her mouth. She was holding a pair of powder-blue suede gloves and carrying a handbag in the crook of her arm, and was probably about to go home to her family in Askim or Billdal where she would sit down with a glass of wine, feel annoyed at her husband clattering in the kitchen – he was always so loud, no matter how she tried to explain that it hurt her ears, that it was painful – and ask her children about school without listening to their answers.

She met his eyes and he looked away, as though he'd just been looking around and happened to linger on her for no reason. He quickly paid for his lamb chops and hurried outside.

The sun was low in the sky. Martin stood in a ray of golden light with his eyes closed until his pulse slowed. He was going to walk home. That usually helped.

The ice was still thick on the canals and cold winds blustered up and down the city streets. Ploughs had piled dirty snow on street corners and in the parks. The ink-stroke branches of bare trees reached up towards a pale-blue sky. Martin passed Hagabadet, where he regularly submitted to strict regimens on various exercise machines. Every time he stepped through the front door, he remembered what the nineteenth-century building had been like before it was converted into a spa and gym, touched the memory the way you'd touch a talisman. Back then, it had housed an obscure record label you could only reach through an intricate back-door route, to which Gustav had dragged him once to borrow money from some mate of his. Since they were there anyway, they'd been allowed to hang out for a bit, nodding along appreciatively to spiky electronic music and sipping vermouth out of plastic cups. The pools down in the spa section had been empty then, and sometimes improvised theatre performances had echoed between the tiled walls.

These days, the courtyards of the Haga neighbourhood were fenced off and tidy, the local children wore striped jumpers, and the cobbled streets were filled with people out for a Sunday stroll and tourists eating oversized cinnamon buns. Sprängkullen was a university building now, not an underground nightclub. His only friends who still lived here had stopped smoking weed and become architects. And the only people who frequented Hagabadet were Martin Berg and others who could afford to pay 1,700 kronor a month to run on a treadmill. At first, he'd felt naked and ridiculous in his gym tights and T-shirts made of synthetic materials that claimed to breathe and wick away moisture (where to?). His gym shoes had been immaculate and looked brand new since he'd never worn them outside. He tried not to think about what his 25-year-old self would have thought. After a while, he'd begun to see the beauty of going to the gym. It wasn't unlike work: the same principles applied. You put in a certain amount of effort, x. That generated a certain result, y. Sometimes, y was just maintaining the status quo – no weight gain, no fall in revenue. It could take quite a bit of work to keep y constant. In fact, keeping y constant was no small feat. In order to increase y, you had to increase x. Annoyingly, the relationship between the two was not linear; in the world outside Hagabadet, you could increase x indefinitely without any effect on y at all. At the gym, the relationship was closer to linear. You sweated on a cross-trainer for thirty minutes and it had a direct impact on your physique. It was a straightforward fact to cling to in a world where such things were becoming increasingly rare.

And afterwards, there was a pleasant kind of exhaustion. He'd read until Elis came home around ten, slamming the door and barely saying hello. Tired enough not to enter into any kind of discussion, only fleetingly note that his son was heating up lasagne in the microwave and bringing it to his room. Tired enough to fall asleep after turning the lights out. Tired enough to sink into a narcotic darkness until his alarm went off again and pulled him back up to the surface.

The cold air cleared Martin's head. He'd always enjoyed walking. He'd walked and walked through Paris until he could get around without a map, and over the years he must have walked tens of thousands of miles through Gothenburg. And yet, despite all that walking, there was one street he never found himself on.

Kastellgatan was actually located at the heart of Martin's walking pattern. He passed Järntorget Square every day. He often walked up Linnégatan or down Övre Husar. Sometimes, he had to get from one of those streets to the other, via Risåsgatan or Majorsgatan, for instance, but no matter what route he chose, he never ended up on Kastellgatan. It had been that way for over a decade, with one glaring exception, that time he accidentally found himself in Cecilia's old flat.

That was many years ago now, during a period when he'd spent a lot of time with a fairly pleasant graphic designer. She kept dragging him to open houses, possibly to demonstrate her independence. "I've been thinking about buying a flat," she'd say, and Martin could never figure out whether she was trying to communicate something else. Either way, there was always something wrong with the flats they went to see. One was on the ground floor, one had a dark-green kitchen. Too expensive, too small, too new. While she talked to estate agents about pipes and balconies, Martin strolled around other people's homes, staged to make them look like someone-lives-here-but-not-quite, amusing himself by trying to identify the algorithms of the open house. There were always pots of fresh herbs with the price tag still on in the kitchens. Certain kinds of cushions had always been placed just so on the sofas. A tealight always burned on the bathroom sink.

His presence was, in all honesty, pointless, and consequently he very nearly didn't accompany her to *that* particular open house. But then he did because if he ever did say no, it would likely be the first no of many.

"There you are," said the graphic designer – whose name was Mimmi – when they met up on Skanstorget. She gave him a stressed peck on the cheek and set off up the street. "I just have to double-check the address," she said. As she rummaged through her handbag, a kind of quiet certainty took root in Martin. *It's going to be number 11.*

"Eleven!" Mimmi said and pulled on him to make him move. "What's the matter with you? It's not one of the buildings sinking into the mud, is it?"

They climbed the stairs, which spiralled upwards like the inside of a seashell. There were three doors on each of the six floors. It was a one in eighteen chance. His pulse quickened and he heard Mimmi's voice as if from a great distance: "I think it's the top floor."

They reached the final landing, and there it was, Cecilia's door. It was held open by an estate agent's sign and a bucket of blue shoe covers.

A young man in a polyester suit appeared and extended his hand, and while Mimmi took care of the social niceties, Martin entered the flat.

Spotlights gleamed overhead and the worn linoleum flooring had been replaced with tiles. Martin popped his head into the bathroom, but of course there wasn't a trace of the cracked sink or the portrait of Haile Selassie and his inevitable lions. Nothing but white tile. A bowl of limes was sitting on the kitchen counter. The parquet floor in the main room was polished and the walls freshly painted. The bed was covered with a mountain of cushions and a white sofa swelled along the entire wall where Cecilia's bookcase had once stood.

But the view – it was like a time warp. Tin roofs and chimneys, Skansen Kronan, the river, the cranes.

He stood by the window while Mimmi inspected baseboards and mullions with a critical eye. She broke up with him a few weeks later, because it was "really weird" that he still insisted on wearing his wedding ring. "My therapist says I have to work on my *boundaries*."

And he'd thought to himself: This whole thing, it's just a waste of time anyway.

3

When he got home, Martin found his daughter in the kitchen. With her elbows on the table and her chin in her hand, Rakel was bent over a book, so absorbed she didn't notice him. Cecilia had been exactly like that, too. It was like they flipped a switch. Heard nothing, saw nothing. There was no knowing what was going on inside. When Rakel was little, he'd had to say her name again and again, and when his voice got loud enough to prompt a reaction, she had glared at him and slunk away to do whatever she'd been asked to do – pick up her toys, make her bed.

Now, she gave a start and offered to help with dinner.

"That's okay," he said. "What are you reading? Freud? *Beyond the Pleasure Principle*? My goodness. For university, I'm hoping?"

She pushed the book away but left it open. "Is that a sceptical tone I detect?"

"Not at all," he said and dumped potatoes into the sink. But he had to admit it: he'd been surprised, not to say leery, when Rakel had insisted on studying psychology a year or two ago. The programme itself wasn't the problem – he'd been told it was as difficult to get into as law or medical school – it was the fact that she wouldn't be using her obvious talent for texts and languages. All that time she'd spent learning German, and what was she doing with it? Reading some old head shrinker's theories about the sexual urges of humankind?

Martin had thought her year in Berlin would nudge her in a more literary and publishing-related direction. He could probably have got her an internship with Ulrike at Schmidt Verlag if she absolutely had to go off to Germany. But even though she almost never turned down the occasional reader's report, that was the full extent of Rakel's interest in Berg & Andrén. Imagine if *he* had had her opportunities at the age of twenty-four! If Abbe had been a publisher instead of a former sailor and if he, Martin, had been able to step right into a world of literature and education…

"Why are you looking so unhappy?"

"There are a lot of green potatoes in here… Hey, actually, I have something for you." He wiped his hands and went to fetch the German novel. "I'm wondering whether this is something we'd want to translate. Why don't you have a read and let me know what you think?"

"I don't know if I have the time," she said, her eyes on the blurb.

"There's no rush." That wasn't entirely true. Knowing Ulrike Ackermann, she would start badgering him about it relatively soon: she needed to know if they were interested or not.

"I have a lot on at uni right now. I'm supposed to write an essay about that." She nodded at Freud.

Martin watched her hands as she flipped through the pages, thin hands with long fingers, just like Cecilia's. Other than the hands, though, she looked more like him.

"*Beyond the Pleasure Principle*," he scoffed. "What is there really beyond the pleasure principle?"

"Humankind's relentless journey towards death and dissolution, it would seem."

"Cheery. Hey, would you mind checking if we have any cream?"

*

After dinner, the little group scattered quickly. Elis slipped out to celebrate his eighteenth birthday again and Martin bit back his objections as he had the unpleasant realisation that the words he'd been about to say – "Should you really be going out again?" – were a direct quote from a prissy old pop song. His mother, Birgitta, who had long since been transformed into Nana, refused to let him call her a taxi since she could just as easily take bus number three all the way home. Rakel was meeting friends at the Haga Cinema.

"A film?" he said. "This late?"

"It's a bar, too, Dad," she sighed.

Their voices echoed in the stairwell until the door slammed shut behind them. Then absolute silence descended. And even after Martin put all the leftovers into various plastic containers, even after he loaded the dishwasher and did the rest of the washing-up by hand, even after he poured himself a glass of wine and played Billie Holiday on vinyl, the hands on the clock seemed barely to have moved at all.

He could watch a film. He could read something. He could, and now he felt the stirrings of something akin to enthusiasm, get back to his William Wallace project.

Standing in the bay window overlooking the cobbled slope and rickety wooden houses of Allmänna Vägen, he formulated his arguments for commissioning new translations of William Wallace. But Per would sigh and take off his glasses, round tortoiseshell frames he'd bought right before everyone else started wearing round tortoiseshell frames. Even Elis had a pair now, notwithstanding that his minute visual impairment hadn't bothered him in the slightest during his spectacle-averse secondary-school years. Per, on the other hand, had a relatively strong prescription, and his glasses always came off whenever he offered criticism or a dissenting opinion. "I'm not sure that's such a wise move, financially speaking," he would say.

"But the old translations are very inaccurate…"

"But would anyone read them even if they were good?"

And then they'd go round and round like they always did: Martin arguing that Wallace was a forgotten genius, Per replying that he was just forgotten, period. Martin offering examples of successful new editions of forgotten works, Per countering with less successful cases. Martin advocating thinking beyond the bottom line, Per pointing out that you have to kill your darlings. Possibly, he'd say, *possibly*, they could consider it if Wallace somehow became topical. If there was a biopic or some such. But at the moment, he was just an interwar writer overshadowed by Hemingway, Fitzgerald and Joyce.

These days, almost all publishing decisions were Martin's to make, but when it came to Wallace, Per was uncharacteristically unyielding.

Martin sighed, and, unable to decide what to do with the time that remained before he was tired enough to go to sleep, he wandered around the flat. When he and Cecilia moved in at the end of the eighties, the building on Djurgårdsgatan had housed at least two communes, their neighbours had grown marijuana in the yard, and the entrance had constantly been covered in graffiti. Since then, their neighbours on the floor below, a family whose fights and parties they'd heard through the floor, had moved away to fight and party somewhere else. When the building became a co-op, the students and the dubious characters in the studio flats vanished, replaced by better-groomed youths who helped out on yard-cleaning days. The alcoholic on the first floor was gone, a direct result of the more tight-laced parents in the co-op (not Martin) making common cause to demand intervention against his mangy but largely harmless German Shepherd because they claimed it "frightened the children". After the turn of the millennium, the number of punk rockers having hungover barbecues in the shared courtyard had hit zero and the garden had become a picture of rural idyll. Around Christmas, there were advent stars in every window. No one had a satellite dish.

Martin wandered from the window to the living room and from the living room to the hallway. The door to Elis's room stood ajar. He pushed it open and paused on the threshold. He could barely remember what it had looked like when it was his study.

Judging from the decor, the room was undergoing a metamorphosis, stuck between one stage of the life cycle (larva) and another (butterfly). The walls were painted the friendly light-green colour he and Elis had picked out almost ten years earlier, and scarred after ten years of ever-changing posters and a confused period in secondary school when Elis was interested in graffiti, a highly unsuitable hobby for someone as anxious as he was. The pop stars of previous years had been forced to make way for a reproduction of Magritte's pipe and two film posters. One was Truffaut's *Jules et Jim*, showing Jules and Jim running across a bridge, jackets flapping, hard on the heels of Jeanne Moreau, whose Cathérine had a pencilled-on moustache and her hair tucked into a man's cap. The other, *Lost in Translation* by Sofia Coppola, featured a disillusioned Bill Murray sitting on the edge of a bed. *Everybody wants to be found* it said above the title.

Martin sat down on Elis's bed, facing Bill Murray.

Elis had always kept his room in exemplary order. When he was a little boy, his comic books had been immaculately stacked and his Transformers tidily lined up. His bed had been made with military precision. These days, that meticulousness showed in his apparel: rows of neat shirts and 1950s trousers with pleats hung on a clothes rack next to a blazer he'd bought off eBay after a week of obsessive indecision and almost never wore.

The desk had been purchased for a shorter, slimmer person. A stapler, a hole punch, a tape dispenser and a pencil holder were standing at attention along one edge. A white, slightly worn-looking MacBook was placed at a right angle to a small stack of books. Martin tilted his head so he could read the authors' names: Arthur Rimbaud and Charles Baudelaire. Imagine that! When Elis was younger, he'd only ever read when he had to, except for Harry Potter, which he liked but seemed to consider an isolated occurrence rather than a sign that there might be other books out there he could enjoy. Consequently, Martin had been surprised the first time – maybe six months ago – he saw his son frowning over *Journey to the End of the Night*, his blackcurrant jam toast tilted at a precarious angle.

"Is it for school?" Martin had asked over the edge of his newspaper.

"Hmm?" had been Elis's reply.

"Céline," Martin had said with a nod to the book. Elis had read something like twenty pages out of four hundred and fifty. "Is it for school?"

"No, I borrowed it from Michel."

Martin poured himself more coffee. Was he supposed to know who Michel was? Was he remiss for not knowing? Was it a boy or girl, even – Michelle? And which gender would be less troubling?

"Who's Michel?" he asked.

"A friend. He studies comparative literature," Elis offered in a fit of communicativeness.

"At university, you mean." It wasn't entirely easy to imagine the teenage Elis in conversation with a literature student, but his son nodded.

"I thought you didn't like Céline," Martin said, opening the paper back up.

"No, this is great."

"But unless I'm misremembering, you thought *Journey to the End of the Night* was 'a bit slow' for you."

Elis looked up with equal parts irritation and genuine confusion. "What are you talking about?"

Martin was just about to inform his son that he'd given him *Journey to the End of the Night* for his sixteenth birthday, well meaning and invested in his intellectual development as he was. Elis had read a few pages before announcing his verdict. Perhaps, he'd said, he needed to be a bit older before tackling that kind of book. "Like… thirty or something like that." And if Elis went to his room and took a good look at that godforsaken floating shelf just below the ceiling, he would find the book there. The first Swedish edition from 1971 (Gebers), with an inscription on the flyleaf.

"Never mind," he said instead.

Elis raised his eyebrows and returned to his book.

This new, Céline-reading Elis seemed to have replaced the old Céline-rejecting Elis more or less overnight. Suddenly, his son was walking around in a ratty old cardigan from a charity shop and letting his hair grow into its natural halo of curls, then one day the tremulous voice of Belgian singer-songwriter Jacques Brel could be heard through his closed bedroom door. New playlists began to appear on his Spotify account. It was Serge Gainsbourg, Françoise Hardy, France Gall, Juliette Gréco: anything with a wavering gramophone sound, the fragile echo of long-gone Parisian autumns and boulevards lined with yellow plane trees.

Even so, Elis showed no sign of wanting to partake of his father's reservoir of knowledge about dead, male, European authors. Elis acted like he was the first to ever read *The Stranger*, as though *The Stranger* were a cool new rock band older generations in general, and Martin, in particular, shouldn't pretend to know anything about. (Martin felt like asking: "Where do you think the song title 'Killing an Arab' comes from?" But it was unclear whether Elis had ever even heard of The Cure.)

The irony was that this Michel, who Elis spoke of as some kind of mythological figure, had led Elis down the same track Martin would have liked to guide him down himself. Elis had shied away and tried to escape, but his flight had led him full circle back to what he'd been running from. He'd accepted the brick that was *Journey to the End of the Night* from Michel only because it was from him.

And Martin watched his son struggle through Céline, put on braces and a waistcoat, do his French homework with his bottom lip slack with concentration – and take up smoking, at which point the whole thing became less endearing.

"They're not mine," Elis said when he was confronted with a packet of Marlboro Lights Martin had found in a jacket pocket. "They're Oskar's. He can't keep them at home because his mum's like the Gestapo and goes through his stuff. Like certain other parents, apparently."

"We've talked about this."

"But they're not *mine*! Ask Oskar. Here. Call him. Check for yourself. But don't tell his mum, or she won't pay for him to get his driving licence."

Martin looked at Elis, at the phone he was holding out, then back at Elis.

"That's Oskar's business," he said at length. "So long as you're clear on our rules."

"I'm not allowed to drink, smoke, do drugs, get a tattoo or ride a motorcycle until I'm eighteen," Elis said. He'd closed his eyes in a very convincing impression of the long-suffering son while he listed Martin's commands off on the fingers of one hand.

"Yes. Once you turn eighteen, you're an adult and, unfortunately, I won't be able to make decisions for you any longer. I can only hope your risk assessment has matured a little by then."

"You're such a weirdo."

He'd thought to himself: *There have to be rules.* No one is going to say I let them run wild. That I didn't look after them.

If the kids had a smoke from time to time, if they did the whole beret-melancholy-cigarette thing, maybe that wasn't so bad in and of itself. (Come *on*, Gustav groaned.) Martin had taken up smoking as a teenager himself, and his parents hadn't even tried to stop him. ("For god's sake," Gustav said. "It was the seventies. The heyday of the ever-glowing cigarette.") Then he'd carried on smoking until he realised he was about to turn forty. It was the kind of epiphany that came in two stages: first, the intellectual stage, and then the emotional, more cudgel-to-the-head stage. His body had reminded him of certain fundamental facts about ageing. He'd been devastatingly out of shape. He'd had the idea that he should grow a beard. So he'd braced himself and quit, all in all a torturous and sad process. Not that torturous and sad processes were necessarily something to fear, but the more torturous and sad they were, the greater the risk of not quitting at all. The only person Martin had ever seen quit cigarettes in that complete, relentless way, without being pregnant or suffering from some kind of lung disease, was Cecilia.

The way Martin saw it, the biggest problem was that young people didn't understand that they were going to die. They operated under the illusion that they had all the time in the world. That nothing could happen to them. That life would continue to unfold before them like an endless red carpet: welcome, we've been waiting for you, flashing cameras, applause. In reality, cigarettes were a small symbolic death, a reminder of the death that comes for us all, but since these young people couldn't wrap their hormone-soaked brains around the concept of DEATH, much too focused on reproduction to have any notion of the polar opposite of procreation – lonely, indifferent death – they were as unable to fathom the inherent destructive power of tobacco as they were to grasp that alcohol and drugs were like physical manifestations of the inevitable disassembling of the body that can only end one way. They were stupid enough to confuse carefree smoking, drinking, and drug-taking with *living*. They were generation upon generation of tiny James Deans, driving towards the edge of a cliff, thinking that meant they were *alive*, when in fact it meant they were just one brake pad away from dying.

The same lack of judgment and thought was responsible for tattoos. What, Martin wondered, was the point of branding your body for all eternity? What did people hope to achieve by it? The question was whether carefully planned tattoos weren't worse than the insipid butterflies and Chinese characters dreamed up on a whim. Spontaneous idiocy was more forgivable than the belief that at any given moment anyone could know something about themselves that was so important to communicate to an older version of themselves that they had to etch it into their flesh. Young people usually thought they were shrewder and more experienced right now than they'd ever been before, which, granted, might well be true. But it rarely occurred to them, despite all their shrewdness and experience, that this belief stayed constant and that they were, therefore, constantly contradicting themselves.

Elis had pinned a photograph to the wall next to the head of his bed. Cecilia on her back on the sofa, reading the paper. A baby sleeping on her chest and her pitching the paper like a tent above it. Her face was turned towards the camera and her eyes shone.

It's just that, Martin mused, the baby in the picture wasn't Elis. They'd got rid of that sofa in 1989. The infant must in fact be Rakel.

Martin studied Cecilia's black-and-white face. She looked on the verge of speaking.

Then he stood up and left the door ajar exactly like he'd found it.

He could call Gustav in Stockholm. As a matter of fact, he could go to Stockholm – he could book a ticket, maybe early tomorrow morning, get on the train, come back Sunday night. Screw it. He could stay until Monday. They could go out for dinner and have a couple of pints and talk. The air would be clearer and colder there.

Gustav didn't pick up, but it was late on a Friday night; he was probably out. He didn't own a mobile phone. Martin left a message. Then he stood by the window, staring out at the dark streets and the park.

HIGHER EDUCATION 1

I

INTERVIEWER: [*clears his throat*] So, Martin Berg, when did you decide to dedicate your life to literature?

MARTIN BERG: [*leans back in his chair, folding his hands around one knee*] Wow – well, I suppose I never really *decided*. It was more like something I'd always known. I guess there must have been a time in my childhood when I wanted to be a firefighter or some such, but other than that it's as though this was the only option open to me. So I never had a choice.

INTERVIEWER: Like fate?

MARTIN BERG: Yes. You could say that.

*

Martin Berg was born in an eventful year. A wall had been built through the heart of Europe. Marilyn Monroe died tangled in her sheets with barbiturates in her blood. Eichmann was hanged in Jerusalem. The Soviets tested nuclear weapons in Novaya Zemlya. At a kitchen table on Kennedygatan, a young librarian by the name of Birgitta Berg was reading about the Cuban Missile Crisis in the morning paper while the column of ash at the end of her cigarette grew longer and longer.

But no one was obliterated in thermonuclear war that year either. Instead, new nations multiplied around the world as colonial powers relinquished their grip on their protectorates. On dance floors, young people writhed rhythmically in a new kind of dance. Astronauts were blasted into orbit, because if we weren't going to blow each other to pieces, we could at least compete for supremacy in space.

And in Gothenburg, new neighbourhoods were sprouting where until then there had been forests and meadows. Dust billowed from demolition and building sites, banging and clanging rang out from the wharves, and a clutch of cranes were silhouetted against the sky. Ships glided out towards the inlet, surrounded by tugboats, the first step of their journey across the seas.

And Birgitta jumped when her son began to wail, as though for a minute she'd forgotten he was there.

*

Martin's father had been christened Albert, but that was a name that only existed in official records and his sailor's discharge book. He was a lean man of average height, dark-haired and brown-eyed, his torso covered in tattoos that over time had turned the same shade of blueish green as the sea itself. Abbe's father had been a riveter at Götaverken who died when an iron girder fell on his head. "A sober man would have had the sense to jump out of the way" was all his mother had to say about it. She became the sole breadwinner, and at fifteen Abbe had to go to sea. After a few years of odd jobs, he found permanent employment with Transatlantic.

Abbe was a quiet man who usually hung back on the outskirts of raucous groups, doing crossword puzzles and enjoying his snus. He was good at every type of board game and known as a wily chess player. He often won at poker but seemed indifferent to it. He rarely read books but frequently read newspapers. He was the person people called on when something had to be translated into English, French, Dutch or German. Languages were as compliant as wrenches and screwdrivers in the hands of Albert Berg.

One night in the late fifties, he met Birgitta Eriksson at the Liseberg dance pavilion. There was something so dizzyingly random about the meeting that eventually led to Martin's existence – that Abbe asked a woman to dance, for once, and that Birgitta accepted, for once – that Martin was never able to think about it without trepidation; they

35

could just as easily have continued down their respective paths in completely opposite directions. Anything could have become of them, but what they did become was a couple.

In the small number of photographs that existed from that time, Birgitta looked vaguely like Esther Williams. She was pretty but looked very proper; there were no dazzling smiles, no coy glances over the shoulder, no sparkling film star eyes. Instead, she wore an absent expression, as though her mind were elsewhere and she'd stumbled into what was happening in the present (the picture-taking) quite by accident. In their framed wedding picture, which was collecting dust on the dresser in the TV room, she was holding an armful of roses she didn't seem to know what to do with. Abbe looked vaguely awkward in his rented suit and a shirt that was too tight around the collar.

One time, Abbe had pointed out the places he'd visited on a globe Martin had been given for Christmas the year he turned seven: Antwerp, Le Havre, New York, Rio de Janeiro. There was an unsettling amount of ocean between the tiny dot that marked Gothenburg and the much larger squares that marked the final destinations. Martin's mother took him down to the docks to watch his father's ship leave, and it was enormous, so large Martin was convinced it was going to collide with the new bridge. Icy terror rushed through him and was made even worse by the fact that his mother looked so calm. But then the chimneys slowly glided under the bridge as if it was nothing and Martin relaxed and didn't even protest when his mum took his hand to go back home.

The word *Atlantic* had a dual ring of adventure and danger to it, while the *Pacific* sounded gentler. The *North Sea* had to be stormy and cold, but on the other hand it was closer, and, on his globe, that sea seemed small enough for land always to be reassuringly near. And the size of the ship was comforting, too, until Aunt Maud told him about the Titanic, thinking her nephew would appreciate an "exciting real-life story". After that, Martin spent his evenings wide awake in bed, thinking about icebergs and shipwrecks, about how easily even big ships could be swallowed by the sea. Tens of thousands of feet it would sink, down to a seabed no daylight had ever reached.

But eventually, the day always came when he heard the heavy footfall in the hallway, the voice that vibrated on lower frequencies than any other in the house, the jingling of coins being emptied onto the hallway dresser. (If he was lucky, he'd find one-kronor coins among all the odd ones that were the wrong size and had holes in the middle.) Then followed a week or two of Abbe being home. He was never loud and rarely angry, and yet Martin played more cautiously when he was around. He would sit in the garden swing seat with his paper and a beer. Martin watched him through a hole in the bushes at the far end of the garden, where there was a leafy cave just large enough for a young boy.

For a long time, that was the way of the world: Mum and Martin, and a dad who came home but then invariably disappeared again. Martin played with the other children in the neighbourhood, learned to read, was served tea every day at five, went to bed and was read a story, though not always one most people would consider a children's story. Consequently, Martin had nightmares several nights in a row about turning into an insect like Gregor Samsa, and for a long time he pondered what was really wrong with Mrs Dubose.

But then one day Mum began to look unwieldy and to wear big dresses he hadn't seen before. One night, Dad told him he was taking a job at a printers and was going to be coming home every night from now on. Mum explained that Martin was going to have a little brother or sister. He pushed his mash around his plate. One Saturday, Aunt Maud came to babysit him.

"They'll be bringing your sister home soon," she said, leaning down from her ominous height.

Kristina, or Kicki, as everyone called her, was at first uninteresting and then, when she got older, mostly annoying. Having followed Martin around like a shadow, she then transformed into a loud girl with a strutting walk who spent hours skipping and playing hopscotch, won at French skipping, and was a master of blowing bubbles with her gum. She wailed and sulked to get out of doing homework but was an expert at vaults, rings and wall bars, and could practise dance moves for hours. She claimed Martin was a hopeless square, but when he brought friends home, she still hid in his closet and ran away shrieking with laughter when she was discovered. Their mother always claimed to love them both equally, but Martin wasn't sure that was true. Because Kicki and she were so different – his sister was actually more like Aunt Maud.

Their mother was the only person in her family to have attended university. Martin didn't know exactly what that meant, but somehow it set her apart from Maud, who was a secretary with a raspy voice and lipstick on her teeth, and their parents, who at Christmas would deliver veiled barbs until they died less than a year apart. Their mum didn't cry at the funeral (unlike Aunt Maud, who sobbed loudly), she just contemplated the stained windows of the church with a slight frown.

Every week, they went to the library, had cookies with her colleagues, and returned home with a stack of books. Their mum kept hers in a neat pile on her bedside table. When Martin came home from school, he often found her at the kitchen table, reading, with an ashtray and a cup of coffee that had long since gone cold next to her. When Martin appeared in the doorway, she would give a start, arrange her face into a smile, put her book aside, and get up to make him a snack.

Birgitta Berg executed all of life's chores with neutral practicality and an even temper. She was rarely upset, and Martin never heard his parents argue. He only saw her surprised a handful of times, once when he was twelve or thirteen and brought an essay home from school. The theme was "My summer holiday", and Martin had written about their annual sailing vacation, which had been trying, as usual. He hadn't planned to show it to her, but he accidentally left it out on the kitchen table with his maths homework.

"This is really well written," his mother said, with a look on her face he'd hardly ever seen. "Really very good."

And with her cigarette forgotten between her fore and long fingers, she read on, without looking up once.

II

INTERVIEWER: So how did it start?

MARTIN BERG: I honestly don't remember. Or, actually... [*laughs*] I started writing what I thought was going to be my first novel very early. I obviously had no idea *how* to write a book. I'd read a lot, and when you read a finished, printed text, it always seems so straightforward, doesn't it? As though it were the easiest thing in the world to write. As though the story just appeared through some process of spontaneous generation. It's lucky young people don't know any better, otherwise a lot of books would probably never have been written...

*

When the SKF head office switched from manual to electric typewriters, Aunt Maud filched one of the old ones and gave it to her nephew. On this office-grey beast, Martin clickety-clacked out the following words about the summer of 1978:

`As close to a limbo of the soul as this earthly existence`
`allows.`

Then he made a line break (*bang, ding*), leaned back in his chair and lit a cigarette.

Since he wasn't used to smoking, a coughing fit followed. Then he discovered he'd forgotten to set out an ashtray, so he fetched the one from his parents' bedroom and placed it on top of a stack of library books. Pleased with this prop, he sat back down at his desk, took a more cautious drag and squinted at the white paper through the smoke.

He was about to turn sixteen and, for the first time ever, he was home alone during the summer. The rest of the family were on the sailing boat his father had purchased after quitting his job with Transatlantic. That was how the Berg family spent their summers: as soon as the holiday drew near, there was a flurry of packing, a search for life jackets, and tinned goods and batteries for the transistor radio were purchased. And then four weeks on the water. Martin was habitually seasick but unable to throw up over the side of the boat because looking into the depths underneath them gave him vertigo. The days were filled with various ropes that had to be tied to things, a sneaky boom that could come flying at him at any moment, a little sister who knew how to tie all the knots and actually liked shellfish. Martin found life jackets uncomfortable and hated swimming in the open sea. Between the bouts of nausea, he usually stayed below decks, reading the cache of comic books he'd brought.

This year, he'd found himself a job at the post office sorting centre to get out of it and was consequently considered old enough to stay in town by himself. He worked four nights a week, cycled home at dawn and went to bed with the blinds closed and postcodes dancing across his retinas. Then he was unconscious until the early afternoon, when he woke up with a stale taste in his mouth and pillow creases on his face. His free time was spent making full use of the empty house: walking around in T-shirt and underpants, playing The Clash as loudly as he dared to without breaking the speakers, having sandwiches for dinner and his friends over to hang out. Aunt Maud had been asked to check in on him, but she was seeing a new man and limited her involvement to bringing him food from time to time. She'd tell him to at least do the dishes, then she'd hurry off, and through the window he'd see her race away in her silver Saab.

Now Martin stubbed his cigarette out firmly – having smoked only half – and turned his attention back to the sheet of paper in the typewriter. That spring, his mum had brought home from the library *Jack* by Ulf Lundell, because she'd noticed it was "popular with the young people". (Her own judgment, having skimmed a few chapters was that it was "sloppily written, but not without charm".) Martin read it in one sitting and then, when a whole new kind of aching emptiness had haunted him for several days, he read it again. The novel made everything seem so wonderfully light. The pavement put a spring in his step as he walked up Kungsladugårdsgatan, the air was rich with oxygen, his blood sung in his veins. A longing he'd never experienced before had taken root in him. It was several weeks before the obvious solution presented itself: he was going to write a novel of his own.

But now, nothing came to him. His mind was as blank as the sheet of paper.

Which was hardly surprising, he told himself. He had no Experience. He had to acquire some and then write about it. He needed to meet more girls. Go to more parties. Leave home and move in somewhere bohemian. But what was the local equivalent to a cabin in Stockholm's Vita Bergen? There were allotments by Godhemsgatan, but only old people ever went there. And they were a stone's throw from home, anyway; it would be like camping in the front garden.

The phone rang, and since Martin had not yet got into the habit of moving it to the desk when he was writing, he had to go out onto the landing to answer. It was Robban, whose brother had bought him beer, and he'd also got his hands on Springsteen's latest, and Sussie and some other people were coming over, did Martin want to come, too?

"Sure," Martin said and crushed the cigarette a bit more to make sure it was definitely out. He had two days off from the post office and was hardly going to experience any bohemian things sitting at his desk all night. "I'm on my way."

Before trying alcohol for the first time, Martin had figured it tasted good, so it was quite a shock when it didn't. This was in eighth grade, when he was fourteen. He'd closed his eyes and swallowed, excitedly waited for something to happen. He'd imagined an instantaneous effect, but noticed nothing much, other than a pleasant, woolly feeling after forcing down the entire can (like when you're little and have to take your cough medicine). He opened another one and tried to think about something else while he chugged it. And a little while later, he was standing on a sofa, jumping up and down, singing at the top of his lungs along with at least five others, and when he wanted to get down (possibly to move in the direction of the crisp bowl) his legs wouldn't obey. He fell on his face, but it didn't hurt. On the contrary, the whole thing was hilarious; he got up but had to lean on Robban, and Robban was laughing, too.

Back then, it didn't take much to make a night a hit. Basically, so long as there was alcohol, they were set. Intoxication was their goal. Granted, a diffuse kind of disappointment surfaced when Sussie unsteadily got to her feet, thanked them for the drinks and slowly stomped down the stairs in the platform shoes she refused to abandon even though they'd caused at least two serious sprains. But on the whole, seeing what happened if you mixed vodka and Coca-Cola, playing every single one of Robban's albums, and reading the lyrics on the back covers was enough.

This summer night was no different. As usual, they met up at Robban's house. As usual, they played Robban's newest albums. As usual, they listened to Robban talking about the band he'd joined and the Rhodes piano he was planning to buy. As usual, Sussie had a few friends who were "maybe coming by later".

"Why so glum?" Sussie said, nudging Martin's arm.

"Mm."

"Want to come out with us later?"

"Sure, why not?"

"Why not?" she mocked and reached for her cigarettes. She usually looked good when she lit her Virginia Slims – shaking her fringe out of her eyes, tilting her head back – but this time he saw her somehow double-exposed over her future self. The soft curve of her neck would soon turn into a double chin, her skin would lose its fuzzy softness and become taut.

He wanted to retort something sharp and witty but couldn't think of anything. He couldn't shake the thought of a party in a swanky flat on Strandvägen or what it would be like to bring a crate of beer out to Djurgården (though they'd visited Djurgården during the customary class trip to the capital and he hadn't seen a single life-affirming bohemian there). The people he imagined meeting were vague to the point of indiscernibility, but he knew they were *different*.

Martin knew exactly how the night would turn out: an aimless get-together in the park, determined drinking until they – fingers crossed – achieved the golden mist of intoxication, which made you invincible and immortal, riding three people on a bike down a hill, thinking it would be a laugh to climb a tree or go for a swim in a fountain, ending up in the bushes with a giggling Sussie, struggling to pull off her very tight jeans. That point where everything hummed with possibility, when you ran across the football field as fast as you could on a whim and collapsed in fits of laughter, lungs burning. Then it always went the other way. You shoved in some snus and the world started to spin too fast. Or the mystery mix of alcohol you'd downed had set a sneaky ambush and suddenly attacked your stomach, making everything come back up again. Someone wandered off, someone else took a leak in a doorway in full view of a police officer, there was a fight, Sussie inexplicably got offended and decided to go home, running across dewy grass with her shoes in her hand.

But when Robban pushed himself to his feet and said: "Come on, let's go to the park," Martin went with them. He didn't mind Sussie riding on the back of Robban's bike instead of his. He looked down at his pedalling legs and they could as easily have belonged to someone else. When they found their friends, the laughter and voices sounded like they were coming from very far away.

"Who are you looking for?" Sussie thumped down next to him.

"Huh?"

"Like, are you waiting for someone?"

"Who would that be?"

"God, you're in a foul mood. What's your problem?"

Later that night, Sussie went on and on about wanting to see the sunrise, so they walked up to Masthugget Church and sat down on a stone wall. Red tin roofs and deserted streets spread out below. The river was mirror-smooth and the cranes by the wharves still. A handful of gulls screeched high above their heads. Martin contemplated his friends. Robban had ambition but no discipline. Sussie got by solely on her looks and had never had to develop any kind of intellectual abilities. (A fact that had become painfully obvious over the past year, as he helped her with her homework and had to try to mimic her illogical and circuitous thinking when some of their teachers had become suspicious about the sudden improvement in the quality of her work. "Don't use words like *relevant* and things like that," Sussie complained, pushing a strand of hair out of her face.) She was so sick of school, she was saying now, she was thinking about dropping out and working instead, like Robban, but Robban said: "Don't be an idiot, Sussie, don't waste your best years slumped behind a till somewhere, get an education, don't be like me when you grow up," and Sussie laughed and punched his arm and said he was only one year older, and Robban tried to calculate what percentage of their life that year constituted, and that kept them busy for a good long while, during which they smoked the last of Sussie's cigarettes.

In the east, the sky was blushing red. Soon the first rays of the sun would slice through the air, bright and cheerful, and Sussie would yawn and put her sunglasses on and find her shoes. They would slowly wander back home along Bangatan, she with a slight limp and Robban yammering on about the keyboardist in The Doors while Martin pushed his bike and thought about something else. Maybe he would walk Sussie home and maybe he wouldn't, but she was blinking sleepily and was moody and sullen, so he was leaning towards the latter, and after they parted ways, he would pedal home, unhurriedly, alone in the streets.

III

INTERVIEWER: What was it about literature that attracted you, do you think?

MARTIN BERG: I suppose it's normal for a teenager to want to be somewhere else. You want to get out. Leave. Go anywhere. Get on the first bus out of the country. But you have no money and there's an exam next Tuesday and, you know… But you actually *can* get out of there through reading.

INTERVIEWER: So some sort of escapism?

MARTIN BERG: Not just that. Reading gives you access to worlds other than your own. You can test out being an adulterous Russian noblewoman or an alcoholic mailman who frequents prostitutes. You can tag along on an outrageous road trip across North America. You can be *anyone.*

*

The first day of upper secondary school, when he was sixteen, Martin was wide awake long before his clock radio came on. He had breakfast and showered with plenty of time to spare (unfortunately, no one else was up to comment on it). He put on the outfit he'd settled on: Levi's, T-shirt, the denim jacket he'd got for his birthday the week before, the fabric of which was still stiff. If he cycled there, he'd arrive sweaty, so he took the tram.

He'd memorised which classroom he was going to but got lost and ended up in a hallway full of older students hanging out in clusters by the lockers, laughing and letting out squeals or bellowing shouts of joy. Martin turned on his heel, tried a different direction, locked onto a flock of confused-looking people, found the right room, and entered as though nothing could be more natural. For a horrifying moment, he almost knocked his chair over, but no one seemed to notice. Safely seated, he studied his future classmates with an expression as indifferent as he could make it.

Top grades in every subject had guaranteed Martin admission to the school of his choice. His dad had put a heavy hand on Martin's shoulder and said: Well done, lad. His mum had given him an envelope containing two crisp one-hundred-kronor notes and Kafka's *The Trial.* Martin changed his official address to Aunt Maud's house in Landala so he could attend Hvitfeldtska. He didn't know more about

Hvitfeldtska than any other upper secondary school, but the buildings, looming at the top of a hill in Vasastan, were surrounded by rose bushes, willow trees and a general aura of historicity. The walls were high, the windows numerous, the hallways endless, the staircases wide and echoing. Martin pictured himself in a not-too-distant future on his way to his locker, carrying heavy books. He'd grown taller and more broad-shouldered. He was wearing new tennis shoes. He took copious notes in class but wasn't a swot. A girl with indistinct facial features was walking towards him across the schoolyard…

A short woman in a grey suit was standing in front of the class, and now she wiped her forehead with one hand, an annoyed gesture that missed a sweaty curl that had escaped her tight bun, glanced at a sheet of paper, looked up at the clock and cleared her throat. When that had no effect on the din (did people already know each other?), she cleared her throat again and added an "All right, then".

She introduced herself: their class teacher who would also be instructing them in maths. "You can call me Miss Gullberg." She wrote the name on the board in the even hand of a schoolteacher, chalk screeching, and then peered out at them, as though she'd be able to tell just from looking whether there were any bright students in her class or not. A pursing of the lips suggested she held out no great hope.

"First, a few rules," she said and picked up the pointer. "No smoking indoors. Don't leave the schoolyard. And for the boys who insist on using snus: it goes in the bin when you're done, *nowhere* else. No running in the hallways. Be on time. Infractions are one strike each, three means detention. Defacing school property is strictly forbidden. Understood?"

A girl's voice spoke a faint yes. Miss Gullberg ignored her. "Then it's time for roll-call. Alén, Marita?"

Martin was near the top of the list, as ever when alphabetic order was involved, and for some idiotic reason, his heart began to race. When Miss Gullberg said her indifferent "Berg, Martin?" he had a sudden fear of his voice not working. But it seemed cowardly to just raise his hand, like Andersson, Kenneth had done.

"Present," Martin replied.

While the rest of the class list was read out, he felt a growing sense of disappointment. The people he was going to spend the next three years with all sported well-groomed hair and impeccably ironed shirt collars folded over V-neck jumpers. Granted, there was a reasonably good-looking girl sitting at the desk next to his, with a ski-slope nose and heavy eyelids that lent her a dreamy, dazed look. As far as Martin could make out, she was the one out of all his future classmates who most resembled the vaguely imagined girl who was walking towards him across the schoolyard in his fantasy, maybe on a chilly September morning, the kind that warmed up around midday, the trees explosions of red and yellow – anyway, she would walk towards him with books (leather bound?) gently pressed to her chest, waving to him...

She noticed him watching and flashed a quick smile; he smiled back. He thought she might have answered to the name Christine.

Then Miss Gullberg said: "Von Becker, Gustav?" and a guy in the second row tipped his chair back and said: "It's just Becker."

The voice was hoarse and quiet. Martin could only see its owner from behind. He was dressed all in black: jeans, T-shirt. Basketball shoes with untied laces. A dark-blue army coat hung over the back of his chair. His arms were pale, his elbows bony.

Miss Gullberg nodded and made a note.

General information followed. Study plans. Schedules. Martin was surprised by the number of free periods, a word he was familiar with in theory but had never encountered in real life. Before, classes had been stacked on top of each other like blocks. On the paper he'd been given now, the dark blocks (free time) and light blocks (classes) were arranged seemingly at random. On Thursdays, they didn't start until 9.40 and on Fridays they finished as early as 2.30. On the other hand, they had class until 4.00 on Tuesdays, but that seemed exotic, too, and Martin pictured himself in a classroom, absorbed in some book, as the sun set outside these windows dating from the 1800s or whatever.

Suddenly, chairs were scraping all around him, people were getting up and talking, sauntering out at the deliberately measured pace characteristic of people eager to end up in one social context and to avoid another.

Martin folded his sheet of paper and shoved it into his back pocket. Then he left without so much as a glance at his classmates.

The only one who had seemed even remotely interesting was that Gustav bloke, but he was nowhere to be found in the schoolyard. He probably had friends who laughed hoarsely and listened to music that didn't sound like music and went over to Christiania all the time to smoke pot and hang out with people who kept big dogs with bandanas around their thick necks. Unfortunately, pot mostly made Martin paranoid and tense, and even though his official stance was that he liked punk rock – he and Robban always got into arguments about that, which usually ended with Martin accusing Robban of liking Elton John and Robban denying it a bit too strenuously – the truth was that he'd listened to *God Save the Queen* three times at most, and at low volume at that. Yet even so, he liked having it in his crate of albums, angrily pink and yellow, and he liked that his little sister never borrowed it without asking.

He shoved his hands in his pockets and tried to look like he was waiting for someone.

"Do you have a light? I can't find my matches."

It was Gustav. Luckily, Martin had a heavy Zippo lighter that belonged to Sussie in his pocket.

"Sure," he said. "Can I bum one?"

Gustav held out a blue-and-white packet with French writing on it and Martin pulled out a cigarette.

Up close, Gustav's eyes were his most striking feature. Anxious and somehow fragile behind a pair of unfashionable, round glasses perched precariously on the ridge of his nose. His nose was a close second for what you noticed most about his face, pointed and slightly red at the tip. Martin's associations took a sharp turn from punk rock – drugs – barking dog to nineteenth century – consumption – candlelit piano music. Gustav's unkempt hair belonged to that undefinable section of the colour spectrum that can be called either mousy or dark blond (depending on your level of generosity) and even though it had been a long, warm summer, he was as pale as cambric, a word Martin had recently learned from Tolstoy. He wore his coat over his shoulders like a robe even though it was warm enough to go without. Martin himself was tanned after spending so much time outdoors, something he'd been pleased with before but was now starting to think looked a bit gauche. This guy gave the impression that he shouldn't be exposed to too much bright light, that he had to be shielded from strong emotions and preferably spend his days at a writing pulpit or some other piece of nineteenth-century furniture. His fingers, which were manipulating the Zippo, were covered in ink.

"I didn't catch your name in there," Gustav said, holding out his hand. "Gustav."

"Martin," Martin said.

They shook hands.

Gustav fiddled with his cigarette, adjusted his glasses, gazed out across the schoolyard and then spent a few moments focusing intently on his shoelaces. Martin tried to think of something intelligent to say, but the more he tried, the blanker his mind went, so instead he took a number of deep drags on his cigarette. The result: acute light-headedness.

"What school did you go to before?" Gustav finally asked.

"Kungsladugård Secondary. In, uh, Kungsladugård." Moron. "What about you?"

"Sam," Gustav replied and nodded several times. It took Martin a moment or two to realise he meant Göteborgs Högre Samskola. "Only took me nine years to escape. Out of the frying pan, into the fire." He gave a low chuckle and tapped the ash off his cigarette with his index finger, a gesture that couldn't be described as anything other than graceful.

"What do you mean?"

"Well, lots of daddy's boys here who are going to grow up to be either exactly what their parents are or what they want them to be. But what do I know – maybe you're planning a future in the, how shall I put it, paternal business, too?"

"Quite the opposite, actually," Martin said, realising he was grinning. Gustav immediately returned the smile. "Though I don't think he'd be sad to see me go to sea aboard some kind of freight ship."

"Oh no?" Gustav sounded impressed. "Why's that?"

"He was a sailor."

"Was? Is he dead?"

"No, he works at a printers now."

Gustav laughed, and Martin laughed too, and just when they couldn't laugh any more without it being awkward, Gustav asked what he was planning to do then, since he wasn't going to conquer the seven seas.

"I don't know," Martin replied. A completely uninteresting response. "Write maybe. Or play music."

"What kind of music? What do you play?"

For each thing Martin told Gustav about himself, Gustav had another question. Why wasn't he doing the arts programme? ("I guess I don't want to play music *that* much.") What did he want to write? ("I was thinking something like *Jack*.") What kind of books did he read? ("The usual...") What was his old school like? Did he know that person or that person? What did he think of Patti Smith? *Easter*? "It's all right," replied Martin, who had listened to "Because the Night" at least twenty times that weekend.

"I've seen her live," Gustav said. "It was incredible..."

It was time to head to the auditorium to listen to the headmaster give a speech; all the way to the ancient pews, and for a while after some grown-up in grey clothes asked for silence up on the stage, Gustav told him about the concert in a low voice.

And even though the headmaster was tedious, and nothing had really happened, Martin could feel an electric current pulsating through him. A steady, driving rhythm that crackled in his veins and muscles.

*

Once the "von" had been struck off the class list, Gustav ended up right before Martin in the roll-call.

Becker? Yes.

Berg? Present.

And if no one responded to Becker, Berg was unlikely to produce a reply, either. At those times, Becker and Berg were off doing something else. Like sitting on the grass in Vasaparken talking, or later, when the weather turned chilly, on a bench. Or they'd gone down to Schillerska Upper Secondary, where Gustav knew some people in the arts programme, killing time in hallways littered with ceramics, watched by rows of self-portraits of varying quality. When winter came, they began to spend a lot of time at a café in Haga. Primarily during free periods and in the afternoon, but also during the occasional class that Gustav insisted he really couldn't attend because there was a risk he might implode. "From tedium and ennui and general inanity." Martin was probably the only reason they went to school at all.

"I don't think I've ever been this *present*," Gustav said, some weeks into the autumn term.

"And isn't there a kind of uptight satisfaction in it?" Martin retorted.

"I don't know…"

"Well, no one's making you go." It came out sharper than Martin had intended. There was a trick to getting top grades, as Martin had discovered. You didn't necessarily have to *like* a particular subject. The central requirement was to be present – physically and vocally – or to do outstandingly on exams. But Martin suspected that if you spent a term raising your hand and asking the right kind of questions (a skill he was always honing to avoid falling into the trap of officiousness) teachers would be more inclined to interpret your responses on the eventual exams more generously, even if they were obscure or abstract or a closer reading would have revealed you did not, in fact, have a solid grasp of the subject matter. Consequently, he'd taken to sitting in the generally shunned seats in the first or second row. It was only pathetic if you were reduced to the front row as a result of social ostracism – like their classmate Gunnar, who had compounded his general hopelessness by admitting to a profound interest in entomology. Gunnar had shot Martin and Gustav a terrified glance and moved his English grammar aside the first time they plonked themselves down next to him. And Martin could feel everyone's eyes on them like a warm golden glow, while he tipped his chair back and waited for their English teacher to enter.

Gustav had skived his way through secondary school and had atrocious grades. And yet he knew about a lot of things in a flippant way, as though they were obvious and not something a person would have to learn. (French word of the week: *savoir-faire*.) His family took annual trips abroad to Italy or France, where his grandmother lived. He casually used words like "misanthropic" or "suggestive". He talked about Dutch painting, Dadaism and *la belle époque*, and Martin nodded as though he knew what they were.

One time, when Gustav declined their usual Friday night activity – chain-smoking at a café for a few hours, walking to Kungsladugård, preferably the long way around to kill time, hanging out in Martin's room while they made calls to gauge the evening's party potential – because he was "going to see a play with my mum", Martin thought he was joking at first.

"I mean, no, she has tickets to *The Wild Duck*," Gustav said.

"All right," Martin said. "The things we do for Ibsen, as I like to say." He was pretty sure it was Ibsen.

Gustav was going to be a painter, he told Martin.

"You mean, like, an artist?" Martin asked.

"Yes, but that sounds so pretentious. 'I'm going to be an artist.' It's not something you can *be* without *doing*, right? In my case, painting. So, painter."

They were on their way up to Skansen Kronan and talking was making Gustav fairly winded. Martin was carrying two warm takeaway boxes from Sjuan's. Gustav was hauling his seabag. The city was enjoying a brief Indian summer and it was their last chance to live a *Jack* kind of life before winter came, and that was worth missing biology class for.

Gustav spread his army coat out like a picnic blanket. Then he pulled out a bottle of vodka and, wrapped in a kitchen towel, two shot glasses that fractured the sunshine into sparkling cascades of light.

"In the words of Baudelaire," he said, filling the glasses, "'Be always drunk. Nothing else matters: that is the only question. If you would not feel the horrible burden of Time weighing on your shoulders and crushing you to the earth, be drunk continually. Drunk with what? With wine, with poetry, or with virtue, as you will. But be drunk.' Personally, I never got the *virtue* part. But horses for courses, I guess. Cheers!"

They clinked glasses. *Les Fleurs du mal* was sitting on Martin's desk, but he'd only read the albatross poem. The ignorant masses who don't appreciate the greatness of the poet and so on. Afterwards, he'd penned a few poems himself, in a notebook he kept carefully hidden underneath a stack of school books.

"So when do I get to see your paintings?" Martin asked. "Or your secret sketch book?"

Gustav smiled. Normally, he looked lost and a little dejected – Martin wasn't sure whether he really was lost and dejected or if that was just the way his facial features arranged themselves when they were at rest. But when he smiled, the sky cleared and Martin thought: If I can make this person smile, I will have achieved something good in this world.

"You can see it right now," he said, and started digging through the seabag.

And while Martin flipped through the sketchbook, its owner set to eating his bangers and mash with intense focus.

It was mostly Indian ink and pencil portraits, predominantly people Martin didn't recognise. But several of their teachers and classmates featured, too, apparently drawn without their knowledge. Martin wondered whether he would come across a picture of himself and was both relieved and disappointed when he didn't.

"They're obviously just sketches," Gustav said.

"They're really great."

"I don't know…"

"Come off it. They're – they're incredible. You're really good."

"A few came out okay."

It was lucky Gustav was talented in an area where Martin was so indisputably incompetent. If he'd had the same aptitude for music, it would have instantly interfered with Martin's toiling with the guitar. Or if Gustav had excelled at writing essays and their Swedish teacher had always expected *him* to answer the question "Is anyone familiar with Strindberg?" Martin had better grades in every subject except art, so it was no big deal to stand aside when it came to drawing. In class, he drew his own stickman art in the margins of Gustav's handouts: Mona-Lisa as a stickman with an inscrutable smile; Venus in what could only with the best will in the world be recognised as a seashell; a square, deconstructed stickman that he had added the caption PICASSO to just to be on the safe side. Gustav suppressed a laugh so violent his whole torso shook. When their teacher asked if Gustav wanted to share what was so funny with the class, he had to compose himself before he could get out that Martin had drawn a stickman version of *The Last Supper* and then he burst out laughing again, and the class rolled their eyes, which only made the whole thing more hysterical.

At the start of term, Martin had hung out a little with some of the other people in the class. He made no real attempts to reach out to them, but he didn't reject them either, like Gustav sometimes did. Whenever their classmates – the few who turned out to be perfectly okay people, after all – came over to shoot the breeze, Gustav would clam up, smoke, look from one person to the other, and reply tersely but politely if asked a direct question. After getting to know Martin, he made no effort to befriend anyone else.

Martin gave him his tattered copy of *Jack*, which Gustav read immediately and said he loved. In return, he gifted Martin his favourite book, a well-read paperback called *Patagonia Days*. It was written by William Wallace.

"Never heard of him," Martin said and instantly regretted it. Maybe Wallace was someone he should know about. He would ask his mum the first chance he got. But Gustav barely knew more than his name either. "It's some English bloke," he said with a shrug. "Or maybe American. I think he was friends with the one who shot elephants."

"Hemingway?"

"Yeah, or one of the other ones. Lived in Paris."

"I wouldn't mind living in Paris," Martin said longingly. Gustav brightened. He'd been to Paris last summer, he said, but only for a few days with his family, which really wasn't ideal. But he and Martin should definitely go. Soon. They could hitchhike. They could take a train. There were probably buses. No big deal. A few hours and you could be on the Continent.

"And what are we going to do when we get there?" Martin said. The Bergs never went abroad.

"We'll have champagne at Closerie des Lilas and observe the giants of philosophy in their natural habitat. Sartre and those guys."

"You saw Sartre?"

Gustav admitted he hadn't spotted Sartre during his philosopher safari. "He must be absolutely ancient by now. But he's going to die with his boots on and a cigarette in his hand, mark my words, and if it doesn't happen at Closerie des Lilas, it'll be at Deux Magots."

Gustav Becker was unlike every other person Martin knew, and even though they spent most of their waking time together, he had a hard time placing his new friend on the social map. His sketchbook and contrary attitude made him a misfit. Their class was geeky enough that it never attracted anything worse than sideways glances from the well-behaved boys and girls in their V-necked jumpers, but Gustav could have easily got beaten up on the night tram just because someone didn't like the way he looked. If that ever happened, he wouldn't be able to defend himself with word or deed.

At the same time, Martin associated him with punk rockers, a group of people that weren't exactly known for their diffidence and timidity. That was partly due to Gustav's crow-like clothes, but also to the fact that he did actually know several punk rockers. It often happened that someone called out "Oi, Gustav" when they cut through Vasaparken, and they would stop for a quick chat while Martin fiddled with a cigarette that mostly just made him feel nauseous. In their stud-and-safety-pin-littered leather jackets, they roved about in groups, accompanied by a general rattling of chains, crushing of beer cans, clearing of throats and spitting. Even though they provided a refreshing contrast to the tanned preppiness (which Martin was royally sick of), the supposedly decadent disco (which he had zero interest in) and the morally superior progg rockers (whom he wasn't politically involved enough to join), there was something about the herd mentality that put him off, because – in all honesty – a herd is a herd is a herd.

"They all wear the same clothes and listen to the same music," Martin said. "I don't know that it really matters whether it's Ebba Grön or ABBA."

"What do you mean?"

"I mean, it's herd mentality either way."

"Yeah, sure, maybe," Gustav said. "But I'm going to take you to Errol's…"

Martin didn't know Errol's and there was no point pretending he did.

"What the hell is Errol's?" he said instead, somewhat defensively.

"A rock club." Gustav had been to the opening a few months earlier. "It was insane. Gothenburg Sound played and the singer cut his own cheeks with razor blades."

"He did *what*?"

"Just slashed away. There was blood everywhere, spattering the audience and whatnot. Someone had to wrestle him to the ground and take him to A&E. And you know what's even wilder? The next day, they played *again*. Even though the bloke needed twenty-two stitches. He looked a bit the worse for wear but, bloody hell, they were tight."

"Hmm," Martin said.

"I think Attentat is playing soon."

"But how did you get in?" It was hard to imagine Gustav passing for eighteen even with a fake ID.

"I know a guy there…" Gustav said. "It doesn't always work, but sometimes."

Martin thought it was paradoxical for a place with an anti-establishment credo to insist on carding people, but Gustav argued that if they let in just anyone, the place would turn into a bloody after-school club. Either way, their visit would have to be postponed until Gustav's friend was working, and since he was currently in Amsterdam it was unclear when that might be.

*

When Gustav was off to a concert with his mother one Friday night ("some Russian playing Chopin") Martin discovered his company had become such an integral part of his life, he didn't know what to do with himself. He killed a few hours rereading his favourite parts of *Patagonia Days* at their favourite café in Haga, but it was so loud and the smoke so thick it gave him a headache. He trudged home and lay on his bed until his sister called him from the landing; he had a phone call. During the short walk from his room to the phone, he was convinced it was Gustav, that the concert had been cancelled for whatever reason. It took him several seconds to identify the voice he heard instead.

"Hiya!" Robban said. "Bloody hell, it's been ages."

Martin remembered several messages (*Robert called Tuesday p.m.*) that he'd noted and immediately forgotten. Now Robban was yammering on as usual, taking forever to get to the point. Did he want to come by, have a few beers, listen to some music?

"Well..."

He heard someone saying something in the background.

"Sussie thinks you should come over, too."

"I would have loved to, but, uh... I have to study."

They hung up after exchanging the kind of polite platitudes grownups use when they run into each other at the shops – let's talk again soon, absolutely, we really have to get together sometime. On the way back to his room, he was intercepted by his mother. Dinner was on the table.

They had meatloaf and potatoes. Abbe's moustache waggled when he chewed. Birgitta cut her food neatly with her napkin on her lap. Kicki nattered on about some gymnastics competition.

"That sounds lovely, sweetheart," Birgitta said and then their parents started talking about Thorbjörn Fälldin's resignation.

Later, after his dad had left for the nightshift, when his mum was doing the washing-up and his sister was in a trance in front of the TV, Martin sat on his bed, unable to breathe. An endless succession of waking hours lay ahead in this room. His chest felt tight. Somewhere, in the hall of some mountain king, Gustav was sitting in a velvet seat and the pianist in his black tailcoat was just striking the first chords...

He stood up abruptly. "I'm going for a walk," he called out in the direction of the kitchen.

"Are you going to be late?" His mum appeared in the doorway. She was wiping a pot lid with the calm demeanour of someone asking purely for the sake of information. She rarely raised objections when he went out; the only time she'd offered any criticism was one time in ninth grade when he'd come home drunk and managed to trip over an awkwardly placed chair, after which he threw up all over the hallway floor. Birgitta had appeared in her dressing gown and said *Martin* in a way that made him feel more ashamed than any scolding ever could have.

He shook his head. "I'm just going for a quick walk."

She nodded and returned to the sink.

The night was cold and damp. Martin turned up his coat collar like Albert Camus. Instead of the bright red jacket he'd been given at the start of ninth grade – at the time it had been the height of aesthetic perfection – he'd bought a black coat from a charity shop. At first he'd felt awkward about wearing someone else's old clothes, but Gustav had been enthusiastic. "My god, you look like Humphrey, if he unclenched a little and had a beer instead of a whisky on the rocks, please." Now, Martin pictured his own coat-clad figure from a distance, a dark silhouette moving in and out of the pools of light around the street lamps in Slottsskogen Park. A handful of solitary shadows were out walking their dogs. He wandered towards the city centre without any real plan. The windows in the large, palatial buildings encircling Linnéplatsen Square sparkled and gleamed. The architecture in Linné was beautiful, but everyone he knew from there smoked pot and was on benefits. The streets were dankly black and the shop windows dark.

He walked down towards Järntorget Square and through Haga. Muffled music could be heard from upper floors, a banner hung between two windows read SAVE HAGA! Voices, laughter from passers-by. They'd reached the intermission now, and Gustav and his mother were letting the tidal wave of concertgoers carry them out into the foyer. Maybe Gustav had popped out for some fresh air and a cigarette and was studying the same sky under which Martin was trudging along – a deep blue dome with clouds like smooth inkblots and the occasional twinkling star.

His feet took him to Magasinsgatan. He walked at a leisurely pace, as though he was on his way home but didn't care overly much about the late hour. Martin identified Errol's from afar by the raucous crowd milling about outside. When he was roughly level with it, but on the other side of the street, he stopped and lit a cigarette. A muffled drumbeat and hungry guitars seeped out through the door. He stood there for a while, and when he'd finished his cigarette, he ground it out against the cobblestones and walked back home.

IV

INTERVIEWER: What was the literary scene like back then?

MARTIN BERG: It was a period characterised by wholesomeness. There was this idea that literature should be edifying and… *principled* in relation to any number of political issues. Which obviously gets dull pretty quickly. And in the end, people started doing the opposite.

INTERVIEWER: Did you?

MARTIN BERG: I suppose we primarily identified as aesthetes, not revolutionaries. Which I suppose might have been revolutionary in itself in the seventies…

INTERVIEWER: When you say "we", are you referring to yourself and Gustav Becker?

*

The one time Martin tried to write about his family and childhood – in a thinly veiled autobiography he worked on for a while in upper secondary school – he was overcome with deep ennui.

> He grew up at the far end of Kungsladugårdsgatan. The X family owned a bland brick-front house with a lawn that sloped feebly towards the street. In the back was a patch of grass with a few depressed lilacs and gooseberry bushes. There was a patio, as well, complete with kettle grill and squeaky garden swing, all under a corrugated plastic roof that frequently had to be cleared of fallen leaves. A dark-blue 1960 Volvo Amazon was parked in the garage.
>
> Other than that, there were windows that revealed nothing and a front door with a mostly silent doorbell.

Even though he'd written the above in a loud pub, the mood came through clearly. The slow ticking of the clock. The smoke from his mum's cigarettes listlessly twisting towards the ceiling. The chequered brown wallpaper in his room, which he would stare at until he wanted to scream. His mum's silent back at the sink. The rustling of his dad's newspaper on the patio. The squeak-squeak of the garden swing. The flickering light from the TV. The six o'clock news. The well-manicured lawn. The asphalt of the street and pavements in the summer. Martin's futile attempts to make time pass more quickly by picking a fight with his sister or heading out on long, aimless bike rides.

The tedium was so palpable he felt he simply couldn't go on.

But on second thoughts, he found Sartre's *The Words* awful, too, so maybe the problem was inherent to the genre.

The von Becker family was something else entirely. They seemed like much more promising fodder for a novel. All in all, Martin visited their flat on the corner of Olofs Wijksgatan and Södra Vägen no more than a handful of times, and in his imagination it quickly took on the diffuse sepia tones and vague proportions of the past. Director von Becker's presence was inescapable – lingering cigar smoke, the hats in the hallway, a dark overcoat – but, in reality, Martin only met him once. It was in the stairwell. They were on their way up. Gustav's father was on his way down. He was in his mid-forties, but had a spring in his step. Easy to picture on a tennis court. Suit and briefcase, tortoiseshell glasses. Martin knew who he was even before he stopped and said something along the lines of, Well, if it isn't Gustav, because ever since the wharves had fallen on hard times, his picture was occasionally in the papers. He was the CEO of one of the shipping companies. Not Transatlantic, Martin would have remembered that – was it maybe Strömberg?

"Dad…" Gustav looked away and his whole body seemed torn between staying where he was and continuing up the stairs as if nothing had happened. In a flash of insight, Martin realised he wasn't the problem, it was the other way around: Gustav didn't want his friends to meet his parents.

"Good day," Martin said, extending his hand. "Martin Berg."

"Bengt von Becker." You could almost hear the signature in that voice, a large, bold signature written with a fountain pen.

"Right, so that's my dad," Gustav said once the door to the street had slammed shut behind him.

Mrs von Becker appeared from the labyrinthine interior of the flat and said it was lovely to meet Martin. Marlene ("after Dietrich") was dressed in a beige suit that couldn't quite hide that she was very thin. Her eyes quickly slipped past anything at eye height to fix instead on something at floor level – feet, the lion's paws of a squat dresser, Gustav's seabag which looked like a tattered refugee next to the polished hardwood floors and Persian rugs.

"I'm taking the girls to dance class," she said, addressing a fringed footstool. As though summoned, two blonde sisters in their early teens joined them, both wearing leotards and carrying ballet shoes. They offered a reserved greeting. "I think there's food in the fridge…" Marlene looked confused for a moment, then she smiled, kind of like when a lightbulb is switched on, and kissed her son on the cheek.

Gustav tugged at the hem of his shirt, looking uncomfortable.

His room overlooked the courtyard, with a view of row upon row of tall windows and cast-iron balconies. It seemed he'd spent quite a bit of time staring out at them, because he pointed out where an old army officer who liked to walk around naked lived and the bedroom window of a woman who spent her days cheating on her husband with what Gustav suspected was the postman.

"You think it's a cliché and then it turns out to be true. When it comes to sinning, I suppose people are less innovative than you'd think."

There was an easel in one corner and sketches littered every free surface. A large piece of oriental cloth was hung up on the wall with drawing pins. The deep windowsills were hidden under piles of paperbacks and magazines, records, empty cigarette packets, a box of watercolours, jars of paintbrushes. A drawer in a chubby rococo dresser was pulled out, as though it had tried to disgorge its contents (mostly socks) but not quite succeeded. On top of the dresser stood a small bronze statuette of a ballerina.

"Nice room," Martin said. Gustav seemed not to want to hear it.

"Come on," he said. "Time to hunt for treasure."

"What?"

But Gustav just grabbed him by the arm, pulling him along.

Somewhere, a clock chimed. Their steps were muffled by plush rugs. In the living room, Gustav stopped with his hands on his hips and looked around, like an adventurer gazing out across an unexplored valley for the first time. The leather sofa and armchairs looked brand new. There were no cigarette butts in the marble ashtrays. The coffee table was empty aside from a vase of flowers. They had a state-of-the-art

TV. Granted, it was possible Mrs and Mrs von B spent their Saturday nights watching talk shows, but it was a lot easier to picture them in the room Gustav called the Parlour, like a buffalo and a gazelle in their natural habitat: nothing but antique furniture, oil paintings and the furtive sparkling of a crystal chandelier.

Martin inspected the bookcase. It held rows of leather-bound books with gilt edges. He pulled out *The Father* by Strindberg. Printed in 1924. The spine creaked and the pages were stiff, unread.

Gustav fumbled about behind the books.

"What are you doing?"

Gustav winked. "*Voilà*," he said and pulled out an unopened bottle of vodka. "Hold this." He did a lap of the room. His T-shirt rode up a little when he scratched his back, revealing a sliver of skin.

"But… won't they know?"

"She would never say anything."

Gustav stuck his hand into a large blue-and-white porcelain urn and pulled out an almost full bottle of cognac.

"In the Ming vase of all places," he said. "She's something else." They carried on. The parlour. The kitchen. A long butler's pantry. The hallway with its small bay window. The only room Gustav didn't search was the study, where the air was heavy with stale cigar smoke and a large desk stood imposingly in the middle of the room. He didn't search his sisters' rooms, either, just went in for fun. Both of them had plastered their walls with posters of horses, ABBA, and Ted Gärdestad with a guitar over his shoulder. Gustav tossed Martin a fairly tatty teddy bear.

"I don't know why she still has this out," he said. "It's probably some shrewd ploy to appear younger and more innocent than she is. Charlotte is a Machiavellian devil, mark my words. She has the entire school, including some of the teachers, wrapped around her finger. Like a puppeteer from hell."

"She looked pretty harmless," Martin said. Though he couldn't remember which one of the sisters Charlotte was.

"Don't be fooled, my friend. Don't be fooled…" Gustav suddenly looked interested, picked up a notebook from the bedside table and flipped through it, only to put it down again with a look of distaste on his face. "*A ledger.* My god. This girl would have become a capitalist even if Castro, Mao and Marx had been her fairy godmothers and Trotsky her godfather…"

A lackadaisical half-light seeped in through the closed blinds in Gustav's parents' bedroom. Their bed was enormous and there was not a single crease in the silk bedspread. It looked like Martin had always imagined a hotel room to look like. Gustav found another bottle of vodka in the drawer of the make-up table, but after considering it for a few seconds, he left it where it was.

He wrapped the loot in a jumper and packed the bundle into his seabag. Then they made sandwiches and drank the last of the milk while Martin quizzed Gustav on their French vocab.

*

One morning, Gustav slipped into his usual seat next to Martin and held out his hand. In it was a key.

"What's that?" Martin whispered.

"My new flat," Gustav replied. "Take it. It's the spare key. I'm always losing mine."

They skipped PE and went over after lunch. The contract was in the name of someone called Joppe, who according to Gustav had left the country to find inner peace on a kibbutz. He was subletting while he was away. The flat was in the older part of town that clung to the slope. Sjömansgatan was basically one long, steep incline lined by worldly-wise buildings in various shades of grey, dirty white and faded red.

"Just one hundred and fifty kronor a month," Gustav said as they stomped up the narrow stairs. He'd been given some money by his grandmother on his last birthday, he said, and she would in all likeliness approve of his decision to move out of his parents' house.

It was a studio. Joppe had left a sofa, a huge plush thing. There was a rickety table in the kitchen. The kitchen cabinets were painted forest green.

They set to finding the cheapest possible furniture. They salvaged an outdated but perfectly serviceable leather armchair from a skip. In the basement, they found four wooden chairs that appeared to be abandoned.

"It's not like they're actually *in* a storage area," Gustav said.

"Maybe someone left them there so someone else could pick them up?" Martin suggested.

To be on the safe side, they carried the chairs up to the flat late at night. Gustav acquired a mattress that he put on the floor. He'd brought his easel and record player from home and so, all in all, he had everything he needed.

After that, Martin rarely went straight home after school. Sometimes, he stopped in to eat and drop off his books before heading out again. The sofa on Sjömansgatan was surprisingly comfortable; he kept a toothbrush there in case he needed it, and more often than not borrowed clothes from Gustav. Striped tops and tattered flannel shirts, the kind of things that put a frown on his mother's face. Though it wasn't so much his outfit she was eyeing now as a rip at the cuff of the shirt.

"But why not?" she demanded when he declined her offer to mend it.

"It's Gustav's."

"But wouldn't Gustav want his shirt mended?"

"Whatever, I have to go now…"

He couldn't remember how he used to spend all those hours that were now taken up by hanging out at Café Moster with a cup of coffee and a patchwork cheese sandwich. He'd probably spent it at home, on the sofa, staring lethargically at endless reruns of M*A*S*H, punctuated by fights with Kicki, who wanted to watch something on Channel Two. His memories seemed fuzzy to him, as though they belonged to a different lifetime. A distant past that was vague and elusive compared to the café's gentle symphony of voices, the soft dinging of the pinball machine, the clanking and clattering of cups and plates, occasionally accompanied by raised voices from the kitchen where the owners yelled at each other behind a barely closed curtain, an orchestral work that eventually (wild waving of the conductor's baton) reached an apogee in the furious revving of the husband's moped as he skidded off across the cobblestones to pick up a few pints of milk. Then tranquillity would envelop the café once more; people stirred their coffee as though nothing had happened. Someone ordered an anchovy sandwich. A semi-famous progg rocker entered.

Before he got to know Gustav, Martin had passed the café on Haga Nygata many times, glancing in through the windows. So when Gustav said: "Come on, let's go to Moster," a few weeks into term, Martin stepped through the door with a sense of occasion that didn't match the atmosphere of the place at all. It looked a bit like someone's cluttered living room, with potted plants and pictures hanging askew on the walls. There was a pinball machine in one corner and next to it a girl with spiky black hair and Siouxsie and the Banshees make-up. Gustav said hi to a group of older guys with guitar cases. It was only a few days after Martin had been talked into buying that coat from the charity shop, and until that day, he hadn't felt a hundred per cent comfortable in it. But walking into Moster in the shiny jacket he for some inexplicable reason had insisted on wearing the previous winter would have been social suicide. These were, he realised, the kind of people Sussie always complained about when she was drunk, because they thought she was "a traitor or whatever" for wearing make-up. (He suddenly remembered Sussie's older sister, an angry 22-year-old who sometimes came home from university to snap at Sussie for being a victim of the patriarchal order and who was she really shaving those legs for? And Sussie's mum told her to dial it down a notch, and when Sussie's sister started going on and on about the proletariat, their mother retorted that at least Eva was getting her education, *she* had worked in the bread factory all her life and then the gloves were off and Sussie sighed and said: "Come on, let's get out of here.")

And now, here he was, dressed in a coat made of graphite-grey wool that Sussie would have dismissed with a look of revulsion (she would have rather died than wear anything second-hand), nodding when someone asked if they wanted to go to see Attentat at Språngkullen in a few weeks.

Then followed a kind of learning period during which Martin worked on figuring out the rhythm and routines of the café's microcosm. They ordered coffee from Margit, who with her gold jewellery and green nylon housecoat didn't quite match her clientele. He learned that you couldn't be in a hurry if you wanted a sandwich because it could be quite a while before you were served, and that considering the general grime of the kitchen regions it was probably safest to stick to cheese sandwiches. You almost always ran into someone you (which was to say Gustav) knew, and depending on your mood, you could join a larger group or sit by yourself. There was an excellent view of the room from the corner, and he liked to sit there with a cup of coffee that was freshly brewed if he was lucky and made from used grounds if he wasn't: one of the cost-conscious owners' less appreciated innovations.

On this day, a damp November afternoon, Martin was at Moster alone. Cigarette smoke billowed like fog up by the ceiling and Martin was turning the pages of *Steppenwolf*, which had been recommended to him by a friend of Gustav's, a good-looking girl from Copenhagen he could have fallen in love with if she hadn't been so obviously out of his league and dating some artist to boot. She'd told him he should read it. At least he was fairly certain that was what she'd said; her Danish was mildly challenging to decipher.

He sensed a presence and looked up to see Gustav standing there with his glasses covered with a fine misting of rain.

"Check out what I just bought," he said, emptying out the contents of a plastic carrier bag onto the table. It was ten or twelve plump tubes of oil paint, each with a small label announcing the shade of its contents. Cadmium red, zinc white, ultramarine. There was also a handful of paintbrushes with stiff bristles.

"Paint," Martin said.

"I have this idea – you know *Livet är en fest*? The cover?"

Martin nodded. He'd always liked that album cover: a table littered with bottles, beer cans and cigarette butts against a black backdrop, the title in white lettering above it.

"Doesn't it remind you of Dutch still lifes, the ones with fruit and food and things? A table full of stuff that's on the verge of going bad, pears that are just a little too ripe and a lobster that's been left sitting out a little too long? Or oysters. And the tablecloth is messed up and in the middle of it all there are some flowers and maybe a human skull?" While he talked, Gustav searched his coat pockets for his packet of cigarettes, found it, and continued to dig around for matches until he found a battered book with two left.

"I guess," Martin replied. He'd always thought the plural was still lives. He made a mental note to add it to the list of things he needed to check at the library: Dutch painting, still lifes, fruit, human skull.

"And always against a dark background," Gustav went on. He lit a match and held it to the end of his cigarette, closing his eyes and inhaling. "Just like on that album… Anyway – are you hungry? I'm pretty hungry. Let's go to the Prague, okay?"

"I'm broke…"

"It's on Nana, she sent me money. I was supposed to use it to buy paint, but there was money left over. I think she enjoys being my patron."

While they walked up towards Sveaplan, Gustav expanded on his idea, which at heart was about combining the skilled but conservative style of the Dutch seventeenth century masters – and at this point he reeled off a number of names that Martin did his best to commit to memory – with a grittier attitude, in the style of the album cover. "A meeting of high and low. Which I suppose is kind of what the seventeenth century blokes were doing too, but no one thinks of it that way any more, they just see Great Art or whatever. And they say that these days people just do nonsense and gimmicks and goats in car tyres and so on."

Martin hoped his face didn't give away how confused he felt.

The Golden Prague was noisy and smoky.

"Two bowls of goulash, please," Gustav said. "And beer. Anyway – in all honesty, I'm not sure how to use oil paint. You have to prepare the canvas and then I guess you just have at it... but I think it takes ages to dry."

"Why don't you ask the art teacher?"

"Splendid idea." Gustav clapped his hands together, as though it were settled, and rewarded the waitress with a beaming smile when she brought them two foggy mugs of beer.

*

Sometimes, Gustav didn't come to school for days at a time, or a full week, even. He'd been ill, he said when he returned. "A proper killer of a cold, fever and whatnot."

While Gustav was off sick, Martin had to make do with classmates who were perfectly all right and whom under other circumstances he wouldn't have minded knowing better. He spent a lot of time in the library. He was pretty certain nothing had changed in there in the past thirty years. The only thing that revealed it was now the late seventies was the slender girl with a mess of curls and dungarees hunched over a tome by the window, bobbing her clog up and down: her casual style would have been out of the question for an upper secondary student in any previous decade.

Martin sighed and turned the page in *Dutch Masters – from Bosch to Vermeer*.

The frailty hinted at by Gustav's constant colds, fevers and various other ailments (shingles, pneumonia) made Martin feel robust in an unexciting way. He'd always been blessed with a good physique, and from time to time he put some effort into PE, to keep his grade from dipping too low. He was average with a ball but a decent runner, especially over short distances, and he did all right with high and long jump. When he was sick, it was an efficient, predictable process, as though his body just wanted to get it over with.

Martin could picture Gustav, wrapped in blankets, nineteenth-century-style, on his mattress.

One time during one of his absences, Martin bought a few tins of pea soup and went over to Gustav's after school. It was March. The sky was leaden, the street covered in slushy snow. The street lamps on their wires swung in the icy wind and Martin shivered as he walked up Sjömansgatan. The front door was locked and as he dug around his pockets for the key, he had a crystal-clear vision of it sitting on top of his dresser at home. He'd taken it out of his jeans when his mother came to collect his laundry.

A ringer with a button for each flat had recently been installed. Martin pushed Gustav's several times, but nothing happened. There was a light on in his window. He waited a while, rang the bell one last time. Then he put the tins of soup down on the ground and left.

V

INTERVIEWER: What were your sources of literary inspiration?

MARTIN BERG: [*running a hand through his hair, thinking*] They came and went, obviously. But I'd have to say William Wallace. Wallace has always been with me. It's funny, actually, because Wallace wasn't a big name in the eighties. He wasn't hip. There was a Wallace renaissance in the sixties when they turned *Patagonia Days* into a film starring Steve McQueen and Pier Angeli. It's not bad, actually. I think the director stayed true to the book's imagery. And they resisted the temptation to turn it into a melodrama. Anyway, Wallace works within a... relatively conservative *literary* tradition. Which fell out of fashion when people started problematising and deconstructing the premises of fiction under the influence of postmodernism. Even if Wallace was innovative in his own time, by then he had become part of the establishment. But he has a unique voice, and his works take an almost epic approach. He took himself very seriously. There's no irony in his writing. Wallace is a very, how to put it – *self-sufficient* author. But I do remember [*laughs*]… at some party or another, I met these people dressed all in black who were studying at the university and felt the only writers worth their salt were Stig Larsson and Mare Kandre. Everything else was just old drivel. We ended up in a fairly heated discussion about it… but I managed to persuade one of them to give Wallace a chance, because obviously he'd never read him.

*

"Do you want one?"

Without waiting for a reply, Gustav tossed ice into two highball glasses he claimed to have nicked from Hotel Eggers by simply walking out with one in each coat pocket. Then he poured a generous slug of bourbon into each, cut a couple of slices of lemon, squeezed in the juice, tasted the result, cut two more and squeezed them too.

"Syrup," he commanded, sounding like a surgeon.

Martin picked up the pot of syrup that had been sitting on the windowsill to cool. Gustav stirred a couple of teaspoons into each glass and held out one of them to him.

Over the years, Martin had tried most kinds of alcohol. Lukewarm beer. Cheap red wine that burned with bile when you threw up. Moonshine someone had bought for next to nothing and mixed with fizzy drinks to virtually no effect. The shit mix from his friends' parents' liquor cabinets. Drinking with Gustav was different. It was whisky that rolled down his throat like a small ball of fire, warming his body from the inside. It was sharp vodka that cut through his brain like a spear made of ice. It was, in the summer months when the top floor at Sjömansgatan was sweltering, cool, cloudy pastis.

"Cheers!"

"To what?" Martin asked.

"To being practically halfway through upper secondary school." Gustav added some more whisky to his glass. "Which honestly is further than I thought I'd get."

"Come off it."

"Can you imagine me *tout seul* in our class? Can you? What would I be doing between classes? Talking to Christine about her boyfriend's year abroad at Berkeley, United States of America? Or maybe" – he pulled hard on his cigarette, squinting as he pretended to think – "delving into the mysteries of business administration with what's-his-face – Olof?"

"Stefan."

"Why is he even in our class? Why didn't he opt for the business programme?"

"Unclear."

"I would have succumbed to despondence and ennui."

There was a pause and Martin seized the opportunity to motion towards the five typed and stapled pages sitting on Gustav's kitchen table.

"So, what did you think?"

"Oh, it was stunning, of course."

A wave of relief washed over Martin. "You really thought so?"

"Yes, yes. The part where they're at the party was particularly good."

Martin snatched up the papers and quickly skimmed the first page. The words jumped out at him, both familiar and new.

"I wonder whether I should flesh it out more. To make it – well, a novel."

The truth was, he'd already been working on his first book for a while. So far, the magnum opus consisted mainly of scribbled paragraphs in a notepad and a stack of typed fragments. He'd calculated roughly how many words were needed for a novel of two hundred pages by estimating the number of words on one page and multiplying it: sixty-six thousand.

Gustav had finished his drink and was making himself another.

"You'd better get another one of these down you," he said. "Novelists always have a very troubled relationship with alcohol."

By then, they'd acquired something of a reputation at school. Martin did nothing to fan it, but he didn't correct glaring untruths, either.

They were seen crossing the schoolyard shoulder to shoulder. Gangly Gustav who apparently was an ace at drawing and Martin who supposedly had top grades in every subject. Who skipped the class party to sit around and listen to classical music and drink wine. Who had found a way to get up into the attic where they'd discovered a cosy little nook. (It was assumed it was theirs because the janitor found well-read issues of culture magazines *BLM* and *Kris*, several empty bottles and two greasy bags that had once contained onion crisps.) Who sat on the wall that ringed the schoolyard with their heads close together until Martin stood up and quoted something that might have been Rimbaud before jumping down the other side and spraining his ankle (a few muffled *bloody hells* were heard) and had to go to the nurse's office. Who turned up five hours later than everyone else to every party. Already drunk and generally unconcerned about how the event was going, they'd nick a few beers and saunter about for a bit, before leaving as abruptly as they'd come. Because they were going to a superior afterparty? An underground club? No one knew.

Martin first became aware of this when he was lucky enough to end up next to Yvonne Pedersen in the advanced French class.

"Oh, it's *you*," she sighed, but she didn't sound too displeased.

"*Moi?*" Martin said. "*Expliquez, s'il vous plaît.*"

Yvonne made a face, but before she could respond, Miss Hoff cleared her throat and started to write out verb forms on the board with a screeching piece of chalk.

Yvonne was known as "the one who looks like Brooke Shields", and after class, she followed him all the way to his locker, asking whether it was true that they'd hitchhiked to Copenhagen, smuggled pot back across the border, and managed to evade the police in Malmö.

"Maybe," Martin replied, opening his padlock.

"What's that supposed to mean?" she said. "Either it's true or it's not."

"Think of it as Schrödinger's cat." Then he walked off, out, towards the schoolyard where Gustav was waiting.

As far as girls went, he'd noticed something interesting: the less effort he made, the better he did. His tepid interest in maths briefly flared up one day as he pondered whether and how one could illustrate that phenomenon with a graph.

"Are you out of your mind?" Gustav said.

"But theoretically speaking – I mean, you can calculate that there are black holes and things... And what do *you* know? You just sit around doodling."

Nevertheless: there was solid empirical data, based on experiments and behavioural observation. Instead of going to this or that party (as he had implied to Helene or Åsa he would), he spent the night at Gustav's, playing guitar and singing bawdy songs he composed himself while Gustav painted. They drank a few dusty bottles of red wine Gustav had liberated from his parents' attic and laughed and horsed around, and somewhere someone was checking her watch for the umpteenth time, wondering: *When* are they coming? And instead of spending the evening with Yvonne, who had made it known she might have plans beyond just the conditional and subjunctive (*la question c'est voulez-vous/voul-ez-vous aha*), he let her sit at home on Kungshöjd and headed down to Errol's, where some discordant punk band was going wild and Gustav was bouncing up and down in front of the stage.

Martin's indifference was feigned, at least at first. He left Yvonne sitting there with her notepads and dictionaries, thinking it might pay off in the long run. (And, lo and behold, when her parents went out of town, she invited him over for dinner and then they fucked on the chintz sofa in the living room, the floral pattern of which hid all incriminating stains.) The only thing he had to do to seem like he couldn't care less was to follow Gustav's lead. Gustav went to parties because he wanted to go to parties. He didn't dress in a paint-spattered denim shirt to seem artistic and interesting, but simply because it had been at the top of the pile. Gustav didn't get entangled in long, abstract discussions about the future of portraiture versus its history because he wanted to impress Sonja from Schillerska, for instance, but because he'd been thinking about portraiture in general and Manet in particular all day and wanted to talk to someone about it. And there she was, fiddling with her beer glass, pushing a strand of hair behind her ear, leaning in closer, and Gustav pushed his glasses up and carried on like nothing was happening.

"This place is dead," he might announce while topping up his silver-plated flask, inherited from his grandfather, with someone else's vodka. "I vote we get out of here."

And if Sonja from Schillerska asked where they'd disappeared to next time they bumped into her at Moster, Martin just shrugged and said: "We went to Errol's."

Those words didn't come close to containing what going to Errol's really entailed – that knot in the pit of his stomach until the bouncer nodded them through, being in a press of people wearing leather jackets, drums exploding on stage and guitars slicing through flesh, accidentally spilling lukewarm beer on himself and probably some other people, a wobbly conversation with an unconvinced girl, cigarette smoke, and, finally, armfuls upon armfuls of cool night air that made you snap back in a little and set your course for the nearest open takeaway, and then they staggered home to Sjömansgatan, where they drank whisky cocktails and smoked, stretched out on the mattress, playing Chopin at a low volume until the sun came up, discussing subjects that felt deep in the moment but dissolved like smoke when you tried to recall them the next day.

Martin rarely made plans without asking Gustav first. And yet it annoyed his friend if Martin said no to playing dominoes and drinking pastis in the early summer sun because he wanted to help Yvonne with her essay on Hermann Hesse instead.

"I see," Gustav said in a voice brimming with *Et tu, Brute*.

"But I'll see you tomorrow," Martin said.

"Sure."

"She really does need help with that essay. She has it in her head Hesse was a Nazi and I would describe the situation as dire."

"Okay."

"Okay?"

"That's what I said."

"I'll see you tomorrow, then."

"Mm."

To say that Martin fell in love during upper secondary school would be overstating matters.

He experienced infatuation, possibly, febrile bursts of emotion, followed by sleeplessness, dizziness and incoherent thoughts. Before long, however, he would snap out of it, and when he did, it left his system, as quickly as it had entered it. That was the case with Anna something-or-the-other, whom he dated for about a month before it became obvious they had nothing to talk about. It was the same story with Yvonne, who was nice and so on, granted, but when he imagined them together three years from now, he felt his chest tighten and his ears began to ring, and a few days later he told her he felt they should stop seeing each other.

"You're breaking up with me?" Yvonne shrieked.

"We were barely even together," Martin countered.

He spent a lot of time discussing the nature of love stretched out on Gustav's green sofa, with a gin and tonic balanced on his chest and a cigarette in his hand. Gustav would experiment with oil painting and contribute the occasional grunt. Some days, Martin concluded love was an illusion created and perpetuated by the capitalist system, "opium for the masses, if you will", and that the idea of two people laying exclusive claim on each other was a virtually baroque notion everyone should break free from.

"So you really wouldn't care if your girlfriend slept with some other guy?" Gustav asked.

"Of course I would. That's why I'm saying we need to *break free*."

Other days, Martin stared thoughtfully at his cigarette, which he had allowed to burn into a long column of ash because in all honesty the nicotine was making him feel nauseous, and said:

"I suppose you meet someone special sooner or later and when you do, you know you belong together. That there's no other option."

Gustav said nothing. "Yes," he agreed after a long pause. "I'm afraid that's how it is."

Of Martin's many flings during upper secondary school, the one with Jenny Halling was the one he would remember best, possibly because he wrote an almost twenty-page short story about it. Gustav dismissed it with the assessment: "Fine, if ever so slightly self-indulgent."

They took the same elective – film studies, one of the few classes Gustav wasn't in – and became friends over a conversation about Scorsese. Martin had no agenda. Jenny Halling wasn't the kind of girl he usually fell for, not even the kind of laid-back *laissez faire* falling that sometimes occurs when you have nothing better to do and it's a long, boring winter. She was originally from Umeå, spoke softly, had a crescent-moon smile and round glasses, not unlike Gustav's. Dressed in a baggy turtleneck jumper, jeans, and flats, she gave a prim impression that didn't entirely align with her character; she shoplifted for fun on occasion and when she was drunk she sometimes climbed drainpipes and fences.

Even before they slept together, he had a vague feeling it would be a mistake. They'd been to see *The Shining* at the Palladium – Jenny approved – and then she'd asked if he wanted to keep talking about the film. They'd gone back to her dorm room in Landala: two hundred square feet, film posters on every wall, a large piece of cloth pressed into service as a curtain.

("Of course you had an agenda," Gustav told him afterwards.

"No, I really didn't.")

It turned out she had a few bottles of red wine. Nina Simone spun on the record player. There wasn't room for a table, so when they ate – spaghetti and fish fingers that Jenny cooked in the shared kitchen – one of them had to sit on the desk chair and the other on the bed. Then Martin moved over to the bed, too, because the wooden chair really wasn't very comfortable and the bed was the only place it made sense to sit.

Jenny was in a terrific mood, laughing, her gestures uncharacteristically emphatic as she talked about whatever it was she was talking about. Joan Baez took over from Nina Simone. Bottle number three was opened. Their faces were inches apart. And at some point, somehow, there was a pause in their conversation, the kind of pregnant pause that can't be ignored, that demands a reaction of some kind.

That was the moment when Martin should have yawned, stretched and said it was time for him to get going. And then he should have put on his shoes and coat and left.

Instead, he kissed her.

Jenny had been happy to set the scene – late night, intimate tête-à-tête, inebriation – and maintain it until his choices became rather limited, but she would never have taken the final step. And wasn't it inevitable anyway? Hadn't the course of events been set in motion the moment he sat down next to her in film class? When they went out for a smoke together during the breaks? Always just the two of them. Which wasn't too surprising, since everyone else in the class was boring or dating each other and only taking film class so they could sit in the back of the dark room and make out while *Seven Samurai* played.

She put her wine glass down and wrapped her arms around his neck. And just like how the chords in a song follow an internal logic, an inescapable progression that your entire being responds to and that is repeated with minute alterations time and again in different songs, the rest inevitably followed.

"I suppose it was just a matter of time," Gustav commented, peering at him over the top of his canvas.

"Was it, though? Because I've actually given that some thought. I'm thinking, you know, that maybe it wasn't the smartest move…"

"I'm sure it wasn't."

"…but that still, sort of… not predestined, but unavoidable. And if that's true, then why not now? Right? Maybe it was just as well. I suppose I should call her. She hasn't called me." He sighed. "Could you toss me my cigarettes, please?"

Gustav got up, set an ashtray down on a stool next to the sofa, and put Martin's cigarettes and a lighter on his chest. Then he returned to his easel, studying his painting with a frown.

"All right," he said. "We have to keep going while there's still light."

Martin had been told to try to look straight ahead so he couldn't see Gustav, only the window and through it the tops of a few trees and a large swathe of sky. He pulled out a cigarette, put it between his lips and lit it. This was something he hadn't known about when he first took up smoking: the pleasure of the coarse smoke, the feeling that at least something was right in the world.

"It's not like she's unattractive," he said, exhaling. "I don't know how I didn't see it at first. But she has the kind of appearance that takes a while to grow on you. Not an obvious knockout. And she dresses like a bloke."

"You're so shallow."

"These things matter. You don't think about things like that? Sure, it's what's inside that counts, blah, blah, blah. But any girl I'm dating still has to be good-looking."

"Lie still."

"Smart, too, I suppose. Remember that girl at Schillerska? I almost died from intellectual tedium."

"Not everyone can rise to your stratospheric heights."

"Oh, come on, she was pretty gormless."

Gustav mixed paints on his palette.

Martin unsuccessfully tried to blow a smoke ring. "Do you think men and women can be friends?" he said after a while. "I mean, have a strictly platonic relationship?"

"I suppose."

"Because clearly Jenny and I *couldn't*. It's weird. It's not like I planned it. It just happened. Still, I reckon it supports the hypothesis that 'men and women can't be friends'. It would have been different if I'd gone into it with ulterior motives, but I swear I really just wanted to talk about Scorsese."

"Hmm."

"And then something like this happens."

Silence.

"It would be great if I could fall in love with her. I don't even know if I believe in love, though. I don't even bloody know if I've been *in love*. I thought I was, you know, with Yvonne? But I was just lying to myself. *Mauvais foi.* I always figured love would be something irrefutable – I mean, *truly* irrefutable. You don't know why, but you know this is it, this is the one, and maybe there's all kinds of obstacles or whatever, but there's nothing you can do. Because it's not a rational process, it's something you can't control, though it would obviously be very convenient if you could… do you know what I mean?"

"Oh yes," Gustav replied darkly.

"Seriously, Gustav: you have to let that thing with the French girl go. You can't mope about forever. Who stands to gain from a thousand years of celibacy?" He threw an empty cigarette packet at Gustav. "Not you, not her."

The French girl was what Martin called her, because Gustav refused to say anything about the person he'd apparently met during his family's annual trip to France. When he got back, he was dejected and miserable for weeks, and it took an inordinate amount of coaxing to finally get him to admit that he'd had a bit of a love affair over the summer. "So what's her *name?*" Martin had demanded to know, but Gustav had just changed the subject. It was in Nice, was the only thing he said. And it was over. At first, Martin had suffered with his friend, who was so obviously having a bad time of it, but then sympathy gradually gave way to anger. "How long were you going to keep it from me, anyway?" he'd snapped. "I'm your best friend. You're supposed to bloody well *tell* me things like this, don't you get that? You can't just go around sulking and acting incomprehensible."

And since Gustav kept mum about the mysterious person who was the cause of his protracted anguish, Martin had started to talk instead. He'd christened Gustav's paramour "the French girl" and knew the scene of their little holiday drama was Nice. Perhaps she had abandoned The Impoverished Artist for some smarmy gambler, like something out of a Wallace novel. Perhaps her upper-class family had refused to let her stay in town when it was time for their yacht to move on, and while the boat glided off towards the open sea, she stood by the railing in a bitter-sweet farewell, watching Gustav, dressed all in black, growing smaller and smaller on the pier.

"There's a lighthouse by the inlet," Gustav said, "but I don't know if you could really call it a *pier…*"

Perhaps, Martin went on, she'd said she'd write. Perhaps she'd put the note with Gustav's address in the pocket of her dress. Perhaps they'd walked along that pier at dusk and—

"I'm telling you, there's no pier. Can you just drop it, please."

But with Gustav having had a fling for once, Martin was determined to make the most of it, as though it would somehow even the score. It was, he realised in a murky and half-baked way, a question of balance. He always had things to tell Gustav about Yvonne, Jenny Halling, or the girl from Schillerska. And what did Gustav have? He talked about hogs-hair paintbrushes, how to mix oil paints, the importance of varnish, and whatever else the art teacher had showed him after class. In the long run, that kind of disparity was bound to upset their dynamic.

Gustav said nothing now either, and Martin hadn't expected him to. The silence that fell between them wasn't really awkward, it was necessary to steer the conversation back to a neutral track now that Martin had brought up the French girl again. For a long while he stared at the treetops swaying in the wind outside the window, thinking about nothing at all.

"If you're not in love with Jenny it's probably not the best idea to date her," Gustav said after a pause.

"No. I suppose it isn't." Martin sighed. "I'll talk to her. But hey, how's that painting coming? I'm getting hungry."

Martin braced himself and had The Talk with Jenny. He was prepared for tears and recriminations, but she behaved completely rationally when he told her he thought it would be best if they just stayed friends. "Absolutely," she said and nodded. "Sure. Yes. So… see you Tuesday, right?"

Except then she was off sick and missed the last class, and Martin had to sit through the class choice (*Jaws*) without anyone to make snarky comments to. A few days later, he spotted her across the schoolyard, but she didn't hear him calling her: she seemed to be in a hurry. Nor did she turn up at Cinemateket that Saturday, even though they were screening a Tarkovsky. Afterwards, he went home instead of to Café Paley, where they used to sit and analyse the films they'd seen over coffee and Budapest pastries.

When he got home, he dialled half her number before hanging up.

4

EVEN THOUGH RAKEL BERG certainly didn't need more books, she had somehow ended up in a second-hand bookshop. It was a dark-blue March afternoon with icy streets and snowflakes swirling in the light spilling out through the windows. They melted on the shoulders of her coat while she weighed a book about fin-de-siècle Vienna in one hand and her phone and the half-finished text on its screen in the other.

Don't know if I feel like going to a party tonight, I'm tired and not up for

For some reason, she couldn't bring herself to finish and send it.

The alternative to going to Ellen's party was picking up pad thai on the way home, retreating to her sofa, downloading a Fassbinder film in an effort to sustain her German, and ending the evening with a few pages of *Beyond the Pleasure Principle* in the German original. Which would inevitably make her think about her mother, who had always insisted on reading in the original. "All kinds of things," Cecilia had said, squatting next to her daughter to help her put on rain clothes, "become warped and distorted in translation." Texts underwent almost imperceptible corruption. Readers had to keep a sharp lookout, apply critical thinking, and always, when possible, choose the original over the translation. It might seem remarkable for a translator to deliver such a sweeping dismissal of translation as a practice, and to a six-year-old of all people. But that was the kind of thing Cecilia Berg used to say, and Rakel could remember her mum frowning – whether at the inherent hopelessness of her profession or at the bright-red rain coat being slightly too big was impossible to know – and in one smooth motion standing back up.

So Rakel would struggle through a few pages of *Jenseits des Lustprinzips* from 1920, fall asleep, and wake up to a new day full of exactly the same things she'd done the day before, which was to say going to the library and writing an essay about Freud's theory about repetition compulsion and the so-called death drive. Which was what she'd done every day this week, and what she would be doing next week, broken up only by more or less vapid lectures about personality psychology.

Not to mention that Lovisa would be calling her within minutes. Rakel had no difficulty imagining how that call would go.

"What do you mean *not up for* it?" On her way someplace, on her bike even though it was snowing and icy out, with one hand on the handlebars and no helmet, naturally. Bottles of booze in her bicycle basket and her mitten dangling from her coat sleeve. Lovisa had lost countless mittens until she realised she could attach them to a piece of string and run that through her sleeves, like a toddler.

And Rakel would say she was tired and didn't have the energy.

"You just don't feel like it, though, right?"

"It's just that—"

"But Ellen's going to be upset if you don't come. And it *is* her twenty-fifth birthday."

When Lovisa had got to know Ellen the previous autumn, she'd done her best to create a Three Musketeers vibe characterised by good will and friendship. Her efforts had been doomed to fail, however, because it had always been the two of them, and two can't become three without friction. Rakel had instantly cast Ellen in the role of wily femme fatale with a film-noir aura; oil-black puddles of rain, neon lights and glowing cigarettes wherever she went, regardless of weather or time of day in the wider world. In a way, the real Ellen had turned out to be a disappointment. Her deliberately reserved air was a poor fit with her sweet face. She had a way of throwing terms like *paradigm shift*, *postmodern* and *hermeneutic interpretation* about like silver pennies for the poor. She changed her hair about once a month, spoke in dialect, and was in a tortured relationship with a guy referred to as The PhD Student. Rakel could never see what was so special about her. Maybe it was just that Ellen never said no to going to an underground nightclub in some warehouse on Hisingen, while Rakel stayed home and highlighted things in her coursebooks or ate ice cream and watched *The Bitter Tears of Petra von Kant*.

Rakel sighed, deleted the half-finished text, and paid for the book. Outside, an Arctic wind gusted along the street, finding its way through her coat and scarf.

*

Lovisa was waiting by the Vågmästareplatsen tram stop, leaning against the railing. The light from a street lamp spilled over her hair, dyed platinum blonde since time immemorial. It was still snowing.

"I swear I saw Alexander getting on the tram," was the first thing out of her mouth. She held her cigarette hand out to the side so she could hug Rakel without accidentally setting fire to her hair. "Have you heard from him? Is he back in town?"

"No idea."

"He can stay in Berlin forever as far as I'm concerned." Lovisa spotted the tulips Rakel had picked up at the supermarket. "Flowers! Genius. Didn't even occur to me. I bought her a bottle of booze."

Muffled party sounds could be heard as soon as they entered the building. Lovisa rang the doorbell, waited one second, then opened the door. The floor was full of shoes, the coat rack groaned under countless jackets and Ellen came prancing towards them with the happy little squeal of an overstimulated hostess. She embraced them both. Close up, Rakel could see each individual powder particle, the contours of acne scars underneath, the precise stroke of eyeliner, the hairpins holding her fifties hairdo in place. She flitted off to put the tulips in a vase and waved for them to follow her to the kitchen.

Rakel thought: I only have to stay for a bit.

"There's drama brewing again," Ellen said *sotto voce*, handing them each a wine glass. "I heard someone wrote to him. Like, an *actual* letter. Left it in his pigeonhole in the department and everything."

"So this is The PhD Student," Lovisa clarified. "He's been receiving love letters."

"Aha." As far as Rakel had been able to make out, the basic plot was that The PhD Student, indecisive about everything from his thesis topic to his relationship with his former student Ellen, blew so hot and cold even Lovisa looked a bit exhausted at the constant twists and turns.

"So now he's both paranoid and smug." Ellen sighed. "I think it's one of the young ones. They're fucking shameless."

After just two years in Gothenburg, Ellen had managed to acquire a social circle as big as anyone who had lived there their entire life. Rakel wondered how she did it. She suspected Ellen didn't like her but had no proof. "You're being unfair," Lovisa had told her several months earlier. "Why would she want to hang out with you if she didn't like you?" Because I'm a *useful acquaintance*, Rakel wanted to say, but she bit her tongue. Lovisa always pretended people were exaggerating. When they got to know each other in secondary school, no one had cared what anyone's parents did for a living. Only as an adult had Rakel discovered that in social contexts she often ended up playing the role of intermediary, opening doors to other, more interesting people – not always, but often enough to make her shift uncomfortably when people realised her mother was *the* Cecilia Berg and her father was the Berg in Berg & Andrén and, first and foremost since he was by far the most famous of the trio, that Gustav Becker the painter was her godfather.

They'd moved into the living room. There were about fifteen people in it already and the doorbell kept ringing. The party unfolded according to the standard house-party pattern. They were currently in the first phase, when people are still greeting new arrivals and conducting more or less civilised conversations with each other while balancing finger food on paper plates. Ellen was holding court to a semicircle of people nodding their agreement.

"You might have thought Norén's diaries would have been enough," she said. "But lo and behold, yet another man who can't resist indulging himself in no fewer than six volumes. I'm not saying it's not *good literature*. It's just that it's a classic example of literary male self-indulgence. Women who behave like that are censured and decried as self-absorbed. Anaïs Nin, am I right? Who reads Anaïs Nin's diary these days?"

"Nin should actually be considered a forerunner to Knausgård," put in one of Rakel's old course mates from the history department, a young man who dressed like an old man, complete with pipe and a burgeoning paunch. Rakel suspected his opinion was directly related to his interest in Ellen.

"Didn't Anaïs Nin sleep with her own dad?" Lovisa asked softly.

"Yes. And two of her therapists," Rakel replied.

"Is it a good book at least?"

"Not particularly. Knausgård's better."

Lovisa pulled a face – she never read anything longer than a hundred and fifty pages – and when she spotted a friend moving towards the balcony, she ran after her to bum a cigarette. Rakel tugged on the seam of her dress, which kept twisting, let her hair down and put it back up, discovered a hole on the toe of her tights and went over to top up her wine glass to have something to do. She felt out of place and the fact that she wasn't, sociologically speaking, only made it worse. In the kitchen, she ended up standing next to a vaguely familiar blonde girl and tried to think of something to say, but she seemed to have forgotten how to talk to strangers. The blonde came to her rescue. "You're studying psychology, too, right?" Her voice was deep and resonant, completely at odds with her angular blonde appearance. A memory surfaced in Rakel's brain: the girl was in the class that had arranged the first party of the year, where she'd played the old piano in the atrium together with a jazz quartet. The piano was usually only used by histrionic people who wanted attention at any cost, even if that attention consisted of the head of the clinical practice coming down to tell them to stop because they could hear it all the way up in the therapy rooms. Hearing this girl play, Rakel had known instantly that *she* would never play chopsticks for a laugh during the lunch break. She was actually good.

"That's right," Rakel said. The pianist's dignified approach to her own talent made her eager to impress in turn. From her dad she'd learned that people feel flattered when you use their names. Martin didn't really have a head for things like that, so he overcompensated by muttering all kinds of details under his breath before meetings. Then, when the person in question showed up, he instantly shifted gears and became all big smiles, open arms and jovial handshakes. He'd exclaim, as if it was the most natural thing in the world: "*Harald*" – or whatever – "long time no see!" and so on. Rakel searched her memories from the party – fuzzy since they'd sold gin and tonics with a lot of gin in them for twenty kronor a glass – and said: "You're Julia, right?"

Julia lit up, surprised. They spent a long time talking about their lecturers, eccentric and/or mentally deranged course mates, the researcher who according to rumour was doing parapsychological experiments in the old rat lab, the insufficient number of microwave ovens, and that all the art in the department seemed to have been chosen to allude to either sex or death. Then Ellen wedged herself between them.

"Sorry to interrupt," she said. "Rakel, I have a friend who's writing an essay in art history, it's about Ola Billgren and Gustav Becker. So I told him you know him and he's dying to talk to you."

As if on cue, a young man joined them and was introduced at length; his name was apparently Aron. Julia mumbled: "See you," and slipped away. Rakel was trapped.

Aron the art historian distinguished himself by having a lot of hair – a big beard, a flowing fringe – while at the same time giving the impression of being impeccably neat and tidy. His shirt was the same shade of blue as an early summer morning. After shaking her hand with cool marble fingers, he described his MA dissertation in excruciating detail, the Swedish art scene over the past few decades, realism in general and hyperrealism in particular. Perhaps, Rakel mused while he rambled on, this was the latest manoeuvre in the fun game known as Set Rakel Up? Preferably with someone with at least three university degrees and a tendency to pepper his conversations with references to Great Men. Step one: an intellectual conversation in a casual environment. Step two: he finds a pretext to get her number that in no way hints at any intentions beyond the platonic – that he wants to talk more about Lacan, for instance. After just a few too many days, he calls as if in passing, asking if she wants to "go for a drink" at Kino. Step three never happened, because by then, Rakel had wriggled out of anything that might be construed as a commitment, usually by not answering the guy's texts and walking in the opposite direction whenever she saw him at the library.

"On closer inspection, I feel like I've seen you before," Aron said, studying her with a frown, as though she were a controversial but interesting piece of art.

Only a complete idiot could ignore the obvious fact that Rakel featured in any number of Gustav's paintings. "The Antibes Suite?" she said. "I'm the child. And the big one from Berlin? That's me in the ushanka, standing in the street. Et cetera."

Aron didn't seem to realise he'd shot himself in the foot. "So what's he like?" he said, leaning in closer. "As a person?"

Rakel thought about Gustav's Berlin visits. Granted, at least one time he'd been there for an exhibition – he was showcased at a posh gallery she'd never felt brave enough to go to on her own – but usually he just mumbled something about happening to be in the area. He took her out to restaurants, nagged her about being too thin, ordered oysters without asking if she liked them and without eating any himself. Rakel squeezed lemon onto one, took a deep breath and swallowed. "The art world," Gustav said while she tried not to gag, "is as spiritually impoverished and sensationalist as everything else in this damn century."

Now, Rakel sipped her wine, mentally casting about for an escape route. "A bit withdrawn, I guess," she said. She caught a glimpse of Lovisa's platinum-blonde mop of hair pushing towards them through the crowd. Whether Lovisa had her course set for the boxed wine on the kitchen counter or intuitively sensed Rakel's desperation was impossible to say. Either way, she tumbled into the conversation. "Ah, you're discussing The Great Artist!" she exclaimed while she reached over Rakel to top up her glass, slopped wine on her dress in the process, set them all to work trying to locate a kitchen towel, left the drying to Rakel, and entangled herself in a confession about how she liked to exploit that "unique connection to the cultural elite" to pick up guys.

"You know what I mean," she said to Aron, a smile spreading across her elfin face. "You meet some poser art guy who wants to drink red wine and show you a film Salvador Dalí and his mates shot while drunk, and you take the opportunity to casually mention Gustav Becker. You have no *idea*, whatever your name is – Aron? – you have no *idea*, Aron, how effective that is."

"Okay…" Aron said.

"It doesn't *matter* that they've spent all that time in the art history department trying to do away with, what's it called…?" She gesticulated impatiently.

"Figurative art?" Aron supplied.

"Exactly," Lovisa said, even though Aron could probably have said anything. "They might have spent their most recent course credits banging on about figurative art being crap. When your average art guy is confronted with celebrity, he's still starstruck."

Without further ado, she pushed her wine glass into Aron's hand and pulled a can of snus from her back pocket. A friend had given her ten cans and economically minded as she was, she insisted on finishing it all. She pressed a pinch of it into a small ball and solemnly pushed it up under her lip. "Want some?" she said. Aron, who seemed like the kind of person who never leaves a hair in the shower or a dirty sock on the floor, shook his head.

"Rakel would obviously never do something like that," Lovisa said. "Would you, Rakel?"

"Oh no, definitely not."

"You're very modest." Lovisa put an arm around her shoulders.

"Extremely modest, if I do say so myself."

"It's the rest of us who employ dubious tactics."

"The common people," Rakel added. "The *hoi polloi*."

"But unlike the rest of us," Lovisa said to Aron, "Rakel has a lot to live up to on her mother's side, too."

Confusion and irritation fought for the upper hand on Aron's face. "Pardon?"

"You have to know your stuff, Aron, *know your stuff.*" Lovisa snatched her wine glass back. "My god. I thought you were writing your dissertation on Gustav Becker? You really should know who Cecilia Berg is."

"Of course. The historian. There are more than thirty portraits of her in Becker's catalogue…"

Maybe, Rakel thought, he'd talked about his dissertation to so many people the phrases just dribbled out of him, neatly packaged, without any thought to his audience. Or maybe he'd spent his whole life being a good student and now found himself in a strange pop-quiz mode, triggered by Lovisa's schoolmistressy attitude. Rakel looked down at her glass. Lovisa used her tongue to poke at her snus. Eventually, it seemed to dawn on Aron the art historian that he didn't need to tell Cecilia Berg's daughter how many portraits there were of Cecilia Berg. He trailed off, ran a hand through his neat hair. A signet ring flashed on one of his fingers.

"There was an essay by her in the last issue of *Glänta*…" he said uncertainly.

Lovisa nodded.

"An old text. From 1995, I think," Aron went on.

"'96," Rakel corrected him.

"Actually, I think it was—"

"'96," Rakel repeated.

"Whatever happened to her?" By now, Aron's eyes were darting nervously this way and that. He was shifting his weight from one foot to the other.

"She disappeared," Lovisa said.

"What?" For the first time, he looked straight at her.

"She scarpered fifteen years ago and never came back. No one knows where she went."

"Seriously?" Maybe he thought they were having him on, because he didn't adopt the shocked/sympathetic expression any mention of

Cecilia's disappearance usually provoked. Instead, he raised his eyebrows in mild disbelief and fingered his ring. "Listen, I actually have to… Rakel, it was nice to meet you. Let's be in touch, yeah?" He slunk off.

"Prick," Lovisa muttered as soon as he was out of earshot.

"I wasn't coming on to him or anything," Rakel said, realising she had stuck her hands up like a gangster in a Lucky Luke comic.

"I should certainly hope not. He must spend at least an hour every day on that beard." Lovisa sighed and shook her head. "Ellen knows a lot of weird people. Hey, don't you think it's 'Happy Birthday' time?" She raised her voice to make herself heard over the din in the kitchen. "All right, everybody, let's sing for the birthday girl. Where is she? Has anyone seen her? Could we maybe send a scouting party out to the balcony?"

5

Rakel fumbled about for her alarm clock. Quarter past nine. She groaned and pulled the pillow over her head. For a long while she lay still, eyes closed, waiting for the soft weight presaging sleep, but unfortunately her brain was busy reconstructing the events of the night before. Someone had made whisky cocktails. Then Lovisa had turned the music up until even Ellen would have told her off, if it weren't for the fact that Ellen was sitting on the balcony, crying over The PhD Student's lack of declarations of love. And Rakel, accidentally caught out there with her, had listened to the countless ins and outs of his irresolute courtship until Ellen blew her nose and announced that they were going to dance, and then they'd gone back into the living room where Lovisa was just putting on Gloria Estefan. Ellen dried her tears while dancing violently to "Conga".

Quarter to ten. Rakel pulled herself up into a sitting position and waited for signs of potential nausea. Apparently, she had dodged the worst of the hangover.

She pulled up her blind with a sharp tug. The sky was bright blue and when she staggered in the direction of the bathroom, she discovered cruel sunlight had filled her whole flat.

In the winter months, when dawn arrived after Rakel went to university and dusk fell long before she left the library, lack of natural light had concealed the increasingly desperate state of her home. On this Sunday morning, however, everything was pitilessly illuminated. Washing-up filled the sink to the brim, occupied the greater part of the kitchen counter, and had established a colony on the kitchen table. A stack of old morning papers three feet tall looked like a very compact fort. The hob was caked in the dried remnants of historic battles. If she retreated to the living room, she would just be confronted with general chaos and big dust bunnies along every wall. Her bookcase had become an overflowing refugee camp that didn't have nearly enough room for everyone in it. There were still traces of previous attempts at *Ordnung und Disziplin* – a hint at a separation of fiction, non-fiction and biographies, a passing nod to alphabetisation – but the constant influx of new titles had long since broken the system's back, and now books were wedged into any space they could physically fit.

The minuscule one-bed flat on the fourth floor could generously be said to have a view of no fewer than two cemeteries. From the kitchen, you could glimpse the clutter of ancient headstones and domed chapels of the Jewish burial ground. Stampen Cemetery spread out beneath the bedroom window, vast and leafy, with a gate topped by a sign that read REMEMBER DEATH. It was an appropriate exhortation to all the secondary-school students who passed it daily on their way to Göteborgs Högre Samskola (stupid brats with no concept of the finite nature of life), and for Rakel an opportunity to compulsively translate the phrase into the Latin. *Memento mori*, she thought to herself every time the tram clattered past the cemetery.

Now she fetched the morning paper from the hallway floor where it lay on top of a pile of envelopes. She found half a packet of bacon that she fried in the last clean pan with an egg and an overripe tomato. The bread was slightly too old but tasted okay toasted. She drank coffee and perused the arts section. The minute hand on the clock was inching towards half past ten. Her body was already itching, and it was only going to get worse. The day spread out before her the way most Sundays did, an endless plain of unbroken time. People would spend the day walking around the park, unwrapping scarfs and pulling off hats, marvelling at snowdrops, sitting by a south-facing wall with eyes closed, faces turned to the newly sprung sun, and then wander back home with glowing cheeks through a blue and pink dusk sprinkled with pale stars.

Rakel decided to go to the library. She got ready with practised efficiency, even though she wasn't really in a hurry. She showered. She brushed her hair and put it up in a ponytail. She didn't bother with make-up. She looked for her warmest sweater and finally found it in the overflowing newspaper rack next to the sofa. She packed up her laptop and books. She checked the thermometer in the kitchen window and discovered it was still cold enough for a winter coat after all. She tied her shoes. Next to the pile of unopened envelopes on the hallway rug she spotted the German novel her father had tasked her with reading and shoved that in her backpack, too. At least it was short. She could flip through it for the sake of having done so and then let him know she really didn't have time. All face-to-face attempts at protest would just end in her acquiescing.

*

The arts and humanities departments were clustered around the Lily Pond, mostly in the main building that dated from the eighties — nothing but brick, linoleum-wrapped hallways and lecture halls indistinguishable from a regular secondary school classroom. Back when Rakel was new, she'd roamed the halls looking for her mother's old office. Memory and reality turned out to be poorly matched and she never did manage to locate the room that was etched into her disjointed memories, as clear as they were fleeting. She searched the signs for the name of the professor who had supervised Cecilia's thesis but discovered that he had retired. She found Cecilia's books in the stacks, bound in the oxblood or chestnut of the university press with the author's name and the title in sans serif fonts. Judging from the state of them, they were still regularly checked out.

In the five years since she graduated from upper secondary school, Rakel had never not been enrolled at the university, because tertiary education seemed to be what she was made for. She had always liked theories: the way they arranged chaotic reality into manageable categories, using abstract concepts to pry open a seemingly petrified world. But sooner or later, you reached the limit of theorising. At some point, theories became insufficient and fell short, so Rakel left the territory of the mind, robbed of everything that had once drawn her to it. After upper secondary school, she'd considered studying maths because the universe of numbers seemed infinite and infallible (and because she'd seen *A Beautiful Mind* and pictured herself surrounded by dark wood panelling, dressed in bottle-green corduroy, nervously chain-smoking and scribbling formulae in white marker on the windows during fits of inspiration). A career in maths was never really on the cards for her, however – she'd barely managed to figure out how to use a graphing calculator in upper secondary – and instead Rakel began her erratic journey through the humanities. She'd done two terms of intellectual history ("Ah – you're *Cecilia's* daughter"), two sleepy evening courses of Latin, several terms of literature and German, first in Gothenburg and then in Berlin. She'd had serious plans to study archaeology when her dad put his foot down ("And how are you going to get a job afterwards, Indiana Jones?"). Instead, she'd applied to the psychology programme. After all, the human psyche seemed like an amalgam of regularity within an infinitely variable space and broken shards of a lost past.

"Psychologist?" Martin had said as though she'd announced she was going to join the circus and spend her days juggling torches. "Why ever would you want to do that? And how are you going to find an outlet for your literary inclinations?" he wanted to know. "Writing reports? Notes for patient files? 'Patient unruly during rounds'? Are you sure you don't want to keep doing history? Or Latin?"

"*Amor fati*," Rakel said, but her father hadn't read Nietzsche since the eighties. He pretended not to have heard.

On this Sunday in March, the library was empty and quiet. Rakel usually went for a seat in the reading room if she was okay with running into someone she knew and one of the out-of-the-way tables in the stacks if she wasn't. Today, she was heading towards the stacks when she passed a deflated figure slumped on a stool among the shelves with a large pile of books in his lap. It took her a few seconds to identify him.

"Emanuel?"

Emanuel Wikner gave a start and looked up at her, his bottom lip wet with saliva. The transition from confusion to recognition took so long Rakel had time to worry he didn't know who she was. That was silly – they'd met as recently as Christmas. But she should have said *Uncle* Emanuel to be on the safe side.

"Rakel!" he said finally. "Dearest Rakel. Imagine seeing you here. On a day like this." Huffing, he got to his feet to give her a hug.

In the past few years, it had become increasingly difficult to guess Emanuel Wikner's age. He was ten years younger than Rakel's mother, and in the past he'd occupied a strange in-between state – not quite grown-up, definitely not a child. Now, his face had lost its sharpness and vigilance. His blond curls formed an ever-thinning wreath around his bald pate. His body, once lanky and slender like his brother's and sisters', was shapeless, as though its contours were redrawn from day to day. He was dressed in various shades of beige and would have given a washed-out impression if it weren't for a deep-red silk scarf, which he wore draped around his neck like a Roman emperor.

"What are you reading?" she asked.

"Oh, nothing, nothing. The arrival of spring always makes me think about that thesis." He heaved his stack of books onto a nearby trolley. It was, Rakel noticed, mostly R.D. Laing and Wilhelm Reich, but also *The Tibetan Book of the Dead*. "Released from death's hopeless grasp, one starts to look to the future. It's a dangerous time of year. Ice melting and whatnot. If you catch me committing to any kind of long-term project, be a dear and remind me I would feel like a king for a few weeks and then spend the rest of the time succumbing to anxiety. And not just about the conditions of creativity, but anxiety about having to think these surely less-than-interesting thoughts through to the end."

"Deal," Rakel said. She couldn't remember Emanuel ever coming close to completing a PhD, or, if so, in what subject it would have been. He'd started medical school at some point long ago, and he'd got into photography after that. His mum had built him a darkroom and, as far as Rakel could recall, he'd mostly taken extreme close-ups of the house. But what was this about a thesis?

"It seems spring has sprung out there," her uncle said. "Are you really going to spend the day cooped up in here?"

She held up her old copy of *Jenseits des Lustprinzips* as an alibi. "For uni."

"Well, well, well! The great Sigmund! I'm glad to see you're getting a proper education. You need all the ammunition you can get. Let me tell you something: *people out there are crazy*. But surely you have time for a quick coffee? You'd be making your old uncle very happy."

Rakel had no choice but to go with him to the café, allow him to buy her a paper cup of coffee and a sugary apple doughnut – since he so clearly wanted one himself – and then follow him into the sharp sunshine. The pond was still frozen, the ice puckered by last year's water lilies. The twisting branches of the rhododendrons were bare down by the roots and the trunks of the giant oak trees were covered with moss. The catkins on the hazels were turning yellow. On the other side of the pond was a small playground; children's voices rose towards the sky, clear and chime-like, divorced from their actual words.

Emanuel claimed he had a favourite bench with an unbeatable location by the water. There were half a dozen benches and Rakel for her part couldn't see any real difference between them, but she nevertheless heard herself say: "Of course, lovely bench, very nice."

"God knows," said Emanuel, who during his uninterrupted rush of words had circled back to his potential thesis, "that no one would have been happier if I'd done something with all those humanities courses than dear old Mum. She calls incessantly, trying to get me to move back up to Stockholm. Trying to lure me with my own damn wing in that swanky flat. I've explained that I'm in the middle of psychoanalysis and can't just take off and she started hinting at a possible future cessation of the financial means I need to fund my divan existence. So to speak."

"Ah," Rakel said.

"Luckily, my therapist is a very wise woman who put her foot down and said, in so many words, that it would affect my individuation issues negatively if I were to regress now by returning to my mother's bosom. I've read up on this, you see, and I have to say there's an inordinate amount of focus on the oedipal, that is to say the triangular relationship, that is to say the one between oneself, one's object of desire and that other person, that is to say the father, or maybe we should call him The Father. The question of whether the individual even is an individual always ends up being overlooked."

"Sure," Rakel said, "the Oedipus Complex is central to Freudian theory…" And in the modern conscience a trivialised formula that people associate with pretty much all twentieth century psychological theory building, she finished inwardly and took a big bite of her apple doughnut to keep herself from speaking it out loud. *He wanted to kill his dad and sleep with his mum,* as though the whole thing were an Agatha Christie novel with the psychiatrist cast in the role of detective, bent on finding the origin of the neurotic symptom; in the final scene, they would all be gathered together – Mum, Dad, Little Hans, the nanny, Herr K., Frau K. and the disciple C.G. Jung wheezing in a corner – while Dr Freud unpicked the strands of the hopelessly entangled family romance.

"I'm glad you know your way around these things. I actually met someone who kept telling me I had to *breathe right* and make all kinds of lists? It was just do, do, do. When the thinking is what we need to get at. That is to say, not the actual thoughts, but rather their shape and structure. On the other hand, it doesn't surprise me, Rakel. You've always had a great head on your shoulders. I suppose you take after your mother. Be grateful for that. You know, Cecilia's the intelligent one of the four of us. Sad but true. I wish I could say it's me. Peter's a master of imitation and Vera gets by okay on her looks and general charm. Aren't you going to finish your doughnut? Oh no, thank you, but I couldn't – okay, okay, since you insist. *Mm*. Magnificent patisserie. What time is it, by the way?"

"Half past eleven."

"Half past eleven! I have to run."

He jogged away with his coat flapping in the wind. Rakel stayed on the bench and finished her coffee. The sun gently lay its hands on her head, her shoulders.

6

After carrying around the novel her dad had forced on her for a week, Rakel sat down in Café Cigar, hoping the geographical proximity to the publishing company would whip up enough of a sense of obligation to make her get started. The reading itself wasn't the problem. Unlike a lot of other people, she'd spent her time in Berlin learning the language properly. The problem was Martin's sudden and therefore suspicious enthusiasm. When she chose German in sixth grade, he'd said: "Sure. All right. Absolutely. A strategic choice." When she decided to do a French elective in upper secondary, on the other hand, he'd dug out his favourite French novels, telling her in detail about when he translated Marguerite Duras back in the olden days, and gave her a stack of VHS tapes with New Wave classics. Rakel only watched *The 400 Blows* before a cassette got stuck in their ancient VCR. Then Martin bought it on DVD instead and discovered that you could stimulate language learning by turning off the subtitles, though at that time, Rakel had only done one term and was still at a stage dominated by sentences like *Je m'appelle Rachel* and *J'habite à Gothenburg*, and consequently didn't understand a word of Godard's dialogue.

But whenever there was something that could draw her into the orbit of the publishing company, it was a different story, and now her language skills were suddenly very important. Nothing seemed to make her father happier than when she did a reader's report. He claimed he valued her opinions, but sometimes Rakel couldn't help but wonder if the primary purpose wasn't to tie her to Berg & Andrén.

She looked at the novel. One good thing about it was that it was only around two hundred pages long. Another that it was handsomely made. Unfortunately, the title was completely uninteresting: *Ein Jahr der Liebe*. "Love" was a hopeless word to put in a title. A hopeless word, period. Overused to the point of having practically lost all meaning, a shadow of what it had once been.

Instead of opening the book, she gazed out across the square. Sitting in the window of Café Cigar, she always saw people from her past sooner or later. That was as true today as any other day: Ellen was hurrying towards the tram stop, her giant briefcase bouncing against her hip. A guy Lovisa had once pulled rode past on a lightweight bike with white tyres and no brakes. There went an old classmate who was rumoured to have tattooed "414" across his heart without taking his nipple into account, with the consequence that it protruded unappealingly from the last digit. And now Max Schreiber, an old friend of her mother's, plodded by, head bowed. He'd always turned up in Cecilia's office and Rakel had been scared of him until he'd given her an orange and made up a silly story she'd pretended to be too old for. Apparently, he'd left academia to practise psychology: his name was sometimes mentioned in class. Maybe, Rakel mused, she could use that fact in one of the recurring discussions about her Professional Future her dad insisted on having with her? Martin's latest angle was that a degree in psychology would be good for the company because sensitive authors had to be guided through the various stages of writing with tact and a gentle hand. He seemed to equate working clinically with being employed at a mental institution. But he did like Max.

Rakel forced herself to focus on the task at hand. The novel seemed to be about a man who had been dumped and didn't understand why.

A few pages in, she pulled out her phone to look up a word she didn't know but found herself googling the author instead. The internet informed her Philip Franke was forty-three years old, looked relatively good in his black-and-white press photographs, and had written three relatively obscure novels before *Ein Jahr*, which had recently been nominated for a literature prize. So it must not be entirely awful.

She read a few more paragraphs and underlined a few expressions she didn't understand, but her chest was starting to feel tight, her feet were tingling and the sounds around her had become very sharp: the hissing and clattering of the coffee machine, the live commentary on the TV above the door showing horse racing, a loud woman at the counter – she couldn't think and every sentence she read dissolved into nothing.

Rakel shut the book and resumed staring out of the window. A whole afternoon lay ahead, and it had to be spent one way or another. She could go to the library. The walk up to the main university library would at least kill thirty minutes or so. But she'd been to the library every day since… she actually couldn't remember a day when she hadn't been to the library. And if you're not going to the library, Rakel Berg? Then where do you go?

On a whim, she texted Martin to ask if she could borrow the car. She could drive out to the summer house. Not that she had any reason to – it would be closed for the winter – but it was something different, a break from the days that rolled by, one after the other with minimal variation, week in and week out. Get up in the morning. Shower. Get dressed. Have breakfast. Take the tram to uni. Lectures between nine and twelve. Queue to use the microwaves. Come up with an excuse to go to the main library instead of the social science library with everyone else. Talk to her classmates when there was no avoiding it. Everyone was so keen to talk to everyone else. They became friends. They threw parties. They went to the pub. They met up at each other's houses to study for exams, would Rakel want to join them? Fucking psychology students, tilting their heads to the side with a slight frown, even though they were only a few terms in and still very far from having patients of their own. *Wow*, they said when Cecilia came up, because she always did, sooner or later, especially among people whose favourite pastime seemed to be to analyse their feelings, thoughts and experiences, in other words every aspect of their inner workings that could be brought out for observation. In the long run, it was impossible to hide the fact that her mother had one day decided to leave her children and her husband, to take off and never come back.

I understand, they said. But what was it they understood? Rakel wasn't sure. And she couldn't ask without coming across as an imbecile. Did they feel like she was traumatised? That this Betrayal had Damaged Her, possibly irreversibly? That she should start seeing a therapist immediately? What was it, Rakel thought, that generated all this warm, sympathetic understanding?

One thing had become clear to her early in life, and that was that there was a difference between absent mothers and absent fathers. A father who left was easy to understand. If a father walked out on his family, he was Dean Moriarty, on the road in a cult classic from the 1950s. He could get high with Allen Ginsberg and take life one day at a time. He could have adventures. He could find another woman and have a few children with her until restlessness rushed through his veins and he had to leave again. Some men were more or less expected to behave that way. The women would yell and slam doors, but there was always someone new who thought she would be the one to make everything right and Reform Him. Which was an impossible equation, because Dean Moriarty's appeal lay in the fact that he was *never going to stay*. Dean Moriarty wouldn't be Dean Moriarty if he didn't get an itch to take off after being sober for a while, knocking up his best girl and seeing the slow, drawn-out death known as Family Life spread out like a desert before him.

Missing fathers were legion. Ne'er-do-wells who drank too much. Artistic types who valued freedom above everything else. Casanovas who couldn't bring themselves to commit. Tortured men driven away by their own demons. You could reproach them for their irresponsibility, but it wasn't incomprehensible. A mother who abandoned her family was *something else entirely*. Once Rakel caught on to this, she felt deceived, as though she'd been running around an open field and suddenly one day she hit on a fence. She'd been eleven or twelve when it happened. That Cecilia had disappeared was known among their friends and in school and it was still recent enough that it was discussed and diffidently enquired about. It was always the same: "How could she leave her children?" Even though the grown-ups rarely said anything directly to Rakel, she gradually became aware that question was always humming and buzzing in the background, unanswered and unresolved, and it bothered her. Why couldn't Cecilia simply be a total prick who got sick of things one day and moved on? From a monotonous, boring life to one that seemed freer and more fun? Why couldn't she be someone who simply couldn't *bear* to stay and take the consequence – divorce, new flat, joint custody? Someone who simply *hadn't felt like* taking responsibility for the situation? Granted, Rakel didn't think that was the case; she had trouble imagining her mother as the Moriarty type, even though she would have preferred a Moriarty type over complete unfathomableness. But – and this was what irked Rakel – most people who had opinions about her mother's disappearance *hadn't known Cecilia Berg*. In other words, *they had no right to say anything* about whether it was in line with Cecilia's character to suddenly point her car towards the sunset and drive off in a spray of gravel with a Springsteen cassette blaring through the speakers. They couldn't just *assume* her actions had anything to with some unspecified mental instability. People were surprisingly stupid. They put on that concerned therapist's frown and you could practically see things grinding into gear in their heads: poor child, a mother like that, what was wrong with her, how *could* she? Teachers, friends, parents, one of Martin's fleeting girlfriends who had been looking to make an ally of sixteen-year-old Rakel.

"But how could she leave her children?" the girlfriend had exclaimed during dinner one night, completely oblivious to Martin shaking his head and making a time-out gesture.

"There are many answers to that question," Rakel had replied, putting her cutlery down. She was old enough to know that words trumped emotion and that if you possessed the words, you could conquer everything else, including other people, discussions and ideas. In reality, she told her father's girlfriend, it wasn't so much about the answers as about the *questions*. People focused too much on the answers. As though they would solve anything. The only way to move forward was through a new question, and each question led to another question, or contained within it a number of subquestions, and then you had to ask questions about the questions themselves. The question "How could she leave her children?" required many follow-up questions. It was by no means unproblematic. It was, for example, a question asked in a patriarchal society and against a background of various things that were taken for granted. Such as what? Probably that women had stronger emotional ties to their children than men. What evidence did the girlfriend have to back that up? Were we talking nature or nurture? Nature: was there a particular gene? Was it a proven fact or a hypothesis? And did genes explain everything? Nurture: if society is to blame for making women seem more strongly tied to their children than men and therefore less inclined to leave them and drive off to the sound of *Born to Run*, then it was a social construct, and if the feeling was a construct, it was possible to imagine it being deconstructed and maybe recast in a different mould. Given all these endless questions, each prompted by the one before, what, Rakel asked, could a person ever hope to understand?

That way, she didn't have to think about the simple question at the heart of it all: how can anyone leave someone they love?

The bell above the door tinkled and one of the louder regulars entered, dragging along a dog and a foldable shopping trolley. Rakel began to gather up her things. Staying here was not an option. She was going to borrow the car and head out to the country.

*

When their old Volvo finally gave up the ghost, Martin bought a new V70, even though he had no real use for the large boot or really the car itself, for that matter. He cycled everywhere in town, without a helmet, his briefcase on the cargo rack, and in the winter he took the tram or walked. But he had the idea that a family needs a car, even if they only use it for fun outings, and he'd started to badger Rakel about learning to drive the moment she turned sixteen.

Turning the key in the ignition made punk band Imperiet roar out of the speakers. Rakel turned the stereo off, checked her seat belt, and slowly reversed out into the street.

Her grandparents owned a summer house less than an hour outside town. It was hardly practical to have what was essentially a dilapidated old manor house so far from where they lived – they had long since moved to Stockholm – but it was a kind of eccentricity typical of the Wikner family. As far as Rakel knew, it had only been their permanent residence for a year or two before her grandfather Lars had hit upon some new idea that had to be realised immediately, which meant he quit his research job at Sahlgrenska Hospital and moved the whole family up to Stockholm. Only Cecilia stayed. They'd kept the house as the setting for holiday get-togethers and summer vacations. The idea was for Emanuel, the only one of the siblings who had moved back to Gothenburg, to "keep an eye" on it, but Rakel wasn't sure he even owned a car.

She drove below the speed limit on the motorway, the subsequent B-road, and finally the potholed gravel road along which the car bumped and jostled for at least fifteen minutes. The house was located in an isolated spot by a lake, surrounded by an ample garden and, beyond that, forest. It was a large, two-storey wooden villa with a tall stone foundation and rows of mullioned windows. The red tile roof slanted past attic windows and chimneys. In the front and back were generous verandas with rows of wooden columns, wreathed in withered honeysuckle. During the latter part of Rakel's childhood, her dad would drop Elis and her out here for the summer. He'd come out for the weekends and spend most of his time walking in circles on the lawn, talking into a brick of an Ericsson mobile sturdy enough to withstand just about anything, even Rakel hurling it against the floor.

"We've hit a snag with the printers," he'd say, resignedly, as though this were just the most recent outrage in a long and complicated relationship everyone knew was ultimately doomed. And inevitably, he went back into town, sometimes as soon as they had finished lunch on Sunday. "I run a *business*, sweetheart," he'd say when she complained. "If I don't work, no one else does either."

Now the driveway was deserted, and the halyard snapped against the flagpole in the breeze. The flowerbeds were full of brown plant skeletons and the trees were bare and black. The greenhouse looked tidy; Nana must have cleaned out last year's tomato plants over Christmas. Rakel fetched the spare key from the woodshed, which was filled to bursting with wood chopped by her other uncle, Peter, who considered wood chopping a type of "high-intensity multi-workout" and spent the better part of the Christmas holiday by the chopping block.

The front door creaked and Rakel called out "Hello" into a compact silence. Her footsteps echoed against the stone floor. She stopped in the hallway, unsure of what to do now she was here.

The house had been built around the turn of the century by a wealthy textile factory owner, whose morose portrait still hung in the library. The rooms on the lower floor were spacious and intended for socialising. When Rakel was little, she'd thought of their names as god-given and unchangeable: The Dining Room, The Main Room, The Main Hallway, The Back Hallway, The Library, The Study, The Studio. It never occurred to her to wonder why The Studio was called The Studio, even though there were no traces of art supplies in there, just leftover junk, like a pump organ and a loom. In every room were rugs from Lars Wikner's brief career as a rug importer – the large number of rugs the family owned were the result of him selling only a handful – and the furniture consisted of antiques and inherited pieces, selected and arranged by Nana Inger. A number of objects were from when Lars had managed a hospital in Addis Ababa: bowl-shaped stools and chairs with straight, narrow backs, each hewn from a dense piece of wood according to the same principle as the rock-hewn churches of Lalibela, which had been carved out of the mountains. How her grandparents had transported them from Ethiopia to the Swedish countryside was a mystery, as was how they had dealt with customs. Inger had also brought back a trove of gold jewellery that she doled out on special occasions. She claimed the Ethiopian jewellery was a symbol of belonging, worn by all the women in the family, but the truth was Aunt Vera would never wear anything that didn't belong to the design canon of the Western world and Rakel never wore jewellery of any kind. Peter's wife Suzanne didn't like "ethnic things" and Inger exacted revenge by complaining that their house in the suburbs was "soulless". Only Cecilia had worn a small pendant, no bigger than a five-pence coin, on a thin gold chain around her neck. It nestled in the freckly hollow between her collarbones, and as a child Rakel had been upset that she had to take off the long plastic-bead necklace she'd made at after-school club to go to bed, while a whole other set of rules seemed to apply to adults. Her mum never took off her gold necklace, not when she went to bed and not when she swam in the sea or at any other time, and to the little girl Rakel had once been, that had become symbolic of the privileges of the secret world of adults.

Now, Rakel went from room to room, pausing for a long time to enjoy the familiar view of the lake before completing a full lap of the first floor. All the beds had been stripped, duvets and pillows tidily folded at the foot of each. All the guestroom doors stood ajar. The crystal chandeliers were wrapped in sheets.

After sitting in the armchair on the landing for a while, looking at the books on the shelf next to it – Paulo Coelho, gardening and female Nobel Prize laureates were the three main genres – Rakel got up. The house had done nothing to soothe her, but then she hadn't expected it to.

On her way back to the car, she popped her head into the ramshackle barn. Back when her grandfather had been into catching butterflies, it had been a No Trespassing zone, and it was with a feeling of doing something forbidden she stepped into the gloom. The windows were covered in grime. Broken nets hung on the walls and sitting on a worktable littered with tools were two long-forgotten containers of ether – all that remained of Lars Wikner's butterfly collecting.

Rakel was just about to close the door behind her when something in the cluttered far corner of the barn caught her eye. It was a bunch of canvases with their backs facing out, leaned against a stack of car tyres. The paintings were covered with a coarse wool blanket that was slipping off. The barn was not a good place to store paintings, Rakel thought, damp and unheated as it was. Inger and Lars should know better. She pulled the blanket all the way off and turned the outermost canvas around to have a look at it. Then she jumped back, straight into some rusty children's bikes that toppled over with a crash.

It was a portrait of Cecilia. A younger but easily recognisable Cecilia, painted in a realistic style with forceful brushstrokes. The painting was signed CW.

HIGHER EDUCATION 2

I

INTERVIEWER: What role did literature play during your teenage years?

MARTIN BERG: Other than that it allowed me do a work placement at the post office just like Charles Bukowski? Well, among other things, I suppose it stimulated my linguistic development. And being able to put word to thought is just priceless, don't you think? People who can't express themselves end up powerless and vice versa. It's frightening sometimes to see the way young people communicate. They don't use *language*. They think you're rude if you don't add smileys and three exclamation marks. Sometimes they skip the words entirely and just send incomprehensible pictures to each other. Some kind of infantilising of our written Swedish seems to be occurring, and the teenagers certainly aren't the only ones to blame. It makes you wonder – but I digress – what was the question again?

*

Martin was woken up by a flood of sunlight hitting his face. His T-shirt was dripping sweat and his cheek was tight with dried saliva. He heaved himself upright. The garden swing squeaked; the newspaper slid off his stomach and fell to the ground. He staggered into the kitchen and drank some water. Apparently, it was four o'clock. And what had he done on this – he pulled the newspaper closer and checked the date – fifth of July 1981? He yawned and downed another glass of water.

A few days earlier his parents and sister had set sail aboard the family boat. It was a blessing to be rid of Kicki, who played Duran

Duran ad nauseam and hogged the phone for hours on end, shut in her room with the cord stretched as far as it would go under the door. On the other hand, he had to cook his own food. (So far, spaghetti and meatballs three days in a row.) And his mum's silent presence had a civilising effect; it wouldn't do to lie in bed until after lunch when she was around. And yet, this was what he'd longed for for months: summer, home alone, endless time to read and write. That being said, he hadn't counted on Gustav disappearing off to France, and Gustav didn't seem to have either.

"Eight weeks," he'd said, hanging his head. "Sentenced to a punishment of family vacation."

"What for? You got good grades in the end."

For three years, Gustav had changed the subject whenever grades came up and secreted his tests away as soon as he got them back, but during the spring term, he'd started to panic more openly. "Not that *I* care," he said. "But Nana does."

In a joint effort, they'd stayed away from the Golden Prague and Sprängkullen. Martin did algebra with a bewildered Gustav in the role of pupil. He staged a dramatic performance of the French Revolution, playing the roles of Marat, a group of angry sans-culottes, Marie Antoinette, Louis XVI and Robespierre, all with a drink sloshing precariously in one hand. He read Gustav's perfectly competent essay on Pär Lagerkvist and inserted phrases like "poetry whose object is the depth of the human soul" in appropriate places. They spent a whole evening on the circumstances leading up to the First and Second World Wars (Gustav didn't pay attention until Martin mentioned the Nazis' *Entartete Kunst* exhibition and Hitler's love of cheap street art). To explain Homer, he drew the whole timeline of the Trojan War using stickmen on a sheet in Gustav's largest sketchpad ("and *this* is Fair Helen – you might not be able to tell from this, but she was super fit"). They slogged through endless irregular French verbs, counted metrical feet in alexandrines and rhyme schemes in sonnets, went to bed on time the night before exams. And considering that they didn't launch their effort until the very last month of school, Gustav's grades weren't half bad in the end. They weren't the unbroken column of fives Martin had netted, but they weren't too shabby.

"They can't force you to go, though," Martin said.

"No, but... you know..."

"I can set you up at the post office. Then you have an excuse to stay."

"But you hate working at the post office."

"You have to make money somehow."

"Sure..."

Gustav raised objections to every single solution Martin proposed, and two days later he left.

Now, Martin returned to the patio, pulled the garden swing into the shade and flipped aimlessly through William Wallace's last novel, *Times and Clocks and Watches*. There was no Swedish translation, probably for good reason – Martin had nodded off after just fifteen pages. He hadn't been able to make sense of the plot and the blurb was no help. Of Wallace's many books, he'd held off on reading *Times* for as long as he'd been able. His mum had had to order it from another library and the most recent date stamp on the due date card was from 1973.

It was too early to call around to see if anyone wanted to come over for a few beers. And who could he call anyway? The other night, he'd run into an old classmate who asked if he wanted to come out for a pint and he'd heard himself reply he had to work. Instead, he went home and wrote a long letter to Gustav. It was fascinating to discover how much he had to say even though virtually nothing had happened. Gustav usually replied with postcards. *Doing* très bien *here in the sun, heavy van Gogh mood minus the syphilis & that ear incident, say hi to Gothenburg from me!!!* Sometimes he sent drawings and sketches so sophisticated it was hard to believe they'd been made by the same hand that had scribbled the virtually illegible words.

For the most part, though, he sent nothing.

Martin stretched out again, let the creaking garden swing rock him. It was a hot, dusty summer, slow and indolent. Just a month ago, he'd been last-minute cramming and taking final exams, early mornings and late nights, black coffee, his mum worriedly scouring her cookbooks for hors d'oeuvre recipes, a graduation ball they didn't plan to attend but ended up at anyway. There had been balloons and streamers and sticky cocktails in plastic cups, and Martin's memories ended around the time they danced violently to Iggy Pop's "Lust for Life" and he fell under a table, pulling the tablecloth along with him, and someone let out a shrill scream. And in the middle of all of that, he had to endure his graduation party, the best parts of which had been his sister's obvious envy and his graduation present from Aunt Maud: a brand-new Facit portable sky-blue typewriter.

"I suppose it will be outdated soon, but it's the kind you said you wanted," she sighed, critically eyeing the contents of the punchbowl.

And so it was that the summer that was supposed to be the start of everything mostly ended up being about waiting. Martin waited for letters from France. He waited for a time when he'd be hungry enough to cook. He waited for acceptance letters from universities. He waited for the post office drudgery to commence. He waited for his pay cheque. He waited for the next issue of *BLM*. He waited for autumn to arrive, though that was too depressing to admit, even to himself. He waited for inspiration. He waited for the postman. He waited, though he tried not to think about that, to be called up for military service. He waited for someone to call, only he didn't know who.

If not for the fact that he'd set his mind to writing a novel, he would probably have imploded.

During upper secondary school, he'd always had other things to do. After graduation, he'd told himself. That's the time. His novel was going to be loosely autobiographical and sharp. It was going to shake the establishment, sweep away the cobwebs and debris. He pictured a room filled with books from floor to ceiling and a desk by a large window. On the desk was a typewriter and stacks of paper, and leaning back in a swivel chair, dressed in a black turtleneck and with long hair and a cigarette burning between his fore and middle fingers, MARTIN BERG.

He started off with a story about a man and a woman in a hotel in Pamplona, vaguely inspired by Wallace. There was an atmosphere of imminent threat in the hotel room he was pretty pleased with, but the dialogue came out long-winded, possibly because he didn't know what his main characters were trying to tell each other. Also, he'd never been to Pamplona; in fact, he'd never been further from home than Denmark. He'd picked the city because of its sun-drenched streets, slow siesta hours, bullfights and humming dusks under dusty, dark-blue skies, and he couldn't shake the thought of what a person who'd actually been to Pamplona would say about his text.

He was happier with the short story *Skansen Kronan, Two O'Clock*. It was more autobiographical in its approach, based on a night when Martin almost got with a girl whose ex got beaten up by some country louts in white jeans. The girl had rushed to the aid of her ex-boyfriend, who seemed strangely pleased despite his gushing nosebleed, and the whole thing had ended with Martin and Gustav sitting at the top of a hill, sharing a bottle of disgusting sherry as the sun came up. In that story he was able to create a kind of tumultuous feeling that was pretty neat, and it had been printed in the school paper, as well.

But it was a short story, and what was a short story but a test of one's strength before the unavoidable novel?

He hadn't come up with a plot, figuring it would work itself out in due course. And either way, the plot wasn't the important thing. The important thing was – hmm, yes, what was the important thing? What did William Wallace actually write about? The things that *happened* in his stories didn't seem particularly momentous. They somehow weren't what mattered.

He told himself he could worry about that later, and wrote about whatever came to mind, mostly recent escapades with Gustav. Martin had given himself the alias Johan, but he couldn't think of anything that really suited Gustav, so for now he was G. Johan and G wandered about aimlessly, went to museums, skipped the graduation party to climb some hill, where they sat on the grass while the sun set, absorbed in a philosophical discussion about the meaning of life that spanned many pages. The phone rang, but he just had to write a bit more about how G shoplifted snus from the corner shop so they had to run like hell and how they'd recovered on the slope below Kungsladugårdsskolan, and how Johan tried snus for the first time, which was fun for five minutes before it ended with an epic fit of vomiting that drew reproving glares from several old ladies.

When he got stuck, he flipped through one of Wallace's novels to see what he'd done. In *Patagonia Days*, there was a section that made him dizzy.

The main character, young Bill, had just arrived in Paris. He was as determined to succeed as he was hungry, alone and recently rejected by a publisher. Bill wandered the streets in what Wallace called the "malaria fever of the ink". Longing for the desk in his hotel room as much as he feared it:

Considering how demanding the writing profession is, it may seem strange that it exerts such a pull on young souls. No one, not even Bill Bradley, could honestly picture himself forever inspired at a desk, drawing on a well that never ran dry, obsessed, feverish, compelled by forces he didn't understand and couldn't control. No, there was always doubt. A balancing act on the edge of a precipice. And some nights he fell asleep on the brink of that abyss, and when he woke up, darkness was the first thing he saw, and he knew: if I fall now, there's no coming back. If I fall now, I'm lost.

Few professions draw luck seekers with such headlines: likely only gold digging and writing. And yet, they find their way to it. They sit down at a table with pen and paper. They search inside themselves for the first sentence, that gossamer lifeline. They understand how long it's going to take, the work that lies before them, and yet they carry on. Why? Because to write, to write is to conquer the world. Making it one's own and oneself a god. Writing grants access to all rooms, to hearts and minds, to the most sacred; the unknown is laid at one's feet. It is a chance to seize eternity. To write is to refuse to die.

In the middle of the slowest, longest week of July, when Gustav's return was still an eternity away and he hadn't heard from him in almost a month, Martin joined a band.

He struck up a conversation with a blond guy at the French Club who introduced himself as Per Andrén and eagerly shook Martin's hand with his own clammy fist. He claimed to recognise Martin from Hvitfeldtska, but Martin couldn't recall ever seeing this Per bloke before.

"Oh yeah, that's right," he lied. Per's body was frog-shaped, with skinny legs and a massive, slightly forward-leaning torso, and Martin was busy committing the shape to memory for future literary use when Per said: "Don't you play the guitar?"

Martin nodded, possibly because he was drunk, possibly because he missed walking down the street with the case on his back. (It had been a year since he last did, since he finally gave up on his lessons with a music teacher who was at least forty-five and never missed an opportunity to underscore his vague connections to progg rock band Blå Tåget.) "Though it's been a while, actually…"

It turned out the guitarist in Per's band had gone off to Italy to tread grapes. They needed a substitute.

Then he was introduced to the singer, Tommy, who wore sunglasses indoors and chewed gum. The drummer had passed out at the pre-drinks.

"Our influences are The Clash, Iggy & the Stooges, early Bowie," Per said.

"What kind of guitar do you have?" Tommy said.

"And let's not forget The Undertones," Per went on quickly. "Ebba Grön, obviously… though possibly more on a conceptual level, because we're really more rock than punk."

"Sounds fun," Martin said. "But my guitar's broken." The truth was his guitar had never existed, because he'd spent his guitar budget on Pernod and records, club cover charges, magazines and a pair of black

Levi's Gustav thought he should cut holes in as a symbolic gesture of resistance against capitalism.

"That's fine, you can use Erik's," Per said. "Where he's gone, he doesn't need it anyway."

"He's sleeping with the fishes," Tommy said.

"I meant in Bologna."

Per envisioned them playing a festival in September. They had to practise at least twice a week, he said. Preferably three. But the first time they got together, the drain in their rehearsal space clogged. The second time, the drummer didn't show up. The few times they actually played, a lot of time was spent discussing what they should sound like. Martin discovered that Erik's electric guitar was more difficult to handle than he'd thought. His fingers kept slipping on the strings, he couldn't find the distortion pedal with his foot, cold sweat trickled down his back, and when someone suggested going for a pint instead, he quickly agreed.

Per and Tommy filled part of the Gustav-shaped hole in his life. Per was all right – he'd roll up in his old banger, nod along with seeming interest, remember what you told him. Tommy, on the other hand, would lean back and talk about himself for twenty minutes straight. It became easier to hang out with them than to not hang out with them, and ultimately, Per and Tommy were who he was with the night before reporting for military service.

Just the fact that he had to go up to Karlstad and waste two days of his life on physical and mental testing was aggravating. Martin had never liked the idea of army life. Doing things as a group. Obeying orders. Suffering hardship. Shaving off his hair, which was long enough to make his mother ask again and again if it wasn't time for a haircut soon, until Kicki groaned: "Mum, it's *supposed* to look like that." (It was one of the few times she ever took her brother's side without there being something in it for her.) Making army friends who would forever call each other by their surname in a forced throwback to a long-gone, sepia-toned past.

They'd talked about it all spring.

"There's always non-combat roles," some people said, but that seemed pointless. He might as well take a page out of Gustav's book and refuse. (Though it was unclear whether Gustav would even be in a position to refuse – with his nebulous sickliness, myopia, chain-smoking and utter lack of muscle mass, he wasn't exactly army material.) They came up with different ways of getting out of it. Could they feign mental illness? Claim to have a drug problem? ("You look too wholesome for that," Gustav commented.) To be homosexuals? Skinheads or Stalinists? To like wearing women's stockings? Turn up rolled into rugs, claiming they were cabbage rolls? Gustav had a friend who had stayed up three nights in a row and shouted at the psychologist that he wanted to be a coastal ranger while banging his head on the table. Another had gone drunk out of his skull. A third had bribed a private psychologist to write an affidavit saying he was unfit for service.

"But that feels a bit – well, a bit immoral," Gustav had said.

"Feigning insanity is more upstanding than bribing someone?"

"It's more like giving the system the finger."

But in time, Martin had resigned himself to the thought. Okay: seven and a half months wasted. Okay: it was going to be uncomfortable and hard. Okay: he was going to have to suffer all kinds of commanding officers. But on the other hand, he'd get his driving licence, and "military service completed" was a common phrase in the job ads he skimmed in his search for alternative sources of income while he established himself as an author. Maybe he'd be posted to Skövde or some other place relatively close to civilisation. Maybe he might even excel? Surprise his superiors by being the first to finish all kinds of tasks and completing long cross-country runs without complaint, despite his intellectual and contrarian air? Once, he'd run all the way home from Gårda at five in the morning, after missing the last tram.

And now it was the night before, the kind of blushing summer night that felt like it had just begun and would continue to do so until it got dark and he went onto Sprängkullen or the French Club where he'd end up in a smoky corner, laughing at what some fit girl said, while lighting her cigarette and inwardly working on his next letter to Gustav. But so far the sky was bright, they'd bought potato salad, deli meats and grapes from the supermarket, and Tommy had brought a case of beer, which compensated for his otherwise fairly enervating presence.

Martin opened a beer and promised himself to drink at most two more after that one, with an eye towards the next day's intelligence test.

"There's no point pretending to be mental," Tommy said, adjusting the bandana he always wore around his neck. "They'll just send you up north as punishment."

"Non-combatant service was all right," Per said.

"If you're lucky, they'll make you a ranger," Tommy said. "Eleven months. Nowhere to go on your leave but the mountains."

Martin swatted at a wasp circling the ham.

"Bloody hell!" The back of his hand smarted; he winced and rubbed the sting. A red welt was already visible. "The bastard stung me. Is it dangerous?"

"Nah," Tommy replied.

"Can be," Per said. "If you're allergic. Are you allergic?"

"How the fuck should I know? I've never been stung before."

"Calm down," Tommy said. "Have a beer."

"Let me see your hand," Per said in an authoritative voice. He had, Martin remembered, done his military service in a medical unit.

"I'm okay, right?"

"Hmm. You didn't have a rash on your neck before, did you?"

"What are you talking about?" He sounded embarrassingly shrill.

Per pushed up the sleeve of Martin's shirt to reveal a number of red bumps like mosquito bites on his lower arm.

"It looks like hives. Listen, we should probably…" Per looked over at the tram stop with a frown. "We should probably go to A&E."

"Well, *I'm* not going anywhere," Tommy announced.

While they waited for the tram to Sahlgrenska Hospital, Per ordered Martin to sit down on a bench. His stomach was churning. It was hard to get air into his lungs and he felt light-headed. Per's voice sounded remote, and when he had to stand up to get on the tram, the world spun.

"Look on the bright side, if you're this allergic to wasp stings, you're probably not going to have a problem getting out of military service. How are you feeling?"

"Not great..."

"What was that?"

But the words were big and unwieldy in his mouth. He tried to lift his head up, but it was heavy, so heavy, he doubled over, trying to breathe, but the more he tried, the less air he got, everything was going dark...

"Is he drunk?" he heard a sharp woman's voice say, and that was the last thing Martin Berg knew before he fainted for the first time in his life.

II

INTERVIEWER: Berg & Andrén have published a fair number of text-books over the years. Can you say a few words about your views on education?

MARTIN BERG: My views on education... [*leaning forward, drinking from his water glass*] *Education* isn't necessarily the same thing as *knowledge*, is it? You can complete a degree without learning any-thing but how to answer exam questions. Knowledge is something else. When it comes to the arts and humanities, young people are inevitably ignorant. It doesn't matter how much they've read or how intelligent they are: they're young and they haven't lived and so they can't be otherwise. Surely there's some aspect of knowledge that... [*trailing off, frowning*]

INTERVIEWER: Yes...?

MARTIN BERG: Well, something that has to do with absorbing one's life experiences. If you don't acknowledge the fact that there are things you don't know, it's very difficult to learn anything at all.

Seven minutes to nine on the first day of the term, Martin Berg was entering the foyer of what he intensely hoped was the Department of Philosophy. It was deserted. He dug out his acceptance letter with sweaty hands. It was the right address. He'd already double-checked since the building didn't exactly radiate academic gravitas: it was a rickety detached wooden house, the kind that gets knocked down to make way for modern blocks of flats or car parks. The foyer contained dark wood panelling, a few upholstered chairs, a rug that was so threadbare only the merest whisper of a pattern could be discerned. The one thing that suggested this was a university building was a noticeboard covered in a whirlwind of paper and not enough drawing pins: *Flat wanted. Selling* The History of Philosophy, volumes 1–5, *used. Join the student union!*

The floorboards creaked. He peered through one of the doors. It looked like an indifferently furnished old-fashioned parlour – sagging sofas and armchairs, low tables – but a blackboard covered one of the walls and there was a pulpit next to it. A plaster bust of a grim-looking old man with a curly beard looked down on the room from a niche in the wall. Everything smelled of old cigarette smoke.

He felt silly standing around with no clue where to go, so, for lack of better options, he went back outside. He wandered along Mölndalsvägen for a while, feeling stupid, as though someone in a window across the street was watching him. He'd planned his arrival time carefully – not too early, not too late. So why was no one else there?

It wasn't until he studied the schedule again that he spotted the tiny footnote about the academic quarter. He was unsure what that meant, but he had a feeling it was relevant. So he walked on, towards the factories in Lyckholm. Smoked a cigarette, which was a bad decision since for some reason he hadn't been able to get most of his breakfast down. Not only were there other students there when he returned to the department ten minutes later, but an older man as well, standing in the foyer with a stack of handouts.

"Philosophy 101?" he said.

Martin was directed into the room with the old sofas. He picked an armchair set slightly apart from the others. Then the man with the handouts entered, introduced himself as a professor and their course instructor. With his alert expression and ironed flannel shirt, he was a far cry from the eccentric type Martin had pictured.

"Right, then," he said from the pulpit. "Welcome."

*

Martin had thought the university was a specific place, a collection of buildings kind of like Hvitfeldtska. In reality, the departments were spread across the city. The art school, Valand, was not by Valand but on Lindholmen, a temporary solution, according to Gustav, but a proper pain because he had to travel out to Hisingen every day. The department of literature was housed in an old building on Stora Nygatan. The department of education, he found out from a girl he made out with on Sprängkullen and then lost track of in the crowd, had been exiled to Mölndal. The business school occupied a hideous box of a building across from the old public library. Chalmers, which did meet Martin's expectations of what a university should look like, wasn't even part of Gothenburg University but rather its own college.

Their teachers never missed an opportunity to complain about the department's facilities – the building was draughty, the boiler was always on the blink, the rooms weren't built for teaching. Martin, for his part, loved it. The classroom that had originally been a drawing or dining room perfectly fit his mental image of what Studying Philosophy should be like, a mental image drawn from what he'd read about Sartre's time at the École Normale forty years earlier. He was surprised at the affection he felt for the worn brocade upholstery of the armchairs, the dark wood panelling covering both walls and ceiling, the ashtrays that the students took it upon themselves to empty before class. He liked that he knew how to close the window that stuck and that the front door was unlocked at eight, so he could come in early and go over the day's readings one more time if he wanted to.

One of his course mates kept talking about the MUL, and it wasn't until he spotted the sign that Martin realised he was referring to the Main University Library. He half expected them to reject his request for a library card, but a bored librarian had it ready in five minutes. He strolled around aimlessly for a long time. There was nothing but bookshelves, jampacked bookshelves with narrow aisles between. No effort had been made to make the books look interesting. They had been stripped of their covers and given new, anonymous bindings in dark brown and maroon. He found the philosophy section and picked up a few volumes mostly because he found their weight reassuring.

He climbed stairs, up, towards the light, and entered, for the first time in his life, a reading room. It was a large room, with a soaring ceiling crowned with wide windows. The desks were arranged in long rows, but each individual one was delineated by a lip and equipped with a reading light and a bookstand. The room was completely silent, the kind of silence that was never achieved at the public library.

He sat down at the end of a row and put his books down on the desk as quietly as he could. But not knowing where to start, in the end, he mostly sat there looking around.

Martin's first introduction to philosophy as a field of study took place in his final year of upper secondary school. Their teacher was relatively young, and all the girls were in love with him despite his oversized jacket, spasmodic body language and tendency to spit when he was fired up, which was most of the time. They covered Plato and Aristotle and Kant – at this point, most of the students were doodling in their notepads – but the most important part seemed to be that they Discuss Things. Their discussions usually devolved into bitter debates in which students accused each other of being communists or lacking political awareness. There was a lot of sighing and chair scraping. Somewhere, a gum bubble burst. Martin's essay on Sartre earned him a top grade.

He'd imagined university as a more civilised sequel, characterised by more reason, note-taking and focused silence. Since he'd been top of his class, he assumed he would continue to be top of whatever class he was in; 'twas always thus.

In their first class, they were given an excerpt from a text. It was full of words Martin had never encountered before, and he had an excellent vocabulary – unlike so many of his fellow readers, he hadn't had to look up the word lugubrious when he read *Gentlemen*. The sentences were so convoluted he'd forgotten how they started by the time they ended. He stared at the paper. He started over, more slowly this time. It made no difference. He'd always sneered at people who said difficult texts were "Greek to them". Then it struck him – this had to be a test. Relief washed over him. It was *supposed* to be completely incomprehensible. The professor was going to offer them some clever angle, something about asking questions or critical thinking. Martin looked around, but the others were still reading. They hadn't seen through it.

And when the professor spoke, it wasn't to let them in on the joke. "You've read," he said, "an excerpt from *The Phenomenology of Spirit* by Hegel." He went on, talking about the importance of going back to the original sources, of not approaching the great thinkers only through secondary literature, which could be of varying quality. If at all possible, they should read texts in the original to avoid potential mistranslations. Was anyone taking German? Several people tentatively raised their hands.

A few weeks later, they were given their first writing assignment. They had to choose an Aristotelian concept and argue for its relevance in the modern world. Martin worked on his essay over several long library sessions and was happy with the result. When he got it back covered in red a week later, he thought there had been a mistake.

Without talking to anyone, he fled, seeking shelter in a remote corner of the library. There, he forced himself to read every last comment. His eyes didn't want to stay on the page and his face was turning red; he violently pulled off his sweater. When he got to the end, he sat for a long time motionless, staring into space.

Some of the comments seemed reasonable, others capriciously critical. Or? Maybe he didn't have a knack for philosophy? Maybe he didn't get what it was about.

He began to pace up and down. Had he simply been smart compared to his indifferent, lazy classmates in upper secondary school and mistaken that for talent? *Please submit revisions no later than two weeks from today.* In other words: he hadn't even passed. Never before had he failed to pass.

Martin was pretty sure the professor discounted some people and favoured others, such as Fredrik, a goody-goody who wore ironed dress shirts and had an annoying habit of incessantly clearing his throat. Fredrik spoke calmly and confidently, nodding almost imperceptibly even when the others had stopped taking notes and gone slack-jawed. Sometimes, the professor addressed him directly, as though the others weren't even there. It went without saying Fredrik had received a top grade, because Fredrik knew exactly what was expected of him. (Martin had never spoken to Fredrik and had no intention of ever doing so.) Fredrik had probably grown up in a family full of academics, felt completely at home in this world, and knew the difference between an adjunct and a lecturer.

Martin painstakingly reread the primary texts and spent a long time pondering what the question was really about. He crossed out several paragraphs he'd actually been pleased with – tangents, granted, but well-written ones – and stuck to the question at hand. In the end, he spent more time revising his essay than he had writing it in the first place. Yet even so, he was unsure if it would be enough when he handed it in. A few days later, it was returned with a simple *Good* in the bottom-right corner, but after the initial wave of relief, he was unable to shake the idea that the only reason he'd passed was laziness, or, even worse, charity.

*

When Martin entered the Golden Prague, Gustav already had an empty pint in front of him. He was looking out of the window, chewing his nails.

"How's it going?"

"Fine, I guess." Gustav signalled to the waitress for two more beers. "Tell me about art school. Is it good? What are your classmates like?"

Gustav shrugged, sucking on the inside of his cheek, and gazing intently out at Sveaplan. "They *talk* so much," he said finally. "What is art? What do I want to express? What do I want to create? Stuff like that."

"And isn't that interesting?"

"I don't know," he said. "I just paint. And several of them went to preschool together."

"Pardon?"

"You know, a preparatory course. I'm the youngest."

"You're probably the most talented, too, as usual."

"We had this seminar where we talked about who we are and what we want to do. One said I was employing 'classical imagery', and I could tell that wasn't a good thing. I don't know. Maybe art school isn't for me." Gustav had been back from France for two weeks. For once, he was tanned. The sun had bleached his hair from mousy to blond and he'd had a haircut in Cannes ("Nana refused to let me do it myself"). In his neat clothes, he could have passed for a regular Riviera tourist, one of the weaker characters in a Hemingway novel or a nervous cousin of Bill Bradley's in *Patagonia Days*. Since he'd been back, he'd been staring off into space a lot, replying "Nothing" when Martin asked what he was thinking. He smoked incessantly and often forgot about the cigarette between his fingers. Even in the middle of the day, he might decide to make cocktails, and when Martin declined, he seemed annoyed, briefly sipped his own and then put it down. He didn't want to go to Errol's. He didn't want to go to Sprängkullen. He didn't want to see Ebba Grön play at the student union. As recently as the previous Saturday, he'd decided to stay in for no apparent reason. Martin had called Per instead. His expectations had been low, but it had turned out to be a great night: they'd had a couple of pints, seen a band, moved on, met a lot of people Per became instant friends with, and then they'd sat with their arms around each other's shoulders and someone had tried to teach them The Internationale in Russian so they could sing it to rile someone, though Martin didn't know whom, and then they staggered home along Bellmansgatan, and tried to get into Bacchus. They didn't have membership cards and the bouncer just gave them a weary look. They stopped further down the street and had a smoke and discussed who among their acquaintance might be able to recommend them for membership.

"Isn't it a gay club?" Martin asked.

"All kinds of people go there," Per said with a significant look at a woman who was just then climbing out of a taxi. Even from afar it was clear she was beautiful in a Fellini way, very unlike any girl they knew. "A friend of mine says that it's as close as you get to New York in Gothenburg. Whatever. I think we have to admit defeat for now. Because Sprängkullen's closed, right?"

They cut across Haga Kyrkoplan. A young man was walking briskly in the opposite direction, his hands in his pockets and his eyes on the ground.

"Gustav?"

He jumped as though a gun had gone off.

"What the fuck," Martin said. "You said you were staying in."

Gustav mumbled something about not being able to sleep. "So where are you going?"

"Just out for a walk. Hi, by the way…" He shook hands with Per, whom he hadn't met yet.

Martin had talked a lot about Gustav Becker and wished he could have made a more impressive entrance. "We're on our way home," he said.

"But we could go for a pint at that place in Haga," Per offered, turning to Gustav. "If you wanted to come?"

"Sure, sounds nice," Gustav replied. That was the last thing he said all night.

Now he flashed a grin at the waitress as she put their beers down on the table.

"Surely if anyone belongs in art school, it's you," Martin said. "What else would you do? Well, I suppose you could get a job like us regular mortals and dedicate your evenings and spare moments to your artistic calling."

Gustav smiled. "At least I get student loans."

*

Autumn settled in. Dusk fell earlier and earlier like vast watercolours and spilled ink. The linden trees on Vasagatan turned yellow and on Allén shiny conkers littered the ground. In the mornings, there was a thin film of ice on his bike seat. Martin took his coat out of the closet, removed all the pin badges from the lapels and bought a scarf he could toss over his shoulder. And he, who had never in his life owned a bag, had to find a way to carry his books around; the cargo rack on his bike was no longer equal to the task. For a while he considered purchasing the same kind of seabag Gustav lugged around, but he couldn't find one and they weren't particularly practical either, come to think of it. A briefcase? He found one in a charity shop, but it looked so out-of-place in his hand he burst out laughing. In the end, he opted for a black leather backpack.

When he cycled past Olof Wijksgatan, he always looked up at the windows of the von Beckers' flat. Several times he passed Marlene, who responded to his waves with a tentative smile, when she noticed him at all.

And in the house on Mölndalsvägen, Martin Berg hung his coat on the valet stand in the hallway. He lit a cigarette and leaned back on the sofa, his eyes fixed on the lecturer. He took notes with a pencil stub he found in his breast pocket. He learned to speak as though a thought had just occurred to him and adopted a careless way of gesticulating. His next essay came back with exclamation marks and encouraging comments in pen. He raised his hand to contribute, and the lecturers learned his name. He read every text at least twice. His copy of *Philosophical Lexicon* was full of dog-eared pages and notes, underlining and marginalia. He read all the secondary literature. In fact, he spent so much time on his studies, he didn't have time to write his novel. It didn't bother him all that much – he'd had the idea of adding a philosophical dimension to the narrative that would set it apart from *Jack* and all the other would-be *Jacks* and therefore felt it was time well spent.

III

INTERVIEWER: With writing, have you encountered any common… pitfalls?

MARTIN BERG: Look, with a pen in your hand – figuratively speaking, I guess no one writes by hand any more – with a pen in your hand, you're God. Every decision is yours to make. In that kind of situation, you might feel tempted to write the world the way you think it *ought to* be. To uncomplicate things. Your hero is flawless and wins in the end. Your antagonist is thoroughly unpleasant and gets his or her comeuppance. Who knows, an author might even want to tell other people how to live their lives. Make his or her characters moral examples or cautionary tales. And by all means, I suppose that's all well and good. It's a free country. You can write whatever the hell you want. Whether it makes artistic sense, however, that's a different question altogether… not to mention whether there's a reader anywhere who will get anything from reading what you wrote.

*

"I have to move out," Martin announced.

"Mm," Gustav replied. He was standing at his easel, busy with what Martin assumed was the first stage of a painting. Unless he was trying out a new style, working in the abstract. Which wasn't exactly unthinkable, given how he'd gone on and on about that bloke Sandor's non-figurative art and his own "unfortunate allegiance to the motif".

Martin was lying on the sagging sofa in Gustav's studio, drinking whisky from their secret stash. It was November. Sharp chill, biting winds. He'd shivered all the way out to Hisingen, standing out on deck (as far away from the railing as he could) so he could enjoy the majesty of the dusk. When he reached the art school, Gustav had been standing out front, contemplating the same sky, his glasses reflecting the last glint of dying sunlight.

Everyone had gone home, or, more likely, to a party. The only ones left in the building were Gustav and one or two other people. Muffled music could be heard from somewhere and light spilled into a dark corridor. Still, hanging out at Valand was better than going home, where Frege's tedious logic waited for him against the backdrop of his boyhood room.

Every time Martin stepped through the door at Kungsladugårdsgatan, a thick, oily film enveloped his lungs, as though the entire weight of history was pressing on his chest, making it impossible to move faster than a crawl. He almost wished there was some kind of conflict he could use as a catalyst. Something that meant he had no choice but to pack his bags and leave. But there was his mum, reading in the light of a softly humming lamp, smoking, eating fudge. His dad was watching some frantic entertainment programme on TV, with the sound turned down low because the printing presses had given him tinnitus. From Kicki's room came the muffled sound of her nattering to someone on the phone.

Now, Martin fumbled for the whisky bottle and stretched out on the sofa. "I can't even write any more," he said. "I think the room's the problem. It's the most inhibiting space in the history of the world. Not even Wallace could have written anything in there. Not even Strindberg, and he wrote all the time, even when he was paranoid and trying to make gold. I promise you my room would have broken Strindberg. It would break anyone."

"So move out, then," Gustav said.

"That's what I just said."

Martin was sure Gustav was going to say he could move in with him on Sjömansgatan. It would have been perfect – he was always there anyway, and the rent would be extremely low. Granted, it would be crowded with two people, but Gustav was always at the art school and Martin at the library, and it would just be temporary, until he found something else…

But Gustav just said: "There's a lot of stuff on the noticeboard out there about communes and whatnot. Maybe you should have a look."

Martin heaved a deep sigh. "Sure," he said, not even pretending to be about to move, "I will."

He called a few people. The first place, a condemned building in Haga, had already been taken. The second required a deposit of two months' rent and didn't have an indoor toilet. The third was a room on Kaptensgatan.

"I'm afraid the guy who used to live in the room didn't do a very good job cleaning it," Anders, the flat's owner, informed him over the phone. "We have an indoor toilet… what else…" He could hear a guitar and a wavering voice singing in the background. "It can get loud around here," he said. "I hope you don't mind."

"Not at all," Martin replied.

"Tried to rent it out to this neat freak once. Disaster. Why don't you just come over and have a look at it?"

The flat was on the second floor of one of the old buildings. There was a Communist Party sticker on the door. Anders opened the door a split second after Martin rang the bell, as though he'd been standing in the hallway, waiting.

"Welcome," he said. Clammy handshake followed by a vague gesture that seemed intended to invite Martin to enter. He looked like someone; Martin tried to think of who throughout the tour through a messy kitchen and a living room that was home to, among other things, a floral-pattern sofa with matching armchairs, a few tired houseplants, and a hookah. He couldn't put his finger on it until Anders opened the door to what would be Martin's room, possibly aided by the slightly pompous gesture which he directed at the thirteen-by-sixteen-foot space overlooking the street: van Dyck's portrait of James Stuart, Duke of Lennox. It was included in a book about Dutch painting Martin had acquired to help him keep up when Gustav talked about Vermeer and Rembrandt. Like James Stuart, Anders had a narrow face framed by golden-red curls that hung to his shoulders, and big, slightly watery eyes, a knobbly nose and a downy moustache. Where van Dyck's young nobleman wore a silk shirt, Anders was dressed in a cotton grandad-collar shirt and instead of a golden pear, he held in his hand a can of snus. From which he now took a pinch before asking Martin what he thought.

With a hand truck and assistance in the form of Gustav, the move only required two trips on the tram. Anders served moving-in dinner in the form of lentil stew and spoke half tentatively, half lecturing about nuclear power ("it's probably going to take a disaster to make people realise how dangerous it is"), the current government ("a sad but logical consequence of the watered-down policies of the Social Democratic Party") and his experience of factory work ("on the assembly line"). When Anders realised his new tenant was studying philosophy, he asked Martin's opinion on Marx, and after Martin answered correctly ("an unavoidable thinker if you want to understand the political and philosophical developments of the twentieth century"), he seemed to relax a little.

Gustav, who was also present at this first meal on Kaptensgatan, said nothing. It made no difference that they agreed on all the important issues or that Gustav looked like someone who spent Labour Day demonstrating and hoped capitalism was on its last legs, in line with the predictions of historical materialism – he still acted stiff and self-conscious, as though he feared he might be the first to be put against the wall.

He sat pushing his lentil stew around his plate, sipping his light beer. Anders talked about his latest attempt to ferment carrots.

*

It took no more than fifteen minutes to walk up the hill from Kaptensgatan to Gustav in Masthugget, and just ten the other way. Yet, even so, sometimes a week or even more would go by without them seeing each other.

"Hey, you should come over," Gustav would say whenever Martin managed to get him on the horn. That always meant Valand, and sometimes Martin did go. Gustav showed him his latest projects and they drank and ate cheese sandwiches. Sooner or later, they were always joined by one or more of his school friends, and the conversation inevitably turned to some Valand scandal or faculty intrigue.

"Are you leaving already?" Gustav would say, but he never sounded particularly disappointed.

One time, they'd made plans to meet up, just the two of them, but Gustav was running late. Martin waited for him on Järntorget Square. It was early April and after a week of sunny weather, he'd traded his coat for a black wool jacket, but now the wind blew cold, and the clouds hung low and grey over the city. He walked several laps around the fountain. He asked a lady for the time. Gustav was ten minutes late. Then fifteen. Then twenty. Scattered droplets of rain began to fall. Martin walked over to the phone booth. He dialled the number of the shared dormitory phone at Valand, and after four or five rings a winded-sounding voice said: "Yes, hello?" In the background, he could hear music and voices.

"Is this Sissel?" He thought he recognised one of Gustav's classmates.

"Yes, who is this?"

"It's Martin – Martin Berg..."

"Hi, Martin!" She sounded bubblier than usual. It was probably what she always sounded like drunk, but he was never sober enough to notice. "Why aren't you here?"

"Uh – so, is Gustav around?"

"Sure – actually, hold on – he just went to get ice. But I can ask him to call you back?"

"Thanks, but don't bother."

Sissel said something that was drowned out by general commotion and subsequent laughter, and they hung up.

Rain was now hammering against the phone booth. Martin walked the three stops home. For once, the flat was empty; Anders was on a university trip to Albania. He hung up his soaked jacket over the bath and put newspaper in his shoes. Then he made himself a dinner of bacon, fried eggs and baked beans that he ate in front of the TV.

The first call came around two the next day. Since Martin didn't pick up, he couldn't be sure it was Gustav, but two was a normal time for Gustav to crawl out of bed and he always waited nine rings before hanging up.

He continued to read. The phone rang again at three, then at half past three, then at quarter to four, then at four, at which point Martin snatched up his books and went down to Hängmattan to study there instead.

That night, he'd agreed to meet some classmates. His jacket was almost dry, and they spent the evening talking about the nature of logic, Karl Popper's white and black swans (Martin restlessly rolled a cigarette) and whether Wittgenstein was a genius or a fraud, gay or not.

"There's no evidence of homosexuality!" exclaimed Fredrik, who had gone so far as to exchange his cigarettes for a pipe, which he was now tapping out a touch aggressively.

Martin told them it was time for him to shoot off.

The next morning, he was woken up by the phone in the kitchen, hurled himself out of bed, and was about to pick up when his determination from the day before caught up with him. He let it ring while he drank a glass of water and fetched the newspaper from the hallway. Anders was suspicious of Martin's subscription to *Göteborgs-Posten* – "It *is* a liberal paper, after all." There had been a brief awkward pause after this comment, because Martin hadn't known how to respond. In the end, he'd said reading the paper was a habit for him, since his dad, who worked at the printers, had always brought a copy home. This blue-collar connection seemed to placate Anders, whose parents were upper secondary school teachers.

Martin made sandwiches and coffee, cleared the worst of the mess off the kitchen table and put plates caked with dried-on food in the sink to soak. He read an entire article about the Falklands, where Thatcher had just decided to send an entire fleet. As far as he knew, the Falklands didn't have much to recommend them in terms of natural resources and such, and the whole thing came off as two children squabbling over a boring toy whose only attraction lay in that the other child wanted it. When he made a mental note to bring the issue up with Gustav, he felt an unfamiliar twinge.

He set to doing the washing-up and then tackled the fridge, which no one had cleaned in a while, even though it was part of the official rota. Originally, the plan had been for Anders and Martin to have two shelves each, but that system had quickly broken down when it became clear you could tell which food belonged to whom just from looking at it. Bowl of beans soaking: Anders. Sausages wrapped in tin foil: Martin. Glass jar full of sprouts: Anders. Half a portion of what was most likely spaghetti Bolognese: Martin. Parsnips: Anders. Open tin of mushrooms…Martin made a face and poured it into the sink. Even those beans were starting to smell a bit funny, and Martin was pondering whether he dared to throw them out when the phone rang again. Nine times.

He took a long shower.

He studied and had lunch at Hängmattan. He returned home late in the afternoon. It was Saturday and he paced around the flat, including Anders's room, where there was nothing of interest to see, not knowing what to do with himself. He could call a girl he'd been seeing and maybe go to the cinema, but there was nothing he wanted to see. He was studying the spines of the books in Anders's bookcase when the doorbell jangled.

For a few seconds, Martin stood stock-still, wondering what to do, but with someone at the door, his options were really rather limited: he opened it.

Gustav poked at the doormat with his foot. A carrier bag full of booze dangled from his slender hand. His cheeks were pallid and covered in scraggly stubble.

"I've been calling every two minutes," he said. He gently set the bag down on the floor and hung up his coat.

"I've been studying," Martin said.

"Good old Descartes, is it?"

"That was months ago. We're doing logic now."

Gustav quickly noted Anders wasn't home ("When the cat's away") and searched the kitchen cabinets for bigger glasses than the normal drinking ones.

"So this exhibition..." He shook his head and rummaged through the freezer for ice. "It's going to be the death of me."

"What exhibition?"

"The Spring Exhibition!"

At Valand, Martin recalled, the academic year was concluded with a big student exhibition. Not only was it a form of examination, which Gustav seemed to consider bad enough, it was also an opportunity to actually sell paintings.

"But it's not until the end of May, right?"

"I have almost nothing ready to show."

"But you've painted loads."

"Sure, but nothing *good*." There was a shrill note of desperation in Gustav's voice. Martin tried to remember what he'd seen of his paintings since the start of the year. As far as he knew, Gustav had continued to pursue his disarrayed still lifes and had also tried his hand at portraiture.

"What's so bad about it?"

Clink, clink, clink as ice hit glass. Gustav pulled out a bottle of whisky.

"There's no concept," he replied. "There's no concept behind them. They just *are*."

"What do you mean by concept?" Martin demanded, fairly authoritatively, because he was the philosopher, after all. Gustav stared at him with equal parts despair and frustration.

"The others always have all these thoughts about what their pieces are supposed to convey," he said finally. "But I don't. I just paint."

"And what's the problem with that?"

"The problem is I don't know what to say when people ask what I 'intend to investigate' and so on." He lit a cigarette, even though Anders insisted on a complete smoking ban on account of his supposed asthma. Martin opened the window just to be safe.

"And I shouldn't have copied those photographs. Now people ask me: 'What's the reasoning behind your work with photography?' and the first time I said it was just easier than lugging the whole table with all the bottles to my studio and they laughed and thought I was cocky or cracking wise or whatever. Then they asked again… I'm considering redoing everything from scratch without photographs…"

"You don't have time to do that."

"You just said I had all the time in the world."

"To finish, sure. Not to start all over again."

Gustav was silent for a while. Then he said it would be easier if Martin could see the paintings in question, and, either way, there was a party at Valand.

They took the ferry across the ink-black river. Gustav wanted to stay out on deck and watch the light sparkle on the water. He'd cheered up and spent the entire ride recounting a convoluted anecdote about one of his classmates. When Gustav talked about his friends at Valand, they'd come off as an extraordinarily funny, intelligent, talented and lovable bunch. Then Martin met them. Sandor Lucács, a long-haired Hungarian with a Zappa moustache, produced nothing like the profound comments Gustav had attributed to him. Sissel, "who has a sixth sense for emotional states", mostly sat in a corner, chewing her nails. Uffe, the mischief maker, turned out to be twitchy and nervous, asked the same questions over and over, and was generally paranoid. "He gets like that when he's high," Gustav said. Uffe's "completely insane" project was a wall made of TVs of which only three worked. His contribution to art consisted mostly of him sitting in his studio, watching horror films and smoking pot.

The ferry docked at Lindholmen. They trudged up the slope towards the university. Gustav hadn't said anything about standing Martin up and didn't for the rest of the night, either. Instead, he kept circling back to the spring exhibition, as though he were stuck in a loop and had no choice but to keep passing that point again and again. And each time, he got more long-winded.

"I mean," he said, slumped on a sofa, "what can I really do? What am I good at? I'm like a poor man's Ola Billgren whose only talent is being precise, but who cares about *precise*? Eh? Since when is *precision*" – he spat out the word – "art?"

"Photorealism," someone put in.

"Which was new and exciting fifteen years ago," someone else countered before being silenced by a girl smacking him on the arm. Gustav seemed not to have heard.

"I mean – can an exact reproduction truly be art? Or does art emerge in the gap between the object and the image?" Someone nodded. "But who fucking cares about reality?" Gustav leaned forward and poured himself more wine. "Reality is the opposite of art, to quote... to quote... well, you know who I mean." A grand gesture with his free hand, scattered laughter.

The conversation around them turned to the question of what really defined postmodernism, and Gustav lowered his voice so only Martin could hear. He'd been to an exhibition of Sandor's friend's art, he said, that Carl Michael what's-his-face, von Hauswolff. Hadn't understood shit. But Sandor said it was good. So it probably was. But on the other hand, Sandor also said Gustav's paintings were in the "Odd Nerdrum school", whatever that meant. Gustav wasn't sure he wanted his paintings to be in anyone's school. Then he'd looked up Nerdrum and sure, fine, there might be some similarities. Especially with the Andreas Baader painting, which did seem like it was something special, even though Gustav had only seen it in books.

At this point, he'd lost Martin, but he kept talking, his eyes ruefully fixed on his glass. "A six-by-nine-foot canvas, that alone..."

The next pass came an hour later, when Martin was discussing the imminent demise of punk from the perspective of a Hegelian dialectic. "Briefly put," he said, "punk is going to be assimilated into mainstream culture – the synthesis, to speak with Hegel. That is to say, the very essence of punk's, well, punkiness, will be neutralised..."

Gustav thumped down next to him.

"You look rather gloomy, my friend," said Sandor with his Zappa moustache.

"Where are your glasses?" Martin asked.

Without a word, Gustav held out his hand. In it lay the thin metal frames, neatly folded. His eyes were big and glassy, unprotected. He looked deflated, sucking on a cigarette whose precarious column of ash was miraculously staying intact.

Sandor laughed. "Shouldn't you put your specs back on?"

Gustav shook his head.

"But you can't see?"

Gustav shook his head again.

"I have all these neat ideas..." he said and started checking the wine bottles on the table.

"Pardon?"

"I have to stop doing the photographs. The photographs just make everything complicated."

"But the photographs are interesting, Gustav." Sandor's voice was kind and gentle. "We've talked about this. You're raising the question of what art is, right? Where to draw the line between, say, art and documentation?"

Gustav mumbled something.

"What was that?"

"*Documentation.* That's what I forgot. I was thinking about it, but I forgot..."

A girl sat down next to Sandor, the conversation shifted, and Gustav said softly, to no one in particular: "...but it's still no good..."

Martin sighed. "Is this about your paintings again?"

"I'm mediocre. Uninteresting."

"Come off it," Martin replied. "You're probably the most talented person I know." He didn't realise that was the truth until he'd said it.

But Gustav just stared at him with sad, misty eyes. "Martin... I always trust you... but you're *biased*. Biased. You would think I was good even if I took a shit on the canvas and smeared it with my own excrement."

"No, I would think you were a disgusting bastard."

"What I need is criticism." He focused on a spot just below Martin's chin. "But I can't get any serious bloody criticism. If you're weird, you're good. If you're not weird, you're boring. Who wants yesterday's newspaper?"

"But you always sulk when people criticise you. Like when that bloke in your class said you were too... what was it he said...?"

"'Tidy and restrained'. Sure, but come on, *that* guy. Like his stuff is anything to write home about. Right? Kitsch, is what it is. Cute animals and whatever... he doesn't even like animals. He kicked a cat once. An innocent bloody cat."

With a look of distaste, Gustav looked around the room for his nemesis, who was doing goofy dancing next to a girl who was writhing sexily by one of the speakers. Then he remembered he was holding his glasses and put them back on with exaggerated care.

Martin suddenly caught a glimpse of a clock – half past one. Fifteen minutes until the last bus. He wasn't as drunk as he would have needed to be.

"Hey," he said, putting a hand on Gustav's shoulder. "I'm off."

Gustav mumbled something inaudible and waved his cigarette about.

He nearly fell asleep on the bus but managed to change at the central station. He had *L'Existentialisme est un humanisme* in his jacket pocket and struggled through two pages.

The flat was dead silent. Martin caught himself missing the sound of guitars being strummed and restrained voices discussing communism versus syndicalism, having someone tell him there was food in the kitchen if he was hungry. He made sandwiches and ate in bed, reading the comic strips, then drank a glass of milk, got undressed, brushed his teeth, collapsed into bed and was out like a light.

It seemed like no more than ten minutes had passed when the phone rang.

Martin blinked at the ceiling, disoriented. He didn't understand why he was awake until the next ring cut through the darkness. The silence seemed to magnify the sound tenfold. He staggered into the kitchen, slamming into the doorpost on the way, had to lean against the counter.

"Martin?" It was Sissel, and she sounded upset. He could hear voices somewhere in the background.

"What's wrong?"

"You have to come get him."

"Who?"

"Gustav! He's completely out of it. He's not talking to us – he's just lying on the ground…"

Martin turned on the lights. They hurt his eyes. "Where are you?"

"Kungsport."

"Okay. Stay there, I'm on my way. Keep an eye on him."

Voices in the background again. "We were actually on our way to a party…" Sissel said.

"Don't you dare fucking leave."

It felt good to curse at Sissel, to slam the phone down. He checked the time – quarter past four. Going to a party *now*. Idiots.

He threw on jeans and a jumper. Checked his wallet – twenty kronor. Pulled out the drawer where he kept his emergency money. Almost had a heart attack when he realised it was empty, until he remembered he'd used it for his share of the rent, which Anders had had to pay before he went to Albania. So, no money for a taxi. And no trams this late. He could take his bike down to Kungsladugård and borrow the car – an idea that seemed brilliant for all of three seconds, until he remembered his dad had probably driven it to work and that he himself was technically under the influence. He felt dead sober and would probably be able to drive no problem, but if something were to happen and he was caught… Martin cursed and kicked a crate of bottles.

Or cycle all the way there? But if they weren't able to drag Gustav to the party, he was unlikely to be able to coax him onto the luggage rack of his bike.

Per, he thought. Per Andrén has a car. Per lived at Mariaplan and worked part-time as a carer. He might be sober even though it was

Saturday. Martin flipped through his phonebook. He had the feeling Per was eager to hang out more than Martin had time to, which was a good thing – he dialled the number – because that meant he might be willing to let him borrow his car.

Four rings. Five. And then Per's sleepy voice on the other end. Martin explained the situation.

"No problem," Per said immediately. "I'll be right there."

Ten minutes later, his Volkswagen Beetle pulled up outside.

A murky dawn was rolling in over the city. Seagulls cried, the streets were deserted aside from paperboys and the occasional late-night reveller. Per indicated before turning and stopped at red lights even when there were no other cars in sight.

"His wonderful mates from Valand, eh?" Martin said and was surprised at how angry he sounded. "Why can't they take care of him, if they're so bloody great? Instead, they're calling me, bloody idiots. Couldn't they just heave him into a taxi or whatever…"

Kungsport Square was empty apart from three people on the steps by the horse statue.

"Did you stop for coffee on the way here or what?" Uffe snapped.

Martin only glared at him.

"Nice jumper," Uffe said and lit a cigarette.

"He said he just needed a rest," Sissel said. She looked tiny and tired and was wrapped in a big Afghan Martin recognised as Sandor's. There was no sign of its owner. "Then he passed out and we haven't been able to wake him up."

Gustav was slumped limply on a step. He wasn't wearing his glasses.

"And it didn't occur to you to call an ambulance?" Per said in his health-professional voice and bent down to check Gustav's pulse. Sissel's eyes went wide and she pulled the coat more tightly around her.

"We didn't think…" she said.

"An ambulance," Uffe sneered.

"This could have been really bad," Per said with his hands on his hips, looking sternly from Sissel to Uffe and back to Sissel again, as though they were a couple of negligent parents.

"We were just going to a party," Sissel whimpered.

They heaved Gustav to his feet. His eyelids flickered and he muttered something incomprehensible.

"I don't love the idea of him throwing up in the car…" Per said.

But there was no need to worry about that, because after just a few steps, Gustav gagged and bent over to emit a cascade of vomit. Martin noted that it was completely liquid and the colour of red wine, no bits of food, and that some of it spattered his shoes.

Sissel made a disgusted sound.

Per pulled out a handkerchief and wiped Gustav's mouth. He mumbled something incomprehensible again but allowed them to lead him to the car and lay him down across the backseat.

"You wouldn't be able to drop us off at Redberg Square, would you?" Uffe called out after them.

IV

INTERVIEWER: You grew up in the seventies, when so-called confession literature rose to prominence. Today, we have autofiction. What are your thoughts on autobiography as a genre?

MARTIN BERG: Equating an author's life with his or her work is always a simplification. Some events can be said to "have happened" [*making air quotes*], I suppose, but there's a difference between text and reality. No matter what you do, there's a gap between them. I believe that gap is necessary for literature to exist. And art in general. Even if I proposed to write something *exactly* the way it happened, I would always fail to some extent. You can't create a perfect reproduction of the world. You can't be completely honest or objective because all experiences are perceived through the filter of subjectivity. And that seems to bother people sometimes – they either want a thing to be *true* or they want it to be *made up*. But literature by its very nature exists at the intersection of the two, and I think we just have to accept that.

*

The summer after their first year of university, Martin and Gustav took an art-cum-festival trip to Denmark. The plan was to go to Copenhagen first, then Louisiana, then Skagen, and finally wrap things up with the Roskilde Festival. Martin wanted to see U2, Ulf Lundell and Ebba Grön. Gustav was more focused on festival life. They'd bought a two-person tent neither knew how to pitch. Martin drove his parents' Volvo and Gustav sat next to him, smoking cigarettes, fiddling with the radio, singing along. At regular intervals, he asked to stop at petrol stations and came out carrying an evening paper, a pair of pilot sunglasses, a bag of onion crisps or ice cream (ice lolly for Martin, Cornetto for himself). Every now and again, he griped about not having a driving licence, but he didn't sound particularly upset.

While they waited for the ferry, Gustav called an acquaintance in Copenhagen and asked if they could possibly sleep on her floor. He was surprisingly good at Danish, or at pretending to speak Danish in a way that didn't offend people.

"Frederikke is a star," he said. They were standing by the railing. Martin kept his eyes firmly fixed on the strip of land steadily moving closer.

"I thought you'd already talked to her?"

"Why would you think that?"

"You said you'd talked to your friend about us coming down."

"I must have meant in general."

"Hmm."

"She lives on a dodgy street somewhere near the central station." He dug around his pocket for the note on which he'd jotted down Frederikke Larsen's address. "You take it. I'm just going to lose it."

"How do you know her?"

"She lived in town a few years ago, dated a friend of mine – you know, Zacke? – and played in a couple of bands and whatever. I think you met her. But Gothenburg isn't exactly Copenhagen and Zacke was in a bad way and didn't care enough about their relationship, so things fell apart and Freddie went back home."

Gustav wasn't much good with maps and his favourite navigation method was rolling down the window and asking passers-by for directions. It took them a long time to find the right address. The building was a monument to past grandeur with its six floors, light-grey plaster facade and tall windows. The door was sky-blue, a handful of abandoned bikes were chained to a drainpipe, and the list of residents next to the entry phone was full of crossed-out and handwritten names.

"Freddie, Freddie," Gustav mumbled, eventually pushing one of the buttons. A few moments later, the lock buzzed, and they trotted up the stairs until a door was thrown open, revealing a woman. She looked vaguely familiar: black hair, striped shirt and harlequin chequered trousers, fingers heavy with silver rings, bright eyes framed by eyeliner, Suzanne-Brøgger style. She was the one, Martin suddenly recalled, who had urged him to read Hermann Hesse.

"Gustav!" she exclaimed, with the more guttural Danish pronunciation. *Gous*-tav. "And you must be Martin." The second syllable was half swallowed, *Mart*-n. "I've heard so much about you. It's *very* nice to meet you." She took his hand in both of hers and smiled, a dazzling smile Martin didn't quite know what he'd done to deserve. Surely he couldn't have made that much of an impression during their discussion of *Steppenwolf*? To his chagrin, he realised he was acting self-conscious and awkward, and when Frederikke led them into her flat, he trooped after her, not understanding half of what she said. When she realised she'd lost him, she changed over to a Swedefied version of her native tongue.

"This is the kitchen, help yourselves to anything you find in the fridge… the bathroom, sometimes one of the taps falls off, just screw it back on. This is my room" – a brief glimpse of Japanese rice-paper lamps and a pale-yellow silk screen – "and this is the living room…"

There were moving boxes and stuff everywhere. The room they were staying in was being used to shoot a film Frederikke had written and was both directing and filming. "Low budget," she said. "It's a kind of chamber play, but through a surrealist filter... most of it takes place in this room. My main character is visiting her parents, though, so I'm not going to get anything done right now anyway. Unfortunately, that is all I have to offer as far as beds go, but you can fit a lot of people on it. I think the current record is five."

The room was dominated by a giant round mattress on the floor. The windows and ceilings were hidden behind red, purple and pink cloth, which created the impression of being inside a circus tent.

"Where does one get one of those?" Gustav asked. "Do I even want to know? Danes. Always so avant-garde."

Frederikke smiled. "I'm hosting a small screening party tomorrow. Eight o'clock. I have to go to work now. Make yourselves at home. Here are the keys." She handed Martin a set of keys and after a minute of intent pottering about, she slammed the front door shut behind her.

"Intense girl," Martin said, pulling one of the cloths aside so he could look out at the street. Judging by the neon signs, it seemed to be home to hotels, prostitution and butcher shops. A street of transience and flesh. Frederikke was wobbling down it on a bike.

"A hundred irons in the fire," Gustav said, fiddling with a group of small figurines huddled on a dresser before picking one up and examining it. "I don't think the film stuff pays. She works in the psych ward to make ends meet. She set this band up with a bunch of straitjackets once, for a gig. But the singer panicked when they strapped him in, and the others couldn't wear straitjackets when they played their instruments, so it all came to nothing."

"Cool idea, though," Martin said.

"One time, she made a soundtrack where she plays the cello, except she doesn't know how to play the cello at all. It sounded awful, obviously. Like a mix of *Psycho* and Ebba Grön, if they were a string quartet." He put the figurine back. "All right, come on. All this driving, not to mention liquorice, has given me a wicked thirst for a shot of Gammel Dansk and a pint."

*

Martin was woken up by Gustav shaking him.

"Good morning! Rise and shine," he said. "There's coffee. Frederikke made some kind of Turkish version. It's good but watch out for the grounds."

"What time is it?"

"Hammershøi time."

"Who?"

"*Vilhelm Hammershøi*. At the Glyptotek."

Martin sat up. His head was spinning and the brightly coloured cloth seemed to billow. It was entirely possible he was still drunk.

The night before had begun with the two of them wandering out into a hot, lazy July afternoon to find a bureau de change. Gustav's primary goals were going to Christiania and, for some reason, a jazz club. On Gustav's initiative, they'd drunk beer and smoked pot and eaten red sausages with mustard like proper tourists. At the end of the night, they'd found themselves in a bar with dark walls and a ceiling obscured by a thick layer of smoke, where they listened to a jazz quartet fronted by a frenzied clarinet player. Then: unknown streets, long rows of street lamps they hoped would lead them right, a Doberman that appeared out of the night like a Cerberus. They got lost trying to get home and ended up in the stockyard district. "*For fanden!*" Gustav shrieked in his best Danish. "We have to get out of here! Swine like us! We're in mortal danger!"

Somehow, they'd managed to locate the blue door at last and made their way up to Freddie's flat, where they collapsed on the round mattress. Probably not too many hours ago.

"I don't feel so good…"

"Who the fuck does," Gustav retorted, and he looked so rough Martin had to laugh: unkempt hair, his T-shirt twisted as though it were on its way somewhere. He was wearing a pair of washed-out long johns. They were slightly too short, revealing a few inches of scrawny, translucently pale calves that looked a little like – Martin thought in his daze – the white asparagus in one of those Dutch still lifes Gustav liked.

He held out his hand and Gustav pulled him to his feet. "Coffee's the ticket, you'll see. And there's always Gammel Dansk."

"There definitely isn't going to be any Gammel Dansk until after three o'clock, at the earliest."

Freddie's kitchen was surprisingly conventional. There were no stacks of dirty dishes, no kitchen table jumble of old newspapers and overflowing ashtrays, no cooking pot forgotten in a corner somewhere with the remains of a bean stew slowly mutating into another life form. Granted, everything was a bit dilapidated – several cabinet doors were missing, and the chubby fridge was probably from the fifties – but clean and tidy. A framed poster with the words 16TH CHICAGO FILM FESTIVAL and a stylised drawing of high rises in orange and blue hung above the kitchen table. A hash pipe lay next to neatly lined-up teapots and tea caddies on a shelf. This was an adult's kitchen. He found himself staring at a grease-stained bag of Danishes on the table. It would never have occurred to him to go out and buy baked goods for two hungover Swedes several years younger than him.

"Told you," Gustav commented. "She's a star. There's sausages and stuff in the fridge, too."

He poured Martin a cup of coffee and himself a shot of Gammel Dansk.

"Cheers, then," he said, knocking it back like it was medicine.

It was a short walk to the Glyptotek, but they could only move very slowly. They'd driven past the big, red building with the arches and the dome while they were looking for Freddie's flat. Ny Carlsberg Glyptotek – you had to appreciate the culturally sanctioned connection between art and beer. The very word *glyptotek* had the amber ring of nineteenth century to it. Martin wasn't sure what it meant.

"That ticket lady certainly looked annoyed, huh?" he said as they walked through the winter garden, where the air was tropically humid.

"She did? I didn't notice. Do you want to check out the mummies?" Gustav unfolded a map he'd picked up in the lobby. "Or the statues with the missing noses? Or should we head straight for old Vilhelm?"

"I'd prefer the latter," Martin said.

Hammershøi, he remembered somewhat hazily from what he'd read about the artist in preparation for their trip, had been active around the turn of the century. A quiet, undramatic life. Married to the same workaday Danish woman from his youth to his death. An incredibly dull biography: no van Goghian breakdowns, no dramatic love affairs à la Picasso, completely devoid of Munch's darkness and demons. Many of his motifs were interiors – rooms so empty they almost seemed uninhabited, filled with diffuse light and heavy moods. His portraits were of women in black with their backs to the viewer. There were also a few dreamlike landscapes, suffused with a lyrical, golden light. Somehow, Hammershøi seemed most at ease when there were no people to interfere with his paintings.

Gustav was particularly fascinated by the interiors. "It feels like you could step right into them, don't you think? And you'd be in this creepy, weird place. Just clocks ticking super loudly. Always early spring outside, you know, that slushy snow. Nothing *ever* happens."

Martin actually liked the building itself more than the art. The winter garden under the dome was beautiful, as were the long galleries with their mosaic floors and dark-red, forest-green and dusty-yellow walls. There were long rows of marble statues everywhere. It made him feel like time was standing still, that he was in a dimension that soared high above the everyday.

"We have art in order to not die of the truth," Martin quoted. They'd barely touched Nietzsche in school. The teachers seemed to dislike anyone who was genuinely interesting – Nietzsche, Kierkegaard, Sartre – as though what they did wasn't real philosophy but some kind of popular version of it, which you might dabble in in upper secondary school, perhaps, but which once you reached university you only had to condescend to cover in overview. Instead, they worked on Russel and Frege, Popper and Wittgenstein.

"Yes," Gustav said. "That's how it is."

As promised, Frederikke screened parts of her film that evening. She'd hung up a sheet to serve as a screen and placed cushions on the floor in front of it, and around nine o'clock a lot of Danes turned up. Freddie swanned around in backcombed hair and a cocktail dress with diagonal stripes in black and a rusty red, a perfect blend of Siouxsie Sioux and true elegance. She introduced them to her friends, and Martin felt oddly confident despite being by far the youngest and barely able to understand a third of what was said.

The film took place in the circus tent room. The light was a muted, shimmering pink. A woman in her thirties lay among the cushions on the giant mattress. For long periods she said nothing, just flipped through a magazine, tried to light and smoke a cigar, or drank absently from a glass she kept balanced on a book next to her on the bed. The camera never moved, and when the woman got up at one point, she simply disappeared out of shot until she returned holding a packet of crackers. Then followed a scene with dialogue, in which her interlocutor was off-screen and didn't speak at all at first. Then he lay next to the woman in bed and the screen was dominated by their faces, in profile. Martin only understood the occasional phrase. There were long silences between lines. "I hoped," the woman said. "I was always waiting for you to understand." The sound was bare and scratchy. No music.

Afterwards, everyone clapped and said it was amazing. Frederikke served wine and Martin ended up seated on a creaky leather sofa with one of her friends from Gothenburg, who talked about synthesisers, cults, black magic and her experiences with LSD. It was a monologue rather than a conversation, and Martin must have listened for an hour, thinking he could use it in his writing somehow. Then he escaped to the kitchen on the pretence of needing something to drink. There, he was waylaid by a young man in a black turtleneck.

"*Are you Swedish?*" he asked in Danish.

"Yeah, yes," Martin replied.

Turtleneck-bloke introduced himself and wondered if Martin had read Stig Larsson, whom he was currently translating into Danish. He'd come across an expression he wasn't familiar with and wanted to ask him about it. What was it now...? He snapped his fingers and impatiently twitched his fringe aside, but no, he couldn't remember. Isn't that just typical, he laughed, when there was linguistic expertise to hand.

And partly because it was a reason not to go back to the cult guy, partly because this Jens was nice – if somewhat difficult to understand at times – Martin stayed in the kitchen for a long time. Leaning against the counter, they talked about Jens's attempts to establish himself as a translator and Martin's struggle with his Novel, which currently consisted of a stack of incoherent notes, half of them typed and half scribbled in various notebooks. Jens understood his frustration, he said, and told him about how he'd been working on a story for more than a year but was now starting to suspect it was terrible. They topped up each other's wine glasses and laughed at the same things. When Martin ran out of cigarettes, Jens went with him to a nearby corner shop and when they returned to Freddie's flat, it was like they'd known each other for years.

But there was something about the other man's unwavering attention Martin couldn't put his finger on: his enthusiastic nodding, the physical closeness, which was, granted, perfectly reasonable, considering how crowded the kitchen was, but still not entirely necessary, a few pauses during which Jens grinned wryly at the floor instead of speaking… Suddenly, Martin realised he hadn't seen Gustav in a long time. He should go find him. Maybe he'd ended up in the monologue man's clutches and needed to be rescued – Gustav would listen to the worst kinds of drivel for hours out of sheer politeness…

As he was trying to come up with a decent excuse to leave, Frederikke joined them. The skirt of her dress rustled when she pushed in between them.

"So, you've met Martin," she said to Jens, who had to move aside slightly to make room for her. Then she added something Martin didn't understand, but her tone was pointed. Jens raised his eyebrows in an expression of simultaneous surprise and understanding.

"I didn't know," he said. Frederikke rolled her eyes and topped up Martin's glass. Jens, whose glass was also empty, but who was not given a top-up, looked like he wanted to explain himself, but then he shook his head and stalked off.

"Trying to play dumb," Frederikke muttered. "When he knows exactly what he's doing." She stepped out of her shoes to rub her toes and was instantly four inches shorter. The make-up around her eyes was smeared and she had a ladder in her stockings.

Martin didn't know how to respond, so he offered her a cigarette.

"I'm so happy," she said, "that Gustav has you. You're lovely together. He's lucky."

"Okay…"

"I've been worried about Gustav, you know. He's the kind of person who could do a lot of damage to himself, I've often thought. But it's nice to be proven wrong sometimes, don't you think?" She tapped ash into the sink. "With you, well – it feels right, I guess. That you're together."

Martin's brain was fuzzy from the wine, and Frederikke's words, barely audible over the laughing and din of voices, reached him as if from a great distance.

"Gustav's a very good friend," he said finally.

Frederikke looked up. "A good *friend*?" There was an alert edge to her voice.

"A good *friend*," Martin repeated.

"Oh." She pulled on her cigarette and squinted at him through the smoke. "I see. A *good friend*."

"Yes."

"I suppose people should be grateful for good friends, too."

"I guess… if you'll excuse me, I just have to…"

With a vague gesture, Martin fled the kitchen.

He found Gustav in the circus room, sitting on the edge of the mattress, rolling a cigarette. The noise of the party was muffled.

"To what do I owe the honour?" Gustav said. "I thought you were going to talk to your new soulmate all night."

"Who?"

"That blond Danish bloke you took off with before."

Martin sat down heavily next to him. He was so tired he could have fallen asleep right then and there. "Oh, right, Jens. We went out to get smokes. I think he might have been trying to pick me up."

"Isn't it enough for you to have all the girls chasing after you in Gothenburg?" Gustav said. "If the gays of Copenhagen are falling over themselves as well, you might want to consider moving to somewhere uninhabited so you can get some peace."

Martin smacked him on the arm.

"*Ow.*" Gustav heaved a sigh. "I guess you can tell him you have a girlfriend."

"But I don't."

"What about Britta?"

Britta, Britta. Cat-eyed Britta whom he'd met a few weeks before they set out on their Danish tour. "It's nothing serious."

"I thought you were rendezvousing at Roskilde."

"And does that mean it has to be serious?"

"You didn't talk to *anyone* else that night at Sandor's." Gustav lit his cigarette and lay back too.

"Everyone else wanted to discuss the nature of pop art. What was I supposed to do? You're going to have to write index cards for me to use when someone asks me what I think about Andy Warhol."

"Come off it, you're fine talking about anything."

"When it comes to Warhol, my repertoire is fairly limited."

"I've heard you go on and on about Warhol for hours."

"Did I say anything smart?"

"Oh yes. Every word will go down in art history."

Martin laughed and reached for the cigarette. He closed his eyes for a while. Probably the best course of action was just to go to sleep and forget all about it.

7

APPARENTLY, IT WAS FRIDAY AGAIN, and when Sanna looked up from a set of proofs and asked about his weekend plans, Martin mumbled something about the theatre. It became a potential truth as soon as he said it: he could go to the theatre. Why not? But before Sanna had a chance to ask awkward follow-up questions, his phone rang, and he could answer it with an important-sounding "Martin Berg" and make a small hand gesture that signalled "I just have to take this" in her direction.

One by one, the employees of the publishing company left. Martin stayed to answer emails. The last sunlight of the dying day slanted into the room, setting the colours of Gustav's large Paris painting alight. The small space really didn't do it justice – the famous realism emerged only at a distance – but Martin liked studying the brushstrokes and the structure of the paint.

Around seven, he turned the lights out and locked the door.

"I'm home."

No answer. "*Les initials, les initials, les initials BB,*" Brigitte Bardot warbled on the other side of Elis's closed door.

His son's school bag lay in a deflated heap on the hallway floor, its contents spilling out. A leather-bound notebook, a handful of mechanical pencils. And – aha! – a Bic lighter. Martin bent down to see what else was hiding inside the bag but stopped himself.

Instead, he took off his shoes, went into the kitchen and started making dinner.

Halfway through chopping the onions, he remembered tearing a recipe out of the newspapers a while ago. It must have ended up in the bookshelf, in the pile where all kinds of loose pieces of paper collected as if by magic. Martin searched, flipping through Elis's ninth-grade transcripts (not terrible, not as outstanding as Rakel's), reviews from the paper, old electricity bills, an issue of *Faktum* he hadn't read, the latest issue of *The 2010s*, which he also hadn't read, the Workers' Educational Association's spring catalogue (last spring), this year's film festival programme with twenty films circled (he'd gone to see three) and a few typed and stapled sheets of paper.

He pulled them out, frowning.

The headline read:

`"Haga Nygata, 2.23 p.m."`

Martin read a paragraph at random.

`She was absorbed in her book and probably didn't even notice`
`him entering. And the question is if she would have noticed`
`his presence even if she'd raised her eyes, which, he knew, were`
`veiled and bright blue, like the autumn sky or the sea in`
`spring, because her entire being seemed to be elsewhere. What`
`she dreamed of, no one knew and`

He couldn't remember writing it. It must have been years ago.

He read a few more lines and put the manuscript back at the bottom of the pile. Then he pulled it out again and tossed it onto his desk.

Elis ate quickly, replying monosyllabically to Martin's every attempt at conversation. Then he disappeared into his room, from which could soon be heard the first trembling chords of Jacques Brel's "Amsterdam". Half an hour later he re-emerged, wearing a shirt, a bow tie, tweed trousers and braces. He was always careful with his boots, did and undid the laces, didn't just step out of them, which would cause them to lose their shape and eventually break.

"Where are you going?"

"Out," Elis replied.

Martin chuckled. Elis looked nonplussed.

"There's a book by that title… Kerstin Thorvall," Martin said, but his son made no reply, just pulled on his anorak. It was little more than a windbreaker, really. Not nearly warm enough for early April. Martin heard himself say:

"Don't you want a warmer coat?"

"I'm taking a scarf," Elis said.

He stood by the window for a long while after Elis's much too lightly dressed figure had vanished from sight.

A line from that short story came back to him: *her eyes were veiled and bright blue.*

You have to choose one or the other. Veiled and bright at the same time, that didn't work. Gustav used to read his drafts and shower them with superlatives. "Marvellous. I really mean that. The only thing missing is for you to… finish it."

Martin pulled out his phone and called again. He must have let it ring fifteen times, in case Gustav was in the middle of some critical artistic moment or had just gone to the loo. No answering machine, either. He was useless with any form of communication that wasn't face-to-face. And always so full of remorse once you did get hold of him it was impossible to stay angry.

Gustav's Luddite attitude to all technological advancements was admirable in theory, but the practical consequences were at times extremely frustrating. He'd insisted on vinyl records long before it became trendy to insist on vinyl records. His home phone was unchanged since 1987; it had big buttons and he liked it because the cord was long enough to let him cradle the receiver between his shoulder and his chin while the phone sat on a chair next to him as he painted. He'd never bought a computer, never had an email address, never a mobile phone. This was sometimes mentioned in articles about him, with, it appeared to Martin, equal parts fascination and pathologising (because who doesn't want to surf the internet on a never-breaking wave?). It wasn't that Gustav was technology averse, though, or that he had some principled objection to new things. He simply had no interest.

"But you can google anything," Martin had told him once.

"What for?"

"Say you want to find out about something. You want to learn more about ducks. Feel an irrepressible urge to go through Dantan's entire catalogue. Whatever."

"If that were to happen, there's always the library. And I might actually have an old exhibition catalogue of Dantan at home. I can read that. And I don't give a shit about ducks."

"Those were just for instances. You could email. Stay in touch with people."

"Can't I just call? Or write letters?"

But Gustav wasn't a reliable pen pal, either. Letters were read and put on the hallway dresser, the mantel, a windowsill full of other missives that had met with the same fate.

The room was dark now, the street outside clearly visible. The occasional patch of ice, pools of lamplight. Elms and horse chestnuts loomed in the park. Café Zenith's sign shone yellow. There was no sign of spring approaching.

Martin pressed Gustav's name again. One by one, the rings faded into the past. Should he reach out to one of Gustav's friends in Stockholm? But the only one who came to mind was Dolores, and there was no point worrying her for no reason. The easiest thing would obviously be to call Gustav's gallerist, KG, but KG might actually know exactly where Gustav was, and Martin didn't want to reveal his ignorance. He was probably just travelling. Probably some art event KG was forcing him to attend. Probably nothing to worry about.

And yet the whole thing made Martin think of an episode several years before. He'd been in Stockholm for work and had had time to kill. He hadn't been able to reach Gustav then either, so he'd taken a taxi over to his studio on Södermalm and managed to slip into the building as a feisty pug exited, followed by a woman wearing headphones. No one opened when he rang the bell, but the door was unlocked. In the dusty gloom of the living room, Gustav was watching TV with the sound off.

"Oh, it's you," he said. He didn't sound particularly surprised.

"I called," Martin said. "How are you?"

"Okay."

"You're not answering your phone."

"No…" Gustav sat up and pushed his fingers against his eyes, behind his glasses. When he looked up, his gaze was clouded.

Martin was about to say he looked awful, but Gustav seemed to have passed the point where that kind of comment came off as refreshingly brusque and instead just became a tragic truth. He was wearing a stained The Smiths T-shirt and no trousers. His legs were very thin, pale. He reeked. But the most worrying thing about him was his facial expression – neutral, blank. As though someone else was hiding behind his features, using them.

What had happened after that? Maybe he'd persuaded Gustav to have a shower. He'd probably been authoritative in a way that masked how distressed he felt. There had been no sheets on the bed, he remembered, just a towel over the mattress, so he'd searched the closet for clean ones. He'd changed his train ticket and forced Gustav to go to bed. The toilet was in a state reminiscent of a student dormitory on a Sunday morning. There were piles of envelopes on the hallway rug. A canvas was sitting out in the studio, but the oil on it was completely dry, and the paint tubes on the work counter were covered in a layer of dust. The fridge was empty aside from half a jar of pickles, a flattened tube of mayonnaise and a tub of butter. Plates covered the kitchen counter, caked to various degrees with dried-on food. There were empty takeaway boxes on the kitchen table. And then there were the bottles. Three paper bags full of empty bottles, lined up neatly along the wall, as though doing their best to look inconspicuous.

"Did you throw a party?" he asked later, maybe the next day, and the edge in his voice made Gustav flinch.

Party. But he meant the party Gustav had always referred to when he ordered another bottle, went to the pub on an ordinary Wednesday, celebrated with champagne. A Baudelairean intoxication, a fairy ring of shimmering golden light in an otherwise grey and barren world.

"No one," Cecilia had commented once, long ago, "has *that* much fun just because it's fun."

*

Long after Elis vanished from view, a familiar figure wandered into it. She was wearing a long coat and a hat pulled down over her ears, but Martin still recognised his daughter instantly.

Rakel looked both ways before cutting diagonally across the street and glancing up at the flat. Martin waved before realising she couldn't see him; there were no lights on in the room.

"I almost thought there was no one home," she said as she stepped through the front door.

"Are you hungry?"

He heated up the leftovers from dinner and asked her about university (she shrugged) and the reader's report (she yawned). As soon as she'd finished eating, she fetched her woolly socks and snuggled up on the sofa under a blanket. She was reading Freud, he noted, not the German novel – *Ein Jahr? Ein Tag?*

Martin opened a beer and sat down in the armchair with a manuscript he had no desire whatsoever to read. The long title was a worrying sign of someone trying too hard. The author was a man whose debut novel had garnered critical acclaim and sold reasonably well; there had been morning shows and interviews and endless reproductions of his pensive author photo in newspapers and on posters for their stand at the book fair, which always, no matter how much Blu Tack you used, insisted on falling down, foreshadowing what their physical counterpart would go on to do a few years later. Martin had practised a cautiously encouraging approach, taking him out for lunch, even agreeing to pay him a small advance. After three years, a new manuscript had arrived and it was pretty much the same story again, just less cheerful.

"I'm afraid we can't publish this," Martin had told him over the phone, closing his eyes as silence invaded the other end of the line, regretting his decision to quit smoking. He hadn't even wanted a cigarette. He'd wanted to want one.

This time, it was one hundred and fifty pages that all seemed to be about The Young Author and his trials and tribulations.

"Oh, dear Lord," he muttered and noted out of the corner of his eye that his daughter took no notice of his muttering.

Mikael stared out across the grey water. Hard. Impenetrable. Surface, nothing but surface. As far as the eye could see. Surface. Depth existed underneath. He was sure of it – he could feel the promise of the depth. But he didn't know how to reach it. It began to rain. He turned up the collar of his trench coat and let the rain caress his hair. He closed his grey eyes and tried to remember that quote by

"Would you like some crisps?" he asked his daughter.

"No, thank you."

"You're not on a diet, are you?"

Rakel lowered her book and rolled her eyes. "No, I'm not on a diet."

"Are you eating enough? You look a bit thin."

"I'm just not a crisp fan."

"Okay." There was a crease at the corner of her mouth, a crease that only appeared when she was in a bad mood.

"So what, you're not having crisps either now?" Rakel said.

"Pardon?"

"Are you not going to have crisps just because I'm not having any?"

"Oh, right – no, sure."

He fetched the bag of crisps.

remember that quote by Strindberg. "Every person has at least one great novel to write – the one about their own life." Or something along those lines. He'd heard it in upper secondary school. His Swedish teacher. He hadn't realised how good she was until much later, and by then it was too late. But maybe he, Mikael, was the exception? He didn't know how to start, he didn't know how to end... the water of the river flowed past. The same colour as granite. As heavy. He had no inspiration. Suddenly, he turned around and strode back towards the city. He needed something to drink before

"Are you staying over?"

"I thought I might," Rakel said.

"You don't have a party to go to? No town to paint red? No dodgy nightclub to frequent?"

Rakel put her arms straight up and stretched until a joint cracked somewhere, yawned, and shook her head. "No. But I did download a couple of films. *Annie Hall* and *Deconstructing Harry*. You pick."

"Do you think Elis has taken up smoking?" he asked later, as Annie was driving Alvy home and Alvy was fearing for his life.

"Probably," Rakel replied. She didn't sound very concerned.

"He only listens to Jacques Brel and Serge Gainsbourg these days. I've even heard some Yves Montand."

"I guess he's trying to emulate you," she said, grabbing a handful of crisps. "These things happen, you know."

Soon thereafter she fell asleep wrapped in the blanket, rolled up like a hedgehog. At rest, her face recalled the child she'd been not so terribly long ago.

When Rakel was little, she'd replied "archaeologist or professor, or both" when asked what she wanted to be when she grew up. Other adults took it as adorable precociousness, but Martin suspected she meant it. She'd always been a curious child. Granted, he had no idea what other children her age were interested in, but he felt relatively certain it wasn't Pompei (covered in ash and lava in 79 CE and turned into a macabre monument for future generations), the Great Library of Alexandria (presumed to have burned to the ground when barbarians sacked the city) or mythological stories about capricious, megalomaniac gods and their escapades (Pallas Athena being born from the head of her father, Zeus, wearing full armour and with her lance lowered). From there, she moved on to the Mayans, Ancient Egypt, endangered animal species, tsarist Russia and explorers. She read historical novels, which were all very thick and had questionable illustrations on their covers. They were called things like *The Sun Queen* and *Daughter of Ra* and were apparently supplied by her school librarian. She arranged a dig on the small strip of beach by her grandparents' summer house, which resulted in seventeen bottle caps, a few shards of weathered glass, and what she hoped was a bone from an iguanodon's thumb. It was beyond Martin how so much information could be stored in a child's brain. "Did you know," she might say, "that the Great Sphinx of Giza is alone? Even though sphinxes always come in pairs everywhere else?" And then she would sigh, a strangely wistful sigh.

This was during a time when Martin desperately wanted to *give* his daughter something – anything, really, so long as it involved giving from him to her. The fact that Rakel didn't *want* anything made it harder. She had handed all her dolls over to Elis and slowly culled the stuffed animals on her bed until only a tattered old seal remained. But she read in the kitchen every chance she got, so he gave her books, which came with the added benefit that he didn't have to pay VAT.

He didn't know how to plait her hair, either. That had always been Cecilia's job. When he tried, the plaits ended up loose and uneven.

"I'll just do it myself," Rakel said and plaited her own hair without even looking in the mirror.

Martin tried calling Gustav again, even though it was past midnight. No answer.

He kept on reading.

8

From the armchair by the panoramic window, she had an unobstructed view of the MUL's entrance. Every time a visitor stepped through the door, Rakel looked up, but what may have looked like the lumbering figure of Emanuel Wikner out of the corner of her eye always turned out to be someone else. At one point, a man with Alexander's sauntering gait and baggy suede jacket entered, and even though she knew instantly it wasn't him, it took her heart several minutes to stop racing. In the past three hours, which she'd spent writing just over half a page of her essay about *Beyond the Pleasure Principle*, she hadn't seen hide nor hair of her uncle. She wanted to ask him about the paintings in the barn. The signature in the corner – CW – had to mean they were self-portraits. Grandpa Lars did use to mutter things like "Cecilia should have applied to art school" when he'd had one too many cognacs, but Rakel couldn't recall ever having seen her mother paint. The received wisdom was that her Talent came from Lars, but no one had seen anything he'd painted, either, at least not for many years. Any genetic artistic ability seemed to have entirely bypassed Rakel, thankfully, and Elis, who had actually turned out to be good at drawing, was too lazy to make anything of it. That said, as a child, she'd been dragged to enough art exhibitions to know that Lars Wikner wasn't too wide of the mark, for once. Even though they were simply made, the five oil paintings in the barn exhibited boldness and sensitivity in their handling of shape and colour. It was the work of an untrained hand, but far above the usual level of an amateur.

Rakel was finding it difficult to focus on her assignment, partly because anyone entering the library could be Emanuel, and partly because the screen of her phone kept lighting up with texts from Lovisa, who was cooped up at home, studying for the medical school entrance exam.

OK, how about this: a small experiment with my friend the adhd drug (Ritalin) during the exam itself?

Obvs in line with medical recommendations

Or could that be a gateway to so-called "heavier stuff"?

NB joke

Just having a fucking hard time not passing out from boredom

Bear in mind that choosing to become a doctor is pretty much a public service

Ne quid nimis, Rakel replied and then put her phone in her bag.

On her computer screen, the cursor was blinking in the middle of a sentence. *Freud describes repetition compulsion in terms of.* Not a single viable way of continuing it came to her. Rakel shut her laptop.

The library wasn't closing for hours yet. Emanuel could still show up. Calling him was obviously an option, but she'd never called her uncle before, and she had a feeling the subject of Cecilia's paintings had to be approached obliquely. A frontal assault could end in disaster.

To kill time, she pulled out *Ein Jahr*. The book was starting to look like she'd read it, at least. But the sentences tumbled about willy-nilly, and Philip Franke's alter ego was so morose she could slap him, even though she was only on page 21. Don't just lie around moping, she wanted to yell at him. Come on, man. Just because some woman left you? How is lying on the sofa staring at the ceiling supposed to help? (Or whatever it was he was doing, Rakel was unsure about that particular phrase and didn't bother looking it up.) Exactly *nothing*. Nothing happens when you lie on a sofa staring at the ceiling. The world stands still. The sun goes up and then it goes down. Shadows move across the wall. Sometimes a newspaper thuds onto the hallway rug. Sometimes there's a rush of water through the neighbours' pipes. But nothing changes. Everything stays the same. You are where you are.

Rakel flipped forward a few pages, but it seemed like more of the same. Fine, let him lie there and mourn. She was going home. Slowly, because her body felt like lead, Rakel gathered up her things and buttoned all her coat buttons.

Outside, the wind snatched at her scarf. Daffodils with smooth, closed buds covered the slope. Just dragging herself down to Korsvägen was an ordeal. It was half past five, far too early to go to bed. She had to get through at least four more hours if she wanted to avoid being pathetic. Four hours, Rakel told herself, you can do that. And the next tram was eight minutes away. Perfect. That means you can kill some time sitting on this bench, staring into space.

If the tram ride had been slightly longer, she might have dozed off. The REMEMBER DEATH sign flickered past at the edge of her vision.

Four hours wasn't too bad. She could do four hours.

There were mounds of unopened envelopes on her hallway rug. Newspapers in a separate pile. Stacks of dirty dishes. No clean pan this time, either, or she could have fried a couple of eggs. Since she should be hungry, she called the Thai restaurant on the corner to order takeaway. And since they didn't deliver, she had to wrap herself in her coat, get herself down the stairs, walk at least fifty yards, wait in the greasy restaurant which was crowded with people who just had to pick up their food at the exact same time as her, walk the fifty yards back with the warm containers in a plastic carrier bag, pull open the front door, which apparently weighed a ton, and then climb up all the stairs. Rakel only realised she could have taken the lift when she was already standing in her hallway. But why make it easy when you can make it hard, Rakel Berg? Why take the easy route? Why go easy on yourself when you can dive headfirst into all kinds of unnecessary hardship, like walking four flights of stairs when you're already so tired you want to cry? Why read in your native language when you can do it in another one, preferably German? Why just be good at grammar when you can spend every Wednesday night for a year studying Latin? Maybe a complete withdrawal from the world would be best, so you can really focus on your tribulations? Stop answering the phone. Or even better, bin the phone so no one can reach you. Barricade yourself in your flat. You have unread books to last you years. Lectures are optional anyway. Write your essay about repetition, compulsion and the death drive, about every human's irrevocable journey towards night. It's bound to impress someone. If you have to leave your home, do it after sundown. Go for a walk in the graveyard. Or find the most remote corner of the library catacombs where you can be sure to be sheltered from daylight and life. Read your books. Write your texts. Stay in your mausoleum and make the best of your funereal existence.

At the back of the kitchen cabinet, she found a clean plate. Better than nothing.

*

After watching half an hour of a TV show she couldn't be bothered to get invested in, washing her hair, and wandering from room to room without achieving more than stacking the post into a pile to be gone through later, maybe tomorrow, she knelt down next to her bed and pulled out a suitcase. The leather was worn, marked by faded stickers – CAIRO, ADDIS ABABA, FRANKFURT – and there was really no reason to keep it hidden. Her dad rarely visited her at Friggagatan and probably wouldn't recognise the suitcase that had transported Cecilia Wikner's belongings from Sweden to Ethiopia in the sixties anyway. It had been sitting in her grandparents' attic for decades until Rakel smuggled it out a few years ago. She'd stumbled across it during one of her teenage attic excursions.

Back then it had contained baby clothes from the seventies that had clearly belonged to one of the younger Wikner siblings and therefore held no interest for her. But on the inside of the lid, someone had written CECILIA WIKNER * 1968 in childish block letters: a five-year-old's preparations for the move to another continent.

Now it held the things Rakel had left of her mother. She undid the locks and picked through the contents. On top lay an emerald-green silk kimono with a white feather pattern. It was worn at the seams and on one of the sleeves there was a dark stain the size of a palm. Rakel had a vague memory of her mother bending over her bed and picking her up in a swirl of cool silk, hushing and murmuring. There was also a T-shirt with STOCKHOLM MARATHON 1992 printed on it, washed so many times the cotton was almost see-through, a paperback copy of *Black Skin, White Masks* that had lost its back cover and from which loose pages were spilling, their margins covered in pencil scribbles, and a pair of worn running shoes from the seventies or eighties.

And then there were the black wax cloth notebooks, eleven in all.

They were the only papers Rakel had found of her mother's. In the attic of the summer house were half a dozen cardboard moving boxes marked *Cecilia's things* in Martin's hand; she had systematically gone through each one. They mostly contained clothes and everyday objects. Her dad had left her books up on the shelves, maybe because moving the thousands of volumes had been too much of an effort, or maybe it would have been too great a violation of their shared history. Rakel had found the wax cloth notebooks at the bottom of one of the boxes.

In the hope of gaining a measure of clarity, Rakel had read everything her mother had published. She'd been in her early teens the first time and hadn't understood much of it. The words held a mysterious power – words from the other side of a chasm – but that didn't make them any more comprehensible to thirteen-year-old Rakel, who was sitting in her room, looking up terms like *paradigmatic* and *discursive* with the feeling of doing something forbidden. She tried again in upper secondary school, armed with espresso at Café Java, but she hurriedly hid the books every time someone she knew came in, which was basically all the time. Over the years, she'd read a chapter here, a chapter there, leaving a trail of dog-ears and coffee rings, read herself to sleep when she was wakeful, been unable to remember where she'd left off, had to start over, referred to one of the texts in a school assignment but changed her mind five minutes before submitting it and removed the entire sentence.

The first of her mother's books, *Atlantic Flight*, was a collection of essays about historical figures Cecilia had been fascinated by for one reason or another. The common denominator seemed to be their uncompromising approach to life and the sacrifices they had been forced to make as a result. The titular essay was about Amelia Earhart, the first woman to cross the Atlantic in an aeroplane, who disappeared somewhere over the Pacific Ocean in 1937. She also discussed Lou Andreas-Salomé, most famous for being the confidante of great men; pianist Glenn Gould, whose eccentricity had devolved into genuine madness: philosopher Ludwig Wittgenstein, whose diaries she had translated, and author Anaïs Nin, whose infamous *Incest* had been published shortly before.

The second book was her doctoral thesis, slightly reworked into a more accessible popular non-fiction form. When it was published, Cecilia had already been gone for more than six months. The photograph on the back showed a serious-looking woman with eagle eyes and hollow shadows on her face.

Of Cecilia's unpublished writings, the wax cloth notebooks seemed to be the sum total of what had been saved. They were full of all kinds of notes, often undated. Her handwriting was straggly and slanted to the right, full of joined letters and capitals with big, sharp swoops. Dots and bars were scattered almost at random. Cecilia usually wrote notes in paragraph form, each with a header, not unlike the method Nietzsche used in several of his works. They were short paragraphs about things that had piqued her interest: the West's relationship with the Soviet Union as expressed in *Rocky IV*, the erosion of classical education in a modern society, the fact that Bach let his *St Matthew Passion* end before the resurrection, when Jesus was dead like any other mortal and there was no light in the darkness for his apostles. The notes rarely touched on her own life. Sometimes, a name appeared, or a phone number or a to-do list, rarely with more than half the entries crossed off. A recurring theme was reminders of things she had to do. *Bring up with M*. Rakel had always assumed M was Martin but considering the nature of certain questions – what type of prefix to use for certain concepts in German or French and so on – it could just as easily stand for Max or someone else. Occasionally, there were even words or sentences written in other scripts, Amharic or Ancient Greek, but even then, the handwriting was sloppy. The Greek letters were dreadful.

There were no dates anywhere, and Rakel had only found one note that resembled a diary entry. It was so hastily written as to be virtually illegible. The paragraph had made Rakel uneasy the first time she'd read it – when she was fourteen – and then she'd forgotten about it for several years, until she came home drunk and upset one night and had the questionable idea of perusing her mother's notebooks. The passage still had the same effect on her – a churning sensation in the pit of her stomach, kind of like nausea.

On the plane: Gustav asleep, don't know how I'm going to get him off at Landvetter. Disgusting flat in Camden. Nice building,

actually, frescoes in stairwell etc, but dingy flat. Smell of old food,
bodies, urine. A Gainsborough on the wall, might have been a clever
rep. (Gustav?) G was sitting on the floor screaming "no, no, not
without L" over and over again, but thankfully, L was completely
out of it. He's supposed to be a writer, was sprawled on the bed, limp
and tripping, making guttural sounds that might have been threats.
G emaciated & weak, confused & angry. Slapped him to sober him
up. Vomited all the way down to the taxi.

9

The dessert plates were covered with cheesecake remnants and crumpled napkins, wine glasses had been topped up, the candles were burning low. Martin Berg leaned back in his chair, hoping he was coming
off as intently attentive to the conversation, which revolved around the
impending twenty-five-year anniversary of Berg & Andrén. In reality,
he was pondering how often Per, who was stoically refusing a decadent second slice of cake, and his wife Sandra, who was cleaning her
glasses with the hem of her dress while squinting near-sightedly at her
dinner guests, slept together these days. What was it like when you'd
been married for so long? When you were tied together by a shared
surname, a mortgage, two children and fifteen years as a couple? There
were so many things no one else would never know about, full-on
Ibsen plays, and then people come over to dinner and study the tip of
the iceberg for a while.

"We were thinking of throwing a dinner party this weekend," Per
had told him a few days earlier. "If you're not busy."

Busy sitting at home, reading mediocre texts penned by men with a
lot on their chests and a fucking straw hat on their heads, for instance,
Martin thought, while I wait for my son to come home and try to hide
the fact that he's drunk, and my daughter is making her weekly good-
Samaritan visit, which she ducks out of by conveniently dozing off on
the sofa. Busy launching a grand project of rereading the collected works

of Wallace, since it's been a few years since my last go. Busy lingering at Hagabadet until closing, running from middle age on the treadmill.

"Sounds great," Martin had said.

It was one of Per's virtues that he enjoyed hosting these kinds of gatherings, which Martin liked to attend but rarely hosted himself. As a young man, he'd had notions of lively discussions and smatterings of intellectuals in nocturnal conversation in his own smoke-filled kitchen: the clinking of ice cubes in chilled glasses, Cecilia with her kimono slipping off her shoulder, surrounded by shadows and swiftly sketched characters… Jazz on vinyl, or, even better, a live trio whose frantic bebop somehow miraculously didn't bother the neighbours. The neighbours might be there, too, as a matter of fact, smoking a joint out of the window, hollering at passers-by on the street below, and the whole thing would carry on until the break of dawn at least.

But Martin never managed to strike the right balance when it came to inviting people over – it was either just two people or every single person he knew – and neither did Cecilia, who adopted an air of deer-in-the-headlights when she was expected to shoulder the hostess role her mother had spent a lifetime honing and performing with Gloria Swansonesque elegance. The few times Cecilia threw a party, things quickly went off the rails: Gustav claimed to have been hungover for three days after celebrating her thirtieth birthday in the summer house and that you could still find beer cans and empty bottles in the blueberry shrubs around the house, like laconic messages to future archaeologists.

Tonight, Martin knew everyone, with only a couple of exceptions. His end of the table was dominated by a discussion about autobiographies. A magazine editor was talking about the contemporary obsession with true stories, regardless of their literary value.

"Real people," someone said.

"That's just class contempt," someone else piped up.

Martin leaned forward. "If it weren't for the fact that people love *true stories*, or, more accurately, a story dressed up as fiction that is assumed to be true in all important respects," he said, "our publishing company would have folded a long time ago."

"Why is that?" the magazine editor demanded. The conversation had died down and everyone was looking at Martin.

They had, he told them, managed to break even the first few years. Hadn't taken salaries. Had worked extra hours and applied for grants. Then the financial crisis of the nineties hit (this was met with an oh from his audience, who had fresh memories of the 2008 reprise). It would have been the death knell for the tiny publisher if a British author who had been big at the time, Lucas Bell, had not, for some inscrutable reason, insisted that his book be published by Berg & Andrén and no one else. It probably had a lot to do with Bell's attention-seeking opposition to the establishment. Why Bonniers or Nordstedts when you could choose a tiny publishing company in Gothenburg that had virtually no marketing budget at all and then, to top it off, fall out with your own agent in London?

"Yes, why?" said Per, who had participated in this anecdote countless times before.

"Because marketing was for people who had adapted to and been cowed by capitalism," Martin continued. "Because he wanted to mess with the status quo. Because he wanted to seem punk when a lot of people who clearly were not particularly punk insisted on praising him. Because it enabled him to ask a performance-style question about the relation of art to commerce." At least that was the analysis he and Per, who had thought the whole thing was a joke at first, had settled on. Because in the wake of his debut novel, Bell had acquired a reputation as an *enfant terrible* and literary rockstar. He featured on the covers of *i-D* and *The Face* under headlines like A RIMBAUD FOR OUR TIMES and was regularly arrested for possession and drink-driving. The novel was peppered with enough details that corresponded to the author's own life that he was forever going to be asked how autobiographical it was, and he would forever answer cryptically. They'd never met Bell in person, because just a few days before he was due to appear at the Gothenburg Book Fair, the bastard overdosed and was sent off to a treatment facility in Wales.

But the book sold well. (Scattered laughs.)

"I remember reading it," said someone who worked in the theatre. "What was it called again…?"

"*A Season in Hell*," Per replied. "Which he straight-up stole from Rimbaud."

"Anyway, then he wrote a sappy autobiography about how he got clean and rediscovered the meaning of life," Martin said. "We didn't publish that one." (More laughter.)

Conversation turned to the newspaper business, which seemed in even more dire straits than the publishing industry, and a woman who turned out to be a journalist delivered a long monologue à la Greek tragedy, like an Iphigenia sacrificed to secure fair winds in the sails of a digital pivot, in a war that was likely to end in defeat regardless.

Then Martin felt a foot brush against his. At first he thought it was happenstance and thought nothing of it, but it was a flirtatious foot; it came back.

Figuring out to whom it belonged was not much of a challenge – Maria Malm, the woman sitting across from him, smiling into her glass, fluttering her eyelashes against her cheeks, whose name he remembered only thanks to its memory-friendly alliteration and because she wrote for *Göteborgs-Posten* sometimes. She seemed remarkably indifferent to the doomsday prophecies aimed at her employer. Martin thought he recalled that she was some kind of author, and before he knew it, he had leaned forward and asked.

Yes, as it turned out, Maria had in fact had several collections of poetry published. Figures, thought Martin, who had never been too up on his poetry. He nodded along to whatever it was she was telling him.

Out of the corner of his eye, he noticed Per giving him a long look. He glared back. All that was missing from this picture was a bloody thumbs up. Over the past few years, Per had tried to set him up, as though he were some kind of eighteenth-century widow with too much time on her hands.

In his youth, it had irked Martin when people coupled up, since it meant they dropped out of his circle. Then he'd had children of his own and had stopped caring. He'd been more or less in lockstep with his surroundings for ten years, as people around him settled down, moved out of condemned buildings, finished their degrees, started families, found jobs, got salaries, stopped buying the cheapest beer, stopped buying beer at all as they struggled to survive life with young children, bought new cars, gained weight, stayed in jobs that weren't exactly what they'd imagined but perfectly all right and financially secure.

Then, after Cecilia, he'd been in sync with another, smaller group: the divorced and separated. The people who suddenly discovered *Tunnel of Love* in Springsteen's catalogue, the divorce album they'd previously ignored in favour of his intoxicated and dizzy seventies period. Who suddenly got in touch when they didn't have the children. Who started going to the pub again and complained about how young everyone was, my god, didn't they have age restrictions any more? Who counted on their fingers and realised to their horror that those people were born the same year they themselves lost their virginity on a corduroy sofa in someone's basement. Who once they finally manged to pick someone up ruined everything by drinking too much and talking about their ex for two hours.

How long had that window stayed open? Five years maybe. Then something had happened. People were on their second go, moving faster this time. Suddenly, they were buying summer houses or getting married barefoot by the sea. Their children began to refer to each other as stepsiblings.

Martin, for his part, had passed the point where loneliness became an anomaly. Something people reacted to and renamed *being single*, an expression people in all seriousness used to describe themselves even though they were closing in on fifty. Being single wasn't the same as being alone, it just meant you were alone-for-now. But if singlehood dragged on for too long, people became suspicious. What was wrong with you? Why had you failed? Why weren't you looking? You were expected to sign up to dating sites. Choose a picture that was flattering but not a lie. Endure people who used smileys in their messages because they were incapable of putting their thoughts into words. Go on dates. Set your course for the land of Sunday conversations over coffee and the arts section of the newspaper, of spending time with other couples in summer houses on beach properties, of the warm weight of having someone by your side in life.

Maria told him about a Norwegian collection of poems she was translating. Muffled by wine, his thoughts on that subject began to move, sluggishly, granted, like some primeval creature, but nevertheless coalescing slowly into a shape that could find its way through his nervous system, past his tongue and teeth and lips, and hopefully impress this Maria Malm, whose alliterative name he now also recalled seeing attached to a couple of articles and columns. He sipped his wine and fleetingly thought about her collarbones. He topped up her glass. He asked some questions. He complimented her texts in the morning paper.

"Briefly put," Per said to him, even though to anyone looking, he would appear busy serving his neighbour a second cup of coffee, "you're flirting with her."

Yes, sure. Absolutely. Let's call things by their proper names. He was flirting. Maybe just to please Per. Maybe because it seemed inevitable. There they were: the publisher and the author. Middle-aged. Half a life, or more like two thirds, behind them. God knows what baggage she's hauling around. And me: Cecilia, the wife who left fifteen years ago, now little more than a strange anecdote to anyone but me, Per and a handful of others who knew her.

And Per hadn't *planned* it, that would be too paranoid to assume, he hadn't planned to invite poor jilted Martin to the same dinner as one of his many hundreds of thousands acquaintances, which is to say this Maria – recently divorced, perhaps? – but when he and Sandra decided to host this gathering, this dinner for a mixed bag of middle-aged cultural sector workers, Maria had come to mind. They both worked with words. He with other people's, her with her own. (Hold on, why does this feel familiar?) They both have impressive bookshelves they can compare and discuss and applaud and gush about – "I can't believe you're looking forward to the new translation of *Ulysses*, too!" – and if they weren't so full of neurotic middle-class shame, they would probably have fallen into each other's arms on a bearskin rug in the warm glow of that very bookshelf, his or hers, it didn't matter which, they both owned the collected works of Foucault for crying out loud. But no, hold on, before we get to that bearskin episode, certain byways need to be travelled. So: coincidentally they decide to leave at the same time. She: "It's getting late," yawns a small cat-yawn. He: "Time to start thinking about heading home." Then they would walk slowly under the whispering trees in Vasaparken, she with her small hand on his arm. It would be a bad time, because it was her week with the children, let's call them Tilde and Vilde, five and seven years old, but this wouldn't be explicitly stated, because that would be forward in a way Maria Malm, the poet, rarely was. Consequently, they would part ways after making plans for dinner just the two of them next week. She climbs into a taxi. He hops on a tram. He wakes up the next morning and goes over the events of the previous evening step by step and finds himself – well, what? Confused? Confounded? Excited? He turns on the coffee machine and reads the paper in his robe and, as it happens, he comes across a small piece by her, which he reads with a diffuse sense of doing something indecent.

And they briefly call to confirm time and place, and he reserves a table at Thörnström's Kitchen or Fond. He irons a white shirt and combs his hair and Elis, who isn't out for once, possibly because he has run out of money, shouts a question about where he's going with that adolescent hoarseness that still breaks through in his voice from time to time. Martin is tempted to reply "out" and slam the door, but suspects Elis wouldn't get the joke. "Work meeting," he says. He's standing in front of the hall mirror, fussing with his tie, and Elis sighs and ties it for him. "Don't be out too late," Elis says with a wink, and Martin is so taken aback by this eruption of humour in his son that he can't think of a witty reply. And then it's time – she's already there, kisses him on the cheek, they're given menus and order wine. She is soberly dressed in black, with pearl earrings and her hair in a low bun. They have "all the time in the world to get to know each other". She tells him about her divorce from Henrik, whom she refers to as *my ex-husband*.

First course: Cisco roe on toast.

He tells a slightly revised version of how his wife, whom he refers to as *Cissi*, left him. "And she just disappeared?" Maria Malm asks, waving her fork about questioningly. "And you never heard from her again?"

Main course: Arctic char and lamb fillet.

She tells him about Tilde and Vilde, who do capoeira and art. He tells her about Rakel and Elis and realises in the middle of a long but explanatory tangent about Rakel's deep interest in ancient civilisations that he might be talking too much about Rakel and Elis; a verbal excursion Maria Malm elegantly parries by tilting her head to the side and saying: "I can tell how much you love your children."

Dessert: crème brûlée, cheese plate.

She tells him about her latest project, a forest-themed cycle of poems. He tells her about the publishing company and their various upcoming titles. They've gone through at least a couple of bottles of wine and over the course of the evening, it has grown increasingly obvious how terrifically well suited they are, this author and this publisher, Maria and Martin, Malm & Berg, you can tell from their names, isn't that just too funny, these coincidences, they laugh about it, her hand brushes against his.

The bill: they split it.

They decide to go somewhere else for a drink, he holds up her coat, he's slightly unsteady, something makes them laugh hard, exit into the night, it's early summer now, they set off in one direction or another in their search for a decent bar, but on the way they kiss, making Project Nightcap superfluous. They wave down a taxi. She lives in a house on Kungsladugårdsgatan with children's shoes and a rumpled rag rug on the whitewashed hardwood floor of the hallway. She fetches glasses and whisky, he locates a CD player and pushes play without checking the disc, and, unfortunately, the music that starts playing on a very loud volume is *Smurf Hits*. Martin quickly turns it off, but the whole thing is hilarious, Maria has to put the bottle and glasses down on a teak sideboard, she's laughing so hard. Martin finds a Billie Holiday album instead, they fall into each other's arms as the laughter echoes around them and kiss again, her body is warm and hums against his, she takes him by the hand, they climb a flight of stairs, she unbuttons his shirt, he pulls off her dress, her breath in his ear, his fingers along her back. And so they sleep together, and for him it's the first time in a long time, and he briefly thinks to himself that he should do this more often.

The next morning, he wakes up in her bed and looks around the bedroom while she sleeps, contemplating its slanted ceiling, the wide bed, so clearly made for two people to sleep in, just like his own. Bought with years of co-sleeping in mind, but subsequently turned into a lonely ghost ship. A kind of *Flying Dutchman* on the high seas of night, he thinks, studying Maria's peaceful face. Her delicate nose, her cute ears.

And then: they have breakfast, they read the paper together, she is wearing a button-down pyjama top and her long hair falls down her back. They continue to see each other. They go for walks and end up down by the wooden dock by Röda Sten where they sit and watch the boats and the bridge and talk even more about themselves and their lives. They go to the theatre together, and the cinema. Martin makes his best pasta dish in her kitchen while she sits on the kitchen table, telling him about some office drama at the paper. He meets her children, who are shy and wear striped shirts. He tells Rakel and Elis that "he has met someone" and Maria Malm comes over for a nervous dinner on Djurgårdsgatan. Everyone's happy. Hooray! they cheer. Especially Rakel and Elis. They're the perfect couple! And they live happily ever after.

Maria Malm, unaware of the future that just shimmered around her like a fourth-dimensional possibility, topped up her glass and was about to do the same for Martin when he raised a hand.

"No, thank you," he said. "I'm good. It's actually getting to be time for me to head home."

"But Martin," Per said, "it's still early…"

Martin closed his eyes and nodded in his best imitation of a wise man. "Sorry. Busy day tomorrow, etc."

Maria looked down at the table and bit her lip. What does she think this is? Martin thought. Some bloody Jane Austen novel?

He thanked his hosts and fetched his coat.

When he stepped out onto the street, the April evening greeted him like an old friend. It was forgiving and mild, spring on the brink of springing. Martin took the route past Vasaplatsen Square to see how the lilacs were coming along, if they were budding or still waiting, waiting.

FURTHER STUDIES IN THE HUMANITIES 1

I

INTERVIEWER: So there's no truth to be found through writing fiction?

MARTIN BERG: Quite the opposite. That may be exactly how to find it. Firstly: What is "truth"? Secondly: Is a human being capable of identifying "truth"? Thirdly: Can she convey that "truth" to someone else, in words? If we're talking on a concrete, everyday level, that's a banal non-question. It is, for example, true that we're sitting here, you and me, in my office. It's true that it's Tuesday. It's true that you're interviewing me for *Svensk Bokhandel* – I hope?

INTERVIEWER: Yes...

MARTIN BERG: It's true the river outside that window is called Göta Älv. It's true tram lines three, nine, eleven and six pass Järntorget Square. And so on. But the moment we go beyond simple, physical truths and try to tackle what we might call *human* truths – it instantly gets harder.

*

The first time he saw her.

Again and again, he'd tried to commit the scene to paper – the pub in Vasastan, the silky-smooth blue of the cigarette smoke, the din, Dylan jangling in the background – and again and again, it slipped away from him. Even though he could see her so clearly. The lights from the bar spilling across her face. Pale fingers rolling a cigarette. The fold across the shoulders of her parka, the rolled-up sleeves. And her eyes, fixed on some point in the distance, focused on something no one else in the room had access to.

It happened at the end of Martin's third year of university. It was a Thursday in a long series of days filled with books he had no desire to read, of soggy sandwiches for lunch, of icy winds hurtling through the streets, of libraries that never quite warmed up fully, of grey skies, a constant lack of money, flat beer, and spaghetti for dinner. In fact, it had been such an unremarkable Thursday the thought of going to bed and irreversibly adding it to the long series of forgotten days that seemed to constitute his life without having done anything of any consequence made Martin depressed. But he wasn't getting his student grant for another week so when Gustav called to ask if he wanted to come out for a pint, he replied, exercising considerable self-control:

"I can't, I'm skint."

As if that wasn't bad enough, he was being mocked by his empty notebook, which lay open on his desk next to a compendium of texts by Frege and Russell. He'd written DISSERTATION in marker on the cover, but that was the sum total of his progress.

The dissertation anxiety of the older students had always seemed so sophisticated. Martin had studied them in the reading room, carrying stacks of unknown books from the university library's basement. He'd listened to their talk about supervisors and dissertation seminars with anticipation and a measure of envy. Now, the prospect of having unlimited time to write twenty pages about a question you barely comprehended didn't seem so glamorous any more. He'd wanted to write about Sartre, but the supervisor he'd been assigned had narrowed his eyes sceptically and polished his glasses in a way that implied he was barely able to contain his annoyance at the student body's inexplicable enthusiasm about existentialism, so Martin had heard himself say: "… or maybe something about Wittgenstein?"

That had made Lecturer Backlund put his glasses back on his nose and lean back in his chair, looking pleased. University faculty, Martin had discovered, had a lot in common with elderly relatives. Just like you had to talk to Dad about boats or the demise of Sweden's social democracy, or about Aunt Maud's friends with Aunt Maud, faculty had to be met wherever their personal interests lay. Backlund's domains centred on analytical philosophy; he treated the Continental school of thought as the delusions of the less informed. There was no point insisting.

In other words, Martin ought to stay home with his compendium, and if he really wanted to liven things up, he could crack open *Tractatus Logico-Philosophicus*.

"If you don't live beyond your means, you live beneath your dignity," Gustav said on the other end. "I'll lend you some money. Nana has taken pity on me."

And the question was if Frege wasn't a worse fate than being slightly in debt.

[s/b]]

By the time Gustav showed up, Martin had smoked two cigarettes, said hi to three acquaintances and performed a strategic evasive manoeuvre around the fountain after spotting a girl he'd slept with once. There was a spring in Gustav's step, and his back was straight and his army coat open, even though it was February.

"I'm not late, am I?"

"Not at all."

"Uffe is at Tajjan."

"You didn't tell me Uffe was coming."

"Don't be like that." With a hand on Martin's shoulder, Gustav pushed him in the direction of Haga. "He's saving us a table and stuff. What about this weather, eh? Feel it? Spring's just around the corner." He smiled up at the sky and pushed his cap back.

Gustav's mood had been swinging wildly up and down in recent weeks. It started when Martin suggested they go get tested for HIV, just to be safe. Gustav shook his head. He refused to read those articles in the papers. If anyone happened to mention a friend of a friend in Stockholm who had just been diagnosed, he got up and walked out. The whole thing was a tad over the top.

"I'm sure we're fine," Martin had said with the confidence of someone trying to tell themselves just that. He had, not for nothing, been pretty good about using protection even before, mostly because he didn't want to be forced into a conversation in which his interlocutor cleared her throat and timorously announced that he was going to be a father. Having children was a terrible idea on the face of it, and for it to happen with the crazy girl with the iguana he'd met at Sprängkullen… He shuddered.

"If I have it, do I even want to know?" Gustav said.

"Knowing is better than wondering, isn't it?"

"It's like finding out you're being executed."

"Women give birth astride a grave, the light gleams an instant, then it's night once more," Martin quoted.

"Pär Lagerkvist doesn't know shit about this."

"It's Beckett."

"Oh. I was thinking about 'Anguish, anguish is my inheritance'."

"That's a very different sentiment," Martin said.

In the end, Gustav let himself be talked into going. In the waiting room, he spoke compulsively about his phobia of needles and tore his numbered ticket into tiny pieces. He was convinced he was going to pass out. They wouldn't be able to find a vein, he said. They were going to have to stick him again and again.

"Good thing you'll be out cold, then," Martin retorted.

After leaving the hospital, Gustav threw up in a bin.

During the two-week wait for results, they went to the pub almost every night. Gustav's intoxication resulted in him either falling asleep or launching into long monologues about death. Death, he said, was his destiny. His family was full of people who had popped their clogs too soon. One uncle had a heart condition and died in his sleep at thirty-five. His grandfather's sister had cancer. His aunt had cancer, too. His other grandfather had managed to drown on a dead-calm sea.

"Surely death is *everyone's* destiny, though," Martin had interjected, but Gustav had just glared at him.

Martin had been forced to study, hungover, as best he could, until their results came back. They were negative, of course. Since then, Gustav had been so elated he couldn't sleep. He'd made a painting of a mother and child that he called "a celebration of life". He'd brought baked goods. He'd insisted they climb up Sjömanshustrun to admire the view, and he'd beamed down at the city from the top of the tower, his ears and nose bright red in the wind.

Their table at Tai Shanghai had been invaded by other people, and Uffe relinquished his chair to a first-year student at Valand with unveiled disgust.

"Let's go somewhere else," he said, nodding curtly to Martin before lighting a cigarette. All the way through Haga and halfway down Vasagatan, Uffe ranted about some teacher who didn't get it and should be shot. Martin stifled a yawn.

"What about this?" Gustav said outside a pub they normally never went to.

"What the hell kind of place is this?" Uffe said.

They ordered pints and sat down at the only free table. Martin ended up with his back to the wall and a view of the bar.

And she just happened to be in his field of vision.

She was nursing a half-finished pint, her elbows on the bar, cigarette in hand. Thin, freckly wrists sticking out of the rolled-up sleeves of an oversized parka. Her dark-blonde hair tumbled down her back in loose curls. She had an attentive way of looking at things. Even though the room was smoky and loud, she seemed enveloped in a sphere of stillness.

At first he assumed she was waiting for someone. A man, probably. Someone older. In a tweed jacket and tortoiseshell glasses who might be doing a PhD on the influence of cubism on some obscure German artist. Or a girlfriend, who would turn up any moment now and crack a joke and the girl in the parka would laugh and the spell would be broken. But no one came. She just sat there with her pint. Ground out her cigarette and set to rolling another.

Just as he was starting to consider going over to talk to her, she put money down on the counter, shot the bartender a quick smile, and then she was gone.

It had been no more than ten minutes. And yet the bar felt empty and meaningless. Martin didn't realise his eyes were fixed on the door until Gustav asked something about that new submarine.

*

A few months earlier, he had ended things with Britta, and it had been a protracted, grand, Wagnerian ending. Britta the soprano refused to get off the stage. Martin, the reluctant tenor, glanced helplessly at the curtain. The whole affair could have easily been told in two acts and would have required no particular effort form the orchestra.

Act 1 took place during the autumn and winter of Martin's second year of university. She talked about (hold on, what had she talked about?). He talked about existentialism, gesticulated, explained what Sartre meant by the term *bad faith*.

"The Swedish translation isn't perfect. In French it's called *mauvais foi*, which means something closer to false or poor faith."

"I see," Britta said. "Mm."

He never felt as intellectual, as insightful, as when she gazed up at him with her dreamy eyes.

In Act 2, spring had turned into summer, and Britta had begun to get on Martin's nerves. The way she constantly smoothed down her hair. Her ditsiness, or, more accurately, the prosaic, grubby sloppiness she tried to cover up with scatterbrained charm, about as successfully as a negligee covers anything. Her vacant stare whenever he talked about philosophy. (Had she ever actually listened?) Her range of affected little noises when she saw something she liked. Her constant nail-biting. Her aerobic exercises in front of the TV, in pink lycra and legwarmers.

Autumn came. It became both harder and easier to pick her out of a crowd. He noted that observing her no longer gave rise to any particular feeling. He realised he'd made a mistake. Britta wasn't *the one*. You might think she was *the one*, at first glance, if there was something in your eye, if the lighting was dim, if you squinted. Britta could be taken for someone else (Britta wanted to become an actor), but she wasn't, simply put, you know, so to speak… and so on.

About half of the time he spent with Britta, he was actively wondering what it would be like not to be with Britta. First hypothetically, because it was in many ways easier to be together than not. Then more concretely. But every time he had an impulse to act on those thoughts, something came up. Her adorable laughter when she was talking to someone, the long looks she got from other men. He'd put his arm around her waist and pull her close, and it felt good to do it. To have the right to.

Early on, it had been so easy to go back to hers whenever they'd stayed out late, and Gustav was slow-blinking with a whisky cocktail in his hand, far too close to the speakers, and Uffe was trying to pick up some girl by repeating the same story three times, and Sissel was crying in a corner. Martin might have got stuck in the kitchen with some old radical going on and on about back when he worked down the wharf, pushing flyers on him. At those times, Britta was an excellent reason to slip out and hop on an eastbound tram, if they were still running. Her window on Danska Vägen was dark but he knew she'd just come home from her shift at Källarkrogen, that she was lying in her bed, warm and soft and mumbling.

And it was easy to wake up there. He could have a shower without the risk of running into one of Anders's sullen communist mates who'd spent the night on the sofa. Britta was a morning person and made amazing breakfasts that they ate on her balcony. She even remembered to buy him the paper. On those mornings, he looked back on vomit and failed one-night stands and sinks full of beer cans and snus, reeking ashtrays, thought about Gustav, who was about to wake up on some stranger's sofa with a crick in his neck, with some bloody fourth-year student staring at him, wondering what he was doing in her studio.

But at some point, there were suddenly evenings when his body itched for something, but he'd promised Britta to spend time with her friends and dip bits of bread in melted cheese. And evenings when the drama Sulky Girlfriend Refuses to Say What's Bothering Her was performed, a farce, but without the laughter.

"You're far too young," Gustav said.

"Too young for what?"

"For commitment."

"I haven't made any commitments."

"Then what do you call this thing with Britta?"

"We're dating. That's not the same as being stuck forever."

"So you're not planning on being with her for all eternity?"

"I don't know."

"I recall you telling me that if you ever have a romantic relationship, you should act as though it were for life, even if it may be doomed."

When Gustav and Britta were together, Gustav was polite as only he could be. He asked Britta how she was doing, about her work, about what she had been up to that day or weekend or week, what she thought of this or that. And Britta was vivacious as only she could be, which is to say that she blathered on about all kinds of things and veered off on tangents or into circumlocution, telling some long and pointless but potentially charming anecdote about someone who had lived next door to her when she was little. And Martin sat between them and looked from Gustav to Britta and from Britta to Gustav as though it were a tennis match between two mediocre junior players. Slice serves were ignored, and the game was at its best when the balls were slow and predictable.

None of Martin's previous relationships had lasted very long, but the one with Britta just kept going and going. Probably because of that simplicity. They had enough fun together. They had enough in common. Enough, enough. *This word of death and ennui*, as he wrote in his notebook.

One Saturday morning in November, they were sitting in Martin's kitchen on Kaptensgatan. Britta was slurping down a bowl of cereal. Martin was eating hönö bread and sipping instant coffee.

"I don't think we can go on like this," Britta said.

"What do you mean?"

"Our relationship. I don't feel like you're interested. We can't be together like this."

"You're right," Martin said, before realising that could easily come across as the opposite of what he meant. (A devious characteristic of language, had Wittgenstein written about that?) He swallowed a bite of his sandwich without chewing it properly and washed it down with coffee. "I don't think we can be together any more."

Britta stared at him, and this was, so to speak, the conductor's raised baton before the final aria.

They sequestered themselves in Martin's room, because Anders had woken up and was shuffling about the flat. Britta sat on the edge of the bed with trembling tears forming a film over her beautiful eyes. Martin stood by the window with his arms crossed.

She took a deep breath, put a hand on her chest. "Martin. We shouldn't throw this away – we shouldn't just throw it away like it's nothing. Do you believe in fate?"

"Metaphysically speaking, no, I don't. I believe fate is a concept people use to, as Sartre said…"

"Well, *I* believe we're meant to be together."

"But you just said we can't go on like this? Make up your mind."

"I just meant that…"

And now she burst into tears, too. He should sit down next to her, should put his arm around her shoulders, mumble something gentle, and then the sobbing would stop, they would kiss, and then everything would be forgotten, as though it never happened.

But Martin stayed where he was. Britta sniffed.

"It's just," he said, "I don't fully share your Tristan-and-Isolde view of our respective roles in each other's lives."

"What does that mean?"

"Britta – you're twenty-one years old."

"So? You're twenty-*two*," she hissed.

"I just mean that there will be, uh, others… who are… better than I am…"

"What are you trying to say?"

Evening had fallen before he finally got her to leave. Martin wasn't really sure which one of them had done the breaking up. He sat down on the floor next to the record player. The prelude to *Tristan and Isolde* spun round and round – he'd bought the record at a flea market after Gustav went to see the opera in question with his mother – and the music blended with the muffled notes of Ebba Grön coming from next door. Thåström braying: "*I just want to feel the lusts of the flesh / not always be what you want.*" Martin poured himself a glass of red wine from a bottle he'd nicked from the kitchen. With his eyes closed, he leaned his head back against the wall and tried to identify the feeling welling up inside him. It felt suspiciously like relief.

"Yeah, I kind of figured that's how it would go," Gustav commented when he found out.

"But why didn't you say something?" Martin asked.

"Would you have listened?"

"You do realise you can't go around saying things like that to people who claim to be in love, don't you?"

In the months that followed, Martin was noticeably gloomy, which people seemed to interpret as grief and separation anxiety. Per put a heavy hand on his shoulder and gave him a kind of I-know-what-you're-going-through look. Gustav tried to talk him into going to Sprängkullen, throwing out the names of bands Martin had no desire to see and pretending to be hurt if he left early.

Martin read *Philosophical Investigations* for the third time and made fifteen pages of notes in paragraph form, which he reckoned was pretty clever. (Kind of like a riff on Wittgenstein's own work," he told a course mate who nodded, impressed.) He stopped jumping every time the phone rang and promised himself to finish at least two short stories, a promise he almost kept. One of them was a story of doomed love between a young author and an equally young actress, and he was particularly pleased with that one.

Every once in a while, there was that kind of flat, steppe-like day that seemed to contain nothing but the constant howling of the wind.

Those were the days that were checked off and promptly forgotten, and when he realised he couldn't remember them, it made him so itchy inside he had to stand up and walk around his room or wander the streets.

*

In the days after their visit to that pub, his thoughts kept circling back to the woman in the parka by the bar. He assigned her the main role in a short story, but didn't know where to go with it, and, in the end, it ended up half-written underneath all the other papers on his desk.

II

INTERVIEWER: In what way can fiction be helpful in... what to call it...

MARTIN BERG: Truth seeking?

*

Every term, new students turned up, upsetting the established order at the university library. They were young and dressed in appropriately eccentric clothes. They moved in groups, too nervous to leave the herd for a solo excursion on the savannah. They whispered in the reading rooms without noticing the disapproving looks they drew. They carried on chirpy conversations in the lobby, with stacks of course books hugged to their chests. During the balmy first few weeks of the autumn term, they spent all their time outside on the lawns, as though they were at a festival, not starting their courses. Martin wasn't sure where they congregated at the start of the spring term, but probably some place with cheap beer and dark walls where they could sit and throw around Buber quotes or do random underlining in some poetry anthology.

They jumped aside when he stomped through the library, looked away when he glared at them. He could feel their eyes on the back of his head. He was the older, more experienced student, working on his dissertation. Hunched under the weight of his backpack, he stalked towards the reading room.

Without even trying to be quiet, he emptied his bag of books and notepads. He hung up his coat but kept his scarf on; it was chilly in there. Perhaps he should invest in a pair of fingerless gloves. After he had poured himself a cup of coffee – a neighbour glanced enviously at his thermos – the moment came when he inevitably had to crack open one of his books.

When Martin first started to study philosophy, he thought he was going to receive a kind of broader, deeper education. Philosophy would fill the gaps he always felt conscious of but couldn't clearly identify. In reality, he kept discovering new areas where he fell short. Instead of feeling enlightened, he felt dumb, first because he didn't instantly understand what they were reading, then because he didn't know how to apply his knowledge in conversation with other people. Several times, he caught himself repeating verbatim what had been said in a lecture. He lacked context, points of reference for his knowledge. What difference did it make if you could give an account of Kant's ethics if you couldn't connect it to anything else? He could always link it to another philosopher, but in the end, that led to circular, suffocating lines of reasoning where x always referred back to x. And what was x good for? (Since the crucible that was the previous term's sojourn into logic, unwelcome variables kept popping into Martin's head when he least wanted them to.) X could possibly be helpful when he was studying x, but x was of little help when it came to navigating reality.

Martin could almost hear one of his course mates objecting: "Can we even talk about a concept like 'reality'?"

After five terms, he still felt something was missing. It might be a class thing. That was a conclusion Martin had become increasingly inclined to draw since talking to a sociology student for five hours at an afterparty where everyone else smoked pot and made out in the next room. (It was at the tail end of the Britta operetta, and Martin had felt a nebulous aversion to going back to hers. He had no idea what the sociologist's excuse was; maybe he was simply incredibly into sociology.) There was no escaping the fact that the people who had *it*, whatever *it* was, often came from academic families or the upper middle class. But strangely, being well read and working class seemed to work almost as well, the first one in a family to attend university, and so on. The Berg family was stuck somewhere in-between. Its attributes were those of the striving middle class (house, boat), but Martin had still always felt like an outsider. He had neither academic tradition nor the bedrock foundation of the working class to lean on.

Frosty light and the rumbling of diggers spilled in through the windows. The old philosophy building had finally been torn down and a building intended to house all the humanities departments was being built where it had stood. Martin tried to ignore the sound of construction. With a sigh, he opened *Tractatus*. He had to sort out his course enrolment for next term, too.

The month of March was thick with slushy snow and ploughed piles of gravel. Anders had met a girl, a grouchy syndicalist with a swooping fringe, and whenever Martin was in the living room or the kitchen, he had to interact with the two of them. He spent most of his time in his room. The floor was covered with open books and magazines. Empty coffee cups and balled-up tissues from a stubborn cold were strewn among old socks and dirty T-shirts. He should wash his clothes. He should get up and answer the phone. He should do a lot of things. Instead, he lay in his bed, under the duvet, fully dressed, reading and dozing by turns. At night, he got up to make himself something to eat, fried eggs with bacon or spaghetti with butter and ketchup. For once, Anders didn't care about the pile of dirty plates that kept growing in the sink.

Martin couldn't be bothered to go on the pull. To go home with someone, to feign interest in the activities that inevitably followed, the exchanging of phone numbers, the sporadic trips to the cinema, and so

on – it all seemed so insipid. It was as though he was only now beginning to reflect on what all that chasing was really supposed to lead to.
Surely the ultimate endgame couldn't be resolute fucking on a creaky
mattress, with a person who kind of bothered you, in a flat that made
you claustrophobic even though it was certainly big enough, until
you finally lost yourself and the rest of the world in a few moments of
divine oblivion?

He tried drinking himself unconscious. He went to parties. He spent
an entire week holed up like a mole in his bed with his books, in the
hope of building up some kind of abstinence in time for the weekend.
Nothing helped. Gustav called daily, nagging about this and that, and
eventually he turned up at Kaptensgatan to drag Martin to the pub.

"But I'm too tired."

"Here, you'll need a jumper."

"I can't go out wearing *this*."

"Why not? What's wrong with it?"

"Where are we going, anyway?"

"I was thinking Sprängis."

"I lost my membership card."

"It's right here." Gustav picked up the annoying piece of paper that
had suddenly materialised on his desk. Martin pulled the jumper on
with heavy movements.

At Sprängkullen, he did his best to keep a low profile while he
waited for the band to start playing. Gustav was going on about a new
place they could go to afterwards, but when Lotta, a girl Martin went
home with from time to time, turned up, he tactfully withdrew. Lotta
seemed genuinely happy to see him, but at the thought of spending yet
another night in her room in an occupied flat in Haga he felt – well,
what?

"Ennui, I think," he said ten minutes later, after escaping and
rejoining Gustav. He was trying to puzzle out the philosophical reasons
for why he didn't want to go home with Lotta, who luckily seemed to
have something going with the clarinet player in the band that had
now showed up and started to clatter, honk, whisk and bray.

"Hmm," said Gustav, who for some reason didn't seem overly inter-ested in the subject.

"I mean – there's nothing wrong with her. She's great. But I'm stuck in a groove. We come here or go wherever and it's the same old story over and over again. Nothing happens. Nothing's new. We're stuck in the same spot. You know? Anyway. This whole thing with Britta. I should have known straight away. I should have seen it. Did you see it straight away?" Martin signalled for two more pints.

"I don't know. You were like most couples."

"What do you mean?"

"An example: we went out for a couple of pints and then Britta showed up. And what happened? Well, she got impatient every time we talked about something she didn't know about. And we couldn't just sit there silently; if we did, we were boring. And then there was always some kind of drama, possibly triggered by you looking at some other girl – probably a completely justified reproach." Gustav covered his mouth with his hand and let out a small burp. "And that was the end of that party. Not to mention all the nights when you didn't get out of the house in the first place, just sat home watching TV."

"*That* is what I don't want to get caught up in again. The rut. The tedium. The feeling that I'm…" he waved his hand in a jerky gesture and almost knocked the bowler hat off a bloke in a dress shirt and chequerboard tie, "…stuck."

"It's not like you were complaining, though," Gustav said. "You cosied up in front of *Dallas* and ate cheese doodles."

"I did *not*."

"I know what I saw," Gustav said.

"How could you have *seen* me sitting in front of the TV eating cheese doodles if you weren't there?"

"It's an expression."

"It is not an expression."

But Gustav had a mischievous glint in his eye, and later on they went to the bathroom and chugged whisky from the flask Gustav had inherited from his grandfather, but sometimes claimed had once belonged to a soldier in the French Foreign Legion. Lotta left with the clarinet player.

*

A few days later, Martin dragged himself to Café Moster. By then, he'd carved out a structure from the alarmingly copious notes he had accumulated.

"It's an interesting question," his supervisor had said when Martin presented his idea about the relationship of language to perception from a philosophical perspective. "You may need to narrow it down slightly…"

Which meant he was probably going to have to throw out his planned digression into phenomenology, which at the moment filled an entire notepad with more or less cryptic notes. He'd been hoping to use it to link Wittgenstein with Heidegger and Husserl, and that his examiners would grunt appreciatively at this bold (but now that they thought about it, obvious) approach, but of course, they'd say, that Martin Berg, he's innovative and unexpected. And then they would chuckle and give him a top grade.

In all honesty, Martin was already pretty sick of Wittgenstein. He'd opted to write about the sullen Austrian mostly because he was infamous for his impenetrability. *Tractatus*, people said, was utterly inaccessible. People argued about whether he was a lunatic or a genius, and, if the latter, what constituted said genius. When he first started, Martin had only read a few excerpts from *Philosophical Investigations* and glanced ever so briefly at *Tractatus*, which was a slim volume, true, but seemed to have the density of a black hole. It sucked in all surrounding energy but gave nothing back.

Since then, Martin's dissertation process had felt akin to digging a massive hole with a tiny trowel. And he had no way of telling if he was even digging in the right spot. It was possible that he was on the wrong track completely and would be forced to start over. He clung to his fundamental idea, which was that language affected how a person experienced things. Or that "the linguistic expression available to an individual has a profound impact on her experience of a range of phenomena" – a sentence he could reel off in his sleep and which made Gustav shake his head. It had to be true, right? Or? He wasn't sure. He told himself being unsure was a good thing. He became suspicious of any sign of certainty in himself and strived to adopt a position of constant doubt. He woke up in the middle of the night, sweating, and decided to radically alter his question. He realised the important thing was not whether it was true or not, but that he was innovative and clever. He began to suspect that he was trying to pass off obvious facts as great discoveries. He read an article about a tribe of natives in the Amazon who appeared not to see a radio sitting right in front of them, behaviour that was ascribed to the fact that they had no concept of the phenomenon "radio" and therefore couldn't distinguish it from its surroundings. He called Gustav and talked excitedly about the articles for fifteen minutes. He spent a couple of days writing feverishly, only to then founder in a quagmire of uncertainty and despondence. What was the point of Wittgenstein anyway? A chill spread through his body at the thought that he wouldn't be able to give a good answer to that question.

Right now, he was in one of his doubting phases. The plan was to read *Tractatus* again, in the hopes of achieving renewed understanding, or, more accurately, understanding, full stop. When he stepped into Café Moster, it was with the heavy steps of a man heading down into a coal mine.

And there she was, in her parka, with a half-eaten meatball sandwich in front of her. He was sure he'd never seen her there before. But now, there she was. Alone. Martin played it cool while he walked by her table, but his pulse was racing and his heart muscles seemed to have taken on a life of their own. When it was time to order he needed several attempts to get out what he wanted.

He sat down and instantly burned his tongue on the coffee. His eyes seemed physically incapable of staying on the pages of his book. They kept sliding down to the floor and across the room until they came to a stop on a table by the opposite wall, as though that particular table were a magnet and his gaze a collection of helpless iron filings.

Oil on canvas, 30 x 50 inches, possibly a lost masterpiece by Renoir ca 1875. Her striped sailor shirt vibrated in starkly contrasted white and mussel-blue. The lines of her nose and jaw were delicately drawn; her skin was rosy pale and slightly freckled in a way that suggested she would get more freckled come summer. Thick hair tumbled down her back – a tousled pre-Raphaelite – and she repeatedly pushed strands of it out of her face, quickly, with a hint of annoyance. She was leaning in over her book, and her eyes, dark blue, moved swiftly across the pages. He could make out the shadow of a vertical line by one eyebrow. She held a fork in her other hand, with which she occasionally skewered a meatball. And even when he glanced at her sort of sideways, so it wouldn't be too obvious he was studying her, she appeared in sharp focus.

Martin turned the page.

Just as he'd managed to wrestle his attention back to the text, he heard a chair scrape against the floor. She was on her feet, gathering up her things. A bell tinkled as the door was pulled open.

He took out his small grey notebook and wrote: *The gentle tinkle of the doorbell – the sound of irreversibility. In a metaphysical sense, it might as well have been the sound of a heavy door slamming shut (forever???).*

*

After that, he began to look for her more actively. He even returned to the bar where he'd first seen her. As they stepped through the door, he'd almost managed to convince himself she'd be there again, alone, in a chiaroscuro of grimy lamplight and blue cigarette smoke. But the room was empty apart from a smattering of old regulars and a man in a leather coat downing Fernet by the bar.

"Can't we go to Tajjan instead?" Gustav said. Then he whinged all the way over there about how Martin had become too geographically liberal about where to go drinking. "Dragging me all the way to *Vasastan*. Makes you wonder what's next."

At first it bothered Martin that he was so hung up on the blonde woman. That his body had triggered an entire battery of reactions without asking his brain's approval. Increased heart rate, muddled thoughts. He analysed the course of events in the notebook where he collected material for his novel. (He'd decided to perform a drastic revision, maybe even rewrite the whole thing completely. As soon as he had finished his dissertation.) Was it simply down to sexual frustration, which he interpreted as a more sophisticated emotion as the result of an evolutionary whim? He'd never believed in anything as facile as love at first sight, but lust at first sight was a different story. But then, she wasn't his type. Too tall, too skinny. When he tried to recall her face, it was blurry like an impressionist painting.

A few weeks later, he caught sight of her in the distance, by Haga Church. Spotting her conjured an unpleasant feeling, a kind of stomach cramp, which he tried to ignore.

"Hey," he said to Gustav, who was in the middle of pontificating on the subject of What is Art, "do you know her?"

"Who?"

"The girl in the green coat."

"No idea."

"Are you sure?"

"Of course I'm not sure. She's really far away. Anyway, like I was saying – he was going to make a copy of the *Venus de Milo*, but, I mean, like a plaster cast of his mate, or, well, some girl he'd picked up…"

She disappeared towards Skanstorget Square.

Martin found that the more he tried not to, the more he thought about her. He thought about her while cycling to university, when he was supposed to reflect on the intellectual kinship of Schopenhauer and Nietzsche. He thought about the way she pushed a strand of hair behind her ear while sitting in the reading room at the library, failing for the third time to comprehend a passage of *Tractatus*. He thought about what she might be doing while he queued at the supermarket, waiting to pay for a clutch of bananas, two pints of milk, three tins of baked beans, bacon, a pound of potatoes and two packs of Lucky Strike, please. He thought about the way her long fingers had rolled a cigarette while Anders talked about the martial big-brother mentality of the United States and managed to spill sauce on his shirt. He thought about her while brushing his teeth and attempting to squeeze a blackhead on his forehead at the same time. And while he dozed off to the muffled sound of a red-wine-fuelled book circle discussing Marx in the next room, he could sense her stretching somewhere else, in a different bed.

*

One of Britta's favourite subjects when she was in her spiritual mood had been Fate. Did it exist? And if it did, was it the same thing as believing in God? It was a hopeless discussion, because Britta had no real arguments for the existence of fate, aside from that it "would be so depressing if nothing had any meaning and everything was just random".

"But that's the fundamental principle of existentialism," Martin countered.

Britta accused him of "always bringing everything back to his philosophy stuff", and if he insisted that she had no rational proof for her belief in fate, that it was an expression of her anxiety at being confronted with the meaninglessness of existence and so on, she sulked.

Chance on the other hand. Martin was completely on board with chance. Chance was a constant factor in human life. Which was why he couldn't think of that day without feeling dizzy. If he'd arrived at the university library five minutes earlier or later. In fact, he'd almost not gone at all.

The leaves on the horse chestnut trees were unusually early, the dry asphalt crunched with winter gravel, and the lawn sloping down towards the Lily Pond was sun-warmed and full of students on picnic blankets, trying hard to tell themselves they were studying for exams. Martin Berg, on the other hand, intended to spend the entire afternoon with von Hartmann, a seemingly forgotten German philosopher with a stripey beard. His *Philosophy of the Unconscious* was really superfluous to Martin's own research, but it would look ambitious to have such an obscure work in his bibliography. As though he'd really got to the bottom of the question of language and perception. He could read one or a couple of chapters and identify a few apt quotes. *As von Hartmann wrote in 1869... Here we see a parallel between Wittgenstein and German thinker von Hartman, in that...* Something like that.

The librarian had written the shelf number on a slip of paper, and now he was trying to orient himself. Sweaty and stressed, he dashed up and down the aisles, close to giving up if he didn't find the bloody shelf soon.

And just then, he found it.

And there she was.

She instinctively glanced over at him and then continued to search the spines. She was taller than he'd imagined, almost as tall as him. Once again wearing the green parka. Her jeans were cut off just above her ankles. He noted with unexpected tenderness that she wore unmatched socks in her tennis shoes: one had a red stripe, the other didn't.

She, too, was holding a slip of paper.

Martin was surprised at how hard his heart was pounding while he searched the titles. His body didn't usually behave this way. Probably his best option was to get out of there as quickly as possible, before he did something stupid, but then she pulled out a book and before he could give it any thought, he blurted out:

"No way!"

She looked up. "Excuse me?"

"No, I mean – god, I'm sorry. I just – the book you're holding, I was looking for that, too." Martin held up his slip of paper as proof. "And I was convinced I was the only person in this town who would want to read von Hartmann on a day like this. Or, well, on any day, really."

She laughed, a pleasant chuckle in her throat. "What do you know. Looks like we have a conflict of interest on our hands." Her voice was deep and slightly hoarse, a jazz-and-cigarettes voice.

"Hey, you beat me to it," Martin said.

"Only just."

"Sure, but…"

"Why don't we flip a coin for it." She pulled a coin out of her pocket, winked at him, chose tails and flicked it into a high arc. It came out heads, and she handed him the book.

"All right," Martin said, "but then I'm buying you coffee."

Afterwards, he wouldn't be able to recall how they got out of the stacks. There must have been stairs. They must have crossed the brand-new carpet in the lobby. When they exited the library, he was so discombobulated by the sharp light he didn't know what to say. He was intensely aware of her presence next to him, but only caught brief glimpses of it: her hand scratching the back of her neck, pulling a pair of sunglasses out of her pocket. The top of her ear, which was glowing, illuminated by a stray ray of sunshine. A fraying seam on the shoulder strap of her leather satchel.

"My name is Cecilia Wikner, by the way."

"Martin Berg," Martin replied.

They shook hands.

"So, Martin Berg, what do you need von Hartmann for?"

Martin had forgotten all about the book in his backpack, even though it weighed at least two pounds.

"I'm writing a dissertation on Wittgenstein. Or about the relationship of language to perception. In philosophy," he managed, as though that explained everything. It didn't, obviously, but he could always tell her about Wittgenstein: one of the greatest thinkers of the twentieth century, wrote his first and completely revolutionary book in the trenches of the First World War, mud-stained paper, exploding grenades, belonged to one of Vienna's wealthiest families, almost all his siblings were mad in one way or the other and most of them died early, usually by their own hand, Wittgenstein himself was a rousing success in Cambridge and revolutionised logic, in fact Bertrand Russell…"

"Old Mr Cheerful," Cecilia said. "What do you think of him?"

"Wittgenstein?"

"Yes."

"Uh – I think it's… interesting the way he, so to speak, subsumes the world into language. The idea that the world, life – humanity itself, as I argue in my dissertation, or will be arguing – I haven't" (he suddenly had an absurd urge to cough and did so) "I haven't written that part yet – anyway, that humans can't exist outside of language."

"*Wovon man nicht sprechen kann, darüber muß man schweigen,*" Cecilia said.

"Exactly," Martin, who didn't know a word of German, replied. He was confused by the turn the conversation had taken – as though they were two old friends meeting on the street and talking about their shared friends, morose German von Hartmann and his more experimentally inclined mate Ludwig W.

They had exited towards the art museum, and in front of them rose Poseidon, clutching his giant codfish, which if you stood in a certain spot between the Concert Hall and the Centre for Contemporary Art looked like something else entirely.

"So, what do you need von Hartmann for?" he asked.

"Well," Cecilia said, "my reading list is German-themed this year. Von Hartmann slipped in kind of like a consolation prize. I'd been looking forward to reading Freud, but then I remembered he was Austrian."

"Tough break," Martin said. He didn't quite understand what she meant but asked what she did when she wasn't reading German literature.

"I study history," Cecilia said.

They sat down at a table outside Paley's. Cecilia told him she was one of three women in a class of twenty-five: the second was a grouchy syndicalist and the third knew everything there was to know about rune stones. The three of them had immediately been lumped together, more or less against their will – an island adrift in an ocean of young, male war aficionados. "The only thing we have in common is that we don't have penises and don't tend to get an engrossed, exalted look on our faces every time the Second World War comes up. Or the First World War, or the Spanish Civil War, or the Vietnam War, or the Thirty-Year War, or any war, really." Cecilia – he hadn't decided if the name suited her or not – gesticulated as she talked, as though her hands had a life of their own.

"What *are* you interested in, then?" Martin asked.

She looked surprised but quickly recovered. "Colonialism."

It was an unexpected answer, and he had to laugh. Cecilia laughed, too, a surprised and happy laugh.

At first, they talked almost exclusively about their studies and intellectual matters. Martin had an unsettling feeling of not being able to think clearly – it was probably the sun, the heat – and worried about saying something stupid. He steered the conversation over to potentially shared acquaintances, because there was always at least one. And, lo and behold, it turned out Cecilia's syndicalist course mate was the girl Anders had recently started dating. Martin became entangled in an anecdote about how Gustav had accidentally ended up at some kind of pre-drinks with Johnny Thunders, and, without really knowing who he was, had challenged him to a drinking game of his own invention, which Martin had never fully understood the rules of. But Thunders had apparently been unable to keep up ("or possibly he didn't understand the rules either") and been forced to knock back shot after shot of vodka, until an extremely stressed-out bloke came looking for him.

"'Johnny, Johnny,' he shouted, sounding incredibly worried, 'you're supposed to be playing right now.' And they dragged him off to wherever. But he only got through two songs, then he staggered off stage and, rumour has it, retired to the bathroom floor. And Gustav made sure to get the hell out before anyone could start pointing fingers."

Cecilia laughed. Martin had left out his own role in the whole debacle – he'd waited and waited for Gustav and had then been enormously annoyed when Thunders called it quits after just two songs. And he'd quarrelled with Britta, who'd wanted to leave early and had sulked when he refused to go with her, and to top it all off, there had been nothing to drink but beer. He'd guzzled down half a dozen bottles, leaving his back teeth floating, and once they left and Martin could finally ease the pressure in a secluded corner on Vallgatan, he managed to draw the attention of a police officer and was nailed with a two-hundred-kronor fine.

They had long since finished their refills, and just when Martin was beginning to wonder what was going to happen next, Cecilia yawned like a lynx and stretched.

"All right, what do you reckon?" she said. "I need to get back."

They parted ways by Valand. Cecilia wrote down her phone number and told him to call when he was finished with von Hartmann.

Then she disappeared along Vasagatan with her hands in her pockets.

Martin's bike was still parked outside the library, so once he was sure she wasn't going to notice, he turned around and walked back.

III

MARTIN BERG: People sometimes want to demystify the art of writing. View it as a craft anyone can learn. It might have something to do with a lot of people wanting to be writers – and yes, maybe "be writers" more than actually write, when you think about it… anyway. There's obviously a crafting aspect to working with text. But there's more to it, the making-things-up part. Where do all those ideas come from that eventually turn into a novel? Where do they originate? Why? *I* don't know, and I've been in this business for twenty-five years.

*

The note with her phone number was sitting on his desk and had been for a week. At one point, Martin thought he'd lost it and frantically rifled through his papers, heart pounding, until he found it under his typewriter.

Six numbers written in pencil.

He wasn't done with von Hartmann. Hadn't even opened the book. Maybe he had to read it, at least part of it. Or maybe he should just say he had? It's not like she was going to give him a pop quiz on it. Or? And if he did call – what was he going to say? Should he ask her out to dinner? But he'd spent most of the month's student loan and was two weeks away from his next instalment, so a restaurant was out of the question. He couldn't bring her home either, since there was no guaranteeing Anders would keep clear, especially if Martin asked him to. He would barge in just for the sake of it, his usual slovenly self. (Martin had discovered that he buttoned his shirts wrong on purpose.) And anyway – dinner? Completely uncalled for? As far as he knew, she just wanted the book. Or? What did "call me" signify? Maybe they could just go for a pint? But would she take that as a lack of interest on his part? That he just wanted to hear the hilarious story of when Germany tried to colonise Ghana? Or would he in fact come off as too eager, making her shift uncomfortably as she cast about for a way to get out of this without being rude?

He couldn't bring himself to do anything at all. Except frequently check to make sure the note was still there.

He recalled the image of her sitting across from him at Paley's, the way you take out a well-worn photograph. The sun transforming her hair into a golden halo, her eyes firmly fixed on him. Serious, focused. And that way she had of suddenly breaking into a smile – eyes sparkling, eyebrows merrily raised.

She could very well be seeing someone.

She hadn't said anything to that effect, but on the other hand she hadn't indicated the opposite either. There hadn't been anything furtive or secretive in her eyes, none of the drawling tone Martin associated with flirting. No allusions. No innuendo. In all honesty, he'd be surprised if she weren't already someone's girlfriend or lover. Someone older than him, an artist or musician. Maybe a professor. Someone whose flat – a converted attic – she walked around wearing nothing but a man's dress shirt, with her long hair loose and a glass of red wine in her hand while the professor/boyfriend played Miles Davis and talked about Buddhism.

"At the end of the day," he said one day as he was frying meat patties in Gustav's kitchen, "there are too many unknown factors." He waggled the spatula.

"I wish you would just call her and get it over with," Gustav sighed.

He was sitting in the window, smoking a cigarette, with one leg dangling out and the other inside the room. Martin hated when he did that, because Gustav was entirely the type to lose his balance in a moment of distraction. He'd promised Martin he wouldn't fall and had casually dismissed his objection that promises like that were impossible to make.

"But what if she says no?" Martin said.

"Then at least you *know*. And you don't have to walk around wondering."

"I don't know if I want to know."

"Hold on – why does this conversation seem familiar?" Gustav held his cigarette up as though he were listening to something.

Martin gave him the finger.

"What would Sartre do?" Gustav said.

"He'd have probably gone for it, even though he was fat and cross-eyed."

"'The coward makes himself cowardly, the hero makes himself heroic, and there is always the possibility for the coward to give up cowardice and for the hero to stop being a hero'," Gustav said. Martin had once used that as the motto of an essay about the existence of free will.

"Yes, but…"

"Just *do* it."

"I'll do it tomorrow."

"Why not now?"

"But it's almost ten. You can't call people at ten o'clock at night."

"I seem to recall you calling Britta at any hour of the day or night just to ask her to pick up cigarettes and milk and god knows what."

"God, Britta. That was completely different."

"It was?"

"She quoted Wittgenstein *in German*. At least I think it was Wittgenstein."

"You said you were swearing off girls for a while after Britta. 'Free' I believe is the exact term you used."

"And I have."

"Several weeks."

"Hey, it's been at least a couple of months. Plus, I don't control these things. They happen when they happen. You just have to roll with it. It can come at the worst of times. The universe doesn't care if I've had an acceptable amount of uninfatuation or not."

"Fine. Whatever."

"She's doing a double degree. Did I tell you that? She does German, too."

"So what is she going to be?"

"Huh?"

"What with all the German and the history. A Nazi?"

"Very funny. No, but, all jokes aside – uh, I actually don't know."

"It's burning." Gustav pointed to the frying pan, took a drag, and leaned back against the window frame.

The next day, Martin was sitting in the kitchen, holding a sweaty receiver. He dialled the first four numbers and hung up immediately when Anders's girlfriend, Nina, entered. For some reason, he'd never told her about the funny coincidence with Cecilia, and now it was too late to do it in a neutral way. She would see through him in a second.

She nodded to Martin, opening the fridge and studying its contents as though it were actually hard to choose. Then she grabbed a beer and spent a long time rattling around the kitchen drawers, looking for a bottle opener. Nina got to see Cecilia almost every day. Sit next to her in lectures, make small talk with her in the hallways, see the outline of her profile in the chalk-dusty sunlight…

"How's university?" he asked.

Nina shrugged one shoulder, maybe because she couldn't muster enough energy to shrug both. "Whatever."

"How are your lecturers?"

"A bunch of old fossils. Consistently terrible as far as Marxist approaches go."

"But…" he was going to say something about how if there was one thing old fossils were usually good at, it was jamming Marx in everywhere. Luckily, Anders appeared, hair damp from the shower, which made him look more seventeenth-century Dutch than ever.

"It's the same thing in the philosophy department," Martin said instead. "They're awful."

The next day he brought Cecilia's note down to the phone box on the corner. This time, he dialled the whole number and felt his awareness sort of rise upwards, towards the ceiling of the phone box, while his stomach pulled downwards, towards the chewing gum-stained concrete slab, as he heard the first ring reverberate down the line. Then another, and another.

After counting to eight, he hung up. Anything else would have seemed desperate.

That night, he was lying in bed when he was struck by sudden suspicion. What if she'd accidentally given him the wrong number? Or if he'd misread her writing?

He pulled on his robe and went out into the kitchen, where a very well-worn phonebook sat on the shelf underneath the phone. With sweaty fingers, he found the Ws.

WIKNER CECILIA, KASTELLGATAN 11.

It was the right number.

He went back to bed.

*

Martin didn't call again, telling himself his best option was to try to run into her. He did his best to shorten the odds. He looked for her at the library. He hung around near the history department. He lingered at Café Moster until closing ("Hello," Gustav said, waving his hand about, "I'm here. Are you waiting for someone?"). One time, he even came up with an excuse to walk along Kastellgatan, but he studiously avoided looking over at the door to her building, and afterwards, he was relieved not to have run into her there.

But Cecilia was probably at the library when he was sitting in the café, and at home when he stayed late at uni, because he didn't catch so much as a glimpse of her for the rest of April.

The turning point came at breakfast one Saturday morning. Martin was hungover after a pointless evening with some course mates and wanted nothing more than to drink his coffee in silence. Unfortunately, Anders and his girlfriend were engaged in a lively debate about the future of the political left. All their attempts to involve him were met with monosyllabic grunts, until Nina swept her fringe aside and said: "So, any fun plans tonight, Martin?"

"A course mate's throwing a party." Martin stared down into his coffee cup as though it could give him further instruction. "But I don't know. It's out in Långedrag. I think I need to study."

"Is it Henke's party?"

"You know him?"

"Doesn't everyone?"

"So you're going?"

Nina and Anders spent a few minutes bickering lovingly on the theme of No, whatever you want: Nina "wouldn't mind going", Anders "preferred a calm evening at home". Martin spread liver pâté on a slice of bread and tried to fish the last pickle slices out of the jar.

"But if it's important to you, of course we'll go," Anders said.

"Look, it's not like I need a chaperone," Nina retorted.

"No, no, I didn't mean it that way…"

"A girl in my class is probably going, I could check with her."

Martin dropped his fork.

"The one who's into runes?" he said. Nina had talked a bit about the rune girl, who for various reasons annoyed her.

"No, the other one. By the way, have you guys read that stuff about second-hand smoke not being all that dangerous, after all?"

By the time Martin and Gustav finally got on the westbound tram, it was already late. That should mean fewer people arriving, Martin the Mathematician thought to himself, clinging to the leather straps, and letting the tram's movements rock him. Which was to say: anyone who was going to the party was probably there already. Except Martin Berg & Gustav Becker. Because Martin Berg & Gustav Becker stepped off the tram only now, at twenty to midnight, and staggered down the winding street in search of the right house. Gustav pulled out his flask. Fire in their throats and fire in their bellies. If Caravaggio had bumbled about Gothenburg one night in May of 1984 with a Polaroid camera around his neck, it would have looked like this. *Click*. Gustav standing under a street light, his skin white like cream and his eyes dark wells. *Click*. Martin Berg lighting a cigarette, the collar of his denim jacket popped, nightlight dividing his face into fields of light and shadow.

"Hey, leave some for me!" Gustav laughed.

The house was lit up, people in every window, and they could just step right into the festivities and say hello to old acquaintances and find a couple of glasses and mix some drinks and start keeping a look-out. They ended up in the hallway, talking to some people. According to the physical laws of parties, she should have passed them by now. Going from one room to another. *Unless*. She wasn't there. And wasn't coming. Unless she was elsewhere. With a boyfriend who was absently stroking her hair. "Weren't you going to some party?" he'd say. "Oops," she'd reply, "it completely slipped my mind."

Martin's heart sank. He drank his vodka mixer, listening to Gustav hold forth about construction cranes. The words seemed to be coming at him from a great distance, like through a tin can telephone.

"Here's something I've been wondering: how do they pee? Do they have little toilets up there in the cabs? Or do they have to go all the way down? Or hold it? How many hours do they have to hold it? Isn't that a, what do they call it, occupational health and safety issue?"

Just then, Cecilia Wikner walked in from the living room. She didn't see him. Several long seconds passed before she disappeared into the kitchen – which, he recalled, had a devious second door that led to a dining room which in turn connected to the living room, which meant she could, in theory, vanish again. Time was suddenly passing both quickly and slowly. She didn't look bored, exactly, but a bit distracted.

And the colours flowed back into the room, the phone wire was reeled back in to the normal party distance of sixteen inches and the mixer sliding down his throat was cold and clear.

"Maybe they pee in little buckets," Martin said.

There was no rush. In fact, he should hang back for a bit. Now she was going to talk to some acquaintance and drink and maybe dance and then, when *she* was starting to feel disappointed, when she was thinking "Is this bloody party going to turn out like every other bloody party?", that's when he would make his move.

He went to take another sip of his drink but discovered his glass was empty.

He bravely set his course for the kitchen, prepared to bump into her, which might require revising his original plan. But he couldn't very well avoid the kitchen. The kitchen was a necessary territory since he had to see if there was any booze to steal. *I have a confession to make,* he'd say. *I'm not getting anywhere with our friend von Hartmann.* Or something along those lines.

But there was no sign of Cecilia. He did, however, find Sandor Lukács, who mournfully waved hello. His moustache was drooping, and when Martin asked how he was doing he immediately launched into a story about how he and Vivi had had a fight. "It was such a stupid thing, really, you know?" he said. She had stormed off, and now he wanted to get drunk enough to go to her house, or possibly stand outside her window and yell if she didn't let him in, either way, the main thing was the getting drunk part. "Girls, am I right? They're the worst."

Sandor barely stopped for breath, and Martin couldn't just walk away. He looked around for Cecilia and thought he saw her in the dining room, but the lights were low, and he couldn't be sure. He zoned out for a second, and when he looked back over, she was gone. The music was turned up in the living room, and maybe that's where she was, dancing to "Kids in America", now that she was drunk and didn't feel a need to go on and on about what imperialist pricks the Americans were.

Sandor went off in search of a phone and Martin ended up on the sofa next to some people he didn't know. He told them he was writing a novel. The sentence slipped out even though it was supposed to be a secret (no pressure, no expectations), but the words felt wonderful to say, they swelled up like a balloon as soon as they'd left his lips, rising towards the ceiling, taking up all kinds of space.

"Wow," one of the strangers said, sounding impressed, "what about? How much have you written? How long is it going to be?"

Gustav came by and assured his audience that if anyone at this party could write, it was Martin Berg.

Martin liberated himself from the sofa, found a beer, and while squinting to see if maybe she was out on the patio, he almost tumbled into her. She briefly put a hand on his shoulder to keep her balance, but at once removed it again.

"Oh – hi."

"What do you know! Cecilia. Champion of dead German guys."

"Pardon?"

"Never mind. How's it going?"

"It's going good. And you?"

"I'd go so far as to say I'm terrific."

"Right." She smiled into her wine glass. "I thought I saw you before."

"We got here pretty late."

"So, what were you busy with earlier?" Polite conversation. She looked tired, as though she had to make an effort.

"Good question… I cooked a simple supper of fish fingers and spaghetti. Gustav was in charge of libations. We listened to *Die Walküre*, and our downstairs neighbour started to bang her ceiling, trying to disrupt our nineteenth-century serenity by playing that song, you know, the one that goes like this: na na na na na na naaa…"

"Total Eclipse of the Heart?"

"Exactly, that one. Anyway, so she put that on really loud, opened the window and everything, so we figured, meh, let's get out of here. Gustav was supposed to deliver a couple of paintings to some gallery bloke who went nuts for his stuff at the student exhibition anyway, so we walked down to Stigbergstorget Square, Gustav, the paintings and I. But the gallery bloke was with some girl. I want to point out that we offered to make ourselves scarce, but he was, like: 'No, come in and have a drink,' so we went in and had a drink…" Martin took a sip of his beer, "…and the girl seemed pretty displeased. I don't think she was in the same festive mood as Gustav and me. Either way, since we're both relatively socially competent, we only stayed for one drink. The gallery bloke was keen to talk more about, and I'm quoting, 'the possibilities inherent in the motif according to postmodernism' and drink champagne with us half the night, but we had places to be. We couldn't just hang around, enriching their interaction forever. And then we discovered to our incredible inconvenience that we didn't have any ciggies."

"Aha."

"Domus was closed, so we set off on a cigarette odyssey around Majorna to find a corner shop. But the first three places had no Gauloises, and I was like: 'Come on, let's just settle for Marlboros, let's settle for Camels, let's bloody settle for Lucky *Strikes*, even,' but you know Gustav, he had to have his Gauloises, so we had to trudge over to that place by Mariaplan Square. *Then* we came here. What have you been up to?"

"Well, I—"

"Hold on – Gustav!" He was coming out of the kitchen, and almost seemed to be avoiding looking in Martin's direction. "*Gustav*. Come here, meet Cecilia."

Gustav turned around resignedly, smiled at Cecilia, shook her hand.

"Nice to meet you," she said.

"Pleasure," he said.

All three of them stood quietly for a beat too long. Gustav recovered first; he asked how Cecilia knew the guy throwing the party. A friend of a friend, she said. Us too, they said. Silence fell again. Apparently, there was no smoking inside, so Gustav was going out for a cigarette. Did they want to come?

"Sure," Martin said. It was possible he'd burned his bridges. But fortune was on his side, Cecilia joined them, and then they stood on the patio in their stocking feet, passing the lighter around. Now he had a full-length view of her: black trousers and jacket, white shirt. She looked like a person who had dressed up as someone with a serious job.

He heard himself talk about Cinemateket, about how lucky they were Cinemateket existed, a watering hole to save the intellectually parched from going under; without Cinemateket, we would be left with nothing but brain-dead American films or depressing documentaries about some village in Romania at the Haga Cinema, and he was deep into his tirade when Cecilia smiled wanly, ground out her cigarette, which she hadn't finished, and said she needed to go to the bathroom.

Gustav said nothing, no "Is this the famous Cecilia?" He just talked about a film club somewhere – Martin wasn't listening too closely – as though the conversation would continue even though Cecilia had left.

Things got in the way. Sandor appeared out of nowhere, wanting to roughhouse with Gustav until they both fell to the ground and had to be helped back up. When enough time had passed, Martin went inside, pretending he had to pee, and queued for the bathroom for at least five minutes, behind two girls with low, intense voices, who were discussing something he couldn't even be bothered to eavesdrop on, and he was convinced Cecilia would step out once the door finally opened. It turned out to be a complete stranger. He gave up his place in line. Cecilia wasn't in the kitchen, either, but Gustav was. Never mind Cecilia, what was the big deal with Cecilia anyway, Gustav put his arm around his neck, so close, his arm was warm, Martin tried to look at him and say something, but he was having trouble keeping his eyes open for some sodding reason.

"Here, drink," Gustav said. A glass with transparent liquid. Vodka? Water? Who cares? It was water. The rushing sound of running water. Another glass. Snus in the sink and soggy crisps.

"Are you okay?"

"*Oui*. I would go so far as to say: *tout va bien*."

"*Fucking* amazing. I would go so far as to say: cheers."

"But I have nothing to cheers with."

"That can be remedied." Gustav opened the fridge and took out a beer, someone else's, it didn't matter, beer is beer, as they say. People were gathering around them, in one of the many kitchens they would leave behind in the same way a rocket leaves its launchpad. People would stare at the place where the rocket used to be just moments before and marvel: *it was right there*. That is how they will leave this kitchen behind, and in years to come, tales will be told of a party: Martin Berg and Gustav Becker were there, they were so young then, it's almost hard to believe, that they were *those* people before they became who they are now. You could see it back then, too, obviously, a seed, the glimmer of what was to be. Does anyone have a camera?

"I need a piss." The bathroom in the hallway was engaged. He should have stayed in line. Those girls were going to take forever in there. Martin walked towards the patio door, found a pair of slippers, too big, stepped out into the garden. Apple trees with dark branches, bright air, he put his beer down on the grass by his feet, opened his fly, steam rose from his urine.

She must have gone home. Gone home or upstairs with someone else. Same difference.

The trees wobbled and maybe he needed to rest, sit down on the sofa for a bit, just close his eyes for a couple of seconds. Just a couple of seconds.

Someone pulled on his arm. A girl's fringe that used to be curly but was lank now, someone he knew but whose name was gone. Used to hang out at Sprängkullen. She laughed, wake up, Martin, come on, let's dance, the room capsized but then righted itself, and he was just going to pour some wine from a bottle that wasn't his own into a glass that wasn't his either, she was holding his hands, his socks slipped so easily across the hardwood floor, he spun her so fast her dress flared. Come on, he said, we're going outside, we're having a smoke. She came with him but didn't want a cigarette, which was a good thing because apparently there was just one little ciggy left in the pack. Her arms were bare in the night, she wrapped her arms around herself, he slouched against the railing and spilled his wine lighting his cigarette, she was warm, he ground the cigarette out in a planter and kissed her and it was unfamiliar at first, like diving, but he got used to it quickly. She pressed her body against his. Everything capsized again.

"Hey, I have to…"

Her hand on his shoulder. He shook it off. Had to get to the bathroom.

"Martin!" Gustav appeared near his face. "Last tram's in five minutes."

"Fuck."

"We'll make it. Or did you want to stay?"

"Bloody hell, no." He could only find one of his shoes, but took another that looked almost the same, tumbled out through the door, the night enveloped him, the music died away, he saw his own feet moving forward, forward in the yellow light of the street lamps, a tram hurtled out of the night, it screeched and hissed, opened its jaws, into the light, free seats. It was so warm, he sank below the surface, was rocked to sleep, they weren't getting off for a while yet. He leaned his head against Gustav's shoulder, said something, didn't even hear what himself.

Then a soft shaking. "Martin? Martin?" A short flight of steps, he toppled forward, hands in grass, dew, retching, like knives in his throat. A hand stroked the hair out of his face.

"Did you get it all out? Do you need to throw up again?"

He shook his head.

"It's best to get it all out, you know."

Another convulsion racked him. Then came his voice, rough with bile, too, had to be spat out. "Just rest a little."

"Sure, lie down right here. No, not on your back, you twit. Remember Jim Morrison." Gustav helped him roll onto his side, moved his arm. Like being a child. Someone else sorts it out. Rocking back and forth in the darkness. Sinking down, down.

"Hey, Martin. *Martin*. Can you walk? We can't fall asleep here. It's going to be bloody freezing. Come one, I'll help you."

His arm over a shoulder, the ground rushing by underneath their feet.

"I have to write about this."

Gustav laughed. "You're not going to remember it."

"I remember everything."

"Sure. So what are you going to write?"

"You know, *this*. Everything. All of it."

"I know you will."

"I will, right?"

"My god, yes. You have to. Watch out for the kerb."

"I actually think that's true. That I have to."

"Of course. You have to write, I have to paint."

"A known fact."

"Exactly."

"Hey, that's a good title. *A Known...* I think I have to throw up again."

Bent legs, hands on knees. The asphalt staring expectantly up at him. "I don't think there's anything left. Are we almost home?"

"Two minutes."

"I promise I will."

"Write?"

"Yes."

Gustav's face in the early morning light. He smiled, squeezed Martin's hand, too hard, really, Gustav had strong fingers, but it was a promise and it had to be sealed somehow and Martin squeezed back just as hard. Something warm welled up behind Martin's eyes and he had to look away, had to blink several times.

10

RAKEL YANKED OPEN the fridge and cursed at the empty shelves. It was going to have to be the most frugal breakfast of the year: a cup of black instant coffee and two pieces of crispbread with butter.

It had completely slipped her mind that she had a psychoanalysis seminar today, and that forgetfulness was a feat in itself. Before every single previous class, she'd read the assigned text several times, made notes, prepared questions, familiarised herself with any secondary readings and made sure she wasn't hungover. The majority of the students attending the seminars were in the last year of their psychology degrees, psychology interns, or fully licensed psychologists. They all kept referring to "the clinic" and seemed to be in psychoanalysis themselves. Rakel knew nothing about the clinic, but quite a bit about German verbs, which seemed to earn her a certain level of respect despite the fact that she was a novice.

She polished off her sad excuse for a morning meal in five minutes flat, then dashed about her flat in search of clothes and her notes. She had even discussed the upcoming seminar with one of her classmates, who was going too. Then, the fact that it was coming up seemed to have been completely erased from her brain, and now she hadn't done the reading, hadn't given it a moment's thought, it was starting in three hours, and she couldn't even find a clean shirt to wear.

Half an hour later, she was sitting at the window table at Cigarren. The TV above the door was showing horse racing. The regulars were already lined up outside and the fountain in the square had been turned back on since the weather warmed up. Its cascades glittered in the morning sun. Rakel lined up her belongings: volume IX of Freud's *Gesamelte Werke*, a notebook, a mechanical pencil, and, for some reason, the by then relatively battered *Ein Jahr der Liebe*, still dog-eared to page 21.

Diligent preparation wasn't strictly necessary. Before each seminar, they read a text and then they discussed it with an invited guest, usually some psychoanalyst or psychologist of the older generation. It was a large class, at least thirty, so hiding behind the others posed no real challenge. She didn't have to say anything at all. And yet, Rakel noted, she seemed virtually incapable of slacking off. She read the text twice, had another cup of coffee, took notes, wrote down her questions even though she probably wouldn't dare to ask them.

On her way to Lagerhuset, she dragged her feet to make sure she was late enough not to have to make small talk with her acquaintances. When she slipped into a seat in the half-moon of folding chairs, she realised another thing she'd managed to forget: today's guest was Max Schreiber. He was sitting at a table facing the room with a stack of books in front of him and was busy rolling up the sleeves of his black turtleneck, a grim look on his face. He was one of the many people who said: "Ah, *Cecilia's* girl," and claimed to have met her as a child. Rakel's memories from the history department were fragmented and irrelevant – a vending machine in a long corridor, the pattern of a curtain billowing in an open window, the texture of the sofa fabric, the endless supply of hot chocolate in paper cups – and rarely included any older men in tweed jackets and glasses. But she did remember Max. "So, Rakel," he'd say, descending from his imposing height to sit next to her in some corner of Cecilia's office. "Your mum claims you're something of a Greek mythology expert. Can you tell me something about it?"

Now he was inarguably middle-aged. His face was stern and grave. His eyes were obscured behind the glare of his round, steel-rimmed glasses. Rakel thought she might avoid detection, but just as the seminar leader – a bloke in a sober sleeveless sweater she knew a little, who always wanted to talk about the impact of Berg & Andrén on the "field of the humanities" – was about to speak, Max spotted her, smiled and nodded.

Then followed two hours of close reading of the Freud text. Sleeveless Sweater Guy, who had taken a seat next to Max, moderated. Some of the attendees asked relevant questions. Others had a habit of presenting a lengthy and abstract problem that they wrapped up with the phrase "Would you mind speaking to that?" Someone wanted to talk about Freud's attitude towards women. Someone else absolutely didn't want to talk about Freud's attitude towards women. One young man spoke in great detail about a text by Lacan that he, but probably almost no one else in the room, had studied. Sleeveless Sweater Guy seemed unable to resist the temptation of showing off how well read he was, and for twenty incomprehensible minutes, the seminar veered off on a strange off-piste tangent during which the term *desire* was repeated a dozen times without anyone involved seeming to know what they were talking about. Then, Max cleared his throat and Sleeveless Sweater Guy, sensitive to protocol as he was, steered the discussion back to the topic at hand.

After a while, Rakel put her pen down. Then it was over, chairs scraped, people stretched and an internal battle was fought inside Rakel between politeness and a wish to be alone. Politeness came out the victor. She went over to say hi to Max.

"Rakel," he said, with a warmth that wrong-footed her flight response. "It's nice to see you."

A stupid and irrational urge to burst into tears washed over her. "You too," she said. Luckily, her voice was steady.

They talked for a while about the psychology programme and things of that nature. Max pointed to the book she was clutching to her chest. "I can see you're reading it in the original," he said. "Cecilia's influence, no?"

Rakel couldn't remember the last time she'd heard her mother's name spoken aloud without hesitation. She nodded.

"Is she still gone?" he asked.

She nodded again. Max pulled on his jacket. He wasn't as tall as she remembered.

"She was always so excessive," he said. "Disappearing like that is a very strange thing to do."

"And not coming back," Rakel said without thinking. "That's almost as strange."

Sleeveless Sweater Guy appeared, thanking Max and asking Rakel if she wanted to join him and some of the others for a pint at Pustervik. Rakel mumbled something about a previous engagement and fled.

*

When she stepped into the hallway on Djurgårdsgatan a little while later, she also stepped into a clash between the other two members of the Berg family. Her dad had decided that Elis had to attend his grandmother's seventy-fifth birthday party. Elis was protesting in part because he felt no one could tell him what to do – he was an *adult* now, he pointed out – but mostly because the celebration in question was to take place on Walpurgis Night. Martin countered that so long as Elis lived at home and didn't make his own money, he had to abide by Martin's rules. Elis had no leg to stand on. The money thing was a sore point. "I just don't get why she has to have the party on Walpurgis," he hissed, slamming the dishwasher closed and storming off to his room. A few minutes later, they heard the muffled sound of the wispy percussion of "Le Poinçonneur des Lilas" by Gainsbourg.

Martin sighed. "You're coming, aren't you?" he said. "Inger sent out the invitations weeks ago."

Rakel recalled the pile of unopened post on her hallway floor. "Absolutely," she said.

Her father pointed at the table. A plate, a glass and cutlery were waiting for her. "I figured we could give her something she doesn't already have from Svenskt Tenn. What do you think? Is that too dull?" He set out the leftovers from their lunch, French potato salad and a plate of smoked salmon, and seeing it, Rakel suddenly realised she was ravenous.

"Sounds great," she said as she heaped food onto her plate and dug in.

Martin sat down across from her. "I've been thinking about getting back to my biography project again," he said casually.

Rakel had already heard most of what there was to say about her dad's plans to write the Great William Wallace Biography, but now she got the whole spiel again. The biography's raison d'être was the "absolutely absurd fact" that there was no "reasonable life history" of the British author, even though he'd been dead for sixty years. Martin refused to believe that was simply because Wallace was passé. He was considered a writer's writer, he said, revered by authors but unknown to most of the reading public. He'd never received the recognition he deserved, because he'd never been in sync with his contemporaries.

In the US, he was considered too determinist, which was probably one of the reasons he never quite made it there—"

"But he didn't really make it anywhere, did he?"

"—but his characters always exhibit impressive psychological depth, maybe because he had an intuitive, rather than theoretical, understanding of human nature. As you know, Wallace poked quite a bit of fun at psychoanalysis, for instance. There's a pretty funny example of that in *Fugue*, where the tormented pianist Fanny ends up at a shrink's office without really knowing why, and—"

"Would you like some tea?"

"No, thank you, I'm good. Anyway – you've read *A Fugue for Fanny*, right?"

"Yes. You gave it to me two years ago. First edition." Rakel put her plate in the dishwasher and turned the kettle on. Elis and Rakel both regularly received Wallace books for their birthdays and Christmas, complete with a small lecture about "Wallace's influence on the modern novel", which Martin seemed to have forgotten delivering the previous year, too. They would unwrap their gift and say: "William Wallace, what a surprise." Rakel had even struggled through the hopelessly experimental *Times and Clocks and Watches*. She'd read all eight hundred and fifty pages and drawn a line in the margin whenever she came across a passage she liked but didn't necessarily understand. She'd even thought, as she reached the cinematic THE END, which were the last words of the book, that maybe *she* could translate it, even though it was considered untranslatable. Just to dip her toes in, she'd transposed the first page of the novel from linguistically wild English to self-conscious Swedish. It had not turned out well.

Her tea steeped while her father rambled on. Tiredness welled up inside Rakel. The thought of going back to Friggagatan made her legs feel limp, like drooping twigs.

"I was going to stay over tonight," she announced in the middle of Martin's rant about what he called "the proto-feminist theme" in another of Wallace's novels. She could spend the evening reading in the narrow single bed in her old room, dressed in the flannel pyjamas that were always freshly laundered, and go to sleep early – she felt like she could sleep for days.

Her dad immediately turned the conversation to his other favourite subject: what they might have for dinner.

"No need to make a fuss on my account," Rakel said, but he was already on his feet, flipping through his grease-and-sauce-stained *The French Cuisine*, which always opened to the beef bourguignon recipe, mumbling something about coq au vin, if they had organic chicken at the shops, and being out of shallots. A regular dinner could balloon into a five-hour project with Martin in charge. A few years earlier, he'd had the kitchen redone and the room that had been a cluttered mess during Rakel's childhood was now a temple of strict order. There was a vast marble counter, soft-closing drawers, a high-tech oven (he'd really wanted a gas hob, since that's apparently what they'd had in Paris, but couldn't be bothered to quarrel with the co-op board about installing a gas line), and Martin himself, with an apron over his black jeans and T-shirt. Since he had a habit of multi-tasking, he was usually talking on the phone, too, with a Bluetooth headset in his ear like some Star Trek cyborg, or shouting commands to his two children if they happened to stray within earshot.

Now, he did an inventory of the fridge and was pleased to conclude that he'd have to go to the shops. The market hall wasn't closing for another hour. Did Rakel have a hankering for anything in particular?

No? Sure? Not olives? Or gruyère? Not even chocolates from Flickorna Kanold?

Rakel shook her head. Elis popped his head out of his room. "I wouldn't mind chocolates," he said.

Then followed a chaotic interlude – Elis was meeting a friend and couldn't find his wallet, Martin discovered it on the dresser, Elis hopped around the hallway on one leg, trying to tie his shoes, Martin searched for a tote bag for the groceries – and then they both left, deep in a heated discussion about whether or not Elis was going to get to practise driving the next day. Rakel went over to the bay window to watch them walk down the street. They lingered at the intersection for a long time, Martin's bike parked next to them. Martin was gesticulating, Elis glaring at the ground. Then Elis talked for a long time and Martin nodded. They parted with a brief mutual pat on the shoulder. Elis, slightly hunched, strode down towards Karl Johansgatan while Martin pedalled up Allmänna Vägen.

There was a narrow door in the living room, framed by cluttered bookshelves. Rakel took a deep breath and opened it. It revealed a steep flight of steps. Each one creaked loudly.

The stairs led up to a small attic nook, with a square window under which stood a desk. It was empty. Even the drawers were empty, despite the unique gravitational pull of desk drawers on faded ticket stubs, paper clips and old tram passes. Empty shelves lined one wall. The other was covered in glass display cases full of butterflies. Each specimen was labelled with its Latin name, written in Lars Wikner's hand.

Rakel pulled out the wooden chair and sat down with her knees pulled up to her chin. She remembered the muffled patter of the typewriter coming from up here. Sometimes, there would be silence, and that could mean the stairs were about to creak under her mother's feet as she made her way down. Or there would be another downpour, possibly discernible only to Rakel, who was an expert at listening for and interpreting the sounds from the study, and she had to resume waiting.

11

Martin dived. Then he surfaced, slicked his hair back, and blinked the water out of his eyes. The clearly visible tiled bottom and clean, chlorinated water of the Valhalla Public Pool stretched out before him.

He was hoping some laps might erase the whole awful day that was throbbing inside his skull. His brain felt feverish, as though he'd thought too many thoughts too fast. When he reached that state, it was almost impossible to make it cool back down. He couldn't just "take it easy, go home, watch a film or something" as the well-intentioned but naive Amir had suggested when Martin's email programme for some unfathomable reason froze, which meant the long email he'd been in the middle of composing disappeared and couldn't be recovered, not even by Amir. "God dammit!" Martin had snapped, kicking his bin across the room. He'd spent at least an hour writing to the author of that manuscript about a young, morose poet struggling with the meaninglessness of existence. The gist was that they didn't want to publish it, but that it had certain qualities and could be reworked. The problem was, Martin had thought as he sat there staring at the computer screen, that not even in its hypothetical, most-perfect form did the novel enthuse him at all. He felt no desire to dig out and bring forth the narrative buried somewhere in the cumbersome manuscript. As far as he was concerned, the stymied poet should just throw himself off a bridge and spare everyone else involved considerable suffering.

Sanna had given it the thumbs down, too.

And then it had just disappeared, all his encouraging phrases and carefully formulated critique. Rage, sudden and searing, surged through his body. Amir had interpreted his reaction as "stress" – which seemed to function as a catchall for practically any state of mind these days – and seemed to believe going home and "taking it easy" would help alleviate it. No, unfortunately not. Martin Berg couldn't just "take it easy". Martin Berg had to go over the list of invitees to the company's twenty-fifth anniversary celebration, since Patricia couldn't be trusted to know and include people who weren't on social media.

He had to get hold of a fact checker who should have been in touch last week. He'd promised the industry publication *Svensk Bokhandel* a phone interview on the occasion of their twenty-fifth anniversary. He had to reserve the laundry room and do a wash, or possibly bribe Elis to do it for him. He had to talk to Rakel about how they were running out of time with that German novel. Readers had to stick to deadlines. From the way she was dragging her feet, you'd think she wasn't interested in publishing in the slightest.

And he had to talk to Per about the offer. They had to agree on a reply. *We are, needless to say, very flattered, but...* Martin Berg can't abandon his only-just-about successful company. Martin Berg can't move away from his grown children and elderly mother, with whom he has spent less time than he should have. Thank you, but it is unfortunately out of the question.

On the other hand, their sales weren't exactly stellar. They were never going to be stellar. They had been stellar for brief, sparkler-like periods, such as when they published Lucas Bell's *A Season in Hell*, but what were the odds of something like that ever happening again? Perhaps doubling down on their relatively niche list was ill advised. Was there even a future for literature? How many people were going to purchase the new edition of Wittgenstein's diaries? A few hundred poor sods who, for reasons passing understanding, were interested in the inner workings of philosophers. A couple of thousand over time. And that was a remarkable work. There was no denying it. Publishing a new edition of Wittgenstein's diaries was nothing to sneer at. And Cecilia had done an outstanding job with the translation.

A gaggle of young teenagers were being loud by the edge of the pool. Martin, used to the quiet atmosphere at Hagabadet, looked daggers at them. This was apparently the price you paid to swim in an Olympic-size pool. He sped up and overtook an old lady in a swim cap.

And Gustav. He still couldn't get hold of Gustav. Prick. He seemed to think he could come and go as he pleased in people's lives. After a few months of silence, he'd call, babbling about how amazing this and that person was, about his trips to this, that or the other place, about some exciting experience he'd had. While Martin had paced in circles as the phone rang unanswered. If he worried, Gustav was peeved. If he didn't worry, he was peeved. And then there was Per with his casual comments about that woman, what was her name? The poet. Read-the-fine-print Maria Malm. "Too bad you had to leave so early." Blah, blah, blah. What next? Another dinner invitation? Would he suddenly have a spare ticket to the theatre, and would Martin want to...?

Martin reached the far end. He braced his feet against the tile and pushed off as hard as he could.

*

Elis was sprawled on the sofa in the manner of teenagers every-where – looking like he'd been dropped from a great height – and greeted Martin with the tiniest of gestures. He'd connected his laptop to the TV, was holding the remote in one hand, and had his phone within easy reach. Its screen kept lighting up with incoming texts.

When Elis began to dress like an old man from the fifties, the clothes he wore at home had changed, too. Gone were the jogging bottoms and washed-out sweatshirts he'd bummed about in the greater part of every day. Let us instead present tartan flannel pyjamas, a soft cardigan with elbow patches, a quality green dressing gown he'd pulled out of a dresser with unadulterated delight. (Martin had been given it for his fortieth birthday but hadn't been able to bring himself to give up his old one.) The next logical step ought to be a smoking jacket. Even his socks had been replaced with versions made of merino wool or whatever it was. And since the occasion when Elis had fished a toddler-sized sock out of the laundry basket, a look of abject horror on his face, and exclaimed: "Why would you put them in the dryer!" his father was no longer trusted to wash them. His son took that upon himself, hanging them up to dry over the bath.

On the TV, a man with a square jaw and a woman in a pillbox hat were talking to each other.

"How was school?"

"Good."

"Did you learn anything?"

"Not really."

"Then what did you do?"

Even in his position of utter relaxation, Elis managed to shrug. "Gave a presentation."

"On what?"

Elis yawned. Mumble, mumble. "…China."

"What?"

"The Cultural Revolution in China. It was" – another yawn – "a special project."

"And did it go well?"

"Yep."

He gave up and went to inspect the contents of the fridge. Not that long ago, Elis had come home from school telling him long, pointless anecdotes, insisting that Martin test him on his homework so he wouldn't get anything wrong.

Martin weighed a cauliflower in his hand and sighed.

And then came those hours. When all the chores of the day were done but it was too early to go to bed.

The dishwasher hummed. Elis didn't want a cup of tea. Martin made one for himself and retreated to his desk.

Many years ago, he'd met a woman who insisted it was bad feng shui to have a desk in your bedroom. "It's supposed to be a space reserved for *relaxation*," she'd told him, her nose wrinkled in the universal expression of revulsion.

She – it was Mimmi, who could never find a flat she wanted to buy – also insisted not using the attic room was sheer idiocy, as it made for the perfect "home office". A home office for Martin Berg, the busy publisher, though he'd have to get rid of those nasty butterflies, obviously. Maybe put up some String shelves and a nice white desk, it has to be white, you know, to make the room feel more spacious.

Now, Martin sat down, opened his laptop, picked up books, and put them back down. William Wallace was peering up at him from the cover of a slim epistolary volume, a glint of mischief in his eyes. His shirt collar was mussed and, even in black and white, his tweed jacket looked like it was stained with red wine and Worcestershire sauce or some such. He was ragged in that unapologetic way only poor people or people who are deeply convinced of their own brilliance can be. Wallace was, for the most part, both.

William Wallace the author had died one night in 1945, from a heart attack, at his desk. He'd been found the next morning, leaning over a sheet of paper on which he had unknowingly jotted down his final, incomplete sentence. His last words were "*He was inevitably*", followed by a wild slash of ink, probably caused by a powerful paroxysm at the moment of death. Martin had decided early on that this would be the title: *He Was Inevitably: A biography of William Wallace.*

He looked for his WW folder, cursing under his breath at his inability to keep his files organised, did a search, and was halfway through a long list of irrelevant results before remembering that those documents had been on his old MacBook, which he had passed on to Elis once its contents had been archived on a portable hard drive. In the lead up to the swap, Martin had spent a few weeks of annual leave writing a synopsis of his latest version of the Wallace project. In a vivid flashback, he could even see himself printing out that most recent document before changing laptops, intending to resume work shortly, placing it somewhere strategic that he would definitely remember. And where on earth could that have been?

First, he searched his desk drawers, even though he was almost certain he couldn't have been dumb enough to put anything important *there*. Then the rest of the room, haphazardly. Then he widened his search, passing his texting son, opening the door to the hallway closet, but closing it again immediately with a sigh. Then back to the shelves lined with enigmatically labelled magazine holders. PAPERS MISC. I. PAPERS MISC. 2. MANUSCRIPTS. MISC. FINANCES 2004.

FINANCES 2005. He emptied a few of the most likely candidates out on the bed and began leafing through the papers.

Then he let out a whoop of surprise.

"What?" Elis called out from the living room.

"Nothing…"

"Then why are you shouting?"

Martin looked at the stack of papers in his hands. Substantial. Double-spaced, admittedly, a trick he'd often employed to make himself feel productive. There was an ambitious title page.

NIGHT SONNETS

A NOVEL

Martin Berg

He remembered this one. The title (vaguely twisted à la Wallace). Parts of the plot (a fumbling man, a helping of comic relief). He'd been working on it before Elis was born. This particular version was, judging by the printout, from the autumn when Cecilia had her book of essays accepted. He remembered the computer: smooth, grey, with a clear-blue screen. The computer was going to make everything so much easier! He was going to make so much progress now that his writing was aided by technology! Floppy discs instead of stacks and more stacks of paper! The only problem was that he didn't quite trust the floppy discs. So he ended up printing everything anyway. And after editing a draft, he didn't want to get rid of it, because what if he changed his mind? And needed to go back? Consequently, the mountains of paper grew even faster than they had during the era of the typewriter, when he'd only occasionally made photostats of some manuscript he was particularly fond of.

The last page was numbered 312 and contained a handwritten note: *What to do with LS??? Need some kind of turning point!*

He opened the bottom drawer, put the manuscript at the far back, closed the drawer and continued his search for the Wallace document.

12

A few days later, Martin turned the page of the morning paper and did a spit take with his coffee at the sudden sight of himself. Or, more accurately: his thirty-year-old self, in furtive conversation with Cecilia. In a painted version, true, but Gustav's paintings were so realistic anyone would have thought it a photograph at first glance. Because the painting had hung in the living room since it was given to them as a wedding present, Martin was exceedingly familiar with the motif, but that only made its appearance in the culture section of *Göteborgs-Posten* all the more unexpected. Usually, one of the Cecilia portraits was used when an example of Gustav's painting was needed.

He let out a curse. He was going to need a clean shirt.

The headline read: GUSTAV BECKER: A LIFE IN INK AND OIL. On the opposite page was a black-and-white photograph of Gustav. He was looking straight into the camera with a cigarette between his lips. His face was lined, his thinning hair dishevelled. The picture had been taken a few years earlier by a British photographer whose name was lost to Martin until he discovered it in tiny script underneath the picture – Christopher Welton. In his memory, the name bobbed around in the vicinity of the Stockholm Museum of Photography. Had there been an exhibition? Was he famous? Either way, Gustav's gallery had insisted on new press photos and the services of the possibly renowned Welton had been retained. Gustav had laughed at the pictures.

"But you do look like that," Martin had protested. "Maybe not quite so Sherlock Holmes-y, but he's caught your spirit. You even wear a turtleneck sometimes. And I seem to recall a beret."

"I've never worn a fucking beret."

"It was in the eighties."

"I didn't wear a beret, even in the eighties."

And so Martin had been forced to fetch one of the photo albums Cecilia had put together and present evidence of the beret.

Now, Martin skimmed the full-page spread. The Gothenburg Museum of Art was putting on a retrospective of the work of Gothenburg artist Gustav Becker (there was no mention of the fact that he'd been based in Stockholm for most of his life). We're very proud, says the curator. One of the most important names in contemporary Swedish art, says gallerist KG Hammarsten. There was no comment from the artist himself – presumably the journalist hadn't been able to reach him, either, and had had to make do with the garrulous KG.

"What the fuck," Martin said to no one at all; Elis was still asleep. He fumbled around for his phone, but no one answered at Gustav's house, as expected. He called Rakel instead. She picked up drowsily after five rings.

"Did you know Gustav is having a retrospective?" he asked.

"No," she yawned. "Where?"

"The art museum. It seems like a pretty big deal." Martin could hear how shrill he sounded.

There was a rustle of sheets and then her voice returned, clearer this time. "What time is it anyway?"

"Seven-thirty."

"But it's Saturday."

"Do you get *Göteborgs-Posten*?"

"I was *out* last night. Celebrating that Lovisa aced her university entrance exam. And now *you're* calling me at half seven. And no, I don't get *Göteborgs-Posten*. I read *Dagens Nyheter*."

He made Rakel promise to read the article, one way or another, but when he moved on to talking about the twenty-fifth anniversary, she told him she was actually planning to go back to sleep.

"How's the German book coming?" he hurriedly asked before she could hang up.

Rakel took a few seconds too long to answer. "I'm reading it now, actually… the one by this…" – her voice faded, as though she were moving away from the phone, then came back stronger – "…Franke. Philip Franke. What a name for a German bloke. I'll get back to you with my psychological diagnosis in due course."

"I do eventually have to tell his publisher something, you know." Martin felt he sounded encouraging, but his daughter just muttered something in German and hung up.

Martin turned back to the article. The cigarette was verging on overkill. Who got away with smoking in a photo these days? If anyone could, it would be Gustav, and maybe Knausgård.

Martin had smoked what he'd sworn was his last cigarette at the turn of the millennium, hoping the symbolism of the act would guarantee its immutability. (It hadn't, but when he fell off the wagon ten months later, he'd felt so pathetic it sucked most of the joy out of the cigarette, which he smoked standing at the bar at Klara.) When the smoking ban was introduced a few years later, some passionate nicotine zealots, like Sanna at work with her bloody Lucky Strikes and a lighter sensibly tucked into the pack, had mourned for weeks. Martin's official stance was that it was a stupid idea. It was, he argued, tantamount to smothering the nation's nightlife, castrating the vitality of a night out. It was political correctness gone mad. Surely people knew that going out involved a few hours of second-hand smoking, but *so what*, and what kind of Big-Brother mentality was this going to open the door for, undermining the Swedish people's last refuge from the endlessly long and frigid winters.

But just a few months later, he had to admit it was a refreshing experience to have a pint at Pustervik without feeling like he was standing in a gas chamber. And then Sanna pulled out a can of snus and confessed she was planning to quit before she turned forty. Vivi and Sandor Lukács swapped their Marlboro Lights and Camels with filters for yoga and cross-country skiing respectively. Not even the young people seemed to be taking up smoking with the same gusto as in the seventies.

They probably got up to some other mischief, online no doubt, but at least their lungs were clean and tar-free.

But in this era of scaling back, phasing out and increased susceptibility to cancer propaganda, Gustav remained unmoved. He still smoked his Gauloises, one or two packs a day. Martin remembered when new neighbours had moved in below him in the early 2000s – a young couple working in media who at first might have felt fancy living right beneath Gustav Becker *l'artiste*, but who a few months into their residency began to complain about the smell of cigarette smoke in their flat.

"What am I supposed to do about it?" Gustav had said on the phone. "They're saying they're going to bring it up at the annual meeting of the co-op."

"Well," said Martin, who just then had been trying to shepherd two children and a bag full of food from the supermarket to his home, "can't you smoke on the balcony?"

"The balcony," Gustav had sneered. "I don't paint on the balcony."

"Have you tried to talk to them?"

"I have, but their approach seems to be that they're right and I'm wrong, and consequently it's not so much a discussion as an attempt at persuasion in which I have been assigned the role of villain. He's all right, but she's a wolf in sheep's clothing. Standing there with her striped top and cropped fringe and I'll bet you anything she won't let her future children play with swords. You know the type. I'm seriously thinking about hiring a lawyer."

"Don't you think that's a bit...?"

The sound of a lighter clicking. "Mm?"

"Nothing. Rakel, could you open the door?"

"You shouldn't be using a mobile phone, Martin. Do you have any idea how much radiation those things generate?"

"No..."

"Exactly. And *no one else* does either. I'll bet you a hundred kronor brain tumours will be the most common cause of death twenty years from now."

"But they've looked into that kind of..."

"How do you know they have?"

"It's the logic of capitalism. Being implicated in a scandal isn't good for business."

"Isn't the logic of capitalism that you sell whatever you can as quickly as you can before anyone realises there's a health risk. Take DDT for instance. Thalidomide. Anything."

"Cigarettes."

"Very funny."

By then, they'd made it back to the flat, and Martin set down the groceries, his arm aching. Rakel and Elis took their shoes off and raced off in an attempt to avoid having to help with dinner. Elis was an expert at going to the bathroom for a really long time, and when you called him, he replied: "I'm pooing!" even though he was in fact sitting there reading the encyclopaedia he kept next to the toilet.

Gustav went on for a good long while about the scourge of mobile phones before circling back to the issue of retaining a lawyer. "Do you know any good ones or what?"

"The only lawyers I know deal with contracts and copyright issues."

"Hmm. I'll have to ask around. Look, I have to go. Have a good one."

He actually did hire a lawyer soon thereafter. "Sahar. Amazing woman. It's painful to realise how little you know about things. It's like living in a Kafka novel, except you don't know it. Like a mix between Kafka and *The Matrix*? I hadn't even considered writing a will. She looked at me like I was an idiot. I was, like: 'It's not like I'm going to *die*, Sahar.' And she was, like: 'I can guarantee that you will, sooner or later.' Tough as nails, that one."

Martin never found out if she actually got involved in the cigarette feud, but Gustav continued to smoke in his flat.

Martin took his coffee with him and sat down in the living room, across from the Wedding Portrait. A few years earlier, he'd agreed to lend it out for an exhibition, where it had hung between a Zorn and a Krøyer. Gustav had been very pleased with that arrangement; he and Martin had gone to see it several times, and one of those times, Gustav had smuggled in a bottle of whisky that they toasted with in secret while the security guard paced back and forth in an adjacent room. Meanwhile, Martin never fully got used to the painting's absence in his home. Every time he stepped into the living room, he felt disoriented, and afterwards he decided never to part with it again.

It was a large painting, three by five feet. It showed the newlyweds alone at a table in a garden. Cecilia on the right, laughing at something Martin was whispering in her ear. There was an empty chair next to Martin and two next to Cecilia, which meant the two of them were positioned slightly left-of-centre. Neither one of them was looking out of the painting: Martin was looking at Cecilia, and Cecilia was looking past any potential spectators, into eternity. The table was littered with glasses, empty or almost empty, plates with remnants of a meal, a couple of vibratingly green wine bottles, silver cutlery. A wasp had drowned in a half-empty pint glass. Behind them, a blooming mock orange filled the entire upper half of the canvas. The top button of Martin's shirt was undone, and his tie was crooked, like a black backslash across the painting. The lace of Cecilia's long-sleeved dress seemed meticulously reproduced, though Martin knew that if he stood close enough to it, it would be nothing but white blobs and lines, seemingly scattered at random. And the whole scene was shrouded in the golden light of the height of summer, and Martin couldn't figure out how Gustav had pulled that off: how he'd painted something that wasn't a physical entity, something as changeable and immaterial as light itself.

"I always knew you'd get married," Gustav had said at the reception, in a moment of lucidity in the otherwise solid intoxication both he and Martin were experiencing. "From the very start."

"You didn't even like her at first."

"Yes, I did."

"You were sceptical and sulky."

"Hey, I was not. I liked Cissi from day one."

"Come off it. You didn't speak to me for weeks."

"*You're* the one who refused to talk to *me*. I called and called like a lunatic, but you were never home. That bloke, what was his name, the one you lived with, would just sigh when he realised it was me again."

"Anders."

"Right. Anders. Whatever happened to him?"

"No idea. I think he became a union man."

"Anyway: my point. Cissi was in a league of her own. Anyone could see that. A league of her own."

FURTHER STUDIES IN THE HUMANITIES 2

I

INTERVIEWER: What are your thoughts on reading?

MARTIN BERG: I'm glad you ask me that. Reading often ends up a bit overshadowed by writing, don't you think? When in fact there are no writers who aren't also passionate readers. I'm absolutely certain about that. A person who says he wants to write but doesn't *read* much... He's a liar. Maybe he wants to be admired. Improve his social standing. I don't know. If you write in earnest, you also read. Ravenously and incessantly.

*

For a long time, Martin's dissertation consisted of a stack of notepads full of scribbled notes, which, when he took a closer look at them, were not at all the almost finished work he'd told himself they were. What had seemed like a brilliant idea was becoming more and more twisted as he strained to straighten it out. And, crucially: did anyone care about the relationship of language to human perception? Was it important? Why had he decided to work on Wittgenstein, this Austrian fellow who was so tangled up in a logical system of his own invention that the world that logic was supposed to be applied to only seemed to exist as an abstract notion, nothing but material for the mind to tinker with?

The end of term was nigh, and Martin had no time for anything but his dissertation, which was just as well, because he couldn't help both looking for Cecilia and dreading running into her at the same time. He barely left the flat. Several days in a row, he walked around in pyjama bottoms, a T-shirt from The Clash's Scandinavium concert in

1980, and, when he felt chilly, his bathrobe. He lived off black coffee, sandwiches with liver pâté and pickles, eggs, bacon and baked beans, and a bottle of cheap wine that he rationed to keep his productivity at optimum level. Occasionally, Anders coaxed him into eating some lentil stew. A handful of times, he trudged up to the hot dog stand on Stigberg Square and ordered a hot dog with mash and prawn salad, which he shovelled down sitting on a park bench between a couple of alcoholics who were griping about their pension.

Gustav, who was in a good mood again now that the spring exhibition was in the past, claimed Martin was "in all honesty taking his studies far too seriously" and should let his hair down a little. "Not even a glass of wine at Pustervik?" he wheedled.

"Not even that."

"Well, well, aren't we the bloody disciplined one."

Martin sighed and shuffled his papers.

At the end of May, he handed in freshly printed copies of his dissertation to his examiners. A week-long respite commenced. The night before, he'd sat up until four in the morning, going over his references one last time, and he left the department feeling at once exhausted and restless.

He was too wired to go home and sleep. From the payphone outside the city library, he called Valand, where Sissel picked up. She would go see if Gustav was in, she said. Martin fed the machine coins while he waited.

Just as he heard Sissel's voice in his ear again, he spotted a familiar figure walking up the front steps, this time sans parka.

"I'm sorry, I missed that."

Sissel repeated: Gustav and Sandor had gone out to eat but would probably be back in a bit. Martin thanked her and hurried into the library.

She couldn't have had more than a forty-five-second head start. She was not at the lending counter or over by the shelves of reserved books. She wasn't walking up the stairs to the first floor. That left only the ground floor or the basement. It was Tuesday, film screening in the auditorium. He reached it just in time to see her buy a ticket at the door.

He followed. A dozen people were spread out inside. He walked down the aisle, heart pounding. Even though he knew she'd be there, his heart skipped a beat when he spotted her. She was sitting near the middle, with her legs crossed and her hands in her lap. Martin squeezed past a prickly, long-legged goth, hoping she wouldn't wonder why he hadn't chosen a more easily accessible seat, and said:

"Hey, Cecilia!" in a voice he had instructed to sound "happily surprised".

She looked up, disoriented. "Oh – hi." She was wearing blue jeans and a man's dress shirt. A thought occurred to him, whining like a mosquito: that the shirt wasn't hers. That it belonged to her boyfriend. That she'd accidentally spilled something on her own shirt and laughingly borrowed one of his. A goodbye kiss in the hallway, he's going to work and she, the Independent Girlfriend, is going to see a film by herself. For a second, Martin thought she'd forgotten his name, didn't remember him at all. But then she moved her bag from the seat next to hers, as though they'd in fact made a date and she'd been holding a seat for him, and said:

"And so we meet in a cultural basement yet again, Martin Berg. I thought people liked to be outside on days like this." She smiled. "How are things?"

Martin heard himself launch into a rambling account of how he'd just handed in his dissertation, how he'd been writing up until the deadline so there hadn't been time to send it in by post, and now he was completely spent, so why not go watch – he realised he didn't know what film he'd just bought a ticket for. "A film," he finished lamely. And the moment he managed to rein himself in enough to ask how she was doing, the lights went out. Martin caught a glimpse of a smile in the dark before she turned towards the screen. The Cinemateket jingle played, the curtains parted and the film began. It was Stanley Kubrick's *2001, A Space Odyssey*. He'd seen it just a few weeks earlier with Gustav. At that point, it had inspired little more than a nebulous feeling of angst, even though he'd later claimed it was "a powerful epic that confronted the banal inconsequentiality of humankind" in conversation with some course mates.

While *Also Sprach Zarathustra* blasted through the speakers, he remembered idiotic things he'd written, pretentious sentences emblazoned across his eyelids.

"Martin," Cecilia said, her hand brushing against his upper arm. "You look pale. Are you feeling okay?"

They were on their way up from the darkness of the auditorium, like a sweaty Orpheus and his concerned Eurydice. Martin noted dimly that she was touching him.

"I'm just anxious about my dissertation," he replied, even though he'd planned to counter with one of the intelligent phrases about the film he'd spent the past couple of hours honing.

"What are you worried about?"

They stepped out into a mild, lilac evening. Martin didn't know what to do with his hands, so he shoved them into his trouser pockets.

"That they're going to think it's shit," he said and tried to tack on a brief chuckle.

"Which parts?"

"All of it. Well, mostly the discussion."

"Sounds like you need a drink," Cecilia said.

They ended up going to the bar where he'd first spotted her. Martin was on the verge of telling her about that but stopped himself at the last second. Now, tables had been set out on the pavement, and they sat down at one of them. Instead of trying to reassure him it would be fine (what Gustav would have done) or whinge about the examiners (what his course-mates would have done), Cecilia quizzed him.

"Is there a section you *know* is weak? Or is it more of a general feeling that it's no good?"

"It *feels* like the whole thing's bad."

"Sure, but which parts would you criticise yourself? Your examiners can't just say 'the whole thing's bad' without looking like imbeciles."

He thought about that for a moment. "There's a section where I compare early and late Wittgenstein. It's pretty decent, but I'm not sure it's entirely coherent."

They went on like that while they drank their first pints. After a while, Martin dug his fairly tattered original out of his bag so Cecilia could read for herself. Trams rattled past from time to time. People passed by on the pavement. She turned the page. He lit a cigarette. After a while, she took one from his pack, too, tapping it lightly against the table while she read.

"There's nothing wrong with this," she said at length. "On the whole, you pose relevant questions and work through them in a coherent way. Possibly you get a bit off track at the end. You could have left out the final paragraph entirely, actually. It's not that it's not interesting, just unnecessary. And it's pretty long" – she flipped through the pages – "so if they insist on you cutting things, you can drop that and tighten up the summary at the start of the discussion. It doesn't have to take up" – more flipping – "a page and a half."

Then she lit her cigarette and blew smoke up at the sky.

"'On the whole'?"

"That stuff about Bertrand Russell wasn't exactly apropos."

"I thought it was elegant."

"Elegant is not the same as relevant, *mein Freund.* Did you find a use for von Hartmann, by the way?"

"What? Oh yeah… he's in there somewhere." Martin waved limply at the sad sheaf of papers that was the result of all that toil. She hadn't said anything about it being original, extraordinary or revolutionary. His only reference to von Hartmann would probably be cut too, if it were up to Cecilia.

"So what subject did you make short shrift of in your dissertation?" he asked.

"The literature on the Second Italo-Ethiopian War."

"I didn't even know there was a *first* one. So, what happened in the second one?"

"Mussolini annexed Ethiopia, turning it into a colony he named the

Italian Province of East Africa. It didn't last long because Ethiopia had the support of the Allies and kicked the Italians out in 1940. Ethiopia usually talks a big game about being the only country in Africa never to have been colonised, but that's not technically true. Though personally, I think it should be viewed as an occupation rather than a colonisation."

"What made you want to study history?"

She squinted at the violet sky. "I had a good history teacher in Addis. I thought maybe I'd become a teacher myself, but I honestly don't know if I can bear having students."

"Addis?" The word meant nothing to him.

Cecilia smiled. "Addis Ababa? Ethiopia? I grew up there."

Martin frantically racked his brain for anything Ethiopia related. The maps he recalled from school were no help – he could see the horsehead-shape of Africa, but where was Ethiopia? Above or below the equator? Jungle or desert? Finally, he recalled a newspaper headline. "There's a famine there now, isn't there?"

She nodded.

"What – why?"

"Partly because there's a drought, but mostly because the president spends all of the country's money on a pointless war with Eritrea. Hey, on a completely unrelated note: what would you say is the most important thing you've learned studying philosophy?"

"The most important thing I've learned?"

"Have you learned *anything*? Has it changed the way you think? Or has it been more like learning things by rote? 'If p, then q'? The ontological argument for God's existence versus Descartes's argument for it? The correct definition of a monad? Because I'm considering doing philosophy next year, it's between that and intellectual history, and I don't want to risk dying slowly on the inside."

Later on, when Cecilia went to the bathroom, a cold realisation washed over him: they were going to be *friends*. Summer happens, they get together from time to time. She introduces him to her mates as "my friend Martin from the library catacombs". They drink wine and talk about intellectual things. Even Gustav likes her. And just when he has mustered the courage to take the next step, she introduces her new boyfriend. He's several years older and has a real job. Possibly a PhD student. He wears glasses but they don't make him look geeky. Black turtleneck. Calls Horace Engdahl and Stig Larsson "Horace and Stig". Has played in a band with Mare Kandre. No. Strike that. There are limits. He has *not* played in a band with Mare Kandre, he's not the type, he's from Örgryte. She looks at him with sparkling eyes…

"You look sad," Cecilia said, setting a fresh pint down in front of him. She asked him to tell her something about himself, and Martin confessed that the only thing he really wanted to do in life was write.

"Write what?"

He told her about the novel he had almost finished, or at least almost, almost finished, but had now decided he would have to abandon. "The whole thing's just a bit too *Jack*." What he was going to start working on in earnest now was about intellectual awakenings in a university setting, but he hadn't come up with a good plot yet.

Night fell, a long, blue spring dusk. After the next round, he admitted he'd thought she was joking when she said she only read German authors. Cecilia laughed out loud.

"But why only Germans?" demanded Martin, who didn't quite get the joke.

"I needed a system. We moved back to Sweden when I was about to start upper secondary. I went to the public library and panicked. I think it was the first time I really grasped how much I didn't know. Like, really didn't have a clue about." Cecilia leaned back in her chair and ran her hands through her hair. "I didn't know where to start. At first, I figured I'd start at A and work my way through the alphabet, but that would have had me reading fiction until I was fifty. So then I came up with the idea of doing it by country instead."

Last year had been her Russian year. She'd tackled Chekov and Dostoevsky. ("Don't you just want to slap Raskolnikov? And that Madonna/whore thing's a bit tired, isn't it?") She'd struggled through a biographical tome about Tolstoy. (How can a person be such a prick and still write so well?") She'd felt unsure about whether to categorise Vladimir Nabokov as Russian or American, since he'd changed both his language and his nationality, but ultimately decided country of origin was the deciding factor. She'd grappled with Mayakovski ("pompous") and Solzhenitsyn ("decent"). The year before that, it had been Britain. Before that, France. With a voice full of laughter, she told him about when she spent a whole month reading *Being and Nothingness* in the hopes of finding answers to "certain fundamental questions about life in general".

When the bell rang for last orders, they'd talked non-stop for five and a half hours. No hands had been held. No knees had touched. No foot had grazed another foot. No long looks had been exchanged, because Martin discovered he was unable to meet her eye for more than a few seconds without being overcome with embarrassment. Cecilia was rosy-cheeked and bright-eyed, and when the waitress had carried every chair except theirs inside, they unsteadily got to their feet and staggered off towards Vasaplatsen Square. The night was an intense van Gogh-blue. The lilacs bloomed in surges and swells.

"All right," she said, squeezing his arm, "what's the next step on our pub crawl?"

He put his hands on her shoulders and kissed her.

II

MARTIN BERG: Though obviously, there are times in life when it's better to do... *other* things than reading...

*

Cecilia's window had no curtains, and the room was flooded with sunlight. She slept with one leg pushed in between his and an arm across his chest. When he freed himself to go to the bathroom, she murmured in her sleep and curled up around her pillow.

Martin drank some water straight from the tap and studied his face in the mirror. Dark circles under his eyes. Stubble. His hair was badly mussed. He feebly tried to tame it. He looked haggard, but haggard, he told himself on the way back to the bed, wasn't so bad. Humphrey Bogart was haggard, and Albert Camus. Haggard was a popped coat collar, a cigarette and worldly-wise nonchalance. In fact – and Martin could sense a possible topic of conversation taking shape at this point – haggardness was downright subversive in this era that worshipped youth and youthfulness so fervently. In the carefree republic of the tanned and fit, the wan, pallid individual was a thorn in society's side, a revolt against contemporary, American ideas of self-actualisation, a counterweight to the vacuous, self-proclaimed happy people who…

Cecilia Wikner groaned and rolled over onto her side.

"How are you feeling?" he asked.

"I'm going to throw up."

She staggered out to the bathroom. Should he be helping her? Hold her hair? Or would she prefer to have her privacy? Before he could make a decision, she was back, collapsing onto the bed, wilted and pasty.

"I don't usually get like this." She picked up her shirt from the floor, slowly unbuttoned it and fell onto her back. "I'm never drinking again."

"I've heard that before."

Martin fetched her a glass of water, and Cecilia took a few sips. "You should leave," she said, eyes closed. "I'm not very good company."

"I'm staying."

"I'm sure you have plans…"

"No plans," Martin lied. He'd promised Gustav they would hang out, but Gustav might not even remember that. He kissed her forehead and went to make breakfast.

She went back to sleep almost immediately, her long hair fanning out across the pillows. Martin was grateful he mostly threw up when he was actually drunk, when people were generally too pissed to care. He placed a bowl next to the bed in case of emergency and then checked the fridge. Scrambled eggs usually worked for Gustav.

Other guys might have jumped at the chance to take off. Might have called later that night to "check in". And what would Cecilia have said? *Great, thanks for asking.* In a cool tone that belonged to a different person from the one sitting on the edge of the bed with bare legs and a sweaty shirt, clutching the phone. Would she maybe want to get together the next day and go for a walk or whatever? *No, sorry, I can't.* Okay, but call me, yeah? *Sure, absolutely.* And then she'd never call, and if he did, she'd be extremely busy just then. She'd have other, unspecified plans. *Maybe some other time*, said with the indifference that made it clear the sentence should be understood as *We're never going to see each other again.*

But he would still be there when she woke up. He would make sure she ate some scrambled eggs. He knew exactly how tedious it was to be hungover and all alone. She didn't have a TV, so what was she supposed to do – read Nietzsche?

While Cecilia slept, Martin acquainted himself with her flat. It was a studio, on the top floor of a six-storey building. It seemed to be in a state of irreversible disrepair – missing cabinet doors in the kitchen, mysterious cracks in the walls, and the temperature of the water from the tap oscillated unpredictably between freezing and scalding. The linoleum floor in the kitchen was warped and discoloured, the hardwood in the main room scarred by decades of carelessness. She'd told him she'd lived there for years, but everything except possibly the bookshelf suggested she had just moved in. She didn't have a lot of plates, and two thirds of the ones she did have were sitting in a dirty pile on a large table by the wall. Aside from the table, which judging by the stacks of books and typewriter served as her desk, there was the bed, a sagging leather armchair and a reading lamp. There was a record player on the floor and a crate full of records. He flipped through them: Chopin, Bach's *St Matthew Passion*, Mulatu Astatke (who on earth was that?), David Bowie, John Coltrane.

The walls were bare save for a portrait of a girl drawn with powerful, confident strokes. He didn't find any revealing notes or old photographs on the fridge. No sentimental knick-knacks. No seashells from a childhood beach. No faded family portraits. After making sure she was still asleep, he opened the door to the wardrobe a crack. In the far back hung a fur coat, the kind Martin's friends would never wear because fur was murder. A pair of running shoes with their laces tied together dangled from a hook. On the floor sat a suitcase, which Martin picked up, half expecting it to be packed.

The only thing left was the bookshelf.

Martin's bookshelf, which, he had to admit, was fairly impressive, often elicited comments. Even Britta had nodded appreciatively, even though her own book collection was limited to a stack of Agatha Christie paperbacks with yellowed pages, which she'd read countless times in various sun loungers and hammocks while chomping on copious amounts of liquorice rope. Britta read to kill time, not for any higher purpose. She would sit sighing on the stairs in the second-hand bookshop, smoking in her slightly-too-short skirt, watching passers-by while Martin wandered through the dusty half-light.

At first glance, there seemed to be no order to Cecilia's books, but on closer inspection, he realised they were in the geographical order in which she'd read them. In the top left-hand corner, he found Strindberg, Lagerlöf, Fröding, Söderberg, Ekelöf, Boye, Tranströmer – all those writers everyone read excerpts from in school – Ivar Lo, Sara Lidman, Harry Martinson. Martin counted on his fingers. The Swedish year must have been 1979. Then came the Americans. He noted that she had both *Pet Sematary* and *Carrie* by Stephen King, and that there was a bookmark a fifth of the way through *Moby Dick*. A handful of Hemingways stood next to Sylvia Plath's *The Bell Jar*, which in turn was next to Vonnegut's *Slaughterhouse 5*, against which leaned a tattered paperback edition of *The Great Gatsby*. And at this point, some non-fiction joined the mix: Noam Chomsky's *Language and Mind*, *Relativity* by Einstein. Then a bold hop across the Atlantic: the United Kingdom. The year was 1981, and Cecilia read Shakespeare's sonnets and plays, went via Jane Austen's *Pride and Prejudice* and Emily Brontë's *Wuthering Heights* to Evelyn Waugh, and there were Locke and Hume, two poor philosophers, surrounded by Woolf, Wilde, Yeats and Keats. (But wasn't one of them Irish?) Then followed a long row of Graham Greene. The British accounted for more than sixty titles; he wondered how she afforded it. But judging by the ageing editions, she habitually visited second-hand bookshops, too.

When the wristwatch pinned to the wall above the desk with a sewing needle showed half past eleven, Cecilia woke up again.

"There's breakfast," he said. "How's your stomach feeling?"

She rolled onto her back and put a hand on her stomach. "I'd consider giving it a shot." Sitting up in bed, she ate a few spoonfuls of scrambled eggs and half a piece of crispbread. Then she slid back down onto the pillows. "Martin Berg, the good Samaritan."

"Stop."

"I'm probably the least charming company you can find in this town today. Maybe any day, come to think of it."

"There's nowhere I'd rather be," Martin said without thinking. Cecilia studied him for a long moment that felt as heavy as lead. Since when was he ever sincere without weighing the benefit of sincerity against its risks? And using such a hackneyed phrase, too?

"Why?" she said finally.

"What do you mean 'why'? Why do you think?"

"I have no idea."

Martin moved over to the bed, snuggling up next to Cecilia. He took her hand.

"You skipped William Wallace," he said. "During your British year."

"Who's William Wallace?"

"Oh my god, Cecilia, this is a serious lapse in your education."

"Oh dear."

"Shocking, even."

"Maybe you could enlighten me?"

"*Patagonia Days,* does that ring a bell?"

"It's a film starring Steve McQueen."

He tutted. "Blasphemy."

"So I don't get any points for having seen the film?"

"Sorry."

"But could it be," she said, "that we have with us here today a leading expert on the subject?"

He put his arm around her shoulders. "I don't know about *expert*," he said in a tone that was supposed to convey false modesty, and she laughed. He ran a finger along her collarbone. She was naked underneath the shirt. He remembered his hands around her hips, the little gasp she had let out when she came.

"It's not a bad film," he said. "But the book is much better. It's unfortunate that your British year is a thing of the irrevocable past."

"This is the downside of my system," she said. "It doesn't leave me free to take the recommendations of well-read young men."

"I imagine you get a lot of those."

"Wallace was new to me."

"Who are the three most often recommended?"

She considered that. "I would say Bukowski, Kafka and Dostoevsky. And domestically there's also Stig Larsson and Monsieur Lundell."

"A charming crew."

"Isn't it? Wax lyrical over a novel about an alcoholic postman who frequents prostitutes. It's definitely the way to a woman's heart."

Martin touched the round pendant she wore on a thin gold chain around her neck. It rested right below the hollow between her collarbones. She had amazing collarbones.

"I noticed you read some of your Frenchmen in French," he said.

"I was given private tutoring," she said. "From an old French lady." She yawned. "She was so unbelievably strict and she hated Addis."

"Then why didn't she move back?"

"She was married to a missionary who was trying to save the souls of the people in Ogaden."

The sun moved across the sky and the room grew cooler. The window was open. There was an unobstructed view across the rooftops all the way to the cranes out on Hisingen. He unbuttoned her shirt, inspecting all her freckles and birthmarks. Her face inches from his, eyes half-open. She had thin wrists. The hair at the back of her neck was damp.

Afterwards, she disappeared off to the bathroom. He heard the shower running. When she came back, she had twisted her hair into a bun, which made her facial features appear more clearly. She had the thick, angled eyebrows of an old-time Hollywood actress.

"We could head down to the Prague later," she said, crawling back into bed. Her skin was cool and smooth like marble after the shower.

"Excellent notion. Assuming you can keep your food down and not cause any vomiting scenes."

She gave him a shove. "I've seen your friend there," she said. "The nervous one with the glasses. He comes in with a loud art school gang."

"Right – Gustav."

"That's the one."

"I'm surprised you haven't seen me." Just as he said it, he realised he hadn't been there in months, not since he looked her up in the phonebook and realised she lived right next door.

"This is better," she said, leaning her head on his shoulder. "All right, then, let's remedy my lack of education. What can you tell me about William Wallace?"

III

MARTIN BERG: Most of us actually encounter the big life questions in books long before we're faced with them in real life.

INTERVIEWER: Can you give an example?

MARTIN BERG: Death, for instance. And love. Love in particular. Some fools imagine love is simple. That love is like floating on a lilo in a lukewarm pool... Which is obvious nonsense. The truth is that love is a very complicated thing. You need all the guidance you can get.

"It's insane," Martin said.

High above them, the foliage of Slottsskogen Park spread out like a series of golden arches. The air was full of birdsong. He was balancing a beer on his stomach. Gustav was sitting a few feet away, like a dissonant chord in a summer hymn, wearing ripped jeans and a striped shirt that was far too baggy for his scrawny chest. Gustav always seemed to have the violet shadows of late nights and hard living under his eyes, whether or not he'd had a solid twelve hours of sleep (which Martin knew for a fact he had), and a proper meal (steak and potatoes with onion gravy at the Prague).

"What's insane?" Gustav said and Martin realised he must have thought rather than spoken the rest of the sentence aloud.

"That people have to spend so much time working."

"That's what I'm saying. Lunacy."

"I'm too tired to do anything at night. It takes me until Sunday to recover from the workweek, and by then Monday's hanging over me like a Damoclean sword, spoiling things. They say you get used to it, but I'm wondering when exactly that's going to happen?"

"Maybe you get used to it, but the question is what *it* is," Gustav replied philosophically.

"Being a slave, I suppose."

"*All in all, you're just another brick in the wall.* Where did I put the bloody filters?"

Due to a newfound urge to pinch pennies, Gustav had switched to rolling his own cigarettes. He'd been given a grant and had immediately gone out to buy canvases and paint, so he wouldn't be tempted to spend the money on other things. He was very pleased with this crafty approach. Money always disappeared from his pockets as though it were actually falling out. Sometimes, when it was time to pay at the end of the night, he'd cheerfully dig around for a one-hundred-kronor note that he was "pretty sure must be here somewhere". He was never embarrassed to find nothing but coins, scraps of paper, receipts and a box of matches. Granted, he didn't mind paying for others – he'd fish out a crisp five-hundred-kronor note after selling a painting or receiving alms from his grandmother, insisting everyone order dessert and cognac with their coffee. To Gustav, money was something that just appeared. When you ran out, you had to roll your own cigarettes and drink cheap wine for a bit, and sooner or later, there would always be more money coming.

Martin, on the other hand, had got himself a summer job as a postman instead of his usual gig at the sorting centre, which meant more time with Cecilia. The first few weeks, his whole body ached after running up and down stairs with post and circulars, and by nine o'clock he was invariably utterly exhausted. If he took a nap now, he'd probably be in better shape come evening, but he had to talk to Gustav about Cecilia. He closed his eyes.

"Slave's the word," Gustav said, as though solid empirical experience had led him to conclude that working for a living was not for him.

"One must imagine Sisyphus happy," Martin said.

"What?"

"Camus. From *The Myth of Sisyphus*. Hey, Cecilia and I were talking about going for a pint later – would you want to come if we do?"

Gustav didn't answer right away. "I was actually thinking…"

"Come on. You have to meet her sometime."

"I've already met her."

"For all of three seconds."

"She seemed nice."

"Why can't you just come out for a pint, then?"

Gustav sighed. "Fine. But just one."

"Since when have you ever had just *one* pint?"

"So you're dating now?"

"I guess so. Or actually, I don't know."

"You don't know if you're dating?"

"I mean…" For weeks they'd been seeing each other regularly. Usually at her place, but sometimes she came to the commune on

Kaptensgatan. (She had pointed out that it wasn't strictly speaking a commune, just two people sharing a flat.) They did typical dating things. They took slow walks through Slottsskogen and fed the mallards leftover baguette. Cooked meals neither one of them had truly mastered (orange-stuffed chicken), while listening to music and drinking all the wine they'd planned to have with dinner. Lay on a picnic blanket for hours under blossoming cherry trees on campus. Went to the cinema. Flipped through albums in second-hand music shops. Cycled to Saltholmen. Went for countryside outings in her rickety old Volvo.

Over time, her contours had firmed up. She'd spent the greater part of her childhood in Addis Ababa, where her father, a doctor, ran a hospital for women injured in childbirth. After returning to Sweden, the Wikners had lived in the Gothenburg area for a year or two but had subsequently settled permanently in Stockholm. Cecilia seemed to enjoy the geographical distance and so did Martin. He'd always considered his girlfriends' families a necessary evil, an appendix that needed to be dealt with out of social necessity. Because what was the point of family? Family hemmed in individuals through arbitrary prohibitions and rules that had to be followed, not for any rational reason, but simply because that's how it was done, which was completely unintellectual. In fact – this was something Martin had been thinking about for a while – in fact, philosophy and family could be thought of as diametrical opposites. Families were collectives that acted according to obscure patterns and irrational justifications. Philosophers, on the other hand, were solitary creatures of the mind, soaring high above the mishmash of family in a celestial craft built of thought alone: by default, a philosopher worked alone. Schopenhauer didn't have to deal with Christmas lunches. Nietzsche didn't have to endure Sunday roasts, except possibly when he hung out with Richard Wagner. Sartre never married. Wittgenstein moved onto a mountain in a grand refutation of all things family.

Mr and Mrs Wikner and Cecilia's three younger siblings thus remained vague parts of her history. At the age of sixteen, she'd moved into a commune in Haga where she set herself up in her room with her books. All around her, people partied, fucked, got high, laughed, played guitar, printed flyers, cooked lentil stew, rallied against nuclear power, occupied places, trudged through the snow in boots, argued about communism, revolted against traditional family structures, stood on the street and howled: "But Micke, you *promised*!" at a closed window. Then the building was torn down. Cecilia found the studio flat on Kastellgatan where she'd lived ever since, and where Martin had spent most of his nights over the past month.

But sometimes days went by without them talking. Cecilia might jump out of bed and get dressed, cursing about being late for work – a nursing home where she could spend large parts of her workday reading while she waited for a chore to announce itself – and leave with just a quick goodbye kiss and no plans having been made.

"Sounds like you're dating," Gustav yawned.

"But we've never *talked* about it."

"Is that really necessary, though? If you're dating, you're dating, right?"

"That's easy to say for someone who never does."

"Well, I can't say you're exactly selling me on the concept. It seems like torture most of the time. So, what's the deal with this pint?"

She was waiting for them in a bar on Skanstorget Square.

"Why are we going *here*?" Gustav said. "We never go here."

"There's nothing wrong with this place. They have cheap beer."

"But why can't we go to the Prague or Tajjan?"

At the Golden Prague and Tai Shanghai they were bound to run into someone they knew, and that was exactly what Martin wanted to avoid. "Cecilia's already here," he said.

"I still think it's a strange choice."

Martin sighed and led the way inside. The air was thick with blue smoke, gently stirred by lazily spinning ceiling fans. Cecilia was sitting by the window. Sharp evening sun set her hair aglow and made her white shirt gleam. When she spotted them, she put away the book she was reading. There was an empty tea mug on the table.

Gustav and Cecilia shook hands.

"We've met before, in passing," Gustav said in his polite voice, which he normally reserved for adults and persons of authority.

"That's right. Långedrag."

A bubble of silence swelled. They all looked down at the table. "First round's on me," Martin said. "Beer? Does beer work for everyone? Or wine? What would you like, Cecilia?"

The girl behind the bar was fumbling and slow. How much damage would be done before he could come to the rescue? If they just sat there in silence, was that good or bad? Bad, definitely bad. He left a crumpled note on the bar and hurried back with their foggy pint glasses.

"...work at a nursing home sometimes, as well," he heard Cecilia say.

"Okay, and is that – fun?"

"I don't think 'fun' is the adjective I'd use. But it's all right. The old people are nice. What about you? Are you working this summer?"

"No, I..." Gustav started to search his pockets, and at length located the case in which he kept his homemade cigarettes. He stuck one between his lips and then began to look for his lighter. Just as Martin was about to speak, he managed to light his cigarette. "I don't work," he said. "Unlike my friend the postman here," he added, slapping Martin on the back. "What do you reckon, Martin? Am I missing out? Does it make you feel like a part of the great machine that is society?"

"Sure. An indispensable cog in the wheel."

"The joys of salaried work," Gustav said.

Cecilia looked from Martin to Gustav and back, with a small da Vinci smile that could mean anything. He had to change the subject, they couldn't sit around and talk about *work*. But Gustav beat him to it.

"But the rest of the year, you study?" he asked, even though he already knew the answer.

"Yes, I've been studying history."

"That sounds interesting."

Cecilia nodded. She pulled a pack of cigarettes out of her bag. Gustav was chivalrously ready with the lighter; she held her hair back and leaned towards the flame.

"But is it, like, *old* history, or…?"

While the hopelessly interview-like interrogation continued, Martin studied his girlfriend, or whatever she was. She was leaning back, the fingers of her unoccupied hand busy repeating a minimal movement: one after the other, each fingertip touched the tip of her thumb, from her pinkie to her forefinger and back again. Every time she took a drag, her eyes narrowed slightly. Her voice sounded normal, but she was unusually terse. Gustav was partly to blame for that, asking all these elderly-relative questions. There – was that her stifling a yawn?

Normally, Cecilia looked like a broke, slightly grubby Katherine Hepburn; tonight, she looked upstanding and proper. The kind of girl who might borrow her mother's pearls and enjoy a cheese plate with her girlfriends in a tidy flat in Tynnered. A passer-by could be excused for thinking the table hid a pair of pleated jeans or a knee-length kilt. Gustav's mates were the kind of people others stared at on the street and every once in a while one of them got beaten up for no other reason than that someone took umbrage with the way they dressed.

Cecilia offered to buy the next round, and before anyone could object, she was on her way to the bar. She was wearing a pair of washed-out flannel trousers, which were too wide and short and swished around her legs when she walked: definitely something a pearl-necklace girl wouldn't wear even with a gun to her head. Martin was relieved.

"I think I only have time for one more pint," Gustav said.

Cecilia returned with their drinks and slipped into her seat. She looked at Martin, but he pretended to be busy drinking. He should take charge of this pathetic conversation, but how? His mind was completely blank. Talking about the post office would hardly be an improvement. Maybe he could bring up his novel. He'd been writing whenever he wasn't with Cecilia, because he was trying to distract himself from the fact that he wasn't with Cecilia. This was a promising thought. Yes: he could talk about his novel. They could be three young intellectuals in a bar, discussing the Conditions of Creativity; that was more like how he'd pictured this evening. While he was trying to think of a natural way to bring the subject up, Cecilia beat him to it.

"I saw one of your paintings at Martin's place," she said with a small nod in Gustav's direction. "It reminded me of Hammershøi, except without that claustrophobic feeling his works sometimes have."

"You're familiar with Hammershøi?"

"My grandparents had a small oil painting by him. An interior, without the wife. Pretty gloomy."

"The wife's important," Gustav said. "Even though you only see her from the back. She adds a kind of…" He gesticulated with one hand, searching for the right word.

"Psychological tension?" Cecilia suggested.

"Exactly!"

"I always felt Hammershøi deserved just as much attention as Krøyer and the rest of them."

"He's not as accessible." Gustav leaned forward in his chair. "Krøyer's an amazing artist, sure, but many of his motifs are banal. It's a hard balance to strike, between the sublime and the banal."

"Getting away with banality requires great talent," Martin put in, since he hadn't said anything in a while. He'd seen Hammershøi at that exhibition in Copenhagen a few years earlier. But Krøyer? He recalled a painting at the art museum that always made him want to get drunk in a garden.

"Anyone can enjoy Krøyer," Gustav went on, making small stabbing motions with his cigarette for emphasis. "Not liking Krøyer is like not liking a cute puppy. It's like not liking *ice cream*."

"Which, granted, is an attitude that's in vogue these days," Cecilia said.

"Absolutely. But we can't forget that Krøyer was a rebel, too, in his day."

"*Was* he though?" Cecilia retorted. "I mean – surely impressionism wasn't exactly new. Was it? In France? It's not like he was a trailblazer."

"I'm buying another round," Martin said.

He watched them from the bar. Unable to hear what they were saying, he saw Cecilia laugh and Gustav gesticulate wildly.

"A toast," Gustav said when he returned to their table. "To the Danes, an exemplary people!"

Several hours later, they stumbled out onto the street. It was a warm night, the sky an electric shade of blue, scattered stars, the moon a silver sickle. Hidden birds sang in the linden trees on Övre Husargatan. Cecilia was swaying slightly and had to lean on Martin. He put his arm around her shoulders.

"Where to now?" Gustav said, dropping his cigarette on the ground.

"I think the French Club is nearest?"

"What's the French Club?" Cecilia said.

"You've never been there?!" Gustav squealed.

"What's so funny about that?"

"You live fifteen feet from it," Martin said. Laughter and applause from Gustav.

"But what is it?" Cecilia insisted, threading her arms through both of theirs so that she ended up in the middle. "What's the connection with *la France? Expliquez-moi, s'il-vous plaît.*"

"Oh my god, don't you ever go to underground clubs?" Gustav said.

"So many lapses in your education," Martin said. "All right, mademoiselle, first we have to sort you out with a membership card…"

For some reason, the French Club was closed; they ended up at Sprängkullen. Cecilia ran into some people she knew and stopped to talk to them for a bit while Martin and Gustav bought more beer. Martin watched her from across the room. Her gestures, the laughter in her shoulders, the way she turned around and scanned the room until her eyes met his, and she smiled, and he smiled, and she looked away, still smiling, and said something to her friends.

Gustav came back with his hands full of bottles. "Where's Cecilia?" he said. "Has she abandoned the sinking ship? Is there mutiny afoot? Is she sailing into the sunset alone?"

"She just ran into someone she knew."

"They're going to steal her away to lands more fertile than these."

"What are you bloody on about?"

"Mind your wife, thou wretched squire, lest she tempt another patruel."

Martin laughed. "Do you even know what patruel means?"

"Isn't it seventeenth century slang for a bloke?"

"It means nephew. But good work with the lest."

"Look, she's coming back. The night is saved! Cecilia! Cissi! Here, have a beer. Does anyone call you Cissi? Do you mind it? No? No traumatic schoolyard associations? No terrifying aunts with piercing voices? We thought we'd lost you to the rabble. You haven't nicked my lighter, by any chance, have you?"

IV

MARTIN BERG: Take infatuation, for instance. Have you ever been infatuated?

INTERVIEWER: Uh...

MARTIN BERG: Of course you have. And aside from being earth-shattering and lovely and effervescent [*making an impatient gesture*] and all that stuff that's usually associated with infatuation, it can also be awful. Right? How do we bear it? How can we even comprehend what's happening to us? Well, we know what's going on because Werther yearned for Lotte, because Catherine and Heathcliff never ended up together, because Arvid cocked things up royally with Lydia. We know because some Swedish teacher forced us to read Sappho and Karin Boye. So when we're overcome with love, to mention but one of humanity's predicaments, at least we're prepared for what lies ahead.

*

"Martin! Phone!"

Stay calm, Martin told himself as he left his room and the notes he was listlessly trying to merge into something that might pass for Chapter One of his new novel. He picked up the receiver.

"Hey," Gustav said, "there's a party here tonight, want to come? There's a band here called – Uffe, what are they called again? Whatever. They seem good."

"I don't know if I'm in the right frame of mind for Valand…"

"You thought it was Cecilia calling."

"No, I just—"

"Come on, admit it. You thought it was Cissi calling, but now it turns out it was just old Gustav."

"I *didn't*, okay?" Martin snapped.

"If that were true, you wouldn't be snapping at me."

"I'm just tired."

"Anyway. There's beer and stuff. Feel free to drop by."

Martin refrained from pointing out that he could hardly just *drop by* Valand, since Lindholmen was across the river and going there involved a decent amount of logistics. It wasn't like Haga or some other place within a reasonable drop-by radius.

It had been four days since he'd last heard from her. Going back to the very first days of their acquaintance, he couldn't recall there ever having been four full days without contact. Nor could he see any obvious reason for the radio silence. Granted, the last time they'd seen each other, something unusual had occurred: she'd cut her hair off. It was a warm, blue night, with wide-open windows. Martin had just drifted off to sleep when he felt Cecilia move his arm aside and slip out of bed. He hadn't roused himself fully until she'd been missing for a good long while. He found her in front of the bathroom mirror, brandishing scissors, the sink full of long strands.

Cecilia's hair was a law unto itself. It seemed to have its own, fairly independent personality. When it got wet, it took ages to dry. No matter how much time she spent brushing it, her curls stubbornly strived to return to their chaotic original state. On hot days, it lay like a blanket across her back and shoulders. Individual hairs got caught in her perspiration, clinging like question marks to her neck and forehead.

"Could you give me a hand with the back?" she said now. She'd cut it off along her jawline.

It wasn't, he discovered, terribly important that he make it dead straight, since her curls had a life of their own, anyway. She stood stock-still while he worked.

"There," he said at length. He kissed the back of her neck and her pale throat, which was now exposed. Something had shifted inside the young woman whose eyes met his in the mirror. The long hair had lent her appearance a girlish prettiness, and without it she seemed ripped out of history, timeless and eternal.

"You're very beautiful," he said.

She smiled. "Mum's going to lose her mind."

The next morning, when he tiptoed off to work, she was still sound asleep. They'd made no plans to meet up; he assumed she'd call. All day, he'd been faint with sleep deprivation – a perpetual state for the newly infatuated – and he went to bed early. The next day, he jumped every time the phone rang. On Thursday, he went straight to the phone, certain there would be a message from her. There was always something jotted down in Anders's tiny, neat hand. *Gustav called at 4.30, wants you to know they're going to "that place on Viktoriagatan by the park". Mariette M called Wed night. Wants you to call back. Fredrik called re wanting to discuss Wittgenstein this week.*

Martin had reassured himself she was working and would definitely call on Friday, which was to say today. It still wasn't too late. Now, he returned to his desk and stared out of the window.

There were three possible explanations:

She didn't call because she wasn't interested in seeing him.

She didn't call *even though* she wanted to see him because she was extremely busy, because a relative had unexpectedly died, because she'd had to leave town suddenly, and so on.

She didn't call because she wanted to establish an emotional advantage over the pacing Martin Berg, who in his desperate attempts to distract himself spent an entire evening playing Scrabble with Anders and one of his mates. (Both were impressed when he put down Marxist for 63 points.)

Not calling as a tactic in some kind of power struggle didn't really seem like her. And why didn't it seem like her? He had a hard time putting his finger on that. A kind of naivety. A surprised laugh. He could picture her face, the blend of interest and concern.

But he'd called her last time. And the time before that. It was her turn.

The first option – that she didn't want to see him – was the simplest and therefore the most plausible. The only problem was that it would constitute an inconsistent behaviour. It lacked logic. There was nothing to back up the hypothesis *Cecilia doesn't want to see Martin*. Or, fine. Maybe there were a few things he wasn't sure how to interpret. For example, Cecilia had recently said with a sigh: "You're probably the kind of guy I should watch out for." He'd wanted to know what she meant by that, but she'd been unwilling or unable to explain. Another time, he'd been woken up by her coming back to her flat, closing the door and walking around in the kitchen. It had been barely half six in the morning. When he asked what she'd been up to, she said she'd gone out to buy bread. But she hadn't brought any bread back and he was pretty sure she'd been gone longer than it took to go to a bakery. She looked anxious and tense – that had actually been around the time when she said she should watch out for him, and when he was annoyed that she wouldn't explain herself, she just looked even unhappier.

Now, Martin methodically went over every single time they'd been together. Had there been signs that she didn't want to be with him? That she was trying to extract herself? And if she didn't want anything to do with him, why had she agreed to meet up? Cecilia probably wouldn't say something like that straight out. She would just neglect to call until the whole thing petered out of its own volition…

Icy cold shuddered down Martin's spine. He walked several laps around the flat, pinched a few dead leaves off the potted plants and watered them, even though some looked beyond salvation. Then he sat down at his typewriter and wrote with genuine inspiration for the first time in weeks.

ON THE WOMEN IN MY LIFE
AND THE WAYS IN WHICH I'VE ABANDONED THEM

I shouldn't have allowed it to drag on for as long as I did. I should have known better. I should have tried to avoid unnecessary pain – I'm not the kind to enjoy other people's suffering, even when I myself have suffered at their hands. Paradoxically, it was likely the fear of causing pain that kept me by B's side for so long. And L's. It was from the very first obvious to me that L and I had very little, even nothing, in common, other than the purely carnal. Which, granted, can take you relatively far. But sooner or later, you reach the burning zenith of tedium and loneliness. The moment you're alone in company. Carnal pleasures expose the blandness of the soul. She was too proud to appear hurt. I realised I had, in my striving for honesty, broken the rules of the game. Instead, I should have not called when she wanted to see me. She would have caught on, and when we ran into each other on the street, she wouldn't have been stripped of her dignity.

He had spaghetti and meatballs for dinner. He tried to read but was only able to take in disjointed sentences. Around eight, Anders's friends turned up for their Marx study group. Martin excused himself, saying he had a party to go to, and fled.

When he got to Valand, the party was already in full swing. Gustav, dressed in a gold lamé poncho, spread his arms wide.

"The prodigal son has returned! Behold, ye doubters, for the Lord hath sent us a miracle!"

"It's nice to see you, too. What's this?" Martin pinched the shimmering fabric.

"Vivi wore it for a performance." Gustav wriggled out of the garment. His glasses ended up askew and he straightened them with exaggerated motions. Martin noticed one of the arms was taped.

"So, what have you been up to lately?" Martin asked. He accepted a lukewarm beer he had no desire to drink.

"No word from Cecilia, I take it?"

"Could you stop?"

"Just a friendly enquiry."

"I think I'd call it insinuating."

"It wasn't. Maybe a little. But I take it as a no. Cecilia W. is shut up in her ivory tower."

Martin shrugged his shoulders. Gustav immediately turned the conversation to other topics. Earlier that day, Vivi had done her performance, which she called *Exposé of the History of Art.* Very successful. Sissel was considering dropping out so she could travel to Iceland and become a hermit. He himself had just sold another painting even though the spring exhibition was weeks ago, one of the afterparty still lifes inspired by seventeenth century Dutch paintings, which the Stockholm gallerist who bought it had thought was terrific, bordering on genius. But shortly thereafter, Gustav had begun to wonder what it signified that his success was happening in the context of pastiche and reprises. The real masters were, after all, Courbet and Manet and Vermeer and Hammershøi. Did Gustav's art exist solely as a comment on their work? And moreover, it wasn't right to refer to Courbet as a "master", or Vermeer, either, because *Girl with the Pearl Earring* was more or less kitsch, too, even though it should be obvious to everyone that it was *real art*. But then, what was "real art"? He was sick of still lifes. No more still lifes. (Never mind that people liked them.) But when he painted interiors and portraits, he always felt the presence of forebears like Ola Billgren, he couldn't shake them, the bastards were standing behind him, looking over his shoulder, but whenever he turned around, there was no one there. And the fact was that *whatever he painted*, someone else would have already done something like it before. Was real art doing what other people considered non-art? Although, the truth was – and at this point Gustav lowered his voice despite the minimal risk of being overheard – that he was alarmingly uninterested in that type of work. Deeply uninterested. Or maybe, intellectually speaking, slightly interested. But emotionally? Indifferent. "Though you absolutely can't tell Vivi."

While he talked, he kept fiddling with his pack of cigarettes, jumping up from the sofa to say hello to someone but coming back straight away, going to fetch more beer. "Or a cocktail, would you prefer a cocktail? Sissel's making piña coladas." Martin accepted a water glass that contained something bearing a vague resemblance to a piña colada, minus the ice.

The atmosphere was electric and tense. People were setting up speakers and synthesisers on a temporary stage. He was going to call Cecilia once he was drunk enough for it to seem like a good idea. He half-listened to Gustav who went on and on about how he was considering no longer selling his paintings, since it felt odd when well-dressed people with shiny shoes surrounded him, clamouring to give him money.

The room was packed. The air thick with cigarette smoke. The band was enthusiastically applauded even though the drummer seemed unable to hold a beat and the singer compensated for his wavering vocals with epileptic dancing. Uffe danced by with his jeans tucked into motorcycle boots. A lot of people, including Martin, wore waistcoats over rumpled shirts. A lot of people, including Martin, had cut off the long hair at the back of their necks but saved the fringe. Fraying knit jumpers adorned with sparkly brooches. Grimy suede jackets dumped in corners and on speakers. Girls in tights, moving spasmodically. It was the kind of party his seventeen-year-old self had always imagined his older self would go to. Except for the fact that he was sitting paralysed on a sofa. Except for the fact that the person sitting next to him was Gustav, not a pretty girl. In order to make himself heard, Gustav had to put his mouth right next to Martin's ear. His breath was warm and moist.

"The selling of art inevitably corrupts it," he said. "Through selling and buying, art is commodified and loses its soul."

"What do you mean by 'soul'?" Martin said. "How are you defining 'soul' in this context?"

He didn't hear the answer because just then someone put on a record at a volume that made the speakers distort. A fast-paced drum machine pumping out a fast, simple, straight beat. A quivering synthesiser slid into the soundscape, followed by a frantic hi-hat and bass.

Gustav leaned back. "I love this song," he yelled, lighting a cigarette.

"Who is it?"

"New Order."

"Never heard of them."

Gustav said something inaudible. He leaned back, looked up at the ceiling, blew out smoke.

Martin went to the bathroom. He stood there staring at his reflection until someone started banging on the door, shouting: "Go fuck somewhere else."

On his way back, he bumped into a girl he knew named Pia. She smiled broadly and ran a hand through her hair, which she'd recently dyed jet black. They'd had something going for a while but for some reason had never managed to take it to the next level. Martin made a pact with fate right then and there: if he didn't end up making out with Pia, he was going to call Cecilia the next day.

"What's up?" Pia shifted to let someone by. She had some sort of art school connection that was escaping him just then. Was she the one who made those sculptures out of wire and yarn that always collapsed in a comical way? "You look a little blue. But this is a *party*." She gently squeezed his shoulder. Strong fingers, long nails.

"I guess…"

"What's getting you down?" She offered him a cigarette – black, vanilla-flavoured. He seemed to remember that they tasted awful but took it anyway.

"If you've been seeing someone for a while and that person doesn't call for days, what does that mean?"

"I suppose it depends."

"On what?"

"Well, lots of things."

"Name one."

"Who called last?"

"Me."

"And the time before that?"

"Also me."

Pia shook her head. "I guess you're going to have to play on her jealousy, that usually works."

"It won't with this one. I honestly don't think it would work on her."

"I see."

"You know, it's like a door that's open a tiny crack, just a sliver, and if you make even the smallest mistake – if you go off with someone else, or whatever – it'll be pulled shut. And stay shut. Other people might slam it and then throw it wide-open again. You know. Storming off, screaming, arguing. But she would just close it and that would be the last you ever saw of her."

"Is that right."

"She's…" He searched for words. "Uncompromising. An either-or person. Right now, she's doing a summer course in sociology without even taking a student loan or relaxing like a normal person. Who does that? The problem is that I don't know if she's either-or when it comes to *me*. You see?"

Uffe appeared, draped an arm around Pia's shoulders, made a comment about the band. Within thirty seconds, they were making out.

Martin stubbed out his cigarette and went to find Gustav.

The next day, he woke up at half past one, pulled on his robe, and shuffled out to the kitchen in a bubble of reassuring certainty. But the most recent message on the pad by the phone was written by him. (*Henke wants you to know that the meeting next Friday is going to be at our place because Katrin's ill.*)

The hours crawled by with monumental sluggishness. Around five, he found himself standing by the phone with his fingers on the dial. If he called now and Cecilia said Sure, come on over, the entire evening would be tainted by the fact that he'd been the one to call, not her.

He hung up and briefly regretted not seizing the opportunity with Pia the night before.

It wasn't exactly that he stayed home to sit by the phone. Rather, the universe was conspiring against him in several ways. Gustav didn't pick up. Per was working a nightshift. For lack of better options, Martin focused on his novel, with the blinds down so he wouldn't be reminded that a lovely June evening was happening outside. Until now, his method had consisted of writing whatever came to mind in the moment, which had resulted in a lot of paragraphs linked only in the sense that they were about the same set of people. "A deconstructed disposition that shines a spotlight on the impossibility of The Novel," as he'd put it to a puzzled Cecilia. There were long dialogues about the death of logic, which might be difficult to fit in. And should he start with the beginning or the end? What even were the beginning and the end? Was organising his writing according to concepts like *beginning* and *end* boring and conventional? Should he just insert a roll of paper into the typewriter and hammer away like Kerouac?

As night fell, he read Wallace's *A Visit to the Museum* for a while, slightly comforted by the way Julie put the raw torment of her beloved's silence into words.

He found one of Cecilia's socks in his bed. He threw it on the floor with all the force he could muster.

*

The phone didn't ring all of Sunday.

She'd grown tired of him. A former lover had turned up, wearing a hat, offering her a spontaneous weekend getaway to Florence and she was at that moment walking through the galleries of the Uffizi, contemplating Botticelli paintings in a state of internal crisis: whom to choose? The urbane man in the suit walking next to her or the penniless philosophy student Martin Berg? Hmm, a difficult choice! What wouldn't a person do for the chance to discuss Wittgenstein every day from now until the end of time?

He was ready to snatch up the receiver, but a tiny, rational voice managed to quash the urge. It was just a weekend. Not a full week. He would give it until tonight and then he'd call. He was going to sound unperturbed, as though it had only just occurred to him to give her a ring. Ask if she felt like seeing a film. Go for a walk. He'd give it until six.

He called at a quarter to. No answer. He called again. No answer. He called a third time and let it ring twenty-five times. When she still didn't answer, he grabbed his jacket and left the flat.

Without proper approval from his head, Martin's feet set their course for Linnéstan. When he reached Cecilia's door, he still didn't have a plan. An old lady exited, and he managed to catch the door before it closed.

With each new flight of stairs, he thought: I can still turn around.

Then he was standing outside her flat. He rang the doorbell before he could think of what to say.

Cecilia opened immediately and looked first surprised, then happy.

"Hi you," she said. "I didn't expect to see you."

Martin entered, stepping over her running shoes. The folding table in the main room was covered with papers and open books and in the middle of it all sat her typewriter, surrounded by coffee cups. The chaos seemed limited to the table, because the rest of the flat was meticulously tidy. Not a drop of water on the kitchen counter. The hob gleamed white. The coffee machine was gurgling; a fresh pot was brewing. Her phone sat on the floor, unplugged.

"You're studying for an exam," he said. "Your sociology course."

"Yes...?"

"I tried to call," he said. "I was worried."

"Oh – I'm sorry, I..."

He pulled her close and felt the warmth of her body, the tapping rhythm of her heart.

"I didn't know you were going to call." Her voice was muffled by his shoulder. "I just… I didn't think…"

He said nothing.

"I'm glad you came," she said quietly.

13

Seen from the outside, very little had changed about the Wikners' summer house since Martin first saw it almost thirty years earlier, and when he parked the Volvo in front of the house – Elis was already yawning demonstratively – the cars were the only clue to what decade they were in. It was possible, Martin noted after closing the car door and stretching his legs, the house was in slightly better shape now. A few summers ago, he and Peter Wikner had scraped and repainted the facade, and it was still blindingly white.

Lars Wikner was standing on the veranda. When the Berg family came driving up the tree-lined road, his arm flew up in greeting so violently it seemed to have been held down by some invisible rope that had suddenly been cut. The wind snatched at his trousers and shirt, which flapped around his body like flags. He was dressed all in white and wore a ceramic bead necklace. His once stentorian voice was full of rattling gravel and could no longer call anyone's attention, except possibly Inger's, since she'd spent a lifetime calibrating it to her husband. These days, his left hand trembled so badly he had to hold both cognac glasses and cigarillos in his right, and he'd turned this one-handed way of living into an artform. Long before he'd needed it he'd acquired a cane, so that now, when he could no longer do without it, it didn't have to be an act of surrender to the ageing process.

Lars kissed Rakel on both cheeks in the French manner and managed, frailty notwithstanding, to slap Elis so hard on the back he staggered slightly.

"I've been reading this book," he said, shaking Martin's hand, "that you should publish. An Italian book. A very interesting investigation of…" – he sniffed – "artistic developments in north Italian monasteries during the Middle Ages."

"What's the title?" Martin sighed.

"I don't remember. I left it inside – remind me later…"

Inger had appeared on the veranda. "There you are!"

Over the past decade, her long plait had greyed while her faced retreated from the inside out; the soft apple-roundness of her cheeks had hardened, the lines around her mouth had been overrun with wrinkles. She was wearing an embroidered kaftan and an apron. Now, she stepped into the yard, chirping about how tall Elis was these days and how beautiful Rakel, embracing them all and ushering them into the house, all the while updating them on the latest goings-on. Emanuel had already arrived. Peter and Suzanne had joined them yesterday. Suzanne was very close to her due date.

The two extant children, Martin noted, were now about knee-high and ran around the garden as though someone had given them uppers.

"Simply *ecstatic* to be here," Inger commented.

Peter was currently out for a run. "And Vera is hopefully on her way. I don't understand why she couldn't come in the car with the rest of us. But you know how it is: drowning in work. I suppose I should be grateful she's staying two whole days."

Inger showed Rakel and Elis to one of the guest rooms. "And you, Martin, you'll be sleeping in the Corner Room."

"The Corner Room?"

She watched a puzzled look spread across her son-in-law's face as he searched all the rooms of the house in his memory, looking for this Corner Room, and when there was no dawning of insight, she added: "*Cecilia's* room."

"Why didn't you just say…"

But Inger had spotted Suzanne and dashed after her, asking how the icing was coming along.

Martin grabbed his bag and went upstairs.

There was nothing left now of the old medallion wallpaper that had been scarred by generations of drawing pins and nails; a wallpaper that in the early hours of the morning had seemed to move, sprouting new lines like some nocturnal flower. Now, everything was painted white. None of Cecilia's paintings had been hung back up after the renovation. The bed was new, too, a basic double bed from Ikea. The only surviving witness was the sideboard. It stood where it always had, probably because it was almost impossible to move. The thing had been put together sometime in the nineteenth century, and by now the pine wood was stripped and worn and the keys to the door and the drawers had long since been lost. Back in the day, Cecilia's stacks of books and papers had materialised on top of it within hours; now, it was topped by a vase full of flowers.

On a whim, Martin opened it. There were clothes on the shelves. At first he figured it was one of Inger's stashes for things-that-needed-storing – bathrobes, spare woollen socks, raingear of every conceivable size. He pulled out a button-down shirt. It was made of blue flannel, worn gossamer thin. The sleeves were still rolled up and there were creases by the elbows. A coffee stain on the chest.

He went through the rest of the clothes. He hadn't thought about them in almost fifteen years, but now it felt as though it had been only days since he last saw her wearing them. She'd left them here so she could travel more lightly. White and blue men's shirts, a pair of jeans, a summer dress of grey cotton. Her bare shoulders under the tie straps, freckly and pale, her face sprinkled with sunlight trickling in through the brim of her straw hat.

He felt a sudden stabbing pain in his gut and had to lie down for a bit.

Sometime later, Martin was standing on the veranda. Inger had shoved a gin and tonic in his hand and fluttered on to see to some kind of food preparation she refused to let him help with. Out here, he wasn't quite so obviously in the way.

Through an open window, he heard Lars interrogating Elis about his plans for the future, but unfortunately he couldn't hear Elis's answers.

A taxi slowly came up the tree-lined road, hesitant like a lost urban animal. It stopped in the middle of the drive. A door opened and a weekend bag thudded onto the gravel, followed by a pair of black heels and two long ankles. Then, in one long, graceful movement, Vera Wikner emerged, slammed the car door shut, and straightened up to her full length while the taxi made a U-turn.

She stood alone in the middle of the drive for a moment, looking around. Garbo arrives at JFK, but where are all the paparazzi? Then she spotted Martin and raised her hand in a wave. *Vera Wikner* – a hard, severe name, full of edges and straight lines in a way the physical VW wasn't at all. She should have been called Isabelle, Laura or Sophie – something billowing, gleaming like silk – but Vera had been Lars's (then-dying) mother's name, and someone had to inherit it. The truth was that she looked a lot like Cecilia, but the likeness only showed up in photographs. They had very different ways of inhabiting their bodies. Vera swayed her hips, lowered her eyes, crossed her legs modestly, wore high heels.

She had to be close to forty, but it was best not to ask. Martin hadn't seen her in years, because she always managed to be travelling at Christmas. As far as he knew, her work consisted of telling rich people what art to buy. She lived ("had her homebase") around the corner from her parents in Stockholm. Apparently, she was good friends with KG the gallerist, if you could call a relationship based on mutual financial interest friendship. Several years ago, Vera had announced she wouldn't mind modelling for Gustav, and, loath to turn her down, he'd agreed to paint a portrait. He didn't think much of it and had tried to gift it to her ("The vibe was off, I mostly just wanted to get rid of it"), but Vera insisted he had to sell it. She found a buyer, too, and gouged the poor sod in the process.

The Wikners were mostly relieved that someone was perpetuating the family's long-standing connection with the arts.

Maybe Inger had heard the car, maybe her social radar was pinging, but seconds after the taxi drove off, she came bursting out onto the veranda.

"You look amazing! Radiant. But I thought you were maybe bringing your gentleman caller…?"

"Who? Oh, Rickard." Vera laughed in Martin's direction. "No, he's been decommissioned."

"But he seemed so nice."

"You haven't even met Rickard, Mum."

"Ginger fellow," Inger said to Martin. "Looked a bit like Prince Harry."

They disappeared into the house, and he heard their high-pitched voices fade away.

Shortly thereafter, Peter came jogging up the tree-lined road, flushed and sweaty, dressed from head to toe in high-performance materials.

"Welcome to the cabin," he said, stretching out his leg against the veranda railing. "Has Dad presented his latest bright idea about the medieval monasteries yet? He talked about it all the way down."

"Luckily, he seems to have forgotten about that for the moment," Martin replied.

"Just wait. Dad has an unshakeable belief in those monks. Isolated in their monasteries without anything to do but make art and contemplate holy writ and whatnot. He thinks it'll be a bestseller. He read it in Italian. I didn't even know he spoke Italian." Peter pulled his phone out of his armband, checked the time, and pulled a face. He was going to have to push himself if he wanted to beat his personal best at the marathon in June, he said. This was okay, but far from as good as it could be. He'd worked on his running step and there was nothing wrong with his stamina, so the question was what he could work on to improve his times. He sighed and went to stretch his other leg.

Like all the Wikner siblings, Peter was tall and gangly. His head was shaved and there wasn't an ounce of fat on his body. His leg muscles were long and sinewy, his hips narrow, his back ramrod straight. Back in the day, he'd been a pale presence at family get-togethers. He'd spent dinners listening to his father while cutting off and not eating various parts of every food put in front of him, and by the end of the meal, most of his porterhouse steak lay dissected in a pool of sauce.

Eventually, he'd stopped coming altogether, because, as Inger would have it, he was "terribly busy". She'd ramble on about being on-call, placements and rotations; on account of which Peter was unfortunately unable, under any circumstances, to come down for Christmas, Easter, Midsummer or whatever it was. But Martin suspected that the white coat served as an excuse and a refuge for Cecilia's oldest brother, and over time he'd grown to like him more and more. Peter was a hub of normalcy among a gaggle of enervating eccentrics. He submitted to his mother's care without batting an eyelid. He never caused drama like Vera *la tragedienne*, or Emanuel *le Pierrot*. His tone was always composed, and he was a man of few words. He immersed himself in physical activity with the zeal of a person who genuinely fears death, and was always cycling up and down the Alps or preparing for some marathon or another. He'd married a fellow surgeon, as loquacious as Inger and with as little distance between thought and action as Lars, but, on the whole, their marriage seemed harmonious.

When Peter went inside to shower, Martin went in search of the third Wikner sibling – he might as well get all three checked off. He found Emanuel in the dimly lit library, where the curtains were permanently drawn and the walls were lined with dark wooden shelves filled with books that had been there since the dawn of time. A ponderous figure, made swollen and shapeless by medication, sat slumped in a leather armchair. Either he genuinely didn't notice, or he pretended not to when Martin entered.

"Hi there. What are you reading?"

"About numerology." Emanuel's eyes turned towards Martin but settled on a point somewhere off to the side. "Did you know the number of inches of half the base of the Cheops Pyramid is the same as the number of days in a year? Fascinating people, those Egyptians." With his hands resting on the open book, he told Martin about various obscure finds from Ancient Egypt, which indicated that their scientific progress was considerably more impressive than previously believed, and, more to the point, inexplicable. "Which is to say," he said, touching his forehead as though the subject were associated with an almost insurmountable mental effort, "inexplicable according to our current scientific paradigm. And that paradigm is humanity's straitjacket. That much is clear. It's a millstone around the neck of free thought attempting to gain altitude. An iron curtain blocking insight and knowledge. It is—" At this point he broke off with a revolted headshake.

"Is that right?" Martin said, wondering if that was enough small talk to satisfy the demands of social protocol. "You look like you're doing well," he added.

In Emanuel's case, that meant something akin to "at least you're not sectioned", but there was no telling if Emanuel himself picked up on that implication. He spent a long time griping about what he was sure must be nascent ischaemic problems, a series of very clear symptoms his doctors were prone to neglect. It was, come to think of it, outrageous how incompetent doctors were these days, he said, struggling to his feet to demonstrate his limp. Patients basically had to do their job for them. Not only did he have to endure the symptoms, he had to diagnose himself and prescribe treatment. The only things doctors were good for was writing prescriptions and, remarkably frequently, they couldn't even manage to do that.

Emanuel Wikner hobbled around the library. Martin could see he was limping, right? It looked serious, didn't it? And yet they could find nothing wrong, bloody quacks, nothing.

*

Eventually, everyone was seated around the table, to the gentle clatter of cutlery and soft din of conversation. Across from him, Vera was pushing food around her plate, not eating.

"I contest," she announced, pouring herself more white wine, "that Ingres is underrated. Very underrated. I mean, those nudes, the *skin*..." She drank. "Phenomenal."

"Wasn't Ingres the one who used to throw in an extra vertebra because he thought it looked better?" Rakel said.

"His entire style radiates a unique eye for beauty that is rare these days. The fact that *beauty* is considered uninteresting – that's just sad. And ironic, too, because it still sells. It sells! Take Gustav Becker, for instance. One of the paintings from his Antibes Suite went for three hundred thousand dollars at auction last month. *Cecilia Reading*, I think it was."

"There must be twenty paintings of Cecilia reading," Martin put in without looking up from his plate.

"Anyway: Becker isn't stuck in this postmodern performance quagmire; he works within a tradition where beauty still matters…"

"Cecilia could have been just as accomplished herself," Lars said, "if she'd just put her back into it." During the coughing fit that followed this pronouncement, Vera changed the subject.

Next to him, Elis was typing a text with quick thumbs, oblivious to the world around him.

"Elis," Martin hissed. "No phones at the table."

"Oskar and Michel are in Slottsskogen," his son retorted accusingly, slipping the phone back into his pocket. "They're having a really good time."

Martin thought about the parties of his own youth in Slottsskogen Park: people wearing denim jackets and T-shirts even though it was freezing out, drinking whatever they could get their hands on, running from the rangers who magically seemed to know when someone was going for an innocent swim in the seal pond, falling into shrubberies, getting lost among the azaleas blooming darkly in the night.

"There will be other parties," he said.

"Not Walpurgis ones. I mean, sure, okay, next year, but I'll be too old by then." Elis stabbed a French bean, studying it morosely. "Some things are only fun when you're young."

On the other side of the table, Rakel had been placed like a buffer between her uncles. She talked to each in turn. Her long hair was plaited and wrapped around her head, the way Cecilia had sometimes worn hers before she cut it short during their first summer together. His daughter looked more and more like her mother with every passing year, as though she had not yet achieved her final form.

Dessert was served. They sang a thunderous "Happy Birthday" to Inger Wikner. Then the group broke up and reassembled in new constellations. The cakes were left sitting on the table like an Acropolis of the baking world, and the candles had almost burned down. Suzanne, Peter's wife, slumped onto the chair next to Martin's. Putting the children to bed, she said, had been a struggle to top all other struggles that day. "Inger has been feeding them sugar since eleven o'clock this morning. They were completely wired. You have no idea how badly I long for the day when they're grown and I can yell at them without someone reporting me to social services." With her hands on her enormous belly, she leaned back and groaned. "The only thing that could top this would be my waters breaking. Which hospital is closest? Borås or Gothenburg? Though come to think of it, nothing would make Lars and Inger happier than the chance to set up a field hospital in the barn. Like the good old days in Ethiopia."

Martin laughed. It was far too easy to imagine.

He'd always liked Suzanne. They moved in very different circles, and he would probably never have met her were it not for the family connection, unless he needed an emergency thoracotomy and ended up on her operating table. That was undeniably one of the advantages of the whole family concept: you were forced to live with people who were not of your choosing, people you might never have chosen in a million years. You didn't choose your children, your parents or your siblings. You didn't choose your in-laws. They were assigned to you at random, blindly, and you simply had to find your place among them.

"What I don't get," Suzanne said now, "is why they didn't just stay in Addis. Lars was doing good work at that hospital. It's still there, you know. I have a friend who works for Médecins Sans Frontières, and she claims he's still considered a bloody saint down there. Maternity care was pretty much non-existent before he came, so I suppose it didn't take much to make him a hero, but I do think it's well deserved. He was a good surgeon. He built a solid hospital. The fieldwork is still being carried out. But after they moved back to Sweden, he just bounced around. Took leaves of absence to catch butterflies and import rugs and god knows what. I don't think he ever spent more than six months at a time at Karolinska Hospital. God, I would kill for a glass of wine."

Then she waddled off to bed, and Martin seized the opportunity to nip out for some fresh air.

The spring evening was chilly. He turned his back on the house and considered the lake, which could be glimpsed between the trees. He'd never swum in it. Lakes were almost as bad as the sea.

"So you're hiding, too?" It was Vera, with her coat over her shoulders, looking mildly unsteady in her high heels. "Would you like a cigarette?"

"No, thank you."

"I thought you went out to smoke."

"I don't smoke. I wanted to look at the water," he said.

Vera set her wine glass down on the lawn and pulled out a packet of cigarettes. The flame lit up her face, so like Cecilia's. She cocked her head and blew out smoke without taking her eyes off him. "The water," she repeated. Her cigarette hissed softly when she took another drag. By means of a very discreet manoeuvre (picking up her wine glass from the ground, shifting onto her other foot, swaying gently) she moved in slightly too close. Then, she shuddered. "It's *cold*," she said, as though the temperature were a personal affront. The fingers holding her cigarette trembled slightly.

Martin moved away and shoved his hands into his jacket pockets.

"You never let me know when you're in Stockholm," she said.

"It's been a while, actually."

"But don't you come up to see Gustav Becker pretty regularly?"

"I do, but you know…" Martin didn't want to admit he hadn't seen Gustav in almost six months. Instead, he said nothing.

Vera could only bear a few seconds of silence. "Do you know if he's up to anything new, Gustav?"

"I assume you've heard about the exhibition at the art museum?"

"Sure, but that's a retrospective. I meant something *new*. Because if he is, I have several interested buyers. I've obviously talked to KG, but he just mumbled something that I unfortunately have to assume means he doesn't quite know what Becker is up to at the moment."

Triumph welled up inside Martin: Gustav's gallerist was as shut out and ignorant as he was. He suddenly felt better about Vera, who yammered on about the scarcity of new works by Gustav.

"It's not a bad strategy, being so inaccessible. Pushes prices up. In fact," her voice suddenly fell into a deeper register, "this kind of abstemiousness is a good tactic for stimulating demand in other areas as well."

"What do you mean?"

She took a long drag. "Nothing."

"You can't just blurt out something incomprehensible and then say you didn't mean anything by it."

Vera blew smoke out in a forceful puff. "You sound like Cecilia," she snapped. "Everything has to be *defined* and *analysed*. Picked apart as far as you're able. Look, in all honesty, did Cecilia ever have fun?"

"Of course she—"

"Such a fucking goody-goody with all those books and her damn thesis. How many years did it take her to put that book together? A diligent worker like her, she should've had it done like *this*." Vera snapped her fingers, swaying ominously. "But it took her a fucking decade. Wasn't she at it for a decade? More or less? And you know – they gave anyone a PhD back then. The eighties: easy as pie. Not like now when you have to secure a research position and grants and whatnot." She made a big gesture, a typical Cecilia gesture. Her cigarette was dangerously close to her hair. "Do you know what the biggest problem with Cecilia was? She was bloody unable to let loose. Everything was always so important. She couldn't just shake things off. You have to be able to do that, don't you think? To live? Shrug and move on. But every time some tiny fucking thing happened, it was that *Erbarme dich, mein Gott* attitude."

"She takes life very seriously," Martin said.

"Tense, Martin, tense!" Vera dropped her cigarette in the grass and stomped it out. "You of all people should be vigilant about things like that. The correct tense in this context ought to be the simple past. 'She took life very seriously.' Whatever that's supposed to mean."

And then she stalked back towards the house, coat flapping behind her.

14

Emanuel Wikner had taken a seat in the far corner of the parlour. Rakel sat down in the armchair next to him. The party was breaking up. Pulled-out, empty chairs were scattered willy-nilly next to the table, the tablecloth was rumpled, and the candles were burning low. Grease-stained glasses gleamed.

"Welcome to my lookout post," Emanuel said, offering Rakel a plate of chocolates he was holding on his lap. "To your left you'll see Mummy dearest, properly fired up after circa one bottle of Amaretto, in lively conversation with poor, sunny Suzanne. I think they're talking about raising children. Suzanne looks a bit cornered, don't you think? There's her mother-in-law, slightly bladdered, with her tiny claw hand around her wrist, pushing some birthing experience from the sixties. And she's completely sober, to boot. Terrible fate. Still, I'm surprised Peter's managing to reproduce at a steady clip. I honestly had my doubts about him. But what do I know? Look, he's even having a second slice of cake. And here comes Vera, sweeping in like some Scarlett O'Hara. My, my, she looks upset. Is she about to lay into someone? Is a confrontation brewing? No… she's only passing through… God, she's stomping pretty hard on those stairs." Emanuel shook his head. "Of course, she always gets prickly when the subject of Cecilia's art comes up."

Rakel saw her chance. "Do you realise I've never seen anything she painted?" she lied. She didn't want to mention the paintings in the barn. She'd snuck out there earlier to have a proper look at them, but they'd gone. The wadmal blanket lay neatly folded on the workbench, surrounded by the old jars of ether.

"Outrageous." His tone was indifferent. "It's part of your cultural heritage. I have some at home; you're welcome to come over and have a look sometime."

"I'd love to."

Emanuel Wikner studied each chocolate with the discerning eye of a connoisseur before popping it into his mouth, one after the other, chewing with a pensive look on his face. Rakel pondered whether to tell him about the barn after all but couldn't bring herself to broach the subject. "Is that one of Grandpa's?" she asked instead, pointing to the lone, green-shimmering butterfly hanging on the wall next to them.

"What? Yes, probably. Butterflies, butterflies. They're everywhere. The butterflies. Do you know anything about butterflies, Rakel?"

"Very little."

"The most important function of the butterfly is to reproduce," Emanuel said, "and I'm citing Wikipedia now. Many species have, for instance, completely lost the ability to eat. They're only interested in finding one or several partners with whom to mate, and if they're female they also have to lay as many eggs as possible before they die. It strikes me now that the butterfly could be easily confused with your average pub-goer at around quarter to three, but anyway, doesn't that speak volumes about human existence?"

"What do you mean?"

"Well, you might call me cynical, or accuse me of presenting a simplified picture of human life, and you would be right on both counts. As my niece, by the way, I'm glad you're such an insightful and critical thinker, Rakel, that you don't just take my word for things simply because I'm an older relative. But I think – and I say this with thirty-seven years of empirical studies to back me up – that all the things we do are convoluted tangents, circuitous detours that inevitably lead us back to where we started, which is the same place as the butterflies…"

He popped another chocolate into his mouth but didn't let chewing slow him down. "You know your Freud, right? It's the uninterrupted journey of an organism towards death. We're headed in the same direction, all of us, but as Sigmund sagely points out at his desk on Berggasse 19: 'the organism wishes to die only in its own fashion'. *Beyond the Pleasure Principle*, page thirty-four. But you have to admit nature really hit the nail on the head with the butterfly. No circuitous detour for them. They just go for it. First life, then death. Existence boiled down to its core essence. Cheers to that, my dear."

"Cheers," Rakel said. She was pretty sure he had that quote wrong.

"Unfortunately, butterfly collecting is a metaphysical impossibility." Emanuel topped himself up from a nearby bottle. "Someone should have told Daddy dearest that before he took a leave of absence to go to the Amazon. Collecting butterflies is a waste of time. Assuming you make the metaphysically possible the lodestar of your life's work."

"I'm not sure I follow…"

"A butterfly, dear Rakel, is by its nature something you can never know everything about. Not fully. Fluttering by, it doesn't simply submit to being studied. You can see what colour it is, estimate its size, and if it sits still for a moment on a flower, you can get an idea of the pattern on its wings. But an inextricable part of the butterfly's nature is that it can flutter off at any second. Escape you. You can't know everything about a living butterfly, because being a butterfly means being in flight. If you catch it, on the other hand. If you crouch down in the grass and lie in wait for it with a net. If you swing the net at once carefully and deliberately. And if you then stick the butterfly in a jar. If you fill the jar with ether to make the butterfly fall asleep, which is to say, die. If you then pin the butterfly to a board – well, *then* you can study it. Then it's completely exposed to your gaze. You can determine its species, document it, catch a few more of the same species for comparison. But, and this is the point, when you have the butterfly pinned up in front of you, you don't have the whole of the butterfly. An important aspect of the butterfly is missing: its fluttering. A butterfly that doesn't flutter away, doesn't flee from you, isn't entirely a butterfly. Thus – no matter what we do, the butterfly eludes us. Whether we let it go or catch it. Listen, I need to take a piss. Save my seat for me, would you?"

*

The curtains were closed, and the room filled with a pale gloom. There was snoring coming from the bottom bunk. Rakel climbed down. Her brother lay wrapped in his duvet, still fully dressed. His face was soft and round-cheeked.

She took some clothes and the German book out of her bag and padded out into the hallway. The rug on the upstairs landing was bunched and a jacket lay tossed over a chair. There were no signs of the night before in the bathroom, save for a glass on the sink with some dregs of wine left in it.

Rakel got dressed and washed her face. The back of her head was throbbing dully.

The stairs creaked even though she tried her best to be quiet. Vera's coat lay in a pile on the hallway floor, as though it had run out of the energy needed to keep clinging to its hanger. A gilded wall clock ticked brusquely. It was half past seven, and Rakel had only had four and a half hours of sleep.

The kitchen had been cleared of all traces of the party. She turned on the coffee machine and spread butter on a piece of semi-dry baguette. Then she tiptoed up the many stairs to the attic.

Once she reached it, she had to walk a few paces into the thick, ancient darkness, because the light switch was set back from the door and the light trickling in through the windows was far from sufficient. The seconds before the fluorescent lights flickered and hummed to life always felt very long. Then, a forgotten world spread out before her: mountains of furniture and boxes, shelves crammed full of all kinds of things, a desk with a rolltop that always got stuck, an old filing cabinet with faded ink on the paper labels on its drawers, a wooden birdcage with plastic flowers stuck through its bars, children's bikes. Skis and what appeared to be an old canoe lay across the ceiling beams. A stuffed crocodile sat on a dresser.

Now, Rakel gingerly balanced her coffee, sandwich and book while she picked her way over to a threadbare corduroy sofa by one of the small attic windows. At no point during the past fifteen years had anyone seemed to have discovered the little lair that had sprung up around the sofa. There was a footstool, a wooden chair eminently suitable for trays of food and coffee cups, and a small rococo table that held a stack of old teen magazines. When Rakel was a teenager, *Starlet* and *Vecko-Revyn* had generously shared nuggets of wisdom like HOW TO GET THE PERFECT TAN (don't worry about skin cancer) and THIS AUTUMN'S BEST BUDGET BUYS (red beret, H&M), and more than once promised more than they could deliver (TANTRIC SEX – THE ULTIMATE GUIDE). On top of the magazines lay Schopenhauer's *The World as Will and Representation* and Jean M. Auel's *The Clan of the Cave Bear*.

The window was grimy, and a number of dead flies were caught between the panes, but it afforded a good view of the drive. From the ground, it looked like nothing more than a small square just below the roof ridge. No one ever so much as glanced up there, the way they might at the kitchen or the study or the studio. A person sitting by the attic window was invisible but all-seeing.

Rakel gazed out at the deserted yard until she could no longer avoid the book she'd been lugging around for a month. She'd brought it thinking she'd have to crack it open if she had nothing else to read. It was possible, of course, to give the misanthropic old German or Ayla, the Cro-Magnon girl who against all odds survives an earthquake, a cave lion and a tribe of Neanderthals, another chance, but that was even less tempting.

And so, she got to it. She skipped words she didn't understand, skimmed some paragraphs, and flipped past others to get a feel for the book, and, above all, so she could tell her father she'd read it.

It was, at heart, a simple narrative. The narrator, who had the same name and profession as his creator, was a relatively unknown author living in Berlin. He wasn't exactly a failure, but definitely not successful either. He felt he'd dedicated too much of his life to writing to change careers, despite bleak prospects and a total lack of ideas for new projects. By chance, he meets a woman. They initiate what he at first considers a fleeting relationship. However, he finds himself deeply affected by her, and in time, his entire being is thrown into a state of flux; their relationship shakes him to the core. What he thought was carefree play turns into something deeply serious. Then, and the reader sees this coming long before the poor narrator does, things begin to fall apart. The woman pulls away and eventually ends the relationship. The narrator is beside himself; his existence and identity lie in ruin, he doesn't understand why and can't go back to the old attitudes and views that used to characterise his life. The way back to his old life is shut. He becomes obsessed with understanding what happened, where it went wrong, why she didn't want him, and all those things jilted people dwell on for far too long. Gradually, a portrait of the woman he loves takes shape – enigmatic yet sincere, self-sufficient and lonely, oscillating between cold rejection and tender intimacy – but without any explanation for her evasive behaviour ever being given. After a while, she vanishes, without a trace, and the book ends in resignation in the face of never knowing.

It had to be said, Rakel thought, that there was a clear, powerful purity to the language, even though it hovered just beyond her linguistic grasp. The chronology was broken up and skilfully reassembled to make the love story between the narrator and the woman – only ever referred to as "she" – exist in a state of constant uncertainty. What she had at first dismissed as a banal break-up story, revenge writing by someone who was dumped, unexpectedly became a thrilling read after the first few chapters. Just like Philip, the reader was hooked, sharing his increasingly feverish compulsion to understand what happened with this woman, who was at once mysterious and unguarded. Rakel had expected a classic portrait of a femme fatale – great beauty, elusive ambiguities, hints of violence – but Philip Franke wrote a completely different type of woman. Her otherwise very spartan flat was filled with books in several languages. When she couldn't sleep, she read Homer in the original. She was a long-distance runner, but didn't make a big affair of it, just slipped out of bed in the morning, laced up her running shoes, and went running along the empty streets of Berlin at dawn. She came across as an independent person with intense integrity, a person who approached the world with a thirst for truth and who would never lie. At the same time, she kept large parts of her life and history hidden, and time and again, Philip would run into closed doors and immutable silence. When the narrator happened to spot his beloved with another man, he couldn't bring himself to believe she was being unfaithful. Even so, he followed them at a distance for a long while, and the unknown man took on virtually godlike proportions in his imagination, even though from afar he appeared to be a fairly haggard man of middle age, dressed in a shapeless army coat of the kind that used to be common in second-hand shops.

While Rakel read, the house woke up. The piercing shriek of a child reverberated below. Water rushed through pipes. Gravel crunched outside, and when Rakel looked up, she saw Uncle Peter walking across the yard, dressed in running tights and a high-vis vest, even though the sun was already high in the sky. When he reached the end of the tree-lined road, he broke into a jog.

All morning, an obscure worry gnawed at Rakel, who ascribed it to being hungover, then to irritation, then to sensory overload. When she went back down to the kitchen, everyone was up. Nana Inger was trying to direct the rest of the family with chirped commands. Suzanne was frying sausages with one hand resting Madonna-like on her huge belly. Elis was spreading generous spoonfuls of marmalade on toast in sleepy slow-motion, apparently unaware that one of their cousins was waving his yoghurt spoon dangerously close to his shirt sleeve. Emanuel was reading aloud from the *Tibetan Book of Death*. Her dad was pacing up and down the hallway, talking into his headset in his boss voice. Vera was complaining that her poached egg was too runny. Grandpa Lars had apparently retired to the library. The older of the cousins spotted Rakel and, having seemingly forgotten his shyness from the day before, insisted on telling her something that had happened at his nursery, or possibly only in his imagination – first, there was someone called William, then a T-Rex, and something about a tree house – while he snuggled in close to her on the kitchen bench, warm and soft in his Spiderman pyjamas, and obediently opened his mouth when she offered him a bite of the croissant that had materialised before her.

A few hours later, they drove back into town. Rakel tried to nap, but her sleep was interrupted by flashbacks of her morning reading. The novel was lingering the way half-forgotten dreams can. Crystal-clear shards of the narrative blended with foggier sections she'd only partly understood.

She was dropped off on Friggagatan and drowsily climbed the stairs to her flat. For a moment, she thought she'd left the book in the summer house and cold fear washed over her while she rummaged through her bag. And yet there was no wave of relief when her fingers closed around the slim volume.

When she unlocked her front door, sunlight flooded her. The air in the flat was stuffy. She dropped her bag on the floor and opened a window. Outside, birds were singing in the cemetery trees, whose light-green leaves were just unfurling. Remember death, Rakel Berg. It was the first of May. The smell of damp earth suffused the air, the fuzzy buds of the magnolias were opening towards the sun, the cherry trees were bursting into bloom, the sky was clean and clear, open towards the heavens, and Rakel couldn't breathe. Spring hit her with full force, square in the chest; she backed away from the window, but there was nowhere to run, or, rather: there was only one path open to her.

She prepared ritualistically and without rushing. Put on a turtleneck and suit trousers. Found a jacket and her German dictionary. Twisted her hair into a bun. The trams had been redirected to accommodate the May Day demonstrations, so she walked.

The library was deserted. Rakel took a seat at the back of the reading room and lined up the novel, the dictionary and a notebook in front of her. Then she leaned in over the books and started over from the beginning.

Taken on their own, the details weren't particularly remarkable, but taken together, they conjured an eerie figure. It was the books in several languages. It was the running. It was the unexpected Ethiopian connection – the first encounter between the narrator and the woman took place in an Ethiopian restaurant, where he noticed how elegantly she ate her injera, a stark contrast to his own messy clumsiness.

But, Rakel thought, leaning back in her chair, her back aching, there was a relatively large Ethiopian diaspora in Berlin. A lot of Ethiopian restaurants. Then again, the narrator noted that the woman conversed with the waitress in Amharic, which was definitely more unusual for a Western woman.

And during the second read-through, she came across a section she hadn't fully understood the first time. It said the woman wore a gold necklace, a thin chain with a small pendant, a sphere to represent the sun surrounded by a wreath of short, dense rays, which she had a habit of running her thumbnail over when she was pondering something.

Rakel left the library on shaking legs. It was early afternoon. The sharp sun hurt her eyes.

Back home on Friggagatan, she found her box of photographs and turned it upside down, scattering its contents across the floor. Most of the pictures were snapshots taken with a disposable camera at some festival, or photos from a week-long stay in Barcelona when she and Lovisa had just turned eighteen, awkwardly smoking Spanish cigarettes in front of the Sagrada Família. But there were also a few family pictures, doubles her dad wouldn't miss when he got up in the middle of the night and flipped through the photo albums. Rakel's favourite was a black-and-white photograph of a very young Cecilia. She was sitting cross-legged, wearing Gustav's round glasses for some reason, and one of her hands was caught mid-gesture. The other held a wine glass. The top buttons of her shirt were undone and the necklace resting between her collarbones was clearly visible. Rakel had played with that pendant as a small child. She hadn't realised it was a sun until her mother had pointed it out, and then she couldn't understand how she'd missed something so obvious. And she had protested when she was forced to take off the long strands of brightly coloured plastic beads she'd made in after-school club, while her mum was allowed to keep her necklace on.

"That's because I'm so sloppy, sweetheart," Cecilia had said, hanging up Rakel's necklace on her bedpost. "I would put it down somewhere and forget where. Best to always keep it on."

PART 2
GERMAN GRAMMAR

A YEAR ABROAD IN PARIS 1

I

INTERVIEWER: Can you say something about your relationship with Paris?

MARTIN BERG: [*leaning back*] I was smart enough to move to Paris in my young, formative years. I think it was a very valuable experience. Incredibly valuable. It was important for me to come back to Gothenburg and make an active decision to live here. It would have been something else entirely if I'd just never left. And never seen the world.

INTERVIEWER: In what way was it valuable?

MARTIN BERG: Well, I had my mind set on writing. The way you do when you're twenty-three, twenty-four. "I'm going to move to Paris and write a novel." Making that kind of decision is a meaningful experience. Staring that empty page square in the eye.

*

They'd been talking about it since upper secondary.

Because one way or another, all roads led to Paris. William Wallace wrote *Patagonia Days* at his regular table at Closerie des Lilas, in a cyclical state of waxing and waning inebriation, smoking those cigarillos that looked so out of place next to his boyish appearance. Hemingway had *Moveable Feast* and Joyce finally finished *Ulysses* and had it published in a binding blue as the Aegean Sea.

The Paris Project was really little more than a vague idea until Per Andrén of all people told them there was a flat he could rent there through a relative.

"An attic conversion," Per said, almost knocking over his pint as he leaned forward, "with a view of the rooftops and the Eiffel Tower. What do you say?"

Was it even *morally defensible* not to go? Wasn't this Martin's big break? His audacious leap into eternity? Wasn't a change of scenery, from Gothenburg (grey, rainy, familiar) to Paris (glittering, jazzy, infinite) exactly what he needed to finally get going on that novel that was still just a pile of notes? Wasn't this the thing that would unleash his inspiration? Wasn't he going to become a Wallace, a Hemingway, a Joyce? Hadn't this been his dream for years?

"I think it sounds terrific," Gustav said.

Without any real hope, Martin sent off a grant application for students enrolled at Gothenburg University. To his surprise, he was awarded 15,000 kronor, which, combined with his savings from working summers for the post office, would last him quite a while, so long as he lived frugally. In a fit of initiative, Gustav sniffed out an exchange programme between Valand and an art school in Paris and applied. Per, the most organised of the trio, had already applied to study French at the Sorbonne.

"Wow. That's – wow," Cecilia said when he told her about his travel plans.

"You could come," he said, because he figured he was expected to.

She shook her head. "I have to write my dissertation. And I can't afford it. I was just…" Her voice trailed off, and Martin quickly filled the silence by telling her about all the practical details. He saved his main argument for last.

"I really think it would be good for my writing. You know, how many chances like this does a person get? You can't just let it pass you by, can you?"

"No, sure."

They'd spent most of the days and nights of the past year together so missing each other was still an abstract concept. Talking on the phone and writing letters seemed feasible, and Cecilia would come visit in the summer. Maybe it was even for the best that there were no distractions. Martin had heard that boxers were celibate before important fights.

Instead of carnal pleasures, he would channel his libido into literature, and this time he was going to finish the damn novel.

"It's like I *owe* it to myself to go," he said. "Otherwise I'll grow old and bitter. I'll be a forty-year-old man who regrets all the things he didn't do. I can't do that to myself. You get it."

"Absolutely."

"Imagine if your whole life had been a lead-up to a particular point, and it's at that point everything will start. Or actually, a door's better. Imagine a door. You step through a door. Your entire life has been about preparing to step through that door. Because the door is a symbol of something more existential. It's your destiny, though Sartre never talks about 'destiny' – in fact, he has a strong dislike of the concept of 'destiny' or, rather, people's belief that this 'destiny' is something that determines and directs their lives, and lies outside their control and ability to take responsibility. Anyway, if we allow ourselves a more everyday understanding of the concept, 'destiny' I mean, just for the sake of this argument, then it's a person's destiny to go through that door. The paths of our existence have brought us to it, and now we have to take the step, or the leap. Kierkegaard, another existentialist, talks about *the leap*—"

"I've read Kierkegaard."

"Of course – uh – where was I?"

"You were leaping through a door."

"Right, so, you have to make the leap through the door. That's the thing. To be brave enough, to throw yourself out, boldly. Existence, when it comes down to it, is nothing but one long exhortation to be brave. To let go and surf uncertainty instead of splashing about at the edge of the water where you know you can touch the bottom and are within safe view of your parents."

"So what's on the other side?"

"Huh?"

"On the other side of the door?"

While they worked on their travel plans, Cecilia got more and more into her running.

At first, Martin had had a difficult time reconciling his girlfriend with Sporty Cissi. His girlfriend never wore a ponytail. She never wore tracksuit bottoms and a T-shirt. She was never so easily mistaken for your run-of-the-mill exercise freak. There was something faintly ridiculous about the way she ran (straight back, slightly raised chin) and she didn't stick to places intended for exercise, she ran wherever she felt like it, usually in town.

Martin had, for his part, realised early on that he had to pick a side in the eternal struggle between Body and Mind. Having sided firmly with Mind, he'd consequently stopped trying to be good at team sports, hand–eye coordination and gross motor skills. But being bad wasn't enough; you also had to demonstrate your contempt in a convincing manner. Martin had done so by sitting on the sidelines with a "sprained ankle", reading Camus. If they'd been outside, he'd have liked to smoke a cigarette, just to really underscore how little he cared about his lung capacity.

Fate hadn't seemed to be entirely on his side, however, because nature had endowed him with a certain talent for running. Since he hadn't been able to resist the temptation of being top of the class, he'd occasionally shuffled down to the four-hundred metre track with his pale legs sticking out of the shorts he wore on average about four times a term, got into the starting position and surrendered to his Body.

The amazing thing about running was that you didn't have to think. You didn't have to keep track of other people or devious, unpredictable balls. You didn't have to gamble everything on a single throw that risked missing the mark. When you were running, there was always the possibility of pushing the pace up a little bit more. Even if you were competing against other people, it wasn't the kind of immediate power struggle that, say, boxing or wrestling was, where you could be so obviously overpowered. You didn't need a rival or a companion, and that meant there was no risk of losing. Martin ran more often than he liked to admit and was therefore able to defend his record in the eight hundred metres three years in a row, which to his PE teacher seemed like a miracle.

Cecilia ran a set number of times every week, gradually increasing the distance until she was pushing fifteen or twenty miles every time.

She ran in the mornings. She ran if it rained. When the days grew darker, she purchased a high-vis jacket.

And then she quit smoking, and Martin wondered if she wasn't taking things a bit far.

It was a Thursday evening in late autumn; everyone was tired. Martin was tired of studying literature, because all he did was read and read and read, and it was never enough. Cecilia was tired because she'd taken on a double course load, German and intellectual history, was writing a dissertation and had just run fifteen miles. Gustav was tired because he'd entered another I-am-a-fraud-as-an-artist phase and spent all day every day sleeping. But they'd gone out for a bite to eat and a few pints at the Golden Prague, and on the whole felt a bit better about life. When they had finished eating, Gustav pulled out the cigarette case that had once belonged to his life-loving grandfather, who had drowned at dawn during a sailing trip off Cap d'Antibes. He offered the cigarettes to Martin, who took one, and Cecilia, who to everyone's surprise said:

"No thanks. I've quit."

"You have?" Martin said.

"Isn't that something you should know?"

Cecilia nodded, though it was unclear what to. "I can't smoke and run at the same time."

"I don't think you're supposed to smoke while you're running," Martin said and felt clever for about one second.

"I obviously don't smoke *while* I'm running."

"So you quit, just like that?" Gustav said.

"Yep."

"Isn't it hard?"

"Definitely. I'd love a cigarette right now, for example."

"Oh, come on," Martin said. "It's hardly a big deal if you have just one. One little cigarette. It makes no difference."

"Of course it does," Cecilia said. "It makes *all* the difference. Because if you take one little cigarette, you haven't quit. If you take one little cigarette, you have, at most, cut back, but you haven't quit."

"But is quitting really that important?" Martin said. He picked up Gustav's case and held it out to her. "You want one, don't you!"

"Leave her alone," Gustav said.

"I just want to know: why is quitting so important?" The discussion was making Martin upset for reasons he couldn't quite explain, even to himself. "I get that it makes running hard, but not *that* bloody hard, which I know from my own experience, since I both smoke and run, if not at the same time. And you can always skip, say, seven out of the ten cigarettes you'd normally smoke and still have three left, three lovely little cigarettes that you could smoke after having a nice dinner out, for instance. What's so wrong with that? Huh?"

"No one said there was anything wrong with it," Cecilia said. "All I said was that I had quit."

"But really, Cissi, you've smoked maybe half a pack a day for as long as I've known you…"

"Not half a pack."

"But at least two, three packs a week. Can we agree on two, three packs a week?"

"Two, three packs a week, sure."

"What does this have to do with anything?" Gustav asked.

"Just hold on," Martin said. "So: you've smoked two, three packs a week for as long as I've known you, which is a year and a half, and presumably for a while before that, too."

"Correct."

"And you've smoked those two, three packs a week with immense pleasure and, so far as I know, little or no guilt about doing something that is, fundamentally, bad for your health."

"Also correct," Cecilia said.

"And now, one day, *just like that*, you decide to quit. Cold turkey. No easing into it. One hundred per cent."

"Exactly. What's your point?"

There was silence around the table for a long moment, because Martin had forgotten what his point was. To hide his confusion, he pulled out another cigarette and lit it.

"I just don't get what's so bad about having *one* cigarette."

Cecilia shrugged. "Because even though it's just one cigarette, it's a cigarette."

"But seriously – you've been smoking all this time and you've been able to run just fine."

"Yes."

"Isn't it a bit, well, a bit…"

"A bit what?"

"A bit over the top. Just quitting like that."

"Why are you so provoked by the fact that I've quit smoking?"

"Have you even quit? When was your last cigarette?"

"Sunday."

"That's," Martin counted inwardly, "five days ago. Five days! You're going to fall off the wagon."

"Don't you think I'm the best judge of whether or not I've quit smoking?" Cecilia snapped.

"Sure," he said. "Absolutely."

"Can we change the subject?" Gustav put in.

"I give you a week," Martin said.

"You're unbelievable," Cecilia said.

He regularly teased her about smoking in secret. Out of pride, he figured, out of pride and stubbornness, she refused to admit to this exceedingly human weakness. He obviously wouldn't have said anything if she'd just admitted to it. He would have let it lie. But clinging to the lie that she'd never taken so much as one drag since the cigarette that she according to the official story had designated her last was just so childish. It was so puerile and obstinate he simply couldn't help ribbing her a little. He delivered his barbs in a loving way, making it an in-joke between the two of them. The only problem was that she didn't seem to think it was funny. He assumed it infuriated her, but she didn't yell or argue with him. Instead, she sulked and withdrew, but there was never an epic scene like the ones he'd experienced with Britta the Wagner soprano, so he figured everything was all right.

Once – a few weeks before he was due to leave for Paris – Martin asked how she was dealing with the withdrawal. They were in his room in Majorna. Martin was packing and Cecilia was sitting on his bed, reading a magazine.

"It's really hard," Cecilia said, sounding completely sincere. "Especially this past week. Every single person I see is smoking."

And then Martin said something about how it wouldn't be as hard if she quit for real and stopped sneaking cigarettes all the time.

Cecilia just looked at him and left the room. Martin carried on with what he was doing, which was sorting all his clothes, which he had laid out on the bed, into a Paris pile and a back-to-Kungsladugårdsgatan pile. He figured she was sulking in the kitchen, and that was fine by him; he'd just told a little joke (granted, perhaps not the funniest joke ever), and he would go out and apologise as soon as he'd found ten matching pairs of socks.

But when Martin got to the kitchen, she wasn't there.

He called out: "Cissi?" No answer. "Cecilia?"

He checked the bathroom and the living room. He even popped his head into Anders's room. He looked in the hallway and realised her boots and coat were gone.

His head began to spin. He went back to his room. He folded up a pair of jeans, then returned to the kitchen. He drank a glass of water and sat down. He got up. He picked up the phone and dialled her number, even though it couldn't have been more than five minutes since she left. He sat there for a long time, listening to the phone ringing unanswered.

II

INTERVIEWER: Back then, you wrote quite a lot yourself.

MARTIN BERG: Well, yes. [*coughing, clearing his throat*]

INTERVIEWER: What was life like for a young writer in Paris?

MARTIN BERG: Well, very stimulating, of course. It was still possible to live cheaply back then. Get by on fairly little. I had time to write.

I hung out with other writers. It was a creative environment in that respect. Genuine. Much of that is gone, now. But *back then*, it was still a piece of the old world.

*

It was a hunched trio that trudged through the slushy snow. Per was lugging a suitcase full of dictionaries and tweed jackets with leather elbow patches his mother had sewn on even though they weren't worn in the slightest. Martin had his travel typewriter. Gustav's luggage, on the other hand, consisted only of his sea bag and his coat from the army surplus store, which almost served as another suitcase, crammed full of necessities (cigarettes, flask) and good-to-have things (mat cutter, pencils) as it was.

They walked in a south-easterly direction from the metro station Saint-Sulpice until Martin, the navigator, stopped outside a door with a rusty number 16 dangling above it. Per pulled out the keys his cousin had sent him in a padded envelope. The staircase spiralled upward like a marble seashell. As they climbed, they passed heavy doors with brass plaques.

The flat was bohemian in theory but in practice consisted of one big room, a converted attic built considerably more recently than the rest of the building. The ceiling was just high enough to accommodate a sleeping loft with an alcove. The other end of the room was dominated by a floral-patterned sofa bed. Roughly in the centre of the room was a kitchenette behind a homemade bar. Next to the front door a cracked porcelain sink had been installed, a round mirror above it, in addition to the bathroom, with its pistachio-green tiles and bath with a ring of grime around the bottom. Someone had left behind an old copy of *Nouvel Observateur* and a packet of mummified madeleines from the shop on the corner. The room was chilly and dank, but outside the four dormer windows the rooftops, chimneys and powerlines of the city spread out beneath a vast white sky. You could even – if you leaned out – catch a glimpse of the Eiffel Tower. With a bit of death defiance, you could climb out onto the roof outside and sit on the tin that cooled in the evening with your *cigarettes* and *vin rouge* and talk about *la vie*, *l'amour* and *la philosophie*. But that would have to wait. Currently, the roof was covered in a thin layer of slush.

As soon as they had dropped off their bags, Gustav insisted on conquering the Left Bank "à la Vilhelm what's-his-name".

The flat was on a narrow side street off Rue de Rennes, which ran, straight and wide, between Boulevard Saint-Germain and Boulevard du Montparnasse. On the train down, Martin had made careful study of his newly purchased map of the city. So this was the Left Bank, which he'd pictured full of shaded avenues and outdoor seating areas, the nights star-strewn and spent at smoky little jazz clubs in medieval basements, not unlike the one Cécile/Jean Seberg visits at the end of *Bonjour Tristesse*. Now, it was January and dusk was falling. They were standing at the intersection with Rue de Rennes. The street was lined with dirt-coloured sandstone buildings with wrought-iron balconies. On the ground floors were shops and other businesses. Display windows, neon signs. A brightly lit laundromat. A café here and there, or a bistro. There were no trees, and cars went by at high speed with tyres hissing through the slushy snow. All the vehicles were small and compact. One glance at the pavements was enough to explain why: with two tyres on the kerb and two on the street, the cars were parked cheek by jowl in long rows, bumper to bumper. To the south, the Montparnasse Tower rose up like the monolith in *2001*.

"Right or left?" Gustav said, gesticulating like an irresolute traffic officer. There was nothing but hunger in Per's eyes and he was shivering in his duffel coat. They both looked at Martin, who said right. Unless he was mistaken, that would mean moving north, towards the Seine.

They went into the first brasserie they found. Martin figured they were lucky to have stumbled across that particular one: it was exactly the kind of restaurant he'd imagined would become one of their regular haunts. The floor was chequered, and the wall-mounted bench seats upholstered with dark-red vinyl. The tables and chairs were made of dark wood, as was the panelling. Sphere lamps hung from the ceiling in clusters. Above a long bar with a mirror stood hundreds of bottles and glittering glasses.

"*Messieurs.*" A woman in her forties appeared with a handful of menus. (He would learn her name, Madame Robert or Madame Dorme or whatever it might be, and joke with her like regulars do, and she would tell him all about her unhappy love affair with a harness driver from the horse racing track outside the city. He would show her the letters when his novels were accepted by BLM or Ord & Bild, even though she obviously wouldn't be able to read them.)

They ordered: schnitzel with chips, sausage with lentils, quiche Lorraine. Madame Robert nodded, making a note, then asked something Martin didn't manage to catch. Gustav replied: "A bottle of house wine." Oh. Martin felt his scalp flush. How could he have missed something so basic?

After dinner, Gustav wanted them to find some kind of bar – Frederikke had shared a few tips, he had the addresses written down somewhere, he searched his many pockets for the piece of paper – but Martin yawned so wide his jaw cracked.

"I think I'd rather just go to bed," he said. His body was still sore after the long train journey, and the past few days were rattling around his head in a tangled jumble. Cecilia had gone with him to the station. She'd been subdued and pale, had looked away but hadn't wanted to let go when he kissed her goodbye. She was probably coming down with something, maybe flu. They'd had a four-hour wait for the Paris train in Copenhagen, so they'd gone for a few pints with Frederikke in a bar near the station. In the end, they'd had to leg it, fairly tipsy even though it was only five o'clock, hauling all their luggage, and only just made it before the doors closed. They hadn't bothered to book a sleeper car, nor, as it turned out, the fastest train. For two days, they were regularly woken up by brusque men who barged in yelling: "Passport!" every time they dozed off.

Snow began to fall as they walked back. Tiny, hard flakes that blew in under their collars and up their coat sleeves.

The next morning Martin woke up with chattering teeth. The only bedding they'd found were three threadbare blankets you used with single sheets underneath. Gustav was used to it; over on the camp bed, a thin foot clad in a woollen sock stuck out from under his blanket. And Per, in the spirit of always being prepared, had brought a sleeping bag.

Without waking the others, Martin pulled on his freezing jeans and woollen jumper. He did a series of jumping jacks to regain full mobility, put on his shoes and coat and left the flat. He was worried about bumping into one of the neighbours, who would be bound to wonder what he was doing there and demand answers he would be unable to formulate, but, thankfully, the stairwell was deserted.

Rue de Rennes was, if possible, even greyer in daylight, but at least there were some people moving about now. He walked until he found a café with *petit déjeuner* written on a blackboard outside. The place was eerily reminiscent of the restaurant from the night before.

When he ordered, the words felt unfamiliar in his mouth. He stumbled over things as basic as *je voudrais*.

While Martin waited, he lit a cigarette, even though he normally never smoked before breakfast. Out of his coat pocket, he pulled an unused notepad and printed *Paris 1986* on the first page. And as he looked out at the street, with its endless stream of cars and buses, people hurrying along the pavements, overflowing bins outside the buildings, and bare trees; as two women stepped through the door, speaking a language of which he only understood snippets; as the waiter set down a greyish café au lait in front of him – he could feel the words moving deep within him. Readying themselves.

But when he put pen to paper, he couldn't think of a single thing to write.

Every morning at half past seven, Per's alarm went off. Gustav resented being woken up by what he'd taken to calling "the death knell", but didn't dare say anything to Per. When it came down to it, moreover, he actually had no problem cocooning himself in his blankets and going back to sleep. Martin, on the other hand, went through the many painful stages of waking up while Per fussed about as quietly as he could and then closed the door behind him at exactly ten past eight. Per always had breakfast on his way to class. He claimed these breakfasts-on-the-go, in the form of a warm croissant and a small espresso, made him feel like a "proper Parisian", but Martin suspected it had as much to do with thoughtfulness. After years in the studio in Masthugget, the commune on Kaptensgatan and the Valand dormitories, Martin and Gustav were used to sharing small spaces with other people. Per had always lived by himself. He picked up his dirty clothes, bought more juice when he drank the last of it, turned the lights off if someone else wanted to sleep.

After Per's footsteps faded away on the stairs, Martin waged a war with his eyelids. It was the hardest part of the day because his bed was warm and the flat freezing cold. The windows didn't seem to be insulated at all. The small heater had no measurable effect. Martin had made a habit of sleeping in long johns, woollen socks and a flannel shirt, and removing these sleep-warmed garments required a special kind of discipline. For the first time ever, he wished he'd done military service.

Then he had to make breakfast to coax Gustav out of bed. So Martin pulled on his boots, coat, scarf and hat and went to the bakery down the street. In there, condensation trickled down the wall mirrors, and if there was a long line, he was inevitably perspiring heavily by the time he put in his order. The feeling of calling out "*une baguette s'il vous plaît*" and tossing a few francs on the counter was, on the other hand, sublimely Parisian. Sometimes he bought *Le Monde* on the way home, too.

Back in the flat, he made coffee and set the table. Gustav grunted and complained, but in the end he always heaved himself off his camp bed, wrapped his robe over his long johns and thudded onto a chair, his hair wild and his glasses askew.

"The elixir of life," he mumbled when Martin handed him a cup of coffee.

Once he'd roused himself sufficiently, he grabbed his art supplies and a foldable stool and went to one of the museums to study. As far as Martin knew, the hours he spent copying other people's portraits to, as he put it, "learn a little something about composition and proportion" weren't part of any assignment, just something he did of his own volition. As a recipient of an art grant, he didn't have to pay admission. He spent most of his time at the Musée d'Orsay ("with Monet and the gang"), but also at the Louvre ("there's something mesmerising about Americans who fall into a trance when they see the *Mona Lisa*") and Centre Pompidou ("that psychotic building"). For a while, he was fascinated with the "Dutchmen" and went on and on about his vision of painting Cecilia against a chocolate-black backdrop, with a white shirt collar and the solemnity of a seventeenth-century portrait. During their first months in Paris, he went to the museums every Tuesday, Wednesday and Thursday, from eleven to three. He was on a first-name basis with the guards, who turned a blind eye when he sold his sketches to the tourists looking over his shoulder while he worked. Gustav had no difficulty parting with his reproductions, and he didn't mind working on commission. An enthusiastic American might pay him as much as 500 francs for a hastily drawn *Olympia*. They went to Closerie des Lilas, and Martin tried goose liver for the first time.

Per quickly became proficient in French, but he spoke it with a heavy accent. Martin's pronunciation was flawless, but since he rarely spoke, no one knew. Even after watching everything by Truffaut and Godard, he wasn't prepared for the way people spoke. He felt like a learner driver who'd been sent onto the motorway for his second lesson. Nor had he realised how quickly other people would grow impatient when he searched for the right word and was unable to find anything but the most basic, most banal building blocks of the language. And even though he managed to get through most everyday conversations without too many major faux pas – ordering, making small talk with the Madame in the café, making small talk with the Madame at *le tabac*, buying vegetables at the market that occasionally popped up on their street, introducing himself, and very superficially discussing the state of the world with Per's Sorbonne friends – discussing Wittgenstein or Wallace was a different matter altogether. The clunkiness of his sentences short-circuited his intellect. Unfamiliar, clumsy words jostled for space in his mouth. The sounds warped and didn't come out right. He couldn't just say whatever came to mind, he had to translate the sentence from Swedish first. All the nuances and ambiguities were lost. It was a relief when he managed to convey the gist of something, order a bottle of wine, or ask where the nearest laundromat could be found.

And yet, Martin could list all the forms of the irregular verbs, even the subjunctive. His high-school French teacher hadn't been able to hide the fact that he was her favourite student in an otherwise hopeless class. But showing off his conversational skills in front of a group of weary high-school students was one thing, getting around Paris with his dignity intact was quite another.

"It might have been easier if anyone was ever even a little bit fucking encouraging," Martin muttered.

"*Bien sûr,*" Per replied.

Martin hadn't been prepared for being treated like a *connard* every time he happened to mispronounce something, and my god, surely it wasn't the end of the world if he accidentally used the second person singular instead of the second person plural form of a verb? He'd watched tons of French film at Cinemateket while the French dubbed everything. He'd been working on his grammar and pronunciation for years. And the French? The French only spoke French. The French thought Johnny Hallyday was bigger than Springsteen.

He could get used to the greengrocers taking offence when he couldn't remember the word for cauliflower (*chou-fleur*). It was worse that he felt stupid every time he tried to read anything more advanced than the paper. Martin read his Swedish copy of *L'Existentialisme est un humanisme* in parallel with the French one to try to gain some sort of philosophical traction. He bought books by Genet and Camus in cream-coloured Gallimard editions and read them with a dictionary and glossary, but it took an eternity to get through just one page. He searched for sentences he could parse and clung to them while he searched for toeholds for the next step, discovered there were none to be had, and had to look up two long words and repeat the sentence to himself, and translate it to Swedish, before finally feeling that it was comprehensible.

He'd pictured himself strolling along the river, rummaging through the bookstands. Martin sighed, tossed Sartre aside more aggressively than he'd intended, lit a cigarette – he was smoking about three times as much as he had in Gothenburg – and checked the time. It was five already. High time to open a bottle of wine.

Martin's first writing effort was to move a rickety but perfectly serviceable little table over to the window at the far end of the room and on said table arrange his typewriter, an ashtray, a stack of blank sheets of paper, his notepads, sharpened pencils and red and blue ballpoint pens. But he had so much to do during the first few weeks after they arrived that he didn't manage to write much. Going to the bank, for example, took several days. Their rent was payable by cheque, and in order to acquire a chequebook you needed a bank account. And so, they walked into the nearest Banque de France branch. But Monsieur wasn't allowed to open a bank account unless Monsieur had a permanent address. No, staying at the address in question was not sufficient, Monsieur also needed a contract to verify his residence. (Then followed several weeks of intense correspondence with Per's cousin, while they slowly ran out of cash.) No, Monsieur von Becker was not allowed to open a bank account under the name *Gustav* since the name listed first in his passport was Bengt. It made no difference that Gustav assured him Gustav was his actual *prénom*, because in France (the bank teller informed him with exaggerated enunciation, as though he were speaking to an *imbécile*) one's first name was the one listed first in one's passport. Consequently, Gustav was given an account and a cheque-book in the name of Bengt von Becker – his father's and grandfather's name – while Martin and Per, who had chosen to order their names in a manner acceptable to the French, were allowed to keep theirs. They really only needed one chequebook to pay their rent and electricity, but the bank teller was completely confounded by this notion. In France, *everyone* had a chequebook, he announced, before asking them to come back in a week's time. When they did, he solemnly presented them with three brand-new chequebooks, and Martin didn't have it in him to point out that the *a* in his middle name had mysteriously been changed to an *e*.

They all agreed they needed to live frugally. Gustav had, in a fit of self-preservation, asked his mother to divide his grant into several smaller instalments. Per received his student loan money every month, but Martin, who was in charge of all of his money and had never before had so much cash on hand, paradoxically became hyper-aware of every little expense. It wouldn't do to eat out all the time, he decided. (The others nodded meekly.) They had to avoid unnecessary costs. ("Just think how much we save on wine, what with it being so cheap," Gustav put in.) For a while, Martin really committed to the spartan lifestyle: he boiled lentils, read Stig Claesson's Paris book in which everyone was hungry and poor, used coffee grounds more than once, and walked past the meat counter at Monoprix with his head held high.

Over time, however, his uncompromising frugality relaxed into what Martin termed "the dialectic of prudence". It consisted of oscillating between feeling penniless and economically limitless, but on a scale adapted to their circumstances. In other words: you went to a restaurant that wasn't the cheap local, you didn't buy the absolute cheapest wine, you paid to get into some jazz or night club instead of taking the metro twelve stops to one of Per's Sorbonne friends, where you crammed into a tiny flat with a bunch of exchange students who were doggedly getting drunk on awful red wine. Then, later, as a rule while hungover, the guilt of such irresponsible behaviour would stir, at least in him and Per. So they made a renewed effort to live cheaply for a few days. Cooked in the kitchenette, which had seemingly been designed for pygmies, and spent the night in. After a few days of thrift – three or four – the restraint shown seemed to call for a reward. And mussels and white wine were delicious, after all, and you couldn't just sit at home forever.

He was always asked: "So, Martin," (pronounced with a nasal French *a*, with a heavy English *ah*, with a half-swallowed Danish *i*), "what are you doing in Paris?"

And every time, he replied: "I'm writing."

"What are you writing, then?" was the obvious follow-up, and at that point things got less straightforward. "Short stories," he said sometimes. He had a pile of disjointed notes that might easily turn into a collection of short stories. Most of the time, though, he leaned towards putting it all into a novel, so then he said he was writing a novel. Novel sounded better.

Just to be on the safe side, he'd brought along the manuscript he'd been working on for several years. The truth was that "manuscript" was an optimistic descriptor. "Notes" would have been more accurate. There was no real plot and no turning point to speak of. In his notebook, he wrote: "PERIPETEIA!!!" But what? He'd had an idea that the turning point would consist of a trip to Paris, but now that he was here, that felt vaguely unappealing. The book was the work of a young man. Immature. Good in places (brilliant, Gustav claimed), but far too uneven. Editing it would be a waste of time.

While he waited for his next idea to present itself, Martin performed what he considered pre-writing. He had long, wine-soaked discussions about the "organically unfolding narrative" versus the "intellectually constructed narrative" with various people. He wandered the streets and jotted things down in his notebook with fingers stiff from cold. He walked to the address where William Wallace had once resided. (It was a bland little dead end, and the only sign of Wallace's existence was a plaque that informed passers-by that British author William Wallace had lived and worked in this building 1918–1938.) He went to Café de Flore, where the coffee was expensive and the staff rude, and filled several pages with a detailed description of its interior: the cream-white china, the waiters in bow ties, black waistcoats and long white aprons – always so many waiters, as though they were in a Soviet republic.

But he spent most of his time at home, alone, trapped by the unique gravitational pull of the typewriter. Martin would hover around it for a while. Do dishes. Make coffee. He'd read *Les Inrockuptibles*. He'd write down words he didn't know from an article about the Smiths and look them up in the dictionary. He'd make his bed. In the end, though, the moment when he had to sit down at his desk couldn't be postponed any longer.

Every keystroke echoed around the room, and silence swelled in the pauses between words. He lit a cigarette and counted them up. But it didn't matter how many he'd written if they weren't any good. And how was he supposed to know if they were good? A paragraph could seem good one day and substandard the next, and a draft he didn't care much for at the time of writing came off as clear and well wrought when he found it at the bottom of the stack a few weeks later. Everyone said to trust your judgment, but Martin's judgment was like a broken compass that pointed with equal confidence to the north and the south in turn. (He wrote that down in his notebook.) He tentatively gave Per and Gustav drafts to read. He brought his stack of papers to the Sorbonne library, hoping the grand surroundings would somehow induce him to create.

Then he wrote *The Chameleons* in a single afternoon.

From the first sentence of the story to the last, it was the result of a state of mind Martin couldn't describe as anything but inspired. They'd been out the night before, and he didn't wake up until almost noon. He stayed in bed, with his eyes closed and his head heavy on his pillow after the previous evening's sampling of the Parisian nightlife. He tried to orient himself in time and space. It was Thursday. The day stretched out before him, completely flat, devoid of obstacles. No times to keep, nothing.

When he got out of bed, he had sleep lines across his chest. His body felt leaden, and he'd grown patchy stubble that unfortunately didn't make him look like a gaunt writer who spent his nights by his typewriter, dressed in a mesh vest, with only a bottle of whisky for company.

Martin made coffee and shaved, and while standing in front of the round mirror with no thoughts of anything but the movements of the razor, the first sentence came to him, like a sparrow appearing out of nowhere, perching on his windowsill and fixing him with its small, peppercorn eyes: *There was a photograph of my father and Marianne that became fairly famous.*

He walked the few steps over to his desk, where he hurriedly scribbled the words down on the first scrap of paper he found. With mounting anticipation, he finished shaving, poured himself a cup of coffee and sat down in front of the typewriter.

He raised his eyes to the rooftops, to the white sky. He continued with the first sentence that came to mind.

Twilight had crept into the room by the time he reached the end, and he could barely make out the text. Martin pulled the seventh and final paper out of the roller and made a neat stack. He was too scared to read it through. That's when he realised the story should be called *The Chameleons*. He liked to think up witty, clever titles in advance, writing them down and waiting for the story to follow. But *The Chameleons* was just there, as though he hadn't come up with it himself. As though he'd just reached out and found it.

III

INTERVIEWER: Tell me a bit about your method.

MARTIN BERG: When it comes down to it, it's all about not giving up. There will be all kinds of setbacks. Bad reviews. Readers who don't get it. Periods when writing's hard. Those kinds of things are enough to make a normal person think "enough already". Which is a perfectly valid reaction.

INTERVIEWER: So how do you deal with that, then?

MARTIN BERG: You carry on. That was one of the things I learned in Paris. I mean, it wasn't always easy. I can't say it was. It was inspiring, eighty or ninety per cent of the time, but it wasn't always easy.

*

Martin wrote a long letter to Cecilia on their second night in Paris, while drinking red wine and trying to make his cigarette dangle from between his lips like Camus. He described, as elegantly as he was able, the journey, their street and their new Parisian life, which while still nascent surrounded them like a whispered promise. His typewriter clattered continually, and the text grew unimpeded on the page.

Their flat had no phone line, which was just as well since the cost of international calls was outrageous. He could make the occasional call from a payphone, but he had to make sure he had enough change and that he was calling at a time when Cecilia would be in. Consequently, Martin purchased airmail envelopes, long rectangles with edges striped in red and blue, and sheets of stamps at *le tabac*. He'd always pictured himself as one half of an epic correspondence. He always made sure to put Cecilia's letters back into their envelopes after reading them and kept them in a shoebox under his bed.

At first, he wrote two to four letters a week. Her replies arrived promptly – often crossing paths with his – and he felt a rush of joy whenever he opened their letterbox in the lobby and saw her handwriting on one of the envelopes.

He wrote that he missed her, but that wasn't entirely true.

Granted, he wouldn't have minded having her there. If they'd had a little flat of their own somewhere. If she'd been studying at the Sorbonne. (She would have fit in nicely at the Sorbonne – in the old library, dressed in slacks and a black turtleneck, her blonde head bent over a biography of Sartre.) But as it was, they were three friends in Paris. If Cecilia had come with them, they would have been three friends and Cecilia in Paris, and that wasn't the same at all. He and Gustav wouldn't be walking home along the empty streets of Montparnasse as the first light of the rising sun enveloped the tops of the buildings in a golden glow. They wouldn't be stopping by a bakery to buy steaming fresh croissants at half three in the morning. They wouldn't be taking a detour, even though their eyes ached with lack of sleep, just so they could see the Luxembourg Gardens at dawn.

"Right?" Martin said to Gustav, who was walking next to him, his coat open, because spring was in the air. "It wouldn't have been *the same*."

They climbed the fence and sat down on a bench. The park was deserted. Vast lawns shimmered with dew. In the flowerbeds, budding tulips bent their heads as if in prayer; the trees had taken on a cautious hint of green, and all the windows of the palace reflected the pale, opalescent sky. Martin lit a cigarette. No, if Cecilia had been with him, he would have been snuggled up in a warm bed, and would have seen no reason why he shouldn't be snuggled up in a warm bed.

"Besides, how is it even possible to miss someone when you're in Paris?" he added.

"And she'll be coming to visit soon anyway," Gustav said.

"Soon? It's only March."

"Time flies."

"Are you going to eat that croissant, or what?" Martin said.

*

One evening, they went to a bar that (according to Per) was supposed to be frequented by artists and writers, but which turned out to be an ordinary bar with ordinary patrons in regular, boring clothes, who probably weren't having a single interesting discussion between them.

"Are you sure this is the right place?"

"It's the right address," Per replied.

"Let's just have a drink," Gustav said.

Martin looked around while Per tried to catch the attention of a waiter so they could order. No raucous bohemian groups. No venal, fatal women in tattered sequins. No sharp eyes darting through the din, observing, taking in, already processing material, kneading sensory impressions into words and sentences, leaving them to prove and grow overnight until they were, so to speak, ready to be baked…

Martin took his notebook out of his pocket. *Kneading sensory impressions into words*, he wrote, *proving, baking.* Was it good imagery or not? It made him want to eat a baguette.

To compensate for the lack of close contact with the French artistic world, they imbibed copious amounts of alcohol. They made new friends in the form of three Germans with whom they bonded over their shared exile. The girl was reasonably pretty and seemed to like Per, and Per made everyone laugh as usual, beaming like the sun, face flushed in an attractive sort of way. Gustav, on the other hand, was quiet and closed-off, mutely chugging wine before going home, claiming he had to get to the museum early the next day.

When Martin needed the toilet, someone was already in it, and after waiting five minutes, he went outside to find a suitable doorway or alley. The street was well lit and he had not yet attained full unperturbedness, so he walked for a while until he found a small park shrouded in reassuring darkness. He pissed on a tree and then turned back. The problem was, he didn't quite know where to go. He walked back along the street, turned, didn't recognise anything, but carried on a bit further anyway, looking for the bar. The bar, the bar. The bloody bar was too bloody bland to be located. Had there been an awning? A few rickety tables with a few rangy women outside? No idea. He checked his pockets and found a packet of cigarettes.

Then he suddenly remembered Per. Per! But Per was with the German girl. Per would be fine. In fact, Per would probably have a better shot without Martin. And now Martin was *tout seul* on this French boulevard, which must have been walked by one or two intellectuals with their hands in their pockets and their thoughts on matters far beyond this paltry, superficial world with its silent facades and brusque streets, but what did that matter (at this point Martin managed to light a match and then his cigarette while glaring challengingly at a small section of Rue du Jardinet) when the slender, sleepy Cecilia

Wikner was in a different country, a different bed, and – this was a thought that hadn't actually struck Martin until that moment, but now really *struck* him – possibly in that bed with someone else. Who wasn't him! Then what did it matter that Martin walked about, okay, fine, staggered about here in the company of a hundred years of authors' ghosts when Cecilia Wikner's silky-smooth neck was over a thousand miles away? What did Paris, whose streets branched out from Martin like spokes from a hub, have to give him when Cecilia wasn't standing on one of those streets, map in one hand and a drunken late-night crêpe in the other?

Martin found himself in front of a payphone, which he could only take as a sign from the universe. He dug through his pockets in search of change and had to focus hard to dial.

"Hello?" Cecilia said hoarsely after seven rings.

"It's me!" Martin said. How amazing it was to hear her voice! "It's so amazing to hear your voice!"

"Martin! Do you know what time it is?"

"*Mais oui, ma chère* – hey, you're alone, right?"

"Of course I'm alone. Are you drunk?"

"Possibly, or probably, yes, come to think of it – but let's not talk about that, that's just par for the course, nothing's happening here, nothing at all, what are *you* doing?"

"Well, I was sleeping, since it's half past two…"

There was a hint of amused scepticism in her voice. Martin launched into an explanation of a theory he'd just come up with (in part encouraged by the fact that Cecilia was sleeping alone), the gist of which was that he and she had something qualitatively different from what most couples had. "Something that makes us, well, that binds us together. *Dans la façon de* Jean-Paul Sartre and Simone de Beauvoir," Martin said.

"I suppose I'm Simone."

"It doesn't matter who's who! What matters is that—" But at this point the phone swallowed Martin's last franc and Cecilia's voice was replaced by a dial tone. Martin had already forgotten what it was that really mattered; he hung up, suddenly feeling more at peace. Cecilia,

Cecilia, sleeping, alone in a bed in Gothenburg. He set his course for home, buoyed by newfound confidence. It took a while because he spent the first ten minutes walking in the wrong direction.

*

At first, just walking the streets was enough. It was as though it didn't matter what he wrote; so long as it was framed by the *rues* and *boulevards*, it seemed successful. After writing *The Chameleons*, he had a strong feeling of being on the right track. He gave himself a few days off from writing, reckoning it would stimulate his creativity.

Instead, he set out to explore the city. With *L'Existentialisme est un humanisme* in his pocket, he wandered through the neighbourhoods Sartre had wandered through not ten years before. He read Henry Miller in a café in Clichy, where Miller himself could easily have sat once. He made a list of every Paris address mentioned in Wallace's *Patagonia Days* and marked them with little Xs on his map. Montmartre was full of American tourists and in the Jewish quarter, where Bill Bradley had rented a room close to Place Renée Vivien, he couldn't shake the thought that everyone he passed was a homosexual. Not that there was anything wrong with that, but he shoved his hands into his pockets and stared at the ground all the same, and when he was stopped by a bloke his own age holding an unlit cigarette and asking for a light, he just mumbled *Non, désolé*.

But when Martin tried to resume writing, he found he was completely stuck.

He spent an hour and a half on a letter to Cecilia and then tried again. The result was three hundred words that had nothing to do with anything. He gave up and left the flat.

It was the same story day after day.

"I've lost it," he sighed to Per, who was home, trying on clothes he'd bought at a flea market.

"How is that possible? I recall you saying you had it just last Thursday."

"That was *then*."

Per enjoyed playing the part of Stable Friend of Struggling Artists and gave him a short pep talk while he changed out of one paisley shirt and into another. Martin listlessly hacked at strands of hair that had grown too long with his nail clippers over the sink.

"Remember how many times you've said that," Per said. "And think about how many times it's come back to you."

"Maybe I don't have it. Maybe I just thought I did."

"What is 'it', anyway?" Per asked.

"Talent, I suppose. Skill. Inspiration."

"But you always say inspiration is a myth and that the only thing that matters is hard work. 'Like digging a hole', I believe is how you put it. 'You just have to keep digging.'"

Martin felt comforted for a brief moment, but then a deep suspicion shook him.

"But maybe that's just something I say to save face," he said. "Because I *don't have any talent*." He underlined each word by snipping the air with the clippers. "So I brandish my only weapon: the shovel. Hard work. Elbow grease. But what good is any of that if everything you write is rubbish? If the only thing you create is a pile of manure?"

"You don't write rubbish."

"How do you know?"

"Because I read it."

"But you're my friend. You're biased."

"Martin, listen to me. *You're a good writer*. I always thought so. But if you want me to keep thinking that, you have to write something I can read and have an opinion on."

Martin decided not to shave. Had Hemingway shaved on days like these? Had Joyce? (Had Joyce even had days like these?) Strindberg? Wallace? They'd probably knocked back a glass of absinthe (*l'absinthe*) or possibly whisky (*on the rocks, please*). But drinking before three o'clock invariably made Martin sluggish.

It wasn't, he thought to himself as he inserted a new sheet of paper into the roller as slowly as humanly possible, that he minded hard work. He was happy to do endless rewrites. He'd read that Hemingway rewrote *The Sun Also Rises* thirty-nine times. It was understandable: he wanted it to be as good as it could be. The question was how a person was supposed to endure the eighteenth, twenty-third or thirty-first time they revised a text and still didn't get it right. Martin let his fingers rest lightly on the keyboard, like a pianist before beginning a concerto. How could a person live knowing they were good but thinking everything they did was bad? How could a person bear to write another short story when they'd just written a really good one? How could a person bear to write at all, come to think of it? There were so many good books. Did he honestly believe he had something to add? Was there anything he could write about that hadn't already been written about by someone else, someone much better?

A key rattled in the lock. Gustav entered.

"How's it going?" He tossed his coat on the nearest chair.

"Horribly."

"I take it you're having a bad day."

"What if I'm having a bad *year*? Or what if I just *am* bad?"

"Of course you're not bad. Look what I purchased from our lovely little *supermarché*." He held up a bag that looked like it might contain a bottle.

"I should be writing…"

"It's after five, you're in the clear."

"I won't write anything if we open that."

"You're not going to be able to anyway, though. Right? You're just going to sit there and type out twenty words that you immediately cross out with that aggressive red pen of yours. Does that make anyone any happier? *Pas du tout*. I'd say your best chance at regaining some hope for this life can be found inside this" – the cork went *plop* – "delightful little fellow."

Would Wallace have said no? Would Hemingway?

While Gustav found glasses and wiped them passably clean, he told Martin about a place where one of Per's Sorbonne friends claimed Serge Gainsbourg always hung out with his new girlfriend, "a virtually underaged Asian". Wouldn't that be something, partying with Gainsbourg? Right? "Come on. You can't just sit around the flat."

"I don't know…"

"Plenty of material for your book," Gustav said, and that settled it.

*

He'd thought he was leaving Sweden for warmer climes, but the first few months, snowed-in cars lined the streets, people were urged to stay off the motorways, pipes burst in the cold, the shops ran out of space heaters. "What is the world coming to?" said the Madame at *le tabac*, shaking her head. "*C'est comme la guerre.*"

And it did feel like a storm was brewing beyond the horizon. In February, a terrorist group carried out three bombings in as many days. One of them was in a bookshop by Place Saint-Michel, not far from their part of town. Martin called home from the payphone on the corner, shiveringly assuring his family he was okay. Gustav didn't see any need to call his parents, but he did contact his grandmother. For several days, they waited for the next attack, claiming to be staying in on account of the frigid temperatures. Martin read *Le Monde* with a dictionary to try to work out what it was all about.

"They're Lebanese," he said. "The CSPPA. Comité de Soutien avec les Prisonniers Politiques et Arabes et du Moyen-Orient. Which is a properly awful name for a terrorist organisation."

"Agreed. And what about the Moyen-Orient?" Per said. "They left that out of the acronym."

"Well, CSPPAMO just doesn't have the same ring to it as CSPPA."

"*We're the People's Front of Judea,*" Gustav quoted Monty Python.

Then Palme was shot. Martin saw the headlines and a strange feeling of unreality trickled down his spine. Even his mother sounded shaken when he spoke to her on the phone.

Even though the bookshop on Place Saint-Michel was a place Martin could theoretically have found himself, Hezbollah and its incomprehensible affiliate organisation that was fighting to free some

320

political prisoners someplace seemed a distant concern. Palme was Palme. Martin couldn't remember a time *without* Palme.

"They think it might have been the PLO," Per, who kept more abreast of the news than the other two, said.

The snow melted and the air grew milder. In the parks, the soil in the flower beds was black and moist. The Seine sparkled like green glass in the sunshine. Doors were thrown open, outdoor seating areas popped up everywhere. Martin put away his woollen sweater and wore nothing but a shirt under his coat; before long, he swapped the coat for a jacket. One day, he had to take a longer route back home because Boulevard Raspail was packed with people. He asked a passer-by if it was a demonstration of some kind and was told it was de Beauvoir's funeral procession. Martin had never read de Beauvoir, but the Paris he would have wanted to visit the most was her Paris: Paris in the fifties and sixties, when philosophers, not tourists, drank coffee at Café de Flore, when the clubs played jazz, not American pop, when the world was still moving forward.

A few weeks later, there was a nuclear meltdown in Chernobyl and radioactive winds blew across Europe. Radioactive fallout was reported and Cecilia, who usually approached the news as though it were all just material for future history books, sounded despondent in her letters. The government had just decided to update Sweden's nuclear power plants, she wrote, so what was the point of wearing a no-to-nuclear-power badge on your jacket any more?

All in all, there was a palpable feeling the world was going straight to hell in a handcart.

"It's not that bad, is it?" Per said. "Think of all the good things."

"If a Hezbollah bomb or nuclear war doesn't kill you, you get to enjoy a more drawn-out death from Chernobyl cancer, is that the kind of perspective you're referring to?" Gustav said. "Or from all the oxygen being sucked out though the hole in the ozone layer?"

"Oxygen is not escaping through the hole in the ozone layer. It might give you skin cancer, though."

"Fine, so you die of cancer."

"The cancer won't necessarily *kill* you. It can be cured. They've made a lot of scientific progress in that area."

But not even Per's optimism could survive HIV. One day, he came home in time for breakfast, pale and with dark circles under his eyes.

"The conquering hero returns," Gustav said, handing him a cup of coffee. Only then did Martin realise Per had been out all night.

"Looks like you had a rough night," he said. "But maybe in a good way?"

"I had sex," Per hissed.

"Congratulations."

"*Unprotected,*" Per added.

"Oh."

"I need to get tested."

"I'm sure you're fine," Gustav said. "But maybe you'd like a little glass of wine? There's whisky, too, I think, and vodka…"

"I should be able to go to a hospital or something, right?" Per's voice cracked. "Why don't they teach you this in school? I don't give a shit about how to ask for directions to the nearest post office. What would have been helpful is knowing how to say 'Where do I go to in this town to find out if I have AIDS?' Am I right? 'I slept with a dodgy girl from Bath, England, and now I think I might be the latest victim of a lethal fucking epidemic.'"

"Calm down," Martin said. "You're going to be fine."

"How could you possibly know that? She could have slept with anyone. She slept with *me*, even though I was utterly hammered and originally trying it on with her friend."

"There's almost no risk of transmission…"

"Dear Father in Heaven, I promise never to have sex again."

One night, they went to a party thrown by a friend of someone Per knew from the Sorbonne. This friend was supposedly a photographer, but it was unclear what he really did, since his artistic integrity was so strong he never showed his pictures to anyone. (In fact, it seemed so strong he rarely even took any pictures.) He had nervous eyes and a smile that lit up and winked out like a child playing with a light switch. On, off, on, off, on, off. They put their bottles of wine down on a table and found a couple of glasses and a handful of people they knew. Martin was at a party in a raucous Paris flat and was suddenly overcome with the vibrating feeling of reality and fantasy merging.

He was so engrossed by this feeling he barely listened to Per's friend, who was talking about an existential crime novel set in New York that he'd just finished reading.

When did he notice her? Hard to say. But awareness of her presence came via a nebulous feeling of guilt.

The brunette in the red top had arrived undramatically with a bottle of wine in one hand, kissing their host on the cheeks before moving off to talk to some people. Martin noticed he found it difficult to take his eyes off her.

He wished he could have told himself it was because she was extraordinarily beautiful. A rare, Catherine-Deneuvean beauty. Someone who drew the eyes of everyone around her according to the flame–moth principle, whether those eyes belonged to men or women, regardless of sexual preference, irrespective of everything. That would have made the whole thing understandable and justifiable. Then, he would have been able to file the episode away under the header STUNNING FRENCH WOMEN I SAW ONCE. But Diane – he obviously didn't know that was her name, not yet – Diane was no Deneuve. She was cute, absolutely. Attractive. But nothing about her really explained the kind of ogling Martin was unable to keep himself from.

Luckily, Gustav wanted to leave. There was a club somewhere, a taxi was waiting. They said goodbye and hurried down the stairs.

And the door to the building slammed shut behind them.

15

ON THE MORNING of the second of May, Rakel woke up with the memory of a story her mother had once told her echoing in her head. She remembered it with sharp clarity, even though she couldn't have been more than seven or eight when she heard it. As a teenager, she'd written it down in a notebook intended for reminiscences and fragments related to her mother.

The story took place when Cecilia was fifteen and had joined her father, the surgeon, on one of his excursions to a field hospital in a poor rural area outside Addis Ababa. Dr Wikner felt it was beneficial for his children to come into contact with Reality, as he put it, and the reality of the capital wasn't enough, it also had to be experienced in its countryside version.

They left Addis at four in the morning. It was pitch-black outside, and a crescent moon hung bowl-shaped over the mountain ridge in the east. Soon, the dogs would begin to bark, and the plaintive cries of the mullahs would ring out across the city – it was the inescapable accompaniment of dawn – and Cecilia sat yawning in her corner of the jeep with a blanket over her to keep off the chill. Their driver was tired. The midwife was tired. Dr Wikner, on the other hand, was on fine form. While they drove through the city, he gave a lecture in Amharic on the many shortcomings of the Ethiopian healthcare system, with at least one grammatical error per sentence and all plosive consonants smoothed out.

They drove for several hours to finally arrive in a small village. Cecilia assisted with the surgery, dressed in a white coat like everyone else. The woman on the makeshift operating table couldn't have been much older than she was. She was malnourished and when the baby was ready to come out, her pelvis had proved too narrow. Cecilia spoke softly to her about everyday things during the surgery, which was not only calming in itself but also served to redirect her attention. For a white girl to be speaking the local language so fluently was always considered astonishing.

"After we move back to Sweden, you won't be able to experience anything like this," Lars Wikner said afterwards as he hung up his bloodstained coat.

"To Sweden?" Cecilia said.

"We're leaving in June," her father replied. "For Gothenburg."

"But we're coming back, right?"

"Bloody hell, no. I've had enough of this shit."

And that was how Cecilia was informed that she was to leave the place where she had grown up and where her whole life was, to go to a country only her parents called "home".

She said nothing else, just stepped outside. A billowing landscape spread out beyond the edge of the village. Occasional acacia trees, dark-green blots of colour against the dry, yellow ground. The air was fresh and clear, and the thin sunshine held a tentative warmth. In a few months, the rains would hopefully come and then summer proper with its oppressive heat, but, for now, the weather was dry and cool.

Without looking back, Cecilia set off at a run, straight into the wilderness.

Every Tuesday and Saturday, she trained with a running club, of which she had long been one of the least talented members. Her friend Rahel, who also attended the international school, was the best. Dainty and light as a gazelle, she sprinted around the athletic field on feet that barely touched the ground. Rahel's running was her body's sheer joy at being alive. She didn't have to try hard, she had the running inside her the way some people have a singing voice inside them. The same could not be said of Cecilia Wikner in her teens. Cecilia had the makings of a runner – a body built like a Maasai and a large helping of grit – but running didn't come as easily to her as, for example, drawing did. She struggled with stitches and blisters, her muscles ached, her lungs felt like they were on fire, she finished last in short races. No one expected anything else from her since she was a *ferengi*, and the Ethiopians were among the best in the world at running. Abebe Bikila had won Olympic gold medals in the marathon two games in a row, one of them running barefoot, and he'd set a new world record. But Cecilia was at least significantly better than the daughter of the American ambassador, who didn't even try.

That said, there were advantages to being one of the worst. Among the underachievers, you could keep trying without having to prove yourself, which provided a certain level of freedom. Eventually, Cecilia made a habit of going to the athletic field to run every day after school and on the weekends. Simply put, she began to work at it. She had neither the desire nor the ability to be the best. Anyone could see Rahel would always be faster. At the time, Cecilia wouldn't have been able to explain why she ran every day, even though she didn't particularly enjoy it at first. It was only after her long solo run through the hinterland, through the wilderness, that she was able to put it into words. It was about *transcendence*.

There's a fixed point that marks what a human is able endure. Sooner or later, she will collapse. Thirteen-year-old Cecilia, who had just joined the running club, couldn't run very far. Her body could probably have kept going; it was her mind that gave up. A person who hasn't tested the limits of their capacity doesn't know what they can do. That person will back away from achievement, held back by doubt and insecurity. That doubt spreads from the brain to the heart and limbs. It paralyses and makes that person unable to act. Fifteen-year-old Cecilia, on the other hand, had lived through all the stages of running, physical as well as mental. She had gradually run further and further, determined to sort out her running step, her breathing, her rhythm. In the end, she'd been rewarded with the complete merging of body and soul that can occur while running, the feeling that one's entire being is in perfect harmony with itself and the world. She had made two important discoveries: that it's impossible to be unhappy while running and that you can always go just a bit further. It was the very essence of running. The American ambassador's daughter who always moaned and sauntered across the finish line last obviously didn't have to stop running with fifty metres left of an eight-hundred-metre race, but she couldn't stand to be last. And since she always quit halfway, she never experienced what it was like to push yourself, she never pushed beyond the limits of her ability. On the other hand, she also didn't have to experience the humiliation of giving something your all and falling short anyway. A runner had to resign herself to failure in both her heart and her mind. Only a person who gave up everything could win everything. So said the Gospel according to Mark, and so it was for runners, such was the place of a human being in this world. Only a person who had reconciled themselves to their own meaninglessness could hope to transcend it.

When Cecilia set off into the wilderness, she wasn't anxious. She knew she could run for miles at the pace she set. She was wearing flat canvas shoes with rubber soles that were eminently suited to running. She paced herself, going slowly enough that she could keep her breathing calm and even. It was a perfect day for a long run. The Ethiopian Highlands averaged an elevation of around seven thousand feet above sea level, which meant less oxygen in the air; visitors from elsewhere became winded at the slightest exertion, but Cecilia's body had long since adapted its production of red blood cells to the local conditions. So she wasn't worried. If she felt anything, it was a searing red heat was throbbing in her head, and there was a pressure across her chest; she had no words; she didn't know what to say; the only thing in her throat was a scream, and you can't scream in front of a temporary field hospital in a poor rural area, especially not if you're the doctor's daughter.

She had no idea how long it would take them to realise she was gone. Some of the children had seen her leave and timidly pointed out the direction. Dr Wikner lit a cigarillo and said he was sure his daughter would be back by the time they'd had their coffee. The coffee ceremony was performed. The hospital's housekeeper scattered grass across the floor, roasted and ground the coffee beans, made the coffee, and served it to the visitors in small, chipped porcelain cups filled to the brim. The doctor was in no hurry. After the third cup, Tesfaye, the driver, called the children over. When had she left? They looked down at the ground and made no reply; they didn't know.

"She'll be back," Dr Wikner said and began to pack his bag.

The driver, the midwife and the village nurse conferred in low voices. The nurse was deeply concerned. It had been a long time. The girl could be hurt, who knew what might happen to her out there? And had she brought water? The midwife from Addis went inside to speak to the doctor again. He insisted his daughter would be back, that they should wait.

Tesfaye went outside and started the Jeep. He drove for a long time and was thinking about turning back when he finally spotted her red T-shirt like a flickering speck of colour in the distance. When he caught up with her, she was still staggering forwards. He helped her into the front seat and gave her water to drink.

Dr Wikner made no comment. During the drive back to Addis, Cecilia pretended to be asleep. Her body ached as though it had been wrung out like a rag. She wondered how far she'd run. She'd considered turning around many times, but she'd kept going, slower and slower, until her running was little more than a slow shuffle, but always forwards. She didn't know why.

It was incredibly stupid, of course, Cecilia had told her eight-year-old daughter, to take off into the wilderness like that. If she had tripped and hurt herself that might have been it. The nights were freezing. There could have been lions. She strongly cautioned Rakel against doing something similar. But, for better or for worse, Cecilia had learned something about herself, something she wouldn't have been able to learn any other way than through the act itself. That act that transformed her in ways she had no way of comprehending at the time.

A few months later, the Wikners left the country. Her parents and siblings settled into the old house in the countryside – this was before the final move to Stockholm – while Cecilia rented a room in Haga and started upper secondary in the city. Her childhood was over. She had ended it herself.

Rakel stayed in bed for a long time, even though her alarm clock indicated she'd already slept for twelve hours. This time the day before, she'd been reading in the summer house attic. It felt like a different lifetime.

Since the only reasonable thing to do was to get up, she got up. The clear morning sunlight really brought out the grime on the windows. Thick ropes of dust clung to the walls. The pile of photographs she'd dumped out the night before still lay scattered on the living room floor.

Rakel emptied a soured coffee filter into the overflowing compost bin, cleaned a frying pan and mixed the last two eggs in the fridge with a dash of milk that was two days past its expiration date but didn't smell funny. She couldn't bring herself to read the paper. She ate sitting on the only one of the four kitchen chairs that wasn't stacked high with old newspapers and books, staring at her wilting plants. The cuttings Lovisa had given her remained scrawny and stunted even though she'd followed the care instructions. It didn't seem to make any difference whether she watered them or not, pinched off the dead leaves or left them on. The problem was that they neither grew nor died. If they'd died, she could have given up on any attempt at cultivating things with a clean conscience: she'd done what she could, but had, sadly, fallen short. As it was, her plants were in a state of atrophic existence that was neither life nor death, as though unable to pick a side. Death meant death. Living meant enduring the trials and demands of growing.

Rakel downed the last of her coffee and went to find a plastic carrier bag. You weren't supposed to throw potting soil in the compost bin. It seemed counter-intuitive, but the printed information on the compost bags was very clear: no cigarette butts, no nappies, no soil. She emptied all the flowerpots into a bag, not caring that soil scattered all over the floor – she needed to vacuum anyway. Then she collected the rubbish off the kitchen counter and table. She tied up the bag and set it down by the front door. In her closet, she found a couple of blue Ikea bags and filled them with every newspaper she could find except the current one. When she had finished collecting rubbish, she lugged everything down to the recycling station on the street outside. It was a chilly morning, the air oxygen-rich and clear.

Then Rakel tackled the washing-up, wiped down all the surfaces, took all the expired food out of the fridge, pulled out the vacuum cleaner for what was probably the first time in a month, or possibly even two. She was sweating underneath her flannel shirt. Moving on to the other rooms, she threw away old papers, cleared off the coffee table, vacuumed the sofa, gathered up shirts and sheets and underwear, carried it all down to the laundry room – she was really out of shape – and ran back up the stairs three steps at a time. She shook out her duvet from the balcony, had a coughing fit dusting, and found an old pizza box under the sofa. She cleaned every last window.

By lunchtime, her body was shaking from the exertion, and she staggered over to the Thai place on the corner. After eating chicken with rice noodles out of a cardboard box, she set to beating her rugs in the courtyard.

It was afternoon by the time Rakel stopped. While cleaning, her actions had been dictated by the logic of cleaning; one concrete task led to another concrete task. Now, she was overcome with emptiness. For a while, she fended it off by showering and washing her hair – she felt as dusty and sticky as the flat had been – but the moment she had done that, it crept back in. Disoriented, she walked from room to room. She'd cleared old PowerPoint printouts and lecture notes off her desk. The only thing on it now was Cecilia's old Olivetti with its long since dried-up ink ribbon. Rakel pushed it aside to make room for *Ein Jahr* and her notebook.

She was, she thought to herself, in a Schrödinger's cat situation.

It was a concept her father referenced sometimes, probably without really knowing what he was talking about since it was taken from the world of physics. If Rakel remembered correctly from science class, Schrödinger's cat was in the precarious situation that it could simultaneously be considered living and dead, according to the laws of quantum mechanics. Schrödinger had been a physicist, not a philosopher;

his thought experiment about the cat was intended to shine a light on the shortcomings of quantum theory, not to explicate a human mental state. And in a way, Rakel's predicament was more akin to that of the imagined researcher waiting outside the cat's box. In Philip Franke's novel, there was a character who might be based on Cecilia Berg. But it was also distinctly possible that Rakel's brain had extrapolated and embellished all by itself, that the similarities she believed she'd spotted consisted of little more than the gossamer foam of imagination, which would evaporate the moment she tried to bring it into reality.

She fetched her phone, thinking she might call Lovisa, but then made no move to find her number. Lovisa was not a doubter. On the contrary, she was dead certain by nature and clung to her convictions with unparalleled stubbornness. She was probably going to decide the person in *Ein Jahr* was Cecilia and bombard Rakel with questions she had no answers to.

For a brief moment, Rakel wished she could talk to Alexander, but she had long since deleted his number.

Instead, she picked up a pencil and opened the book to one of the paragraphs she'd circled. Yesterday, it had seemed indisputable that the sum of these fragments was a portrait of her mother, but Rakel had been sleep deprived and even temporarily insane in an abandoned library. It remained to be seen whether her conviction would stand the test of translation.

16

Her lungs began to burn after less than a mile. Her legs felt like concrete and her running shoes, which she'd found at the back of her closet, chafed. Also, her body seemed oddly disjointed. What in other runners looked like harmonious motions to Rakel felt like a snarl of disorganised limbs that in some mysterious way still managed to propel her forward. Her sports bra was too loose. Her leggings itched. Every step sent an aggregation of pain surging through every part of her body – from budding blisters on her feet to sandpapery breaths – and she slowed to a hobbling shuffle by Trädgårdsföreningen.

She spotted Emanuel Wikner from afar, dressed all in beige corduroy with his red imperial shawl draped around his shoulders. He was busy photographing the newly opened tulips with a digital camera. When he looked her way, Rakel ventured a wave, but his gaze slid past her without a flicker of recognition.

She took a few deep breaths and sped back up.

All day, Rakel had translated sections of text about the nameless woman whom she increasingly thought of as Cecilia. Every time the name popped into her head, Rakel tried to banish it with a barrage of common sense: you don't know, it could be coincidence, you're projecting your own not particularly subconscious wishes onto this text, it's a novel, not a documentary. And yet, the woman in the novel took on her mother's gangly form, forever frozen in time at the age of thirty-three. Rakel wrote by hand, because as long as she wrote by hand it wasn't an entirely serious endeavour. Even she could barely read her scribbles. After so many hours bent over her desk, a desire to move had flared up inside her, powerful and sudden like a gust of wind.

Now she jogged on, with at least a measure of dignity, down the tree-lined Södra vägen, fighting her way up Olof Wijksgatan, rounding Artisten and running the last few hundred yards down towards Götaplatsen, fuelled by sheer stubbornness. There, she leaned against the shady wall of Stadsteatern, the stitch in her side bending her double, sucking in long, shaking breaths until her heart rate began to slow. Strands of hair had escaped her ponytail and were clinging damply to her forehead. Her back was dripping sweat. Her thighs were trembling and her knees buckling. She slid down into a crouch with her back against the wall, checking how far she'd run: less than two miles.

Rakel burst out laughing. A marathon was twenty-six.

When she looked up, she saw the enormous poster on the wall of the Museum of Art advertising Gustav's upcoming retrospective. The motif was a detail from a painting of Cecilia. The focus was on her stern, beautiful face. Her mother's grave eyes stared at Rakel.

Thanks to Gustav's paintings, there was no risk of Rakel forgetting what her mother looked like. But despite the almost eerie realism that had made him famous, Gustav's Cecilia portraits were different from the photographs of her in some ineffable way. It had been a long time since Rakel last looked through the Berg family's photo albums, but the way she remembered it, the oldest pictures were of a young woman who was almost always laughing, or moving so that she came out blurry, or pulling a face the very moment the picture was taken. Remarkably often she was in positions that required significant flexibility – sitting cross-legged on a chair, lying draped over a garden swing with one leg dragging on the ground and the other thrown over the back at a ninety-degree angle. There were countless precariously sloshing glasses and cigarettes that seemed dangerously close to setting something on fire. Her curls were always wild and when she wore shoes, they always seemed on the verge of falling off. But the living, boyish girl parading through Martin's photographs – because he'd almost always been the person behind the camera – seemed in Gustav's paintings to have been transformed into a light, focused being. Gustav's Cecilia appeared timeless and exalted in her regal strictness. If she ever smiled, it was a da Vinci-like smile, enigmatic and restrained, and quiet power characterised her bearing.

Cecilia's self-portraits in the barn had been something else again. They were different from both Martin's photographs and Gustav's flawless portraits. Rakel regretted not having had the presence of mind to take pictures of them with her phone before they disappeared. The neatly folded blanket that had been left behind pointed the finger at Nana Inger, but Rakel didn't want to ask her. On the rare occasion that Inger mentioned her missing daughter, she referred to her as "your mother", and a vertical line invariably appeared between her eyebrows.

Her heart rate and breathing had returned to normal. Rakel pushed back up onto shaking legs and began to trudge homeward. Cecilia's gaze followed her down Avenyn.

*

While Rakel showered and got dressed, a plan for her immediate future began to take shape. First, she was going to go over to Djurgårdsgatan. Partly because she wanted to have a look at the photo albums, but primarily because she had to face her father sooner or later. Better to get it over with. She didn't know whether she should tell him or not. Nor was she clear on whether she *wanted* to tell him or not.

On the one hand, Martin very rarely mentioned Cecilia. On the other hand, he still wore his wedding ring. The latter fact had caused trouble in his half-hearted attempts at relationships. During a period when Rakel was a teenager, several women she would have liked if they'd been her Swedish teachers, librarians or cello instructors came and went. (At the time, Rakel had nurtured a misguided notion that she possessed a hidden musical talent and insisted on learning to play the cello, an instrument she associated with the nineteenth century, slanted light through tall windows, velvet, flickering candles and letters sealed with wax. Her father had refused, probably out of sheer self-preservation.) If they'd been her Swedish teachers, librarians or cello instructors, she would have admired their shiny hair and silk blouses. Their smiling attention would have made her feel warm inside. She would have wanted their eyes to linger on her and for them to occasionally say: "Very good, Rakel," with suppressed admiration. But they weren't, they were regular women, sitting at the Berg dinner table with nervous smiles. They invariably turned out to be the more enthusiastic half of the relationship. Over time, they grew increasingly frustrated and discontented, and they complained in creative ways about what they called Martin's indifference, lack of initiative or indolence while Rakel eavesdropped through the door. She'd been reading a book about the Incas with a torch under her duvet and, upset about the conquistadors – greedy Spaniards who sanctimoniously dragged their alibi Christianity along to wherever there was anything to pillage and conquer – who always came in and destroyed things, she'd found herself unable to sleep. The fluorescent hands of her alarm clock told her it was quarter past eleven. Outside, a muffled quarrel was taking place. The word *indolent* was new. Rakel tiptoed over to her bookshelf as quietly as she could to look it up in the Swedish Academy's dictionary, which she'd asked for for her thirteenth birthday.

1. Having or showing a disposition to avoid exertion; slothful.
2. Pathology. Causing little or no pain; inactive or relatively benign.

"I don't know what you *want*," the woman had said. "It would be a lot easier if you could just say what you want out of this."

It seemed true that her father didn't take his romantic entanglements very seriously. Rakel had repeatedly noticed him pulling a face when he saw the number on his ringing phone and after a moment of hesitation answered. "Hi, hi, sorry – I haven't had time to call. Super busy. I'm at the summer house with the kids."

There had been a number of such liaisons, which had all fizzled out without anyone seeming too upset about it. It was, on the whole, a relief. Over the years, the Berg family had set in the shape of dad, two children and an absent mother.

Martin seemed content to be alone. He had none of that desperation some older single people seemed to exude. His relationships with those women – in Rakel's memory there had been a gaggle of them, but in reality it was more like three or four – seemed more like a concession to convention. Any insinuating comment about how he should try to meet someone was met with his standard response, "Things are just so busy at work," and then he'd change the subject, usually to something book-related. He'd been busy at work for the past twenty-five years, and he wasn't showing any sign of slowing down. In fact, he seemed at his happiest when there were deadlines and meetings and non-stop activity. Rakel couldn't remember him ever complaining about his job.

She felt queasy on the tram ride over. It was early evening; it was perfectly possible that her dad would still be at the office or that he'd gone to the gym. Elis could be anywhere, but then he was completely unaware of almost everything that happened around him.

For the first time, it occurred to Rakel that her discovery in *Ein Jahr* involved her brother, too. For days, she'd walked around with this knowledge as if she was in a secret, painful bubble, impenetrable to the rest of the world, worrying about how her dad would react if she decided to tell him. That Elis had a stake in the matter, too, had apparently slipped her mind. And what – she hadn't thought about this either – about her reader's report? Berg & Andrén did, after all, have to make a decision about whether or not they were going to buy the rights, and from what little she'd read online, Philip Franke seemed well on his way to some kind of success. While Rakel walked down Allmänna Vägen, icy cold washed over her, not unlike the first and only time she'd forgotten about an exam and had to take it completely unprepared. (Ironically, it had been on the subject of Europe's colonial history, and she'd aced it, writing what she recalled from her mother's writings.) It was a banal kind of terror, but it was still terror, the terror of a child – all eyes were on her and her brain became blankly unable to produce a plausible alibi.

If *Ein Jahr* was successful on the German market, it wouldn't escape the notice of publisher Martin Berg. Granted, Rakel the reader could certainly advise them not to acquire the book, but if another publisher picked it up – not exactly an unlikely scenario if it did well – she would look like an idiot. Rakel's understanding of the company's finances was, truth be told, fairly hazy, but she knew they weren't great, and she'd heard countless times how that novel by the Decadent Romantic saved the publishing house from bankruptcy in the nineties.

Rakel's heart was racing. More than anything, she wanted to be alone and read more about Philip Franke to form an opinion on just how bad the situation was, but she'd already pulled open the heavy door. The ancient lady on the second floor was tottering about on the stairs, watering the plants that had annexed every available windowsill, so not even there could she google in peace. Rakel said hi and quickly slunk past her to avoid having to participate in polite small talk about the recent arrival of spring.

"To what do we owe the pleasure?" Martin shouted from deeper inside the flat.

All her strength drained out of her, and she collapsed on a chair to take off her shoes. There wasn't usually a chair in that spot; it was probably a newfound solution to Martin's vague back problems. He claimed they had nothing to do with age, but were more likely the result of overly enthusiastic exercise or his sedentary job.

Her dad appeared in the hallway. At home, he wore Birkenstocks to complement his all-black apparel, which had that feeling of a uniform that older people who embraced an alternative style in their youth seemed prone to developing. They still cared about their clothes but had become so deeply mainstream they could no longer signal a rebellious detachment through their sartorial choices. They retreated to small but familiar islands in the boundless sea of fashion – in Martin's case black jeans, T-shirt and a jacket, and every once in a while a bold, white button-down – and stayed there, year after year.

"Trendy sandals," she said, nodding towards his feet.

"Are you being sarcastic?"

"Not at all. They're in this year."

"I saw a girl wearing ones exactly like these the other day, but I figured she was poor. So you're saying it was just a regular hip Majorna girl thing?"

"Probably. Like there are poor people around here anyway. Everyone's wealthy, even the alcoholics down the pub draw a solid pension. At least that's what Lovisa tells me. You seem in a good mood. What are you up to?" She was paying her shoelaces an inordinate amount of attention.

"I'm just pondering this Wallace book. I reread the so-called biography his granddaughter's husband wrote. It's hardly objective. He's far too entangled with the Wallace family, and ninety per cent of the Wallace family are lunatics. They've hoarded every scrap of his correspondence. Refuse to let researchers anywhere near it. Don't seem to care one jot about the fact that they're keeping a pivotal part of the literary history of the twentieth century from the world. They claim to be protecting him from 'sensationalist wolves'. It's an outrage."

"*Du hast wahrscheinlich recht, lieber Vater.*"

337

"Don't be cheeky. You should have taken French instead. If you'd gone to Paris, you wouldn't have had to learn everything from scratch and live in that mould-infested place that gave you insomnia. On the other hand, I suppose I should be grateful your only teenage rebellion was to learn German." He sighed. "When you could have become a Nazi, or a junkie, or god knows what. But you really miss out, you know, if you don't go to Paris while you're young."

"I reckon I'm still young enough to go to Paris while I'm young, don't you?"

But Martin had already moved on; she could tell from his raised eyebrows and index finger. "Speaking of which," he said, "how's that reader's report coming? That novel, what was it called, *Ein Tag…*?"

Just then, Rakel stood up, which was a bad decision, because she wasn't sure her legs would carry her.

"Right," she said. "I read it. Just the one time."

"Ah! And what did you think?"

"I would really need to read it one more—"

"Of course."

"But it's – not *bad*. It has something."

"High praise, coming from you. What did you like about it?"

"It's well written and cleverly constructed. Suspenseful, even though it's just a love story."

"No murders? No terrible secrets? No mysterious main characters fleeing justice?"

The opportunity to confess lay wide open before her. She had to either lie or tell the truth. Whichever she chose, it would set the course of her future. She opened her mouth and heard herself answer in a completely calm voice: "No, not so much, no. It's a love story gone pear-shaped."

"A fate the majority of the population can relate to." Martin sighed. "Take another week and write a report, and we'll see what happens. Are you hungry? There's lasagne. You look like you've lost weight. You haven't gone vegetarian, have you?"

17

Passing headlights flashed through the blinds. A tram rattled down Karl Johansgatan and from the flat next door he could hear a muffled conversation. Martin rolled onto the diagonal so that he was partially occupying the cool, unslept right side of the bed and stared into the darkness.

He'd read that it was pointless to spend more than thirty minutes awake in bed. You had to, as some peppy psychologist had put it in a newspaper article, "reset" your sleep. You needed a calm, stress-free environment. To refrain from judging yourself too harshly. To accept the state of things. And so he spent a while pacing around the flat, eating a banana and staring out at the dark courtyard while he, as was his habit, took inventory of the children's whereabouts and status.

Rakel had wandered about like a restless spirit all evening before finally retiring to her room, where he hoped she was reading that German book. He would never have accepted this kind of delay from anyone but her. He'd considered pointing out to her that he had to give the German publisher an answer pretty soon, but that could easily have backfired. At least she was working on it now.

Elis, for his part, was "sleeping elsewhere," information he'd relayed via a text message whose iceberg technique would have impressed even Hemingway. Martin sighed. As a child, Elis had clung to him, been prone to nightmares, unwilling to go on sleepovers at his friends' houses. He'd worried about his dad being kidnapped ("I honestly don't think anyone would be dumb enough to think that would be lucrative," Martin had told him) or that their flat would be burgled while they were away ("they probably didn't take your Lego"). After the Backa fire, he came home from nursery school, insisting they check the smoke alarm was working correctly. He was often ill or thought he was. Pale and tiny, he would sit on the nurse practitioner's examination table, telling her his tummy hurt, no, no problems pooing, it just, like, *hurt*, and sometimes he felt sick, as though he needed to throw up but then he never did throw up? Elis wanted to stay home from school so often Martin called his teacher to ask if he was having problems with his classmates, or…? But his teacher, a young woman with the plucky cheerfulness of a heroine in any number of girls' books from the forties, had assured him all was well, Elis was a happy and well-liked child, played during recess and was very conscientious about his schoolwork.

Sometimes, when Martin was sitting on the edge of the bed, listening to his son telling him he thought he was coming down with a fever, he'd stroke his head and ask if he missed his mother. "Because it's perfectly normal if you do, you know," Martin had said. "When you miss someone, you can feel… sad… and stuff." But Elis always just shook his head, rolled himself into his duvet, and waited for Martin to read him another chapter of *Harry Potter*, which he was possibly too young for but absolutely wanted to have read to him anyway.

After what he hoped was an appropriate amount of time, Martin went back to bed. He'd suffered periods of insomnia before, but there was no reason to think this was the start of anything like that. Nothing new had happened. It was probably nothing to worry about. A one-time occurrence. He lay down on his side and closed his eyes to try to persuade his body it was already asleep. In the past, he'd rejected the idea of taking sleeping pills, because if there was a situation with the children, he had to be switched on. In the hopes of getting sufficiently bored, he'd reread the Hemingway novels of his youth instead, taking comfort in the fact that Elis's unconscious role model when it came to cryptic writing had experienced plenty of sleepless nights in the Paris of the 1920s. Hemingway's tactic had been to close his eyes and rest – he'd told himself that he at least got something out of all the long sleepless hours that way – until morning, when he could get up and get back to work.

The main challenge seemed to be not to think. In the silence of his bedroom, all kinds of ponderings surfaced, unstoppable and disorganised. Somewhere, probably in that newspaper article, he'd read that you were supposed to acknowledge and accept your thoughts, but not assign any value to them, and, after thinking them, release them, allowing them to vanish. Apparently that helped. He'd also read something about visualising placing his worries on a leaf and letting it float away. But first, he was irked by the trite conceptualisation of nature inherent in those kinds of strategies, whose peacefully babbling brooks and sunny glades full of birdsong seemed conjured by a subpar nineteenth-century nature poet. Second, the idea of trying so hard to forget your worries didn't sit right with Martin. Worries were worries for a reason. They were problems that had to be solved one way or another, usually by him. In the past, Martin had disliked the idea of being bossed around, but these days he saw the advantages of a hierarchical corporate structure. The buck had to stop somewhere. Young people seemed to associate senior positions with opportunity and freedom. Maybe they also recognised that there was a level of responsibility involved, but what that responsibility consisted of was abstract and speculative. The realities of responsibility seemed to lie in a series of unglamorous practical tasks and often involved sacrificing something – a Friday night, people's approval – and no one ever thanked you. Per and he could keep going for another twenty years if neither one of them had a bloody heart attack, but unless they wanted to sell the company, they would eventually need a plan for its future. The publishing industry was going through rapid change, and Berg & Andrén had probably peaked in terms of size and direction. True, it could be allowed to dwindle as the publishers themselves became more focused on summer houses and hobbies or whatever it was people turned their attention to when they began to drift away from working life, but that was not an attractive thought. The publishing company Berg & Andrén was not the same as the individuals Berg and Andrén; it was a business, and it was the nature of a business to want to perpetuate its existence. Rakel would actually be a very good successor. She was dutiful and hard-working, her love of literature unadulterated by any artistic ambitions of her own. She was a lot like her mother: analytical rather than artistic, propelled through life by a powerful thirst for knowledge. Granted, Cecilia had been a gifted painter; they were different in that respect.

There had been a lot of nagging for a while about her applying to art school at Konstfack, which is to say Lars Wikner had nagged and Cissi had silently rolled her eyes. For her to apply to Konstfack in Stockholm rather than Valand in Gothenburg was, come to think of it, a strange idea.

Suddenly, the doorbell rang, making Martin jump. He heaved himself out of bed and hurried through the flat. There was no one to be seen through the peephole and when he opened the door, the landing was deserted in the grey light of dawn. It was four o'clock in the morning.

Last time around, he'd learned something about sleeplessness: sooner or later, you reached a point of no return. Back in his bedroom, Martin pulled on his robe and turned on his desk lamp.

*

At nine o'clock the next morning, Martin Berg greeted his colleagues, striding towards his office with a firm hold on his briefcase and his handsfree in his ear. Per was on the phone and waved to him through the window in his door.

Martin tossed his briefcase on the sofa, hung up his jacket because cycling over had made him warm, slumped into his office chair, decided a sitting position would only exacerbate his mental lethargy, and therefore pushed the button that raised the table to appropriate standing height. In the middle of his computer screen was a Post-it: *Frilagret doesn't serve alcohol??!!!*

Martin popped his head out into the hallway. No Patricia in sight. "Patricia!" he bellowed.

Patricia appeared from under her desk and limped towards him. "Blisters," she explained. "Right, okay. I talked to the people who rent out the place. Apparently, there's some problem with the bar. Or they don't have a bar. And I figured a twenty-fifth anniversary bash without alcohol would be less than ideal."

"Sounds like a spot-on analysis."

"So, what do we do?"

Martin stared at the offensively pink Post-it as though it might be hiding the answer. Where thoughts usually moved, he now found nothing but the barren wasteland of sleep-deprivation.

"Sort it out," he said. "You're going to have to fix it. You're in charge."

Patricia looked doubtful. "Okay…"

He knew how to delegate. No one could claim otherwise. "Speaking of which, have the invitations gone out?"

Patricia's expression morphed into outright suspicion. "We sent them last week, don't you remember? You double-checked to make sure everything was correct?"

"Yes. Sure. Of course." He did remember. Of course he did. The cream envelopes with the handwritten addresses. Slipping a note into Gustav's envelope, because it felt odd to address Gustav in the general, slightly formal tone of the invitations. But did he even open his post? He still hadn't called back, even though Martin had left several messages.

Patricia gently took the Post-it from him and limped back to her desk.

The first thing Martin saw when he opened his inbox was Ulrike Ackermann's name. The subject line read "Philip Franke?"

Instead of opening it, he went to get coffee and drank it standing by the window. A ferry pushed off from the Rosenlund quay, setting its course for Lindholmen. Where docks had once sprawled there was now a sea of steel and glass, Chalmers' buildings and private businesses. The old wooden houses on Slottsberget had been refurbished and sold for obscene sums. The building that had once housed the art school had been turned into a psychiatric clinic. There were no more parties. No students fighting over the best studios, and no Gustav Becker sauntering down the hill with a cigarette dangling from the corner of his mouth and the sun in his eyes.

There was a knock on the door and Amir appeared. "Martin? Do you have time to have a look at the cover now?"

"Absolutely." Martin tried to recall which cover he was referring to. The day had begun. All he could do was top up his coffee and surrender to the forward motion of the workday.

They all went to Bombay for lunch. The topic du jour was summer plans. Patricia's boyfriend wanted to go hiking up north, but Patricia feared that would be the death of their relationship. Sanna was going to have a new roof installed and not read a single book. Per intended to spend as much time as possible on Orust but wasn't sure what they were actually going to do there now that the house was, after many trials and tribulations, finished. Amir mumbled something about not having made any plans yet, and everyone tactfully refrained from asking follow-up questions; he'd recently been dumped by his girlfriend of seven years.

"What about you, Martin?" Sanna asked.

"I was going to work on the Wallace biography," Martin said, busying himself with his lamb stew.

"Oh yeah? How's it coming?"

"Well, you know – a lot of material and never enough time to put it all together." Martin once again had the feeling his mouth had taken on a life of its own. "I might rent a house in France with the kids... work there..."

"Have you read Wallace?" Sanna said, nudging Amir.

"Remind me, what did he write?"

Sanna let out a raspy laugh. "Let's hope you're not representative of the younger generation," she said.

Later that afternoon, Martin was flipping through a book that was fresh from the printers. It was about Swedish colonialism, particularly Saint-Barthélemy in the West Indies. The author was a well-known professor at Lund University, and even though it wasn't going to be a bestseller, it was the kind of book that ended up on university reading lists and thus generated modest but steady revenue. He was admiring the wide margins, made for note-taking, and the felicitous choice of font when his eyes caught on an in-text reference: Berg (1997).

For one confused moment, he thought it was a reference to him and he quickly flipped to the bibliography, as if to rip the mask off his unknown namesake.

"Berg, C. (1997). *Terra Incognita. An intellectual history of colonialism.* Gothenburg University."

He had to sit down. His jacket felt tight across his shoulders, he was having trouble breathing, the air in his office was stuffy, he had to remember to call the property owners and ask them to have a look at the ventilation.

A YEAR ABROAD IN PARIS 2

I

INTERVIEWER: How do you decide what to write about?

MARTIN BERG: I think the subject chooses you. You don't choose what to write about. You have as much control over that as over whom you choose to love, your children or whatever. To paraphrase Söderberg: "You have them and sometimes you lose them. But you don't *choose*."

INTERVIEWER: It sounds like in reality you believe the author of a novel has very little say over his or her subject?

MARTIN BERG: It's an interesting question: is there free will, and so on. People and philosophers have debated that for centuries. The question was obviously problematic from a religious perspective, but after we did away with God it became *truly* interesting. What makes us do what we do? Do we do things because we want to or because capitalism wants us to? Or society? Subconscious forces? So, when I choose to write about a certain subject, for instance, who is doing the choosing? Is it "Martin Berg"? Is it preordained? Is it the market? Is it [*chuckling*] suppressed trauma?

*

Martin forced his eyelids open, blinking a few times. The chugging rhythm of the train was soothing. The other passengers in his compartment were a middle-aged man rustling a paper and two American ladies who, thankfully, had stopped reading aloud to each other from various travel guides and settled down with their own books.

He found his notebook in his shirt pocket and scribbled two words across an entire page. *Night Sonnets.* Dazed and drowsy, he pondered this potential title for his novel when the compartment door opened, and Cecilia thudded onto the seat next to his.

"Honestly, I don't know why people have children." She used the bottle opener on his keyring to get the caps off two bottles of Orangina.

"What do you mean?"

"There was a group of three-year-old delinquents in the restaurant car. They discussed little George's toilet habits for fifteen straight minutes."

"The three-year-old delinquents?"

She made a face. "Their mothers. There was a line and a rude teenager behind the till. There was no avoiding them. Didn't they have anything else to talk about? What did they talk about before *petit* George arrived on the scene?"

"Women," Martin said in jest, but Cecilia wasn't listening, just staring out at the ochre-and-rusty-red expressionist landscape flying past outside.

"Not everyone's like that," he added after a while, but he could hear the hesitation in his voice. He had no close friends with children. When he pictured his future, it's not that there weren't any children it in, he'd just never thought of them as anything more than a shadowy presence in a far distant future. When he was older. Like, thirty. But he could see himself as a grandfather: Martin Berg, author, in his fifties, in a wicker chair on the veranda, fussing with his latest manuscript, joking with the little ones toddling about in the background.

"I'm not against the concept of children," Cecilia said. "If anything, it's the parents. My mother insists it's a biological thing that kicks in in due course, but I believe people have children for psychological reasons. To have another go at whatever they failed at. Or" – she laughed mirthlessly – "just to lend some purpose to their small lives."

"Or because the meaninglessness of existence causes existential angst." Having gone through it several times, armed with both a dictionary and a close reading of the Swedish translation, Martin now had a fairly good grasp of *L'Existentialisme est un humanisme*.

"That's what I'm saying. Are we almost there yet?"

For two weeks, they'd travelled the length and breadth of Europe. Martin's back ached from nights spent on station benches and in cheap hotel beds. The last time he'd showered had been at a hostel in Zürich four days earlier. True, they'd gone for a swim in Lake Geneva, but it was doubtful whether that had had any measurable effect on their cleanliness. Their backpacks were full of dirty clothes, tattered paperbacks and rolls of film he had to remember to put in the fridge when they got back. When they set off from Gare de Lyon, he'd felt like a pioneer, but the train stations were teeming with young people with Interrail tickets. Hung over, greasy-haired, they had sat on their backpacks, squinting at the sky from behind their sunglasses, waiting for the 11.45 to Florence. And what were they going to do in Florence? Walk around. Get blisters. Get drunk on cheap wine. Snap blurry pictures of the Arno. Pay a dutiful visit to one single museum.

They arrived in Antibes on time.

"I never want to get on another train ever again," Cecilia muttered as they climbed down onto the platform.

At first, Martin didn't recognise the figure that stepped out of the shadows.

Gustav was tanned, the skin on his nose peeling, and his hair had assumed a shade of blond that conjured images of tennis, white shorts and British cheerfulness ("jolly good"). He embraced Martin, kissed Cecilia on both cheeks and talked non-stop while they walked through the station building and out to the taxi rank, where they shoved their backpacks into a dusty Mercedes. Gustav took the front seat and gave the driver directions in his shaky French.

"*Là! À gauche!*" he hollered, and the car turned and jostled down a winding road that gleamed like silver in the sunshine.

"You look good," Martin said.

"I feel good. Like a prince. But as a matter of fact, life was getting a little bit lonely. Marie's brave attempts – that's the housekeeper – to talk to me are... well, brave, and I think she has been trying to establish a line of communication through food instead, because every day there's different pâtés and terrines and bouillabaisse, and plates full of peaches and melons and grapes that I consider still lifes but that she insists I'm supposed to *eat*. Nana's orders, I suspect. She's off visiting her daughter now, but she has left the fridge crammed full of pots and things with little notes on them that I can barely read. And I have to say she seemed relieved when she realised my *amis suédois* were coming." He pointed the driver the right way and then turned back to them. "I'm working on an amazing painting, by the way, amazingly alternative-kitsch, I'd love to have your thoughts on it..."

Ten minutes later, they were there. Once the car had disappeared down the road, they could hear the sea and the screaming gulls.

"*Bienvenus*," Gustav said.

The walls of the house were so blindingly white it was impossible to look straight at them, save for the one that was entirely covered in bougainvillea. There were lemon and palm trees in the garden. Stone steps wound down towards a small sandy beach. Gustav told them he started every morning with a swim and felt like a whole new person as a result.

"My mind has never been this sharp," he said. "I really recommend it. Look, I can't say it enough: it's *phenomenal* that you're here."

*

They had decided to make it a summer of work.

Gustav was engaged in what he called a "painterly love affair with the light". Cecilia was going to write an essay about Joseph Conrad's *Heart of Darkness*. Martin had his stack of notes.

He'd made it so far as to settle on a main character that was a-bit-similar-but-not-quite-like himself: Jesper, a literature student doing his PhD on – Martin hadn't worked this out yet, because he couldn't decide whether he wanted Jesper's thesis subject to *seem* interesting, while in reality it was soul-crushingly dull, or whether it should simply be dull, full stop. Jesper was renting a room in a commune where he'd ended up by sheer happenstance. He'd moved to town from the countryside… Or maybe not. Maybe he'd in fact lived in town his whole life. Either way, Martin wanted to include the commune and the wayward souls living within its walls, the lively, bustling atmosphere. And then something would happen – marked with an X on the timeline he'd made – which induced Jesper to break out of his routine. For some reason, he would travel south, meeting interesting people along the way. There would be a woman, for instance – at this point Jesper's path veered away from his creator's – who in Martin's mind looked quite a bit like Lena Olin. Possibly on a train. In a compartment. A number of scenes would be set on the Riviera, naturally. In the tradition of Wallace's *Patagonia Days* and that one by Hemingway that was published posthumously not so long ago. And *Bonjour Tristesse*, of course, which Martin had read in French and found delightfully juvenile. It was going to be a fairly long book, he figured. In fact, it would have to be, since he already had fifty pages written, and it had not yet crossed his hero's mind to leave his winter-dreary Gothenburg.

Martin sat down at his desk. A cup of coffee next to him, a pack of Gauloises, an ashtray. There was a blank sheet of paper in the typewriter. If he looked up, he could see the ocean and the sky through the open balcony doors.

From the veranda below he could hear a *tacktacktack tack tack… tack tack. Tack-tack-tack-tack.* Ding. *Tacktack tack tack tack.*

It had been Cecilia's idea to send their typewriters down ahead of them before they left Paris. And so, his Facit and her Olivetti had been waiting for them at the post office in Antibes, in a worn leather bag and bright-orange plastic case respectively, with address tags tied to their handles. Electric typewriters, word processors and computers were all well and good, but how could they compete with the portability of a travel typewriter? Just the words *travel typewriter* set off a cascade of mental associations that *word processor* could never evoke.

Martin was overcome with a sudden need for absolute silence. He closed the balcony doors, which erased much of the Riviera feel.

He stared at the blank sheet of paper.

Maybe he should start by reading what he had so far. Yes.

He picked up the stack of paper and went out to the hammock.

Their life in Antibes soon took on rhythm and direction. Frederikke came to visit for a week and even though everyone came to life while she was there, both Gustav and Cecilia seemed relieved when she left and they could return to their routine.

Mornings were for writing. Cecilia got up first, went for a quick run, made breakfast and coffee. Gustav woke up last, around ten, and spent some time on the veranda with coffee and a cigarette before stretching so hard his chest could be seen under his Imperiet T-shirt, yawning big, shouting "*Au travail!*" and disappearing around the corner. He usually painted outside, with rolled-up shirt sleeves and a lumpy straw hat pulled down low "to protect himself from van Goghian insanity".

"I've really never been much of an outdoorsman," he said. "Given as how being outdoors is difficult and traumatic for the most part. Remember when we went camping, Martin? In Skagen? And it rained? It was a bloody deluge, and we had no idea how to pitch a tent, so it got in everywhere and we were soaked through. I had a sketchbook, I remember that, which like an idiot I hadn't left in the car; it was beyond salvation. Anyway. This is something else entirely. You can trust the weather here. It doesn't change schizophrenically from one moment to the next."

He took a large number of Polaroids of Cecilia and used her as the model for several elaborate studies for paintings he was planning. Cecilia herself was so engrossed in her Joseph Conrad essay she barely noticed him. His studies that spring had yielded results – Gustav had distilled and refined his style, excluding elements that clouded the motif and, by so doing, emphasising what it was he was trying to convey. What had once been an intuitive sense of composition was now conscious decision-making.

Gustav's work was usually associated with what he called "a certain level of anguish". He sketched, pondered, crumpled up paper, paced to and fro, and claimed that even though he'd made good art before, that was in no way a guarantee he could do it again. He was especially prone to gloom and doom after making something he was pleased with, since that meant his next painting would invariably be worse. He refused to listen to reason and when he approached a canvas again, it was with the sagging shoulders of a person walking down Via Dolorosa towards certain death on Golgotha. Then followed the actual painting. While that was taking place, he didn't care how it was going, just kept at it, once for a memorable sixteen-hour stretch, with a packet of biscuits and carton of expired milk as his only victuals. Then followed relieved joy. "This didn't turn out too bad, after all," he might say, studying his work with his hands on his hips. "Not too shabby, eh?"

But happy or not, Gustav always gravitated towards doubt. It was inevitable. Doubt seemed to be his default position. It didn't matter what they said. It didn't matter that he always proved himself wrong. Sooner or later, that's where he ended up. He was willing to accept that he had a gift – to claim otherwise would be outright delusional – but what difference, he asked them, did that make at the end of the day?

"Having a gift isn't the same as having something to say," he muttered, stubbing out a cigarette in the overflowing ashtray. "It's hardly a fucking guarantee that what you make is any *good*."

Now, Martin was braced for the comedown, like a seasoned general who refuses to be taken in by the notion that the battling forces have found inner peace and harmony and put down their arms once and for all. But during all those days, vibrating in their sun-seared stillness, Gustav continued to work for at least eight hours a day, with a productivity that should have generated at least a quick round of the old refrains: *Who am I to be doing this?* and *Will I ever be able to produce anything of substance?* But Gustav just whistled along to the reedy racket from his transistor radio and carried on painting.

Martin was always the first to stop working. Someone had to make lunch, and after grappling with his book (it felt more real now that he could call it *Night Sonnets* and not just The Novel, which was hard to say without built-in quotation marks) for a few hours, he was grateful for the concrete and well-defined task that was cooking. More often than strictly necessary, he cycled into town to visit the marketplace in the old quarter. He bought cherries and apricots, artichokes, aubergine and potatoes, olives, eggs and large hunks of cheese that survived the ride home only because there was an ice pack at the bottom of each pannier. It was thirty minutes each way, if you kept a brisk pace, and Martin told himself he used the time to think about his writing, but the truth was that for the most part he thought of nothing at all. The sharply glittering sea with its scattered white sails and yachts bobbing at anchor off the coast, the burnt sienna palette of the cliffs, the rustling of dry palm fronds, and the singing of his tyres against the asphalt – all of it contributed to erasing any attempt at thought. What remained was the motion of his legs, the rhythm of his heart, his breathing, the sweat trickling down his back, and the sun against his skin. Martin hadn't spent that much time outside in years and discovered that his ever-darkening tan made him look like his father. Gustav was the first to point it out – "Blimey, you look just like Abbe!" – and Cecilia agreed. With their fair skin, the two of them had to be careful, and the sun mostly turned them even blonder.

When Cecilia had done the washing-up after lunch, they went to the beach. She was the one who insisted on it. Martin had never met a person who loved the sea as much as Cecilia turned out to, except possibly Abbe, though Abbe preferred to be on it, rather than in it. Cecilia dived from the edge of cliffs and swam until her head was just a tiny dot. Then she returned and came walking out of the surf, squinting against the sun.

"Do you have to swim that far out?" Gustav complained. "What if you have a cramp or something?"

She assured him she had been given a solid aquatic education in the pool at the Addis Ababa Hilton.

Gustav, for his part, spent their beach sessions reading Simenon novels, dressed in a button-down, in the shade under the umbrella, with his long, pale feet burrowed into the sand and a cigarette smouldering forgotten between his fingers. When they were ready to leave, he gathered up the considerable number of butts he'd accumulated so he could deposit them in the nearest bin. "Still a conscientious Swede," he noted.

Come to think of it, he probably spent the whole summer working his way through just one book, because every time he came across a word he didn't know, he asked Martin, and there was never more than five minutes between these interruptions.

"What does *langoureux* mean, anyway? Toss me a peach, would you? Look, there's a proper old Riviera lady over there. Burnt to the likeness of a car tyre. A pastis would be just the ticket right now, don't you think?"

Much like the dubious hero of *Patagonia Days*, Martin had tasked himself with giving Homer a proper read; he had an idea that the main character of *Night Sonnets* would serve as Odysseus's contemporary heir. That obviously meant he had to read Joyce, as well, but there were worse fates than having to read Joyce. Now, he closed his paperback Homer and rolled onto his stomach.

"I would guess it means 'languorous' or some such," he said, throwing a sun-warmed peach to Gustav, who caught it with both hands, his cigarette dangling from between his lips. "A word no serious writer should let anywhere near his or her text."

"Then a terrible mistake has been made. Call Detective Maigret."

Martin laughed. Waves lapped against the shore and gulls screeched overhead. The sound of a lowing boat siren rolled into the bay.

"Where is she?" Gustav said. "Can you see her?"

"She's out there, look. She's on her way back now. I think you need new glasses."

"The pool at the Hilton. She doesn't stand a chance if there's a shark."

"There are no sharks here, Gustav."

But the relief that washed over him every time he saw her brace her feet against the bottom and straighten up out of the sea was palpable.

They spent their evenings playing cards and watching whatever films were showing on TF1. When Cecilia grew tired of the dubbed dialogue, she made up her own lines, which she delivered in different voices. And so, throughout *King Kong*, Jeff Bridges had a thick German accent while Jessica Lange's Dalecarlian twang was a poor fit with her constant shrieking, and in Cecilia's version each character had a different view on the Western world's relationship with its African colonies.

But for the most part, they stayed at the table under the lemon trees long after dinner was over. While cicadas sang in the balmy night, they talked, smoked and drank in the light of a couple of flickering candles. Martin assumed the never-ending supply of alcohol came from the house's wine cellar, and one night he let slip a comment about how they should return it to its original state before they left.

"What? No, no." Gustav waved his hand dismissively, drawing glowing lines in the dark with his cigarette. "Nana hasn't drunk a drop since that business with Granddad. But I stocked up a little before you came. It would have been unbearable to find ourselves completely dry."

"What business with your granddad?" Cecilia asked.

"They had a small boat. One morning, he wasn't here, and when Nana looked around with a pair of binoculars, she spotted the boat drifting about abandoned out there. He'd fallen in. He was probably hammered, because it was dead calm, and he'd forgotten to take the nets with him."

"That's terrible."

"It was before I was born. He drifted ashore eventually. Anyway, Nana's a bit sensitive about 'inebriants'. But you only live once, right? You can't live your life in the shadow of a drowned drunkard. *N'est-ce pas?*"

"Wise words," Martin said.

"Besides, this is Homer's sea," Gustav went on, pointing with his cigarette at the vast ocean beyond the cliffs, which in the gloom had taken on the purple shade of wine and ox blood. "Homer knew, like some of the more skilled painters, that *blue* is a grossly oversimplifying word to use to describe the colour of the sea. And so he never let Odysseus or the sirens or any of those sexy girls on that island, whatever they're called—"

"Nymphs," Cecilia put in.

"Can't someone just put you on Jeopardy so we can use the winnings to go to Greece?"

"*Volontiers.*"

"Where was I? I've forgotten what I was going to say."

"But I know," Martin said. "You were going to tell us that nowhere in the *Iliad* or the *Odyssey* is the sea described as blue, even though the sea is ubiquitous in both works."

"It sounds like I might have made this observation before."

"You have."

"But I'm right, though, no?"

"Not sure about that," Martin said. "But I can add an observation I made today: his hexameter is reminiscent of the rhythm of the waves."

They unanimously asked him to recite a passage to see if that was true. Martin performed a small scene on the theme of No, I don't think I should, then raised his hands to silence them, took a deep drag on his cigarette and said: "This is when Achilles is told about Patroclus's death. The messenger is called Antilochus, but that's not important. Anyway." He read:

Son of warlike Peleus,
you must hear this dreadful news—something
I wish weren't so—Patroclus lies dead.
Men are fighting now around the body.
He's stripped. Hector with his gleaming helmet
has the armour.

356

A black cloud of grief swallowed up Achilles.
With both hands he scooped up soot and dust and poured it
on his head, covering his handsome face with dirt,
covering his sweet-smelling tunic with black ash.
He lay sprawling—his mighty warrior's massive body
collapsed and stretched out in the dust. With his hands,
he tugged at his own hair, disfiguring himself.

It was a rather dark passage, but Gustav and Cecilia clapped and whistled. Gustav decreed him the next great poet of the Mediterranean, on the brink of making history with his magnum opus about the futility of existence. They discussed which historical fate would have been most appropriate for each of them. Gustav, Martin decided, should have been a court painter at some Spanish or Italian Renaissance court.

"Unlimited wine and feasting. Of course, you'd have to immortalise some noble lady or other from time to time, but on the whole, a fairly pleasant existence."

Martin, Gustav countered, should have been around when Gutenberg was active and gone off to some remote corner of Europe to peddle his marvellous new printing machine. "You'd find great success producing bibles, thereby melding religion with nascent capitalism, or, in other words, becoming a self-satisfied and appreciated member of society."

"I would probably have joined a convent," Cecilia said.

"You sound worryingly pleased at that prospect," Martin said.

"Well, think about it: peace and quiet. All the time in the world. Free access to a decent library. Walks in the rose garden. Hearty meals served three times a day."

"You would probably have attracted the virtuous admiration of some poor knight," Martin said, "and been remembered by posterity as the lady of some medieval ballad."

"Oh, I don't know. Knights aren't usually very interested in me."

"You never know."

"So far, I seem to do better with reprobate jesters."

They laughed; Gustav so hard he got hiccoughs. Then Gustav wanted to go for a nocturnal swim in the Homerian sea and it was all they could do to stop him.

*

Life was in every way paradisical, but the question was whether it was conducive to writing a novel. After all, William Wallace had written *Patagonia Days* under generally miserable circumstances, and Martin was starting to feel that his main character Jesper was growing a bit too contented with his sunny Riviera existence. Something new had to happen. One night, he talked Gustav and Cecilia into going into town. Cecilia sighed, washed the salt out of her hair and put on a dress. Gustav muttered something about being happier at home but swapped his paint-stained shirt for a clean one and washed his hands with turpentine. Martin called a taxi.

They had oysters at a restaurant with white linen tablecloths, strolled through the old quarter, found a quayside bar, drank rosé, drank more rosé, laughed so loudly people stared, but who cared – Martin topped up their glasses and almost dropped his cigarette – it was just a bunch of tourists who had nothing better to do than to ogle people who knew how to live. Cheers, then, chin-chin.

Then, suddenly, Gustav was gone.

He'd got up – to go for a piss? – and it was unclear how much time had passed since then. Martin and Cecilia had been absorbed in a discussion about Milan Kundera.

"Where's Gustav?" Cecilia said, which Martin at first took as a ploy to distract him because she could sense she was losing.

"You're claiming," he said, slurring his words ever so slightly, "that his descriptions of women are objectifying, but isn't it rather that woman, or maybe we should say 'woman' in Kundera's writing represents the access to…" Martin gestured vaguely, because somewhere along the way, he'd lost sight of his thesis.

"He's been gone a really long time."

"He's probably studying the way the lights are reflected in the harbour or something." Martin hiccoughed.

"But his cigarettes are here."

That, Martin had to admit, was strange.

Cecilia called the waiter over. Had he seen their friend? He shook his head. In that moment, swaddled in the pleasant cotton wool-haze of intoxication, Martin didn't consider it a very serious situation. Gustav always turned up sooner or later. But Cecilia had sobered up and asked for the bill. Martin wasn't sure it was right and wanted to argue with the waiter, but Cecilia grabbed him by the arm.

They looked for Gustav for at least an hour, in the streets and alleyways and every last bar in the neighbourhood. Cecilia had lost all interest in discussing literature. In the end, they returned to the bar, hoping to find him waiting for them there, but no one had seen him.

"I'm sure he's fine," Martin said. "Gustav always does things like this."

"Really? Always?"

"Okay, maybe not always. But it's definitely not the first time. He probably fell asleep somewhere."

"He might get robbed."

"I'm ninety per cent sure Gustav has nothing worth robbing."

They agreed it was possible he'd gone home. Cecilia stared out of the window all the way back, chewing her nails.

But the house was empty when they got there, and he still hadn't turned up the next morning. Cecilia wanted to go back into town, but Martin talked her into waiting until after lunch.

She didn't write a word all morning.

Around noon, a figure could be seen walking up the road towards the house. Gustav had tied a bandana around his head and wore a pair of sunglasses they'd never seen before. Aside from being awfully thirsty, he felt all right, he claimed. He'd been given a ride part of the way and walked the last bit.

"Where were you?" Cecilia said.

"Honestly – no idea."

"Where did you wake up?"

"In a fairly pleasant park."

"But why did you leave?"

He shrugged. "Don't remember. Maybe the oysters were bad."

"Bad oysters don't cause blackouts."

"Well, I'm here now, aren't I? In fact, I wouldn't half mind a drink and a round of Scrabble. What do you say? Who's going to accept my challenge? Martin? I can tell you'd enjoy trouncing a ne'er-do-well like me."

II

INTERVIEWER: So an author's ability to choose his or her subject is limited. What are your thoughts on choosing more generally? Are we ever free to choose?

MARTIN BERG: Yes, well – there are situations in which you don't really have a choice. Or in which your only choice is to act in accordance with your nature. If you live with one eye on your deathbed, there are some things you might not be able to refrain from doing. And given that, the question of whether you ever... [*trailing off, seeming lost in thought*]

INTERVIEWER: Yes...?

MARTIN BERG: Whether you ever really have any choice at all.

*

It hadn't rained for a month in Paris and the plane trees were grey with exhaust fumes. The metro clattered. Cars honked and revved their engines. People tumbled into each other and hurried on without apologising. Rows of grimy facades rose towards a hazy sky. The sluggish, murky-green Seine flowed lethargically towards the sea between quays covered with broken glass, graffiti, discarded chewing gum and American tourists taking pictures of each other.

The studio was smaller than Martin remembered. Someone had forgotten to empty the ashtray. Bird droppings were smeared across one of the windows. He sighed and pulled out the sofa bed.

While Martin and Cecilia were travelling through Europe, Per Andrén had been on a cycling holiday with a British girl – the one who hadn't given him HIV – and he returned from it several cheese-and-wine pounds lighter and with the tan of a character by Hemingway. Lizzy from Bath, it turned out, didn't let flat tyres or hangovers hold her back. Which had aroused Per's gentlemanly competitiveness. Their record had been covering nearly a hundred miles with heavy packs in one day. They'd already made plans to tackle Spain next summer.

"*Mais d'abord, le trimestre d'automne*," Per said, shaking out his tweed jacket, which had been hanging in the wardrobe all summer. "Has anyone seen my briefcase?"

This was Martin's favourite time of year: the start of the academic year. The phrase stirred up memories of cold morning air during his bike ride to university, deep-cleaned lecture halls with shiny blackboards and neat boxes of chalk on the shelf underneath, sharpened pencils and blank notebooks. Between classes, he smoked cigarettes with his course mates, leaning against brick walls in the sunshine, talking about the new lecturers. Afterwards, he did the usual second-hand bookshop crawl in search of the term's course literature. Then he had coffee at Paley, and Cecilia came walking with her coat thrown over her shoulders, she smiled and waved, bent down for a kiss, and slipped onto the chair across from him…

"Seriously. Has either of you seen my briefcase?" Per said.

"Pierre, *mon ami*. Calm down," Gustav said. "It's on the hat rack."

And Per pulled on his jacket, even though it was warm enough to go without, grabbed his briefcase and went off to the Sorbonne.

Gustav stayed in bed, a cup of coffee balanced on a book next to him and the latest issue of *Les Inrockuptibles* splayed across his stomach.

"We had such a nice time down there," he said, out of the blue. "Imagine living like that all the time."

"I suppose that would get old, too," Martin said without looking up from his typewriter. He hoped his tone would convey that he was very busy with his Novel.

He'd written another thirty pages of decent quality in Antibes. His protagonist had stumbled into various entanglements on the Riviera. There was a woman, but Martin wasn't entirely happy with how she was working out. She was a bit too evasive. It wasn't particularly clear why Jesper was so affected by her. She needed something… Well, *something*. To define her. To elevate her textual status from woman to Woman. A bowler hat?

"I don't know." Gustav reached for his cigarettes. "I guess Cissi would have to finish her degree first. But if she were writing, too… When we got bored, we could pop over to Marseille. Or Nice, hit the casinos."

"You'd probably be skint as usual, and Cecilia would give a short lecture about how all gamblers are losers in the end, and that casinos can be thought of as microcosms of capitalism," Martin said.

"I bet Nana would let us use the house. She's always talking about how her French old-lady friends leave much to be desired."

"And how would we make our money?"

"I could always sell some paintings. It would be fine."

"I would have to have a job," Martin said. "And probably a car, too, so I could get to said job every day. It wouldn't be like it is now. I've almost used up my grant and *unfortunately* tourists are unlikely to want to pay me for my art. In fact, *no one* pays me for my art. So I honestly don't quite see how we could pull that off."

"There's no need to get upset," Gustav said.

"I'm not upset."

"You sound upset."

"I just need to get somewhere with this… crap."

"It's not crap. Stop saying it's crap."

"I'm going out for a bit," Martin said, snatching up a notebook and pen.

Instead of going to his usual café on the corner, Martin walked on, towards Montparnasse.

He'd grown used to talking to Cecilia whenever he got stuck. Now, Jesper had just arrived in Cannes by train. He tried to conjure Cecilia's voice. *Okay. So, what is he doing there? What's the first thing he does? Who does he meet?*

At Closerie des Lilas, he ordered coffee and flipped through his notebook.

Just like at that party in the spring, he didn't notice her entering. It was more as though he became aware of her presence gradually. When he looked up from the page for a split-second, she was just there, seated a few tables away. At first, he couldn't place her, but then he remembered: she was the girl in the red top at that snobby photographer's party.

Martin tried to focus on his text again.

But now that he'd recognised her, he couldn't ignore the sound of her voice when she ordered. She pulled a magazine from her bag. There followed twenty minutes during which she read and Martin smoked four cigarettes and scribbled furiously in his notebook.

Then she stood up and left. Martin stared at her back until it disappeared in the crowd.

Tremblingly, he lit his fifth cigarette.

*

Martin hadn't wanted to make a big affair of his birthday, but Per and Gustav threw a party in their attic studio. It was exactly the kind of party Martin had imagined throwing as a young, struggling writer in Paris. The room was packed with people of whom he knew less than half, music from Per's new portable cassette player vibrated in the background, loud conversations were happening in at least four languages, clouds of cigarette smoke were billowing up by the ceiling. There was an endless supply of wine. Martin talked to everyone, and someone topped up his glass with champagne. In his mind, he was already composing a letter to Cecilia. *Since there were only three cassettes, Bowie and some kind of jazz, they were played over and over all night long. Per was*

on fine form and served as party photographer – I'll show you the pictures.
Gustav was the epitome of The Artist as a Young Man, the only thing miss-
ing was a beret...

Then it was late, and everyone had left. Gustav had passed out. Per had taken off with Lizzy, who was going back to England the following week. Martin poured out half-finished drinks, emptied ashtrays and collected empty bottles. When the place looked decent, he topped up his glass and sat down on the window ledge. The metal roof under his feet was still warm. The lights of Paris glittered.

Before the summer, there had still been long stretches of time spreading out before him, but now he'd crested the peak and was rolling rapidly downhill towards the new year. He counted on his fingers – in just three months, it would be December. True, he could stay longer, but he'd have to find a job. And work things out with Cecilia. She could join him. They could live together in a studio flat with large windows. It might be a bit draughty in winter, and they might have to settle for a communal bathroom, but they would have a bohemian landlady everyone called Madame and never be without freshly baked croissants for breakfast. Except how was he supposed to find a flat? How much would it cost? Did Cecilia even want to come? He tried to recall how far along she was in her studies, but it was hard to keep track since she was taking a double course load and was going for a bachelor's degree in one subject and a master's in the other. She'd written a dissertation last spring, but had it been intellectual history or German? And what about sociology? Could she do a term abroad? Maybe she could write, too? No, Cecilia didn't want that kind of life. But maybe if she wrote her master's dissertation here?

If time kept passing this quickly, he would soon be on a slippery slope towards thirty. It was an age that had until now seemed like a purely theoretical construct, not unlike the logical concepts he'd been forced to learn about when he studied philosophy.

He drank the last of his wine even though he'd begun to feel sick. Inside, Gustav was sawing logs on his camp bed.

Martin had decided he was going to be returning to Gothenburg with a finished manuscript. He could almost feel the weight of the book in his hand and see the name MARTIN BERG in print. But the same stack of ink-scribbled papers was still sitting on his desk and page 105 was gathering dust in the typewriter. He'd scaled back his daily quota from a certain number of words to a certain number of hours, because surely the important thing was not how much he wrote, but how good it was. James Joyce hadn't managed a lot of words per day, either. William Wallace had toiled over a single page for weeks before he was satisfied. Hemingway rewrote the first chapter of *The Sun Also Rises*—

"Thirty-nine times," Gustav said. "I know. Sounds sensible. Hop to it."

"Aren't you going to the museum or whatever?"

"Maybe later. We'll see."

He was still in bed, writing what he called his "monthly report" to his mother, an incomplete and smoothed-out account of their Parisian life, in which Martin often played a prominent role. Gustav's parents considered Martin an upright person and were convinced he was a "good influence", which was no less annoying for probably being true.

Martin returned to his typewriter. He'd managed to name the woman – Laetitia after an old Gainsbourg song – but her contours remained vague compared to Jesper's. Jesper, both Gustav and Per said, was believable. He jumped off the page. But this Laetitia… Martin sighed, stubbed out his half-smoked cigarette, stared at the paper. The words looked good. It looked like a proper paragraph. He lit another cigarette and squinted through the smoke in a way he'd seen Per's friend the photographer do.

He needed inspiration, something to work with. Someone like the girl in the red top. *La Femme avec le Pull Rouge*. Maybe she could be his model, the way Gustav used a model for painting. He would need to see her again, observe her more closely, take note of those tiny details that he could then make use of. Gather material, simply put. He needed material for his book. Nothing wrong with that. Every author before him had needed material for their books. And how did one come by material? Not by sitting at a desk in a stuffy attic flat, trying to make stuff up, that much was certain. Material had to be collected, then processed and rendered into artistic form. That's what writing literature *was*. Gathering, processing.

This was the first interesting idea Martin had stumbled across in days, and now he couldn't stop thinking about it.

"Where are you going?" Gustav called after him. "Could you pick up some wine on your way back?"

"*Sur ma Remington portative j'ai écrit ton nom Laetitia,*" he hummed under his breath on his way down the stairs and out onto the street, his notebook in his pocket.

In the days that followed, Martin wandered around Montparnasse, seeing the city with fresh eyes. The streets glowed in the autumn sunshine. A wind shook the plane trees. The crowded scenes were lively. He went to La Rotonde. He went to Le Select. He went to Closerie des Lilas and if he squinted and turned his head just so, he could almost believe it was still the time of Wallace, especially now the Americans had gone home and the only language he heard around him was French. He didn't see her anywhere, but what were the chances of that anyway? In his text, he recreated the image of her. Her soft, pale wrist. The dark hair tumbling down her back. The little flourish with which she opened her newspaper. He imagined their first conversation and wrote it down for Jesper and Laetitia.

She bowed her head, bending her vanilla-white neck. Then she looked up: a quick glance, furtive, full of promises but gone in a second. Had he imagined it? Her red jumper shimmered in the dark. "I recognise you," she said. "I've seen you in that café by Vavin, haven't I?" And since she very well might have, he had to admit he often frequented that café. She nodded and told him she'd passed him several times. He was flattered she recognised him but didn't want to let on. He cast about

for something to say and seized on the first thing that came
to mind: did she live around here? "Non," she replied with a
smile.

It was one o'clock in the morning when Per gently pointed out that he
was having a hard time falling asleep what with the sound of Martin
hammering on his typewriter.

"But you seem inspired. And that's great, really."

*

September brought a new wave of terrorist attacks. Bombs went off in a
casino in La Défense, a restaurant and City Hall. Planted by Hezbollah
or whomever. Some were *morts* and even more *blessés*. Martin flipped
through *Le Monde* with fingers greasy from a breakfast croissant. There
was some connection to a Lebanese man who was in prison. He tried
to stay informed, since it was a subject he might bring up with his
Laetitia, if he ever saw her again.

Gustav stepped through the door with a carton of Gauloises under
his arm. "Have they blown something up again?"

"A restaurant on the Champs-Elysées."

"Lucky I'm never there. Would be just like me to die in some
bloody political attack."

"Well, from a career perspective, dying young has always proved
beneficial," Martin countered.

"True. But you have to die from hard living. Like Jim Morrison or
Janis Joplin or Jackson Pollock or... I can only think of people whose
names start with J."

"Didn't Pollock die in a car crash?" Martin said.

"Sure, but he was hammered." Gustav took a seat across from him.
"Jimi Hendrix. Brian Jones. Bloody hell, have you ever noticed that –
they all have names that start with the letter J? We're onto something
here. Jones, Jim, Jimi, Joplin, Jackson. Could there be some kind of
conspiracy?"

"I think the common denominator is that they did a lot of drugs."

"True. What did people do before drugs, anyway?"

"Contracted syphilis."

"Of course. Syphilis. Van Gogh. Munch."

"Nietzsche," Martin added.

"I wonder if AIDS is going acquire the same cult status as syphilis." Gustav took the last croissant out of the bag and ate it by tearing it into thin strips.

"AIDS is too horrible," Martin said. "Plus, it's not the artists dying, it's the gays."

"And Michel Foucault."

"Foucault was gay."

"Syphilis is better," Gustav said. "A slow descent into an undefinable type of madness. Or is it actually the flipside of genius? Is it Icarus being punished by the gods? Or is it just what happens when you're less than careful about fucking prostitutes from the provinces?"

Martin laughed.

"I prefer it to being blown to bits because someone's grumpy about someone else being in prison," Gustav went on. "No one has ever become a recognised artist after dying in an incomprehensible terrorist attack."

"Maybe if it was the Red Army Faction who killed you," Martin said. "If you were offed by Gudrun Ensslin."

"We'd better steer clear of *la rive droite*," Gustav said. "So we don't miss the chance to pop our clogs in a way more suited to our artistic dignity and become unbelievably big posthumously. Though we might have to brave it. Pierre's friend over by République is throwing another party."

"What friend?"

"The one who thinks really highly of himself. The photographer. If we sneak over there under cover of darkness, we might make it out alive."

"The place we went to last spring?"

"We could get a couple of those ski masks, too."

"That time when we left early because you wanted us to go to some club, which we couldn't find at first and then realised was ridiculously expensive to get into, so we went home and drank whisky instead?"

"That could be any old night. What difference does it make? Pierre's friend is throwing a party. The only problem, the way I see it, is figuring out how to get to the right bank and back in one piece... maybe taxi?"

They did go in the end, and Martin was almost relieved when he didn't see the brunette in the red jumper anywhere. He poured himself some wine. He talked to some of the Sorbonne gang. He was in the middle of a story about how Foucault had been rejected as a PhD candidate by Uppsala University because he was considered too odd when he saw her enter the room.

And this is when the sword falls, this is three strikes and you're out, this is the universe announcing its will, this is Martin giving her a light and asking her name, this is the opening lines to a brief but intense short story with commas as the predominant form of punctuation, followed by ellipses. This is Martin Berg on a sofa next to Diane Thomas, with an arm around her shoulders, his left leg pressed against her right, and someone raises a Polaroid camera and Martin raises his glass, *click*, and there's no way back from this.

III

INTERVIEWER: How autobiographical are your texts from this period?

MARTIN BERG: [*sipping his water, coughing quietly*] As in what percentage?

INTERVIEWER: [*gesticulating*] Are there autobiographical elements?

*

Since they didn't have a phone, there was no absence of ringing to obsess about. Nothing to wait for. When Martin woke up the morning after the party and discovered after looking at his alarm clock that it was less than ten hours since he'd stood against a wall with his hands under Diane's shirt, around her warm waist; less than twelve hours since he'd heard her laugh quietly right next to his ear – it might as well have been twelve years. No phone numbers had been exchanged. They would never meet again. And that was probably just as well, because that meant he could write home to Cecilia with a clean conscience. (Or at least cleaner.) He didn't have to leave out and obfuscate the way he'd already imagined needing to. Almost everything was harmless.

So when Martin opened their letterbox a few days later, he wondered innocently who the small white envelope could be from. He didn't recognise the handwriting.

It turned out to contain the Polaroid picture of him and the brunette in the red jumper, along with a short note. An address, a date and a time, and it was signed *Diane*.

*

He didn't come home from their first meeting until two o'clock the next day. The flat was empty. He lay down on his bed and was asleep within seconds.

A few hours later, Gustav came back and began to fuss about, clinking bottles together and eventually slamming the door shut needlessly hard. Martin blinked, disoriented. His body was sore and ached, like that time he ran a half-marathon and then went out partying.

"Where were you last night?" Gustav asked without making eye contact.

"I passed out on the sofa at Paul and the German's place."

Gustav nodded, the suspicion on his face breaking into a smile.

"Hungover?"

"As fuck."

"Want to get a pizza?"

"*Bien sûr.*"

Since they'd been back, Gustav had lost the pounds he'd put on over the summer. His legs were twigs in black denim. His fraying sailor's shirts looked baggy around his chest. His denim jacket was too big. He'd swapped his straw hat for a Greek fisherman's cap and his sandals for trainers that were quietly falling apart. Old ladies routinely tutted at the sight of Gustav, and Martin felt their reproach was somehow aimed at him for not looking after his friend properly. But how was it his fault that Gustav's breakfast consisted of two cigarettes and that he often forgot to have lunch?

And now, he only ate half his pizza before putting down his cutlery and ordering another beer.

"Written anything?"

Martin's mouth was full so he shook his head. "Not in a while," he said after swallowing. "You?"

"No. It's been getting steadily worse since we came back."

And thus, they were doomed to wander through the valley of the shadow of death until Gustav perked up again. Martin must have made a face, because Gustav said: "What?" in a fairly annoyed tone.

"No, I was just thinking… it's always like this. At first, everything's going great and then it goes poorly. And then it starts to go well again. But you always panic and think the bad periods are going to last forever."

Gustav pinched the ridge of his nose with his thumb and forefinger. "It's not just that."

"Then what is it?"

"Never mind. I'm just low. Let's talk about something else."

A couple of days later, he had a letter from Cecilia. He left it sitting unopened next to his typewriter for several days.

"What news from Gothenburg?" Gustav said when he spotted the airmail envelope. "It must be bloody hard. That the person you're with is so far away."

"It is," Martin replied.

When Gustav went to the bathroom, he opened the letter and skimmed it. Lucky for him, because, moments later, Gustav wanted to know how the *Heart of Darkness* essay had fared. "Did it get published?"

"Uh – yes, it did."

"That's fucking great!"

"Yes. Amazing."

"Tell her congrats from me the next time you talk to her. Or why don't I call her myself? Do you have any change?"

Martin watched him through the window. Gustav stepping out onto the street. Walking to the payphone on the corner. Gesticulating with one arm, his shoulders shaking with laughter. Walking back.

Martin inserted a new sheet of paper into the roller but couldn't think of a word to write in response.

The next day, CSPPA, or maybe it was Hezbollah, set off a bomb at Tati, just a few blocks from the flat. It was a Wednesday, and the children had the day off school. Seven dead. Rue de Rennes was full of ambulances and police cars. When Martin walked past a few days later, there was still broken glass on the pavement.

"Good thing I'd never sink to eating at Tati," Gustav said.

"Gustav!" Per said reproachfully.

Martin lay on his bed, wondering when he would see Diane Thomas again.

*

After it was over, their affair would feel more protracted and substantial than it really was.

Martin could list every time they'd met, including dates and the number of hours they'd spent together. He remembered how many times they'd gone to a nameless bar by Canal Saint-Martin (four). How many times they'd slept together in her flat in Belleville, a mythical place with chequerboard floors and red scarves over the lampshades (five). And he could give an account of the entire course of events, line by line, the times she told him it was over and then changed her mind (two and a half in all).

She was a waitress but wanted to work with literature. A friend of a friend worked for a publishing company, and she was waiting for him to help her get a foot in the door. In the meantime, she slaved away at a restaurant in the sixteenth arrondissement. Good tips but very stiff vibe, she said. Martin never saw her in her work clothes – she changed there – but he pictured a black dress and white apron, possibly some type of cap. Otherwise, Diane's most prominent item of clothing was that red jumper, which was slightly too short, revealing a sliver of stomach when she raised her arms. The skin there was as white as cream. She had a carefree way of dressing, a result primarily of her habit of grabbing literally whatever was nearest, often a pair of 501s that were regrettably similar to Cecilia's.

At first, he derived a unique pleasure from the thought of Diane, but over time, it became more like torment. He zoned out in conversation. He stared vacantly at the blank sheet of paper in front of him while smoke from his cigarette rose idly towards the ceiling. He thought that the only thing that could alleviate his utter obsession with her was to see her. Just one more time, to get it out of his system. But he always ended up in the same eternal feedback loop: Did she want to see him again? Didn't she? If so, why? Had he done something wrong? How was he supposed to interpret *that* word choice, *that* look?

He stubbed out his cigarette and tapped out a sentence. He wanted Jesper and Laetitia to end up together, but from a literary perspective that was probably a bad choice. It would make his book a melodrama. He certainly couldn't write a *happy* love story.

Gradually, he gave up even trying to write, grabbed his jacket and wandered about the city instead.

Every time they met up, they had sex.

That first time, she brought him back to her studio in the east part of town, not far from the cemetery where Jim Morrison was buried. This – he thought as they fucked on the kitchen table – wasn't the moment he betrayed Cecilia. (Or, more accurately, Martin wasn't thinking all that much while it was going on; that came later, when Diane quickly pulled her 501s back on and asked if he wanted a drink, a beer maybe?) He'd betrayed her the moment he went to meet Diane. When they took the metro together. When he followed her up the stairs. And in the name of complete accuracy, hadn't the betrayal occurred long before then? At Lucien's party. When he lit her cigarette and introduced himself. Or a while later, when he slid his hand in under her shirt and she smiled.

So against the backdrop of all those betrayals, big and small, what difference did intercourse make? Hadn't the damage already been done? From a moral-philosophy perspective. Would it be considered an extenuating circumstance if he'd taken all those other steps and then backed out at the pivotal moment when Diane unbuttoned her trousers?

And since they'd already had sex once, they might as well do it again.

After a couple of weeks, she stopped answering her phone. He called and called for days, but the signals might as well have been relayed straight into space.

Just as he was pondering whether to write her a letter, Per came home and asked if Martin wanted to go with him to a mate's house for a drink. Martin was disinclined until he realised which mate Per was referring to: the stuck-up photographer.

All three of them went. Per had aced an essay and was trying to cheer up Gustav, who was still low. Martin walked half a pace behind them and said little.

They got there. They rang the doorbell.

It was almost too much to hope for.

But there she was. He recognised the back of her neck immediately. She turned to see who had just arrived, but because Martin was trying hard to pretend he hadn't noticed her, he missed her facial expression.

After a while, she came over. They kissed each other on the cheek, made small talk. Martin felt Gustav's eyes burning holes in the back of his head.

"I've been calling you," he said when he was sure Gustav couldn't overhear.

She stared into her glass. "I've been away."

Of course. So simple.

And then he asked where and she said La Rochelle, and she asked if he'd written more of *le roman*, and he said *Oui, naturellement*, and she asked if it was about her, and time passed both very quickly and very slowly, and he gazed into her eyes, brown and moist, and the future seemed, in that moment, physically tangible, he saw her pull her jumper over her head, every day, every morning, felt puzzle pieces fall into place, and for a second, Cecilia's face flashed past, but he pretended not to see it, what happens in Paris stays in Paris, oh my god, I have to be allowed to live, don't I, you're only young once, sometimes you have to just take the plunge.

"Maybe," he said.

Per left early, but Gustav insisted on staying. He sat in the kitchen, rolling cigarettes, drinking vodka and discussing art. And then he'd suddenly called a taxi and was telling Martin it was time to go, and Martin felt his body get up off the sofa where he'd been talking to Diane and some other people.

He gave Diane and the others some kind of farewell salute.

"*À la prochaine*," he said and then they were on the steps, on the street.

Is it about me?

He could wait.

*

Shortly thereafter, Diane made it clear that the two of them having a relationship was a bad idea, that they were on a course for disaster, and that it was largely her fault.

"*Je suis impossible*," she said, not particularly regretfully. Unfortunately, there was nothing to be done about it. "*Rien.*"

But then, a few days later, she wanted to meet up again.

Without writing anything that could be misconstrued as a diary, Martin tried to sort through what was happening with Diane. Per took it as him finally getting into the writing groove. Cecilia, Martin wrote, was his soul's companion. She represented the kind of love that wasn't threatened by the love he practised with Diane. Which was more of a Love of the Flesh. But for all he wrote, long essay-like paragraphs in which he referred to Sartre/de Beauvoir, transcendent/contingent love, and such, Martin's being seemed unwilling to get used to the idea of two women at once. When his heart focused on *one*, it seemed to forget the *other*. He wished he could talk to Cecilia about it. Philosophically.

He tried to write *I love Cecilia* again and again, and it didn't feel like a lie.

He could hear her voice, objective and dry: *What if I had been with someone else?* Not even now did that thought feel particularly bearable.

Diane only ever said *See you* when they parted ways. Never a word about when.

And Martin discovered how much time could be spent waiting.

He woke in the morning and the thought was instantly there: Maybe today. He waited while he ate breakfast. He waited while he wrote without finding any purchase in his prose. He admitted he was waiting when he decided to leave the library just in time to catch the postman. When he tore open the letterbox and riffled through the post.

Then it started all over again. He waited for the time when he'd decided it was acceptable to call. He waited while he talked to his friends, waited while he tried to think of something intelligent to say back.

He waited while the phone rang and rang.

She didn't pick up and he stared at the receiver.

But maybe she was writing a letter in this very moment? Maybe she was just now going out to post it so she wouldn't forget? Or maybe both those things had already happened, and now her letter was one among thousands in a sack somewhere, waiting to be sorted? Maybe it had already been sorted and was sitting in his local post office?

He waited to get drunk. He waited to go home. He waited for sleep. He was on the verge of giving up when she finally called.

And then a new kind of wait commenced, a feverish wait for a date and a time. He waited for the moment he spotted her face in the crowd. He waited for when they were going back to hers together. For her to take her clothes off. For there to be no distance between himself and her.

Time began to behave erratically. Just a few days earlier, everything had been fine, but from one moment to the next, he could be thrown into a chasm of despair. The present stretched out in every direction. He couldn't see beyond it. Time expressions that used to mean something were stripped of their referents. Next Saturday? This Christmas? He shrugged. Sure, sounds fine.

The leaves fell from the trees. The sky lay heavy above the rooftops. The Seine was shades of slate and lead. The churches of the city rang their doomsday bells. The pavements were covered in dog shit. Plastic carrier bags bobbed in Canal Saint-Martin.

*

Cecilia wrote. He couldn't bring himself to open the envelope.

IV

MARTIN BERG: It's important to remember that fiction is always fiction.

INTERVIEWER: Can you say a bit about how fiction relates to lived experience?

*

For two very long weeks in November, he heard nothing from Diane. Afterwards, he thought: I should have known.

She was going away for a while, she said. How long? Oh, just *quelques jours*.

The conversation took place while she brushed her hair and got ready for work. They were taking the metro together to Châtelet, a journey Martin hated so intensely he sometimes said goodbye to her above ground and walked to the next stop. Anything to avoid the distance that grew between them in the presence of other people, the moment she said goodbye with a fleeting kiss on the cheek as though he were just anybody. But that particular day, he wasn't worried. Quite the contrary. He wished her a good trip and then went home to sleep.

It was unusual for him to have stayed the night. Ironically, his evasiveness when it came to sleepovers was one of his few psychological advantages. Diane sighed demonstratively when he got out of bed; she took her clothes off at the same pace he put on his. But so long as Martin went home, no matter how late the hour, he didn't have to endure Gustav's looks. Propriety seemed satisfied so long as he spent a few hours of each night alone in his own bed. An entire night's absence, however, aroused suspicion.

"Aren't you the busy bee these days," Gustav's voice came from the alcove. He was lying on his camp bed, smoking. The cassette player next to him was playing a scratchy tape of what sounded like "Ashes to Ashes".

"I missed the last metro."

"That sucks. Where were you?"

"By Porte d'Orléans."

"I meant at whose house?"

"Honestly, no idea. It was some friend of—"

"Let me guess. Paul and the German bloke."

"Just Heinrich, actually. Paul wasn't feeling well."

"And why wasn't I invited?"

"You weren't here when I left. Besides, you don't like Paul or Heinrich."

"So he's been upgraded to Heinrich."

"I seem to recall that your assessment was 'typical pretentious German fruit'. Whatever that's supposed to mean. *I* think he's nice. But what's the point of bringing you if you're just going to sulk in a corner?"

Gustav pulled off the feat of shrugging while lying down. A long, tense silence followed, during which he busied himself with rolling a cigarette. Martin suddenly wished Per was there. Per hated when the mood turned frosty; it rarely took him more than five seconds to find a way to thaw the ice.

He pulled out the sofa bed and began to fuss with his sheets and blankets, even though he wasn't particularly tired any more.

Gustav blinked first. "Fine," he said, "so did you have fun?"

"Not particularly."

"The place wasn't buzzing?"

"Some stoners smoking up in a corner. The guy who threw the party spent most of the night in his bedroom, arguing with his girl-friend. Heinrich wanted to hit a club but then we drank a bottle of Fernet instead."

"Hmm. Doesn't sound like I missed much."

"You can say that again."

The genius part of the lie was that it was all true. Martin really had met up with Heinrich, a.k.a. the German (originally a friend of Per's). The party really had been rather dead – the only reason Martin had gone was that he wanted to meet more real French people and because it was near Diane's flat. And there really had been a bottle of Fernet. The difference was that Heinrich had done most of the drinking. Once he'd passed out in the bath, Martin had slipped out.

Gustav seemed to accept this redacted version of the truth. He ami-cably moved over to the sofa bed to play cards.

When the sun set, neither one of them could be bothered to get up and turn on the lights, so they lay there in the gloom, talking about nothing, smoking. The tape ended. They fell asleep.

And not even in hindsight, when Martin went over the events of that day, since it was the last he would hear from Diane in a long time, could he remember if he'd sensed it coming.

After Cecilia had sent three letters in as many weeks without him replying to any of them, there was no fourth.

At first, it was a relief, because it meant one less unopened envelope in the shoebox under his bed. But it wouldn't surprise him if Gustav, the world's worst pen pal, had managed to scratch out a couple of lines to Cecilia. Which would underscore the fact that Martin was alive and well and simply *not answering her letters*.

His only hope was that Gustav hadn't caught onto the fact that he wasn't writing, and that Gustav had a poor sense of time. But that wouldn't stop Cecilia from writing to Gustav to ask why Martin wasn't replying. Which would be just as bad. Possibly worse.

At that point, Martin struck a deal with fate: if he read her most recent letter and wrote back, he'd be allowed to call Diane from the payphone.

The letter contained a gentle rebuke for not being in touch, some talk about university and gripes about her family, whom she'd visited in conjunction with one of her brothers' birthdays. But it wasn't even a page long and the tone was bland; it could have been a letter to anyone.

Martin made himself a cup of coffee, emptied the ashtray, dusted off his keyboard, pulled out the old paper and put a new one in. Then he stretched his arms, cracked his knuckles and set to.

He wrote that he'd come down with tonsillitis and been in pretty poor shape until he dragged himself to the clinic and was given some powerful French pills. He wrote that he was thinking about her (true, though not quite in the way she probably assumed) and that he missed her (also true, on a kind of metaphysical plane). Then he padded the text with a few lines about Paris and Gustav. But even though he tried his best, the letter didn't even come to a page and a half. He signed off with a *I'll write again soon! Lots of love, Martin*.

Satisfied with his work, he trudged down to the postbox on the corner, which was conveniently located right next to the payphone.

No answer. He let it ring at least twenty times and immediately regretted it.

It was far too easy to picture Diane's expressionless face as she waited for the phone to stop ringing.

Ironically, he did get sick not long thereafter. It wasn't tonsillitis, but a very bad cold. He was completely drained and couldn't do anything but lie in bed. Per brought him tea with ginger and Gustav nagged him about not smoking. He read the first half of newspaper articles and listened to the radio on a low volume, slept most of the time, and occasionally forced down a few spoonfuls of soup. Life beyond his messy bed, the bin full of used tissues, his glass of water, an open *Paris Review*, a plate holding a dry half-eaten croissant from the corner shop, his woollen socks and his pyjama bottoms temporarily ceased to exist.

When a reply to his deal-striking letter arrived, he made sure to write again while he was so numb he couldn't really feel much of anything.

And then two weeks had gone by with no sign of Diane.

Martin tried to call one more time, promising himself it was the last. This time, there was an out-of-breath *'Allo?*

What did her tone imply when she realised it was him? Surprise, guilt? She was evasive and curt; Martin realised he'd twisted the phone cord into a tight spiral.

"Do you want to meet up?" he said, fairly aggressively. "Or don't you?"

"Sure, sure, absolutely…"

"Because it doesn't seem like you do."

"I've had a lot on."

"Hmm."

"Tomorrow?" she said. "Around seven?" She mentioned the bar by the Canal. After they hung up, Martin stared at the receiver. He felt vaguely nauseous.

Over the next twenty-four hours, he wondered if maybe he was coming down with something again. For a while, he even considered calling to cancel. Instead, he took a long shower and put on his least dirty jeans.

Diane was already there when he arrived. She was wearing her coat.

They ordered and exchanged bland pleasantries. After ten minutes, Diane said: "I'm sorry. I just don't feel like this is going anywhere."

"But I don't understand…"

"Us. You and me."

He didn't know what to say. She didn't say anything either.

"But you can't just…" Martin said after a while.

"What can't I do?"

"But you said you…"

But he couldn't quite remember what she'd said.

Diane put money down on the table. She hadn't even drunk half of her wine. He'd thought they were going to sit there for a long time, that they were going to talk it through, that things would be explained, that they would order more wine, become slightly tipsy, reach for each other's hands across the table.

"I have somewhere else to be," she said. "See you."

See you.

A few days later, however, she got in touch again. She'd been thinking and so on, maybe he'd like to meet up again after all?

Martin waited several days before calling her back. It would have been better if he'd been determined enough to avoid all contact, but apparently his character was of the more pliable kind.

Their next meeting did nothing to clear things up. Diane was upset about something she didn't want to explain. Then she kissed him, said: "Let's not talk about sad things," and tugged at the waistband of his jeans.

The dignified thing to do would have been to break things off at that point. To push her away, grab his coat and leave. As it was, he had to leave her among tangled sheets and with as curt a goodbye as he could manage.

*

He received a letter with the address on the envelope written in an unfamiliar hand. When he took it out of the letterbox, his heart began to pound madly, mostly out of habit.

It turned out to be a letter informing him that *The Chameleons* had won first prize in the short-story competition he'd forgotten he'd submitted it to.

"This is amazing," Per said.

"We have to celebrate!" Gustav said.

His arm draped itself heavily around Martin's shoulders. Their smiles stretched the corners of their mouths, clown smiles.

Per mobilised their social circle, they met up, champagne was ordered, glasses clinked. Martin's arms moved in various drinking motions; he said the kinds of things that were expected of him; his tongue seemed to take charge and take care of things by itself, *cheers*, yes, thank you, who knows, maybe the start of a long career?

*

One day, he wandered all the way up to Sacré-Coeur, without even a hint of annoyance that the Montmartre that had once belonged to the painters, home of decadence, absinthe and abstinence, had now been overrun by tourists and kitsch. He walked with his eyes on the ground and his hands in his pockets. Like so many doubters, he was drawn to the church.

She'd started it. He'd been completely content to leave it at innocent fantasies. Silly dreams that would have been forgotten if she hadn't pulled him in and then pulled back out again so cruelly. Why had she even started anything? What was the point? Had she even liked him? She'd evidently wanted to see him, because why else would she have sent that Polaroid? She must have liked him. And if she'd liked him, what had made her stop? Had it been something he did, and if so, could it be undone? Compensated for? Was there someone else? If so, who?

He reached the church and turned to behold the vista, as was expected of him. A milky fog shrouded the city. Through it, he saw rooftops and boulevards, the Eiffel Tower and the train stations like scattered building blocks.

*

"Hey, what's with you?"

"With me? Nothing much."

"Come off it, Martin. I can tell something's up."

The bar they were in was loud with cackling and chattering that grated in his ears, and Gustav's face seemed to be floating out like some kind of experimental oil painting.

"Have you looked in a mirror recently?" He sounded concerned. "You look like you're on the brink of collapse."

"I guess I just have the winter blues."

"Is it about Cecilia?"

"Cissi? God, no."

"Writer's block again?"

Martin saw his chance. "Yes," he said. "I'm actually properly stuck right now. You know, you keep at it and keep at it and the more crap you write the worse you feel." He sipped his wine, somewhat encouraged by his own words. "Like walking straight into the darkness."

He'd left his notebook at home. He had to remember that. Straight into the darkness.

Life was slipping through his fingers. These days, he usually woke up hungover around lunchtime, and if he left the flat at all, it was only to go to a bar or the cinema. In November and early December, he spent hours upon hours in the blessed darkness of the theatre. He bought tickets without caring what was playing. *Top Gun* and *La folle journée de Ferris Bueller* flickered past with French dubbing. The same day a student was killed during a demonstration, Martin watched *Karate Kid, le moment de verité II* as though in a trance, and when he walked home through the Quartier Latin, he barely noticed the tense mood in the streets.

And yet, Gustav was the one Per worried about.

"He looks a bit haggard, don't you think?" he said one day, when Gustav had dragged himself out of the flat for once.

"Isn't 'a bit haggard' Gustav's default state?"

So when Gustav woke up fully dressed on his camp bed, reeking of alcohol, and started the day by throwing up in the toilet, Martin didn't give it a second thought. Nor was he particularly worried the time Gustav disappeared and didn't come back for several days. It hadn't been a particularly great evening. Martin got too drunk and Per took him home. Gustav insisted on staying. The next night, he was still out. Martin tried to explain that this wasn't all that unusual and started to tell Per about the time last summer when he'd taken off from the restaurant in Antibes and not reappeared until the next day. But the mere mention of last summer triggered stabbing pains in his stomach, so he quickly returned to the topic at hand. "He probably met some people who seemed all right and then they lived all the way out in some suburb or whatever. If we had a phone, I'm sure he would have called."

"But what if he's lost, or…"

"Well, at least it's fairly mild out. It's not like he's going to freeze to death."

He'd meant it as a joke, but Per just nodded thoughtfully.

The next day rolled around. As if on cue, the outside temperature had plummeted overnight, and their windows were covered with frost. They didn't exchange many words; they were both listening for footsteps on the stairs.

"Maybe we should tell the police," Per said after lunch.

"I'm sure he'll turn up any minute now."

"But what if he doesn't?"

They agreed to do something about it if Gustav wasn't home by seven. He stepped through the door at quarter to.

"What a fucking night," he said, throwing himself down on his bed without taking his coat off.

"Last night or the one before that?"

"Both."

"See?" Martin said to Per. "No need to fret."

V

INTERVIEWER: I read one of your early short stories while I was preparing for this interview…

MARTIN BERG: Is that right.

INTERVIEWER: You write with great feeling about a young man's search for love and validation. What did the act of writing mean to you during this period?

*

December came. The streets and buildings were like dark tunnels. Martin tried to talk the others into going to Marseille over Christmas, arguing that unlike tidy, museal Paris, Marseille was a working-class town marked by seafaring and hard living, a bit like Gothenburg, in other words. "Except probably more dangerous. Come on, it'll be fun. Or at least it will be different." But Per had exams and Gustav didn't want to go anywhere. He was skint, he said, and had no desire to be robbed of the few francs he had left.

Tant pis – Martin went by himself. He quickly made new friends: Leonard, a twitchy, trilingual Frenchman with very pale eyes, one of which was lazy, Katja, a quiet Russian, and her fiancé-or-maybe-not, an American whose name Martin never learned. He told them he'd come to Europe to Interrail, but hadn't realised how cold the winter would be, and now he was trying to make the best of it. They'd ended up in the same compartment on the train down and Leonard had offered everyone wine from an unlabelled bottle. "*Une fête internationale, quoi*," he'd chuckled, running his long fingers over his shaved, lumpy scalp. Martin thought they might have said they'd met in a restaurant at Gare de Lyon, but he wasn't sure. A bloke like Leonard could probably turn up anytime, anywhere and attract new friends like fly paper attracts flies, and before Martin knew it, they'd tumbled off the train and staggered down to a basement bar by the docks. There, they toasted with absinthe (Leonard's suggestion) and sang Soviet drinking songs (Katja's suggestion). Diane was lightyears away. Cecilia was lightyears beyond that. For a while, Martin floated in a pleasant bubble of serenity in which nothing really mattered.

Then a series of sharply illuminated fragments, followed by a compact darkness.

Martin woke up with a throbbing headache, a stomach on the verge of turning itself inside-out, and a mouth like a hot, sandy cave. In addition to these familiar agonies (which he had no problem with, which, indeed, he welcomed in the same way monks sometimes flagellate themselves) there was also a new and unknown pain localised to his left upper arm. Only after taking a piss and running freezing water from the tap over his head in the cheap hotel room he'd checked into pre-absinthe, did Martin investigate its cause. When he pulled his undershirt up over his head, the pain intensified.

His upper arm was red and swollen. In the mirror, he saw the unmistakeable contours of an anchor.

He didn't even know the word for anchor in French.

Down at reception, he asked if there had been any sign of his friend Monsieur Leonard. The receptionist pointed towards a café twenty yards down the street. He found Leonard inside, drinking coffee from a very small cup with his coat on.

"*C'est quoi ça?*" Martin said, showing him his arm.

"*Un ancre*," Leonard replied.

"Fuck," Martin said in Swedish.

Leonard laughed. Martin asked where he'd got this idiotic idea from. Leonard admitted he wasn't sure, but that they'd been walking past a tattoo parlour when the spirit had suddenly moved Martin.

"At one o'clock in the morning?" Martin said.

Leonard shrugged. "Marseille," he said. "Sailors and so on. You never know."

"But why didn't you stop me?" Martin demanded.

"How was I supposed to know you wanted to be stopped?" Leonard said. "Come on. It's not even that big. Would you like anything? Coffee?

A beer? You have to make sure you put some lotion on that, too. To keep it from getting infected. And if I were you, I'd go get tested."

"Tested?"

"AIDS," the Frenchman said, as though it were completely obvious. "The needles are usually clean, but you never know."

Marseille was cold and faded like an old postcard. The sky was an icy blue, the wind howled incessantly, and the white buildings pressed themselves against the hills as though they were cold. Martin wandered up and down the streets but couldn't get a sense of how big the town really was. He was probably walking in circles. The second night, he went out with Leonard to eat and get hammered. It was Christmas Eve, and on the way from one bar to another, he mustered enough change and presence of mind to call Sweden. He didn't expect her to pick up, and she didn't. She was probably at her summer house. But at least this way he could say he'd tried to call.

The next morning, he felt all right, as though the alcohol had stabilised his body and put everything back in its rightful place. After breakfast – espresso and buttery brioche at the café, no sign of Leonard – he found a pharmacy and bought a salve.

The anchor was about four inches long and not particularly sophisticated, which was probably a good thing, because it didn't seem particularly well executed, either. Fewer details to fail at. With time, it would turn blue, like his dad's tattoos.

*

When Martin returned to Paris, there was a note on his desk, written in Per's neat hand. Gustav had gone to visit his grandmother without saying when he'd be back. Per himself was on a trip with some people from university and was expected back on the thirtieth.

Martin hadn't heard Cecilia's voice in over a month.

He went to *le tabac* for change and called from the payphone on the corner. There was a raw chill in the air he hadn't thought Paris capable of.

"Hello?"

"It's me. Martin," said Martin, who had just been skewered by a sharp arrow of concern that Cecilia might not instantly understand that *he* was the *me* in that greeting.

"God, I thought it was Mum again… How are you?"

"I'm good, I'm good. Hey," he said and fed the phone another franc, "I might run out of money. I just wanted to tell you I've bought a ticket back home."

"Oh." She sounded surprised. "When?"

"Day after tomorrow. I'll be back Friday."

"Wow – but I thought you were staying for New Year's? And maybe even longer?"

"Huh?" Martin suddenly recalled having implied something along those lines a while ago. He might be staying a few more months, he'd written. Spring in Paris and so on. "Right. No. No, I miss you."

She promised to meet him at the station.

"Thanks. You're a star," he said. "And Cecilia? I'm—"

The call cut out.

*

France was covered in snow, as was Belgium, and all the way through Germany, the train raced across endless white plains. After changing in Berlin, Martin slept through most of the last leg of the journey. It was a restless, shallow sleep. He woke up in Halmstad and stared out of the window the rest of the way. Earth and sky blended together, indistinguishable in their whiteness. His stomach ached, but he could barely get half the sandwich he'd bought in the restaurant car down. Despite long johns, double sweaters, coat and scarf, he was shivering. To distract himself, he tried to read a newspaper someone had left behind on the seat next to his. *Record cold snap*, the front page shouted. *Coldest winter in 20 years*.

By the time the train pulled up to the platform, snorting and hissing and screeching and then finally falling silent, his stomach was cramping and twisting so badly it doubled him up.

He was one of the last to disembark, scanning the crowd with panic building in his chest. Then a figure stepped out of the crowd and started towards him. She was wearing a long fur coat with the collar turned up like a Russian princess, and no hat even though it was almost fifteen below. There was something about her face Martin didn't recognise, and when he went to meet her, he thought about a coffee cup that has been broken and meticulously glued back together.

He wrapped his arms around her. They stood like that for a long time without speaking.

"I'll never leave again," Martin mumbled into her hair after a while. He didn't know if it was true or not, but it felt like the right thing to say.

"Okay," Cecilia said. "Good."

18

THE PSYCHOLOGY DEPARTMENT was housed in a right-angled, red-brick colossus whose design seemed torn between ambition and self-effacement, like the architectural expression of an inner conflict common among the students who frequented the building daily. Its centre was dominated by the airy space of a wide atrium, but the lecture halls were all cramped and stuffy. The large windows were hung with bespoke curtains with the Greek letter *psi* woven into the pattern, but the lunchroom was tiny and the number of microwaves vastly insufficient. The building was full of art, but none of the photocopiers ever worked.

Rakel Berg was sitting in one of the undersized classrooms, attempting in vain to focus on the PowerPoint presentation on psychometric testing flashing before her. Someone raised their hand to ask if this was going to be in the exam. Another asked if the PowerPoint could be emailed to everyone. The girl who asked about the exam raised her hand again to tell the class about a manager she'd had working in a nursing home, saying that manager had had clear psychopathic traits. Rakel's notebook remained empty.

Instead of studying, she'd scoured the internet for any and all information about the author of *Ein Jahr*. A scanty Wikipedia entry informed her Franke was born in Munich, lived in Berlin and had published four novels since his debut in the nineties. *Ein Jahr der Liebe* was his most recent and most acclaimed. As far as Rakel could tell, the book's success had been unexpected and had snowballed. Philip Franke's fame had been waning, or, rather, had never actually waxed, which meant the launch of *Ein Jahr* had not been accompanied by much of a PR campaign. The book had simply been published, without fanfare, and only briefly mentioned by the papers. But after a few months, something had happened. The novel was held up by several influential critics, Franke was praised for "the vibrant and powerful prose with which he describes the inevitability of a doomed love affair" and such. A long interview with him featured in a renowned culture magazine; he was nominated for a literature prize, ended up on a couple of best-books-of-the-year lists just in time for the Christmas shopping season, and appeared on a TV show. Words like "bestseller" began to be bandied about in the newspapers.

Her image search showed a man in his early forties with wild hair and a clear aversion to smiling in press pictures. He was good-looking in an undefined way, as though he looked like someone you knew and liked. In some older pictures, taken to promote previous publications, he looked younger and happier. He sat perched on a crumbling stone wall in an autumnal landscape, smiling at the camera with a red scarf over a herringbone coat. In a YouTube clip from last year's Frankfurt Book Fair, he spoke for ten minutes about how the German novel had dealt with reunification. His voice was sonorous, and he formulated his words with precision and clarity.

Rakel had considerable difficulty imagining her mother, or the person she remembered as her mother, having anything to do with the man staring out of the black-and-white author portrait. Middle-aged men anxious to come across as very serious always seemed to be precariously close to being ridiculous without realising it. There were some really good press pictures of Gustav, and they were good because Gustav's face was so relaxed and naked, completely devoid of the mask people lock their features into when put in front of a camera. The photographer was a friend of Gustav's, and when Rakel met him at a gallery opening in Berlin, she'd been struck by his probing, mildly investigatory manner, as though he were constantly searching for chinks in people's armour, tenderly on the lookout for the hidden, the ugly. In his presence, she'd felt exposed but not judged. Philip Franke's photographer had not been able to pull that off. The photographs were closed off in their flat muteness. It wasn't until Rakel heard the author's voice and saw his facial expressions in the interview at the book fair that understanding began to take shape inside her. His gaze was steady, his entire being focused; he breathed heavily when he paused to think and winced at his own words when he found them insufficient. His jokes were archly self-deprecating, and he would suddenly crack into strangely embarrassed smiles.

Chairs scraped around her; class was over.

Rakel gathered up her things and left the building.

She wandered the streets at random. Cecilia's eyes followed her from every advertising column. By Vasa Viktoria, she absent-mindedly stepped into the street and had to jump out of the way of a tram. The city suddenly seemed so small. There was nowhere to go but sitting still was impossible. After zigzagging through Vasastan and Johanneberg, she reached Näckrosdammen, where she sat down under a mossy oak tree. She spread her coat out and lay down on her back. The light under the trees was a golden haze, the grass was warm, the swelling buds on the rhododendron bushes were on the cusp of opening, and from the hazel shrubs she could hear the buzzing of bumblebees and chirping of birds. It was, Rakel realised, the first time she'd ever skipped a lecture. The first time she'd ever skipped anything.

She closed her eyes and the world fell away. She thought about Philip Franke and she thought about her mother. If Philip's novel was even slightly based on a true story, it seemed he might be a brother in misfortune: Cecilia Berg had appeared in his life, had an intense guest run, and then vanished irrevocably. Confusion and anguish filled the space she'd left behind, and nothing was ever the same. When Rakel tried to imagine the woman Philip might have encountered, she pictured 33-year-old Cecilia, but she must have been at least forty-five.

Human memory is unreliable, that was one thing all subfields of psychology agreed on. An individual's life story was a morass of fragmented recollections, other people's narratives, unconscious incitements to direct one's attention this or that way. Experiences and events were forgotten, invented, merged and warped. Cecilia had always belonged to the past, an inaccessible and grand continent from which Rakel was banished. She was a shadow who came and went in Rakel's remembrances, appearing suddenly in sharp focus, then slipping once again out of reach. Among the clearer sections of Rakel's life story was the very long summer spent in the summer house; it must have been right after Elis was born. It had been a wondrous and special time full of events that were out of the ordinary, which was probably why it was prominent among Rakel's childhood memories. Something had always seemed to be going on at the edge of her vision. Every time she tried to look at it, it slipped away, only to reappear at the corner of her eye a little while later. All the grown-ups were busy and just like that, Rakel had been promoted from Child to Big Girl, which was associated with a long list of privileges. She was allowed to play alone in the woods, stay up longer at night, and ride her bike up and down the tree-lined road. She was expected to keep track of dinnertime with the aid of an old wristwatch her dad had found in the basement; he'd made a new hole in the leather strap with a hammer and a nail so it fit Rakel's downy little wrist. No one checked the age rating of the films she watched, and even though she was strictly forbidden from going down to the lake without an adult, no one had said anything about wading in the little stream, fishing for tadpoles with the butterfly net her grandfather had given her.

Her mum was locked in a room upstairs and absolutely not to be disturbed. There was no running in the hallways. She had to pick up her toys. Sometimes, her dad would fetch her and let her into the room, closing the door behind her with an almost inaudible click. And there was her mum, propped up against her pillows, still wearing pyjamas even though it was the middle of the day. On the bed was a tray table with a teapot and a plate of untouched sandwiches. Rakel didn't know what she was supposed to do, so she studied her legs, which were fairly dirty. There was a plaster on her knee from a fall, she was learning how to ride a bike on the big bike which according to her dad was for children nine and up, not seven-year-olds like her. But fuck it, her dad had said, apparently forgetting that swearing wasn't allowed, just wear a helmet, I'll give you twenty kronor if you make it all the way down the lane and back.

"Hi, sweetheart," her mum said. "What have you been up to today?"

Rakel had saved a wasp from being killed by her dad by catching it in her net and releasing it outside, while her dad turned the whole house upside down, looking for his injection thing, even though he hadn't been stung. She'd built a fort in the woods. She'd explored the dry water feature at the far end of the garden. She'd gone over to the meadow to look for ladybirds and discovered timothy, daisies with tough stalks, yarrow that was easier to pick, tangly bird vetch, blue and white lupins, pink lovage – she wiped her hands on her trousers – and the dangerous foxglove flowers you mustn't touch. *Digitalis purpurea.* Very toxic.

She shrugged. "Not much."

"Emanuel tells me you played chess."

Rakel nodded.

"He didn't tell me who won, so I'm guessing you did."

Rakel nodded. She shifted her weight onto her other foot. She scratched a mosquito bite with her toenail. Her mum patted the duvet with one hand and Rakel crawled onto the bed with her.

"Did you know the Ancient Greeks had two words for time?" Cecilia said. Her eyes were half-closed and her hair, longer than Rakel had ever seen it, fanned out across her pillow. She was envious of her mother's hair on principle, since it was the kind that the other girls in Rakel's class prized: blonde and curly. Rakel knew it had been very long once – her dad had indicated about halfway down her back, and her mum had laughed and said he was exaggerating – but she'd never seen it below her shoulders. Unlike Rakel, who had to go to the hairdresser's, her mum cut her own hair in front of the bathroom mirror, usually while listening to music from a cassette player she'd plugged into the outlet by the mirror, even though electrical devices weren't allowed in the bathroom. But now her hair had grown long, framing her face like a saint's halo. Her white pyjama shirt was open at the neck, revealing a patch of pale chest. There was an old book among the sheets. It looked like it was from the library, but Rakel hadn't seen her mother downstairs once since they arrived. Maybe she'd asked someone to fetch it for her.

"Two separate words," her mum said. Her voice was hoarse and weak, but since Rakel's head was pressed against her ribs, she could feel the vibrations of her words, their resonance. "*Chronos* and *Kairos*."

"Which is which?" Rakel asked. She had to keep her mother talking.

"*Chronos* is chronological time," Cecilia said, still without opening her eyes. "You can tell from the name, right? Do you know what chronological means?"

"No."

"That something happens in a certain order, starting with what happened first and then moving forward in the order the events took place. *Kairos*, on the other hand, is a situational concept that refers to the right time for action."

"And when is that?"

"Oh, I suppose part of the point is that you have to learn to recognise it."

He mother's body was warm and sleepy under the duvet. She stroked Rakel's hair and Rakel lay stock-still to keep anything from changing. The curtains billowed into the room like white sails. On the sideboard was a vase that held peonies, irises and white roses. Rakel knew their names, because she'd spent several days studying a botanical encyclopaedia she'd found in a bookshelf. For lack of anything better to do, she'd memorised the names of virtually every plant in the garden, which in her world was divided according to children's book rules into wild/unruly and cultivated/dignified flowers. Now, she wished her mum would ask her something so she could show off her botanical knowledge, but unfortunately her mother only wanted to discuss Greek words. It was warm and soft under the duvet, and her mum's familiar prosody was making her sleepy. When Rakel opened her eyes again, dusk had crept into the room. Her mum was rolled over on her side, breathing very heavily. Rakel's arm bumped into the old book. She put it on the bedside table and slipped off the bed. Everything was carrying on as normal downstairs. No one seemed to have noticed she was missing. All the grown-ups were gathered in front of the TV, shouting every time the blue-and-yellow players had the ball.

Her mother spending all day every day in the closed room on the first floor seemed to have something to do with Elis being born. Rakel's little brother had dedicated the first few months of his life to causing trouble. More than anything, he screamed, a drawn-out, razor-sharp infant's cry that sliced through the serenity of the flat. A big advantage of the summer house was that he simply couldn't be heard in every part of it. When he started to scream, someone, usually her dad, picked him up and walked him around and around in the Studio, the least used and most sound-proof room on the ground floor, and Rakel just had to move over to the other side of the house to keep reading in peace. Granted, Elis had toned it down, but he was still the absolute centre of everything. Only Emanuel seemed unmoved when Elis rolled over on his blanket, lifted his head up, obediently took his bottle, or performed other, completely basic activities. Everyone else was impressed.

Emanuel Wikner stayed in the house the entire time Rakel and her family were there, but the other Wikner siblings came to visit, too, bringing a sense of happy excitement in their wake. Peter was doing his residency somewhere; Rakel wasn't sure what that meant, but she gathered from her grandmother's tone that it was terribly important. He only stayed for a few days and was busy with various practical things most of that time. When the others were scoffing crisps during the football games, he munched on neatly cut cucumber and carrot sticks. Vera stayed longer and immediately transformed her room into a realm of mystery. The curtains were always closed, silk scarves were thrown over the lampshades, her bedside table was crammed full of boxes and bottles, there were clothes strewn everywhere and no one made her pick them up. Emanuel stared suspiciously at all those clothes, particularly the short sequined dress hung on a hanger on the closet door. "What do you need *this* for?" he said. The clothes really did seem pointless, since she wore a silk nightgown until lunch and spent the rest of the day sunbathing. Maybe she, too, was looking for Reception, because with all of the giant garden to choose from, she always lay down on the lawn where Martin was walking round and round on a path shaped like the delta sign her mum had shown Rakel in her book, the only spot where his mobile phone worked. Dad was on one of his Important Calls, she could tell from his hunched shoulders and grim expression, and didn't notice Vera or anyone else for that matter.

If it rained, Vera stayed in bed, reading the glossy fashion magazines that had gathered in a pile at the foot of her bed. Then she sighed, asked if Rakel wanted to play dress-up, and of course Rakel did, but Vera tired of the game after five minutes and there was no point unless you were two people playing. After a while, she left again, and the room felt strangely empty without all the amazing things that had been in it just the day before.

That summer was also the only time Frederikke visited the summer house. Since she was associated with their trips to France and the sunny, sugary town of Copenhagen, which they went to sometimes, it was strange to see her there, and Rakel felt very shy when she first showed up. Frederikke talked funny, laughed often, and brought presents. Mum came downstairs and wore a regular shirt and tights instead of her pyjamas and kimono. They had coffee on the veranda for so long it became tedious.

And Rakel was angry, despite the light, happy mood. She was angry because her mother was suddenly behaving like a normal mum, because Frederikke had somehow coaxed her out of her room, because Elis was allowed to lie in her arms, because everything had changed, because her dad wasn't making everything go back to normal, because her grandmother hadn't so much as glanced at her drawings, because she was expected to be grown-up and well behaved even though no one noticed when she was, because of everything, really, so she got up and wandered off into the garden, waiting for someone to call her back, but no one did.

Rakel sat up and blinked. The sound of wordless voices growing louder around her indicated that the morning's lectures were over. Her stomach grumbled and ached.

While she trudged up towards the cafeteria in the Humanities building, she thought about the fact that the Cecilia who had read about Greek words had been only thirty-one years old. She'd been twenty-four when Rakel was born; the same age Rakel was now.

Today's lunch was grilled salmon with risotto. Once Rakel had mopped up the last of the sauce with a piece of bread, she looked up Philip Franke's contact details. He didn't have a website, but his publisher listed an email address and a PR contact. Rakel began typing an email but immediately deleted it. Instead, she just sat there, motionless, staring out at the grassy slope, the blooming horse chestnut trees, the early summer unfurling in the sunshine, beautiful and fleeting like a poppy.

19

The schoolyard at Schillerska lay deserted. Rakel leaned against the warm stone wall, squinting at the sun. The doors opened and a stream of students poured out. Their appearance brought to mind a pop band in which each member maintained a strictly branded style: there was the girl with pink hair and silver jacket, there was the one with a peacoat and her grandmother's satchel, there was the bloke in the leather jacket and skinny jeans, and there was Elis, dressed like an extra in an American college film set in the fifties, which had scored an average rating of three stars. During the spring, he'd launched Project Visual Impairment, insisting he needed glasses. An examination showed that he was minimally myopic, so minimally that there really wasn't much point in correcting it, but Elis complained about headaches and their dad benevolently paid for the round tortoiseshell frames he now wore whenever they went with his outfit.

When she called his name, Elis turned around, completely disoriented, exchanged a few words with his friends, and quickly came over.

"What are you doing here?"

"I wanted to talk to you about something."

"Why didn't you text me?" For someone so hung up on the aesthetics of the past, he was surprisingly obsessed with technology.

"I was in the area anyway."

He sighed but waved goodbye to his friends. "Okay," he said. "So, I assume this is about dad's fiftieth?" When Rakel shook her head – Martin's impending birthday had completely slipped her mind – he seemed genuinely surprised, as though there were no other subject the two of them could possibly want to discuss.

For days, Rakel had pondered how to put it to him. Her best option, she'd decided, was to take him somewhere private to talk. Calmly and methodically, she would go through the novel's eerie parallels with reality, without arousing any unwarranted hopes, presenting the whole thing as an unlikely and very curious possibility, which maybe, possibly, if they wanted to, could be followed up on.

As it was, though, she simply blurted it out: "I've been reading this book and I think it's about Mum."

"Pardon?" Elis's face was such a study of incredulity. Rakel felt a sudden urge to rip off his useless glasses and stamp on them.

"I think the author knows Mum and based his main character on her."

"Okay…"

At least he sat down on the stone steps, after pulling a free newspaper out of his tote to sit on. Rakel sat down next to him. The granite was cool. She decided not to say anything else until Elis did, and so silence settled between the Berg siblings.

"What makes you think that?" Elis said finally. He'd always been the least stubborn of the two of them.

The presentation she'd prepared was gone. Instead, she handed him the book as proof of her credibility, and he gingerly flipped through the pages, full of circled paragraphs and marginalia. She gave a general summary of the plot – the random encounter, the initial infatuation, the growing cracks, the narrator's attempts to tie himself to his beloved through confrontation and demands for the truth, followed by the inevitable end – and then moved on to all the details that taken separately could be considered inconsequential, but together conjured a familiar shape. The marathon running, she said, carefully avoiding his eyes, the multilingualism, the reading, the life in exile, the Ethiopia connection, the necklace.

Elis didn't interrupt once, just stared at the ground, smoking several Lucky Strikes, one after the other, and ripping the lid of the cigarette packet into tiny pieces.

"But it might all be coincidence," Rakel finished.

"No, it sounds reasonable. How many people speak, what's it called…"

"Amharic?"

Rakel refrained from noting that over twenty million Ethiopians spoke Amharic. "Maybe he just made that up," she said instead.

"But why would anyone make that up? That would be a really weird thing to make up."

"What do you mean?"

"It's so random. Why would a made-up person in a book speak Amharic?"

"Maybe to show that there were all kinds of important things the narrator didn't know about her."

"But why *Amharic*? Why not something else? Fine, so there are probably several thousand white people who speak Amharic. Missionaries and what not. But how many of them also run marathons and read Ancient Greek? It's so implausible it has to be true." He ran his finger down the book's spine. "Has it been translated into English?"

"No, there's only German."

"Shame. I'd like to read it."

"I've translated part of it, I can email it to you."

"Into Swedish? Wow!"

"Are you being sarcastic?"

"No!"

Rakel had expected more resistance and persuasion, and when there was none, she instead started to feel Elis had accepted the whole thing a bit too easily.

"But it's still pretty unlikely," she said in a severe tone. "I could have imagined the whole thing."

"But why would you do that?"

The answer just slipped out. "Because I miss her."

"But she left." Elis squashed his cigarette against the steps. "And I doubt *she* misses us. If she did, she would have come back."

Even though Rakel didn't remember any of it, the story of Cecilia's disappearance was so deeply etched into everyone involved they could recite it like a well-practised alibi. One Saturday morning in April, the Berg family had woken up to find Cecilia missing. It was just a few weeks after she successfully defended her doctoral thesis, and the plan had been for her to take up a position as a lecturer in the department the following autumn. She'd left a letter addressed to Martin in which she informed him she'd left. The police dropped the investigation since there were no signs of anything untoward having taken place. Everyone had figured she'd come back eventually, or at least be in touch, but they'd turned out to be mistaken. Thirty-three-year-old Cecilia Berg, mother of two and promising scholar, had vanished without a trace.

"I actually don't remember her," Elis said. "I remember nursery school and that. I remember turning five. You and me and Dad went to see a film and then we had burgers. I remember going to that cottage with Gustav because Dad was always so happy then. We took swimming lessons, and I was afraid of jellyfish, but Gustav stood on a rock and shouted if he saw any. I remember a lot of things about Gustav from when I was little, but nothing about her."

Rakel hadn't heard her brother say that many words at once in at least the past five years.

"Nothing at all?"

"Sometimes I think I remember, but it's probably mostly from photos and stuff other people have told me. I was three years old. Is it even possible to have memories from when you're three? Or is it kind of like a suppressed trauma?"

"Well…"

"Maybe it would help if you walked me around the playground in Zenitparken like Thomas Quick and fed me lots of benzos."

It took Rakel a moment to get the joke, but once she did, she couldn't stop laughing.

"All right, it wasn't that funny," Elis said after a while. "So, what do we do now?"

"We're *not* telling Dad."

"Agreed. He always gets so worked up about everything." Elis mimicked their father's voice with surprising accuracy: "Elis, we have to practise driving on Sunday. Elis, you haven't taken up smoking, have you? Elis, do you have any French homework?" He fished another cigarette out of the pack, even though he'd barely touched the last one. "What he doesn't know won't hurt him."

"I'm not really sure what we should do," Rakel said. "But I'll think of something."

Her brother nodded, seemingly satisfied with that. She should know what to do, after all, she was his big sister. Since he'd always been the baby, she had to be the big girl. Such was the inescapable dynamic of siblinghood.

Rakel had figured he'd want to be alone after this earth-shattering revelation – wander around empty streets, find a lookout spot, gaze over the city, contemplate existence – but Elis was meeting his friends at a café.

"All right, so, see you," he said and hurried down the tree-lined street.

*

It was too early to go home and the mere thought of spending the evening with her dad, who would nag her about the reader's report, was enough to give Rakel a headache. Not to mention having to listen to another jeremiad about the trials and tribulations of his William Wallace biography. Considering what a self-starter he was when it came to the publishing company, he was surprisingly apathetic about his own manuscript. Other people's books he shepherded from idea to reality with a firm hand, rarely hesitating, identifying problems and making sure someone solved them, and when one book was finished, he was already busy with the next. But as far as his own project went, Rakel mused, he might prefer a stack of notes and a clutch of vague ideas – every door still open, the motorway stretching off into the golden haze of infinity, the first chords of a Springsteen song reverberating, and the future ahead of him.

She plodded along towards the Haga Cinema, where Lovisa was sitting, according to a series of frantic texts, "completely abandoned and alone". That Lovisa had been on her own for more than five minutes struck Rakel as unlikely, but she hadn't seen her in weeks, and she had completely stopped answering her phone, so having a pint was really the least she could do. But every person she saw was another person she had to tell or not tell about Cecilia. Without being able to put her finger on a good reason, Rakel felt she should keep it to herself, at least for now, apart from Elis, who did have an inherent right to this particular secret.

It turned out Lovisa really was sitting alone at a rickety table next to the verdant hops wall. Her face was turned skyward, a pair of enormous sunglasses on her nose and a pint in front of her. It was one of the smaller tables in the outdoor serving area, just big enough for two or three, and in other words not conducive to a gathering of a merry group of friends and loose acquaintances. A level of spring immediately returned to Rakel's step.

"You look like you've seen a ghost," Lovisa exclaimed. "Is it my hair? Does it look hideous?" She'd bleached her roots again and it was white and friable like spun sugar.

"Eighty per cent Debbie Harry and twenty per cent Marilyn Monroe on the skids," Rakel said.

"Perfect. What a relief. You need a beer, I could tell from a mile away. Go buy one."

The only thing rattling around Rakel's brain was the question Elis had asked – what now? – to which she had no answer but it was silenced by the din and noise and alcohol and, above all, Lovisa's various conundrums. The final results of the university placement test were in, and she had, as suspected, achieved a perfect score of 2.0. This feat suggested her friend Ritalin, which she'd taken before the test, had a beneficial effect on her, which had in turn made Lovisa contemplate seeing someone about an ADHD diagnosis.

"There's amphetamine in Ritalin," Rakel countered. "Of course you felt switched on and generally terrific."

"But how can you tell if you felt good because you have ADHD or because people feel good when they take amphetamines?"

Rakel couldn't answer that, and Lovisa went off on a tangent, comparing her previous experiences with amphetamines.

"And that time we went to Berghain? When you were so miserable, and I had to pry you off the sofa and pretty much manhandle you out the door? Granted, you looked like a depressed dyke, and that might have been the only reason they let us in. It could hardly have been my charming enthusiasm. Remember that? And I wanted to find out if that thing about the golden showers was true? Anyway, *that* time – hello, what's with you?" She snapped her fingers in front of Rakel's nose. "You're sleeping, you're not listening."

"You were high when we went to Berghain?" Rakel said to prove she was paying attention.

"Well, he *said* it was uppers. But what do I know? I was merely a simple tourist. Anyway…"

What Rakel had in fact been thinking about was that Cecilia hadn't had any female friends. The closest to it was probably Frederikke, but that was more on the level of sending each other obscure books with some cramped dedication on the flyleaf. As far as Rakel knew, there had been no equivalent of Lovisa in her mother's life. She was surrounded by melancholy men like Gustav and Max Schreiber – nothing but dark jackets, Cecilia's fair figure – and it was all just German grammar or Nietzsche's view of art. Lovisa had been there when Rakel got her period, had shared a stolen sixpack of beer with her in eighth grade, had played the role of pimp when Rakel lost her virginity to a guy from Schillerska, and so on through all the initiation rites of youth. Rakel's discovery of Philip Franke's novel was the first major life event she was excluded from. Over the past couple of weeks, Lovisa's texts had lined up on her phone in a long series of unanswered bubbles. And yet, she kept texting, again and again, and if too much time had passed without a sign of life, she would without a doubt have turned up on Friggagatan, with her arms crossed and her foot tapping, warped by the fish-eye perspective of the peephole.

Lovisa tore off her sunglasses, staring intently at a point behind Rakel. "Don't turn around," she hissed. Rakel immediately turned around, and, for the first time in two years, saw Alexander in the flesh.

He was standing at the bar, waiting for his pint. With a human being's reflexive sense of murderous glaring in his immediate vicinity, he turned around and spotted them, but unfortunately he didn't interpret Lovisa's hostility as hostility: he waved, looking genuinely happy, and set his course for them. He called their names long before he reached them. "Long time no see!"

Awkward hugs followed. He had, Rakel noted, a new backpack but an old sweatshirt. She asked how long he'd been back, and Alexander gave an account of the past few months. He'd finished his course and was working now; he was subletting on Hisingen but about to take over his sister's flat in Högsbo. When they'd talked so long it was rude not to ask if he wanted to join them, he gestured towards the other end of the outdoor seating area. He was meeting some friends, he said, but it was good to see them, and did they want to go for a pint sometime? Sure, Rakel said, and he scrolled through his contacts list to see if he still had her number. His phone was new, too – a shiny iPhone, not the beat-up Nokia that had always woken her in the middle of the night with its dinging – but it turned out the number had successfully migrated.

"Great, amazing, I'll give you a ring, then!" he said and strolled off.

Nothing in his demeanour hinted at the circumstances of their break-up, to the fact that Rakel had packed her things one day and left their flat in Kreuzberg without even a note, only the following month's rent in cashpoint-crisp euro notes on the kitchen table.

"All done," Rakel said and sipped her drink.

The evening sun shone on the climbing hops and Lovisa's skin was as pale as cellar sprouts. Around her, the world marched on, and she found something had shifted. She sensed an absent-minded interest in Alexander's current life, but had no real desire to talk more to him about it.

"All right, Marilyn," she said. "Other than that time you were possibly high in Berlin, what experience do you have with stimulants?"

20

Gustav still hadn't replied to his calls or letters, and when their twenty-fifth anniversary party was only two weeks away, Martin dropped a line to the only one of Gustav's Stockholm friends he knew at least a little – Dolores, whose name he'd always suspected was assumed. She replied within hours.

> Hi Martin!! Nice to hear from you. Everything's good here. Actually haven't heard from Gustav in a while, but I know he went to London in April. Will remind him the next time I talk to him!
> Love!
> Dolores

No doubt Dolores was also waiting anxiously for a phone call or gnomic postcard, even though she was putting on a brave face through the extensive use of exclamation marks. How many people were at this moment united in their waiting for Gustav to be in touch? A curator was very probably pacing about nervously up at the art museum, unsure whether the main attraction was going to deign to show up to the opening of their exhibition.

And Martin thought about the last time he saw Gustav.

It was last winter. Perpetual deep-blue twilight, people scurrying up and down the pavements, hunched against the frigid wind howling through the streets. Snowflakes whirled around the street lights and Strömmen, or whatever that body of water was called, gleamed like onyx. Gustav had been waiting on the platform, leaning against a pillar, a cigarette in his hand. His brow was deeply lined, his cheeks coarse and sunken, and there were violet shadows under his eyes. His hair had faded into something in between ditch-water blond and grey, thinning into sad, lanky strands. There was a bald spot exactly where Gustav couldn't see it himself, just behind the crown of his head. He'd put on some weight, but all his body fat was concentrated on his belly. If his physiognomy spoke of the relentless progression of middle age, his clothes signalled the opposite. His black jeans looked new and were well fitting in a way that suggested he'd encountered a particularly determined shop assistant, and despite the cold his old greatcoat was open to reveal his T-shirt.

He didn't notice Martin approaching until Martin said his name, and then his face broke into a positively radiant smile. They embraced.

"Don't you look all business."

"I do what I can." Martin could tell his dialect sounded thicker than usual.

"We're donkeys among horses," Gustav said.

His studio was on Södermalm, that much even Martin with his limited knowledge of Stockholm had figured out. Gustav had once claimed Martin's inability to find his way around was a symptom of old-fashioned Gothenburgian aversion to the capital, but that wasn't true. Martin had been unable to find his way around Paris, too, but after months of walking around with a map in his hands, he'd eventually been able to visualise the city to some extent, even in moments of mapless confusion. The difference was that he'd never had a Stockholm map. Consequently, the relative location of land and water was unpredictable and surprising, streets appeared where you least expected them to and then disappeared as irrevocably, you wandered down into the metro and back up again without having any idea of where you had travelled.

It was an old building, turn of the century. More or less unusual surnames on the other doors in the stairwell. Gustav rattled his keys for a long time before discovering that he'd left the door unlocked. Inside, it was neat like a hotel room. Gustav explained that he had engaged the services of a cleaning lady.

"Or is it called something else? Janitor? Or is it only a janitor if it's in a school? Either way, it's a wonderfully nice woman who comes once a week and keeps everything at a reasonably sanitary level… Hey, would you like a drink? Wine, whisky?"

"A glass of wine would be good…"

Martin was on his way up to the studio when Gustav stopped him. "Bloody hell, can't the paintings wait? I need a break from myself."

So they sat in the living room for a while, Martin on the sofa and Gustav in an armchair that looked like the only piece of furniture in the flat that ever saw any real use. It took Martin a moment to identify it – it was one of the pair they'd once salvaged from a skip to furnish Gustav's studio flat in Masthugget. It was the kind of fifties or sixties armchair that had felt woefully outdated in the early eighties but was now back on trend. All other surfaces in the room were clean, untouched. The TV was large and shiny. Even though Gustav was wearing brand-new jeans, he fit in poorly in his own home. He shifted uncomfortably in his armchair, patted his pockets, got up to fetch a packet of Gauloises. He opened the window and lit one.

"Want one?"

"I quit."

"Oh. Right." He laughed, a brief, raspy laugh, full of rattling and gravel. "*Quit*. Everyone's quitting these days, taking up yoga instead. You haven't taken up yoga, have you?"

"I have no intention of doing yoga," Martin said, even though he'd been considering signing up for a session at Hagabadet after determined lobbying by Sanna at work, who claimed it would be good for his blood pressure and general stress levels.

"Glad to hear it. I suppose people are free to do what they want, I just resent their attitude. People get all holier than thou. It's like pregnant women. Walking around thinking they're a little bit better than everyone else." He turned towards the street, blew out smoke. "At least Cecilia wasn't stuck-up when she was knocked up. Though in all honesty, she wasn't exactly a good time, either."

"You're not smoking indoors any more?"

"Well. It just makes everything kind of dingy."

"So your neighbours won in the end, did they?"

"What neighbours?"

"They ones who complained?"

"Oh, *them*. No, they moved. They had another kid and moved to Bromma or one of the other toddler reserves. Their flat sold for over four million. A tiny two-bed! People are out of their minds – they borrow and borrow and buy and buy without realising the bank owns it all. Another financial crisis and they're toast. When you can rent."

"But you own your flat, too...?"

"Sure, yes, but I don't have a sodding mortgage." Gustav flicked his butt out of the window and closed it. "Where were we going for dinner again? Operakällaren?"

As usual, Martin had made the reservation, and when they entered the restaurant, he tried not to let Gustav's oppositional sartorial defiance annoy him.

It's not that people were looking – the places they went to were upmarket enough that no one would. Besides, the ARTIST GUSTAV BECKER could get away with wearing anything, even a T-shirt with a punk-rock print and an inside-out Helly Hansen sweater, like tonight. The problem was, rather, that Martin was automatically assigned the role of well-adjusted and boring citizen. Martin was the one with the Acne jacket and wristwatch, who deposited his wool coat and scarf in the cloakroom, who lied to his son when he asked how much his Italian loafers cost. Because Gustav had laid claim to being the bohemian, it was the only route open to him. How would it look if Publisher Berg turned up in a threadbare flannel shirt, too?

Gustav eyed the wine list, ordered a bottle of Bordeaux that cost nine hundred kronor and began to fiddle with his napkin the second the waiter left. The soft lighting reversed some of what the years had done to his face. The furrows were transformed from haggard to soulful. But he'd barely smiled since Martin stepped off the train.

"How are the kids?" he asked.

Martin got entangled in a fairly protracted description of Elis, who had begun to stay out late, was generally sulky and seemed to think he knew more about life than he really did, and how frustrating that could be. Rakel had been completely different, he'd never had to worry about her. Rakel, on the other hand, was completely engrossed by her psychology studies, and not particularly interested in the publishing company, which, honestly, was a fairly strange attitude for her to take, because—

"I'm going out for a smoke," Gustav said.

Gustav did most of the talking that evening, and whenever anything interrupted his stream of words, he seemed annoyed. He pontificated about things that bothered him, primarily Stockholmers, old friends who had never cared when he was a nobody but wanted to be best friends now that he'd made something of himself, contemporary art, which was "superficial and banal", not to mention the art market, "capitalism's glittering brothel where we're all whores".

"But no one's forcing you to sell your paintings," Martin tried to object, but Gustav continued his diatribe, which somehow came to include his gallery, people who used the word "network" as a verb, the conservative government, the management at the Thielska Gallery, and the protracted construction around Slussen. The only subject he couldn't be drawn on was that of his own work.

Time and again, he broke off with the chorus "I'm just going for a quick smoke". Martin joined him the first couple of times, but it was cold out, so the third time he stayed. A largely uneaten portion of venison with mushrooms was sitting on Gustav's plate, his cutlery neatly placed at four and eight. When Gustav returned, he moved between the tables like a man on a mission, bumping a chair in his hurry. He stopped to right it. He handled the chair as though it were an unusually unruly object, and one leg got entangled with some other leg, hidden underneath the white tablecloth, so he had to pull the chair all the way back out and try to fit it back in again. He didn't quite manage – it was still askew – and eventually walked away from the scene of the crime without looking back.

"Did you know," he said, sitting back down, "that there's a person writing their thesis about me. That's something to write home about, no?"

"What's it about?"

"No idea."

Martin laughed, choked and began to cough. "What, no idea at all?" he said once he could speak again.

Gustav made a vague gesture. "It's some girl, an art historian. It's about gender and... the female subject as depicted in something something." He shook his head. "She was nice, but angry, too. Not at me, of course. But at the world. At men. Why are feminists always so angry?"

"I suppose they're upset at being the losers in a patriarchal society."

"She got properly, you know, fired up talking about it. How the objectification of women blah blah blah. But she liked me, because I've done so many paintings of Cissi working. When the simple truth was that if I wanted to paint Cissi, I had to make do with her working." He stabbed a chanterelle and studied it, his face unreadable. "And now I'm some kind of feminist hero."

"Far from all middle-aged men in the cultural sector can say they..."

"But she's not going to write about all the other things. My spiritual kinship with the Dutch painters of the seventeenth century, for example. Vulgar people think it started with Ola Billgren, but that simply isn't true. It started with Vermeer and Rembrandt. And a few others. She might mention Zorn, but probably only to give him a swift kick for objectifying some poor peasant women who didn't know any better." He flagged down the waiter to order another bottle of wine.

"I'm good," Martin said. His thoughts had grown clouded, indolent. Pleasantly wrapped in cotton wool. He would be able to go to the bathroom without tripping over his own feet. He would be able to sign his name on the receipt without it coming out like an illegible scribble. And they had to get back somehow, too. Were they going to take a taxi? Walk? He had no idea where they were in relation to Gustav's flat. Were they still on Södermalm? He reached for his inside pocket to check Google Maps but thought better of it; Gustav took offence when you used your phone in front of him.

"Oh, come on, let's have another glass," Gustav said, clapping his hands. "You're here, aren't you? We need to mark the occasion. The way I see it, we need to mark the occasion. Another one of these, please. We can't just let this event pass us by unobserved, can we, Martin Berg? That would be sacrilege. The way I see it. What are you laughing at? What's so funny? Huh?"

The wine was brought. They drank.

"I think they might be closing..."

The other dinner guests had slipped away unnoticed. The restaurant was a Renoir painting of dreamy, diffuse outlines in shades of umber and mahogany. The waiters moved on the periphery, probably eager to go home, but Gustav just laughed, knocked back what was left of his digestif, which was to say virtually nothing, "*rien*", Martin said, and Gustav laughed again. He waved for the bill, and they bickered chivalrously about who should pay it. Martin triumphed, the little card on the silver tray, the little signature – a swish that bore only a glancing resemblance to his usual signature – and then off to the cloakroom; they pulled on their coats, where were his gloves, had he left them somewhere? – no, one in each pocket – and out, out into the snowy night, black and bitter, the cold lunging at their exposed throats while they fumbled with their coat buttons. Hadn't he had a scarf, too?

Gustav wouldn't hear of them going home.

"Martin. *Martin.* The night is young. As I like to say: never waste a good opportunity. Before you know it, it'll be Monday and you'll be back to business, working on your life puzzle and your slow-cooked meat..." He waved down a taxi. "Being outside in this weather is probably dangerous. People get lost, end up in snow drifts, freeze to death."

"Only if they're drunk."

"And who isn't, in this country? Maybe the Muslims. Get in." He held the door for Martin and tumbled in after him. Gave the driver an address. Outside, the lights of the city trickled past in the dark. Gustav continued: "This country was built on alcoholism. Take the nineteenth century. Everyone, including the children, were on the sauce. A fifth of the population emigrated, which makes a lot of sense. And only through the extreme paternalism of the state could the ship be turned around, transforming the poor man of the Nordic countries into the snobbish welfare state we know and love. And now! What are the idiots doing *now*? They've voted in a government that's trying to *dismantle* the nanny state. Apparently, they've forgotten that when people were free to make their own decisions, they drank themselves to death and didn't lift a finger to contribute to financial growth or anything else... Here's good!"

Back out onto a pavement, he should try to stop this, but Gustav had the momentum of a runaway freight train. Red, glowing windows. A loud crowd of people standing outside. A queue. Cigarette smoke and laughter. Twisted red velvet ropes. A bouncer waved them in, heartily greeting Gustav. New cloakroom, tag in the inside pocket of his jacket.

Inside, it was hot and humid, the din and music deafening. Grenade-red light. Crystal chandeliers and mirrors glittered. It was cramped and crowded, his body always pressed against someone else's, everyone looked like each aspect of their appearance was under strict supervision and control. Bare shoulders, short skirts. The air was thick with the potential for transaction: smiles, drinks, numbers, business cards changed hands.

Gustav, an alley cat among Persians and Siamese, ordered champagne and gazed out at the crowd.

"Look at them," he shouted. Speaking at a normal volume was impossible. "People are so fucking driven these days. They know what they want and think they have a right to get it, too. Because they *deserve* it. It doesn't occur to them that they don't deserve a sodding jot more than anyone else. They're pleasant on the surface, I mean, really bloody nice, but everyone here wants something from you. Sometimes, I wonder if the reason they get miffed is simply because I don't mess about with the internet, which robs them of the chance to prove that they know me online... It's not real, you know. It's just games, for show, the whole thing." A thread had come lose in the neckline of his shirt. Martin pulled it out.

"Then why don't you move back home?" he shouted.

"Good old Gothenburg," Gustav said and suddenly burst out laughing, a snorting laughter.

"I'm serious."

"We had a bloody good time, didn't we?"

At that moment, a girl came up to Gustav, putting a hand on his shoulder to make him aware of her presence. She was wearing a black leather T-shirt, which must have been ridiculously hot, you almost had to admire the grit of someone who willingly subjected themselves to wearing leather in a place with a tropical indoor climate. She had to be sweating profusely, though you would have pegged her for someone who didn't like to sweat, with her shiny bob cut and that air of being immaculately clean like everyone else in here. As though they were clinically free of body hair and skin imperfections, blackheads and spots, bodily fluids of any kind.

"Martin, this is Nina," Gustav shouted. Nina seemed to have brought with her an entourage of people Rakel's age or a bit older. They greeted Martin with bland, quickly forgotten handshakes. One bloke was wearing a baseball cap, another a hat perched like some kind of kippa on his pate.

The champagne set off fireworks and balloon-drops in his brain.

"So, what do you do?" Nina yelled.

He wished she'd asked him anything but that. He couldn't bear to talk about his work, so he asked about hers – it turned out she worked at KG's gallery – and tried to remember to nod with interest while he contemplated throwing one of Cecilia's favourite theses into the conversation, just for kicks: that capitalism, which was to say the *raison d'être* of the art trade, was the most efficient economic system the world had seen to date, and probably utterly unstoppable. But that there was only one possible final destination for its locomotive-like progress: the total depletion of the planet's resources, with war and famine its inevitable consequences, and then (and she'd say this with all the Hegelian seriousness she could muster) the end of history.

Instead, he told a hilarious anecdote about Gustav. Nina laughed and nodded, and even though he paused at appropriate moments to give her ample opportunity to elegantly slip in an excuse and leave, she stayed.

The compact noise of the bar pressed against his eardrums, his thoughts rose like helium towards the ceiling, refusing to be corralled, and this person Nina found his dialect exotic (she herself spoke in a Stockholm accent even though she was apparently from Västerås), so when Gustav made the sign for *cigarette?* Martin nodded and excused himself. They stumbled outside, staying on the right side of the ropes, people were still queueing, my god, and when Gustav handed Martin his packet, he took one and let Gustav light it. Then Gustav fumbled with his own, dropped it in the snow, laughed, fished out another, lit it, almost fell over, and had to lean against Martin. He'd brought a drink with him.

"Who are those people?" Martin said, nodding back towards the bar. "Your friends?"

"Just some people I know."

"I imagine we were their age when they were born."

Gustav shrugged. "They're all right. They're all right…"

"So, do you see much of Dolores?"

"Dolores, Dolores. Have you ever noticed that if you say that name over and over again, it doesn't sound like a name? I mean, sure, I guess I do… she stops by… but she works for the municipality these days, so we don't exactly keep the same hours, if you know what I mean."

Martin tried to recall any other old mates of Gustav's. "What about Vivi and Sandor? I heard he comes up here for work quite a bit…"

"*Sandor*. One hundred per cent market-adapted nowadays. And still" – Gustav gestured vaguely with his glass – "and still, he could have made a decent artist."

"They're asking about you."

"I'm not surprised. The prodigy who made it. Stop the presses. Listen, I'm freezing my arse off."

"I need some more air."

His cigarette had gone out. He was going to go straight in and drink a glass of water. Yes. A glass of water, then home. A gaggle of girls tumbled out, someone howled with laughter, spindly heels in the grainy snow, phones in hand.

At the bar, Gustav was ordering shots and distributing them among his friends, and it was easier to take the glass than to turn it down, easier to toast than not, easier to knock the booze back and wipe his mouth with the back of his hand, and when Gustav said something inaudible that made everyone laugh, he laughed, too.

Later – how much later? – Martin managed to flag down a taxi. Gustav had to be led up the stairs, a slow climb during which he mumbled that Martin was his one true friend, none of the others could be trusted, would they have helped him like this, they would just as soon have left him in the gutter like some bloody Carl Michael Bellman, where was his key? He was sure he had the key… and he took off his coat, patted every pocket several times, at length. Martin sat on the steps with his head in his hands until Gustav found the key under the doormat.

FINAL EXAMS

I

MARTIN BERG: Just like reading can be a means to understanding oneself and the world, writing can be, too. An author can intend to write about X, and then, when the book is done, it turns out to be about Y. It's not unusual for a text to somehow *know more* than the person who wrote it. When one renders one's experiences into fictional form, something happens, but what exactly that process entails, I don't know. I rather think no one does. And maybe that's not what matters.

INTERVIEWER: Then what is it that matters?

*

The snow kept falling. People skied through the city. The rows of parked cars were covered with a blanket of snow. Pipes froze and sometimes there was no hot water. At first, Martin thought the thermometer outside the kitchen window was broken, since it always showed twenty-three below. More than once, he woke up to a room where his breath came out as smoke. They pooled their money to hire a chimney sweep to sort out the tiled stove at Kaptensgatan, and Martin found himself in the distinctly nineteenth-century situation of having to spend the last of his scholarship money on firewood.

There was no trace left in Martin's room of the previous year's temporary tenant, other than a condom among the dust bunnies under the bed and a handful of issues of syndicalist newspaper *Arbetaren*. When he visited his parents, his mother said he looked like he was doing well (which was a dubious interpretation of the state of things) and his father mumbled something about the docks in Marseille (Martin scratched his arm where his anchor tattoo was hidden under three layers of clothing). He couldn't be bothered to get in touch with anyone. Per had returned a week or so after he did, and Gustav was still with his grandmother. The only person he saw was Cecilia.

In the mornings, he wanted her to stay under the down duvet. He held her, hard, for a long time, until her rigid body relaxed. Sometimes, she cried. If he started to say something, she just shook her head, and eventually they both fell asleep. During his absence, she'd acquired a fourteen-inch TV and a VHS player, and for several days they stayed in bed, watching films, drinking tea, peeling oranges and eating crisps until the sheets were grungy and full of crumbs.

One of the first things Martin did was to go get tested for HIV, and, since he was at it anyway, every other STD. His anchor tattoo was an excellent alibi. It lightened the mood a little, too, because Cecilia let out something akin to a small laugh when he pulled up his shirt and told her about Marseille.

"Martin Berg, the sailor," she said in a voice that sounded almost normal, amused and deep. "I actually never imagined that."

He wanted to tell her about Diane. Long after she fell asleep, he lay awake, formulating a confession in his mind. At one point, he went over to her flat on Kastellgatan with the intention of coming clean. The studio flat was cold and more reminiscent of a monk's cell than ever: bare white walls, empty windowsills, naked daylight. There was no food in the fridge. She mostly ate at the Golden Prague, she said. Her face was pale, Vermeerian, her eyes anxious, searching, the lines of her cheekbones and jaw clearly visible underneath her skin. The belt holding up her flannel trousers was cinched to the innermost hole. She hadn't had her hair cut in months and her curls were pulled taut across her skull and held in a low bun. In the blue fox fur coat she'd inherited, she looked like a forlorn Russian princess. You wanted to put her in a sled and drive her somewhere you might find a warm hearth and borscht and the Bolshoi Ballet.

In the end, he didn't tell her. Instead, he waited for the verdict of his blood test. When the results came a few weeks later, he'd had time to picture his imminent death a hundred times over, and the fact that all the tests came back negative put an anticlimactic end to his fantasies about funeral processions, white lilies and posthumous fame for his unfinished masterpiece *Night Sonnets.*

*

While Cecilia worked on her dissertations – she was going for an MA in intellectual history and a BA in language – Martin cooked in her neglected little kitchen. He found a clay pot and Julia Child's French cookbook for virtually nothing in a charity shop. He chose dishes that took a long time to prepare and involved many steps. Buying an entire chicken, he discovered, wasn't too expensive, but it had to be stuffed, and seasoned, and carefully supervised in the unreliable oven, and basted. He whipped mayonnaise. He learned to poach eggs. He wished it were crayfish season, because eating with her hands always made Cecilia happy, but he could get cheap prawns and mussels from Feskekôrka. He made aioli according to Child's recipe. He pan-fried plaice. He simmered a tomato sauce with red wine for three hours. He learned how to bake bread. Since he woke up at four in the morning anyway, he got up and made the dough, then waited for the paper to arrive, drank coffee and read while the dough proved. The oven glowed in the gloom.

When Cecilia wasn't writing, she wanted to sleep. As early as nine o'clock, she'd curl up under the down duvets, rolled up like a hedge-hog. She woke up when he came to bed, straightened out at the touch of his hands, they had sex without saying a word, he held back until he could tell she was losing control; those sounds she only ever made when she lost herself, that quiver running through her body.

The alarm clock was barely able to wake her in the mornings.

A week or so after coming home, Martin trudged up to the university library to borrow books for his next literature class. He didn't even have to renew his library card. After this term, the only thing standing between him and a master's degree was a dissertation. And after that, he'd be almost out of student loans. And what was a poor humanities student supposed to do for a living? He could do a PhD. He could take a few more courses and become a librarian. He could use his credits in philosophy and literature to get a degree in education. And become an upper secondary teacher… Martin pictured his old class at Hvitfeldtska. Surely you needed at least a decade between desk and blackboard, or life would feel too bleak.

As he walked home, the city seemed to fit in his cupped hand. The tree-lined street was cold and white. Here and there, solitary figures in dark overcoats trudged slowly up and down the ploughed furrow running down the middle of the pavement. At this time of day, he'd usually been walking through Saint-Germain, on his way to some café with chequerboard floors and mirrors on the walls. Here, it was the same people in the same bars, the same topics of conversations, the same food in the shops, the same view from the window, the same cracks in the ceiling.

But one thing was different: he was a published author now. A book had been waiting for him in the banana box full of his post. The anthology's cover was cornflower blue and dominated by the words THE EIGHTIES in black. Underneath were two columns, each five names long, and MARTIN BERG was one of them.

He read his own text and skimmed the others. It was, in fact, a good short story. He didn't need to feel ashamed of it. But he would need to follow it up with something. Anyone could write one good short story. You have to strike while the iron's hot, he thought to himself and immediately rebuked himself for resorting to such a cliché. You had to pull your finger out – never mind, you had to finish the great, sprawling debut novel which was well on its way to being done.

At the end of January, a package he'd posted before leaving Paris arrived. It contained the past year's notebooks, all kinds of papers, letters and manuscripts, a box too heavy to take on the train. Normally, he would have worried about the contents getting lost – kind of like when Hemingway's manuscript was left in a taxi by his wife Hadley and lost forever – but this time he hadn't given it a second thought.

Martin dug out the draft of *Night Sonnets*. Then he wrote PARIS on the box and shoved it in the cupboard.

One day in February, Gustav turned up at Kaptensgatan with a bottle of wine and a bag of saffron buns he'd found in the freezer. They hadn't seen each other in almost two months. The only sign of life had been a postcard a few weeks earlier: *Aloha! Still held captive by Nana while I convalesce. See you in Feb. probably!*

He might have gained a little weight, but it was hard to tell under all the clothes. After taking off his coat, he pulled off a woollen jumper, revealing a sober black shirt that was not frayed in the slightest and had nary a hole in it.

"Christmas present from Nana," Gustav explained. "She insists on giving me these cashmere things. Not really my style, obviously, but bloody warm. So, where's the commune?" He opened the fridge.

"Anders is at work, I guess."

Gustav nodded thoughtfully, as though Martin had said something extraordinarily profound and insightful. Then he took out a piece of cheese and sniffed it.

Martin busied himself with the coffee machine. "How was your Christmas?" he asked.

"Tolerable. Nana was a bit overbearing. Said I mustn't exert myself like that and insisted I stay a while. So I did." Gustav closed the fridge door and sat down on one of the kitchen chairs, immediately pushing it up onto its back legs. One of his socks had a hole in the heel.

Martin scooped coffee into the filter. "So, what are you up to now?"

"Back to school. Final push. It might be good to finish something, I guess… You?"

While the coffee machine gurgled, Martin told him about his literature course in general and that day's tutorial in particular. It had been the first of the term, and he was rusty. Sluggish. They'd discussed Auerbach, and he'd given the text a quick glance, assuming that would be enough. But there were fewer students in the advanced course and every one of them was the well-read, pompous type, children of academics who'd used expressions like "relevant criticism" in primary school. They saw through you if you shot from the hip and simply had to point it out, too.

"So it didn't go great," he summed up.

They'd finished their coffee, and it was after four, so it felt reasonable to locate the corkscrew and tackle Gustav's bottle of wine.

"But isn't the real question: is this what I want to do for the rest of my life?" Martin said. "Break things down and analyse them? As opposed to creating something myself. I can't help but wonder which is more rewarding in the long run."

"Sure." Gustav said nothing for a while. "So, how's Cecilia?"

"Good, I guess."

"Where is she?"

Martin almost said *I don't know*, but that wasn't true. "She's at home, working on her dissertation. I told her she should come over, her place is freezing, and we have the tiled stove here and all, but she says there's nowhere for her to work here. You know what she's like. Needs her own space."

"The tiled stove's a pretty big plus, actually," Gustav said.

"It does add a certain Dostoevskyan dimension, doesn't it? And, speaking of which, guess what happened in Marseille?"

"Do I want to know?"

"Let's put it this way: *you* probably want to know, while my parents, for example, would prefer blissful ignorance."

"Sounds promising."

Martin pulled off his jumper and rolled up the sleeve of his T-shirt to reveal the anchor tattoo. "*Voilà*."

"Bloody hell," Gustav said. "It was sheer luck, I guess, that you weren't kidnapped by a bunch of Moroccan sailors and ended up in the Foreign Legion like Rimbaud."

"Rimbaud became an arms dealer in Ethiopia. But sure. It's sheer happenstance that I'm sitting here in a wood-panelled kitchen and not living out the rest of my days as a prostituted morphinist in Algiers."

"What would Cecilia have said about that?"

"*Tant pis.*"

"At least make sure you get a good book out of it."

They laughed. Gustav topped up his glass.

"Right," Martin said. "I suppose we're back now."

"Pah. We'll always have Paris."

II

INTERVIEWER: Have there been any pivotal moments in your professional life?

*

It dripped and thawed and from time to time wet lumps of snow fell from the branches of the trees in Slottsskogen Park, sliding down the backs of unsuspecting passers-by. The asphalt was bare and black, the storm drains gurgled, the evenings were growing lighter. Cecilia pulled on her running shoes and went out for her first run in months. She came back rosy-cheeked and clear-eyed, announced that she felt human again, downed two glasses of milk and disappeared into the shower. But as her viva drew closer, she increasingly often felt dizzy, complained about nausea and claimed she'd lost her appetite. Could the dizziness and tiredness possibly be symptoms of a brain tumour? Martin bet her one hundred kronor that her brain tumour would be gone the second her dissertation was approved.

At least she wasn't as skinny any more, and she slept deeply through the night in his arms. He would have given, well, maybe not anything, but quite a lot to be able to get nine hours of carefree sleep like she did. Instead, he woke up around four every night, having dreamed something unsettling he couldn't remember, stared at the ceiling, and listened to her slow breathing.

To give Cecilia space to work, Martin retreated to the commune on Kaptensgatan. Granted, Anders worked all day, but since he was the generous type, he'd offered the sofa in the living room to a mate whose girlfriend had kicked him out. The Society of Wayward Souls was less fun when its latest representative was in his underpants popping spots in front of the bathroom mirror when you needed the loo. Or when he'd eaten the last of your homemade hollandaise ("I figured it was bound for the bin"). Or rediscovered a Love of Life in general, insisting on red wine-fuelled dinners that resulted in mountains of washing-up and a girl with hennaed hair who argued with you about the lack of a feminist perspective in Goethe. Shut up and go home, Martin wanted to tell her, but he couldn't, because their new lodger most likely wanted to sleep with this girl, or he wouldn't have been sitting there with a drunk grin on his face, constantly pouring her more wine. And lo and behold, they insisted on shagging on the living room sofa, separated from the other residents of the flat by nothing but flimsy doors. Martin put his pillow over his head.

Sitting on his desk was the *Night Sonnets* manuscript, a stack of paper two inches thick (he'd measured it). But he could always write tomorrow. Why torture yourself when you had no inspiration? Had good literature ever come out of self-flagellation? He was young. My god. There was plenty of time. First, he had to finish his degree. He had to find his own flat. He had to finish this vegetable stock. He fished out an onion with a slotted spoon, this indispensable tool whose existence he'd been unaware of two months ago. Julia Child's cookbook lay open on the kitchen table, alongside *À la recherche du temps perdu*. He had a tutorial on Tuesday and was a quarter of the way through. But he had an infinite number of hours to spend on Proust. In fact, the hours were lining up before him. All the hours today, all the hours tomorrow, all the hours this weekend. What was he supposed to do with all of them?

He put the lid back on, leaving a small gap to let the steam out.

Gustav was back at Valand and was having one of his battles with "painting as theory and practice", an expression that could probably be traced back to Sandor Lukács with the Zappa moustache.

He paced around his studio, gesticulating. He'd been painting the same motifs for years, he said. Mostly portraits. Especially portraits of Cecilia. It was either Cecilia or his "postmodern still lifes" (Sandor again). His boldest departure had been some Parisian exteriors. Buildings. He'd painted *buildings*. He'd painted buildings and roofs and the sky *in Paris*. "Could someone please give me a beret? A striped shirt? Where's my baguette? Where's Picasso's old mistress?" Gustav waved his hand about so wildly ash went flying everywhere. Even worse, he almost exclusively used a single technique: oil on canvas. What about watercolours, ink, good old charcoal, etching, gouache, pastel crayons? Not to mention collage? Sculpture? Or why not an "installation" or a "performance"? Sure, oil painting was his thing. He was good at oil painting. It wasn't a bad idea per se to play to your strengths. And he had an idea about a Rembrandt-inspired thing with Cecilia in a white collar and black blazer, where the textures of the black would appear, sort of, three-dimensional. But on second thought, he wondered if that was his own idea or if he'd nicked it from Nerdrum's self-portraits, which were skilfully made, true, but – Gustav took a drag and shook his head – far too nostalgically backward-looking. Pastiche. And did it even matter if it was his own idea or not, since Nerdrum had got there first?

Meanwhile, he'd been trying to get around the whole portrait problem by simply removing the people. He emptied a folder onto the sofa where Martin was trying to open a bottle of wine using a hammer and nail since someone had nicked the corkscrew. They were sketches of a studio interior.

"I've drawn my own sodding studio. It's like navel-gazing, but with drawing. You think so, too, right? It's self-indulgent. It's like images turning in towards themselves. And, in case I'd missed it, it's extremely eighties, and not these eighties. Could someone please transport me to the previous eighties? Let me paint my reading women in bright rooms in the right bloody century."

"Hypothetically, if you had to choose between no wine or wine with cork in it, which would you pick?" Martin said.

"Definitely option number two."

Martin pushed the cork into the bottle and filled two water glasses. Then he gathered up the sketches Gustav had thrown about so carelessly. "It's not like they're bad," he said.

"Of course they're not *bad*." Gustav picked a piece of cork out of his mouth.

"Ah, Monsieur *le génie* defends his works."

"All I'm saying is that they're perfectly fine."

"I meant it as a good thing. Leave the false modesty to Sissel or some other semi-talented person, okay?"

"Sissel's really good…"

"It reminds me of that painting on the stairs at the art museum that you always have me staring at. The one with the sculptors and the naked girl."

Gustav nodded. "Édouard Dantan, 'A Casting from Life', 1887."

"So, a hundred years of Dantan this year, I guess."

"That's what I'm telling you. If only someone would give me a time machine and some absinthe."

"Talk to Cecilia, maybe she'll sit for you again? She could do with the distraction. The only thing she talks about these days is Frantz Fanon and that she has developed an ulcer, or possibly a hitherto unknown, undiscovered intestinal disease. Listen, it doesn't exactly taste great with all this cork in it."

Gustav agonised for weeks about his canvases from France getting lost in transit. Once they arrived, the crate sat unopened in the hallway.

"Don't you want to have a look at them?" Martin said.

"Nah. Some other time."

"I don't get why you're so nervous about the exhibition. You have loads of paintings."

Gustav just gesticulated vaguely, as though that were a debatable fact.

As Valand's spring exhibition drew closer, Gustav spent more and more time at home. He was too broke to eat out. He couldn't stand the thought of "a lot of people", which was to say Anders and the new bloke at Kaptensgatan. School had a "depressing vibe". Martin still had a spare key to his flat on Sjömansgatan, and sometimes he stopped by when Gustav was out. His feet made crunching noises when he crossed the floor. The kitchen was full of washing-up and empty bottles. There were drawings everywhere, pinned up sheets on the walls, stacks of sketch pads, rolled up canvases, empty paint tubes, messy palettes. The easel was empty. The question was whether the windows had been washed once since – Martin counted the years since Gustav moved in and found them to be shockingly numerous. He binned a withered houseplant, pot and all. There were no towels in the bathroom. He found them in a pile of dirty washing on the floor. A few silver fish skittered away. Ashtrays, ashtrays, ashtrays. Martin found more bin bags in the bottom kitchen drawer.

"Stop that," was the first thing out of Gustav's mouth when he opened the door. He was carrying bags full of clinking bottles.

"Don't you have a vacuum cleaner?"

"No, I don't have a sodding vacuum cleaner."

Martin straightened up, emptying the pan. At least the place looked decent now. "I put all the post on the table. There are quite a few of those manila envelopes you might want to open. And someone in France sent a bunch of postcards with pictures derived from Catholic iconography."

"Probably someone worried about my immortal soul again. Are you cooking? Jesus."

"Just pasta with tomato sauce."

After dinner, they watched a TV programme in which a chain-smoking Kristina Lugn, Jörn Donner and someone else interviewed Siewert Öholm.

"Cecilia's coming over on Wednesday," Gustav said, lighting a cigarette, too.

"What?"

"For the painting. You know. The Dantan painting."

"Oh, good."

The April sky darkened. Gustav did the washing-up. Martin found the old record with Chopin's piano sonatas.

"What are you doing this summer?" he asked.

Gustav topped up his glass, looking away. "No idea," he said. "I'm sure it'll work out."

Martin wanted to scream: How the fuck is it supposed to work out? Maybe it'll work out for *you*, someone always buys a painting, someone always pays for dinner, sooner or later you always find a couple of crumpled banknotes in your pocket. But what are the rest of us supposed to do?

He took the bin out, slamming the door to the rubbish chute so hard the crash echoed up and down the stairwell.

What are the rest of us, who aren't bloody prodigies, supposed to do? Who's going to hire a humanities graduate with one published short story? And to do what? Was he supposed to take a job at the printers with his two hundred university credits? Was he supposed to work down the docks? Or what? Volvo, maybe? The assembly line at Volvo? He was no working-class hero. Unfortunately. No flat cap in his back pocket. He simply wasn't made to toil all day and then come home and read Dostoevsky. Was he supposed to go back to the post office? If he did, fifteen years would have passed before he knew it, like some bloody wormhole on Star Trek, suddenly it's 2002 (he chuckled at the ridiculous year), it's 2002 and he's standing there, making jokes about working hard or hardly working with some poor summer temp who's inwardly swearing to himself he's not going to end up like Martin Berg, who published one good short story and then took a job at the post office.

*

These days, the literature department was housed in the new buildings by Näckrosdammen that people had taken to calling Humanisten. Martin attended every lecture and tutorial. Sitting there in his black turtleneck, he heard himself start sentences with phrases like "when

I lived in Paris". What he really wanted was to write his dissertation on William Wallace. His supervisor, a weary docent who had written a thesis on *Le Chanson de Roland* a few years earlier, scratched his beard and furrowed his brow.

"Wallace, you say? Well, okay… And have you thought about how to approach his authorship? Do you have a specific question in mind?"

And he went out and got drunk. Quite a bit of time could be killed that way. He had a few pints. Four, five. Okay, seven or eight. With Gustav and Gustav's friends. With Per and Per's friends. With Fredrik from philosophy and Fredrik's friends. Did Cecilia want to come? No, Cecilia was polishing the final draft of one of her dissertations, she was defending it in two weeks, she was convinced she was going to fail, and she was tired, too. She wolfed down a large portion of bouillabaisse. She was going to go over her reference list and then get an early night, she said, politely stifling a burp.

Her bibliography was twice as long as his had been for that essay on Wittgenstein or whatever it was he'd written about. And she'd read everything in the original, too. That would have been expected if she'd been writing a doctoral thesis, but for a bachelor's or master's dissertation there was no such requirement. It was as though she was striding into a pole vault competition for middle schoolers, clearing two metres even though the bar was at one metre sixty. There was no need to show off. As long as you had a master's degree and a subject, it appeared they let anyone who wanted do a PhD. Fredrik (who had swapped his pipe for cigarillos) had similar intentions and was currently discussing thesis topics and potential supervisors with the prefect. Fredrik's friend, who claimed to have met Martin at some party in Långedrag a hundred years ago, was working on his master's dissertation in sociology and didn't feel ready to jump into the rat race, which made writing a thesis and thus lingering in the warm bosom of academia a while longer seem very tempting.

Martin lit a cigarette, looking back and forth between the two of them. He was the first person in his family to attend university. His dad nodded and hummed along, then asked if Martin wanted to play a game of chess, but Martin didn't, because he was terrible at chess. His mother just sat there with her Camels and *Anna Karenina* or whatever it was she was reading this week. How many times could a person read *Anna Karenina*? And Cecilia was no help. Cecilia had that prophetic look in her eye she always got when she was deeply engrossed in something. Cecilia walked around her flat wrapped in a kimono, talking to herself, writing a dissertation that was obviously going to be legendary and—

"Cecilia?" Fredrik's friend said. "Cecilia *Wikner*? She's your girlfriend?"

"Yes…"

"That explains a lot."

"What do you mean?"

The friend shrugged. "A friend of mine has been trying to get with her for six months to no avail."

"Glad to hear it."

"I took two courses with her. If teachers remember anyone's name, it's hers. She's the kind of person who could make professor before thirty-five. Is it true she speaks six languages?"

"Five. And she's not completely fluent in French."

Cecilia was dead asleep when Martin came home. He wasn't too drunk to make a dough. Easy as pie. Sourdough in a bowl. Warm water. Fuck, too hot. Start over. Stand by the hob, watching like a hawk. Come on, Martin Berg! Snap to! Thirty-seven degrees is what we need. He tested it with his pinkie. Perfect. Salt. Oil. Flour. He didn't even use a measuring cup. Stir, stir, stir with the wooden spoon. Cover with a kitchen towel. If our calculations are correct, the dough will have doubled in size just in time for when you wake up, horribly hungover, wanting nothing more than to go back to bed.

In April, Cecilia defended her dissertations. She wasn't overly concerned about the German one, but her master's dissertation in intellectual history still caused heavy sighing. At first, she didn't want to show it to Martin. Then she did, pacing to and fro while he read.

It was a sophisticated piece of writing, anyone could see that. A well-thought-out topic. Obviously well supported. Clearly and cleanly written, without compromising on complexity and nuance. Her formulations were elegant and independent from her source texts.

He told her to go over the discussion one more time, because some of the themes were inadequately defined. Generally speaking, he said, handing back the stack of papers, her writing could use some improvement.

*

Shortly thereafter, Martin was woken up by Cecilia jumping out of bed and running to the bathroom, where she proceeded to throw up loudly.

It took him a while to orient himself in space and time. The day before, Gustav had sold a painting to "a fairly brash lady working in banking", after which he went and bought a couple of bottles of Moët & Chandon just because he could. They'd drunk them at Valand. Then they'd ended up in a club by the Rosenlund Canal called something that conjured an image of a Viking-era villain – Draupner? – where they drank German beer. A band was playing synth-pop. Martin didn't normally like synthesisers, but this sounded like machines had come alive and begun to create monotonous factory music, there was a certain kind of sharp evil to the music that was pretty uplifting, and they'd danced in a sea of smoke-machine smoke, and at some point around there, his recollection grew hazy. He'd lost Gustav. How long had he stayed? Until three? Four? A hot dog with relish at Järntorget Square. Then he'd staggered up towards Linnéstan, to Cecilia's.

And so, while listening to her retching in the bathroom, his thoughts moved sluggishly. Food poisoning? Some kind of stomach flu? Could he feel any hint of the latter beneath the regular hangover?

"Cissi? Are you okay?"

She flushed the toilet and shouted something unintelligible.

A while later, she collapsed onto the edge of the bed. "I feel pretty rotten, actually."

"Maybe it's a stomach bug?" He shifted over a little to make more room.

She nodded but seemed unconvinced. "Maybe."

"I don't feel great either."

She smiled wanly in reply. "I reckon you feel as good as you deserve," she commented. "But I wonder if I should cancel my appointment…"

"What appointment?"

"My doctor's appointment."

After a period of protracted stomach trouble, she'd finally made an appointment to see a doctor.

"Of course you shouldn't cancel."

"But what if I'm contagious?"

"Pah. They're immune. They're around bacteria and whatnot all day every day."

And so it was that Martin spent the last few hours of his youth eating crisps and watching a rerun of some police procedural. Sven Wollter was naked and Thomas Hellberg wore a tight, white turtleneck not unlike the ones Martin's classmates had sported in the seventies.

Cecilia came home in the middle of the final scene and sat next to him in bed while everyone tried to shoot each other, and Sven Wollter lowered the wounded Detective Beck down through a window. When the credits began to roll, she turned the TV off.

"Okay," she said. "So, I'm pregnant."

III

MARTIN BERG: That being said – sooner or later, life inevitably intrudes into literature.

*

The foetus, they'd told her at the clinic, was by now as long as the palm of a hand and weighed about seven ounces. Brow furrowed, Cecilia inspected her stomach in the mirror. A gentle curve. Martin wouldn't have noticed if he hadn't known.

He knew she'd gone off the pill after their summer in Antibes. Then she hadn't started taking it again because he'd planned to stay in Paris a few months longer. She'd never liked the idea of messing about with her hormones, but on the other hand, she loathed having her period, which hadn't come until she was sixteen and had been irregular ever since, but when she was on the pill she barely bled at all, which was why she preferred it to a copper IUD, for example. She hadn't thought twice about missing her period, didn't even know when she'd last had one. Possibly early January.

Cecilia had never talked much about her body before, and now it all came pouring out as, perched on the very edge of the sofa, she tried to explain how she could have failed to notice, in fact *not even considered*, that she might be pregnant. Martin marvelled at this secret life that went on entirely without his knowledge or involvement. A series of memories, clear as could be, of times when he couldn't be bothered to fiddle with a condom immediately came to mind. At the time, he'd figured they could "be careful" instead. He'd had a vague idea that Cecilia would somehow, mystically, know whether she could be impregnated or not. But Cecilia, sleepy and lovely and warm, had mumbled something like "Remember that I'm not on the pill any more" and he'd said "Absolutely" but he was already inside her, and honestly, how much is a person expected to think at a time like that?

The pregnancy had progressed just beyond the limit of a legal abortion. Which meant there was no decision to be made.

*

"Oh wow, congrats," Abbe Berg said, shoving some snus in under his lip.

"Amazing news," his mother said, taking off her apron. And she, who rarely touched anyone, put a hand on Cecilia's arm. Was she feeling sick? Tired? And how had her dissertation defence gone? She even showed pictures of Martin as a newborn. "I can't believe how *fat* he was," he heard Cecilia exclaim in the bedroom.

Martin was sitting on the patio. His dad had gone off to buy the evening paper and baked goods from the bakery at Mariaplan. The lawn was full of flowers he felt pretty sure were crocuses. His mum had planted some bushes since his last visit. The earth around them was black, moist. Birds were singing in the trees. On the table lay a half-solved crossword puzzle. He pictured himself in a long succession of fathers. His father had travelled all over the world and now spent his days with crossword puzzles and coffee. His grandfather had been a booze hound who died when an iron girder hit him in the head. And his great-grandfather – did anyone even know anything about him?

He stood up and went inside.

On the table in the living room was a chessboard with the pieces suspended mid-game. "Who's he playing?"

"It's correspondence chess," his mother said. "He's waiting for a man in Borås to move."

"*I am Death*," Martin quoted Bergman. "What did Dad's grandfather do for a living, by the way?"

"He was a sailor, too." Birgitta turned the page in the photo album. "He lived to eighty-five. He supposedly had an ear for languages. He'd manged to accumulate some savings, but your grandfather gambled it all away."

"So every other generation is screwed."

"Well, that's good news for this one, at least," Cecilia said with a hand on her stomach.

Cecilia held off on telling her own parents until they came down from Stockholm to celebrate Easter in the summer house. She wore a loose dress, and her stomach, which was by then a smooth, oval bump, was only obvious to those in the know. During dinner, Dr Wikner talked in detail about the common blue butterfly, "fascinating little scamps" who, granted, were protected, but what the hell, it was his property, what was anyone going to do about him catching some butterflies in the meadow behind the house, of which he was the rightful owner? He was deep into a *Polyommatinae* project, which, in brief, was intended to map the colour and pattern variations of the blues. "It requires the undivided attention of a scientist," he said, scratching his beard, which was streaked with more grey than the last time they'd seen each other. In the candlelight, the doctor's straight nose and intense blue eyes had a touch of Russian nineteenth century about them, of tsars and Rasputian devilry. Martin didn't quite know how to deal with these entomological monologues. Lars could at any moment burst into sudden laughter, a staccato *ha-ha-ha*, slap Martin's arm and in some unclear way make him the butt of the joke.

Halfway through the chocolate mousse, Cecilia said: "We're having a baby", just like that. Inger dropped her dessert spoon onto her plate. Lars topped up his port glass to the brim, talked extensively about obstetricians of his acquaintance, offered Martin a cigar, and then disappeared out to his butterfly collection in the barn.

Inger ran up to the attic to find a box of baby clothes she was sure was there. Peter, who was a few terms into medical school at that point, discreetly asked his sister about various pregnancy symptoms. Vera prodded her chocolate mousse, looking bored. Emanuel watched, wide-eyed. He was apparently in one of those periods when he only spoke when necessary, and even then only in a low, whispery voice.

Martin nudged him. "Would you like the rest of my dessert?"

Emanuel nodded, plunging his spoon into the chocolate mousse.

Inger spent the rest of the evening talking about her own pregnancies, which had been smooth sailing.

"I put on twenty-five pounds and then boom! – gone within weeks. But then, I had a figure back then. In fact, I did some modelling." At least until Emanuel was born, when a series of complications occurred and the delivery was a protracted affair full of blood, sweat and tears, and she'd needed stitches afterwards. "And what do you know, after that, it was as though I just couldn't get the weight off. I was good, I fasted, but it just *wouldn't* come off."

She talked about clogged milk ducts and pelvic girdle pain, about colic and diarrhoea, and when Cecilia said she was tired and going to bed, Inger launched into a lecture about the pros and cons of breast-feeding versus formula.

It was close to midnight when Cecilia fell into bed. The mattress springs squeaked. She stretched out on her back with her hands on her stomach.

"What if I can never run again?" she said.

*

Neither of them wanted to tell Gustav.

"You do it. He's *your* friend," Cecilia said.

"He's just as much your friend, isn't he?"

"But he was your friend first. I'm your girlfriend. That puts you at the top of the loved-ones list."

"You're the one who's pregnant."

"I reckon we're both equally bloody pregnant."

"It could be interesting to see how long it takes him to notice."

"Don't be an idiot."

They agreed to do it together, over lunch at the Golden Prague.

When they'd covered Gustav's anxiety about his graduation exhibition and he asked how things were on their end and Martin replied: Yeah, good, and launched into a detailed account of how his studies were going, Cecilia cut him off.

"As a matter of fact, we're having a baby."

Gustav's hand, which was holding a pint glass, stopped halfway to his mouth.

"What?"

Cecilia looked at Martin with her eyebrows raised in a *help-me-out-here-will-you* way, but when he opened his mouth, no sound came out.

"I'm pregnant," she said.

Gustav put his glass down, picked up his cutlery, put it back down. The he shook his head and said: "*Wow*. Or what is it people say? Congratulations."

"Thanks."

"But seriously, wow. How did this happen?"

"Well, you see," Cecilia said in a faux-pedagogical voice, "when a man and a woman – or in our case an ambitious author-to-be and a distracted historian – meet and take a liking to one another, some-times, it happens that—"

Gustav threw a balled-up napkin at her. "Should you even be drink-ing beer?"

"It's low-alcohol beer."

"Bloody hell."

"It's what I get from giving into carnal desires."

"It's due in October," Martin said, because he felt he had to contrib-ute to the conversation.

Gustav leaned forward to get a better view of Cecilia's stomach. "I can't tell," he said.

"We figured you could be the godfather?" Martin said. "If you want."

"If I want? Of course I do."

Martin had brought his camera, and now he snapped a picture. The photograph, developed a few weeks later, showed Gustav's pale face overexposed against the dark decor of the restaurant. He was smiling in that wide, surprised way that touched something soft in the heart region of anyone who saw it. His glasses had slipped down his nose a little and if you looked closely, you could see one of the arms was taped. One of his earlobes shone bright red after a failed attempt to pierce it the weekend before. On the table sat a half-eaten schnitzel and an empty pint glass.

*

A friend of Valand-Uffe's was moving to Noresund, and Martin and Cecilia were able to take over the lease of his flat on Djurgårdsgatan.

People seemed to feel a special kind of goodwill towards parents-to-be, or possibly the rent was simply so high Uffe couldn't afford it.

The flat was on the third floor and had until recently housed the Marigold Commune, judging from a piece of paper taped to the front door, which listed five names, one of which was Moon, next to an upbeat *Stop imperialism!!!* and a more prosaic *No circulars, please*, all written in neat cursive letters. When Uffe's friend decided to realise his dream of rural communal living, the members of the Marigold had, like seeds in a pod, scattered to the four winds without giving the place a proper clean. Between the hallway and the living room hung a tangled beaded curtain and in one of the smaller rooms, one of the walls was adorned with an amateurishly painted sun with long, undulating rays. There was a soiled mattress on the floor in the attic room. A picture of Chairman Mao was taped to the fridge.

"Well, it certainly needs work," Cecilia said. She studied the walls and the ceiling, touched the peeling wallpaper. "A new coat of paint and whatnot. I'm sure we could get rid of this, too." She tapped her toe against the linoleum in the kitchen.

"We can each have a study," Martin said. He pictured a desk, light flowing in through the mullioned windows, stacks and stacks of book...

Cecilia looked around at the empty rooms, the dead flies on the windowsills, the dirty wooden floors, the left-behind flowerpot holding the cadaver of what appeared to be a marijuana plant. Then she burst out laughing. She laughed and then she grabbed Martin's face and kissed him.

Cecilia knew quite a bit about home improvement, which was fortunate, because Martin did not.

Growing up, she'd been subjected to her mother's Projects – first in Addis Ababa, then in the summer house – and therefore felt at home in the world of Polyfilla and scrapers and primer and brushes Martin had been so careful to avoid. In fact, he'd been so successful at this, he couldn't help but brag a little. *I don't know how to fix a leaking tap,* he'd say, spreading his hand. *I* don't know what to do with a crow-bar. Don't ask *me* if I have a spirit level. He'd categorically refused to hammer in a single nail, even though he was perfectly equal to the task. It was a matter of principle. He'd had to fight for those principles more than once, primarily in pitched battles with his ex-girlfriend Britta (whose handling of a drill had something at once dejected and salacious about it).

"Seriously?" Britta had said in her most disappointed voice. "You can't put this shelf up?"

"Why would I be able to?"

"Isn't that something you just know?"

"Are you saying the ability to use tools comes with the Y-chromosome, or what are you implying?"

"But have you never, well, drilled anything? When you were a child?"

"I read books as a child."

"But didn't your dad..."

"Why don't you just put it up yourself? Female empowerment and all that?"

"Yes, but I told you, I don't know *how*."

He'd shrugged. "Neither do I."

And maybe she would have resented him for it if it weren't for the fact that Martin had defended his right to know nothing about drills with such sullen aggression. Apologising for his ignorance, or trying and failing – drill crooked, bend the nails, miss with hammer – would have been deeply humiliating.

"You're going to have to sort it out yourself," he'd told Britta, lighting a cigarette even though she didn't want him to smoke in her flat. "Or get yourself another boyfriend."

At first, Martin was unequivocally pleased that Cecilia was so capable when it came to DIY. He liked that she owned a big jangly toolbox made of scuffed blue metal, which was full of screwdrivers, tiny nails, wrenches and a bunch of other things he didn't know the names of. He liked that she had a special type of flat, red pencil with thick lead that she sharpened with a knife. He liked her self-assured way of handling a folding rule. He liked that they were a Modern Couple, which was to say not like his parents with their laughably stereotypical division of labour and areas of expertise. No, he and Cecilia were not burdened by the yoke of the nuclear family. They could deconstruct assumptions taken for granted by previous generations. They could look at the world through the revealing lens of postmodernism and see that "male" and "female" (Martin inwardly made quotation marks around the words) were constructs, not natural laws. They, Martin and Cecilia, were representatives of this yoke-free generation, which had learned to view the human body as a politico-historical arena rather than destiny. And so: let us be deeply grateful for the fact that Cecilia Wikner handles her new role with such grace and confidence! Besides, she looked sexy in dungarees and a paint-spattered tank top.

He was good at other things. Twentieth-century philosophical movements, for instance. Sartre hadn't painted ceilings, either. Heidegger had never held a hammer. Wittgenstein may have chopped wood up at his small Norwegian cabin on occasion, but he was bloody weird. In other words, it was fine that Martin was the one who listened while Cecilia explained how to go about removing the yellowish-brown medallion wallpaper, or how they were going to repair the wall and then paint it a sober shade of white. It was fine that she tore down the wallpaper three times as fast as him and that her movements were efficient and precise while his were hesitant and clumsy.

The first few days of the renovation passed in perfect harmony. All the windows were open, they listened to the radio echoing through the empty rooms and when lunchtime rolled around, Martin went out to buy pizza that they ate out of the box. But they were working hard and were under a degree of time pressure because Anders had found someone to rent Martin's room. And Martin began to feel Cecilia was telling him he was doing things wrong *a bit* too often, and true as that may be, she could be a bit more understanding, or at least use a different tone.

And so, they had their first big fight, if it could even be called a fight.

Martin and his sister had fought like cats and dogs growing up. They'd gone through every type of conflict there was. Furious fisticuffs. The more sophisticated icy silence. Teasing, also known as the verbal version of Chinese water torture. Political machinations involving their parents. Theft/hostage-taking of possessions. The throwing of various items at each other. The yelling of creative invectives and the slamming of doors in general. Later in life, he'd fought, as people are prone to do, with his girlfriends. (Britta, for instance, had seemed to prefer a good row to living in placid harmony.) But Cecilia was always so reasonable, so cool and rational, she never raised her voice, things could always be discussed. Logically and thoroughly.

It had started with some triviality neither one of them could recall after the fact. It probably had to do with paintbrushes not being put in turpentine or paint cans not being closed properly, and the fact that whoever had failed to perform this task, whatever it may have been, was Martin. And when the first hint of snarky irritation vibrated though the air after a full day of hard toil, painting walls and ceilings, Martin had probably been unable to let it slide. He might have said: Well, excuse *me* for not being as bloody fast and amazing as everyone else in here. He might have said: Bloody relax, will you?

And she'd said something along the lines of: But I didn't mean, and he said: Of course you bloody did, you can't take back the fact that you meant it, and she said: But, and he said: I'm so fucking over this.

And that was how it happened that Cecilia was left standing in the middle of the room with a wallpaper scraper in her hand and a strange look on her face, as though she were suspicious and afraid. Damp strands of hair clung to her forehead and her eyes were brimming. When she opened her mouth to say something, all that came out was a cut-off gasp. Instead, she shook her head and carefully put the scraper down on the floor and silently left the room.

"You can't just walk out!" Martin shouted. "You can't just leave before we've sorted this out! Cissi – what the fuck. *Cissi!*" He stayed where he was for a minute, listening. Not a sound. "What the fuck," he muttered.

He cleaned the paintbrushes and washed his face and hands before going to look for her. The door to the attic room was closed and when he climbed the stairs, he found her rolled up on the mattress.

"Hey, Cissi," he said. No answer. She was fast asleep. When he touched her face, he could tell she'd been crying. Martin squatted next to the mattress for a while, unsure what to do.

IV

INTERVIEWER: What is your relationship with success?

MARTIN BERG: Success? God. [*puffing up his cheeks, sighing, scratching his hair*] I suppose success is a necessity if you want to write. [*laughing*] Would people have the drive to keep going if no one cared? I don't know. Some people seem to think writing is so rewarding in and of itself that it doesn't matter if there's a reader. But if it's all adversity and rejections and that... If you never find any kind of success...

INTERVIEWER: ... then...?

*

At the Valand Academy degree show, Gustav's last exhibition before graduating, they found their friend in a corner of the Museum of Contemporary Art, drinking red wine out of a plastic cup.

"I'm hiding from Mother," he said. "She's wandering about, uncritically admiring everything she sees."

Marlene von Becker was, indeed, standing in front of one of her son's paintings, head tilted back, arms crossed, handbag dangling from one wrist. The painting in question was of Cecilia in her armchair

443

in front of her homemade bookshelf. Her feet were crossed on the footstool, and she was holding a pen. A look of utter concentration on her face. On the floor next to her a notepad and some loose sheets of paper. It was a motif typical of Gustav's style, like a snapshot but on a grand scale and with realistic clarity. It was also the last painting from Cecilia's flat. She had cancelled her lease and her books had been moved to Djurgårdsgatan, where they were standing next to Martin's in a real bookshelf they'd bought at Ikea and assembled with unexpected ease.

"Martin!" Marlene's hand was cold and clammy. "And you must be Cecilia." Her eyes flickered almost imperceptibly to Cecilia's stomach, which protruded slightly under her shirt, followed by a moment of weighing her options. "Congratulations. How far along?"

"Four months," Cecilia said and smiled the way she smiled at all parents except her own.

"That's wonderful. I know Gustav's art is always lifelike, but he has really captured you. I'm no connoisseur, but... to my eyes... of course, he doesn't listen to *me* when I tell him he's in a league of his own." Marlene swayed ever so slightly but immediately parried the movement by pulling herself up and smiling. She was wearing a silk dress with broad shoulders and a belt cinching her tiny waist. She had aged as discreetly as she did everything else, and her face was to youth as a dried rose was to a freshly picked one. Martin wondered what Marlene got up to now that her children were grown. He knew Gustav sometimes went to plays and concerts with her. Afterwards, he would turn up in his Sunday best, looking exhausted, and head straight to the bar, fridge or wherever alcohol was to be found.

"I've been told every last piece is already sold," Marlene said, her voice lowered, businesslike. She fumbled with her handbag, pulling out a packet of Camels. Martin found his lighter. Her cigarette touched the flame. Marlene tilted her head back and squinted through the smoke. "Every last painting. And I heard Galleri 1 is very interested. Don't tell him I said that. He hates it when I brag. But how can I not? You know, he's been drawing since he could hold a pen. Of course" – she took a deep drag and tapped ash onto the floor next to her – "my father was also very talented, he takes after him. But then my dad died. The son of one of Gothenburg's most prominent shipping families *drowned*." She snorted derisively. "Our ships have been crossing oceans for decades, but he manages to *drown* one morning in dead calm. Isn't that funny? You know what. It's very crowded in here. I think it's time for me to retire. Bengt wanted to be here, too, of course, but then he had to pop off to China on business…"

Martin couldn't remember a student exhibition ever being so busy. He wondered who all the people were. The art students themselves were easy to spot, as were their parents: sober-looking couples at the upper end of middle age ambling through the room with their features arranged into expressions of interested goodwill. And then there was the category of people to which he and Cecilia belonged, friends and acquaintances. But outside of that? Martin's eyes were caught by a tall man in a beige suit who had taken up post in front of Vivi's giant wall hanging made of crocheted wire, which she had explained was a "feminist comment on the crafting tradition within the world of art". The man was accompanied by a young woman who was also wearing a suit and carrying a shiny briefcase, and who was nodding at something he was whispering in her ear.

"Art collectors, maybe," Cecilia said when she noticed him looking.

"Here?"

"What could be better than buying someone currently unknown who could become a big name? It's the kind of things traders do. Art is like stocks – buy when it's cheap and sell for a profit."

Martin considered a series of paintings that had to be Sissel's: deer, foals and baby rabbits in bright colours, like a poppier Bruno Liljefors slipped into second childhood. That a finance bloke with any level of self-respect would mistake them for investments was hard to imagine.

"It's no wonder, really," Cecilia went on, wedging her arm in under his. "The moment something acquires value, it can become the object of speculation. But the value per se is something we just make up, isn't it? Somehow, we all agree that object A is worth this or that much while object B isn't."

Martin put his arm around her waist. Her taut, warm stomach under the fabric of her shirt still felt like a new and unexpectedly pleasant discovery.

They picked their way through the crowd, looking for Sandor's paintings, when Uffe intercepted them. The room where his TV sets were flickering was, Martin had noted, the least popular in the exhibition.

"So, you're knocked up?" Uffe nodded at Cecilia, pulling out a cigarette. "Nicely done. Do you know if the so-called prodigy has fled the scene? Because they're asking for him again. That woman from Galleri 1" – the mention of the gallery was followed by a studiedly indifferent wave of his lighter – "was apparently keen on the portraits of you, Cissi. So make sure you don't let the fact that you're popping one out ruin your figure. Well, anyway. Let him know he's the most wanted in here when you see him." He sauntered off.

After a while, Cecilia wanted to step outside for some fresh air, and up under the arches of the Museum of Contemporary Art, they spotted Gustav. He was sitting slumped on the front steps, smoking. When they approached, he looked up and nodded to them.

"They're looking for you in there," Martin said, sitting down next to him. Cecilia sat on the other side of him. Avenyn spread out before them. Sitting at the top of the steps, you always felt like you had the city at your feet.

"What year did we start university?" Gustav said. "Was it '82?"

"I think it was '81, actually."

Gustav flicked his cigarette away. "Right. Five years plus one in Paris." He sighed. "I need to be out of my studio by the end of July."

"So, where are you going to work?" Cecilia asked. "Are you going to rent a place? Vivi was talking about the new studio spaces in that old epidemic hospital – they're calling it the Art Clinic."

Gustav shrugged. "Something'll work out, I guess," he said. Then he sighed, took his glasses off, and pressed his fingertips against his closed eyes. "One way or another."

*

Cecilia went to the library and borrowed every book she could find about pregnancy. She frowned at Lennart Nilsson's *A Child Is Born*. She studied her bump in the mirror. She noted kicks and foetal movements and reported them to her midwife at the clinic, whom she thought of as an eccentric academic supervisor whose idiosyncrasies she sometimes had to be tolerant of. She made sure she ate properly, abstained from alcohol completely, and asked Gustav to smoke out of the window. When she was offered a spot in a group for first-time mothers, she went to every single session even though she hated it.

That summer, she decided their baby was a girl and was going to be called Rakel. Martin protested: first of all, it could just as easily be a boy, and surely no one under the age of seventy was called Rakel? Cecilia graciously told him he could pick the name if it turned out to be a boy, but Martin never managed to come up with a name for their potential son.

One morning in June, Per called to tell him he'd found a start-up course run by the Job Centre.

"I mean, how hard can it be?" he said in the receiver Martin had wedged between his shoulder and his ear while he prepped the coffee machine. "You and me, a small but highly curated list, modest revenue but on the other hand no outrageous overheads… The way I see it, and I've been looking at the numbers, we could absolutely make it work. It might not make us rich, but it could work, and over time we could expand, depending on how it goes, obviously."

"What are you talking about?"

"The publishing company? Look at it this way: what's the worst that could happen? The thing fails and that's obviously not great, but on the other hand it's not the end of the world either, is it? Especially if we start slow. It's a risk we'd have to take. Anyway, I reckon it's worth a shot."

"Absolutely," Martin said, still unsure what he was agreeing to. He cut some cheese and put it on a slice of Skogaholm loaf.

"And I think this bookkeeping course is a good place to start," Per said. "You'll go with me, right?"

"Sure," Martin said around a mouthful of bread. "When is it?"

The whole thing had started when Martin *l'écrivain* and the still-searching Pierrot were walking through Paris, talking about the future. Per didn't share Martin's authorial ambitions. He claimed to have not one jot of Talent for such pursuits and that he was at his best when working behind the curtain. He just wasn't sure what kind of curtain it was going to be yet. And Martin had to admit that it was possible the first few years of his career could turn out pretty lean. That was common, expected even, and it meant he'd need a side gig. One of the ideas they'd bandied about, with cigarettes dangling from the corners of their mouths and legs dangling off a Seine quayside, was that they could start a publishing company.

"Think about how many books there are," Per said. "That never get published. Or that get published but not translated."

"We'd need some kind of manager," Martin said.

"We'd *be* the managers. Let that sink in for a second," Per said with his eyes lost somewhere above the rooftops of the fourth arrondissement. "Because, like, why not? It has evidently been done before."

Martin had assumed this idea would go the way of all their other ideas: after an initial burst of energy and a period of intense theoretical planning, it would cool off, be put on ice, and finally forgotten. It was the natural life cycle of ideas. Therein lay their charm. He'd completely forgotten about it, and it was with tepid enthusiasm he trudged after Per into a stuffy office to learn about the basics of self-employment.

He'd always imagined himself on the other side of the publisher's desk, or whatever the spatial arrangement was – he assumed there was a desk involved – anyway: on the other side, in the visitor's chair, while the publisher, an older man (distinguished) or why not a woman (wearing a suit) touched the fingertips of one hand to the fingertips of the other as he or she leaned forward, saying: "You see, Martin Berg, we think your book is good – very good, even – and we'd be honoured to publish it."

He'd never even considered being that publisher himself, that person with a desk and business cards, and, who knows, maybe even a secretary? He'd never pictured himself as particularly successful either, at least not in the remunerative sense. Running a successful business was a prime example of the kind of thing that was Worthwhile and Desirable according to Martin's father and which Martin had consequently spent all his life up until that point classifying as Not Particularly Worthwhile or Desirable. No, he wanted to step into that office, which wasn't his but rather embodied the antithesis of his very being, possibly wearing a leather jacket, place his latest manuscript on the desk, make some small talk with the distinguished or besuited publisher and then leave again, head out into the sunshine, light a cigarette, squint at the sky and feel the freedom of the freelancer spread out around him like the tundra around Attila the Hun. He didn't want to be the person who *stayed in there* until the clock struck five and he could pick up his jacket and briefcase and start his journey home while hundreds of thousands of others did the exact same thing.

"I mean, I don't know…" he said to Gustav because he didn't want to voice his doubts too loudly in front of Per, who was so happy and had already brought by a stack of books he figured they might translate.

Gustav shrugged. "You do need a job."

"*I* need a job? What do *you* do for a living, if I may ask?"

"I sold every last piece at the exhibition."

"I don't think starting a publishing company is the most watertight approach to this fatherhood thing," Martin said.

"Then get a job at Volvo. Or SKF. Decent salary. Or why not the printers where your dad works? At least you'd be in close proximity to printed text being disseminated. That's not too shabby."

"Are you serious?"

"Of course I'm not bloody serious."

And then daydreaming began to spin its mother-of-pearl threads around the idea of a publishing company. Every day, Cecilia's bump grew a little bit bigger, and there was unmistakeably a child inside it, and that child had to be supported somehow, and the modest cheque Martin had received for his participation in the anthology was far from enough to support even himself. Not even if he brought in one a month. (Martin had figured children didn't cost anything the first few years, but after going into a pram shop one day for no particular reason, he'd been forced to revise that notion.)

He could rock his baby's pram with one foot while he read manuscripts. He could talk on the phone with various important people. He could read tons of untranslated English literature, and maybe French, too, he did have to keep his French alive somehow, and acquire the Swedish rights. Maybe even translate himself? They would have bright offices with floor-to-ceiling bookshelves and shiny black Bakelite phones on their desks. Hire people to do various things.

The fact was that Martin, who just a few weeks earlier had been sitting in the lunchroom at Humanisten arguing that privately owned companies were morally defunct, now envisioned his and Per's little publishing company growing and growing, thanks to his infallible instinct for text and Per's infallible business nous. He would belong to an *industry*.

So after the course at the Job Centre, he went with Per to the Tax Authority to talk to a caseworker about how one went about starting a company. He found himself taking notes and subsequently filling out forms for a start-up grant. He bought a decent black jacket. For the first time in his life, he considered wearing a tie. He cheered when Per called to say that his grandfather, an Estonian exile entrepreneur who was rumoured to own a port south of Helsinki, had been so proud – "and touched – he actually used the word touched" – to learn of his grandson's audacious initiative that he'd called to offer to lend him a hundred thousand kronor.

"He says we can pay him back once we're in the black, and if that never happens, I can consider it an advance on my inheritance."

In October, their daughter was born.

During the delivery, Cecilia was quiet and determined, and when she awkwardly received the newborn, she studied her sceptically at first, then with a wan smile. The little one screamed through its miniature throat, probably in shock or maybe just offended at having been born. She was so tiny and weighed so little, Martin's intense happiness was mingled with abject terror, because what if he dropped her, or something happened, or she suddenly stopped breathing? But the baby just peered up at him with eyes that were very dark, almost black, and afterwards he would never fully believe people who assured him newborns were short-sighted, because she met his gaze openly and curiously.

A few weeks later, Gustav announced he was moving to Stockholm. He claimed to have been thinking about it for ages, but Martin couldn't recall him mentioning it even once. Anyway, he kept the flat on Sjömansgatan, and a good thing, too, because he'd just officially taken over the tenancy and it would have been so exactly like him to blow a solid rental agreement just like that.

V

MARTIN BERG: Well, of course. Success is a double-edged sword. It is.
INTERVIEWER: What do you mean by that?
MARTIN BERG: Well. I suppose there's a certain kind of freedom to being unknown. Successful people are slaves to the rule that they're only as good as their latest book. Unfortunately. And sooner or later, you end up in that place where your biggest successes… [*coughing, clearing his throat*] are behind you…

*

They were the last people off the Stockholm-bound train, because unloading the pram turned out to be extremely tricky. Just as Martin paused to make sure his little family and their accompanying luggage were all accounted for, he heard a familiar voice rise above the din of the station.

"Hoohoo! Cecilia! Martin!" And Inger Wikner was rushing towards them, heels clattering, arms spread wide, Jesus-like.

"Oh, Mum… I told you you didn't have to…"

"Yes, but Emanuel was just dying to come. Weren't you, Emanuel?"

Instead of her usual kaftan and long plait, Inger Wikner wore a Klein-blue coat and her hair in a bun, and Martin had barely recognised her at first. Emanuel, lurking right behind her, said nothing.

"Can I help you carry anything?" Inger asked with a vice-like grip on Martin's arm. "Would you like me to take Rakel?" She emitted a cascade of cooing sounds aimed at the child on Cecilia's hip.

"That's okay," Martin replied.

Inger ushered them all into a taxi and gave the driver the address. Squeezed into the middle, Cecilia closed her eyes in a give-me-strength pose worthy of a martyrdom painting in an old Catholic church.

Emanuel stared intently at his eight-month-old niece. Rakel seemed to deal with changes in her immediate environment by simply nodding off, and she slept through both Emanuel's staring and her grandmother's chirping attention.

Martin's knowledge of Stockholm came courtesy of a school trip in ninth grade (the Old Town, the Royal Palace, Kaknästornet) and one time when he and Gustav had hitched up to visit a friend (Södermalm, confusing metro rides, a flat in which people sat in groups, smoking weed). He remembered it as a beautiful city, but that could just as easily be thanks to Söderberg and Strindberg. And Eugène Jansson's twilight-blue paintings of Riddarfjärden, which Gustav had dragged him to the Thielska Gallery to see. He didn't know his way around and his Gothenburg accent had never seemed so blue-collar-dock worker, so underground-club-and-porkpie-and-low-rent as when it was spoken next to its snappy Stockholm counterpart. If not for his year in Paris, he would have felt lost. Because what was Stockholm compared to Paris, in the grand scheme of things? *Pas beaucoup.*

During the short drive to the Wikners' flat on Östermalm, Inger pointed out the most expensive streets on the Monopoly board. Maybe they should go out to Djurgården, she said, it's always nice this time of year—

"I don't know if there'll be time," Cecilia cut in.

"The marathon doesn't take all day, does it?"

"It does, actually. And then we're seeing Gustav."

The street was lined with tall buildings with the mocha-cake facades and cast-iron Haussmann balconies of the nineteenth century. There was an ancient lift the pram just about fit into if no one else was inside; Emanuel had to run up ahead and be ready to open the door. While ushering them into the flat, his mother-in-law went on and on about how ill-advised it was to run a marathon "so soon after giving birth".

"What if something were to happen. Hmm?"

"Like what? That I get shin splints?"

"For example. Yes. Or something worse."

"You're going to have to be more specific."

"It's unnatural to subject your body to that kind of exertion. Dad had a friend who died playing tennis."

"But he was fifty and obese. His heart gave out."

The flat was smaller than their summer residence, true, but it was nevertheless imposing. There were butler's pantries, hallways, nooks and window seats, wall sconces, crystal chandeliers, end tables, cut flowers. Doors and more doors. Inger tidied away any visual disturbances as soon as they appeared. A well-worn phonebook was consigned to a drawer. Wilting tulips met their fate in the bin, glimpsed for a fraction of a second behind a cupboard door. She picked a loose thread off Cecilia's shirt and smoothed down the corner of a collar that had turned up. Cushions were picked up off the floor. Rugs were pulled straight. Magazines were arranged in neat stacks. She snatched the hat Emanuel was wearing despite the warm early-summer weather off his head, but he snatched it back just as quickly and put it back on, deaf to her admonishments about it being rude to wear hats indoors.

Martin was thoroughly up-to-date on the Wikner family's goings-on, because whenever Inger called, her daughter would perform a pantomime conveying the message "I'm not here" so Martin had to listen to her status updates instead. Apparently, Emanuel still didn't feel at home in Stockholm. He spent most of his time in his room. What he was doing in there, no one knew, though Inger did her best to coax him out. She snooped around when he was at school, but never found anything of interest. He either had nothing to hide or was smarter than her; she didn't know which was worse.

"Can you imagine, Martin," she said with exalted dejection, "being shut out like that? Hmm? By your own son. And he was always such an intelligent boy. Sensitive, but intelligent. And now he won't even talk to me... Dad" – this was what Inger called Lars Wikner – "does manage to snap him out of it on occasion, but that's hardly sustainable, is it? For him to need us there, helping him..."

Vera, on the other hand, was doing well, after slipping seamlessly into the role of New Girl in Upper Secondary, which she'd played with panache. Now, she'd just graduated and was waiting to hear back from the Royal Dramatic Theatre. (She hadn't deigned to apply to the Academy of Music and Drama in Gothenburg.)

Lars, for his part, had been "talked into" returning to his job at Karolinska, after a sabbatical spent importing rugs from Iran, Pakistan and Turkey. She'd said nothing about how he'd fared in that business, but judging from the large number of rugs in the family's flat, Martin concluded that the doctor had not been a terribly successful rug merchant.

"I *really* tried to get Peter to come home for dinner now that we're all together for once," Inger said, setting down a plate of steamed vegetables on the table. "I called him weeks ago. He told me then he couldn't commit at that point, that it was 'too far into the future'... and when I called him again this week, he apparently had an exam. But I do think he should have made time, now that you're here and all… it's not an everyday occurrence, I mean…"

She finally sat down.

They were having dinner in the dining room. Vera glanced at her reflection in the gravy boat. Emanuel had smuggled in a comic book that he kept on his lap. Rakel quietly spat out puréed carrots. Lars Wikner opened a bottle of wine.

"What did you have to eat yesterday?" he asked Cecilia. "The night before is the most important meal."

Cecilia told him what they'd had for dinner, and he nodded approvingly.

"I read knee injuries are common," Inger put in. "The most important thing is to have *fun*, remember that."

"Isn't the most important thing to run fast?" Lars objected.

"It doesn't matter how fast she runs if she gets injured, does it?" Inger countered.

"She's not getting injured. She's in excellent shape."

"I'm just saying having fun is the point, not winning."

"It's not about winning." Lars cut a potato in two. "I never said anything about winning. Some Kenyan is going to sprint around the course in two hours flat. She has no chance of *winning*. It's about challenging yourself, exploring your capacity."

Inger frowned and raised her eyebrows.

"Why would anyone want to run a stupid race?" Vera said. "It makes you sweaty and ugly."

"I take it you didn't apply to Konstfack this year, either," Lars said to Cecilia.

"That is correct," his oldest daughter replied.

"All they want is samples of your work and a personal letter. It's no big deal. You just send it in. If you were half as ambitious with your art as you are with your running, your paintings would be selling for good money by now. Like your friend Becker's."

There was a pause, filled with the clattering of cutlery. Lars levelled his fork at Martin. "And how is the publishing company doing?"

Martin had been expecting that question. Before answering, he took a sip of wine, set his glass down and wiped the corner of his mouth with the linen napkin, leaning into the drama. Conversing with Lars was a peculiar kind of sport. His father-in-law preferred an even stream of words at a fast clip, preferably coming from him. But since he also wanted to know everything that was going on within his social sphere, he sometimes had to condescend to listen, which he did while fixing his interlocutor with his pale, raptor-like eyes that blinked far too infrequently.

"Our first book is coming out in a few weeks."

"And what kind of book is it?"

Martin had been asked all the publishing questions so many times he'd developed a fully automated spiel. Sometimes, he varied the dramatic pauses and tone just for kicks. And so, he told them about the First Book (an incisive debut by a young woman who could in all likeliness have had her book published by a bigger company if she'd sat on her hands a bit longer, but who was so happy anyone at all was interested in publishing her work that she didn't care one bit that the print run would be minimal and that they couldn't afford to do any real promotion). He told them about Upcoming Projects (manuscripts that seemed promising, their plans for publishing philosophical works and other non-fiction). He lingered for a while on the "so-to-speak aesthetic and intellectual standard" Berg & Andrén were determined to cleave to. He dodged the question of economic sustainability with a *que-será-será* attitude that intimated he was on top of things but didn't want to bore his dinner company with tedious details. He praised his co-workers: Per had the entrepreneurial inclination Martin himself lacked, Cecilia was doing a wonderful job with the translation of Wittgenstein's diaries.

"Do you really have time for that?" Inger asked her daughter. "With little Rakel and everything?"

"Tell us about your research," Lars commanded. "How much do they pay PhD candidates these days?"

The next morning, Martin was standing in the crowd on Strandvägen, behind a sagging strip of plastic tape that separated runners from onlookers, together with a mute Emanuel dressed in a heathered grey gym outfit and his mother-in-law, who insisted on pushing the pram. At the sight of the runners, something shifted in his chest. They weren't really running all that fast. It didn't look that hard. It seemed like something anyone could do. There was nothing monumental about them in any given moment, nothing grand; they were just regular people running, spending a few seconds in his field of vision.

*

They'd been waiting in the outdoor serving area for twenty minutes when they finally spotted Gustav walking towards them with a girl in tow. If he'd looked up, he would have seen Martin and Cecilia from afar, but he picked his way between the tables with his head bowed. Only when he reached them did he look up and envelop them both in long, fierce hugs.

"God," he mumbled. "It's been a long time."

Next to Cecilia's rosy-cheeked post-marathon Botticelli face, Gustav was a blurred pencil sketch. His eyes were shadowed and his nose seemed drawn with careless strokes. His temples were greying; a process that had begun at twenty-five, a gradual shift towards the colourless. He was dressed all in black.

"The only thing missing is a beret," Cecilia teased, pinching the shapeless blazer that seemed superfluous in the balmy June night.

And at that, Gustav smiled. Martin could feel something inside him that he hadn't even known was tense relax.

The girl he'd brought looked like a sullen Liza Minnelli who'd cut her own hair with nail scissors. Her name was Dolores and she introduced herself as a poet. With studied indifference, she took out a short cigarette holder into which she somewhat ceremoniously inserted a cigarette that Gustav then lit. Once that was done, she complained about the marathon making it virtually impossible to get around town, saying she couldn't understand why people would want to do something as idiotic as run twenty-six miles in a group – "I mean, if that's not an expression of human folly, I don't know what is" – at which point Gustav and Martin were suddenly very busy reading their menus. Dolores looked around, irked by the lack of response.

"I ran the marathon," Cecilia said in a stage whisper, and then the waitress arrived to take their orders.

"Do you have Trocadero?" Gustav asked. "I have a terrible craving for Trocadero."

Martin expected Dolores to comment on this peculiar choice of beverage, but she was engrossed in the list of first courses.

Gustav hadn't told them he was bringing someone, and it was never quite the same when other people were present. Things had to be explained. Irrelevant details had to be dusted off ("I actually grew up in East Africa," Cecilia was just saying to Dolores, who pushed out her lower lip and nodded as though that were an admirable feat). For social reasons, matters that were deemed too in-group had to be either excluded or clarified. As a consequence, the conversation moved slowly and unevenly through general topics. They talked about the Picasso exhibition at the Museum of Modern Art (which Dolores hadn't enjoyed). They talked about the latest gruesome murder trial (which Dolores had read all about). They talked about the Ebbe Carlsson affair (Dolores yawned).

Gustav was the one who talked the least. His eyes rested on Cecilia and Dolores in turn but seemed to slide past Martin. He cut his steak into tiny pieces and focused on his food as though eating it were a challenging task. As soon as he finished his fizzy drink, he ordered another.

But Dolores had no problem carrying the conversation by herself. She seemed younger than them, around twenty. It was eminently possible that she would, later in the evening, try to foist a rumpled script covered in ballpoint pen on him, so that he'd have to give his little speech about how they "unfortunately aren't publishing any poetry, it's just not financially viable for us right now". At regular intervals, she inserted comments along the lines of "Since Gustav is always doing this or that" or "Isn't that just so, Gustav", as though Gustav himself weren't there, which indeed he seemed not to be, spiritually – he was leaning back in his chair, holding a cigarette whose column of ash grew longer and longer and longer until Dolores held out the ashtray to him. Those comments awakened a competitive instinct in Martin, and he found himself countering with anecdotes from their decade-long friendship. At one point, he took a cigarette from Gustav's pack, and when Gustav gave him a light, he ached with the memory of all the hundreds of times Gustav had given him a light, when their bodies had been in these exact positions – both slightly hunched over, fingers lightly touching, in the sphere of stillness surrounding the lighting of a cigarette.

Gustav's hand was ice cold. His fingers trembled slightly as they fumbled for the opening of his pocket to return the lighter to its rightful place.

"We passed your gallery on the way here," Cecilia said. "It looked amazing."

For the second time that evening, a smile flickered across Gustav's face. "Aha. Then maybe you had the dubious pleasure of meeting the great K.G. Hammarsten himself."

Not long after moving, Gustav had been snapped up by a gallery in Stockholm. He'd talked about it as a purely practical arrangement, because handling the selling part on his own was complicated, waved aside Martin's questions about how it all worked, financially. When Gustav mentioned the gallery owner Klas-Göran, known as KG, it was with equal parts irritation and respect. Martin assumed galleries were similar to publishing companies – some were more prominent than others – but he knew nothing about the taxonomy of the art world and he could never get a good read on KG's place in the hierarchy. Then he hadn't given it another thought until Cecilia suggested they stop by.

The gallery turned out to be located very close to her parents' flat, on the ground floor of a nineteenth-century building. Behind big, arched windows they could glimpse white walls and paintings hung at very dignified intervals. You had to ring a bell to get in. Martin had mumbled something about how it was probably closed, but Cecilia had grabbed his hand. "Nonsense," she'd said, "come on."

Inside, the room was dead silent and cool. The vast stone floor gleamed. The sound of muffled voices was coming from another room. Martin was intensely aware that they were too young and too simply dressed to fit in, and when Cecilia marched further in, he hovered near the door. At first, he thought her confidence came from growing up the daughter of a doctor, but then he spotted one of the paintings. A Cecilia dressed all in white with a book on her lap was gazing down at them from the wall, oil on canvas, 60 x 40 inches. In an adjacent room hung another enormous portrait. When a tan middle-aged man in a dark suit appeared, she smiled at him, saying: "You must be KG," in her deep voice, and then calmly waited to be recognised.

Now, she assured Gustav the gallery owner was very nice and that the exhibition was great. "Your still lifes really came off well. They gain something from being shown all together."

"Those old things," Gustav replied. "They're really kind of imma-ture and half-baked, aren't they?" But he looked pleased.

During this segment of the conversation, Dolores took impatient drags on her cigarette. Then she abruptly stubbed it out and excused herself to "go to the ladies' room". Martin regretted that they'd already talked about the gallery, and for lack of something to say, he cleared his throat. Gustav blinked, iguana-like. Cecilia shifted in her chair, winced at the pain in her sore muscles, and finally asked: "So, where did the two of you meet?"

"Who? Dolores? Oh, you know. Around. She recently moved here, too. From Östersund or whatever. Two exiles from the provinces."

Again, Cecilia was the one to break the silence. "Do you like it here?"

"Sure. Absolutely."

"How – how have you been?"

"Great. Just great."

At that point, Dolores returned, dropping into her chair, announcing drily that they should have gone to Prinsen instead. "It's all yuppies and tourists here."

They parted ways as soon as they'd finished their coffee. Gustav and Dolores were going to a party and invited them to come, but Cecilia wanted to go home to get some sleep. Martin hesitated but found himself shaking his head.

So they said goodbye and he watched them disappear down the street. The glow of Dolores's cigarette flitted about like a firefly, and Gustav didn't turn around once.

21

AT FRIGGAGATAN, all the windows were open to the train tracks and cemeteries. A gentle breeze was blowing through the flat. Sitting at her desk, Rakel stared at what until now she had considered a decent translation of various excerpts from the novel *Ein Jahr der Liebe*. Handwritten text was different from text typed on a computer. The provisional nature of the handwritten provided excellent protection against having to stand by your work. Confronted with the blinking cursor in her Word document, she was left sitting there with her chin in her hands, unable even to make herself go to get coffee. She should have been at a lecture on sociocognitive perspectives on personality, whatever that meant. But she had to translate this for Elis, because until he read it for himself, he couldn't be expected to take her words as truth, even though he purported to find her claims "pretty plausible". It was a strike against his judgment, Rakel mused, that he trusted her so implicitly. She could have convinced him of anything. He'd always been easily swayed. If he could read part of the text, he at least had a chance of combating her wild fancies.

Besides, she'd promised her dad a sample translation when he called for the third or fourth time to nag about her reader's report.

"*Wonderful*, yes, do that," he'd said.

"But that obviously means it'll take a bit longer to..."

But Martin had just kept talking about all the opportunities the publishing company could offer an aspiring translator, apparently in a future-oriented frame of mind to which one or two weeks more was nothing to bicker about. And thus, Rakel had bought herself more time, but sooner or later she was going to have to show him something.

The scribbled translation in her notepad had been done without any thought to a readership. It was full of approximations and skipped phrases she hadn't fully managed to pin down. Transposing each sentence into a Swedish faithful to Franke's inflection and thrust turned out to be something else entirely. As soon as Rakel had transcribed a line from her notepad to the computer, all the power and shine seemed to drain out of it, like fool's gold sparkling in a stream turning into ordinary rock when you lift it out of the water. She scrutinised each word, unable to figure out where the failure lay. If anything, she thought, the text was too correct.

All her life, Rakel had been told she was "good at languages", partly because she was and partly because in the Berg family, linguistic talent was expected. And not only because of Cecilia; the polyglot line could be traced back through the generations to Rakel's paternal grandfather Abbe. When he'd had a stroke a few years earlier, he'd greeted her in fluent German when she entered his hospital room. "You're the very picture of your mother," he'd also said, even though everyone agreed Rakel favoured the Bergs. At first, she thought his German greeting was a nod to her year in Berlin, from which she'd only just returned, but it had more likely just been a lucky draw in some neurological lottery. "He started speaking Dutch to me earlier," her dad had told her, pacing up and down the hallway outside. "I called for the nurse because I thought he was having another stroke. You know, Dutch sounds a lot like Swedish, prosody-wise, but the words are completely different. But no, apparently, he's just slightly 'disoriented, time and space-wise'. What does that mean? That Albert Berg is in Antwerp in 1965?"

"He knows Dutch?"

"Drop him off on a beach in Polynesia and he would instantly pick up whatever bloody language they speak over there. Have you seen Mum? She left to pick up a paper half an hour ago. And where is Elis?"

On a June day not long thereafter, Abbe was buried at Västra Kyrkogården. "For some unfathomable reason he didn't want to be cremated," her dad had muttered at the reception afterwards. "You would have thought he of all people would have wanted his ashes scattered at sea and all that jazz. Romantically backlit archipelago or whatever. But no, he just has to be left to rot in Majorna." Then he stood up, tapped his glass, pulled a folded piece of paper out of his inside pocket and gave a speech to the small gathering of family and the occasional colleague from the printers and Transatlantic. He talked about his ear for languages, knack for chess and love of the sea, the latter in a way that made it hard to believe it had been at least thirty years since he himself had set foot on a sailboat. Martin didn't say: What would have happened if Abbe had ended up in the department of Romance languages instead of on a freight ship? If he'd been given the Rosetta Stone instead of a crossword puzzle in a week-old *Corriere della Sera*? Even though none of that was said, his speech conjured the image of an alternative grandpa. An Abbe wearing a sports jacket, on his bike, on his way to the university, instead of Abbe in a T-shirt with a logo on the back, in his Volvo, on his way to the printers.

And so, it was impossible to work with languages without ending up in the shadow of other members of the Berg family. And even though Rakel was good, she was, no use denying it, hardly a genius. She sighed. Resisted an urge to get up from the desk. Next to the wall sat her mother's old Olivetti. Rakel inserted a sheet of paper and tapped a few keys. The types left only shadows of letters on the paper, but there was nothing wrong with the keys. It took a lot more force than typing on a laptop and every keystroke rang out in the silence. Rakel tapped out a row of invisible letters until she got to the ding that marked a line break. When her mum wrote, there were regular dings, instantly followed by the swishing sound of the carriage being pushed back.

One of Cecilia's stock phrases suddenly popped into her head: "How hard can it be?" She'd say it with a furrowed brow, as though she were really trying to understand what the problem was. It wasn't meant as criticism – Cecilia accepted other people's shortcomings with transcendent calm, as though she hadn't really expected anything different – but a matter of principle. Running a marathon, for instance, she'd said, was not all that *hard*. It wasn't some kind of Übermensch thing attainable only by a select few. Of course, if you hadn't trained for it, it wasn't easy, but any weak-willed sod could train for a marathon as long as they possessed the basic physical prerequisites. If you wanted to run a marathon but didn't run a marathon, it wasn't because it was *hard*. There were other reasons, like laziness or fear. Fear was probably the stronger of the two. Fear of failure was a heavy yoke for humanity, preventing us from taking action. People's lives were full of aborted attempts and abandoned efforts. An aborted attempt allowed a person to cling to their dreams; a failed attempt always entailed loss of some kind. You could go all your life with a potential marathon in your future, until old age freed you from the risks and exertion of actually running.

Since Rakel had been very young and very literal-minded when her mother talked about running marathons, she hadn't imagined it could have been about anything other than running marathons. But over the past week, she'd gone for a few more runs and things had begun to appear in a different light. Her body was constantly in various stages of soreness. She ran slowly, almost at a shuffle. Her chest heaved with laboured breathing. Bile burned in her throat. No one could claim it was even close to pleasurable, except maybe when it was over and she was walking the last stretch home on trembling legs, her T-shirt soaked. Lycra-clad runners zipped past her with inhumanly springy steps.

She was free to stop running, just like she was free to stop translating. All she had to do was walk away. If she did, the pressure across her chest and the shame of struggling with something other people did with ease would instantly be alleviated.

The phone rang, making Rakel jump. It was several rings before she could pull herself together to answer. It was her dad calling, to tell her the books had arrived. "What books?" she was on the verge of snapping – they had to establish some limits for this reader's report business, she did have a paper about compulsive repetition to write and she had lectures to attend – but then she recalled asking Martin to order Philip Franke's earlier novels. The reason she'd given was that she wanted to familiarise herself with his language and style, but above all, it bought her more time.

"Do you want to pick them up at the office, or should I bring them home?" Martin asked.

She was so sick of his helpfulness. "I'll come pick them up," she replied.

*

Over the years, Berg & Andrén's offices had expanded and became more functional – no dangling wires, no windows that stuck – and their current location was a bright, cosy place with a view of the river.

"Hey, Rakel," Sanna hollered. Her desk was piled high with neat stacks of paper, her pencils were always sharp, and she had a special tin for paper clips. "Your dad's in a meeting, but I'm sure he'll be out any minute."

Through the glass door to Per's office, she could see her father, sitting with his elbows on his knees, leaning forward. He was running his hands though his hair and saying something with a dejected gesture. Per was standing up, leaning against the desk with his arms crossed, and now he nodded, and kept nodding to himself even after Martin had stopped talking.

"I heard you were working on some German novel?" Sanna said.

"Well – yes…" Maybe her dad's new strategy was to tell everyone she was doing some work for the company, so she couldn't pull out without looking like an indolent shirker. A craftily set hook aimed at her sense of duty. She could have said no to the *Ein Jahr* assignment, but for unclear reasons, she hadn't. It was becoming increasingly rare, she suddenly realised, for her to say no to anything. Everything she did or didn't do seemed focused on not inconveniencing other people. It was a good way to make yourself liked, but questionable as a central life principle. What would become of the upstanding, reasonable Rakel Berg?

In Per's office, her dad got up, a tired, heavy movement. Per said something and it was Martin's turn to nod. They kept talking for a long time while Martin stood with one hand on the door handle. When he stepped out among his employees, his posture metamorphosed over the course of a few paces: his back straightened, his shoulders were pulled back and his steps grew determined. He spotted Rakel, insisted that she wanted coffee, and talked incessantly while the coffee machine dripped espresso into a chunky little cup. The anniversary party was his main subject, with Elis's driving lessons and some kind of problem with a graphic designer they'd hired to do a cover a close second and third. She trudged after him into the office where Gustav's big Paris painting hung. The colours were shiningly pure as though he'd painted the exteriors of the buildings right after a spring rain. In his paintings, a film seemed to have been ripped from the world.

Martin picked up a paper and shook it open. "Seen this?" he said, holding up a full-page advert for Gustav's retrospective. The picture was the same as on the posters: Cecilia's solemn face, her eyes looking straight at Rakel. Her stomach flipped. She couldn't think of anything to say.

"They're certainly not skimping, anyway, the art museum people," Martin continued. "Do you know what a full-page ad costs? I'm look-ing forward to the opening. Quite the affair. He really deserves it. Oh, right – your books."

While he rummaged around the jumble, he began to talk about a book by some Austrian philosopher he'd been thinking about, appar-ently there was some psychoanalytical connection, maybe Rakel could have a look at it, and if she wanted to have a go at translating…

"It's too hard," she broke in. "I can't do philosophy." It was as though she was just learning to walk, and he wanted her to leap out onto a slack tightrope fifteen feet above the ground. Martin dealt with professionals all day; he should know she was an amateur and couldn't be expected to produce anything other than amateurish work.

"How can you know when you haven't tried?"

"Ask Max Schreiber," she said.

Martin snapped his fingers. "Excellent idea. I'll ask Schreiber. I've never met anyone more interested in German grammar."

"What about Mum?"

Martin stiffened. When he answered, he spoke more slowly, with a wary undertone. "Your mother, yes."

He shuffled some books around and Rakel knew she only had moments before he'd composed himself enough to change the subject. "Do you still have that letter?" she said.

Martin looked straight at her, wild-eyed. "What letter?"

"The letter she left when she took off."

"Oh, I see, *that* letter. Well, I'm not sure. I suppose it must be around here somewhere."

"Can I read it?"

He was silent for so long she repeated her question.

"Rakel, it was a very long time ago, I don't know where it is, if I even still have it, I might have thrown it out..." He pushed three volumes into her arms. "Here are your books. And would you mind getting that report to me sooner rather than later?"

The wind had picked up. It snatched at her hair and shirt and whipped up waves on the river, breaking up its normally placid surface. In the west, the arc of the Älvsborgsbron bridge swept across the harbour inlet, and beyond the bridge, oil tanks glinted in the sun. The sky on the Hisingen side was marred by the silhouettes of several large cranes. Rakel sat down on the edge of the quay, resisting a sudden urge to throw Philip Franke's three novels into the river just to watch them disappear through the impenetrable surface.

Instead, she pulled out her phone, ignoring the sudden image of hurling that into the river, too – it had superior sinking potential compared to the books, which were sure to bob around in a highly unsatisfying manner until they'd absorbed enough water to slowly drift down to the bottom – and found the tab with contact details on the publisher's website. She opened a new email, pictured the recipient as a German version of Sanna and wrote that she was a journalist who would love to sit down for an interview with Franke. And then, with an impossibly simple little movement of her forefinger, she hit SEND.

22

The worst thing you could do was fear the sleeplessness. You had to act as though you couldn't care less. Through an indifferent attitude, you could trick it, at least keep it from claiming even more territory. At the same time, you had to tend to what the newspaper psychologist had called "sleep hygiene". Martin had googled the article even though the clichéd descriptions of tranquil forest clearings and babbling brooks that were supposed to provide a calming haven were so provoking. It was worse than he remembered. What was he supposed to get up to in a forest clearing? He couldn't imagine a more stressful situation than being in a forest clearing. Who would make sure things were getting done? Per? Per was phenomenal as far as marketing and admin went, but he was no longer particularly involved in the literary side of things. As the publishing company grew and it became unnecessary for everyone to pitch in across every area, Per had, with some relief, transitioned to focusing on the company itself. The books were Martin's responsibility. He was their last line of defence. Without him, it would all come crashing down.

Which was why he would, despite his misgivings, consider implementing some of the pompous sleep psychologist's advice. A sleepless brain was evidently not as functional as one that had benefited from sufficient REM sleep and deep sleep and what have you. And so, he imposed a strict coffee ban after three o'clock. And so, he shunned all forms of technology for a full hour before bedtime, even though he really should have answered some of those emails. And so, he sipped a sensible cup of tea and read Wallace's *A Visit to the Museum*, which he knew by heart, and which therefore wouldn't risk triggering any unexpected ideas or emotions.

But once he was in bed, he tossed and turned as much as ever. His brain was overheated and frantic. Jumbled impressions were catapulted through his consciousness. His conversation with Per. Rakel's visit, her questions about that letter. The rambling interview with a trade magazine he should have prepped for. And that evening, his mother had called to ask for help with her unreliable internet connection. And in the middle of the call, she'd had a violent coughing fit that never seemed to end.

"Have you seen anyone about that cough?" he'd demanded.

"It's fine, I have my lozenges," Birgitta had replied.

"Well, have you cut back on the cigarettes like the doctor told you to?"

"Well, sure." Translation: she still smoked a pack a day.

He was going to ask Kicki to talk to her, too. Maybe his sister could exercise some of that nurse's authority. But Kicki had lived in Norway for years and was probably going to keep a safe geographical distance from their mother's proliferating age-related ailments.

He stared at the ceiling for a long time.

It was pointless. Martin Berg, ever the obedient student, turned on the light and read for a bit longer. How skilfully William Wallace described young Julie's restrained anger towards Professor Matthews! The dialogue was pure pleasure: every politely formal line crackled with rage, kept within the narrow confines of convention. When he started going cross-eyed from exhaustion – after all, he knew how Miss Julie's love story with the professor would end: badly, of course – he turned out the light and closed his eyes.

Around four, he woke from a muddled dream. He turned his alarm clock to face the wall. What felt like ten minutes later, he checked it again. Half five. He rolled onto his stomach, woke up again around seven and heaved himself out of bed. He and the sleep psychologist agreed on one thing: it was crucial not to accommodate the insomnia during the day. If you began to adapt to your sleeplessness, you were done for. The only thing that truly worked was a strict, fascist approach. The day after a sleepless night was a long torturous journey towards bed, but your chances of actually sleeping once you got there improved markedly if you allowed yourself no reprieve. No naps, no cancelled meetings. It was possible, he'd discovered, to accomplish a surprising amount on only three hours of sleep. Even a sleep-deprived zombie can keep up an appearance of normalcy.

He shaved, only cutting himself a little. He ate a couple of pieces of toast standing by the kitchen counter. He packed a towel and work clothes. He put on tracksuit bottoms and a sweatshirt. Here's a middle-aged man full of pep who cycles to the gym at seven, before work! Order and discipline.

They hadn't even opened yet when he got there. A woman his age was waiting outside the door. She was clutching one of those white Hagabadet bags people dragged around everywhere to let everyone else know they were members. After parking his bike, he recognised her: it was one of Gustav's sisters.

"Morning, Charlotte," he said, hoping it wasn't Helene. As far as he knew, one of them lived in Örgryte with her family while the other had married some semi-nobleman in the Scanian countryside where she ran a horse stud farm.

"Hi, Martin," Charlotte von Becker said. "Up early, too, eh?"

"When you're as old as me, you keep infirmity at bay any way you can."

"Quite right. I'm here for the very same reason."

"You don't look a day over thirty-five." It was almost true.

Charlotte smiled and said she was training for a Classic. "I did Vasaloppet last March and the Vansbro Swim a few weeks ago. Now I'm running Lidingöloppet in September, but I can't get over the fact that running's just so boring. I listen to audiobooks, that helps a little."

A girl in a polo shirt unlocked the door from the inside. They walked towards their respective changing rooms. "Say hi to Gustav from me," Charlotte called as they parted ways.

*

Martin was pacing in his office when Patricia, the intern, appeared in the doorway.

"Did you listen to the band?" she asked.

"Huh?"

"I sent you a link to a band I thought we might book for the party." He must have looked confused, because she clarified: "They apparently play, like, jazz, and sing harmonies?"

"Sure. Sure. I'm sure that's fine."

"So you want me to book them?"

He made a gesture intended to convey *you're in charge*.

"Don't you at least want to check them out?" Patricia said.

"I know who you mean," he lied. "They're great. Go for it." He wasn't some kind of control freak with a compulsive need to supervise every single aspect of the anniversary party, what they published or his children's lives. He wasn't the type to keep some poor graphic designer awake with emails about how the white should maybe be just a touch warmer. Sometimes, he avoided staying up until the wee hours poring over blurbs. He wasn't afraid of millennials who had no sense of work-life balance and therefore stayed at their desks late into the night instead of going home.

He scrolled through his contacts list, looking for the person who was dealing with the party venue. Then he stopped himself and put his phone down at an appropriate distance. Instead, he googled summer house + Gotland. Outrageous prices for a week's rental. Recalling that Stockholmers traditionally annexed Gotland during the warmer months, he changed the search to summer house + Koster instead. Or why not Denmark? Maybe he could persuade Gustav to come. Or France? The Riviera would be fun. They could rent a house, the kids could come. Several long weeks under that dizzying sky.

His hand reached for the phone again and he dialled Gustav's number. He let it ring at least twenty times before hanging up.

The room was hot. The sun was beating down. Every detail in the room appeared in sharp relief: the mess on his desk, the thin layer of dust on his computer screen, the ring left by a cup on the coffee table.

The colours of Gustav's Paris painting glowed, seemingly soaking up the light and re-emitting it.

Martin pulled off his jacket with sweaty hands. Sweat was trickling down his back, too, his entire torso was overheated. And he was slightly light-headed. The air seemed to contain no oxygen. He opened the window. The sun hit him full force. Razor-sharp reflections from the river. His heart was pounding. His pulse was refusing to slow. Anxiety was spreading like a chill from the pit of his stomach. The world went dark, his head spun. He closed the door and collapsed on the sofa. He was having trouble breathing and a wave of nausea was pushing up his throat. He forced himself over to the computer, typing "heart attack" in the search field. Common symptoms of heart attack, the public healthcare system's information service informed him in its dry prose, included strong and persistent chest pain that may radiate into one or both arms; an unpleasant sensation in the chest that may radiate into the throat, jaw and shoulders; nausea; breathing difficulty; cold sweats; fear; and anxiety. Martin closed his eyes and listened inwardly. Granted, there was no radiating pain in his arms, but apparently it was possible to have a heart attack without chest pains.

What would happen if he called emergency services? There would be an ambulance, a big scene in the lobby, robust paramedics in green clothes would burst into his office with a stretcher...

He scrolled down to the next header. "When to seek medical attention." From the jumble of words, he managed to pick out "fifteen minutes" – if the pain didn't subside within fifteen minutes, you should call an ambulance.

It was twenty to two. Martin lay back down on the sofa, breathing as calmly as he was able. He considered calling Rakel but decided to hold off until after he'd called an ambulance. Possibly from A&E. He counted the number of windows in the Paris painting, and then the chimneys. Those chimneys, the black tin roofs, the hazy sky, the countless antennas! The muffled cacophony of traffic drifting in through the windows of their attic flat! His French had been pretty good by the end. It may have been hubris to translate that Duras novel, true, and it had taken much longer than he'd expected, but the fact was that his translation still held up. Skimming it recently, he hadn't detected any traces of himself, just Duras and his unmistakeable Duras language. Maybe he should consider taking up translating again...

After a while, his pulse slowed. Nothing hurt. His body was more or less back to normal, though every muscle felt completely wrung out. He glanced at the clock: seven minutes. So, no ambulance.

He had a meeting at half past two.

Martin went to the bathroom and spent a long time standing with his hands on the sink and his forehead pressed against the cool glass of the mirror.

The flat was deserted when Martin got home late that evening. He turned on the TV and texted Elis to ask where he was. His son had been unusually quiet, barely saying hi before spending the whole of the previous evening ironing all of his shirts, listening to Jacques Brel's most accordion-heavy songs. When he'd finished his shirts, he'd moved on to Martin's, which he normally left in a wrinkled heap at the bottom of the hamper. Then he'd taken out the shoe-shining kit and thoroughly cleaned all their shoes. When interrupted, by, for instance, a gentle question about whether he might like a cup of tea, he'd spat out a "*What?*" to which there was no possible civilised response. That morning, he'd been looking for his keys in the hallway, muttering something about going to a flea market before slamming the door behind him. Martin had had to clean up after him, all the photo albums were scattered across the living room floor. Elis's fussiness was apparently highly selective, he mused, making a mental list for an impending discussion about Responsibilities and the Division of Labour in their home.

The room was stuffy. Martin opened the windows and closed the curtains. There was a Danish crime show on. Two detectives were sitting in a car with a rain-streaked windscreen. Maybe they should publish more crime. Even bad crime sold. What would future scholars think of the early twentieth century's obsession with crime novels? A faint spark of interest came to life somewhere at the back of his mind.

"A symptom of cultural degeneration and a lack of intellectual rigour more generally." Martin only had to close his eyes to hear Cecilia's voice and feel her presence beside him – the depression in the sofa where she was sitting with her legs pulled up under her, the rustle of her cotton shirt. For some reason, Cecilia's accent, which was otherwise a hodgepodge best described as standard Swedish, always became more pronounced in her prosody when she was criticising contemporary culture. "That's *one* hypothesis. Generous interpreters sometimes claim crime literature is an arena for social critique, which I'm sure is true of some authors. But in ninety-eight per cent of cases, it's an arena more akin to the Colosseum, which is to say an arena for entertainment of the fatal and destructive kind." She pushed a strand of hair behind her ear. Her long fingers were always moving, like those of an idle pianist. She turned her wedding ring round and round or fiddled with her necklace. "On the other hand," she said, "crime literature is also a symptom of our times, and, as such, very interesting. You might compare it to these so-called BDSM narratives. Why are they so incredibly popular? What need do these types of text satisfy in the thousands of women who read them?" The publishing company, she giggled, should maybe consider refocusing their list on crime and erotica. And then they could buy a summer house in France and retire. "Death and sex – isn't that what all cultural expression is about at the end of the day? And maybe God, too. But then God is inextricably linked to both death and sex. God is our last chance to avoid the eternal problem of death and sex." She got up to fetch something from the kitchen. He could hear the clinking of glasses as she whistled an aria by Bach. Once, long ago, she'd recited parts of the *St Matthew Passion* in German. He'd always liked hearing her speak languages he didn't understand.

*

And night after night, Martin failed to sleep. Outside, the birds sang like lunatics, because it was early summer and life was beginning anew. He threw off his duvet, put his pillow over his head, put his pyjama bottoms on, took his pyjama bottoms off, got up to drink some water, peeked in on Elis. His son was snoring open-mouthed with a white arm draped over his head. It would make sense to sell now. Better to get it done while Berg & André were at their peak. *We obviously value your experience and would love to see you stay on as publisher.* He could move to Stockholm. He could rent a house on a rocky headland some-where and finish his book on Wallace. The world was his oyster.

The days trickled past. He found the Spotify link Patricia had sent him. He bought a new suit. When an unknown Stockholm number called, his heart skipped a beat in the middle of the street, but it was just a telemarketer.

"I'm not interested," he snapped and hung up.

He went to the doctor and was examined with the cold steel of a stethoscope against his back. The doctor informed him there was noth-ing wrong with his heart.

23

Franke's publisher didn't get back to her. Not a peep from Elis about the excerpt she'd sent him. She hadn't even heard from her dad, who usually called incessantly.

Rakel stayed up late, translating, and in the mornings, she woke up long before her alarm. Having decided to stop attending lectures, she'd also forgotten about the personality psychology assignment; she'd discovered it was the last day to hand it in only because she'd been flipping through her calendar in search of Emanuel Wikner's phone number. It was strangely exhilarating to be so last-minute. She made herself a thermos of coffee and sought out the most remote corner she could find in the maze that was the university library, and proceeded to work intently for several hours straight, without giving so much as one thought to her mother or Philip Franke or anything else. When the essay felt reasonably finished, she sent it off to her course lecturer without reading it through. She was instantly back on her feet – she couldn't bear to stay another second – and went outside. The early evening was hazy and mild, and she stood at the top of the hill, lost, unsure which way to go and what to do.

Emanuel lived nearby. And he'd invited her to come over for a look at Cecilia's old drawings, but that was weeks ago now. He might easily feel stressed if she turned up unannounced. On the other hand, he could always pretend he wasn't home if that were the case.

Rakel trotted up the stairs. Even though she was well aware that he lived in town, she always pictured him in the environs of the summer house, and she had never visited his home on Lundgrensgatan.

When she thought about her uncle, it was always the Emanuel of her childhood summers that came to mind. With a pierced ear, always smelling faintly of sweat, hanging blankets across his windows to plunge his room into a ruddy twilight. Emanuel rode the flatbed moped to the village and he didn't mind her sitting in the flatbed, he solemnly promised not to crash, he swore on his mother's future grave that no traffic violations would occur, but perhaps it would be a good idea to get permission from her legal guardians. ("You're going *nowhere* without a seatbelt, young lady," her dad had declared.) He was an inherent presence in the house and, unlike all the other adults, he had time for her. "I heard you're a chess whizz," he might say, lighting a cigarette on the veranda. Nana objected to his smoking but had nevertheless set out an ashtray in the form of an upside-down flowerpot on a saucer.

"Grandpa taught me," Rakel replied.

"Excellent, excellent. *En garde, ma petite cousine.* Show me what you've got. Be ruthless. Hit me with your craftiest moves. No mercy."

"I don't know French."

Emanuel emptied the velvet bag of chess pieces onto the board and started setting them up. "You will, in time," he said. "Just look at your father. Exceedingly well versed in the Romance languages. And your mother. Between you and me, she's the true genius. Phenomenal instincts when it comes to syntax and the conditional and all that. Some people are wizards with a ball. Now imagine a person doing with all those tiny words what famous football players do with a ball. And that's the poly-talented Cecilia Wikner. All right, you start."

Rakel moved the same pawn her grandfather usually opened with.

"Ah, this idyll," Emanuel would say, placing his cigarette on the edge of the flowerpot to clap his large hands together and rub them against each other in the universal gesture of excitement. "Soon, Mummy dearest will bring us squash and biscuits. The convalescing patient is sleeping peacefully. Your father, the successful publisher, is having a terribly fruitful conversation with a prominent author. The baby is resting in his manger. The three wise men have seen a new star in the sky. The nuclear family is complete! Long live the nuclear family! Fanfares and parades. You're moving your rook *there*? Very bold, if I may say so."

Emanuel had been around twenty at the time. As the years went by, he spent more and more time on the computer in his room, shuffling out onto the veranda to smoke only at night. Rakel grew up and it had always felt like a peculiar kind of betrayal, as though she'd promised to remain a child companion forever and had broken that vow through the inevitable progression of physical development. Emanuel himself stayed more or less the same. Every once in a while, he signed up for courses in the humanities, but he never finished any of them, for unknown reasons. Then, he was going back to photography, but only for his own personal pleasure, he stressed, as though it was all he could do to fend off hordes of people clamouring for his works. He planned a trip to Japan that never happened, and then there was the ever-recurring talk about "a thesis".

Lundgrensgatan was a short rump of a street, and it didn't take Rakel long to find a Wikner at number 10. Emanuel lived on the third floor. When she rang the doorbell, nothing happened; she was just about to leave when the door finally opened. As usual, Emanuel was dressed in all-beige. The only detail that stood out from his otherwise colourless appearance was a ring with a large red stone on his pinkie.

"Rakel! What an exceedingly unusual surprise. I thought it was the cleaning lady, but she comes on Tuesdays. And today's not Tuesday, is it? A wormhole of possibilities opened up – all of them, I'd have to admit, fairly unpleasant. And then it turned out to be you! And all is well again. Come in, come in."

"When I last saw you, you told me about Mum's drawings – I was wondering if I could see them?"

"Drawings? What drawings?" Emanuel looked so nonplussed the icy cold of misunderstanding began to spread through Rakel, until he – after a little bit too long – burst into a high-pitched, barking laughter. "I'm joking, I'm joking," he said. "Don't look so scared. Cecilia's drawings. Absolutely. No problem. Aye, aye, Captain. Would you like a cup of coffee?"

"Please…"

She followed him into the kitchen. The flat seemed furnished with antiques from the summer house attic, far too large and cumbersome for a one-bed. In every room hung a crystal chandelier and on a dresser in the living room she glimpsed what appeared to be a stuffed peacock.

"Your flat is lovely," she lied.

"Thank you. A bit old-fashioned, perhaps, but I can't abide chaos." Emanuel turned on the coffee machine. "I tried it for a while, in a commune in Christiania. I didn't even need to do drugs. A girl from Odense had painted mandalas on the ceilings and kitchen cabinet doors. She was on the run from some kind of bourgeois fate and was fighting tooth and nail not to be pulled into the awful maelstrom of assimilation, the Charybdis of a workaday existence… Yellow, orange, purple, the works. No one ever did the washing-up and I, with my sodding upper-class upbringing, was the only one who cleaned the bathroom every once in a while, though that was more an act of self-preservation than of bowing to convention. So no, chaos – no. Ostindia or Mon Ami?" He pulled open a cabinet, revealing stacks of Rörstrand porcelain. There were at least two full services, including tureens and serving dishes.

"Uh – you choose."

With his hands on his hips, Emanuel studied the contents of the cabinet for a long moment before taking out two delicate cups and filling them to the brim with black coffee. He didn't ask if she wanted milk. Rakel slurped down some of the scalding coffee so she'd be able to carry the cup without spilling.

He led the way to the living room. There was, indeed, a peacock in there, standing on a chubby rococo dresser inlaid with intarsia. The blinds were closed, casting the room in a dusty half-light. Every inch of the floor was covered with rugs. The only thing that indicated the arrival of the twenty-first century was a surprisingly modern TV.

"Mum and Dad obviously loved that Cecilia had 'artistic talent'," Emanuel said, settling into a well-worn leather armchair. Rakel took a seat on the edge of the sofa. The brocade turned out to be hiding a sneaky collection of hard springs. "Or at least Dad did. You know him. He has spent a lifetime fighting mediocrity. Despising the way it's content with the little things. Challenging the imperatives of the Jante Law. We had better turn out special if we knew what was good for us. Whenever they had people over, he always fetched her sketch book for an improvised red-wine exhibition. Everyone cooed over her: she was so young and yet so uncompromising in her visual expression, a true talent, and so on. Anyway, Cecilia left all her old things here. 'Don't tell anyone you have them,' she said, 'if anyone asks.' Why would anyone ask, I said, but she just told me she trusted me. And if you think about it, I suppose I was in fact the only one she could trust." At this point, Emanuel seemed to choke up and closed his eyes. His face was mild and martyrlike.

Rakel waited for him to go on, and after he'd sat in silence with his eyes closed for quite some time, she deliberately clattered her cup against its saucer to remind him of her existence. Her uncle gave a start. "She left them in my care," he said. "She asked me to keep them safe, to look after them…" His voice trailed off, in another pause that severely tried Rakel's patience.

"What kind of things did she actually give you?"

He laughed his abrupt, barking laugh. "You're thinking: Why is he telling me *now* if Cecilia swore him to secrecy?" He stood up, with obvious difficulty, and set his course for the door to what had to be his bedroom. From her seat on the sofa, Rakel could see it was, if anything, even more cluttered than the rest of the flat. Every wall was lined with overflowing shelves. On the floor were stacks of newspapers and documents, separated by narrow paths. The blinds were closed in there, too, and everything was bathed in the thin light from an ancient crystal chandelier. Emanuel rummaged around for a long while before emerging with two paper bags from a local supermarket.

"The answer to your questions," he said, "is that I thought she'd come back. That's normal, right? You trust that the sun will rise and that the laws of gravity will apply tomorrow, too."

With a gentleness that belied the careless storage method, Emanuel held up a self-portrait drawn with charcoal. Cecilia had drawn herself in half-profile, a wary expression on her face, as though she didn't trust the person she saw.

"How old was she there?"

"Sixteen. Seventeen, maybe. For a period, she drew one self-portrait a day. I think she only saved the ones she was happy with, because she usually burned anything she didn't like."

The drawings were mostly self-portraits made with every possible technique: ink, pencil, charcoal, pastels. There were some watercolours, too, and several rolled-up oil paintings on canvas. They varied in terms of likeness, colour palette, size and technique, but the eyes looking out at the viewer were always the same. Aside from the self-portraits, there were some still lifes and interiors, and several drawings of very young Wikner siblings. Emanuel also found among the drawings an aerial photograph of a deep valley ploughing through a misty landscape.

"The Great Rift Valley," he said. "Cecilia loved it. Dad knew some-one involved in the digs, so we went there to see it. This was just after they found Lucy. It was grand. Dad almost fell down one of those archaeological holes. Mum tried to get in with the Leakeys."

Rakel asked if she could take one of the self-portraits with her, and Emanuel dug around the bags, mumbling to himself. "This one, per-haps... or no, not that one..." Perspiration appeared on his forehead.

"Here we are!" he exclaimed at length, triumphantly, handing her an unassuming slip of paper. It was a faint pencil sketch, probably a preliminary study for one of the more serious portraits. Rakel placed it between the pages of her notepad.

"When exactly did she come by to drop all of this off?" she asked.

"Oh, I remember exactly. It was the fourth of April 1997."

Rakel put her cup down; her hand was trembling slightly. "And what did she say?"

"I remember it well, very well." Emanuel looked up at the ceiling and put his hands together. "She said I had to look after her works because I was the only – the *only* – one she could trust, and that I had to take them to my grave if required, and that it was a privilege to be able to entrust something so dear to her to someone on whose unwavering loyalty she could rely."

"But didn't it strike you as odd that…?"

"She had her reasons."

"And she didn't say anything about those reasons?"

Emanuel broke into a giggle. "She quoted Wittgenstein, actually. *Warum man nicht sprechen kann* and all of that. Ah, typical, typical Cecilia. Wittgenstein." He laughed to himself, by all appearances unperturbed by Rakel not joining in his mirth. He had the quote wrong, Rakel noted. *Warum* had no place in it; it was supposed to be *wovon*.

"Do you remember anything out of the ordinary from the time before she disappeared?" she asked.

"I was in my second term of med school… Peter's name was in all of my books."

"How was Mum feeling?"

"Good, I guess. Normal."

"It was the spring she completed her thesis."

"Is that right? Wasn't that the year before?"

Rakel shook her head. "It was the same year."

Emanuel counted the years on his fingers because he could have sworn, he said, that she defended her thesis the year before, but on the other hand, the year before had been the year he started medical school. "Hmm," he mumbled. "'96, '97 – if she finished her thesis in '96…" When he couldn't make it come out right, he stood up with a groan and went to find a copy of her thesis to double-check. He disappeared into the bedroom once more and it was a long while before he returned.

Rakel's fingers and arms were tingling, itching. She had to get off the sofa and walk a few laps around the room. Why Emanuel took issue with a simple fact was beyond her. She wanted to snap at him that he could probably trust that Rakel had her timeline right – after all, she was the abandoned daughter – but since he hadn't given her words any weight the first time, he would hardly do so now. The chronology was clear and indisputable. That autumn, Cecilia had worked on her thesis, her viva had taken place in March, and in April, she'd left. And his assertion that she'd been "normal" during the months before she submitted was hardly accurate. That winter, all the adults had kept telling her: "Your mum's working on her Thesis," in hushed tones, meaning her mother was absent and moody and Rakel mustn't cause trouble. Once she had finished, everything would be well again. She just had to grin and bear it until then.

An episode detached itself from the recesses of Rakel's memory, rising to the surface like bubbles from a lake bed. It was winter, snowball fights were happening outside, and the children of the neighbourhood didn't go home until it was too dark to see. Rakel's mittens were soaked through, loose strands of hair from her plait clung to her forehead, and her hat had been pushed back. Music was coming from inside the flat. Her dad didn't appear to help her with her boots and there was no sign of Elis.

Rakel put her hat and mittens on the radiator and her boots on an old newspaper that was warped from melting snow. She hung her coat on a child-level hook. Then she padded into the living room and snuggled up next to her mother on the sofa.

Her mum ran a hand across her eyes. Her smile flickered like a broken light bulb and her voice was hoarse when she asked how school had been.

"But it's Saturday. I was outside."

"How was outside, then?"

"There was a snowball fight."

"Ah. Snowball fight."

"What's this music?" Her mother would probably be more interested in talking about the music than the snowball fight.

"The *St Matthew Passion* by Johann Sebastian Bach."

"What is she singing?"

"Something like this: have mercy, my God, for my tears' sake. See how my heart and my eyes weep bitterly before you, have mercy."

"Is it German?"

"*Das ist richtig.*" And now, my love, could you by any chance count from one to twenty in German?"

Rakel counted completely *richtig*, except that she left out *zwölf*. Her mum stroked her hair. "Fetch your hairbrush and I'll fix your plait," she said.

And for a long time, Rakel sat on the floor by her feet, with her mother's long legs on either side of her. Cecilia combed out her long hair, brushing it in sections. Her hands were gentle and careful, it never hurt when she took care of tangles, and when she had done that, she made a razor-sharp centre parting and began to plait. The plaiting was always a melancholy process, because it signalled the imminent end.

Now, Rakel's thoughts were scattered by Emanuel who reappeared with his nose in a book.

"It actually appears that you're right," he said. "1997, it says here. Very odd."

"Thanks for the coffee," Rakel said. "I need to get going."

"I would have bet my right arm on it being 1996. What do you know."

Back out on the street, she took several deep breaths. The evening air was fresh and clear. She had a feeling Emanuel was watching her through the gaps in the blinds as she casually walked down the street. Not until after she'd turned the corner did she lean against the wall of the building and look up when Lucy was found. It turned out the three-million-year-old hominid named after a Beatles song had been dug up the same year Emanuel Wikner was born. For her uncle to have such clear memories of the dig was therefore unlikely.

Her phone dinged to announce an incoming email, but it was just the university library, informing her that several of her books were now overdue. Rakel stayed where she was until her heart rate returned to normal.

THE PHD CANDIDATE

I

INTERVIEWER: What attribute would you say is an author's greatest asset?

MARTIN BERG: I would have to say perseverance, I think. You have to be good at many other things, too, of course. You have to have a way with language, dramaturgy, all of that. But lots of people are. To actually see a project through from the first word to the final full stop, that requires a very special kind of perseverance. Like a marathon runner. Any old sod can run, but to run twenty-six miles – that's something else entirely. Anyone who has ever done long-distance running knows it's all right at first. But sooner or later, resistance inevitably rears its ugly head. The going gets tough. There are blisters. Your legs feel like concrete. You want to quit. But for an author, the race has only just *begun*.

*

Thirty had always seemed like an absolute demarcation, a River Styx once crossed, never to return. Martin had imagined that some pivotal, internal change would occur just in time for his thirtieth birthday, but if anything, it was external factors that marked the passing of time. Per bought a flat. Frederikke finished her psychology degree. Vivi from Valand became an art therapist, whatever that was. Cecilia secured a PhD position at the department of intellectual history. It seemed like yesterday that he himself had been sitting in those lecture halls during his first term at university, listening intently to the PhD candidates, who all seemed to be sallow men with corduroy trousers and glasses. And now *his wife* was one of them. He wasn't quite used to thinking of her that way yet, and when he called her "my wife", he almost expected people to laugh at him, but no one ever reacted. Cecilia Wikner became Cecilia Berg, and Cecilia Berg immediately got a new driving licence, passport and sign on her office door. She asked the landlord to change the name on their letterbox and recorded a new message on their newly acquired answering machine.

Martin's business cards said *Publisher*, though in reality, he did whatever needed doing at a publishing company, except design covers. There was already a substantial row of titles lined up on the bookshelf at the office, which was located in an old factory in Kungssten, more were on their way, and unread manuscripts were piling up in tall stacks. Per muttered about the financial section of the newspapers and no one could honestly claim the future looked bright for Berg & Andrén, but, for now, they were getting by, partly due to a grant from the Swedish Arts Council and some other stipends. Maybe this wasn't the time to publish the most niche of philosophers, but somehow, Martin told his sceptical colleague, surprised at the enthusiasm in his own voice – somehow, they would find a way to steer their small ship through this downturn.

And even though he'd always felt like part of the younger generation, he was eventually forced to face the fact that the next generation was now old enough to buy alcohol and go to bars and turn up at after parties, the few he attended. They talked about bands he hadn't heard of, played albums he didn't listen to, and Martin was overcome with the simultaneously liberating and mournful feeling that he was not part of their value system.

"You're still *young*," Cecilia said. "Just compared to different people."

One day, Martin opened his notebook and realised his most recent entry was dated six months earlier. He sat there staring, pen in hand. He recalled his mother's journals, blue vinyl, one column per day, intended for brief daily notes. The limited format didn't encourage longer reflections or accounts. Those books had always depressed him, their pointless notes about birthdays and the first windflowers of the season.

He turned his attention to the dusty stack of papers that was *Night Sonnets*. It was a Saturday afternoon and for the first time in a long time, he had nothing to do. Or, more accurately: there was nothing he *had to* do. His wife and daughter were at a swimming lesson, everything was quiet, and the office was flooded with encouraging spring sunlight. What was Martin Berg to do except flip through the fragile, typewritten pages?

The last paragraph read:

He wasn't sure how he'd ended up in this predicament. He tried to trace the threads of consequence back to their source, but the sun was too strong, and maybe he'd had one gin and tonic too many and his brain was sedated, numb, battered by this cruel sunshine, and fields of colour danced before his eyes, and he was thinking – or, more accurately, he wasn't thinking at all. Even though he was vaguely aware that it would lead to consequences down the line, he was in a carefree frame of mind characterised by the maxim "Bah, what the hell" and so he jumped into the boat with the others.

"Sedated" and "numb" were synonymous, "cruel sunshine" was hackneyed, and the word "consequence" was used twice in consecutive sentences. (Martin reached for a pen, found a red ballpoint, and marked these shortcomings with swift strokes.) More troubling was that he had no earthly idea what predicament his hero was referring to, or whose boat he was jumping into. The paragraph conjured images of oppressive heat, lukewarm Pastis, and sand in his shoes, which would suggest it was written during their holiday in Antibes a couple of years ago. But could it really be true that he'd written nothing at all since?

He had to stand up and walk a few laps around the room. He'd obviously been writing *something*, he just couldn't recall what, right this second. On some floppy disc somewhere. But maybe not *Night Sonnets.*

He tried to continue to work on the text for a good fifteen minutes but couldn't come up with a single idea. His feet shuffled restlessly, he cracked his knuckles, his neck was tense. Inside, a white emptiness spread out in every direction.

Martin took his manuscript with him to the sofa, where he lay down, red pen in hand. He'd barely got through the first page when the phone rang.

"It's me," Gustav said on the other end. It sounded like he was eating something. In fact, he told Martin without prelude, he was at Gothenburg's central station, contemplating what to do during his "shore leave from the capital".

"When did you get in?"

"Five minutes ago. What are you up to? When can we meet?"

Martin was about to tell him it was pretty short notice. But Gustav would take offence and call Uffe, who never turned down a pint, and then they would go on and on all night about the degeneration of art in the era of capitalism or other well-digested topics. He stifled a sigh.

"Järntorget in fifteen minutes?"

Martin bought cigarettes at a 7-Eleven, took up position by the fountain and lit one. Cars everywhere. He was unused to smoking, the nicotine went straight to his head.

Even though five years had passed since Gustav moved to Stockholm, Martin couldn't sit at Pustervik or Tai Shanghai without expecting him to come through the door every time it opened. He would stand there, glasses fogged up, hands in his pockets, scanning the room, and when he spotted Martin at the table in the back, he'd fire off a big smile, raise a hand in greeting, pick his way between the tables. "I've had it," he'd say. "No human being in their right mind could ever want to live in Stockholm."

And the waitress would recognise him, because waitresses always recognised him, and he would smile at her, that big, amazing smile that made people want to do anything and everything for him. He would order a pint, and everything would be back to normal.

Martin was just pondering whether he should brave another cigarette so soon after the first when Gustav crossed the street, ten minutes late.

"There's construction at Kungsport," he shouted.

"They're always building somewhere."

"And yet, nothing ever gets better. Take this bloody street, for instance. What genius came up with the idea of having a street run straight through Järntorget Square..."

He was wearing his greatcoat, black jeans and basketball shoes with bunched-up socks, an ensemble that was taking on the status of uniform. One of the arms of his glasses was held together with tape.

They stood there in silence for a moment or two. "So, you're in town," Martin said. "How are things?"

"Well, you know. Same, same. What do you say, want to go to the Prague?"

They walked up Landsvägsgatan. The cinema on Lilla Risåsgatan was gone. Below Skansen Kronan was a new brick building with rows of empty windows. Gustav nodded towards the new buildings, square and sensible with orange-and-yellow plaster facades. "A monument to the idiocy of the municipality," he said.

"A lot of the old buildings were pretty dilapidated," Martin said.

"They could have done them up, though, right? It can't have been cheaper to tear everything down and start over than to renovate?"

"I actually think it was."

The building that housed the Golden Prague had been demolished years before, but luckily the restaurant had been resurrected in the exact same spot when the new building was completed. This early in the day, only a few regulars lurked in the corners. Gustav brightened up slightly when they were handed the menus; the restaurant's offerings hadn't changed much.

"So, what's new with you?" Martin asked while the waitress set down two foggy tankards on their table. He was trying to figure out when they'd last seen each other. It was the kind of question he wouldn't ask out loud, because it was a sore point with Gustav that he never came to visit.

"Not much. People don't buy art any more. Apparently, the Great Depression's going on out there and all the yuppies are nervous."

The Valand degree show still felt like just yesterday – Martin remembered the crowd, the upbeat mood, how dizzying it had seemed that all of Gustav's paintings had sold. But, he reminded himself, five years had passed since then. And Gustav had been lucky. Less than six months after the exhibition, the stock market had crashed, taking the art market down with it. By then, Martin had been busy with his newborn daughter, only glancing ever so briefly at the newspaper headlines – uninteresting messages from a world that at that time had nothing to do with him. Now, Rakel had become a solemn, gangly child who scratched her mosquito bites until they bled and read comic books with intense concentration, and Gustav Becker was no longer an unknown artist whose works might make you a fortune someday.

"But you didn't want to sell your paintings to yuppies anyway, did you?"

Gustav stuck a cigarette between his lips. "Hard to avoid in Stockholm."

Then Martin found himself talking about the publishing company: were they going to make it through the financial crisis? What was he going to do if they didn't? A few laconic jokes and phrases were similar to ones he'd used in other conversations, but he was unable to change course. It was a relief when their food came, because Gustav was thrilled to see that his schnitzel plate "looked exactly the same as ten years ago". Martin refrained from pointing out that there were probably only so many ways to arrange a plate of schnitzel, and they drank a toast to the fixed point the Golden Prague represented in an ever-changing universe.

After pint number two, Martin went to call Cecilia to tell her he was going to be late. He half wished Cecilia would ask him to come home, like other men's wives sometimes seemed to. But she just sighed enviously and told him to send Gustav her love.

Gustav became more talkative after the third or fourth round – he was drinking at twice Martin's pace – but also more indignant.

"Everyone's gone over to the dark side. It's all dinner parties and flowers and shit. And children. People are having children. Vivi's knocked up, you know, and I haven't heard from them in months. They've disappeared into the black hole of family life." Gustav peered suspiciously at Martin through the cigarette smoke, as though he were a potential traitor, too. Children stressed him out, he said. Rakel was the exception, an "intelligent and sensitive person".

Another subject he kept circling back to in endless retakes and repeats was the city he came from and the city he lived in. "*Gothenburg,*" he spat out in an exaggerated, dock worker Gothenburg accent. That "Little London" crap was just a euphemism for a godforsaken hole built on mud. The World Athletics Championship had proved just how justified their inferiority complex was. Avenyn was a joke of a parade route. People had no sense of style. The club scene was neglected and uninteresting. The art scene in this provincial backwater was languishing. The Göteborgskalaset festival was a sad bacchanalia for bumpkins. Gothia Cup was the only international effort of any importance – to the middle-school children of this world, that is.

"You should move up there, too," he said, pulling out yet another cigarette. "Who runs a publishing company out of Gothenburg, anyway? It's like trying to hawk oysters at a football game."

"Cecilia thinks it's too close to her parents," Martin replied.

In reality, they'd never discussed it.

As his blood alcohol level rose, Gustav swung over to the opposite position. Stockholm, he said, missing the ashtray, was full of people who were only interested in you if you were someone important. The day you ended up on a park bench, they wouldn't give you so much as a glance. You got elbowed in the back if you took your time in the metro. Everyone was stressed, the gallery owners snobbish, there were no real friends to be had.

"And things are different here, I assume," Martin said.

"At least there are *real people* here," Gustav said, his voice shrill. "Real people. I mean it."

"So come back, then."

"I've been thinking of moving to Berlin for a while. Or London. All right, sod it. How long have we been sitting here? It's only midnight? Where to next?"

"I should probably be getting on…" Martin was unsure how many of the glasses on the table were his. New ones kept coming all the time.

"You can't give up now! The night's young, Martin!"

"I don't know…"

"Come on. What about your work hours? What about your fading youth?"

"Sure, but I'm actually pretty tired…"

"Valvet is the antithesis of tiredness."

"Does Valvet even exist any more?"

"You're asking *me*? Martin, I'm disappointed. Who's holding down the fort in this town? Huh?"

They walked briskly down Linnégatan and it almost felt like old times. But Valvet was indeed closed, and the line outside Magasinet was impossibly long. Martin recalled a new place on Kungsgatan and suddenly they were crammed onto a packed staircase leading down into the underworld. He didn't recognise a single face. Girls with tangled hair and big boots. Blokes in tartan flannel and ripped jeans. A camera flash in his face blinded him.

"I'm too old for this," Martin said.

"Come off it. You have at least ten good years in you before the great tedium sinks its claws into you."

"It's possible that's already happened."

"Pah. You're young in all the ways that matter. Forty, though – bloody hell," Gustav said. "I hope I die before I reach forty."

"Don't say that."

The group ahead of them suddenly started wobbling precariously, laughing loudly; someone fell and the girl closest to them was pushed into Martin. Giggling, she apologised. Her eyes were curious, holding his, and the hand she'd put on his arm lingered there a few seconds too long. In a split-second sequence he saw: her body moving slightly off-beat on the dancefloor – a pair of thin arms around his neck – the paling sky – laughing at silly jokes in the harsh light outside a 24-hour hotdog stand – a shirt being pulled off – the slightly too-narrow bed in her run-down studio flat in Gårda…

"No worries," he said, turning away.

II

MARTIN BERG: But then, the author is always at a disadvantage, too.
INTERVIEWER: What do you mean?
MARTIN BERG: If he's unknown, no one expects him to be of interest. He constantly has to prove himself. If he's written something good, on the other hand, everyone will be waiting for his next book to fail. And the better he writes, the slimmer the chance of him living up to expectations. Like Nabokov after *Lolita*. Joyce after *Ulysses*. So things are always against you.

*

Of all the things that happened in the early nineties, one of the more positive was that a publishing company far bigger than Berg & Andrén wanted to publish Cecilia's essays.

"But you obviously have dibs," she said.

As it happened, however, Berg & Andrén had limited ability to publish niche subject-oriented prose. In fact, it was far from clear Berg & Andrén were going to be able to publish anything at all. Plus, Martin noted, it wouldn't be terrible if some external money entered the Bergian financial ecosystem.

But it had to be said: he was surprised.

Somehow, her writings had made their way out of the university.

An article here, an essay there. She submitted them to various magazines, and whenever something was accepted, she came to him with surprised glee. Of course he was *happy* for her. The first time he saw her name in print, he felt proud. Of course he did.

It started with a text she wrote about Amelia Earhart, the first woman to fly across the Atlantic, whose twin-engine plane crashed into the sea in 1937. For a while, Cecilia was deeply fascinated with Amelia Earhart, reading the autobiography she'd written shortly before the crash and pinning a photograph of the plucky aviatrix on the corkboard in her study. And then she had, sort of just in passing, written a short essay about it. The angle was women who followed their own path and met their doom because of it, and Cecilia drew parallels to Antigone in Sophocles' tragedy. (Martin, for his part, had never fully understood why Antigone would risk her life to bury her brother, whom the king had denied proper interment. They'd gone to see it at Stadsteatern, one night with a babysitter and wine during the interval, and afterwards his questioning of Antigone's psychological believability had led to the closest a person could get to a row with Cecilia. Which was to say: on the tram home, she'd delivered a forcefully argumentative mini lecture on the individual, the collective and fate in Ancient Greece, and Martin had heard himself say: "Cissi, if this is our annual fight, I absolutely refuse to have it about bloody Sophocles.")

The text was published in a renowned cultural magazine. Cecilia received a small cheque and apparently developed a taste for it, because she wrote more, resulting in a collection of essays entitled *Atlantic Flight*. It was published that autumn and garnered surprising praise from critics. Cecilia herself claimed not to even know which day the reviews were coming out.

"No one gives a toss about that book," she says. "Save a handful of wannabe intellectuals who take a special interest."

But as sometimes unpredictably happens, *Atlantic Flight* was in the right place at the right time. CECILIA BERG, not yet thirty years old, PhD candidate in intellectual history and translator, had revived the essay genre, making it funny and topical. CECILIA BERG wrote in the interstice between Montaigne and Bang and apparently no one else did, and suddenly *Atlantic Flight* appeared in the end-of-year literature round-ups in the big papers.

"Her style is at once light as a butterfly and relentless as Jake LaMotta's right hook," *Dagens Nyheter*'s reviewer wrote. Martin magnanimously pretended not to remember that the same man had unabashedly tried to pick Cecilia up during the Gothenburg Book Fair a few years earlier as he carefully tore out the article and put it on the fridge.

*

Martin was undeniably the one who kept pushing for a second child.

But they agreed that only children tended to be brats. Rakel seemed perfectly content walking around with her chin in the air, holding her mummy by one hand and her daddy by the other. She made a big deal of having learned to read at the age of four and feigned incomprehension at other children who were just learning the alphabet. In conversation with adults, she used words like *relevant*, and, on the whole, her existence at nursery school was characterised by exalted self-satisfaction.

"Maybe when I'm done with my thesis…" Cecilia would say. But they both knew that would take years.

Martin pictured their offspring taking over the publishing company, so that a greying and distinguished version of himself could retire to focus on his writing. Then they all got together for boisterously bohemian Sunday dinners, completely unlike the pushing around the plate of a dry roast to the sound of his father's throat-clearing and the ticking of the clock on the wall that he himself had grown up with.

"Everyone says the first child is the hardest," he'd say. "Number two is easy as pie. You don't have to buy a pram and all that. And it's not like you're getting any younger, exactly," he'd add. It was meant as a joke – it was the kind of comment her mother would throw around – but Cecilia just glared.

She was turning thirty that year. Cecilia insisted this new number meant nothing, but she was growing exasperated with the younger students ("a shiftless, pleasure-seeking bunch of seventies kids") and one night he caught her going through the box of unsorted photographs.

"Look how little I was," she said, holding up a picture of a sullen teenager with tousled curls, sitting fully dressed by a pool in Addis Ababa.

"Almost like Rakel," Martin said.

She laughed. "I was at least seven years older than Rakel."

"Well, what's seven years? Before you know it, you'll be the one with a sulky teenage daughter who refuses to go swimming."

She snatched the photo out of his hand and went up to her study.

So far, Cecilia's big thesis consisted primarily of countless piles of paper and notes stuck between pages of books. The intellectual history of colonialism had turned out to be a subject of almost infinite scope. Where to start? When? In what part of the world? Or should she – at this point, she was walking in circles in the living room, dealing verbal machete blows to her hypothesis – maybe write about the intellectual history of *post*colonialism? About the concatenation of thoughts and ideas that had spread through the philosophical space in which the Western world's colonies had once existed? (She wrote that sentence down in one of the notepads scattered about their home.) She reread Fanon, dug deeper into Said, contemplated whether she should read everything by Foucault and approach her subject armed with the tools of discourse analysis. Her supervisor pointed out that her material-gathering was getting out of hand. "He's probably right," Cecilia sighed.

Gradually, she went from saying "if we have another child" to "when we have another child". When she turned thirty, she threw a big party, a rarity for her. "A wake for my fading youth," she said. Then, for the first time in a long time, she got so drunk she threw up magnificently in a planter, after which she insisted that someone give her another glass of whisky.

"My period's late," she announced not long afterwards. Then she kept forgetting to buy a pregnancy test, and when she came out of the bathroom with a blue plus sign on the stick, she seemed more bewildered than anything else.

Martin wasn't prepared for the wave of warm delight that welled up inside him. He remembered the insignificant weight of a baby in his arms, the downy head, the miniature hand grabbing his forefinger. The explosion of joy when your child smiles back for the first time, when it sticks out its tiny tongue in an ancient, innate reflex to mimic, when its eyes focus and meet your own. He embraced Cecilia and tried to take her for a spontaneous spin across the floor, but her body was rigid and uncooperative.

"What's the matter?" he said. "You're not happy about this?"

"Yes, sure… I just thought it would take longer…"

"When is it due?" He counted. "It should be March of next year, right? When do we tell Rakel? We should call the doctor."

"I think I need to sit down."

"See, your mum didn't know what she was talking about when she said you weren't the fertile type."

*

That September, Gustav came to visit again, and this time he stopped by Djurgårdsgatan. He turned up two hours late, blamed the trains and handed Rakel a gigantic bag of sweets that she raced off with before either of her parents could intervene. If they were lucky, Martin thought to himself, gluttony would make her pass out in the middle of *Asterix and Cleopatra*.

Cecilia had made it out of bed, combed her hair and put on slacks and a freshly ironed shirt. Her belly was a discreet rounding above the waistband of her trousers. Her condition was primarily revealed by her cautious, slightly leaned-back way of walking.

"What do you know," Gustav said. "The expectant mother. Congratulations!"

When Martin told him over the phone about the new addition to the family, Gustav had sighed: "I see. I guess it was just a matter of time." Now, he was in every way chivalrous: taking her by the elbow, leading her into the living room, firmly declining the offer of a cup of coffee. Or rather, insisting he was "fully capable of fetching one himself". He said she looked radiant, which was an obvious lie, and asked if they knew whether it was a boy or a girl. That made Cecilia laugh for the first time in a long time.

"I'm fifteen weeks along," she said. "It's the size of an orange. Its eyes only just moved into their correct positions."

Martin dug a bag of cinnamon buns out of the freezer. Gustav ate half of one and Cecilia three.

"I'm moving to London," Gustav said without preamble. He picked at a loose thread at the hem of his shirt. "Just for a while. Nothing permanent."

Cecilia put her cup down. "I see," she said, one eyebrow cocked.

"Sweden's too small," Gustav continued, as though he'd prepared a little speech in his own defence and was now unable to change course. He was withering away spiritually, he said. If things carried on the way they had been, he'd be painting kitschy foxes or taking up mosaics before they knew it. Plus, KG was opening a British branch and had this idea about exhibiting his paintings from Antibes. "He feels they 'constitute such a powerful unit'. And it would make sense for me to be in London for 'PR purposes'. He says he might be able to finagle an interview with *Art Review*."

Speaking of which," Cecilia said, "what have you been painting recently? That trip to France was years ago."

"Nothing. A bunch of nonsense. That's what I'm telling you. I need a fresh start. Not that anyone buys art any more, but still."

Cecilia studied him for a while, hands folded on her belly. "But you must have been working on something? What do you get up to in Stockholm?"

"A few portraits of Dolores and some other people. And I've been working on an interior of this bar I go to a lot, but we'll see how that turns out. At first, I thought it'd be fun to do a giant trompe l'oeil thing, but I don't know." He sighed. "I don't know if I've done anything properly good since that one with you and the books. *The Historian.*"

"That was outstanding, though," Martin offered. "And you can't be expected to turn out masterpieces every day of the week, can you? Would anyone like another bun? Cissi? Come on, you know you want one. Remember that you're eating for two."

After Cecilia went to have a quick lie-down, Gustav and Martin walked towards the city centre. The sun was perched just above the cranes on Hisingen, casting sheets of light across the streets. The horse chestnut trees lining the street had turned yellow. The air was clear, with an edge of brine on the breeze.

"I wouldn't mind Pustervik," Gustav said. "Or where do the kids go these days?"

"C von," Martin replied. He wasn't completely out of the loop, even though he could count on the fingers of one hand the number of pub crawls he'd been on in the past six months. The publishing company took up all his waking time. In the face of hopeless prospects, you could choose to lie down and die or to roll up your sleeves and try some more, and, apparently, Berg & Andrén had opted for the latter.

"To Linné, then," Gustav said. "How's Cecilia really doing?"

"They've put her on sick leave. Apparently, she has pelvic girdle pain. She went to see her supervisor and when they had finished, she couldn't get out of the chair, so he made her go see a doctor."

Just a few months into the pregnancy, Cecilia had started complaining that climbing stairs "hurt like the devil". Martin retorted with common sense: it couldn't be *that* bad, she was only three weeks along. He reminded her about when she was pregnant with Rakel and was ripping up linoleum weeks before giving birth. "You know, the one with all the scorch marks from the hookah coals?" That made her smile, but the smile winked out almost immediately and she collapsed on the sofa with a groan.

Then, she began to fall asleep everywhere. Several times, he found her slumped over her desk, with her head on her arms and a potentially interesting passage in *Black Skin, White Masks* marked with dried saliva. If they watched a movie, she passed out during the opening credits. Once, she fell asleep on the tram home and was woken up by the driver at the last stop; she took the tram all the way back again and only just managed to stay awake until their stop.

He assumed she was just overworked.

Cecilia tried to relax by reading novels. For some reason, she chose *War and Peace*, and after just three chapters she hurled the book at a wall and screamed: "But I can't remember who all these fucking Russians *are*." Martin suggested switching to short stories. Chekov, perhaps?

A few days later, he found her in the foetal position on the floor of her study, surrounded by papers and open books. She just couldn't focus, she sobbed. She kept forgetting what she'd written, couldn't bring any order to anything, all her thoughts kept falling apart. Martin pulled her up into his arms. Together, they rocked back and forth while she wept. He mumbled comforting nonsense words until she had calmed down.

"She seemed pretty the worse for wear," Gustav was saying now, digging through his coat pocket. Lighter, pack of cigarettes.

"I guess that pelvic thing is pretty hard on her," Martin replied.

"What is pelvic girdle pain, anyway?"

"It's like something in the pelvis..."

"Pain, by any chance?"

Martin slapped his arm and tried to recall what Cecilia had told him in her exhausted, unstructured way after seeing the midwife. "It's to do with the pelvis," he said. "Joints getting looser or something. It hurts."

"Sounds awful. Hey, do you mind if we go to Tai Shanghai, on second thought?"

Even though it was a Tuesday, Tai Shanghai was almost full. They got a table by the door. The air was hazy with cigarette smoke. There was a large, rowdy group of people sitting at one of the long tables, musicians, judging by the guitar cases leaning against the wall. And there were some people from Cecilia's department, younger scholar types in baggy tweed jackets. They waved. Martin waved back. For a moment, he saw himself through their eyes: Martin Berg, the publisher, an unambiguously grown-up man, father of almost two, married to the beautiful, intelligent and for everyone but him completely unattainable Cecilia, stepping through the door in the company of famous painter Gustav Becker.

"How is this place always full?" Gustav said. "It's been bloody packed since 1981."

They ordered beef with bamboo shoots and a pint each. Gustav presented a theory that far fewer pints per capita were drunk in Stockholm than in Gothenburg.

"So what do they drink instead?"

"Fuck knows. Champagne. Cocktails. Maybe wine at a pinch."

"And yet you insist on living there."

Gustav stifled a burp. "Art requires sacrifice, my friend. Besides, I'm moving to London, aren't I? Why don't I know anyone in here?" He put his cutlery at twenty past four even though he'd eaten barely half and chugged the rest of his beer. "Feels like there should be people I know here. Hey, miss – could you bring us two more of these? Thank you, thank you. So, Martin, where do we go from here? Want to go to Valvet?"

"Valvet closed, remember?"

"Right. Well, they didn't sell any decent beer, anyway. And there's nothing going on at Draupner?"

"Sad to say, but Draupner's gone. They tore down the building."

They sat in silent, gloomy thought for a while. Martin hadn't been to Draupner since the eighties and remembered labyrinthine meandering between drunk people dressed in leather, lukewarm beer, a grinding band whose long-haired heads bobbed up and down on a stage on the other side of an audience that could just as easily have been a bunch of hooligans.

"Then let's grab a few pints at C von," Gustav said eventually.

"It's getting kind of late..."

"Sure. I get it. I get it. It's the whole breadwinner thing."

"It's not that," Martin began and then felt suddenly exhausted. Tomorrow was Wednesday. There was a pile of unopened post on his desk. Among other things, he suspected, a few alarming invoices. He had to call their accountant. He had to make preparations for the book fair. He had to check if those boxes in the basement had flooded or not. He should have called at least five different people yesterday, at the latest.

Gustav made a gesture as if to say, Let's talk no more about it, lit a cigarette, and gazed out at the room.

"They don't have places like this in Stockholm," he said. "I mean it, there's Tranan and Prinsen and KB" – he pronounced the names in a Stockholm drawl – "but what they don't bloody have is a Tai Shanghai. If you'll excuse me, I just need to make a call..."

Over the thirty minutes that followed, Gustav walked over to the payphone in the corner several times. He wedged the receiver between his shoulder and chin, shook out a cigarette, popped in another one-krona coin, ignored the girl chewing gum with her arms crossed, waiting her turn. But Uffe didn't pick up, nor did Sissel, and he no longer knew anyone else's number by heart.

While he waited, Martin leaned back in his chair and thought about his thirtieth birthday party the year before. Gustav had been excited weeks in advance. "Do you know how long it's been since I went to a proper party?" he'd said over the phone. "I mean, not just a few mates having a pint but a proper *bash*? Decades. It hasn't happened since the dawn of time. I might bring Dolores. I want to show her the best of what Gothenburg has to offer, party-wise."

"That might be expecting a bit much..."

"Nonsense, Dolores is happy so long as there's a kitchen table and an ashtray and a few like-minded souls she can bemoan popular culture with. Pleased as punch. You can't tell from looking at her, but on the inside, she's happy as a clam at high tide. So long as she gets to dump on the times we live in and so on."

Martin hadn't thought so many people would come, but the flat was packed. You could barely hear the music over the sound of talking and laughing. There was drinking, cake and coffee, "Happy Birthday" was sung. Gustav and Dolores didn't turn up until close to eleven. Giggly and wobbly, they took their coats and shoes off in the hallway. Dolores was wrapped in an enormous fake fur coat. Gustav almost knocked over the valet stand.

"Happy birthday," Dolores said. Her hand was cold and clammy.

"We stopped by Eggers for a couple of drinks," Gustav said. "Because it looked so nice, coming in on the train. You'd like it. Leather sofas. Hemingway. That vibe."

Dolores clapped a hand to her mouth, eyes wide. "We forgot the painting," she said.

"What?"

"The painting. We forgot Martin's painting."

Gustav burst out laughing. "And after you went to all that trouble wrapping it so neatly," he said.

"It's not *funny*. God, god, I hope it's still in that sodding hotel."

"Calm down, it's just a painting."

"But it's Martin's *present*."

"Pah. Worldly things. I'll make another."

Dolores and Martin exchanged a look.

"May I borrow your phone?" Dolores said. The rotary dial turned. She was calling Information. "Yes, hello," she said in an authoritative voice, "could you please connect me to Hotel Eggers on…"

"Drottningtorget Square," Martin put in.

"Drottningtorget Square in Gothenburg? Thank you." She drummed her fingers against the dresser while she waited.

"It's just a painting," Gustav mumbled before disappearing towards the kitchen.

Dolores's fur coat had fallen to the floor. Martin hung it back up. Someone answered at Eggers and Dolores explained the situation. "It's wrapped in blue paper. About fifteen by twenty-five inches… Sure, but I guess you'll have to go have a *look*… By the window. Yes, I'll hold…

Are you *sure*? Look one more time. To the *right* of the door… Exactly! Thank *god*. Thank you so much – we'll pick it up tomorrow."

She hung up and shook her head. "Being around Gustav tends to have a sobering effect, don't you think?" she said.

While Martin made Dolores a gin and tonic, she told him she'd had a collection of poems published by a minuscule press. "But, to be realistic," she sighed, "I'm hardly a Lugn or Frostenson." She was thinking about going back to university, she said. At the moment, she was working part-time at an addiction treatment centre, and working with people was actually rewarding.

The evening wore on. Empty bottles and sticky glasses covered tables and dressers. The ashtrays were constantly overflowing. In the living room, Cecilia and Frederikke were sitting with their heads together. "What kind of secrets are you two talking about?" Martin said as he staggered by and topped up their wine glasses.

"Structuralism's relationship to psychoanalysis," Cecilia laughed. He kissed her on the head and moved on.

As usual, no one really knew how the fight started. Martin was collecting cups and dessert plates in the living room when he heard raised voices in the kitchen. Uffe from Valand, who Martin didn't recall inviting, but who had somehow found his way there anyway, was sitting by the open window. One arm casually draped over the back of his chair, the other holding a cigarette that he was now pointing at Gustav.

"…with all the money, then?" he said. "Put it in the bank, or what? A nice little nest egg?"

"Come off it," Dolores said.

"Maybe a little trip to the Bahamas?" Uffe continued. "To get away from the press? It must be tough to be, how did they put it again…" He frowned, pretending to search his memory. "'*One of the most promising names of the new generation*'. Quite a thing to have to live up to, eh? What are you going to do when you can't just steal all your ideas from Ola Billgren and that Norwegian bloke?"

"He *doesn't*."

"Sounds like no one's shagged you in quite a while, sweetheart," Uffe said. "But that's hardly surprising, considering—"

Dolores threw her drink in his face.

Up until that moment, Martin had only ever seen drinks thrown on film. And there was, in fact, something slow-motion-like about Uffe's surprise, his big hand wiping gin and tonic off his face. The room went dead silent.

"Cheers and welcome," Martin said, tossing Uffe a kitchen towel. "I'd like to remind everyone that there's still cake left if anyone fancies it and that all of this wine needs to be drunk." A champagne cork popped; Per, his trusty second, took a small bow. Relieved laughter. Conversations resumed.

The hours went by. Some people went home. Per and Frederikke danced in their stocking feet. Cecilia laughed and spilled wine on herself. Martin's sister Kicki had nodded off in an armchair, tired after her shift in the Sahlgrenska A&E. Dolores and Uffe were nowhere to be found. The only one who didn't seem to be enjoying himself was Gustav. He'd taken over the chair by the kitchen window, where he sat chain-smoking in silence. Apparently, they were out of clean glasses, because he'd mixed himself a drink in Rakel's Pippi Longstocking mug.

"How's it going?" Martin said, taking a seat at the kitchen table.

Gustav shrugged. "*Ava.*"

Martin pulled a cigarette out of Gustav's pack. Since he quit smoking during the workweek, he hadn't bought cigarettes in ages. "I guess I'm thirty now," he said. "Does feel a bit a weird, after all."

"But you're the epitome of adulthood," Gustav said.

"What do you mean?"

Gustav waved a hand vaguely. He had difficulty focusing, his eyes wouldn't rise above floor level. "You, with your tiled stoves and your own, private washing machine, which is just so prat-, practical when you have *kids*."

"Guilty as charged," Martin replied.

"And business cards and briefcase and the whole to-do."

"I don't actually own a briefcase."

"Give it time. You're inches away from a briefcase. You heard it here first, don't forget."

"All right, Nostradamus."

"*Inches*. No one's drinking here. Have you seen Dolores? We were going to stay in a hotel. We'd said we'd stay in a hotel."

Martin recalled seeing Dolores and Uffe in the hallway earlier, his arm around her waist. "I think it's a bit late for a hotel now," he said.

"But I promised." Gustav topped up the Pippi Longstocking mug. "We were going to have breakfast..."

"Dolores is a woman of action. She'll sort out breakfast wherever she is."

"She says I'm always promising things but that I have to start *keeping* my promises."

"You can sleep here if you want. Rakel's room is free."

"Why did she have to get so bloody angry about the painting. I can always make another. Right? I just have to paint and then there's another painting. You're probably pissed off about the painting, too."

"I'm really not. We'll pick it up tomorrow."

"Everyone just wants more paintings all the time. Gustav, Gustav, paint another fucking painting." He hiccoughed and shook his head. "I'm not spending five hours on a fucking train tomorrow. If she thinks I am, she's out of her mind. We're flying back."

III

MARTIN BERG: Most of the writers I know are stubborn bastards. They don't give up. You can't be a quitter in this industry.

*

Martin put his keys on the dresser and took his shoes off as silently as he could. His wife was sitting on the sofa with milk stains on her flannel shirt, staring straight ahead, rocking Elis's bouncy chair with one foot. The moment she stopped, he would start to whimper, his miniature face scrunching up and a scream shattering the temporary peace on Djurgårdsgatan.

"How are you feeling?"

She just shook her head.

"I can take over for a bit," Martin said.

She reached for her crutch, and he helped her up. He heard her turn the shower on in the bathroom. She always showered hot, so hot it steamed. Several times, he'd scalded himself because she hadn't remembered to turn the knob back down.

Their son seemed to have fallen asleep. Martin got up to get some pasta water boiling, but Elis began to whimper almost instantly, and by the time Martin was putting the pot on the hob, the boy was screaming at the top of his lungs.

"Colic," the doctor said. "It'll pass in three to four months."

At first, they were relieved to learn there was an explanation for why their one-month-old son was crying inconsolably for hours on end, but after a week of nonstop screaming, he might as well have said "three to four years". For weeks, Martin was dizzy from sleep deprivation and lay passed out on the sofa in his office for a couple of hours around lunchtime. Over time, he came to associate the lumpy piece of furniture with the height of comfort and serenity. In fact, being at work began to feel more and more like time off. Nothing but quiet office sounds. Nothing but adults with whom he could communicate verbally. Nothing but intellectual and aesthetic matters to deal with. Nothing seemed particularly troubling, so long as it took place outside the Bergs' flat. He was blessed with the same carefree attitude a pleasant inebriation brings. They bought a PC. They hired an editor-cum-general administrator, Sanna Engström, on an hourly basis, and granted, she kept threatening to find a better-paid side gig, but for now she was there, chain-smoking and going over texts in her feistily efficient way. So what if Berg & Andrén had to fold! So what if the spring catalogue was a flop! They'd have to drive it all to the landfill, he supposed. But he was only thirty-two. He'd never set out to become a publisher. He could just come up with a new plan.

So Martin Berg poured himself a large cup of black coffee, rubbed the sleep out of his eyes, and answered the phone as clearly as he was able. He made difficult calls to the printers without hesitation. He read manuscripts as though they could actually be published. He started to translate a foreword from French to Swedish and discovered it was easy. You went from sentence to sentence and then you had a page of text, and that page was something tangible. He'd made something out of nothing. And he himself – Martin Berg, *le traducteur* – was at once invisible and indispensable. He weighed the nuances and connotations of each word. He allowed his mind to orbit particularly elusive concepts. He took delight in an elegant verb form. He topped up his coffee, clicked his pen, reached for the dictionary. He was the humble servant of the text. As the weeks went by, he began to stay later and later.

"Don't look so accusatory," he exclaimed at one such late homecoming, but Cecilia just continued her endless pacing through the flat with Elis on her shoulder.

There were piles of sheets everywhere, soiled shirts and vomit-stained baby clothes. The kitchen counter was covered with washing-up and the hob crusty with baked-in spills. No matter how often he vacuumed, the kitchen floor was sticky and covered in crumbs. No one had cleaned the fridge for at least six months. The only presentable space was Rakel's room, where the desk was meticulously organised, the comic books neatly stored in their drawer, and the stuffed animals lined up on the bed.

Rakel was in first grade, and the rest of the class was apparently learning the alphabet. That autumn, she'd come home with a notebook in which she was expected to write long rows of letters even though she'd been writing for years. (Martin had a sudden flash of chalk dust, the pencil sharpener screwed to Miss Karin's desk, the vast asphalt plain of the schoolyard, the reassuring rattle of marbles in the pocket of his corduroy trousers. His even handwriting had always earned him gold stars.) Rakel's As and Bs had used to be neat at first, before losing their zest and shape as she went on. However, since the birth of her younger brother, she'd begun to produce long rows of perfect, right-angled letters. She spent hours doing her homework, bent over her desk like a tiny medieval monk. Otherwise, she could usually be found sitting on her bed with ear defenders on and a book on her lap. She didn't react when Martin opened the door, only looking up when he stepped into the room.

"Didn't you read the sign?" she said. "It says *Knock before entering.*"

"I did knock. Maybe it was heard to hear because you were wearing ear defenders."

Rakel shrugged, a gesture too big for her seven-year-old body.

Then Elis started up again. Rakel put the ear defenders back on, and Martin went to relieve his wife.

For the wellbeing of everyone involved, Rakel spent the weekends with Martin's parents.

Martin's impression of those weekends was that they were equal parts child-level hedonism and a training camp for his Intellectually Precocious child. Grandma and Grandpa had both TV3 and Channel 5, which meant a slew of new children's programmes, endlessly more tempting than the ones Rakel was allowed to watch at home: bright, sparkly, animated worlds flickering past, impenetrably cryptic to an adult. They'd also acquired a VHS player, so could consequently record potentially interesting programmes that Rakel missed during the school week. Within ten minutes of being dropped off in Kungsladugård, she was in a trance in front of *My Little Pony* (or "my little pony, my little pony, may all your days be briiiiight" as the demented theme song kept hammering into his sleep-deprived brain.) What would Cecilia say? Cecilia would frown, she who had never been exposed to the spellbinding lure of television, growing up in Addis. But why worry her needlessly? Besides, Birgitta also took her grandchild to the library and read aloud from *Jane Eyre* at night. Abbe's main interaction with Rakel consisted of the two of them driving down to a sweet shop on

Sveaplan and swinging by the video store on the way home. But he also taught her to solve crossword puzzles and play chess, even letting her win every once in a while. They had a game that consisted of Rakel spinning the old globe and stopping it without looking, at which point Abbe would tell a story about the spot where her chocolate-sticky finger had landed. He wasn't too cautious about the age rating, either, possibly because he'd only been sixteen himself when he went to sea. Sometimes, Martin felt a pang of what had to be envy: Abbe had never told *him* the story about the tranny in Antwerpen, certainly not when he was seven.

When he came to pick up Rakel one Sunday afternoon, everyone was deep in a round of bridge. Aunt Maud was the fourth player.

"You're here already?" Birgitta said, winning a trick.

Maud studied him over the rim of her gigantic glasses, which had been on trend ten years earlier. "You're looking down in the doldrums."

"Their little boy has colic," Abbe said.

"I see. Well, they need a reason to cry, don't they?"

"We're almost done," Rakel said, shooting him the very briefest of glances before turning her attention back to her cards.

Martin poured himself the last of the coffee, which was lukewarm and tasted like tannic acid, and contemplated the people who happened to be his closest relatives.

Abbe's hair and moustache had turned grey. He wasn't fat exactly, but his torso seemed to have expanded over the years, making his body completely incompatible with the slim sailor in the old photographs. Aunt Maud had permed her hair and dressed in calf-length skirts and baggy lace blouses, an awkward match with her salty manner and Camel-raspy voice. She always brought sweets for Rakel, but since they were sweets no child enjoyed – liquorice allsorts, After Eights, Finnish marmalade jellies – Maud eventually ended up eating them all herself.

His mum had wrinkles around her eyes and mouth and looked like someone young people might call "ma'am" in a knee-jerk remnant of rapidly eroding politeness. Now, she lit a cigarette, regally unmoved by the cancer propaganda, and studied her cards, her face inscrutable.

Martin sighed, snatched up a marmalade jelly from right under Maud's nose and wandered off through the rooms. Very little about the house had changed. The brown patterned wallpaper and the pervasive smell of tobacco gave the impression of being inside a cigar box. The bathroom with its pistachio-green suite had passed Dated and was on its way to Kitsch, but he could hear his mother's retort to any such comment: "Why fix what's not broken?" The bookshelf in the living room still contained *The Bra Böcker Lexicon* from 1974 and the kind of glass ornaments people give you when they have no idea what to buy you for your birthday. One shelf held books, every last one published by Berg & Andrén and a gift from him. Otherwise, everything was as before, except that an oversized recliner with accompanying footstool now stood like a bizarre interloper among the slender teak furniture. And there was an exercise bike in the middle of Martin's old room.

He lay down on the bed. It was made up with the same crocheted bedspread he used to leave in a heap on the floor an eternity ago. Outside, the wind shook the birch trees in the garden. Somewhere, a clock was ticking. Muffled voices could be heard from the living room. Not even the tram rattling by towards Marklandsgatan bothered him as he sank into the cool darkness of sleep.

*

When Elis was three months old and still wailing like a foghorn, Cecilia said:

"It's been a year."

"A year since what?"

"Since I became pregnant."

One year: that had to be true, a calendar would back it up. But when Martin tried to recall the events of the past year, they blended together with other years. Long swathes of time vanished to make space for some clearly illuminated fragment of dubious relevance. If he'd been forced to give an account of the past months, he wouldn't have been able to. He had a great talent for forgetting. It was doubtful whether this was a good quality for an aspiring novelist to have; William Wallace had once said his primary tools were "memory, this unfaithful bride, coupled with the urgent wish to escape the dingy dreariness of everyday life", a quote Martin could (ah, the irony of fate!) repeat verbatim at the drop of a hat.

Cecilia was standing by the bay window, studying the street below. "I've barely left the flat," she said.

"Isn't that just what it's like when you have a baby, though?"

"Not for *you*. You go to work. I've been lying about like a paraplegic, barely able to make it to the bathroom by myself. Everyone said it would get better once I gave birth. I figured I could grin and bear it for nine months, that things would improve. But it was all bullshit."

She was, in fact, standing up without her crutch, but it probably wasn't the right time to point that out.

Martin hugged her, wishing she would yield and soften the way she sometimes did in his embrace, but her shoulders remained stiff and angular and through the fabric of her shirt he could feel every vertebra of her spine. She'd actually grown ever thinner and paler since she gave birth. She fried bloody steaks but only managed a few mouthfuls. (Martin would put the meat back in the pan, leave it to fry a while longer, and then eat it himself.) All day every day, she shuffled about in pyjama bottoms and one of his washed-out T-shirts. With slow underwater movements, she slogged through the daily chores. Before, her desk had been the gravitational centre of Cecilia's life, now, everything revolved around their bed. At the first opportunity, his wife would crawl in under the down duvet. She slept like she was unconscious, always with a line between her eyebrows. The sheets were stained with breast milk and baby vomit, but she didn't seem to notice. Their nightstands were cluttered with children's books, water glasses, a plastic thingamajig that was part of the breast pump, plates with half-eaten sandwiches. On the floor was a high tide line of dirty underwear, toys, more books and balled-up tissues. The room slumbered in eternal twilight behind closed blinds.

Some late nights, Martin came home to find all three of them there: Elis on his back, miniature fists closed, his face troubled in sleep, Rakel snoring quietly with the tip of her nose against her mother's shoulder. Those nights, Martin slept on the sofa with earplugs in his ears, which at best meant several hours of uninterrupted sleep.

Only sometimes did he wake up to the sound of infant crying and sense Cecilia's shadowy figure in the room, hushing and rocking, a black silhouette against the brighter rectangles of the windows.

At least once a week, Inger Wikner – who since Rakel's birth referred to herself as "Nana" –called and offered to come down. "To help carry some of the load. That would be good, wouldn't it?"

They could go out to the summer house, she said. Nana would help with baby Elis. She would make her special chicken soup. Cecilia would be able to rest and take restorative walks in nature. Fresh air would do her good, wouldn't he agree?

Cecilia just silently shook her head at Martin, who was standing there, receiver in hand. She shook her head every time until Martin, to his own great surprise, threw the phone down so hard it broke.

A few days later, they drove out to the Wikner summer house. It was early June and nature was in full bloom. Martin had barely noticed summer arriving.

"Oh *my*! *What* a sweetheart. *What* a little dumpling!" Inger leaned in over the car seat making cooing noises. Elis was quiet for once, maybe out of shock. "You have Daddy's eyes, don't you? Yes, you do. Want to come to Nana? Huh? Want to come to Nana?"

Martin was about to say Elis didn't have his daddy's eyes – they were blue, like Cecilia's – but realised "Daddy" probably referred not to him but to Lars Wikner.

"You can't have someone else's eyes," Rakel objected. "You can only have your own."

"Absolutely right, sweetie," Cecilia said, heaving herself out of the car with some difficulty. She'd been quiet most of the drive.

Having extricated Elis from the car seat, Inger expertly picked him up, one hand behind his neck. She murmured something that sounded like "Do you have colic, yes, you do", then turned to her daughter. "*You* screamed. How you screamed. Not a moment's peace for months. Your father had to move into one of the hospital's overnight flats to catch even a wink of sleep. Darling, you look like a labour camp inmate. Go upstairs and get into bed this instant. Martin will see to the bags. *Go on.*"

The hallway floor was cluttered with vacuum cleaners and buckets. In the dining room, the crystal chandelier was still wrapped in a sheet, as was the grand piano. Rolled up rugs leaned against the walls. Martin briefly wondered how the potted plants survived when his mother-in-law wasn't there to give them her overbearing care.

Cecilia and he made the bed together. It was the first thing they'd done together in a very long time.

"Rakel needs to eat something," Cecilia said, sitting down on the edge of the bed. "And Elis is probably about to snap out of the kidnapping trauma down there…"

"I'll take care of it," Martin said. It was unexpectedly restful not to be within the needs-radius of an infant. And if he knew his mother-in-law, their daughter would soon be fed more healthy crispy rolls with homemade blackberry jam than she could possibly eat.

"The nappies are in the red bag and his clothes are in the backpack…" Cecilia's voice was already fading, and she pulled the duvet up to her chin.

Over the hour that followed, Martin was updated on the goings-on of the Wikner family. Lars was going to be working for at least another month before joining them. He was terribly busy because most of his colleagues were incompetent and/or secret alcoholics. Peter was working as an assistant physician over the summer and had even managed to get into the good books of the veteran head nurse. Vera was doing a language course in Italy and had, naturally, been discovered by a modelling agency within days of arriving, so now she was going to be photographed for some fashionable brand the name of which Inger couldn't recall at the moment.

Then, they heard the coughing sound of a moped, and Emanuel Wikner rode up to the house with overflowing bags of food in the flatbed. Moments later, he stepped through the back door.

"Hello," he said.

Over the past few years, he'd stretched out and become hunched, as though apologising for his new height. His hair was in a ponytail, and he'd had his ear pierced. All of which Martin already knew from the thank-you card from Emanuel's graduation reception, and now, comparing the besuited young man on the card with the cowering teenager in front of him, he concluded that Emanuel Wikner looked better in photographs. There, he was someone else, a person with a determined jawline and direct gaze. In reality, every part of his being seemed to shy away. His foot tapped, his fingers drummed, his eyes darted this way and that. He smelled faintly of sweat and his T-shirt, advertising the name of a band Martin had heard of but couldn't place musically, was grimy.

Rakel came in from the garden, ran over and hugged Emanuel, studied his shirt and said:

"What does 'nirvana' mean?"

"It's the ultimate goal of Buddhism," her uncle replied solemnly. "It entails being released from the endless cycle of rebirth and becoming one with the universe."

"Okay," Rakel replied, sounding uninterested. Her questions about what things meant were, Martin suspected, primarily a way of making it clear to her interlocutors that she knew how to read and was paying attention.

"It's also an American rock band my mum dislikes."

"That's not very fair, Emanuel. I don't 'dislike' them. I just think they're not – well, skilled musicians. I don't think what's-his-name is a very good singer. I think they have an unhealthy relationship with drugs."

"Mum's worried I'm going to start doing heroin," Emanuel said to Rakel.

"What's heroin?"

"It's drugs."

"Emanuel, I really don't think—" Inger said, but was interrupted by a thin, piercing infant's wail.

It was a relief to see Inger go through her entire repertoire of consoling motions without result: rocking Elis, offering him a bottle, changing his nappy. Elis had been so quiet since they came, it had begun to seem like they'd been exaggerating.

"I'll take him for a walk in the pram," Martin said. "So we don't wake Cecilia."

Inger assured him there was no need, she would take him herself. Martin offered a few lame protests for the sake of appearances.

"I don't know how you're still sane," Emanuel said after they left. "I honestly ask myself sometimes why anyone would choose to have children. It seems to involve a constant balancing act on the edge of insanity."

Martin sighed. "It's not as bad as all that."

"I suppose it's evolutionary," Emanuel said. "The perpetuation of the species and so on."

"What's evolution?" Rakel said.

Cecilia slept for sixteen hours straight.

Martin was having breakfast when he heard her coming down the kitchen stairs.

"Where is everyone?" She was wearing pyjamas and went straight to the coffee machine.

"Rakel went fishing with Emanuel. Your mother has fashioned a kind of sling out of a shawl, strapping Elis to her body."

"My god."

"It seems pretty effective. He hangs there like a baby monkey. They're in the garden."

And for a few moments they both listened, in unison, for their screaming son. Nothing but silence.

"Was Rakel wearing a life jacket?"

"I think the plan was to ambush the old pike from the jetty."

"Emanuel actually caught a pike once," Cecilia said with a laugh. "Mum boiled it. It was full of bones. Tasted awful. Major disappointment."

They sat at the kitchen table together for a full fifteen minutes. At first, Martin didn't know what to say, but Cecilia seemed content to just flip through the paper. She made a comment about Rwanda and asked him to pass the cheese, but aside from that, she was quiet.

He remembered back when they'd first met and he'd catalogued every detail about her: birthmarks, freckles, the shape of her hands, that spastic way her arm shot out when she wanted to underline something, the way she chewed her cheek, ran both hands through her hair, making her curls go every which way. Over the past year, she'd grown stiller, as though she no longer had any energy for superfluous action.

Then, Inger burst in wearing muddy boots and commanded breastfeeding. Cecilia took the child into the parlour for some privacy.

*

Martin wrote a letter to Gustav, seated at the giant desk in the library. It wasn't particularly long, but it took him several hours and four discarded drafts.

They hadn't heard anything from London in months. Right after moving, Gustav had written from time to time, but the correspondence had soon dwindled into the occasional postcard. The last sign of life had been a message of congratulation on Elis's birth, two weeks late and formulated with jaded politeness. The newspapers were probably a more reliable source of information at this point. That spring, *Göteborgs-Posten* had run an article under the headline GOTHENBURG ARTIST GUSTAV BECKER THE TOAST OF LONDON. Something called the Antibes Suite – that had to be KG's marketing ploy for the paintings from France – had met considerable success, receiving high praise. The Museum of Modern Art in Stockholm had bought no fewer than two works for its collection. "Delighted," says Klas-Göran Hammarsten, gallery owner. The journalist also managed to squeeze in that the young artist was the son of Bengt von Becker, CEO of Strömberg Shipping, and a paragraph on the trials and tribulations of the shipping company after the precipitous decline of Swedish shipbuilding. All of it illustrated with a grainy photograph of a smiling Gustav which must have been taken years earlier.

Martin sighed and twirled the pen between his fingers.

The difficulty was to strike the right note in the letter: cheerful, but not insincere, truthful but not nagging. At first, he wrote far too much about the colic and the sleepless nights and the publishing company that was unlikely to make it past next year. Then he tried excising all the self-pity, but that made the letter dry and sterile. He had an unpleasant vision of Gustav skimming the letter the day after some kaleidoscopic club night, without the words resonating at all.

The final version contained everything essential, but briefly and unsentimentally described: the three months of constant screaming, that Cecilia was in pieces, the decline and likely doom of the publishing company. The Wikner summer house became the backdrop of a bourgeois circus, their temporary move an exile, Martin himself a James Joyce in Trieste.

He typed out the final version on an abandoned typewriter with dried-up ink ribbons, couldn't find any stamps, put it in a plastic bag with a tenner for postage, and walked all the way down to the road where he fastened it to the letterbox with the clip intended for that very purpose.

IV

INTERVIEWER: What would you say an author should be wary of?

MARTIN BERG: The Tax Authority.

INTERVIEWER: [*laughing politely*]

MARTIN BERG: All jokes aside – fixating too much on their own ambitions. Having something in your head is one thing, it's quite another to get it down on paper. It's child's play if you're Mozart, you know, like in the film. But most people aren't Mozart. Most people are regular mortals, which means they may need some guidance to avoid getting lost among their own intentions.

*

Martin had planned to wait until July to take annual leave, but it made no real difference whether he was physically present at work or not. Granted, both he and Per went in every day, but it was more for morale than anything else.

He used the rest of the week to finish up what needed doing in town, left the number for the summer house on the answering machine, and arranged for their post to be forwarded. With the excuse of tidying up the flat, he stayed a few more nights than he really needed to, and afterwards he couldn't remember when he'd last felt so rested. Before heading back out to the countryside, he even gathered up the stacks of paper that constituted *Night Sonnets* and threw them in a bag along with manuscripts and proofs from work.

He drove no faster than he had to, stopped for petrol, bought the evening papers and a hotdog that he ate leaning against the bonnet. The June sun was warm and mild, the newspapers brand new and uncreased. In Falun, some crazy army lieutenant had killed seven people. An opinion piece listed reasons why Sweden should join the EU. The national football team was presented, a group of upstanding young men with full fringes and grave faces.

When Martin pulled up at the house, his daughter came running out to meet him.

"Dad," she exclaimed before pausing for breath, "can you drive Emanuel and me to the video store?"

"Sweetheart, I just arrived..."

"Please!"

"You know, it's almost twenty miles away." It was barely ten.

"But I'm bored."

"Read a book."

"I *have* been reading."

"I'll take you tomorrow."

Satisfied, she ran off.

During the five days he'd been away, the house had taken on the air of a convalescent hospital. White curtains billowing in sunny rooms. Martin felt a strong urge to keep his voice down. Inger had removed her jangling necklaces and swapped her kaftan for a simple dress and apron. In the big cast-iron bed on the second floor, his wife lay tucked in, pale and drawn, wearing freshly ironed cotton pyjamas.

According to Inger, the diagnosis and cure were simple: Cecilia was "overworked" and now had to "recuperate" by resting. She, the veteran mother of four, was going to look after Elis in the meantime. Granted, the child occasionally needed breastfeeding, but in between feeds, Cecilia should be in bed. Or at most take a turn about the garden. In any event, she was not to be disturbed by Rakel, who had to be a good girl and leave her mum be, and Cecilia was not to give her thesis on the intellectual history of colonialism any thought at all.

A chaise longue had been set up on the veranda, and when Cecilia said she felt like Castorp in *The Magic Mountain*, it took Martin a second to realise she was joking. It was the kind of joke that went right over her mother's head, which meant it was a joke intended for the two of them.

Martin never fully figured out what his role was in this sanatorium play. He made awkward attempts at helping out in the kitchen but was driven out by his stressed mother-in-law, who was frying meatballs for five while watching her sleeping grandchild. He went to check on Cecilia, but she was waited on hand and foot by her brother. Emanuel had been given the task of raising the alarm if and when Cecilia needed anything and took it very seriously. Would she like a cup of tea? A book? To play cards?

"No, thank you, I'm fine," she said, eyes closed.

"We could play cards?"

She shook her head.

Martin had brought some books from town, fantasising about how moved she'd be at his thoughtfulness, but they stayed in his bag. Cecilia read only the paper. Her crossword puzzles were abandoned halfway through, and she missed easy clues. The next day, when he drove the youngest members of the house to the village on a rent-a-film expedition, her only wish was for salt liquorice and possibly the Rocky films.

In the car, Emanuel tried to find any other radio channel than P4 and from the back seat Rakel counted grazing cows, after extracting a promise of new comic books from her father if she reached five hundred.

"Seventeen, eighteen…"

"Sweetheart, would you mind counting in your head?"

When they got there, Rakel said: "I only saw thirty-two."

"Well, you've shown great courage in battle. You can have a Donald Duck anyway."

*

Until then, Martin had mostly seen Inger Wikner's efficiency manifest in pointless hostess tasks – setting out biscuits, pinching off a dried flower from a bouquet – but now her restless moving through the house had been given purpose and direction. She acted like the head nurse at some private health clinic in the early twentieth century, whose staff (Emanuel and Rakel) were sadly not to be trusted with any real responsibility and required constant supervision. Emanuel soon forgot about his nursing duties and returned to his room, the windows of which were hung with blankets. Muffled rock music could be heard through the door. Rakel was relatively uninterested in sprinkling pearl sugar onto biscuits and snuck out at the first opportunity. And on top of that, the sailor's dress Inger had put her in got torn when she decided to play in the blackberry brambles.

"That dress was an *antique*!" Inger shrieked.

Rakel's face scrunched up and she ran off again. When Martin finally managed to locate his daughter, she'd fallen asleep behind a sofa.

If Inger was everywhere at all times, there was barely any trace of Cecilia's presence in the house. Her footsteps creaking on the upstairs landing. A breakfast tray with half a cup of cold tea and eggshells carried back downstairs. Evening papers brought to her room. A pair of leather slippers with trodden-down heels left out on the veranda. He heard her muffled voice through the bedroom door and found her sitting up in bed with Rakel by her side and a book on her lap. The girl was sitting stock-still, as though the slightest movement would get her sent away.

For a long time, their stay in the country seemed to do nothing for his wife. At least in town, she'd maintained a minimal level of normalcy; now, the slightest task seemed overwhelming. She steered clear of any situation where she'd have to interact with more than one person at a time. Breastfeeding took forever and afterwards she was out for the count, as though she'd been bled. Half an hour with Rakel was followed by a two-hour nap. The few times she walked around the garden, she moved slowly, like a very old person. She spent the majority of her time dozing, either in her Castorp chair on the veranda or in bed. The rest of the house was bustling (clattering in the kitchen, Rakel running across the lawn, Emanuel revving the moped), but Cecilia's cool, twilit room was a place of restrained movements and hushed voices.

Martin sat on the edge of the bed, unsure what to do. She was always too tired to talk, so he rambled on aimlessly about the events of the day: Rakel had swum fifty yards in the lake after he bribed her with ice cream, Elis had rolled over, which according to Inger was "incredibly early". He brought tea she didn't drink and sandwiches she didn't eat. He finished the abandoned crossword puzzles sitting on the nightstand.

"Have you heard from Gustav at all?" she asked at one point. Her eyes were closed, as though it required significant effort just to formulate the words.

"No, but I wrote to him just a week or so ago. I'm sure it takes time, what with the post being forwarded…"

In reality, it had been a couple of weeks, and the post arrived with a delay of no more than a day or two.

But Cecilia nodded, satisfied with his reply.

One night, when the house was dark and the sky had taken on a deep shade of blue you never saw in the city, Martin took out his novel and placed it emphatically on the desk.

Over the years, his magnum opus had undergone a series of name changes. Via *Au Revoir Antibes* (pretentious), *Project X* (an uninspiring provisional title) and *Youth* (nondescript), he'd circuitously returned to the incomprehensible but tantalising title *Night Sonnets*. The majority of the manuscript had been penned during the summers he'd spent with Gustav in Antibes, which he recalled in an exposé of sharp sunlight, sparkling seas, sandy feet and freckles on Cecilia's shoulders. It didn't need too many more pages, really, but what was to happen in those pages, he had no idea. He knew what the ending was supposed to *do* – lend the narrative existential weight, bring the dark undercurrent of the rest of the novel to the surface – but not how to make that happen.

He wasn't even remarkably young any more. He hadn't been remarkably young for an author for eight, ten years, and unless he was given a Nobel Prize or a professorship soon, which was unlikely, he'd never be remarkably young again. Ulf Lundell debuted with *Jack* when he was twenty-seven. Stig Larsson wrote *Autisterna* at twenty-four. Klas Östergren was only twenty when *Attila* came out and twenty-five when he wrote *Gentlemen*.

And Martin Berg was sitting at his desk, thirty-two years old, not knowing where to begin.

*

Over the course of the weeks that followed, two unexpected things happened.

The first was that Frederikke came driving up the tree-lined road in a shiny black Saab 900, gravel spraying from the tyres. Cecilia hurried outside so fast she lost one of her slippers, laughingly hobbling over to hug her. When Frederikke had finished greeting the other inhabitants of the house, she told them she'd bought a car and had been in the area.

"How did you know we were here?" Martin asked.

"Cecilia wrote to me," Frederikke said, seeming surprised at the question. Her backcombed frizz had been replaced by a short, tidy hairdo that kept blowing into her eyes. Gone was the leather jacket and the silver rings, the striped trousers and the spats; now she was dressed in slacks and loafers.

"Would you like a cup of coffee?" Inger hollered from the veranda.

Martin said nothing while they had coffee, just fiddled with his cup, his napkin. Granted, Cecilia looked exhausted and wan, but she was smiling and there was a certain bounciness to her movements. If she could barely read the papers and was exhausted by a walk down to the lake, when had she had time to write to Frederikke? The thought annoyed Martin until he realised it was probably during that first week, when he was still in town. Cecilia must have felt lonely and trapped and had made a desperate attempt to establish contact with the outside world.

The two women set off on a long walk around the garden, and afterwards, Cecilia sat up a bit straighter in her chair.

A few days later, Martin walked into the bathroom to find his naked wife cutting her own hair in front of the mirror. He remembered her doing the same thing one blue summer night many years earlier. The sink and the floor had been covered with strands of hair.

"Let me do it," he said, taking the scissors from her. And standing right next to her, so close he could feel and smell her body, he cut her curls off just above her shoulders.

Cecilia stood stock-still. "Not too short," she whispered.

Afterwards, she returned the scissors to their rightful place on a high shelf in a cabinet and ran a hand through her hair. Martin kissed her downy neck and watched her disappear down the dark corridor. He sighed and returned to the guestroom to which he'd been exiled.

When he stopped by to drop off the post the next morning, she was propped up against her pillows, rosy-cheeked and bright-eyed, absorbed in an old book that seemed far too heavy for her thin, pale hands. Martin took a seat on the edge of the bed. The breakfast tray, he noted, was empty for once. All the coffee gone, the sandwiches eaten, aside from a single piece of crust.

"What are you reading?"

Cecilia handed him the book and he handed her the letters. He'd already checked the senders' addresses to see if any of them were from Gustav, but it was just Frederikke, Cecilia's supervisor and a few people whose names he recognised from her department.

What she'd been studying so intently turned out to be a half-bound Ancient Greek textbook from 1935. Martin recognised it from the downstairs library. The books had been left by the previous owner when the Wikners bought the house in the seventies, and had remained on the shelves ever since, unread but regularly dusted. He'd long since gone through them all to see if there was anything of interest. Apparently, his wife had done the same, but with different results.

"Greek?" he said. "You're not taking up Ancient Greek now, are you?"

But Cecilia wasn't listening, too busy with her post. She'd spread out a few typewritten sheets on her lap. "Max Schreiber has translated a small text by Weber," she said. "Pretty good, it looks like. Read this."

Martin hurled the book away so hard it bounced against the foot of the bed. He'd been pushing Elis's pram up and down the tree-lined road all morning. If they were lucky, he wouldn't wake up until lunchtime. Then he had to be fed again, changed and carried around while his screams vibrated against his long-suffering eardrums. He was going to throw up half of what they managed to get him to eat and howl incessantly while Martin had another attempt at making him go to sleep in the pram. And meanwhile, Rakel was – yes, what was their daughter doing? He hadn't seen her since breakfast.

"It would be extremely helpful if you could agree to deal with the realities of life every once in a while," Martin said.

Then he left her in bed, surrounded by her papers.

*

The second unexpected thing was that Per Andrén called to ask if Martin knew anything about a Lucas Bell. He sounded at once excited and sceptical.

"The name sounds familiar," Martin said, even though he'd never heard it before. Or had he? Maybe he was thinking of Quentin Bell? And who was Quentin Bell again? Virginia Woolf's nephew, who'd written a biography about his famous aunt. Martin had bought it at a second-hand bookshop because he'd wanted to read about the Hogarth Press.

"…in the *Times Literary Supplement* a few weeks ago," Per continued. "Completely nuts. But in a good way. Kerouac was mentioned. It's always Kerouac, am I right? And Rimbaud. Anyway, his agent just called – he sounded pretty tired, actually, I would have expected more verve since this bloke is apparently a rising star – anyway, this what's-his-name, Mr Goldman…"

Rakel had padded up to him and was now staring at him intently. Martin put a hand over the receiver and whispered: "What?"

"Can I watch a film with Uncle Emanuel?"

"What film?"

"It's about a robot from the future, and he's nice now, but before he was mean, and there's another robot that—"

"Ask Mum."

"But she's asleep."

"Sweetheart, I'm on the phone with Per right now…"

"Please."

Martin sighed. "Okay. Fine." And as his daughter skipped off, he turned his attention back to Per's voice.

"…no bidding yet from what I understand, but it's probably only a matter of time. The thing is: apparently, for whatever reason, this guy wants *us* to publish his book, no one else. He thinks big publishers, and I'm quoting, 'are the lapdogs of capitalism, corrupting art'."

"Sounds like Gustav."

"It's ours if we want it."

"Aren't we the lapdogs of capitalism, too?"

"God, I wish. Capitalism seems to want nothing to do with us."

"What did you say the *TLS* wrote?"

Papers rustling on the other end. "Blah blah blah, *a clear and relentless voice.* Comparison with Salinger. *Black humour and a nihilistic gaze upon society.*"

"Wasn't it Kerouac a second ago? Is it both Kerouac and Salinger?"

"And Rimbaud."

"Sounds a bit sophomoric. What did you think?"

Per admitted he'd only read the excerpt in the *Times Literary Supplement* so far, but that the book in its entirety was on its way by post.

"All right. So what we have is a tired English agent, one – *one* – pretentious review and no competition. Sounds like a winner."

"You could at least read it."

"Oh, I will. Reading's the only thing standing between me and losing at chess to my own daughter."

"But I think we'll have to move quickly on this one, Martin."

"Has it been translated anywhere at all? Or would we be the first?" Per's silence spoke volumes. Martin sighed again, more heavily this time. "It's like going into an empty club, where the only people are the bartender and a desperate DJ."

"At least read the thing."

"Do we even have any money? I thought we were bankrupt."

"Read the book. I'm sending it to you. Then we'll talk."

*

Lars Wikner arrived on the first of August.

He revved up the drive, leaning on the horn to get Emanuel to come out and move the moped, even though there was plenty of room for him to park. Within three minutes, he'd inspected Elis and declared that the child had his nose, taken a seat on the veranda, sent for a bottle of cognac, lit a Spanish cigarillo, asked why Martin hadn't thought of publishing biographies in novel form, and shouted to no one in particular that there were four pounds of fresh mackerel in the car.

"Where's Cecilia?" he said. Then, so loudly everyone gave a start: "Cecilia!"

No answer.

"She's probably out," Martin said. Since it would have seemed rude to leave, he sat down, too.

Lars accepted this explanation without further ado, stretching out his legs and placing the cigarillo in the ashtray. He was dressed all in white, a casual shirt and wide trousers that looked like some kind of Indian formalwear. A gold chain around his neck glinted in the sunlight. Martin was pondering how aware of the convalescent nature of their stay his father-in-law really was (for some reason it was hard to imagine Dr and Mrs Wikner discussing serious matters in private, as though the two of them were puppets that only came alive on stage and spent the rest of the time in a box) when he realised his father-in-law had circled back to what he called "fictionalised biographies". To Martin's alarm, he told him he'd just written one, about Leonardo da Vinci.

"My first thought was that this, this is something for Martin's publishing company."

That was his cue, and Martin had had plenty of time to prepare his regretful face. He laid out the company's precarious financial situation, saying he wasn't sure they were able to publish anything at all, and Lars nodded graciously.

"Of course. Of course. I understand. But at least have a look… Emanuel? *Emanuel!* Fetch me the green suitcase from the car."

That Dr Wikner's butterfly obsession and failed rug import business was now being followed by a megalomaniac novel-writing project was hardly surprising. Even though he was apparently a skilled surgeon, he seemed incapable of being merely a physician for very long at a time. He was constantly taking sabbaticals to chase some bright idea that inevitably led nowhere. And this time, it was this – a manuscript of almost six hundred pages, split into three faux-leather binders, written with his son-in-law's publishing company in mind. Martin retreated to the library. He might as well get it over with.

The first few pages set the scene in fifteenth century Anchiano. A Ser Piero didn't appear until page five, after an endless description of olive groves, peacefully grazing goats and stone houses, all illuminated by a sun whose "strong, clear, irreproachable light" was probably supposed to symbolise the main character. Leonardo himself, however, didn't turn up until – Martin skipped ahead – page forty-two, and then in the shape of an infant. He opened the second binder to a random page.

"Alas," Isabella d'Este exclaimed, in a well-modulated voice heavy with sorrow. "I cannot believe that humanity is predestined to such a fate. It would be too terrible. There must be something else that can be done!"

The pathetic existence of man only acquires meaning in its meeting with God," the cardinal rumbled, stroking his long, well-groomed beard with a hand adorned with rings and gemstones, studying the lady with veiled, yet critical, eyes.

After an hour with the Leonardo manuscript, Martin had never been less tempted to visit Italy. The subordinate clauses were sticky and maudlin, everyone talked like they were in *Ivanhoe*, Leonardo himself was constantly mild, inventive, sharp-eyed, righteous, ingenious and myriad other adjectives that taken together ceased to mean anything at all. He did not, however, seem to be at all homosexual; his friendly relationship with his students was unequivocally platonic. Martin skimmed several chapters, looking for hints to the contrary, which could have livened up this unintentionally bathetic work a little. There was not one typo or instance of errant punctuation to be found anywhere. There were no notes.

It was at once infuriating and sad.

Martin stood by the window, pondering how to deliver the rejection to Dr Wikner, when Cecilia appeared in the doorway. Something about her was different, but it took him a moment to pinpoint what. Instead of pyjamas and kimono, she was wearing running clothes.

"There's post for you." She handed over a package – it had to be that book Per had been talking about. As suspected: cheap paper, awful cover. On the back, a long-haired bloke with tattoos on his crossed arms squinting at his potential reader with a look on his face that said: Fuck the book, go home with me instead.

"What's that?" Cecilia asked.

"Something Per thinks we should publish, though I'm honestly not sure how that's supposed to happen…"

"No, I meant the binders."

"Oh, right – well, that's your father, trying to sell me on his extremely tedious novel about Leonardo da Vinci…" The blurb contained no fewer than two exclamation marks as well as the words *sex, drugs and rock'n'roll* and seemed penned by a seventeen-year-old boy stoned out of his mind.

"Don't tell me he wrote it himself."

"*Mais oui, ma chérie.* Will he disown you if I decline?"

"I will lose all respect for you if you don't." She leaned forward quickly and kissed him fleetingly on the cheek. Moments later, he heard her footsteps on the gravel outside.

Martin read the first few pages of *A Season in Hell* with narrowed eyes and red pen in hand, poised to make up for what he hadn't dared to give voice to in the Leonardo script. The paper was grey and rough, the font ill chosen. It already irked him that the young man on the back was posing like a rock star.

But after the first chapter, he still hadn't made a single indignant note in the margin. Instead, he went to get coffee and find a dictionary. When Rakel came to tell him it was dinnertime, he shooed her away. An hour or so later, he turned on the reading lamp, and it wasn't until its bright light swept away the dusk that he realised how dark the room had become.

It was past ten by the time he finished and looked around for the phone. He wedged the receiver between his ear and shoulder, and it took forever for the dial to turn back after each digit.

V

INTERVIEWER: Speaking of novel writing as a marathon. I was thinking about writer's block, what are your experiences with that?

MARTIN BERG: Yes, it can be a scourge. People become blocked for different reasons. Things just grind to a halt. Stop working. In that situation, your only option is to keep at it, I think. Despite everything. It's mostly psychological.

INTERVIEWER: But what if your work's no good? If you're not happy with it?

MARTIN BERG: Even if you only manage five lines, at least it's a start. You can't afford to develop a fear of the blank page. That's the most important thing. You can't let uncertainty intimidate you. You have to give yourself over to it and see where it takes you.

*

Autumn came again. Rakel brought home new exercise books and with a measure of trepidation, Martin read the story on the theme "My Summer" she had produced in a neat hand.

I had a great time. My mum slept and my dad worked. My little brother is really awful but my uncle whose name is Emanuel is nice. We rode his moped without helmets and bought sweets from the newsagent in the village.

Cecilia met with her supervisor at the start of term. She came home talking about her thesis, a course she was going to audit, some conference where a fellow student who had just finished his MPhil was going to present his work. "And I have far more material than he does, so I mean – how hard can it be?"

She spent an entire morning cleaning her study. Several binbags were filled with papers and when Martin went up there to ask if she wanted a cup of coffee, she was sitting cross-legged on the floor, reading, distractedly chewing her thumbnail.

"This," she said, nodding at the text, "is pretty good in places."

She took up running again, though "running" might have been an overstatement – she told him she'd made it less than a mile in Slottsskogen Park before having to stop and bend double. Then she'd plodded home, noting the number of minutes she'd run on their wall calendar (nine). The next day, she did it again. She never complained about her lack of stamina or about how her runs were so short they were barely worth writing down. Instead, every achievement was recorded.

Their long summer in the country had served one important purpose: it had divided things into a *before* and an *after*. Everything before it could be blamed on the difficult pregnancy, the colic, the chronic sleep deprivation. Eventually, the period was encased in a mother-of-pearl-like wordlessness, even though only a few months had passed.

Once the colic subsided, Elis was calm and easy-going. He made adorable gurgling noises, tentatively returned smiles, and liked to travel through life stretched out along Martin's forearm like a very small sloth. There was even a certain charm to the stream of warm urine that would suddenly trickle down his arm and drip onto his jeans. ("Dad, he's peeing!" Rakel would shout, probably to highlight the fact that she'd been in control of her bodily functions for years.) Elis meekly took his bottle and then delivered magnificent burps over Martin's shoulder. He learned to grasp things and amused himself by rolling over whenever he had a chance.

Taking a few months of parental leave in the spring might not be such a bad idea after all. He could write in the mornings, go for a walk with the pram, meet up with friends. Sit next to the wall of a building, squinting up at the sun, sipping coffee while the boy slept…

And Cecilia could write her thesis, and everything would be back to normal.

Per was still fired up about Lucas Bell. Martin, for his part, considered the facts with cool objectivity – it was a good novel, they'd been lucky to acquire the rights – but for some reason he was unable to muster the same bubbling enthusiasm. It was a gamble. Something could always go wrong. Worst-case scenario, they'd be standing there with stacks upon stacks of unsold books and the company would fold.

To compensate for his pessimism, he went over the translation with a fine-tooth comb, spent hours choosing the font, and bombarded the graphic designer with his opinions about the cover. And even though he couldn't bring himself to share Per's passionate conviction, he did experience a feeling of clarity and naturalness, working with the book. It was like when you've been studying for an exam, sit down for the paper and realise you know the answer to every last question.

Unfortunately, that feeling of certainty didn't extend beyond the walls of the office. He wouldn't have complained if there had been some left over for *Night Sonnets*. Martin had no idea how to continue the story. He should let someone read it but couldn't bear the thought of criticism. And good wasn't even enough, that meaningless little word. It had to be interesting. It had to resonate. It would have been one thing if he'd had nothing to lose, but since he was now claiming to know a thing or two about literature… He could imagine how the talk would go: "Have you heard about Martin Berg's novel? He wrote six hundred pages, every one of them rubbish."

The Leonardo book from the summer had insinuated itself into Martin's consciousness: it had become the epitome of a grand failure. Asking for silence, clearing your throat, making sure everyone's eyes are on you, and then making an utter fool of yourself.

They bought Rakel new wellies and the shoebox was exactly the right size for a stack of A4 pages. Martin shoved his manuscript, which was now so full of changes he wasn't entirely sure which version was the current one, into it and stuck it in a drawer in his desk. Just for now, he promised himself. Just to let it mature.

*

Martin's last letter to Gustav remained unanswered and when he called the number he'd given them, a recorded woman's voice informed him the number was out of service. When five months had passed without any sign of life, Cecilia called the people who might know something, but without any real success. KG had talked to him at the opening of the Antibes Suite vernissage just over six months earlier, but hadn't heard from him since. He assumed, he said vaguely, that Gustav was "working and doing his thing", and if they managed to get hold of him, would they mind telling him to give his gallerist a call?

Cecilia hung up with a sceptical look on her face. "'Doing his thing' isn't necessarily the same as painting, now, is it? Should we call his parents?"

"They definitely have no idea."

"What about his grandmother? Or maybe that would just make her worry?"

Martin wondered why he hadn't thought of calling Nana Edith. He found the number scrawled on the inside of the cover of his address book, and she picked up after three rings (Cecilia reflexively said *bonjour* before switching to Swedish). After hanging up, she heaved a heavy sigh.

"Apparently, he was supposed to visit last summer, but he never showed. Then he called from Scotland, rambling on about a friend who was renting a castle. Was going to drink whisky and wear a kilt. His grandmother apparently thought that sounded like a reasonable plan, so she didn't give it a second thought. But now, she's worried, obviously. I said he's probably just travelling. And what do I know — maybe he *is*."

"For five months?"

Martin was about to mention the polite, weirdly formal message of congratulations he'd sent after Elis was born, but maybe Cecilia had managed to forget that.

"He can be pretty forgetful." She didn't sound like she believed it herself.

"No, seriously – who does he think he is?" Martin said. "I'm certainly done trying to reach him."

"Still, it's odd…"

"Hardly. It's exactly like him. Doesn't lift a finger to keep in touch but is mortally offended if you do the same to him."

Even though Martin decided not to care from that moment on, the thought of Gustav's nonchalance kept gnawing at him. When he was in the shower or brushing his teeth. When he was drying the washing-up. When he was cycling to work. It irked him so badly he kicked his bike over when the lock wouldn't cooperate. A few days later, he ran into Vivi from Valand, who was searching for the best bananas at the supermarket, looking extremely pregnant. They chatted for a bit, and when she asked how Gustav was doing – why did everyone always ask *him* how Gustav was doing? As though he were some kind of information relay hub? – he gave her a very detailed account of the situation. Vivi nodded and her brow furrowed with concern, but when Martin started in on the theory that their friend had simply upped and moved without so much as a sodding word to anyone, he could tell her mind was elsewhere.

Cecilia called him unfair and Martin made a mental list of Gustav's communicative shortcomings over the years.

"And there's a clear trend, let me tell you. *I'm* the one who reaches out. *I'm* the one who calls. Then he pops up, expecting me to go out drinking with him and for everything to be like it was ten years ago. He gets drunk and sulks about everyone judging him, and I just want to say Gustav, no one's bloody *judging* you. Who's judging you? Huh? Who in here is judging you? And then he mutters something about everyone else's 'grand titles', which I assume refers to our BAs and MAs – I don't even have an MA! – when he spent five years at bloody

Valand Academy. And he thinks 'everyone' is always 'overanalysing everything'? As though he's some kind of innocent child, just bobbing around the intuitive uterine existence of art, just *creating*, while the rest of us sully the purity of art with our analyses and our critique? As though being unintellectual is some kind of virtue, just because he hasn't bothered to lift so much as a finger to learn anything? As though intellectual endeavours are some kind of second-rate work in the constant shadow of... of I don't bloody know. Art. Life. Right?"

In the end, he tried to put it out of his mind completely. And yet, he woke up some mornings with three words echoing inside his skull: *Gustav is missing*.

Not long after that outburst, things happened quickly. Cecilia's supervisor called about a conference, the London Congress of Humanities and Social Sciences, with the theme "A Changing Europe". One of the PhD candidates who was supposed to go had got his bicycle tyre stuck in the tram tracks and broken his leg, would she like to take his place?

"Absolutely," she said, clutching the receiver, trying to catch Martin's eye. "Or do I have to present? I don't have anything to – okay – yes... yes... no, that works. Let me just check with my husband."

She hadn't called him *her husband* in god knew how long. It was unexpectedly nice to hear.

"...just a few days," she said, pacing round and round the kitchen. "Two nights maybe, three at most. If that's okay with you? We could call Mum to help out with the kids..."

"Sure, if it's important to you."

She looked at him as though he were missing the point. "I don't care about the conference. I'm talking about Gustav."

Cecilia's plan was simple: at some point, she would go to Gustav's house, and if he wasn't there, maybe someone at the gallery might know something, and if not, she'd have to give up. "But at least we will have tried."

And the next week, she went to England. The moment the taxi pulled away, Elis began to scream. Rakel fetched her ear defenders from the colic period and sat down on the sofa with a stack of *Asterix* from the library.

"Thanks for the help," Martin muttered.

A day of low-intensity warfare followed. Elis transitioned to refusing to eat, a less exhibitionist form of protest. Rakel happily wolfed down her food and nattered on about dinosaurs, her most recent passion. Tyrannosaurus Rex was primarily a scavenger. Dinosaurs lay eggs, just like birds. The brain of a stegosaurus was the size of a walnut, but it was enough because all it did was eat grass and leaves. All dinosaurs came from birds and weren't exactly giant lizards, even though they looked like they were. How big did he reckon Elis's brain was?

Then followed a walk through Slottsskogen, with a pram and an eight-year-old on a bike, squashed bananas in his backpack, some protracted drama about a lost hat, and an exhausted chat with Uffe, of all people, who was strolling through Azaleadalen wearing an unseasonably thin denim jacket.

"Any news on the great artist?" he asked. "Now that he's no longer the darling of the establishment?"

"He's been painting some really great stuff recently," Martin lied. "So I guess he's all right. Getting on with it. No, no, Elis – don't eat that stick – I said *no*. Rakel, could you – Uffe, I need to deal with this. Nice to see you, bye, goodbye."

The next morning, Cecilia called to tell him she'd found Gustav. "We're coming back tonight. Could you make sure the kids are in bed and make up the guest bed?"

"Okay," Martin replied, because her voice had that please-don't-ask-questions edge to it, and international calls were expensive, too. "Absolutely."

Martin spent several hours cleaning the kitchen – he'd tried to work, but for some reason found it impossible to focus – becoming more and more irate as he wiped down the cabinet doors. Then he heard a key in the lock, and there they were, standing in the hallway.

At the sight of Gustav, all the things Martin had planned to say vanished. Instead, he tried to catch Cecilia's eye, but she looked away, unbuttoning her coat.

During their fifteen-year friendship, Gustav had always looked much the same. Granted, he'd adopted a certain art-student style while attending art school, and he'd looked more haggard at thirty than sixteen. But it was always the same round, steel-rimmed specs, the same lack of a haircut, the same seabag, the same greatcoat. (You had to give it to the army: they made ridiculously durable clothes.) And that was why his clothes were the first thing Martin noticed. His coat was a bizarre deep-red velvet affair. Underneath, a black silk shirt hung askew. There was some kind of fringed shawl happening. He wore leather trousers that were a size too big and held up by a belt lined with flat studs. His glasses were the usual round model, true, but tiny and with shaded lenses.

And after that, there was no avoiding his face. His eyes were sunken and unfocused. His skin seemed to have grown a size too big for his cranium. Between his nostrils and the corners of his mouth ran two sharp lines, and sparse stubble covered his grey cheeks. Now, he bashfully scratched the back of his neck. His hair had grown into a lanky ponytail.

And he reeked.

Gustav cleared his throat. "All right, mate?"

"Hi."

"Where are the kids? Rakel and…?"

"Elis," Martin replied. "They're asleep."

Gustav nodded slowly. He went into the kitchen, still wearing his coat. He studied the kitchen table, the counter and the fridge in turn, all the while nodding to himself. Then he asked if he could have something to drink.

"Tea," Cecilia said. She'd taken off her coat and joined them in the kitchen.

"What the fuck, Cissi, come on…"

"But you're going to have to shower first."

"Do you have to be so Gestapo?"

She pointed towards the bathroom.

Gustav glanced helplessly at Martin, who made a she's-the-boss gesture, but then he retreated to the bathroom, muttering to himself. "It's not that fucking easy. I won't have them thinking it's all that fucking easy."

While he was gone, Cecilia asked Martin to find him "some sensible clothes". Then she opened the bathroom door – Gustav protested feebly – and came back out carrying the leather trousers and all the rest. She shoved the clothes into a binbag, and before Martin could ask what she was doing, he heard the rubbish chute in the hallway slam shut.

Instead of talking, they busied themselves with practical tasks until Gustav emerged, wrapped in a towel. His ribcage was skinnier than Martin remembered. His arms looked like twigs. Without comment, he put on the clothes he was given: a pair of jeans Martin hadn't been able to wear since '82, a T-shirt and a flannel shirt. When Cecilia ordered him to eat his soup, he slurped down the entire bowl. And he did actually drink some tea.

In the middle of all this, Rakel appeared, standing silently in the doorway, fiddling with her nightgown. Cecilia ushered her back to her room, speaking calmly and soothingly. Rakel's clear child's voice was easily heard through the wall: "But I want to be with Gustav."

Gustav just stared straight ahead.

24

"SOME PEOPLE HAVE SAID they're coming but haven't RSVP'd," Patricia said, studying the guestlist she'd stuck to a clipboard. She'd walked into the party venue with the self-assuredness of a person who has watched too many TV programmes set among Manhattan Career Women. The sound of her heels made everyone in the vicinity, including Martin, snap to and look around for anything that might need doing, but unfortunately they seemed to have run out of meaningless busy work. Everything was in order. The party was set to start in thirty minutes.

"Okay," Martin said. When the meaning of her words sank in, he added: "How does that work?"

"They didn't email. There were clear instructions to RSVP by email."

"Rakel's probably one of them," Martin said. Truth be told, he doubted his daughter was going to make an appearance. He hadn't heard so much as a peep from her since she stopped by the office the other week to pick up those books. They were going to need that reader's report very soon. An email from Ulrike Ackermann had sat unopened in his inbox for several days, and even though it had turned out to be exactly what he'd assumed – a gentle prodding about Philip Franke's novel – it had taken him half an hour to formulate a reply consisting of three apologetic lines which on the one hand indicated they were interested, but on the other hand didn't make any promises.

Patricia's voice pulled him out of his German reverie. "No, she emailed. Rakel plus two."

"And what about Gustav?"

"Becker, Gustav… also good."

"What?"

"Why? Did you hear otherwise?"

"No, no… Do I look presentable?"

"Very dashing."

Per joined them, tugging at his tie. "Does it look okay? I don't ever wear a bloody tie any more."

"Looks fine to my untrained eye. You'll have to double-check with Elis when he gets here. He helped me with mine."

"Elis?"

"He's started dressing like a Cambridge student circa 1955."

"Wasn't he into that unidentified hip-hop style? Baseball cap with a straight visor and baggy trousers."

"You're not keeping up with the times."

Over the past few days, Martin had begun to regret his decision to throw this party. Watching the bar staff making their preparations, the jazz quartet swirling their cymbals and discreetly testing their microphones, and Per, whose jacket was slightly too tight across his shoulders even though it was very expensive, he suddenly had the feeling that a celebration of this magnitude was hubris, bordering on arrogant. What did they really have to celebrate? That they'd been lucky? That they hadn't folded? That they'd done their jobs? That they'd likely reached the highest peak of success a publishing company geared towards non-fiction and more niche, high-quality fiction could ever hope to achieve, and that it was downhill from here? That he'd been surprised to find two actually decent authors on last year's bestseller list, while ignoring the four books that advocated a bizarre diet that revolved around eating everything that had been known to be unhealthy since the dawn of time, while fearing the dangerous potato?

"What if no one shows up?" he said to no one in particular.

"If that were to happen," Per said, adjusting his cufflinks, "we have fifty bottles of champagne and a limitless supply of wine to help us deal with it."

That particular worry turned out to be unfounded. By half past seven, Martin had moved on to worrying about being confronted by angry vegetarians about there being only chicken canapés left, or that his son would get too drunk and make a fool of himself; Elis was downing wine with the urgency of someone fearing it'll be dumped out by the police in Kungsparken. The venue was packed to the rafters. Uffe from Valand was standing by the bar, talking to a slightly harassed-looking cover illustrator. Vivi and Sandor turned up, the latter's Zappa moustache intact but greying, already on the lookout for Sissel, who apparently didn't do well with crowds and had therefore taken a double dose of sedatives. Now, they worried she might have passed out in a corner somewhere. Martin directed them to Patricia, even though there was a risk she might kick out anyone who didn't live up to her ideas of dignified publishing party behaviour. They disappeared into the crowd and instead Jenny Halling, Martin's old friend from upper secondary, appeared, shaking his hand and saying he'd done himself proud. She looked the same, with a razor-sharp bob and thick black glasses; she was now the director of the Gothenburg Film Festival. Johannes Anyuru was hanging out in a corner with some people from the cultural magazine *Glänta*. UKON was eating peanuts. For some reason Sven Wollter, whom Martin didn't recall seeing on the guestlist, was engaged in a lively debate with one of the company's young first-time novelists. And there was Max Schreiber, to whom he had to remember to talk about that translation, standing with old people from the Department of Intellectual History. Mummy Birgitta and Aunt Maud, who looked like old ladies and wildly out of place, were hugging the wall. Even Martin's sister Kicki was there, despite insisting only the day before that she absolutely couldn't get out of work; for the past few years she had worked as a locum nurse in the backwaters of Norway. But there she was, studying the culture crowd the same way a person might observe a huddle of penguins in a zoo when there's absolutely nothing else to look at. The few times Kicki read anything at all, it was books about barefoot running or healthy cooking, but Martin doubted she viewed that as a shortcoming, even in a context like this. Her forte, he knew, was emergency care – gory traffic accidents, injured mountain climbers, childbirth miles from anywhere – and maybe her intimacy with life and death served as her protective shield.

He should go over and talk to them, but to his relief he saw his son appear by their side. Aunt Maud's wary expression changed in the blink of an eye. Elis had always been her favourite.

Martin was just about to set off on a greeting tour when he felt a featherlight touch on his elbow.

"Congratulations." It was Maria Malm, the poet from the couples' dinner. "Twenty-five years. That's a long time…"

"Thank you. Yes, it is. It's a bit frightening, when you think about it."

He could touch her hair, push a stray strand out of her face. He clutched his glass.

"I don't think I've been able to stick with anything for twenty-five years," she said.

"You will once your children are grown. You know: suddenly you realise you've had them for longer than you'd lived before they came."

"Yes, I suppose…" She changed the subject, asked about the company, when they'd started it, why. Martin gave her his usual spiel: they were both passionate about publishing a certain kind of literature that they felt was missing on the market, they were young and reckless enough to think "how hard can it be", and so on. Maria listened attentively, nodding in all the right places. Then, in the middle of an account of the absurd market monopoly of crime fiction, Martin spotted Rakel entering.

"Excuse me," he said to Maria, "my daughter just arrived… I have to…" and with a vague gesture in Rakel's direction, he strode off.

Rakel pretended not to see him waving. She was dressed like Hermine in *Steppenwolf*, in a black, three-piece suit with a snow-white shirt and velvet bow around her neck, and for once she had her hair in a neat low bun, instead of the usual messy bird's nest on top of her head.

"Hi," she said curtly when he was so close he couldn't be ignored.

"I'm so happy you came."

She said something in German he pretended not to hear and added: "It's a lovely party." Then she scurried off after her friends.

The rest of the evening, he only ever saw her from afar. Rakel nodding solemnly in conversation with her aunt, having her velvet bow straightened by Sanna, talking to the pianist while the band took a short break, giggling with Patricia and Amir, exchanging a few words with Max. She had a sunny smile for everyone but him, and whenever he came near her, she immediately slunk away, her eyes stubbornly averted.

Martin continued to shake people's hands, repeating the same empty phrases. He was surprised at the turnout.

"Martin!" Vera Wikner emerged from the crowd, with Emanuel following slowly in her wake. Vera kissed him on the cheeks, saying the place looked great. Her eyes kept glancing restlessly around. At the first opportunity, Martin mused, she would ditch her brother and professionally mingle her way over to whoever was the biggest celebrity. Emanuel was dressed in a pale linen suit, with a ruby-red pocket square. He was perspiring slightly, a few damp strands of hair clinging to his forehead.

"Good day," he said. "Mum called to say we had to represent the family at this celebration of a major milestone in your career. Unfortunately, she and Dad were unable to make it, but they're going down to the country in a few weeks and you and 'the children' – Mum's words, not mine – are, needless to say, more than welcome. Between us, they've started to talk about selling it and 'buying a nice little place a smidge closer', so this may well be your last chance."

"It would be terrible if they were to sell," Vera said, sipping her champagne.

"I guess…"

Something about Vera always made him feel like a B-list actor who had forgotten his lines. He recalled the odd scene on the lawn about a month ago. Apparently, they were going to act as though it never happened. Which was good because his memories of that night were fairly foggy. Not knowing what to say, he stayed quiet. Vera began to talk about some gallery, then spotted someone she knew and disappeared.

Martin, the exhausted general, took stock of his troops: a laughing, talking, tipsy mass uniformly dressed in black. His eyes almost roved on without taking any particular notice of the middle-aged, bespectacled man who had stopped just inside the door. In fact, if you cut out the image of Gustav Becker, who was just then patting his pockets, probably in search of the cigarettes he would moments later realise he couldn't smoke inside anyway, and separated it from its unmistakeably twenty-first century surroundings, he would have been nigh impossible to date.

Later that evening, Sandor slipped in next to Martin, poking his tongue under his top lip, making his moustache undulate up and down, and commenting without preamble that Gustav seemed to be "in fine form". Per dropped a comment about how he'd "put on some pounds – in a good way", and Vivi, who with age had developed certain New Age tendencies, felt he "had really great energy".

Gustav even said so himself. "It's all good. I feel *good*, Martin." And he squeezed Martin's arm firmly, as if to underline his statement. His hands, those thin nineteenth-century hands, were clean, no paint stains.

"How was England?"

"Great, just great. I decided to go see the countryside. Amazing landscapes. You'd think you were in that Kate Bush song."

"I always thought of you as an incorrigible urbanite."

Gustav chuckled – yes, well, he supposed he was, at heart – and immediately launched into an account of his visits to Tate Modern and the Saatchi Gallery.

They talked about generalities for a while. Yes, he was excited about the retrospective, but maybe it was a bit – you know – stressful being the centre of attention? And lately, he'd been pondering his priorities in life, and success was pretty far down the list, at the end of the day, wouldn't he agree? He was thinking about making like Lundell and buying a farm somewhere in the middle of nowhere. Paint. Go for walks along the sea. He'd taken up tennis.

"Tennis?"

"Yes, though I'm not sure you can rightly call it that, considering the shape I'm in... but you should try it sometime. It's fun."

Gustav spent most of the party in a corner, shyly fiddling with a glass of unidentifiable contents. He was constantly surrounded by a group of people whose members changed at regular intervals, as though in silent agreement about the proper duration of an audience. He had the kind of forcefield around him that famous people sometimes develop: a sphere of rapt attention, quick sideways glances, self-conscious postures. Granted, there were several authors at the party who had to be considered "famous", but (and for Berg & Andrén this was a lamentable fact) their fame was not of the same calibre as that of the painter in the corner. Perhaps, Martin thought, it was about the sums for which his paintings exchanged hands? Or was it Gustav himself? Was it because he was a prodigal son who had "put Gothenburg on the map"? Would the head of the municipality suddenly appear and try to lure him back with the promise of a rental flat in Haga?

Then, just under two hours after he'd arrived, he was standing in the doorway, wrapping a scarf around his neck. "Let's meet up next week?" he said to Martin. "I'm inspecting the hanging on Monday and then I have a few interviews, but other than that, I have no plans. Call me, and we'll go for a bite somewhere."

And then he was gone.

Around midnight, the mood of the party changed. The jazz quartet kept playing, but upped both tempo and volume. A gentleman with thin white hair and his wife struck up some kind of ballroom dance and were soon joined by others. Maria Malm goofed around with an unknown man. One of Martin's gloomier authors was sitting at the bar, drinking too much, flanked by one of Rakel's friends, who was gesticulating in a way that suggested the subject matter was something along the lines of the Human Condition in a Postmodern Society. On the other side of the room, he spotted his children in a corner, and for once they were talking to each other, their heads close together, each wearing a facial expression typical for them: Elis indecisive, Rakel determined. Martin was just about to head over when a hand was placed on his shoulder, and there was Per Andrén with his tie untied, introducing him to a young man who was working on a doctoral thesis about postcolonial perspectives on – the young man spoke unclearly and exactly what he was investigating through the lens of postcolonialism was drowned out by general noise. Martin wondered if he should say something about Cecilia's work. Patricia came to his rescue: with her hairdo askew and a harassed look in her eyes, she asked him if this was a good time to bring out the late-night snacks. After a moment's hesitation, she added that Lisa Ekman had passed out in the accessible bathroom. Since the same thing had happened at the launch party for Lisa's first novel, Martin knew from experience that the best thing to do was to find a pair of scissors and pry open the lock (*not* to go into hysterics and call Securitas). Which was what he calmly and quietly did, after banging on the door for a while. Granted, Lisa was in the foetal position on the floor, but she looked up at him and said a wan hello. While he helped her to her feet and gathered up her things, she rambled on about how she was almost done with a first draft of her new book, she was going to go away for the summer, to a house in the woods with no internet, and she was going to write – and then she gagged and threw up in the toilet.

After putting Lisa in a taxi to Bergsjön or Hjällbo or whatever godforsaken suburb in the northeast it was she lived in, Martin went straight to the bar and asked for a gin and tonic. He knocked it back faster than he should have and ordered another. Why was he always the one people turned to in emergencies? Why did he have to pick his way through dissolving paper towels in a bathroom in order to rescue a virtual teenager who had somehow managed to land the *Borås Tidning*'s award for best first novel, and who would sooner or later produce an anaemic second novel that was the literary equivalent of a deer in headlights? Unless she got it in her head to write prose poetry? And when he didn't want to publish her experiments in prose poetry, he would be a cowardly capitalist who was too scared to make art his top priority.

She would deliver a lecture in the kind of quavering Poetry Slam voice everyone born in the late eighties used for readings and such. Why insist on this affected tone and its timbre of indignation? Couldn't they listen to Krister Henriksson?

The band was replaced with a playlist with a decent number of Madonna songs on it. His children went home, possibly out of fear of seeing their father let loose to "Vogue". (Martin tried to assure them that wasn't going to happen, but Elis just said: Yes, *yes*, Dad.) Patricia ran around collecting used paper plates. Per had switched to non-alcoholic beer and confessed that he'd spoken to you-know-who earlier that day. The decorations drooped. Somewhere a glass broke. A middle-aged couple was having a row in a corner. The bartender yawned, mixing his cocktails on autopilot. Maria Malm appeared at his side, asking if he'd had a good time.

And then he was in the back of a taxi, the city flashing by outside, long streaks of light in the dark-blue summer night, eastbound, and across the seat, Maria Malm's hand was in his, he had to stop thinking of her as Maria Malm and start to think of her as Maria. *Maria.* But it was hard, Maria Malm had sort of stuck, her surname an integral part of the whole.

They had arrived. Car doors slamming in the night.

Maria Malm didn't live in the city, as he'd thought, but in a terraced house in Kålltorp. She fumbled with her keys while Martin studied a flowerpot on the front steps.

"Here we are," she said, letting him into a hallway where drowsy lamplight blinked itself awake over wooden floors and original radiators. Did he want something to drink, whisky, maybe? Martin said yes, realising as he did so that he'd have to be an idiot to drink more. He asked for the bathroom and was pointed to a door, didn't really need to pee but did it anyway to gain some respite and to fix himself sternly in the mirror, which would have been easier if he hadn't found it so very difficult to focus. What were the others doing right now? Where was Gustav? Did they know he was here? Had they seen them leave and if so, what had they thought about it?

To get out of drinking the whisky she'd already poured him, he kissed her. *Maria Malm.* Don't forget.

25

An unfamiliar ceiling was slanting away from him. The grainy light of dawn. A feeling of whiteness. White walls, white curtains. White sheets. Martin looked down at his chest, which was bare. One of his legs was in contact with warm, soft skin. He turned his head and saw a tangle of dark hair.

He could close his eyes again. Go back to sleep. In a few hours, she'd wake up, make a breakfast they'd eat on the small patio out back. Warmed by the June sun, he would begin to feel human again. Another cup of coffee. Orange juice from some complicated kitchen gadget. Then, well, why not seize the opportunity, they'd have sex again, sober this time and in full possession of their faculties…

Infinitely slowly, he moved one leg towards the edge of the bed. Then the other. Then he heaved himself up and when she rolled over, he stood stock-still until he was certain she was fast asleep.

He found his clothes and put them on, keeping his movements as small and silent as he could manage. He tiptoed down the stairs – also white, there didn't seem to be a single surface in this house that wasn't white – and found his jacket thrown over a chair in the kitchen. His phone and wallet were in the inside pocket. It was 06.41. No missed calls, no messages. Which was oddly upsetting.

In the hallway, he tied his laces with clumsy fingers, listening for creaking floors or anything else to indicate that she was awake. The house was completely silent. Martin closed the door with the faintest of clicks and hurried towards the tram stop.

The flat on Djurgårdsgatan was desolate the way only flats nobody has slept in can be. The bed was made in Elis's room. Martin reached for his phone to send an accusatory text about Elis not having informed him of his absence – as required by their agreement – before realising that would entail admitting his own.

Instead, he took off his suit, threw his shirt in the hamper, downed two glasses of water standing by the sink, and took a third with him to the bedroom. In bed, he spent a long time formulating an apologetic but non-committal text to the MARIA MALM who had appeared in his contacts list overnight. Then he opened the window to let in a cool waft of air, lay down on the duvet, and closed his eyes. He fell asleep almost instantly.

*

Martin must have heard the front door, but since he often thought he heard the front door opening and closing in the liminal space between sleeping and waking, he didn't pay it much heed. Instead, it was the stubborn buzzing of a fly that finally roused him. He stared out into the gloom, taking inventory of his existence. It was Sunday. The anniversary party was behind him. Gustav had showed up. They were going to talk, maybe even see each other sometime today. He'd forgotten to talk to Kicki about their mother's cough, but she was in town for the rest of the weekend, so there was plenty of time. He should go over there and have coffee later. Elis had slept elsewhere and his current whereabouts were unknown. He himself had – and at this point Martin felt his face contract in a grimace – snuck out of Maria Malm's terraced house in Kålltorp. He reached for his phone: no reply. Relief washed over him. She must have read his text by now. If she hadn't replied yet, it was very possible she might never.

With some effort, he wrapped his dressing gown around his body, which ached as though it had been put through the ringer. He couldn't remember the last time he'd been drunk. Probably with Gustav at some point. Now, he could in good conscience spend a few weekends reading in peace, with the excuse of needing to recover.

He found his daughter sitting on the sofa with a photo album open on her lap.

"You're awake," was all she said.

Martin told himself Rakel's presence was a good thing – her aloof attitude during the party must have been caused by shame at not having delivered her reader's report – even though somewhere in his mushy brain, there was an undercurrent of unease.

"Yesterday went well, right?" he said. "Don't you think?" He continued through the living room to the kitchen, expecting her to follow. The kitchen was where the Berg family did their talking and socialising. People made sandwiches, checked the fridge, scoured the pantry for a stray bag of nuts, and so on. But Rakel didn't join him, so after turning on the coffee machine, he went back and sat in the armchair across from her.

Rakel studied him. She was sitting very still, wreathed in a flowing early-summer light that Gustav would have loved. The silence stretched.

"Some people were pretty hammered, I suppose," Martin offered, as though there had been no pause in their conversation. "Things were getting pretty wild at the end there. But on the whole, a good party. Did you have a good time?"

"Absolutely. But I'm actually here for a completely different reason." Her tone was cool and businesslike.

"Okay," Martin said. A chill was spreading from the pit of his stomach. He wondered if she had somehow found about this business with Maria Malm. "And what might that be?"

Rakel turned the photo album towards him. "Mum," she said.

It was the last album with any pictures of Cecilia. He'd taken most of those photographs himself. A thirty-year-old Cecilia Berg at the lectern during her viva, a figure all in white, radiant, whose face was so powerfully illuminated it disappeared in a haze of light.

"Let me just get a cup of coffee," he said after a moment that felt longer than it probably was. "Want some?"

"No, thank you."

"Are you sure? It's no hassle. I have a virtually endless supply here. Just say the word."

His hand was trembling slightly when he put the cup on the saucer, but he forced himself to carry it one-handed, as usual, the few feet back to the living room.

"Have you seen your brother, by the way?"

"No."

Martin stood up again, this time to fetch his phone. It took him a while to find it among the sheets, and when he did, he discovered a message from Maria Malm on the locked screen. He flung the phone away as though it had burned him. Once again, he returned to the room where Rakel was waiting silently on the sofa. His cup rattled and he spilled coffee on his dressing gown.

"All right," Martin said.

"I didn't want to ask you before the party," Rakel said, and now there was a hint of tenderness in her voice.

"Ask me what?"

Rakel turned the page in the photo album. Martin knew what she was looking at: two empty pages. The album was only half-full.

"The only thing I remember from the day Mum disappeared," she said, "was that you let me stay up late and that Gustav came by with a lot of suitcases. And then we went to that cottage on the coast for the first time."

"That was later." Martin's voice seemed stuck at the back of his throat. He cleared it. "The cottage was later. That summer."

Rakel ignored his comment. "And I remember you telling me and Elis about that letter. That Mum had left a letter before leaving. The one I asked you about a while ago."

"What are you getting at?"

"What did she actually write in it?"

"Rakel, it was fifteen years ago. As I believe I told you, I don't recall. And it wasn't a long letter. I guess she wrote, well – I don't know. That she was leaving."

His daughter was quiet for so long Martin thought he was free to stretch and go to the kitchen to make himself a slice of toast. He hadn't eaten anything since a collection of rushed finger foods the night before. He looked for a way to guide the conversation back to the realm of harmless topics, but just as he was about to say something about Gustav's upcoming retrospective, Rakel spoke again.

"Why didn't you try to find her?"

Martin shrugged, realised it was the wrong kind of gesture, and reached for his coffee cup to mask the movement. He cleared his throat again. There seemed to be something wrong with his throat; maybe he was coming down with something.

"I tried to report her missing," he said. "But the police wouldn't let me since she'd left 'of her own volition', if I remember the phrase correctly."

"That's not what I asked. I want to know why *you* didn't try to find her?"

"Where was I supposed to look? Where was I supposed to even start? I had nothing to go on. She wanted to be alone. I had to respect that."

"People who run away want to be found," Rakel sneered, tossing the photo album aside. "Everyone knows that."

"But what was I supposed to do?"

"*I* don't know. I'm not the one who's married to her."

"It would have been pointless. Cecilia's stubborn as sin. She has always gone her own way."

"And you just accepted it? You just left it at that?"

Martin raised his hands the way he liked to do when he wanted some headstrong author, or, indeed, his headstrong children, to listen to him – a conductor in front of his orchestra – but couldn't think of anything to say. His brain was empty and when he opened his mouth, no sound came out. He let his hands drop.

"A person might almost think you were happy with how things turned out." Rakel's voice was low and deep. "That it suited you just fine. That you, when push came to shove, weren't all that interested in her coming back." She was sitting up very straight on the sofa, her legs crossed and her hands folded around one knee. Her knuckles were white and the tendons of her forearms taut. She was staring straight at him, unblinking. Those eyes: brown, like his own, like Abbe's, like the sailors and dock workers of the Berg family.

"Rakel – I got four hours of sleep last night." In reality, he'd had at least nine. "I would at the very least like to drink this cup of coffee before you throw all kinds of accusations at me."

His daughter stood up without a word. Then she was in the hallway, the front door slammed shut, and the sound of her footsteps died away on the stairs.

26

The art museum was swarming with people and Rakel's first impulse was to turn around and leave. She'd barely left the flat in days. At this point, she was four-fifths of the way through *Ein Jahr* and after her last read-through, she had at least not felt the need to lower her eyes in shame. Now, the din seemed ear-splitting, and sudden movements caught out of the corners of her eyes made her head swivel this way and that. But her dad and Elis were here, and even though she would have preferred to avoid them – at least her dad, who had kept complete radio silence the past few days – convention dictated that the Bergs behave more or less like a family unit in contexts such as these.

The vernissage visitors were clustered in small groups, sipping wine, waving at each other or maybe at Rakel. Even though she could only catch glimpses of the paintings through the milling crowd, she was aware of the eyes that followed her from portrait to portrait. She tried to make herself as unnoticeable as possible as she picked her way through the throng, but ended up in a dead end of black-clad backs, tapped a shoulder to be let past, and found herself face to face with Frederikke Larsen.

"Rakel!" Frederikke exclaimed, and for some reason Rakel wished she could have kept her voice down. As so often with her parents' friends, she felt shackled to her status as child: they always marvelled at the fact that she had achieved perfectly normal things like getting her driving licence, finding a flat, attending university. She hadn't seen Frederikke in years and now she suspected the Danish woman, like everyone else in this place, to some extent still lived in the frozen time of the Antibes Suite, where an eternal sun shone, and nothing ever changed.

Frederikke explained that she was sorry to have missed the publishing company's anniversary party, but that she'd been unable to get out of a conference organised by the Danish Association of Psychologists. Now, she was looking forward to seeing everyone, it really had been much too long. And how was Rakel these days?

"Fine, thank you," Rakel said, dizzy and disoriented by the flood of words.

"What a lovely kimono," Frederikke said, pinching the fabric. "Green suits you."

Searching for her family, Rakel zigzagged through the crowd until she found her father, deep in discussion with a man with long grey hair and a denim jacket. Elis was standing next to him, looking deeply bored.

When Martin spotted Rakel, he instantly looked away, just for a fraction of a second. Then he raised his hand in greeting, though pretty stiffly, she thought.

"Uffe, you remember Rakel, right? Rakel, this is Uffe."

"Old mate from Valand," Uffe said, shaking her hand. "The last time I saw you, you were about yay tall. Time flies, it seems. Bloody terrible. Where did you find that wine? Was there more of it? I'll be back, ladies and gentlemen. See you."

He left a bubble of silence in his wake; Elis checked his phone and Martin looked up at the ceiling and whistled a little tune. Then, the curator, standing on a temporary stage at the far end of the room, began to test the microphone, setting off waves of howling reverb. A tech guy jumped up on the stage and fixed something. The curator tugged awkwardly on the cord before bidding them welcome and calling the evening's main attraction up on stage.

Gustav blinked at the lights, nodding awkwardly at the applause. He said something into the microphone but there was no sound.

"Turn it on," someone shouted. The curator stepped forward again and began turning the microphone over. More reverb.

"There," Gustav said, "is it working now?" His voice rang out across the room, raspy from thirty-five years of two packets of Gauloises a day.

"Nope," Uffe called out. A wave of laughter rippled through the audience.

Gustav grinned, and it was easy to see why everyone always forgave his tardiness and unanswered phone calls: he had a big, beautiful smile.

"I'm not a man of many words, but…" he said. More laughter. "Seriously, though. If you're looking for a speaker, Martin Berg's your man. He's a man of words. Where are you, Martin?"

"Over here," Martin hollered.

"I would ask that you direct all questions about my so-called oeuvre to him. He has been subjected to it, up close, since the seventies. It's that bloke over there" – Gustav pointed from the stage – "the one in the slate-grey jacket. See him? How are you doing, Martin? Do you mind acting as my spokesperson?"

"Not at all."

"You can send me an invoice later. Just joking. Anyway, you can also behold Martin as a young ne'er-do-well in several of the paintings assembled here. Right, what else…"

He went on to say that he was very happy about the retrospective, it was an honour, truly, and great to see such a big turnout, and a big thank you to Anna who had done such a wonderful job curating the exhibition. Then he slunk off stage. He was succeeded by a man in his sixties, who waited calmly while the curator introduced him, standing with feet shoulder-width apart, gazing out at the audience.

"KG," Martin muttered.

"…KG Hammarsten," the curator echoed. "Gustav Becker's gallerist since the eighties."

Applause.

"Just a few quick things," KG said. Then he went on for at least fifteen minutes about how he'd been there right from the start ("More like since Gustav started to *sell*," Martin said to no one in particular), that it had been an unadulterated pleasure to watch Gustav Becker's development over the years, that his works demonstrated unusual integrity and truthfulness, and so on.

Rakel looked around for Gustav, but he was nowhere to be found.

"At least they managed to get Gustav up on stage," her dad said when the din of conversation resumed. "No small feat."

Rakel made a noise that with some goodwill could be interpreted as a yes. Her surroundings seemed to consist of blurry splotches of colour and fields of light – definitely more Monet than Becker – and it took her several seconds to make out who the waving arm in the crowd belonged to. It was Ellen, Lovisa's friend. She was accompanied by the young man with the tidy hairdo from the party. His name was spinning just out of reach. Anton? Adam?

"I just have to…" she mumbled. And without looking at her father, she bolted.

Ellen hugged her and said: "Well, you've already met Aron," and Aron and Rakel shook hands and exchanged pleasantries.

"How do you like the exhibition?" Rakel asked, realising as she did that she couldn't bear to listen to the answer. Too late: Aron stroked his beard, adopting a thoughtful expression.

"Very well executed," he said. "Experiencing Becker's body of work this way is just…" he spread his hands as though he were lost for words, which Rakel seriously doubted he was. "It highlights the way he has been pursuing and developing his unique expression from the very first. The works from his youth, by which I mean the works from before his breakthrough in '87, are surprisingly bold and articulated."

"Totally," Ellen put in.

"Another interesting thing, of course, is that Becker so often depicted women engaged in intellectual work, as opposed to women whose main function is to be aesthetic objects, a vessel for the artist's projections and views on 'Woman'." Aron straightened up, gesticulating in a measured, precise way, as though he were standing in front of a much larger audience than just Rakel and Ellen. He was of the opinion, he said, that Becker examined humanity beyond gender and sexuality, an idea he based on the artist's many explorations of reading and writing women. These motifs in turn posed questions connected to Becker's use of live models, an outmoded method in itself, as well as the field of psychological tension that inevitably arose between painter and painted.

"Hmm," Rakel said.

Aron's use of the plural, *women*, wasn't entirely accurate, since almost all the paintings were of one and the same person. True, Frederikke figured in the Antibes Suite to great effect – dark and raven-like next to the fair Cecilia – but in more conventionally idle poses. The same was true of the rest of the portraits. Gustav had always painted his loved ones – as a way of showing his affection, Rakel suddenly thought – but Cecilia had been his model *par excellence*.

With an effort, she refrained from commenting and instead kept smiling as normally as she could, wishing she had a prompter to help her get through this conversation. "I'm going to have a look at the paintings," she said, possibly a bit too abruptly, because Aron had just opened his mouth to continue his lecture.

Rakel had hoped it would get easier to breathe once she was alone, but, if possible, the pressure across her chest intensified.

It was the largest collection of Gustav's paintings she'd ever seen. Hung side by side like this, they were overwhelming. Rakel counted twenty-five Cecilia portraits, spanning just over a decade. On several enormous canvases, Cecilia was pictured full length, like in old royal portraits. Remarkably often, she was dressed in light colours and looking grave, like a Pallas Athena of the north, gazing out at the regular mortals before her with silent wisdom.

Since every painting was accompanied by a plaque with a year, Rakel could organise them chronologically – a word her brain reflexively associated with the two Greek concepts of time, like a devil and an angel sitting on either shoulder – as well as in relation to her own life history. She found one from the year she was born, but it was impossible to tell if Cecilia was pregnant. The title was *Cecilia in the*

Studio, and with a flash of insight and a concomitant impulse to show off (she looked around for Elis), Rakel recognised the motif from a nineteenth-century painting in the museum's permanent collection. It showed three people in a sculptor's studio. Against a backdrop of clay pots and half-finished sculptures stood a naked model on a table, from which she watched with idle interest as two men were making a plaster cast of her legs. According to the catalogue, Gustav's painting was "a comment" on this work by Édouard Dantan. It, too, showed three people in a studio: Martin, Cecilia and Gustav himself ("a rare self-portrait", the catalogue informed her). Cecilia was in the same pose, wearing the same expression as Dantan's model, but was standing fully clothed on the floor. One hand leaning on a table and her eyes on an open newspaper. Martin and Gustav were sitting on chairs a bit further away. Like Dantan's artists, they were leaning forward, busy, engaged in conversation, you had to assume, since they were holding nothing. The room was suffused with a clean, beautiful light, but also the everyday mess that was so typical of Gustav's paintings – an overflowing ashtray, empty glasses, balled up turpentine rags.

As Rakel wandered through the rooms, it suddenly seemed so obvious: the central motif of Gustav's oeuvre was Cecilia Berg. Granted, there were some early still lifes, exteriors, nature scenes and portraits of various acquaintances, but from painting after painting, Cecilia's face turned to the onlooker with a vibrating presence, as though she might at any moment blink and let her deep, amused voice echo through the decades. But a picture, Rakel mused, is always created at the expense of another picture. The Cecilia of Gustav's paintings pushed another Cecilia out of the frame. There was an unseen figure in the dark, locked out of history, exiled to the shadow world of the invisible. And who was she?

The sound level had risen higher than ever. The oxygen seemed to be running out. Rakel tore herself away from the paintings and set to doing what she had known all along she would have to do – find Gustav.

Everywhere, she saw people she recognised but couldn't place. She passed a lady leaning on a crutch, whose raw silk suit hung loosely from her stooped form. She could tell she must have been a beauty once, but now her eyes were runny and unfocused, her lips fixed in a befuddled smile, and one corner of her mouth kept twitching. Next to her stood a bored-looking woman in her forties, typing on her phone. She was fit and blonde, dressed in tight jeans and blindingly white canvas shoes. They both looked vaguely familiar and Rakel realised they had to be Gustav's mother and sister. Further away, her dad was talking to a woman who looked like the kind of fictional character who keeps "forgetting" to eat and subsists on green apples from the first page of the novel to the last. She steered well clear of them and eventually found her brother lounging in a corner, flipping through the exhibition catalogue with a sceptical look on his face.

"Is this really what she looked like?" He held up the *Historian* portrait. In thumbnail-format, it could have passed for a photograph.

"I guess that depends on who's looking. Have you seen Gustav?"

"Nope. Have you heard back from the German yet? No? Seems dodgy. I think he's hiding something."

"Why would he be? I didn't write anything about Mum. I just asked if he would have time for 'an interview'."

"Maybe he can sense that something's fishy."

"That something's fishy? Maybe he can smell a rat too? Maybe he thinks something's rotten in the state of Denmark?"

Her brother ignored her. "I think his book's pretty good. Hey – is she *flirting* with Dad?" He nodded towards the Green Apples Woman who was tilting her head back to laugh at something Martin had said.

"Good luck to her," Rakel said.

She'd almost given up hope when she spotted Gustav across the room. He was hugging the wall, seemingly about to make his escape. Without taking her eyes off him, she said goodbye to Elis and followed.

When she cut him off, Gustav jumped so high he spilled the contents of his glass. "What the fuck – oh, Rakel, it's you. It's so unusual to see you in..." he pointed to the kimono. "Colour. My god, this place is packed. What are these people doing here? Were they just passing by? Don't they have lives? I figured it would be friends and family only." While fiddling with his shirt buttons and adjusting his glasses, he asked if she was having a good time, if she needed a drink of any kind, and what she thought of the exhibition.

"It's strange to see Mum everywhere," Rakel said, fully aware it was the wrong thing to say. She studied her godfather closely during this dangerous departure from the script, but he just took off his glasses to see if they needed cleaning.

"I would imagine," he said.

Deep inside Rakel, something quavered, like when tectonic plates move over magma and the fault lines chafe and creak. Cecilia Berg's eyes were watching her from every direction.

"I wanted to ask you something," she said. At first, her voice didn't carry, so she had to repeat the sentence.

"Go ahead," Gustav said, his face impassive.

"Why do you think she left?"

There was a long silence before he answered. "I have no idea. Not the foggiest. But there's no point dwelling on it, Rakel. Leave it be. It is what it is." He sighed, as though the topic were awkward and tedious, and then tried to change the subject.

"You were one of the people closest to her," Rakel interrupted.

"And I still don't know. People do what they do. You have to take a page out of Dylan's book. Don't look back."

There was something wrong with her field of vision, it was going dark at the edges, the world was turning into a tunnel. "You all want to confine her to how you see her," Rakel said. This time, her voice was distinctive and sharp and unstoppable. "Anything that doesn't fit, you cut off, leave outside the canvas. And we're all supposed to help you pretend. And anyone who contributes really well to this pretend world gets patted on the head. This" – she made a sweeping gesture that took in the paintings – "isn't the *truth*. It may look like her but it's not the truth. But it's the only story anyone will ever tell me about her. Can't someone just tell it like it *is*?"

Gustav had been staring mutely at the floor while she spoke, and when he looked up his big, winning smile broke out on his face as though everything in life was good and wonderful. Rakel's own face felt stiff like a death mask and tears were burning behind her eyelids.

She turned around, marched down the stairs, not moving aside for anyone, crossed the lobby and pushed open the doors, the kimono billowing like a sail in her wake.

Rakel had only made it to the other side of Götaplatsen Square when an incoming email dinged. She quickly pulled out her phone.

Philip Franke apologised for the slow reply; he'd been busy relocating to Paris. He would love to set up an interview with her. Why didn't she get back to him with some suggestions for possible dates.

Her legs buckled. For five minutes, she sat on one of the benches ringing the fountain without anyone coming after her. The moment her hands stopped shaking, she wrote back.

THE VIVA

I

INTERVIEWER: So one shouldn't be too intimidated by the blank page?

MARTIN BERG: There's really only one way to overcome writer's block, and I'm quoting William Wallace now: "Work, and do it at once like an ox and a goldsmith, a mountaineer and a street musician." There's no point waiting around for inspiration to strike. Sure, it's heavy going sometimes. You hit a rut. You can feel it drying up. Suddenly, it's just not happening, and you stare at your papers and you're, like: What the fuck? You know. The worst part is that you don't know how long it's going to last. Maybe a few hours. Maybe a few days. But you don't *know*. Maybe longer than that, and then there's really only one thing to do. You have to keep going, like some kind of *Aniara* spaceship.

*

When Cecilia couldn't make Gustav move into his flat in Masthugget or agree to admit himself to a treatment facility, she found Vendela, a widow who lived in Vaxholm, and arranged for Gustav to be her lodger.

Martin said nothing. Sure, Gustav was looking decidedly the worse for wear, but he'd probably just partied too hard for too long. Now, there would be a period of fizzy drinks in the fridge and then he'd snap out of it and start to paint again and have another exhibition and feel like of course he could have just one drink. A snifter of whisky or why not a lovely little Jäger to accompany his beer. It was the eternal cycle. There was no need to overreact, was there?

But Gustav let Cecilia take him to Vaxholm with only token protests. When she returned to Gothenburg the following evening, she poured herself a glass of wine and sat down in the living room without turning on the lights.

"So, how did it go?" Martin said, happy for the excuse to turn off the TV. The news was reporting on a cruise ferry that had foundered in the Baltic. The thought of a ship like that capsizing and pulling hundreds of people with it into the depths filled him with a strange sense of dread.

"She seems reliable. I think staying with her will do him good." Cecilia paused before continuing. "We stopped by his flat to pick up some of his things. It looked like a place where old people have lain dead for two years while the rent kept being paid by direct debit."

"He was never one for domesticity."

"There were no paintings in London, either. Not one. Brushes and paint and canvases, but no paintings. All I could find was a few ink self-portraits."

She reached out to turn on the floor lamp and a golden glow fell around her. For some reason, she looked like the Cecilia he'd never known, only imagined: the teenager in the Haga commune, sitting in her room reading while everyone else smoked weed and raucously discussed politics, who slept in woollen socks and a cardigan because no one paid the electricity bill, who never realised she was being hit on when men wanted to talk about historic materialism, but was simply eager to discuss *Das Kommunistische Manifest*. Then, when someone put an arm around her shoulder, she went stiff and uncomfortable, found an excuse to pull away, and before you knew it, she was gone, had left the party without saying goodbye, walking home through the quietly falling snow with her hands in the pockets of her duffel coat.

"Has there ever been an extended period of time when Gustav didn't paint?" she asked.

Martin pondered that. First, there had been his sketch books in upper secondary. Not long after, he'd started to experiment with oils. He'd made several paintings of Martin, who particularly recalled one where he was sprawled on the green plush sofa on Sjömansgatan, smoking.

"I've seen that one," Cecilia said. "Very Ola Billgren."

"Don't tell Gustav that. Right, and then he started doing his still lifes." Martin chuckled. "One time, I went to rinse out two dirty glasses sitting on his kitchen table, so we'd have something to drink out of. Gustav panicked. 'No, no, no – don't move them.' What I'd taken to be just his regular mess was in fact a carefully arranged motif. And after upper secondary, what did we get up to…"

"Valand," Cecilia said.

"Right. And Paris. No, I actually can't think of a substantial period of time when he wasn't painting. Except now, I guess."

His wife sighed. "That Vendela woman had a pretty decent art collection. There was an oil painting by Eugène Jansson – a friend of the family apparently – in the dining room. That made Gustav wake up a little and he started talking about painting water." She knocked back the last of her wine. "So I don't think it's a completely lost cause."

*

That autumn, Cecilia went back to work. Through his early-morning drowsiness, Martin heard the clattering of the coffee machine, followed by the creak of the stairs to the attic study. At first, her shifts lasted no more than thirty minutes, but she gradually added time, much the same way she had when she was training for the marathon. Before long, her warm weight was gone from their bed by four in the morning.

But as she resumed work on her thesis, she also grew more self-critical.

"It's not *wrong*, but it's not relevant, either," she'd say, throwing her papers down. "Clearly, I thought it was important, but I honestly have no idea why."

There were too many perspectives, too many references, the themes were too broad. The project was groaning under the weight of its own ambitions. Something had to be done, and it probably didn't involve reading a peripheral French text from the nineteenth century. "No matter how exciting that would be." She shoved piles of papers down the rubbish chute before she could change her mind. She brought down the washing-up and apple cores that had collected on her desk. She biked over to the department to see her supervisor. She went for runs. Afterwards, she fried steaks, poured the juices over her spaghetti, ate standing up at the kitchen counter.

When Martin was about to leave for work, she emerged from her study. And like when a well-respected general enters the room, the lowly privates instantly snapped to: Rakel dashed off to pack her school bag, Elis stopped fussing with his bottle, obediently sucking the contents down. Before Martin left the battlefield, she would give him a distracted kiss.

She completed her MPhil before Elis turned one.

And in large swathes, weeks and months were ripped from his life. No one chore was particularly time-consuming in itself. He went to the shops. He cooked. He attended parent–teacher conferences with his daughter and humbly accepted her teacher's paean about her pre-cocious intelligence. He read *Curious George* to his son for the eight hundred and fifth time. He started a wash. He discovered he'd for-gotten to pay the bills and had to go through the envelopes that had accumulated in a pile on the hallway dresser. He expended quite a lot of time and energy transporting his entire family to Stockholm and settling them in with his in-laws, so that he could go to his best friend's first solo exhibition in years. He went to work. He reserved a stand at the book fair. He talked on the phone to the barely English-speaking owner of a printer in Riga, trying to make the man explain what in the world was keeping them from printing a sixth run of a book everyone wanted to read, which was "one of the twentieth century's major liter-ary sensations" (*Aftonbladet*), "a dizzying, raw, and searingly beautiful depiction of a person's descent into addiction" (*Dagens Nyheter*), in short a "bestselling cult novel for our times" (*Svensk Bokhandel*). His wife scattered used teabags and leaking red pens everywhere. He found a manuscript under the sofa. He chased his son through Slottsskogen Park because apparently he'd learned how to run on his trembling, cherub-like legs and had now set his course for the duck pond. He bought shin guards for his daughter, who had announced she wanted to play football. He passed out the minute his head hit the pillow.

When had his own father found time to sit on the veranda or paint the boat? All those hours spent on the boat – where had they come from? But then, Birgitta Berg had never slammed down a book on the table in front of her husband, saying: "So, have you read this one, or what?", forcing him to admit that while he'd read Sartre, Camus, Lévi-Strauss, Merleau-Ponty, Barthes and Foucault, his campaign to conquer French philosophy had completely overlooked the book now staring belligerently up at him. Nor had Birgitta Berg demanded that her husband then read that book, once and for all, and his father hadn't had to make an honest attempt at it, but for various reasons not get further than page 133 (out of 840) only to then be haunted by *The Other Sex* for six full months before surreptitiously sneaking it back onto the shelf.

They received sporadic postcards from Gustav that autumn and winter, but with the arrival of spring, roughly six months after Cecilia brought him back from London, came a letter. It was handwritten over several sheets of paper, and probably the longest missive Gustav had managed during their almost twenty-seven years of friendship. Gustav told them about how he and Vendela had pruned trees, dug flowerbeds, sowed, visited a nursery and purchased six big sacks of topsoil. After lugging the bags from the car, Gustav had been completely knackered the rest of the day. Having never participated in the many preparations for spring before, he now saw spring in a completely new light, he wrote. A few months earlier, he'd reluctantly knelt down and aimlessly poked lumpy bulbs into the ground because Vendela had a back spasm and was unable to do it herself. Now, he watched crocuses, hyacinths and daffodils sprout with all the pride of the creator. When the apple trees bloomed, he went on an inspection round, like some kind of lord of the manor. For weeks, he was trepidatious about how some newly planted irises and anemones would fare.

"Are anemones really flowers?" Martin called to his wife.

"Yes."

"I thought they were things that lived in the ocean?"

"That too."

"Is this general knowledge? Do people know this?"

Cecilia appeared in the doorway, asking why on earth he wanted to know; Martin gave her a dismissive wave and turned his attention back to the letter.

Gustav had, above all, viewed spring as the time when drinking outside became more socially acceptable and less painful, he wrote, but Vendela's involvement in the botanical life of her garden had changed his perspective. Now he was working on some paintings on that theme.

That surprised Martin, because they'd always made fun of nature scenes and landscape painting. The only thing that had met with their approval was Carl Fredrik Hill's post-psychosis works. But now, Gustav Becker was sitting in an old widow's garden, painting flowers and waxing lyrical about the Stockholm archipelago.

"So long as he's painting," Cecilia said.

"But it's not *him*. Gustav paints portraits and still lifes with ashtrays and old socks. What's the next step? 'Lady with poodle'?"

That August, there was another exhibition. In the spirit of internationalism, KG had changed the name of his operation from Galleri Hammarsten to Hammarsten Gallery. Stepping into the cool venue, Martin for some reason wanted to be anywhere but there. The latesummer heat shimmered above the asphalt, and they'd spent all morning on a train with no air conditioning. Elis had enthusiastically smeared yoghurt all over Martin's shirt. Once they got to Lars and Inger's flat, it turned out he'd neglected to pack a spare, and he didn't want to go in a T-shirt, even though that was probably what Gustav would be wearing. Inger immediately ironed one of Lars's shirts, but Dr Wikner was a bit taller than Martin and the shirt consequently a touch too large, and now Martin couldn't decide whether to roll up the sleeves. Needless to say, everyone else in the sodding place was wearing perfectly fitted shirts. And they had Vera Wikner trailing in their wake, too. After one term of art history, she'd announced that she was going to become a gallerist or possibly an art trader. "There's an awful lot of people with money but no taste, and I have taste but no money – an excellent arrangement for everyone involved." When she'd asked if she could come with them to the exhibition, Cecilia had just sighed and said fine, if it was that important to her. Martin wished Vera had worn a longer dress and significantly less make-up. She was probably trying to look older than twenty, or however old she was now, but the effect was the opposite, if anything. She sashayed through the gallery, blissfully ignorant of the fact that she looked like a student on a field trip.

"Martin Berg, long time no see." KG appeared, insisting on shaking his hand too hard for too long. "Everything good with you? Wonderful, wonderful. I hear the publishing company's doing well? And here's Cecilia. *Really* great to have you here."

Despite the heat, he was wearing a black suit. He rambled on about Gustav Becker's new "sphere of motifs" and the Stockholm Art Fair. When Martin felt a familiar hand on his shoulder, his entire body gave a start.

Gustav was tanned and straight-backed and beamed like the sun. He'd been away from the city for so long all the impressions were making his head spin, he told them. Just stepping out into the street was a veritable shock. Vendela had said he could stay as long as he liked (at this point he introduced them to very small, very Chanel-clad old lady with squinting peppercorn eyes) but he was going to try to move back in the autumn, because nowhere was autumn more amazing than in Stockholm, wouldn't they agree?

Vendela and Cecilia exchanged a quick look.

It turned out he had, in fact, painted his art-collecting landlady and her dog – a fox terrier, someone informed them. Everyone except Martin seemed to find the portrait moving. Until that point, Gustav's canvases had grown larger from year to year, but now, the largest was twenty by thirty inches. Not even the Vendela portrait was particularly large, even though the background, a cluttered drawing room, could have given the painting a satirical edge if he'd emphasised it more – the desiccated old lady in her gigantic, lavish home, a modern Medici, the playing-card getup with the lace collar and gold embroidery swapped for a sober suit and pearl necklace and so on.

There were about ten smaller paintings as well. Half of them were of black spruce trees reflected in a silvery sliver of water. A few of the skies were the gas-flame shade of blue Gustav had used in his early urban landscapes, while others tended towards absinthe-green, a new colour for him. The rest of the paintings were studies of plant life, organic and grotesque in the colour palette of early spring and late autumn. Close up, they were hyper-detailed, but take a few steps back and they appeared almost abstract.

"Like a reverse Monet," Cecilia commented.

It was the first time there was no portrait of her.

A few days later, the exhibition was reviewed in *Dagens Nyheter*. Martin read it with a racing heart and a churning stomach. It was a positive review, and when Martin put the paper down, he didn't quite know how to feel.

*

People slapped him on the back when the first edition of Lucas Bell's book sold out in a month, as though it were his achievement and not the author's. They congratulated him when another author on their list was nominated for a literary award. Some people thanked him in their forewords. "My publisher Martin Berg, whose guidance has been invaluable." But when Publisher Martin Berg thought back to what this invaluable guidance had consisted of, he could find nothing beyond perfectly normal input like "strike that", "flesh that part out", and "maybe we should consider a different title". He had a nagging feeling anyone could do what he was doing.

When he complained to his wife, she said: "So write, then. Finish your novel."

He protested: it was virtually impossible to write a novel while working full-time. And with two children, too. Writing fiction wasn't like writing scholarly texts, you couldn't just bang them out, you had to process and—

"Then why don't you work less?"

How was he supposed to "work less" when he was running a business? There was no one to pick up the slack. It would eat away at him the whole time. He needed peace and quiet, ample time and space; he wouldn't get anything done in a few random hours here and there.

"Then use your parental leave," Cecilia said. "Elis is still entitled to four hours of nursery, even if you're home. Or is four hours not enough to get anything done, either?"

Martin pointed out that, in his case, taking parental leave was no different from working less, it simply meant Per and Sanna would have to do more, or that Martin would have to work at night, and consequently it wasn't a sustainable solution, but the further he got, the more sceptical she looked.

"But you shut yourself up in your study and wrote…" He remembered Elis knocking over his porridge, Rakel completely uncontactable with her nose in *Kitty Drew and the Secret of Shadow Ranch*, the coffee getting cold on the kitchen counter, and no waterproof trousers to be found anywhere.

It was the wrong thing to say, he could tell from the way she tossed her hair and the hardness of her mouth, so he immediately added: "And I can't multitask like you can. I have to do one thing at a time. *Cissi.* Come on. Don't leave – what the fuck, you can't just *leave.*"

He had lunch with Per Andrén and found himself talking extensively and angrily about how lack of time was keeping him from writing.

"Isn't half the point of running your own business that you can spend your time as you see fit?" Per said. "You don't have a boss. You don't clock in and out. There's nothing to say you have to be here at eight."

Martin objected: there was work to do, and that work would still be there waiting for him if he chose to come in later.

Per countered: how much time did Martin spend drinking coffee, having very long phone conversations with his feet on the desk, flipping through literary magazines, or going over proofs just one more time, even though someone else had already gone over it one more time? Did it make a book better if its author had infinite time to tinker with it? Had anyone ever completed anything without a deadline?

"Here's what you do," Per said. "Tuesday, Wednesday and Thursday, you get up like you normally would in the morning. Then you write until lunch and come in for the afternoon. Give it a month. Starting next week. If it turns out to be unsustainable, we'll regroup. Okay? Great. It's a deal."

"I don't know if it works that way."

"It almost seems like you don't really want to write that novel."

"Of course I do." Martin waved for the bill. He suddenly felt hot. "Of course I do. So okay. Let's do it. Why not."

Unfortunately, a series of practical problems soon presented themselves. First – what was he supposed to write on? Cecilia was very attached to her Olivetti. It clattered and banged and dinged and then she pulled the paper out of the roller and inserted a new sheet. Martin had tried to make her see the wisdom of switching over to a computer, but she didn't like, as she put it, the aesthetic aspect of it.

"But it's very convenient," Martin said. "You can save what you write on floppy discs. You wouldn't need all these stacks of paper."

"It may be practical, but it's ugly."

"If this were the nineteenth century, you'd be banging on about how cosy candles are, and why switch to electricity when you already have perfectly serviceable kerosene lamps?"

He'd been sceptical about computers himself. It was one thing at work; he had a hard time imagining his professional life without a PC. But at home? For a novel? Text from a typewriter had a very particular physical quality. It radiated achievement, toil. He'd had long discussions with Per, embracer and advocate of all things technological, in which he himself had been cast in the role of Luddite. He had to ask himself *what* aspect of typewriting it was he was clinging to, since no one could deny that the computer was superior in every practical sense.

Besides, he'd just purchased a computer for home use, tax-deductible, and he had to use it for something.

The next problem was trickier. What was he going to write? He read through *Night Sonnets* with a nagging feeling he'd have to rewrite large parts of it. Maybe the whole thing. Should he keep working on it? Or start something new? But he had no ideas whatsoever, and there was some good stuff in *Night Sonnets*. He decided to give it one last chance.

And so, the following Tuesday he sat down at his desk after dropping the children off at school and nursery. The cursor blinked. He wrote a few words. Deleted them. Wrote some more, deleted them, too.

It was certainly an advantage not to have to see how much you'd deleted.

But half an hour later, when Martin still hadn't got past a stubborn *tabula rasa*, he turned the computer off and put the monitor on the floor. He fetched his typewriter from the cupboard and set it down in the computer's place.

He inserted a sheet of paper.

He stared at the paper for a while.

He went to fetch a cup of coffee.

It really was no wonder he found it hard to focus with such a messy desk. He jumped up and began to tidy, getting rid of all the papers, the stacks of books, the envelopes. Some of the envelopes had to be opened, since he'd apparently neglected to do so before. He had to organise his work papers. He put everything he didn't know what to do with on the floor for further consideration down the line, but the floor turned out to be dusty. He had to vacuum. There was something ineffably depressing about dusty papers. The window was filthy, too, now that he thought about it. The sunlight showed it up clearly. He spent half an hour cleaning it.

When he sat back down at his desk, he stared for a long time at the William Wallace quote he'd pinned to the wall in front of him:

To write is to refuse to die.

The problem was that somewhere between Martin's interior and the paper's exterior, something went awry. The words warped, morphing into something else. He no longer recognised what he'd written as what he'd felt. And he knew he could do better. That within him lay the means to create something grander. If he could just draw it out. If *someone else* could just draw it out. Because what was the point of creating something mediocre? The world was already full of half-felt emotions, of trifling love stories, of poorly worded melodramas. They found their way to the publishing company at regular intervals, this paltriness of human existence, squeezed in between a foreword in a cursive font and a teary epilogue, and the copy was always terrible, too. (Why couldn't they put some effort into typing up their manuscripts neatly? Did they imagine he would find their texts so brilliant he wouldn't even notice the white-out, pen scribbles and outright typos?). He read them listlessly, thinking about all the work that had gone into the sheaf of papers in his hands, about all the dreams it held within it, and about how he read two chapters and then, with what had to be sheer ill will, put together a personal rejection letter. Those letters tended to start out critically but grow gentler towards the end, because, as he wrote, he was inevitably struck by the bottomless tragedy of all the time the author had wasted. On something that was pointless in the grand scheme of things. All those hours sitting at a desk. *Thank you for your interest, but.*

It was an effort that could only be made up for by triumph.

Martin stood up so abruptly he knocked his chair over.

He paced around the flat. From his study to the kitchen through the hallway into Rakel's room and the living room. He still had hours before he was supposed to be at work.

It hadn't occurred to him that Cecilia would be home, too. Or rather: in his fantasy, the two of them took coffee breaks together, discussed their work, the sun slanted in across the kitchen table, casting prisms through their glasses, and he was a man in his thirties who ran a publishing company and was writing a novel and she was his beautiful wife and together they had two children with turn-of-the-century names, and they lived in this spacious flat on Djurgårdsgatan in Majorna, this gem of a neighbourhoods, a stone's throw from the lazy river with its majestic ferryboats.

He hadn't given any thought to the constant click-clack of her typewriter. It was nigh impossible to enter a proper trance over the whiteness of the white paper, over the whiteness of his own awareness and the empty, desolate whiteness of existence in general, and then maybe smoke a cigarette to see if that triggered some kind of interesting thought process, when you had to listen to someone else's typewriter clattering upstairs.

He went back to his study and closed the door.

He sat down and stared at the paper. He stared at the keys. He stared at the desktop, now cleared of every last object. (Maybe that was the problem? Maybe he needed to surround himself with some kind of creative chaos?)

Strindberg went through his Inferno crisis alone. He wandered around Paris, drinking absinthe and hating life all by himself. He did *not* share a flat with an insanely productive academic. And when James Joyce was wrestling with *Finnegan's Wake*, he was at least spared from having to see Nora Joyce's stack of finished pages growing and growing.

Martin picked up the last chapter again. At some point, he must have stumbled into a dead end. Perhaps the easiest solution was to rewrite it – yes. He was going to rewrite it and see if he could get it right.

From the attic came a faint patter, like rain.

*

A month later, *Night Sonnets* had once more been consigned to its shoebox sarcophagus, and Martin had begun work on synopses for at least three new novels. Several times he thought he'd hit upon a promising subject, but each time it turned out to be too abstract. Countless

Post-it notes had in the moment of scribbling seemed to hold within them whole books, but closer scrutiny inevitably revealed that it was just a bunch of words.

He knew full well one should write what one wants to read. But what did Martin Berg want to read? That hadn't already been written by someone else? The only thing he could think of was a thorough and clear-eyed biography about William Wallace, something along the lines of Ray Monk's book on Wittgenstein. He cycled to the university library to establish beyond doubt, with the aid of a still-bleary-eyed librarian, that the only Wallace biography in existence was a book written twenty-five years earlier by Wallace's nephew. Martin remembered it as a series of disjointed, idealising observations that painted a picture of a harmless writer of puns whose literary works were mentioned only in passing, like a backdrop against which Wallace's delightful eccentricities played out. There was absolutely a gap in the market here. And given that Wallace was a much bigger name in the English-speaking world, it might even be translated. The book would be printed on thick, cream paper and lavishly illustrated with photographs. Its publication would be accompanied by new editions of Wallace's most important works. Maybe they could even sort out a translation of *Times and Clocks and Watches* – which would be big since it was considered untranslatable. The newspapers would write about the rediscovered Wallace. Martin Berg, a Howard Carter of literature, would go on all the most prestigious culture shows and give interviews about an undeservedly forgotten author. He wouldn't be surprised if he was nominated for the August Prize.

"That's a pretty good idea," Cecilia said. "But I thought you wanted to write a novel?"

He was going to be an Author of Biographies. Eternally stuck writing about the lives of others. If he ever managed to squeeze out a novel, it would happen in the massive shadow of what he had written about writing.

Martin rifled through his papers and took his notebook with him to Java but the espresso and the cigarettes he smoked mostly for the sake of it made him so wired his thoughts rattled around his skull like the worst kind of experimental jazz. (A sentence he wrote down with a slightly trembling hand before giving up and going home.)

*

Such was Martin Berg's life, when on the first day of the Gothenburg Book Fair, he heaved a box of books up on a table and straightened back up.

It was the first quiet moment he'd had in weeks. He'd been so busy preparing for the fair he hadn't had time to write a single word, but that could hardly be expected of him, could it? The floor of their stand was covered with Persian rugs from Dr Wikner's rug import venture in the eighties. On the table were stacks of Berg & Andrén's current titles. A storage cupboard held several boxes of hot-off-the-press copies of *A Season in Hell*. There was no Lucas Bell, however, even though he'd promised to come over for a book signing – he'd been admitted to a rehab facility just days before. "He couldn't hold off on overdosing for just a few more days?" Per had snapped. Now, Martin had to surrender to the rhythm of the fair. Sell books. Talk to industry people. Wolf down a baguette in ten minutes. Drink wine after closing. It was all he had to do; Cecilia had taken the children to the summer house.

Martin contemplated the slow stream of visitors. For the first time in a long time, he felt completely content.

And then he suddenly found himself face to face with Diane Thomas from Paris. Diane, who ten years earlier had turned away as though he'd never mattered, looked confused for a split second. Then her face broke into a big, carefree smile.

II

INTERVIEWER: How do you maintain that kind of work ethic?
MARTIN BERG: You have to not let yourself be distracted by trivialities. Stay focused. Not go off on tangents. You have to resist all the

distractions life constantly offers. In a way, it's very simple. Abstain, and work instead.

*

With a degree of surprise, Martin noted that the passage of time had reset the balance. They were two old friends, improbably running into each other. They laughed brightly the way people do when that happens. They asked: "What are you doing here?" and "How are you doing?" Diane was the one who supplied the superlatives ("*quelle chance, c'est fantastique*"). Diane was the one who asked if he wanted to meet up later. Diane was the one who unfolded a tourist map to show him where her hotel was.

They had a glass of wine and there was nothing wrong with that.

He didn't really have the time or inclination to meet up with her for *un verre* and tried to come up with a good excuse until the very end. But when she appeared again just before closing, he heard himself agree to meet outside the main entrance in fifteen minutes. They went to Klara. Martin Berg's main focus was to keep things as brief as possible. If he'd had any ulterior motives, would he have gone to a place where he was virtually guaranteed to bump into someone he knew? One of Cecilia's fellow PhD candidates or colleagues? No. He didn't give it a second thought. He was a man without guilt.

Mademoiselle Thomas (no wedding ring) was nearing thirty-five, but aside from having cut her hair short, she looked the same. If anything, the short hair made her look younger. An annoyed Irène Jacob. She shook her fringe out of her face, ordered a bottle of red wine, lit a cigarette, and said it was a relief to get away from Hélène, who was a bore. Then she told him about her professional life, which was confusing and labyrinthine. Every job seemed to have ricocheted her off to another – sometimes in a completely different field – which was how she'd ended up working for Alliance Française, whom she was now representing at the fair, together with this Hélène. Because this year's theme was cultural diversity, she reminded him when he looked questioning. Their stand was on the second floor. You could sign up for language courses and so on. She waved away his follow-up questions. She asked about his life, but when he told her about the publishing company, Cecilia and the children, her eyes began to flit around the room.

"This is a nice place," she said.

"Yeah, sure…"

He mostly welcomed the opportunity to speak French. It was hard going at first, but became easier as he went along. When they ran out of wine, he hurriedly took his leave before she could order more. He made his excuses, reminded her that he'd told her he couldn't stay long, that he was meeting a colleague and so on, but this was his card, if she wanted to give him a ring – yes, well, that's it, isn't it, more cheek kisses.

Martin stepped out into the September night. It smelled like rain and rotting leaves. He walked towards Avenyn. Only then did he realise it had been pointless to give her his office number – since he wouldn't be there. He supposed he should buy a mobile phone, like Per.

The next day, everything reminded him of Paris. A whirl of dancing leaves suddenly brought to life an autumnal Jardin des Tuileries. The coffee that burned his tongue brought to mind the feisty Madame who ran the café on the corner. Back then, life had fit around his writing, not the other way around. He'd woken up when he felt like it and had still had hour upon hour of undisturbed writing time ahead of him. But since he'd been so young, he hadn't had the sense to appreciate it, hadn't realised it would one day change. He'd taken it for granted that he could spend four hours in a café and still have most of the day left. He'd never had to make much of a distinction between workweek and weekend as far as wine-drinking went. And if he'd been able to see ten years into the future, he would almost definitely have been horrified by the 34-year-old Martin who opted for a small beer because he couldn't bear to be hungover, who fell asleep at ten on a Friday night, who worried about affording a new car.

A young man in a baggy turtleneck, who spent a good long while carefully examining the books they had for sale, made him recall himself at the second-hand bookshops lining the Seine. (Martin had just decided to give him a discount when he slunk off without buying anything.) After lunch, he had a sudden urge to smoke, but they didn't sell Gauloises at the corner shop. He settled for Lucky Strike.

At closing, he invented an excuse to go up to the second floor and spent some time looking for Alliance Française. When he found their stand, she wasn't there. He left without leaving a message with anyone.

That evening, he went with Per and some other people to a party at Scandic. Per looked euphoric and inexhaustible; he discreetly pointed out people to Martin.

"And there – hey, you, you're not listening?"

"I am, I am. I'm just tired."

"Here, have some champagne."

"No, I'm fine…"

"Drink! There. Now where was I? Oh, right…"

It was far too late when he cycled home, slowly and carefully so as not to wobble. The flat was empty and quiet. It was tempting to fall asleep in his clothes, but he at least managed to pull off his jeans.

On Saturday, he barely had time to think, and his distraction passed for a becoming hangover coupled with sleep deprivation. After scarfing down a limp pasta salad, he once again set his course for the stand on the second floor, this time with determined steps.

*

According to the calendar, it was over in a week, but in the lived experience, time behaved capriciously and unpredictably. Days stretched to breaking point. Hours were either endless or flew by like minutes. 1986, which had long since faded to a safe distance, became tangibly present. Afterwards, he could never be entirely sure how long it went on for, not even after double-checking the offending week in the calendar. There was no trace of her anywhere. Not the tiniest of notes. He'd had no need to note down the times of their meetings, even if he'd been brazen enough to chance it. Those times, nonchalantly agreed to and continentally negotiable, were constantly lit up in his mind. That other people could be indifferent to them was incomprehensible.

They went to a restaurant he'd read about in the paper but never visited. He'd prepared an explanation that wasn't even a lie about how he was meeting someone he knew: she was an old acquaintance from Paris he'd run into at the fair.

They must have talked about something. They gazed into each other's eyes. Crystal prisms sparkled. White tablecloths and the din of conversation. Her pale neck. French fish soup. Bill, please. A short walk along a rain-soaked street. Lingering steps. Cognac in the hotel bar, like amber. A leg against his leg. A hand on his hand. The lift. The jangle of keys. A room full of nocturnal light. Wide bed, neatly made. The white, silent hotel sheets.

*

He was convinced Cecilia would know instantly. That his face or voice would somehow betray him. But when she acted the same as ever, he started to worry about her finding compromising evidence. A hair? A letter steamed open by a worried wife's trembling hands?

Yet even so, he met up with Diane two more times.

Her plan was to go to Stockholm that Monday, on holiday. They'd said goodbye and he was proud of the unsentimental way he'd handled it. While she climbed aboard a northbound train, he went back to the office. He was busy counting money and organising receipts when the phone rang. She'd decided to stay a few more days. Stockholm could wait. She'd been walking around the city, through the 'Aga neighbourhood, it was *très jolie*, would he like to have dinner later?

But he'd promised to look after the children so Cecilia could go for a run. He forced himself to say no. Just then, Per entered, so he asked her to call him back tomorrow and quickly hung up.

Tuesday passed in slow motion. He made coffee in the kitchenette. Sat down at his desk, shuffled papers. The phone rang but it wasn't her. Went to the bathroom, fetched the post. The phone rang again, a nervous individual asking if they'd had a chance to read his manuscript. Back to the desk, drumming his fingers, staring at the phone. Opened his post and sorted it into piles. Went to fetch another cup of coffee.

Obviously the best thing would be for her to leave and never come back. He wasn't the adulterous type.

He pictured a solemn conversation with the children, a flight during which he studied the tops of clouds and miniature Belgian villages, disembarking the RER at Châtelet. And there, Martin Berg emerges from the underground into the sunshine, throws his jacket over his shoulder, blinded by the harsh light. *Au revoir*, Sweden, grey, stagnant old Sweden with its slushy streets and cold springs and silent shadows across the pavements, where Gustav Becker paints close-ups of autumnal meadows and everyone talks about how much fun they had in the eighties.

She called around two, and they agreed to meet up an hour later.

The next day, he went to her hotel around lunchtime. He hadn't planned to. But it's what happened. He stayed until five. Before he left, he took a long shower and was careful not to get his hair wet, in case Cecilia asked about it. But she hurried up to her study the moment she could hand over Elis and stayed there for several hours; she wouldn't have noticed if he'd been wearing a tuxedo and top hat.

On Thursday, a "French girl" had called the office several times, asking for him. But Martin Berg was very busy with various tasks and didn't have time to call back. Not until Friday night did he shut himself in a payphone booth and insert enough coins to call the hotel front desk, which informed him that unfortunately, Mademoiselle Thomas had checked out.

INTERVIEWER: So, to wrap up, do you have any advice to people who want to write?

MARTIN BERG: Don't shy away from the truth. That's important. [*laughing*] I think that's the only piece of advice I have to offer.

*

"Martin? Is that you?" Gustav's voice was hoarse with sleep.

"Good morning," Martin said.

"Why are you whispering?"

"I'm not whispering, am I?"

"It sounded suspiciously like a whisper, if you're asking me." A yawn, then the click of a lighter.

"It... I... it's been so long," Martin said. "I wanted to see how you're doing?"

It had been a week since Diane. It already felt unreal. Maybe because he hadn't talked to anyone about it, nor written about it, nothing. It was beyond words. A thought can be forgotten and hidden away, but once it's spoken aloud to another person, there's no way back. He'd begun to worry about being alone with Cecilia, because the unspoken was always there between them. In bed, it felt like they were lying on thin ice. Underneath, a black, cold abyss. Words would have weighed too much.

He was sure she had no idea. She couldn't possibly. And Cecilia, you had to give her that, wasn't the jealous type. The notion that he might be interested in someone other than her had never crossed her mind. She just sat upstairs, typing away, expecting the world to be exactly how she'd left it when she came back down. She absently twirled spaghetti around her fork and told Rakel to put her book down, absently asked him about work. And then she answered I see, oh dear, hmm, okay, and it made him even more annoyed that she wouldn't spare him more effort than that. Responding like some dutiful stay-at-home mother when she was certainly capable of actually helping him with his problems.

"Hello? Are you still there?"

"What? Yes – I'm here. What were you saying?"

"I was just asking about Cissi and the kids."

"They're great. Just great."

"Rakel wouldn't happen to be around, would she? So I can get an update on what's new in the world of dinosaurs."

"I think she's over dinosaurs."

"My god, yes, she's almost a teenager."

"She's nine."

"That's what I'm saying. Four more years, then she'll be sneaking cigarettes behind the school and hooking up with some moped guy."

"I don't think that's Rakel's thing…"

"That's what they all say, my friend. That's what they all say. But seriously, is she around?"

*

Life went on. Make breakfast, get dressed. Nursery, school. Don't forget to take the bin out. Go to work. Come back home. Cook dinner, help with homework. Children's programmes, baths. Flip through the paper, watch the news. Read for a bit in bed. Meanwhile, October's foliage rained away and November came, a grey and slushy month cast in semi-twilight. Cars spattered through puddles, the trams were full of moist heat and stuffy red noses. Advent candelabra appeared in windows and Rakel came down with tonsillitis. Everyone reminisced about last year's snow, and, just like the children, Martin hoped something similar would happen again, fathoms of snow blanketing everything, making the world new and unwritten.

The urge to write returned. He couldn't remember when he'd last felt it. He shoved the Wallace project aside and sat up straighter at his desk.

SYNOPSIS. The main character, a middle-aged man in the cultural sector (dramatist, director?), leads a humdrum life with
his wife (culture journalist?) and their children. (Or maybe
they don't have children yet? Children clearly add a certain
measure of moral complexity.) The man is putting on [A play]
and one of the people auditioning for the role of X is a woman
who exerts a mystical, magnetic pull on the director. At first,
he tries to tell himself it's because of her dramatic talent,
but he soon accepts that it's more than that. The life he is
building with his wife fragments and collapses

A classic tale, sure, but he could write it with intensity and verve, film
noir-esque, like a thriller. All black and crimson. The only problem
was that he wasn't sure how it would end. The ending that appealed
to him the most – the Director and Actress end up together and all is
well – was also the one that possessed the least (not to say zero) literary
quality.

He wrote for about an hour, then just sat there, staring out of the
window that only showed his own reflection.

One of the questions they'd debated in his upper-secondary philosophy classes was this: if a tree falls in the woods and no one hears it, did
it make a sound?

If no one ever finds out about X, can you really say X happened?
Martin swore Cecilia would never find out. He would shield her from
this. He was almost moved by his own resolve. At the same time,
people had affairs all the time. Literature was full of infidelity. In films,
people were constantly cheating. Just because normal people didn't
advertise it didn't mean it didn't happen. Probably more often than
you'd think. And life went on. It didn't necessarily end like for Emma
Bovary or Anna Karenina, or even T.S. Garp and Helen Holm.

Maybe Cecilia, too…

The moment the thought occurred to him, it began to leak acid.
Cecilia and one of her fellow PhD students. Or an old course mate.

Or Max with his German translations. Though Max was only twenty-four or twenty-five. The professors and docents were more worrying. Martin tried to recall the people behind the names that flashed by when she talked about her work and the fact that they were no more than shadows only made things worse. For days, he was haunted by visions. Men had always been more interested in Cecilia than she in them. Lethal combination. She could easily end up in some kind of situation and for her own inscrutable reasons decide to go through with it.

At night, he held her close. Without knowing what he was looking for, he flipped through her address book. He tried to see her the way other men might. Her beautiful but slightly weary face, her long neck, the sweeping line of her chin. Slender and fair, she leaned against the kitchen counter, deeply absorbed in the newspaper, pushing a strand of hair behind her ear. One time, they'd agreed to meet up in town – they were going to the bank – and he didn't recognise her until she was just a few steps away. Before Cecilia materialised, she'd been an unknown woman in a camel hair coat.

He developed a bad habit of constantly asking her what she was thinking. Wasn't she more closed-off than usual? Tenser? Inaccessible? She often said: "What?" as if she hadn't been listening. She pulled away at night. Sometimes, he woke up to find her gone. He told himself she was just in the bathroom, and went back to sleep. When he asked if she was okay, she nodded, said she was just stressed out about her thesis. The deadline was approaching. She might have to rewrite some sections.

And she ran a hand through her hair, making her curls even unrulier, and stared into space, disappearing into her mind.

*

Just as the Director decides to take charge of his life and take The Leap, he finds out the Actress is having an affair with another member of the cast, a handsome but smug young man in some minor role. He goes back to his life with the Culture Journalist and observes the torrid yet incredibly clichéd love affair between the two actors from a distance. He knows it will end in tears and is not surprised when the Actress comes to see him, bitter, her eyes red from crying. But it's too late: /.../

*

Diane had left an address, and for a long time he carried it around in his wallet. Then, he crumpled it up and threw it in the canal.

*

A date was set for her viva and Cecilia's workdays grew longer and longer. Martin encouraged her to take all the time she needed, he picked up the children every day, did the shopping, cooked, sent her to her study, suggested she stay on campus so she could work in peace. That winter, they rarely went to bed at the same time. She was up before anyone else in the mornings. Despite the weather, she laced up her running shoes and disappeared out on runs that lasted for hours. And yet she was almost never tired. There were dark circles under her eyes, but her face shone with febrile intensity. She ate her food in a fast and focused way, but it was as though the food could find no purchase. Her shirts hung from bony shoulders. She used a hammer and nail to make a new hole in her belt. They were having sex again, but always in complete darkness, in the borderland between sleeping and waking, and without saying a word. Afterwards, she always fell asleep instantly.

They spent Christmas in the Wikner villa. Within days, the library was cluttered with stacks of paper and open books, forgotten orange peel and dried-up teabags, plates with what was left of the Christmas fare she ate bent over the desk.

He asked her to take it easy, but she just shot him a hard smile, stony-eyed.

IV

INTERVIEWER: Thank you, and on that note, I think it's time to wrap this up.

MARTIN BERG: Thank you.

*

In hindsight, every detail seemed sharply illuminated, as though by the light in an interrogation room or a museum display case, the kind of light that casts no shadow, leaves nothing hidden.

It wasn't just the day it happened, it was the weeks before it, too, days that would undoubtedly have faded into obscurity had he not kept going over every hour again and again. The hours flickered past so quickly he had to shut his eyes: a parade of everyday events that with each iteration seemed more and more absurd and incomprehensible. He scoured every corner of his recollection for signs he might have missed that could have alerted him to what was about to happen.

There was a period of two weeks between her viva and the night she disappeared. As Martin would later tell the police (not that they were really asking) nothing of note happened during those weeks. Cecilia worked on preparing her thesis for publication, but not at the same frenzied pace as before. She no longer forgot what she was supposed to buy from the shops. She aired duvets, changed sheets and gave the flat a thorough clean. One time, he came home to the cosy, lingering warmth of the tiled stove. Cecilia liked their tiled stoves in theory, but rarely made use of them in practice; now, she'd both lit a fire and given the rugs a good beating. She dropped off and picked up Elis from his nursery, helped Rakel with her homework, went out for her runs.

True, he often asked her what she was thinking, and she replied: "Nothing," without meeting his eyes. And true, she sometimes stood by the window for longer than she had reason to, gazing out at the blue light of dusk enveloping the park and the puddles of light around the street lamps, unapproachable with her arms wrapped around herself as though she were cold.

But he didn't know how to convey that to the mildly sceptical police officer, who seemed to think his wife had simply taken off, the way wives sometimes do. So he said nothing.

*

The night before, a Friday, they'd had dinner as usual. Cecilia spent a long time reading to Elis and then sat with Rakel for a while. When the children had turned their lights out, she thumped onto the sofa and started watching *Rocky*, which was on TV, with great interest.

He kissed her goodnight.

At half past seven the next morning, he was woken up by Elis crawling into bed with him, asking for Mummy.

Martin blinked, trying to orient himself. His body was heavy and his brain slow. He checked the time: he'd had a full eight hours of sleep. How much sleep would it take for him to wake up feeling like a human being?

"I'm sure Mum's in her study," he said. They'd installed a gate to keep Elis from attempting precarious feats of climbing. "Why don't you watch some TV?"

"I'm hungry," Elis said.

Martin pulled on the first T-shirt he could find over his pyjama bottoms and hoisted his son up onto his hip.

On his way to the kitchen, he called up the stairs to the study. No answer.

"Mummy's probably out running," he told Elis. "Go to the kitchen and I'll be there in a second."

Elis slipped out of his arms like a small fish.

Rakel shuffled into the kitchen in her nightgown, sleepy, her hair one big tangle. Martin made scrambled eggs and semolina porridge. Rakel reminded him she had a game that afternoon.

It wasn't until Elis had finished his protracted eating process and sat down in front of the children's channel that Martin began to feel annoyed. She could at least have left a note. It was, in fact, so bloody like Cecilia to head off on some kind of morning odyssey and not give a toss that someone else (which was to say him) would have to deal with making breakfast and getting the children ready. Hopefully, she was planning to take Rakel to her game. Hopefully, she would appear in the hallway any moment now, sweaty and apologetic. Hopefully, he wouldn't even have to mention the fact that she'd dumped the whole morning routine on him.

With Elis glued to the TV, Martin was able to drink two cups of coffee and read the entire culture section from start to finish without being interrupted. By the time he reached the film reviews, it was ten o'clock.

At first, he spent a good long while working himself up by preparing a righteously annoyed speech on the subject of Responsibility and Communication. He recalled other times when she'd disappeared without a word and then been surprised when he was worried. "I didn't realise you would even notice," she'd said once, as though she were an invisible person who could come and go as she pleased. When he was angry with her, she was devastated. And even so, something like this happened – she took off somewhere, without a peep, without even leaving a fucking *note*, how long did it take to write a note to say where you were going – but then, it wasn't that it would have taken too long to write a note, it was that it didn't even occur to her that this was a textbook example of information she should share, because she walked around with her head in the clouds, distracted Docent Cecilia Berg, who was apparently too intellectually advanced to spend a Saturday morning with her family.

He folded an entire load of laundry, mostly to have one more thing to reproach her with.

Around eleven, annoyance gave way to something else. It started as vague nausea. Over the next half hour, it slowly spread through his body, becoming harder to ignore. With every minute that passed without Cecilia's steps echoing in the stairwell, he inched closer to the core of his concern.

She should have been back by now.

The coffee, his fourth cup, tasted of nothing. The sound of children's TV reached him from what seemed like a mile away. (Normally, Elis wasn't allowed to spend this long in front of the TV.) Maybe she'd run into someone she knew and… stopped for a cup of coffee? Maybe there had been a family emergency and she had to get on a train to Stockholm right away – but if that were the case, she would have told him.

He went into the living room, to check on the car. It was parked in its usual spot in front of the building.

"Where's Mum?" Rakel asked.

"I don't know," he snapped.

Martin got dressed, brushed his teeth, shouted to Elis that he had to brush his teeth too, did the washing-up and stood looking out of the window, staring at the maple tree outside.

Then he asked Rakel to watch her brother for five minutes and shut himself in the bedroom with the phonebook.

He called every hospital in town. No, they had no patients that could be Cecilia Berg. Martin didn't know whether to feel relieved or worried.

He called the police and talked to a bored woman at the switchboard who seemed to fail to see the seriousness of it all.

"And how long has she been gone, did you say?"

"Since this morning…"

"Well, it's far too soon to do anything, then. You're welcome to call back…"

He tried to explain that this was highly irregular, but she cut him off.

"When the missing person's an adult, we can't do anything until twenty-four hours have passed."

When Martin hung up, he realised he hadn't actually seen her since the night before. He dialled half the number to the police switchboard to amend his statement, but then stopped himself and hung up.

He used the bathroom and when he went to wash his hands, he realised they were trembling slightly.

Elis sat hypnotised in front of the TV. Rakel studied her father with the inscrutable eyes of a ten-year-old. "When's Mum coming back?" she asked. She was already wearing her black-and-orange Azalea BK kit.

"Any minute now, hopefully… Hey, would you mind watching Elis a bit longer, please."

Rakel sighed.

Another thirty minutes went by, during which Martin began to make lunch, even though no one was feeling particularly hungry. At one point, he heard footsteps in the stairwell – light, quick – and for several seconds he was euphorically convinced it was her. When he heard their neighbour's doorbell ring, he went back into the bedroom again, out of sight, and called Gustav.

He answered after eight infinitely long rings, his voice hoarse, full of gravel.

"If I've heard from Cecilia?" he said with a yawn. "Why would you ask me that?"

"Because she's not here."

"What do you mean 'not here'?"

"She hasn't been here all morning."

"What did she say when she left?"

Martin wanted to scream. "But that's the fucking problem. She *said nothing*. She was just gone when I woke up and now it's been *five hours*…"

"She's probably out running then." The click of a lighter. "Or hanging out with some friend or whatever, I don't know."

"Cecilia *doesn't have* any friends."

"Come off it, of course she does."

"No one she spends Saturday mornings with, anyway. Frederikke maybe, but she's in Copenhagen."

After they hung up, it struck Martin that there was a very straight-forward way of finding out if she was out running – which was theoretically possible if she'd taken the tram to Skatås, run twenty-five miles, stopped somewhere for breakfast and was currently on her way home. The apprehension was so overwhelming as he went out into the hallway to check if her running shoes were there that he completely forgot that she would most likely have driven to Skatås.

No shoes. The relief crashing over him was so tremendous he had to shut his eyes.

When he opened them again, he noticed her black Chelsea boots were also missing.

And her camel hair coat.

Martin started to wander about the flat aimlessly. Her toothbrush was missing. His arms and legs went cold. He climbed the stairs to her study, had to hold onto the banister.

Her desk had been cleared. For the first time, he noticed the grain of the wood: he'd never seen it before, because the desktop had always been covered with papers and old newspapers, notebooks, open books, letters. Now, there was nothing, just a single envelope leaning against a mug. Written on the envelope was the word *Martin*.

PART 3
KAIROS

27

PHILIP FRANKE HAD ALWAYS dreamt of success, but he didn't tell journalists that. He told them all kinds of other things, though. He talked about writing as exorcism. About literature as solace and refuge. About his characters' relationships with one another, as though they really were born of his imagination.

He said so many things to so many different journalists that eventually seeing his own picture in the paper brought a stale taste to his mouth. This was one of the main reasons for his temporary relocation from Berlin to France, a country where he was not published. ("*Yet*," his publisher corrected him. "Not published *yet*.")

Why not be honest about his naked ambition for once, Philip thought, studying the row of shirts hanging in his wardrobe. Now that he was having them dry-cleaned, they were always uncreased and snow-white, and by eliminating the need to iron them, he'd freed up a bit more time to write. It was just a pity he wasn't making use of that time. Why not admit that a few years ago he would have been hyperventilating with ecstatic shock at learning that he was about to be interviewed by a journalist who had travelled from a different country to meet him? *Ein Jahr der Liebe* hadn't even been translated into Swedish. Ulrike claimed to have a deal in the works, but he hadn't heard anything in months and couldn't find it in him to care. "Well, Rakel," he might say, for once, "I think I'd have to name the thirst for success my most important motivation."

He dreamed of success throughout middle school, when he was always picked last, regardless of the sport. He dreamed of success when his first girlfriend broke up with him and there seemed to be little reason to keep breathing except possibly to pull off something extraordinary enough for her to want him back. He dreamed of success when at seventeen he submitted a short story to the school paper and saw his name in print for the first time. (A less than impressive feat since he was also the editor.) He dreamed of success when the following year he took part in a poetry competition arranged by his local library, and with trembling hands read what had, until that moment, seemed like a good poem. He dreamed of success when he took a journalism job at an ambitious culture magazine, though "job" might be a misnomer since he didn't make a penny in his seven years there, but on the other hand he did have the recurring joy of seeing his name printed above blocks of text he called "prose poems" or "fragments". He dreamed of success when he took another job, as a substitute teacher in secondary school, to fund his work for the magazine. (He dreamed of success more than usual just then, because he loathed those little bastards.) He dreamed of success as a means to get through the winter when he lived off nothing but beans and pasta and wore a scarf and slippers at home to save on electricity so he could abstain from paid work and continue to write. Write, write, write, write a novel which one day he put in the post, along with a pre-paid envelope, and which was then returned to him again and again, accompanied by pro forma rejection letters. *Thank you for submitting your manuscript. Unfortunately, we must decline publishing it.* He dreamed even more hotly of success while he wrote his second novel, a book that was in every respect shorter, angrier and more high-paced, and sent that off, too. It was published and sold four hundred and fifty copies, at least half of which were hawked by him at various humiliating events. Even though no one seemed interested, he appeared at yet another not-for-profit literary festival in some draughty suburban library and talked to some poet. Salted peanuts, sour red wine.

And if he hadn't dreamed so much about success, he would probably have called it quits there. He would have got himself a proper degree instead of soldiering on with his unpaid work at a magazine that was slowly but surely digging its own grave with the help of ten-page interviews with obscure authors.

His second novel was a flop, but that was almost expected. His third, a family saga spanning from the late seventies to the present, earned him some attention and racked up decent sales. His publisher praised it and there were some positive reviews, but no one seemed to feel it was an indispensable account of Germany's modern history, which had been Philip's aim.

So he kept dreaming of success, about reviews and culture sections, about regular appearances in prominent magazines, about literature programmes on TV. And he dreamed, there was no denying it, about money. His hunger for success had been his constant companion through every stage of life. Until now. Now, it seemed to have been severed like an amputated limb. Sometimes he had phantom pains, or, rather, phantom pleasure – a moment of flaring joy at the news that his book was being translated, warm pride at the sight of his name in print – but the old aching, nagging hunger for success was gone.

While Philip got dressed and tried to tame his hair, he imagined the journalist saying something along the lines of "And why is that, do you think?"

"Well, Rakel," he'd say, "you might think it has to do with *Ein Jahr*." That the longed-for success had lost its appeal the moment it was achieved. But in reality, the withering and eventual death of his yearning for success had begun long before then. The question was when. At what point had the rot set in? Or finally begun to recede, depending on your perspective?

Perhaps it had started the moment he met the woman who had now indirectly catapulted him into success. Right *then*, he hadn't noticed, of course. It had taken him months to detect it, and by then it was too late to do anything. Such was the irony of fate. Only once the process had run its course could he observe with any clarity the phase that had begun a few years earlier, on the day when he dived into a restaurant to escape a downpour and since it was dinner time decided he might as well eat, even though he didn't usually go for – he glanced at the menu a young waitress handed him – Ethiopian food.

Six months had passed since the publication of his family saga and since then he'd started work on a new novel every other month. An arts stipend and the occasional stint of paid work kept him afloat, and he could spend an entire day on the sofa with a bag of crisps and a good TV show without consequences. When he was hungry, he ordered takeaways. When he was tired, he dozed for a while. Hours passed in the gloom behind the closed blinds, and suddenly it was evening. Philip would turn on some lights, find his reading glasses, make a pot of tea, sit down at his desk, clear his throat, run a hand through his hair, furrow his brow, and take out whatever it was he was working on right then. That particular day, he'd forced himself to go for a walk to expose himself to some new impressions, and, of course, the sky had opened.

The restaurant was deserted. Aside from him and a family at one of the window tables, the only guest was a woman sitting by herself, bent over a book.

Philip was seated at a table near the reading woman. He ordered a beer and what he hoped was chicken stew. The sight of a deeply absorbed reader cheered him up; it was so unusual to see people reading books in public these days, when almost everyone had their noses in their phones. He had deliberately left his own at home the better to observe his surroundings.

The woman tore off a piece of bread and mopped up some sauce in one graceful movement. Her long fingers moved with tentative precision across her meal. Her shirtsleeves were rolled up and the slender muscles of her forearms danced as her hands moved. At regular intervals, she turned the page.

His chicken stew and a basket of rolled up bread were set down in front of him. Philip considered asking for cutlery but realised that would be admitting defeat. He busied himself with his food. The woman a few tables over didn't even know he was there. Because her fingers were unadorned, and because she was sitting there alone, even though she was beautiful, he decided she must be single.

She'd finished her injera and was talking to the waitress. Her voice was a deep, slightly hoarse alto – the part Philip's mother used to sing in the church choir – and he was so enthralled by the timbre of her voice it took him a minute to realise he didn't understand the language they were speaking. The waitress was clearly Ethiopian, and the blonde woman clearly was not, but they were laughing about something, and Philip felt an unexpected pang of emptiness when he didn't understand what it was.

The waitress returned with more bread and left again after a last comment in the unknown language.

"What are you reading?" Philip said without thinking.

While the woman finished chewing, she held up her book to show him the title. Horror spread from the pit of Philip's stomach. It was his own novel, the grand family saga he'd worked on for years and considered his best book yet. He both hoped and feared she'd recognise his picture from the inside cover.

"Is it any good?" he said. An infinitely long second passed before she swallowed and nodded.

"It's a multigenerational narrative written with considerable psychological insight," she said. "And a sizeable helping of gallows humour."

To his immense chagrin, Philip realised he was blushing. He said that was good to hear and that he had to confess he was the author. Her face brightened and she asked how he had gone about doing his research. After a few minutes, he picked up his beer and moved over to her table.

And thus, the story began.

Much later, Philip would bring out all the nuances and phases of their relationship with ice-cold precision. When he wrote, the dramaturgical arc came through so clearly he couldn't understand how he'd been so blind to how things were developing. But it had started out well. At least well enough that he'd been able to convince himself all was as it should be. That first period turned out to be the hardest to put into words. Perhaps it was because the pure, dizzying infatuation of the story's beginning was sullied by the bitterness and vitriol of its ending. He didn't want to remember the beginning. He definitely didn't want to think about the fact that he'd thought a life together with her was possible, within reach, almost fated and inevitable. No, the novelist Philip Franke had zero desire to think about that; all he wanted to do was be angry and write. But since a one-sidedly spiteful narrative was less effective than one in which love and hate fought for dominion, he sadly had to.

From the first, it was unclear what kind of relationship they really had. Philip never knew what to call her. The words "my girlfriend" had connotations of meek normality that fit poorly with her actual appearance. She herself seemed uninterested in defining him, and since they never spent time together around other people, there was never any actual need.

The conversation that had begun in the Ethiopian restaurant lasted for hours, continuing down the street, into a bar, and back to her one-bedroom flat nearby. She lived on the fourth floor of a 1920s building on Grünburger Strasse, just a few blocks from Philip. Aside from books, she had very few possessions and barely any furniture.

"You don't have a sofa?" he exclaimed.

She laughed and shook her head. Philip wanted to know how long she'd lived there.

"A while," she said, eyes lowered. If he'd been a painter, Philip thought to himself, he could have spent decades on that face.

She didn't talk about her past but gave him to understand that she'd worked as an interpreter. What she was currently doing for a living he didn't know, because any questions to that end she weaselled out of with the elegance of an escape artist. Several days a week she went to the university, where she studied Ancient Greek. Philip wasn't sure what she did there or if it was in some way connected to how she supported herself. On her nightstand lay a well-worn copy of the *Odyssey*. Whenever she was unable to sleep, she told him once, she'd read her favourite books aloud to herself. Hearing the dead language in the silence of the night was a wondrous experience, and sometimes she had to get up and look at the street outside – the cars, the street lights, the blue flickering of TVs in windows – to anchor herself in the right time and place.

She spent most of her time reading and writing – at that point, a work about the conditions of exile. When he offered to read it, she laughed again and handed him a sheet of paper. The text was in a different language. Swedish, he guessed. Correct, she said.

Sometime during the first few months of their relationship, he went with her to the concert hall even though he found classical music tedious. He suffered through an eternity of – he checked the programme – Bach's *St Matthew Passion*. How long was that soprano going to howl about God's mercy? He had to fight an urge to pull out his phone. He tried to catch her eye to pull an ironic face, but she was intently facing the stage. Her cheeks, he noticed, were wet with tears.

During the interval, he noted men's eyes lingering on her back, which was exposed by a lowcut dress. He touched her arm and she let him. She rarely touched him, never took his hand, would never sit on his lap in a public place or succumb to any other vulgar show of affection. The only thing he could do to mark his territory was this light touch that she didn't pull away from.

Back in the darkness of the auditorium, he thought to himself that maybe the shortcoming was his, not the music's. He leaned back and tried to let everything else fall away, to open himself up to the experience, such as it was.

"What did you think?" she asked as they strolled homeward.

Philip was not normally hampered by any particular need to be honest with people. On the contrary, he found things usually went more smoothly if you adjusted your stated opinions to your interlocutor and the context. Writing was different, because he could write in the belief that only he and the text existed in this world. Besides, a text aimed at concealing or manipulating something painful rarely turned out well. Real-life interaction was another story. People rarely said what they meant. Nor were they necessarily interested in others doing so. They wanted to hear all kinds of things: that they were doing well when they were mediocre, that they were beautiful when they were plain, that you were just fine when you were falling apart, that Saturday was going to be sunny when in fact rain was more likely.

But with the woman walking next to him, it was different. Secretive as she was about her past, she was unguardedly open about other things, like her tears during the concert, and she was by nature honest and direct. She took an interest in all kinds of things, and when her interest found a foothold somewhere, she didn't let go. By and by, methodically and sensitively, she probed at the heart of matters. Philip knew she'd worked as an interpreter in war-torn African countries, and he made a connection between her relentless search for the lowest substrates of existence with this experience. *Nothing human is alien to me*, as Marx and Terentius would have put it. It was an attitude that stimulated honesty in him in turn. And, he mused, the price of abiding within the sphere of her light was truthfulness. She would see through and dismiss pleasantries and blandishments. Not to mention attempts at being clever.

"I don't think I understand Bach," Philip said at length. It was a banal comment, but it was the only assessment he was prepared to stand by. He made an effort to expand on it. "I noticed that you were moved by the music, but for my part I felt nothing even close to that. I've thought that maybe it's a matter of taste, that you either like or dislike certain kinds of music, but now I wonder if I simply lack the capacity to appreciate some types of artistic expression."

"What usually moves you?" she said. "Has music ever made you cry?"

Before they met, Philip had figured he could talk to anyone, assuming they were of reasonable intelligence. Now, he was beginning to sense that had been a grave misunderstanding. This was something else. It wasn't easy to explain to other people what it was about, because a conversation was hard to recount or describe. By necessity, any recounting was succinct and summarising. Even worse, you often had to paraphrase your interlocutor's words, which you could rarely recall verbatim, using your own, and something was inevitably lost in translation. The wondrous thing about their conversations was that he never knew what she was going to say. They could start off with Bach and go from subject to subject for hours, and he never knew where it would take them.

Their conversations gave him a feeling of belonging, of having found a place in the world. This was what he refused to remember afterwards, what he absolutely didn't want any part of but had to deal with lest his sad excuse for a novel become a project of lies characterised by malice and vengefulness. With her, doors to something hitherto unknown opened. Philip had always wanted to be somewhere else, but now, all he wanted was to be with her. Much later, he would cast about for fixed points for that experience of contact and closeness, but at the time, while it was happening, it was unassailable and absolute. He was absolutely convinced they shared it. That it was the two of them. Two lonely people who had found something together.

During the first few months, they spent hours and hours talking, but then came the silence. It gradually crept in between their conversations, like the first chill winds of autumn dispersing the summer heat. He couldn't see any immediate reason for it and came up with various rationalisations. She was tired. She was busy with her work. She was wrestling with a particularly difficult translation. It was nothing to worry about, he thought. All was well. She was just – well, he didn't really know what, since she told him nothing, but soon enough things would be all right again. Since it happened so infrequently at first, he was able to forget it between occurrences.

More and more often, he asked her if something was wrong. More and more often, she denied it. More and more time passed between her calls. If he pointed to her avoidance, she denied it. She didn't do things like that, she declared, even though she hadn't answered a single phone call for a full week and was barely meeting his eyes now. Like a black hole, she closed up around herself, in a wordlessness whose gravitational pull upended his entire existence. "I have nothing to say," became her most common line.

On one occasion, he randomly ran into her on the street; they did live just a few blocks apart, after all. She was walking briskly, shoulders pulled up and hands shoved into the pockets of her camel hair coat. At first, she just gave him a curt nod, as though he were some distant acquaintance. Then she relented, gave him a quick peck on the cheek – a concession to convention, he thought, a matter of good breeding – and asked how he was doing. Her face was closed and her body rigid. Philip fled after a few dutiful words about giving her a call that night.

Then, just as suddenly, things changed back. She sought him out, laughed and talked, and all was well in the world once more. Until the next time she turned on him. And so it was, on and on, as the pendulum continued to swing between intimacy and aloofness. Every time he thought the closeness would last, but when the cold detachment reared its ugly head once more, he was unable to reach her. If they could just talk, he figured, they'd be able to reach an understanding, a shared narrative. But what was the point of him talking when she was closed-off and blocked? Philip came to realise she would rather say nothing at all, that he was the one who insisted on conversation, that all this bloody talking was his idea and that she would have preferred to cover their affair with silence like the salt with which the Romans according to legend covered the fields around Carthage to make sure nothing ever grew there again.

Philip walked and walked through every part of Berlin until his feet ached and he collapsed on a park bench in a remote part of the city. His weight plummeted precipitously, his eyes were hollow, and he had to dig through his wardrobe for jeans he hadn't been able to wear for years. When he went back home to Munich over Christmas, his mother took one look at his pathetic state and asked in a low voice if everything was all right. Philip would probably have broken down and told her everything if his rowdy nephews hadn't tumbled in just then.

He never set his phone to silent in case she called. He kept his evenings free in case she got in touch. He tried his very best when she actually did. He formed a habit of walking down her street to see if the lights were on in her windows. On was as bad as off. If they were on, she was at home and had no interest in seeing him. If they were off, she was out and anything could happen. He tried to tell himself that off meant she was out for a run, and running was harmless, but the lights were out a lot, and there was a limit to how many times a week even a marathon runner could be out running.

The linden trees on her street shielded him from discovery. Once, when he was standing there, looking up at the golden rectangle of her window, he saw the light go out. Heart racing, he dived into the nearest doorway. Moments later, the front door across the street opened and there she was, a bright figure in the blue twilight. He followed her at a distance, feeling like a total psychopath. When they reached a nearby city square, he hid behind a falafel stand while she paced around the statue. Before Philip could muster enough willpower to leave, a gangly man in a dark coat appeared, greeting her with an embrace. Like a friend, Philip told himself. Like friends happy to see each other. The dying sun was reflected in the man's glasses, that was all he could see from so far away. Unable to control his own feet properly, he followed them until they disappeared into a restaurant that was supposed to be good and they'd talked about going to.

In the throes of his subsequent self-reproach, he told himself their relationship could have continued if he'd just had the sense to keep his mouth shut. If he'd just surrendered to the motion of the pendulum. If he hadn't insisted on anchoring their relationship in the real world. If he'd allowed it to live in its own parallel universe. But he just had to tell her he'd seen her with that man. (Thankfully, his impulse to confess didn't extend to telling her he'd stalked her.) And then, as if to really hammer the nails into his own coffin, he had to insist that she come with him to a friend's birthday party, and when she demurred, saying she was meeting a friend, he demanded to go with her. And what had he gained from that? An embarrassing meeting with a wary woman – he'd expected the man with the long coat – and the dawning realisation that he was acting like a lunatic.

Afterwards, when it was over, he spent a considerable amount of time trying to identify his mistakes. Those two incidents were at the top of his list of idiotic blunders. If he'd done this or that, things would have turned out differently. If he'd stayed mum and not talked. If he'd refrained from confronting her. If he'd confronted her sooner.

If he'd just left well enough alone. If he'd acted cool and aloof. If he'd pulled away and been less open about his feelings – and so on. There was no end to his sins, and he rebuked himself for each one in turn. He'd ruined everything. Through his infinite stupidity and incessant demands, he'd annihilated her love.

When he hadn't heard from her in three weeks, he finally went over to her flat. By then, he no longer had any hope of her wanting anything to do with him. All he wanted was an explanation. When he got there, Cecilia's door was wide open and construction workers were going in and out. For a split-second, he actually thought he'd been the victim of a conspiracy, like Nicholas Urfe in John Fowle's *The Magus*, a novel Philip reread every time he went on holiday to Greece. Were secret forces bent on forcing him to change from a cocky egocentric to a humble doubter through the staging of genuine heartache? He sat in Cecilia's stairwell with his head in his hands, with no way of telling truth from fantasy, until, eventually, the landlord appeared. Frau Berg had moved out, he was informed. There had been a problem with the pipes, nothing serious, a renovation had been scheduled, and as he could see – he gestured towards a man bringing in a toolbox – it was now happening, but Frau Berg had unfortunately had enough of minor plumbing incidents and terminated her lease. Philip asked if he knew where she'd gone. The landlord shrugged.

A few days later, he pulled himself together and called, even though he'd promised himself he wouldn't. She'd changed her number. At first, he thought it was an attempt to avoid him, and that made him feel strangely elated because it was proof that he'd at least been a factor in her life. Then he recalled that she'd had an ancient phone with a pay-as-you-go SIM and had been talking about buying a proper phone with internet connection.

He deleted her number from his phonebook.

After she disappeared, he listened to the *St Matthew Passion* from start to finish, doubled over on the sofa. He could see no logic to it. In the only comprehensible narrative he could construct, their relationship had never meant anything to her and was therefore something she could leave behind without sadness or grief. On the other hand, that meant their moments of closeness and contact had only existed in his head. That she, briefly put, had never loved him.

Philip was shaken by a hard, vibrating urge to provoke some kind of reaction. Writing was as close to violence as he could get. It was redemption and accusation, a scream and an act of retribution. The worst part wasn't that she'd rejected him; he'd been dumped before. The worst part was that he hadn't left even the tiniest of marks on her life, while she had affected him so deeply a book was born of their relationship. What fit into a parenthesis in her narrative was a love story to him.

She'd been gone about a week when he stopped leaving his flat. The World Cup was on, and he watched every single game. Between games, he wrote. He moved between his bed, the sofa, the computer and the corner shop, where he purchased coffee filters and individual fruit yoghurts. The bloke who delivered the Chinese food gave his unshaved chin and stained hoodie a sceptical look. He wrote one page at a time. He couldn't be bothered to go over what he'd written the day before. He opened a bag of crisps. Germany scored four goals against Argentina in the quarter-final, and he felt a small surge of happiness. He forced himself to watch the semi-final in a sports bar with some friends. He couldn't remember the last time he'd worn normal clothes. "Are you doing okay?" his friends asked. I'm all right, Philip replied, even though he still woke up every morning with a ton of concrete pressing on his chest.

As a novelist, he'd always counted his understanding of cause and effect as one of his greatest assets. As part of one of the haphazard university courses he'd taken in his youth, he'd read Aristotle's *Poetics* and had, to his own surprise, been genuinely moved by a section about the impact of tragedy. The greatest tragic effect was achieved when the elements of the plot developed according to their own inherent principle towards an inevitable climax. The story had to follow its own logic to the bitter end. Because the end, that much even the then-young and innocent Philip knew, was bitter most of the time. None of his novels had a happy ending. The endings weren't necessarily unhappy, either, but they unfolded the way they had to.

Unfortunately, all sense of cause and effect seemed to have abandoned him in this case. It was only now, when writing forced him out of his obstinately self-absorbed perspective, that the voice of reason turned his attention to the only plausible trajectory of his narrative. Hey, Philip, it said, it can't be *happenstance* that she lived without a past and without a family. And it can't just be *bad luck* that she's never found lasting love, despite all her obvious qualities. That kind of loneliness must have very deep roots. She's a solitary creature, and a story centred on a person so removed from life can hardly end happily, regardless of how badly the author wants it to. For a while, you accompanied her on her lonely space flight into emptiness, but now it has continued without you. She has left you behind the same way she leaves everyone and everything.

It was over and done, and that was all it was ever going to be.

Before, he'd spent a lot of time coming up with good titles, but this time he just wrote down the first thing that came to mind: *Ein Jahr der Liebe*. Without reading the text through, he emailed it to Ulrike, his publisher. Then he showered, went out and got hammered.

A few weeks later, Philip was busy with more hands-on methods of forgetting. Somehow he'd managed to pick up a good-looking sociology student and they'd gone to a club. He'd popped a small pill and danced for fourteen hours straight. He'd felt amazing. Then, he'd woken up in a strange bed in the commune where the student apparently lived. His body ached. His phone was ringing in the pocket of his jeans, lost in a chaos of clothes. When he didn't pick up, it rang again. He found it and managed a gravelly hello. It was Ulrike.

It took him a while to understand what she was talking about. He was distracted by movement in the bed. It was the student, lifting her head up and blinking like an owl. She had hennaed dreads.

"...really the best thing you've written in a long time. I have genuine faith in this. The family saga was good, but this is something else entirely. From seven hundred pages to two hundred – I must say I'm surprised, Philip, surprised and *pleased*..."

At that point, Philip hadn't given any thought to success in a very long time, and he didn't now, either. He thought: I need a cup of coffee. He thought: How do I get out of here? He thought: Where are my underpants?

28

Even though he was now officially a "success", Philip hadn't been able to lose the habit of being on time to every meeting. He was fifteen minutes early for his interview with the Swedish journalist. He contemplated the café where they'd agreed to meet. Unfortunately, fifteen minutes wasn't enough to find a different meeting place.

He'd asked his girlfriend Nicole if she knew anywhere good to do the interview, and this had been her recommendation: a newly opened place on Boulevard du Montparnasse, where young people with horn-rimmed glasses that looked suspiciously like the ones his history teacher used to wear were sitting with wafer-thin computers open in front of them. Philip lingered by the door for a minute to see if anyone noticed him – Swedes were known for their punctuality, too, right? – but the only thing that happened was that a Japanese girl in a lace blouse snapped a picture of her raspberry tartlet with her phone. He sighed and chose a window table. Nicole would have fit right in. That morning, she'd been walking around the flat wearing nothing but knickers and a tank top, and even though he found it sexy that she smoked as though lung cancer was something that only happened to other people, the whole flat reeked. He made a show of opening the windows. By the time he left, she'd put on some clothes, set up her tripod and was busy taking pictures of herself with the remote.

Philip had had high hopes for his move to Paris, but after a few months in the city, he was starting to worry it had been a mistake. He'd tried hard to work up something akin to homesickness, but to no avail. He'd visualised his new flat in Mitte, with its sound-proofed study and big desk. His previous novels had all been written at an old table whose original purpose was unknown; he guessed it had been intended for a hallway. The teak veneer of the tabletop was scarred by decades of coffee-cup rings and had space for little more than a laptop and a manuscript stack. When he moved, he'd personally heaved it into a skip and heard its rickety legs break. He'd purchased a new printer and computer. He'd acquired an espresso machine and been struck by the realisation that he would never have to drink instant coffee again. Everything was new, white and clean. He had a view of a small park. He wanted for nothing. Everything was great. Everything was out-standing, aside from the fact that he couldn't focus. The document on the big screen remained blank.

"Philip," Ulrike said, pretty firmly. "Go away for a while. It's been an intense time. Take a few months off and get some distance. And peace and quiet."

He'd been considering the Caribbean and Mexico but then he'd met Nicole at Berlin Fashion Week and well, Paris was as good as anywhere, right?

Now, Philip Franke glanced at his watch. He'd brought an empty notebook that he placed on the table, then put back in his pocket, then back on the table. He took out a pen and placed it next to the notebook. He sat facing the street, amusing himself by guessing which of all the passers-by might be the journalist.

It was hard to say what identified her to him. It was a very young woman whose features would have fit in anywhere in Europe, but whose sartorial style was unmistakeably Scandinavian. She carried her belongings in a tote instead of a handbag, her hair was pulled up into a messy bun on top of her head and she was dressed in a loose shirt and thin, billowing trousers. She walked resolutely down the pavement, stepped into the café, spotted him instantly and waved.

"*Guten Tag,*" she said. "I'm Rakel. Nice to meet you." She looked around and said: "Nice place," the way someone might say someone's ugly kid is cute. A waiter fluttered up to them. She ordered coffee in French and asked Philip in German if he would like anything. He asked for a cappuccino in English.

He waited for Rakel to launch into the usual spiel about how she'd really enjoyed his book, to take out her phone to record their conversation and so on, but she just studied him with a furrowed brow and pursed lips. Philip had a sudden feeling he mustn't break eye contact.

"I have to confess," Rakel said at length, "that I'm not really a journalist. I'd planned on doing a proper interview, but now that feels like a waste of time." She reached for something in her tote bag. "I read your novel and it was a strange experience. Your main character seemed so very familiar. I had to find out what's real and what might just be figments of my imagination."

The young woman placed a photograph on the table between them. Philip knew instantly who it was.

"How do you know her?" He didn't recognise his own voice.

She smiled and leaned across the table, hands folded.

*

Philip had discovered literature at the age of thirteen, and it was doubtful if he could have made it through puberty without it. He still sometimes wondered how people who didn't read handled life. Before Philip became a reader, his existence had been filled with more or less meaningless activities the primary purpose of which was to keep tedium at bay. He'd collected stamps. He'd played floorball. He'd built model aeroplanes. He'd played the trumpet. He'd learned to shuffle a deck of cards in various flashy ways. By eleven, he'd been worryingly good at solitaire, and that was probably the same period he'd excelled at building houses of cards. Hunchbacked, he'd sat bent over the table in the living room, placing card after card on a tapering tower. It was a task that required great precision and could take up an entire morning. One second of distracted hesitation and it was over. The vibrations of insecurity almost seemed enough to set the cards swaying. It was rarely possible to pinpoint the exact cause of a collapse. Suddenly, the structure just came crashing down. He could still remember the sound of playing cards falling into a pile; it wasn't loud, but it was irrevocable.

Now, as Philip studied Cecilia Berg's daughter, he could sense the same kind of collapse.

It had never occurred to him that she might be a mother. Nowhere in his carefully catalogued facts were there children or marriage. He only knew disjointed details about Cecilia's background, things he would barely have noticed about anyone else, but that in her case shimmered like a pinned butterfly or a burial-chamber scarab. He could have listed every last one of those details, and had in fact done so in *Ein Jahr*, in a chapter that demonstrated how painfully little he really knew about this person he'd felt so close to.

After telling him her story in one fell swoop and in good German, Rakel fell silent. Porcelain clattered all around them and the coffee machine roared; the noise was deafening. People seemed to visit this café in large groups, several people wore hats, someone had on sunglasses indoors, they were taking pictures of each other, electronic music was playing in the background, the singer sounded high.

"Let's get out of here," Philip said. "Let's go for a walk."

The day was dusty and hot, the sky smoggy, the air stagnant. For a moment, he was unsure where they were and in which direction they should go. The city was spinning around him, buses and taxis rushed past, the foliage of the plane trees rustled in an imperceptible breeze, the voices of some passing Americans sliced straight through his brain.

"I don't know where she is," he said in answer to the question Rakel hadn't asked.

She let out a long breath, swaying slightly. "Oh," was all she said.

"It happened pretty much like it says in the book. After three weeks, I went over to her place, and she'd moved. Gone. If I'd really wanted to find out where she was, I probably could have, but..."

"What was the point," she finished his sentence. "More of the same."

They'd turned into the Montparnasse Cemetery and were walking down a tree-lined path. When Philip first arrived in Paris, he'd spent a few days visiting the graves of old literary heroes. Now, that seemed like a perfectly pointless thing to do.

"One thing I've been wondering," Philip said, to distract himself from the agony of the break-up. "What was her problem with Lucas Bell?"

"Lucas Bell?"

"A British author, big in the nineties. He wrote a novel…"

"I know, I know. *A Season in Hell*. Dad's company published it. But I don't get it. Why would she have a problem with him?"

As long as he had things to tell her, Cecilia's daughter would stay, and Philip noticed himself embellishing the tiny episode, stretching it as far as it would go. It had happened something like this, he began. Granted, he wasn't particularly keen on Lucas Bell's later works – that sentimental junkie-coming-clean-autobiography *Notes from the Edge* was in all honesty not very impressive – but he was still curious about the man who'd written the perfect, black pearl of a novel that *Season* truly was. So when Bell was doing an event at one of Berlin's larger bookshops, which was trying to kickstart commerce, Philip had wanted to go, to feel nostalgic, to have his tattered copy signed, and then to leave with the pleasant knowledge that Bell, despite his genius, was passé. The future belonged to a younger generation, to hard-working young authors who would sooner or later come to celebrate literary triumphs and general success.

"Lucas Bell?" Rakel's mother had said when he asked if she wanted to come. "I'd rather not. I've met him. He's an idiot. He might be a talented writer, but he's an idiot."

Philip had obviously wanted to know in what way. As usual, Cecilia had been evasive. It didn't matter, she'd said, it was a long time ago, a good friend had been in trouble, she wasn't really personally involved, could they just drop it, it was unpleasant to think about.

In the end, Philip went to the event by himself. A pasty man was sitting on the stage with the lanky remains of the wavy mane of his youth, greying at the roots. He seemed to have put on quite a bit of weight only to have lost about half of it again. His skin hung in bulldog-like folds around his jaw. He would barely have recognised him if it weren't for the tattoos on his arms – a faded row of what might be birds, and a sagging quote written in cursive script. His answers were rambling and full of tangents. Afterwards, when the microphone was passed around to enquiring audience members, Philip asked a question about autofiction. Bell had looked uncomfortable, thinking about it for a long time before producing a trite answer.

Philip hadn't bothered to queue for an autograph. He went straight to Cecilia's. "How was it?" she'd said. "What was he like?" She'd wanted to hear every detail about Bell's decline and had seemed almost excited to hear him describe the dullness and banality of this former *enfant terrible* who had burned out his own talent on pronouncements of decadence.

"That's odd," Rakel said. "I can't remember ever hearing much about Lucas Bell. Dad tells the story of when he overdosed two days before the Gothenburg Book Fair. He's still bitter about it, I think. But Mum's not exactly the type to hold a grudge. I can't imagine her holding *that* against him."

It was true – Cecilia didn't hold grudges. If anything, her problem was that no one ever made a mark on her life.

"Is there anything else," she said, "that you think might help me find her?"

Philip noticed her soaking up every detail about her mother with a hunger he was only too familiar with. His friends had long since tired of hearing about Cecilia and the slightest mention of her annoyed Nicole. She felt writing an entire book about *cette femme* was more than enough, obliquely implying that maybe he could write about her next. Nicole didn't understand the elementary principle of writing: people write to alleviate pain or loss. Sometimes, Philip wondered if *Ein Jahr* might not simply be an attempt to silence the questions tearing at him. Writing had been the only way to allay the storm inside him, and once the book was finished, it seemed to have died down for good. Now, he was no longer so sure.

"There's the Bird Woman and the man in the greatcoat, I suppose," Philip said. "I know nothing about them, but maybe you know who they are."

That episode, too, he told her, had happened pretty much the way he'd written it. Philip's best friend was throwing a big party to celebrate his fortieth birthday. Everyone had been excited to meet his new girl-friend, or whatever she was. The new girlfriend in question had prevari-cated until the last minute and then finally said she couldn't make it. Philip had demanded to know why, of course. When Cecilia claimed she was meeting "an old friend", he didn't believe her. He'd demanded to meet this "friend". He'd also demanded an explanation for why she prioritised this "friend" over going to the party with him. Cecilia had agreed to the first demand, possibly to get out of the second, and a few days later, he'd gone with her on a dreary walk to a nearby square. The friend whose existence he'd doubted turned out to be a foreign woman with a sharp nose, dressed in a loose black coat that billowed in the wind. She'd reminded him of a raven, ominous and remote. She'd seemed to know he was coming, because Cecilia just said: "Right, so this is Philip." They shook hands, exchanged a few words, and then parted ways. Philip had gone to the birthday party alone. Only later had he realised the birdlike woman hadn't told him her name. What's with these people, he'd thought, for the first time more weary than upset. Given all the secrecy, you'd almost think Cecilia was running from the law.

"How old was she?" Rakel asked.

"Around fifty."

"And how tall?"

He indicated with one hand.

"And dark-haired, right? Short bob with a fringe?"

"You know who it is?"

"I might." Rakel's voice was dark. "But tell me about the man with the greatcoat, too."

617

Philip described the episode more farcically than it had felt at the time, with himself in the role of mentally unstable private eye and Cecilia the mysterious *femme fatale*. For days, he said, he was obsessed with that man. In his memory, his face, posture and gait had been reassembled into a jerky newsreel with no sound. He looked for him everywhere, and every time he spotted a gangly person with round glasses he jumped, he even followed people on the street, even though he knew how insane it was. At the first opportunity, he'd searched Cecilia's entire flat while she was in the shower. It was quick work because there wasn't a single object that tied her to her past. Not one memento. No photographs in her desk drawer, no newspaper clippings, no old calendar, nothing.

The man in the greatcoat wasn't important *per se*, even Philip could see that. He could have been anyone, he really did look like someone's friend from back in the day, a down-and-out old punk rocker. He became a symbol of Cecilia's silence and elusiveness, of the vast unknown on which their relationship was built. What could grow out of that uncertainty other than confrontation, demands and revenge? What could such reticence—

"Rakel? Are you okay?"

She had collapsed on a bench. One hand was clutching the armrest and the other was pressed to her stomach. Philip sat down next to her. Rakel took a few laboured breaths and then pulled out her phone, looking for a picture with businesslike speed. Without a word, she handed over her phone.

"Who is he?" Philip zoomed in on a painting in the background. The portrait looked eerily like Cecilia.

"My dad's best friend." She stared straight ahead.

They were quiet for a long time. Philip didn't fully understand, but then, he thought to himself, he didn't really need to. The feeling was the same as when an idea for a novel begins to take shape: disjointed images and fragments floating up out of the dark without any clear connections, a dreamwork operating according to its own rules in the unknown recesses of the brain, only to eventually surface as a narrative.

Rakel's hands were the same shape as her mother's. She kept picking at a peeling piece of skin on her thumb.

"Stop that," he said. "You're going to make it bleed."

"I should get back to my brother," she said.

"I'll walk you to the metro." Philip offered her his arm, and she took it. Rakel's straight shoulders were drooping now, her neck wilting like a poppy. She looked like a child who has tricked everyone into thinking she's an adult and now despises the adult world for being so easily fooled.

They left the calm of the cemetery, stepping out onto Boulevard Raspail. The rumble of traffic, exhaust fumes hanging unmoving in the heat.

He was going to leave Paris. There was nothing for him here.

"Your novel's beautiful, by the way," Rakel said when they reached the station. "I'm translating it."

"You'll have to let me know how it turns out."

"Absolutely. There's a paragraph in chapter three that—"

"I meant with Cecilia."

She laughed, a ray of sunlight across her face. "Of course." And then she hurried down the steps into the underground.

29

"So the house is no longer available?"

"As far as *I* know, it's been let." The young man at the travel agency could be heard typing on his keyboard.

"But yesterday, I was told—"

"I understand. There must have been a misunderstanding."

Martin pictured himself hurling his phone at the wall. "What's the point," he said, "of using a travel agency, if one day you're told you're practically set and the next day you have nothing? How hard can it be?"

"I can see that we have a flat in Nice, if you'd—"

"But I don't want a flat in *Nice*, I want a house outside Antibes." He was having trouble breathing, needed to sit down, fumbled about for a chair, heard the agency bloke talking but couldn't make out the words. His phone hand was slippery with sweat.

Silence on the other end, following a question mark.

"I didn't quite catch that," Martin said.

"I was saying that I can keep looking and call you back in a while. So to confirm: what you're interested in is the Mediterranean coast?"

After he hung up, Martin stayed seated with his hands on his knees, leaning forward slightly as though he were about to stand up.

It was Saturday morning. He'd woken up early. He'd been waiting outside when Hagabadet opened and had run on the treadmill until sweat drew a V on his back. Now, he was back home again. It had just gone eleven. He wanted to see Gustav, but Gustav had interviews. Since when did he give interviews? GUSTAV BECKER BREAKS SILENCE, STOPS PRETENDING TO BE A BROODING ARTIST. They'd agreed to meet up the next day instead.

When his children announced they were going on some kind of Interrail odyssey through Europe, he'd felt – "Upset, it sounds like?" Gustav said over the phone.

"But *Rakel and Elis...*"

"Aren't you happy they're doing something together?"

"But they never do anything together."

"As I recall it, Rakel was always coming up with shenanigans that she then dragged Elis into," Gustav said. "All kinds of games and fort-building." There was loud clattering in the background.

"What are you doing?" Martin said. "Are you cooking?"

"Just making an omelette."

"I didn't even know you owned a frying pan."

"You used to fry beef patties for *pannbiff* in it, unless I'm misremembering. What I can't find" – more clattering – "is a spatula."

"You can get pretty far with just a cheese slicer."

After their conversation, Martin had hit upon the idea of renting a house on the French Riviera. The thought had popped into his head with such clarity it was hard to understand how it hadn't occurred to him sooner. In his memory, their summers in Gustav's grandmother's house were bathed in the lyrical light, as *Dagens Nyheter*'s reviewer had put it, that illuminated Becker's legendary Antibes Suite, which was now available to view in its entirety at the Gothenburg Museum of Art.

Sometime in the first few years of the new millennium, his grandmother had passed away, and Marlene von Becker and her siblings had sold the house to a British TV producer who'd made his fortune filming ordinary people locked in a house together with an unlimited supply of alcohol. "Or, in other words, a concept not too different from the family get-togethers on my mother's side," Gustav had written in a long letter from an outdoor serving area in Cannes, where he'd sought refuge after the funeral to, according to the letter, enjoy white wine, a plate of oysters and communication with the wider world.

But there were plenty of other houses on that long coast, Martin thought to himself, and set to finding some suitable place to rent. A vision of the summer welled up inside him. The landscape would be drawn in shades of ochre and sienna. The sea a study in azure. Gustav would sit in the shade under a lemon tree with a pastis, fanning himself with a days-old copy of *Le Monde*. When Martin closed his eyes, the only sounds would be the sea, distant gulls and the buzzing of a bumblebee coming closer. They would bring the children. They would go into Cannes to eat shellfish and walk along the Croisette in opal-blue twilight. And since he was there anyway, Martin would take the opportunity to find the house where William Wallace had once lived and worked. With a bit of luck, there'd be a concierge who knew about the building's history and could show him around. He would – right then, he was completely sure of it – work on the Wallace book every day, while Gustav set up his tripod to snap pictures for new paintings, whistling all the while. The biography would not turn out to be a work of genius, perhaps, but what biography was? It would be well researched and solid, its notes and sources unimpeachable, written with the lightness and authority that comes with a complete command of the material. William Wallace, who had undeservedly spent so many years in the shadow of Hemingway, Fitzgerald and all the rest, would appear in all his spirited, elusively double-natured glory. The radiance of his prose was still intact beneath decades of dust. Martin had no difficulty imagining himself leaning back in an armchair on Babel, the premier culture show on TV, saying: "As a matter of fact, Wallace wrote complex and compelling female characters," in reply to one of the interviewer's questions. "He often listed Emily Brontë's *Wuthering Heights* as one of his most profound reading experiences, and he was a great admirer of Emily Dickinson. Among his novels we find, to take just one example, *A Visit to the Museum*, which tells the story of a woman's struggle against her desire in a social context that suppresses her sexuality and longing for freedom. Wallace approaches the trope of a young woman in a relationship with an older man in a position of authority with an incredibly fine-tuned understanding of women's social and psychological environment." (It was true, too. It was almost enough to make you think Wallace was in love with that indecisive professor himself.)

It was a brilliant idea, this Riviera thing. And if he couldn't find anything in France, there was always Italy.

Martin was about to call Gustav to get him on board but recalled yet again that he was busy giving interviews. Instead, he began to clean the kitchen, even though there was no real need. For years, he'd fought to keep it from tipping over into chaos. Crumbs, marmalade stains, toys on the floor. The rag rug bunched up in a corner. Washing-up stacked up on any open surface faster than he could run the dishwasher. Now, everything was exactly how he'd left it. He didn't even have Elis's mess to clean up. He moved on to inspecting the fridge. Should he get started on lunch? There were leftovers and unopened things close to their expiration dates, gravlax he'd bought for Rakel, which he'd have to eat himself unless she returned from this Interrailing business within a relatively near future. No, he wasn't hungry.

Should he text the children? But he'd talked to Elis just the night before and had ended up in a typical Elis discussion: he'd reminded his son to turn off the roaming on his phone, sharing a slightly long-winded anecdote about the cousin of one of his co-workers, who had come home from a holiday abroad to a gigantic phone bill after forgetting this one simple task. His son had groaned that he knew that, but he was at a Starbucks at the moment because he needed to use their free wi-fi to check something on Google Maps. Martin had asked why he didn't just use the map. "What map?" Elis said and Martin had felt cold sweat break out on his back. He shouldn't have let him borrow his Paris map. He should have known something was going to happen to it. He should have known that just because something meant a lot to him, that didn't mean Elis understood – but then Elis had said, "Oh, *that* map, I left that in our hotel room."

No. He would hold off for now and call them later.

Martin's pulse was still racing. At the doctor's office, a lost-looking foundation doctor had claimed there was nothing wrong with his heart, that he was in good shape, and his blood pressure was fine; if anything, he should have a look at his work–life balance to try to pre-empt any work-related stress reactions. Martin had tried to explain that work was the least of his problems, notwithstanding that the industry was unstable in general, that several paradigm shifts had taken place recently, that the digital revolution had changed everything, the readers' consumption patterns, the breakthrough of audiobooks, and sure, Berg & Andrén's revenue was down in the past few years, but it wasn't a question of a proper *crisis* – at which point the doctor had glanced discreetly at his watch and given him a prescription for anti-anxiety medication to be taken as needed.

Maybe he should change doctors? Get a second opinion? The healthcare system should have an interest in keeping him alive, given how much money he'd paid in taxes over the past twenty-five years. Could they really justify letting a man of working age who still had decades left of a highly productive professional life die from an undiagnosed cardiological problem? What if he had a heart aneurysm? Martin wasn't sure what that was, but somewhere in his brain, a cool voice argued that he might be better off not looking it up. The moment he opened the door to the ailments of middle age, he'd be done for. Prostate cancer, cardiovascular disease, those sneaky aneurysms, whatever they were: they would invade his existence, make life unbearable. All he wanted was for an experienced doctor to assure him he wasn't dying from an overlooked heart attack.

To distract himself, Martin opened his text conversation with Maria Malm. Over the past few days, it had taken on the tone of light, fleeting shuttlecocks soaring over a sagging net. He could spend half an hour formulating something completely bland that struck a precise balance between aloofness and engagement. When he heard the little sound that announced his message had been sent, he invariably wondered what he was doing.

Her latest speech bubble hung there unanswered. It was the kind of text a person could reply to, but didn't have to. Before then, they'd talked about Gustav's exhibition. MM thought it was amazing. MM thought the pencil and ink drawings, and especially the self-portraits, were intriguing. MM had immediately identified Martin in some of the early paintings. (MM did not, however, mention a certain recurring person.) Maria Malm, Maria Malm. Let's imagine Maria Malm: Maria Malm has done a spot of yoga on her patio. Maria Malm contemplates her garden while sipping a kale and kiwi smoothie. Maria Malm is, in other words, a guardian of the little things. Seeds, shoots, birthmarks. Her poems are simple and stripped down. Her words carefully weighed. Everything about her is carefully weighed. Thin hands, slender wrists. Starting a relationship with Maria Malm would be a reasonable thing to do. It would mean long weekends in European capitals, a classically decorated summer house, and, generally speaking, a thousand things for him to get up to once Elis had finally had enough and moved into a commune in Biskopsgården and only came home at the end of the month when he was skint and hungry.

Martin annihilated a particularly stubborn stain on the hob, scrubbing until the enamel was immaculately white.

30

The day passed in slow motion and the silence grew ever more compact. Martin played Thåström at a loud volume. He listened to P1 Kultur on the radio. He turned the TV on to play in the background while he answered emails. Nothing helped. In the end, he called Gustav, even though he'd promised to wait, and when Gustav actually answered, relief washed over him.

"Oh, hi, it's you, hello…" He couldn't meet up tonight, he said. He was tired after all the interviews. Tomorrow would work better.

"Sure," Martin said. "Tomorrow's great." He'd wanted to tell him about his holiday plans, but Gustav didn't seem in the right frame of mind. Tomorrow. He'd have to wait until tomorrow. He pictured them having a couple of glasses of wine at one of the more decent bars. He was going to present his Riviera idea and Gustav was going to break into a smile and propose a toast to this genius idea, which would save them from the verdant Swedish summer and its accompanying requirement to enjoy all things in moderation. They were going to make plans, set dates…

Tomorrow.

With restlessness buzzing inside him, Martin pulled on his jacket and left the flat. It didn't help much. Silence still pressed against his temples as he plodded up Allmänna Vägen. There wasn't a street in this town he hadn't walked a thousand times. There was nowhere he could go without risking tumbling down a rabbit hole to the past. One advantage to selling the company was that he'd be able to move away.

It was a sunny afternoon, full of cherry blossom and flowering horse chestnuts – those sodding lilacs on Vasaplatsen were probably still in full bloom, too – and truth be told a bit too warm for wearing a jacket. He kept it on anyway. It was tailored to his measurements, and Martin needed its reassuring grip around his shoulders as he meandered aimlessly towards the city centre. Every outdoor serving area he passed was full. Where all these people were to be found in the winter months was a mystery. Colourful clothes shone against the dirty-white stone of the buildings. Loud laughter rose towards the bright sky. Lipstick-stained cigarette butts were ground into ashtrays. Someone stumbled in high-heeled sandals and was caught with a shriek by a girlfriend.

At Kungsport Bridge, he spotted Max Schreiber. Max! A gift from the heavens. If there was one person in this world who wouldn't be lured by worldly pleasures, it was him. German vocab always came first.

"Hi, Max," Martin said. They'd spoken briefly at the anniversary party, but he hadn't been able to tell him about the small collection of essays Rakel had sensibly declined, suggesting Max could translate it instead. Her judgment was, at the end of the day, sound. She would be able to chart a sensible course through the thousands of decisions involved in publishing. People who thought they knew everything couldn't be trusted. But she did need to learn to focus. As it was – this psychology degree of hers, going interrailing on a whim – she was too distracted.

Max gave a start and his grave expression morphed into happy recognition. He'd just attended a lecture, he said, and now he was heading home to watch the game. Yes, of course, Martin said, even though he had no idea what game he was talking about, or even what sport. Probably football. Aside from those steel-rimmed glasses, Max had always looked more like a former football player than a scholar. Martin approved.

He suddenly felt a wave of warmth and goodwill towards this man he barely knew. He remembered him as an angry and intelligent young student Cecilia had absent-mindedly taken under her wing. She was really just five or six years older, but that had been a lot back then. Their friendship seemed founded on a shared interest in German grammar, of which Max was a master. Outside of that, Cecilia didn't really have much reason to hang out with a young man who was still working on his BA in intellectual history. He remembered her soft laughter on the phone, the way she leaned her head against the wall and scratched at a peeling piece of wallpaper while they talked. Several times she'd told Martin that Max's father, who had immigrated from

Germany in the sixties and had children with a Swedish woman, hadn't taught Max his native language. He'd grown up with a German name but hadn't learned the language that should have been his birthright until he was a grown-up. Martin never figured out why she was so stuck on that.

"Hey, I was just thinking about you," Martin said, which was only sort of true. "You still translate, don't you?"

They walked through Kungsparken together. All around them, people were sitting on blankets, having picnics, pouring boxed wine into plastic cups, and playing music on tinny speakers. While Martin told Max about the book and its author – an Austrian philosopher who worked in the spirit of Slavoj Žižek, but sadly enjoyed none of Žižek's fame – he was filled with a familiar excitement. Over the years, he'd learned to trust that rush of adrenaline, to think of it almost as a barometer.

They kept talking for a good long while, standing in the spot that marked the parting of their ways, until Max realised he was about to miss kick-off. Martin watched him disappear through the park. He suddenly recalled an episode from his old life. Cecilia and he had been invited over for dinner by one of Cecilia's fellow PhD students. There was the PhD student, his girlfriend, Max Schreiber and his girlfriend. The dinner party was a civilised affair. No one got too drunk. No one launched into a twenty-minute monologue. Cecilia was held in a certain esteem that Martin found difficult to understand. Everyone left at a decent hour. As they were walking to the tram, Martin said it had been nice to meet her friends and colleagues, that they seemed, well – he searched for the right words but his mind moved sluggishly under the influence of the red wine – they seemed *nice*.

Cecilia laughed. "There's nothing *wrong* with them." The PhD student, she said, was hard-working and determined, but not particularly bright. He was another brick in the wall in the academic project. He would do what was expected of him and slowly climb the ladder thanks to persistence and reliability. The PhD student's girlfriend bossed him around and was never satisfied. When she told people about their life, she always expunged any objectionable details – the fact that "a job" in this place or that was in fact a temporary gig, that the magazine *90-tal* had only accepted that essay on the fourth attempt, that "their flat" on Kungshöjd was actually sublet from a half-senile old lady. Max, she continued, was talented and promising, true, but he thought so highly of himself he would allow nothing but perfection, which left him blocked and stunted. Besides, Max was inherently passive, and that combination – talent and passivity – was a dangerous one. He might do well, but he might also make it just far enough not to feel like a complete loser and settle. Max's girlfriend wanted Max to be more interested in her than Hegel, a perfectly understandable but unrealistic wish. The two of them had no future together.

And at the same time, she said, these couples depended on each other. They would cling to the idea of love for as long as they could. The alternative was loneliness, a fate worse than death in their eyes. With the possible exception of Max, who seemed to think this other-people-thing often got "too complicated". Cecilia made quotes in the air and accidentally whacked Martin with an unintentionally sweeping gesture. They laughed at the fact that she was drunk.

"People engage in a lot of self-deception," she said with a firm grip on his arm to keep her balance. "They have this need to write books and get a PhD and become professors and noted intellectuals. But almost everyone's mediocre. They're intelligent enough to recognise genius and excellence, and with a bit of luck they may achieve something above average themselves. But the vast majority of people are middling. And they don't want to accept that. Instead, they buy houses and build patios and have children, which serves as a watertight alibi. I never got to write that book, they say. Because I have the house and the patio and the children to take care of. And besides, they like it just fine at work. Next summer, they're going on an extended vacation to France. They say they love to read, but how much do they really read? A book a month, if that. They say they wish they had more time to read. They say they wish they had more time to *write*. That they would love to write that book, but *time*. There's not enough *time*. Because of the patio and all the other things they have to spend their time on. But maybe next year, or when the children are older, or – hey, is that our tram? Should we run?"

They ran. Once they'd stepped into the warmth and light and were clinging to the leather straps with laughter in their throats, he kissed her, touched her glowing face.

*

It was just as bad, if not worse, over by Järntorget. The air was thick with the smell of blooming horse chestnut trees. Outside Pustervik, laughing people in summer clothes jostled for space. The cascades of water in the fountain sparkled in the sunlight. In the square and along the tree-lined street, people moved about in groups, the evening was still young, people were buying cigarettes at the 7-Eleven, jumping out of the way of screeching trams, taking pictures under the cherry trees. In a few hours, there would be long queues outside Burger King and Grillen.

Since he was in the area anyway, he might as well stop by the office and do some work.

Martin disarmed the alarm and went around closing all the blinds. Not until gloom filled the rooms and the only sound was the humming of the ventilation and the coffee machine did something akin to serenity begin to spread through him.

When the children were little, he'd always looked forward to his evening shift: a few undisturbed hours when he didn't have to be awake and alert, didn't have to be liked, didn't have to make any decisions. Reading without interruption was a blessing. People sometimes worried about the pace he kept, saying he should "take it easy" and "look after himself" – whatever that meant. None of the activities vaguely suggested by these well-intentioned souls interested him much. At the end of the day, few things were more fun than working on his books. So why forgo that kind of pleasure?

Martin kicked off his shoes. His feet were warm and swollen after his walk. Against his better judgment, he made coffee, sat down on the sofa with his computer on his lap and his feet on the table. Ten or so emails had come in during the afternoon, one of which was from Ulrike at Schmidt Verlag. He went through them in the order they'd come in, saving Ulrike's for last. Then he remembered he had to post the book to Max, go to the bathroom, clean his desk, and print out a recently submitted manuscript to keep him busy the following day. Only once that was all taken care of did he return to his computer and open Ulrike's email. As suspected, she was writing to ask how things were going with the novel they'd talked about in London. *Ein Jahr der Liebe* – he made an effort to remember the title once and for all, it was *Ein Jahr*, not *Ein Tag*; he repeated it to himself again and again as if he was cramming vocab while going to top up his coffee. Were they interested, Ulrike wanted to know. Otherwise, she had to put out feelers elsewhere. She included a link to an article in a culture magazine that Martin skimmed even though he only understood the odd word here and there. The margins (generous) and the pictures (one full and one half-page) were enough to make him itch all over: if appearances were anything to go by, this Philip Franke was rapidly emerging from his earlier relative obscurity.

Before she left, Rakel had promised him an excerpt and a report within a week. It was a mystery how she was going to pull that off during her European odyssey, when she'd already had half the spring and had produced nothing, but there was no point nagging her. Martin quashed the impulse to forward the email as a gentle reminder that things were coming to a head. Instead, he wrote back to Ulrike, promising an answer shortly.

Berg & Andrén could really use a hit, to boost both their finances and morale. Being a small publishing company, they could never compete for the big names, but rather had to gamble on unknown and promising authors that might one day turn into something. When they published Lucas Bell's book in the nineties, it wasn't just that the book had sold well, it was also that it had been proof positive that they, Martin and Per, were doing something right. One's ideas had to be calibrated against reality at regular intervals. It was an outstanding novel, the kind of book literature-loving upper secondary teachers recommend to their students, and it was still selling well to this day. The supply of lost young souls was, thankfully, constant, and you could buy a paperback for the same amount of money you'd spend on two pints on Andra Långgatan. The only miscalculation they'd made with Bell was his subsequent books. He seemed to have burned everything he had on his debut, and the thinly veiled autobiography that followed had had a sentimental, self-righteous tone to it, full of long paragraphs about various slights suffered, which inevitably made the reader take the antagonist's side because Bell's alter ego was so misanthropic there was no identifying with him. Today, it could possibly have been published as autofiction, but Bell had given every character a made-up name, not bothering to flesh them out to make them seem at least somewhat real to the reader. After some agonising, they'd declined to publish it. No other publisher had picked it up, either. It was a tragic tale, in a way, and not at all a suitable lesson for the upper secondary students: write a fantastic novel on drugs and a terrible one in rehab.

Martin was seized by an urge to remind himself how dismal it really was. Against all odds, he found it at the bottom of one of the book-shelves. The night was, in other words, not a total waste: he had a fresh manuscript and a trite old recovery narrative to amuse himself with, he was going to pick up crisps and beer, there had to be something decent on TV, and tomorrow he was seeing Gustav.

31

Elis Berg was sitting on a park bench outside the Musée des Arts et Métiers, cleaning his glasses with a cloth made for that purpose, and then busying himself with taking out and lighting a cigarette in a fairly punctilious fashion. He hadn't wanted to go with Rakel to meet Philip

Franke. While she was gone, he'd taken in an exhibition about haute couture from 1900 to 1950.

"It's her," Rakel said as soon as she was within earshot. Her brother stared at her like a goldfish. The cigarette, which he hadn't yet learned to smoke with any measure of credibility, smouldered forgotten in his hand.

"Fuck," he said at length. "So where is she?"

"He doesn't know. She ran out on him, too."

"So we came all this way just to hear that she's gone *again*?"

"Well, there was a bit more to it than that. Do you have any water? I feel sick."

He handed her a bottle. The plastic creaked as Rakel drank. Even though they were sitting in the shade, her back was sweaty. An oppressive heat lay heavy over the city. Dry leaves rustled across the cobbled courtyard. Rakel was experiencing a strange sensation of weightlessness, as though the world order had been disturbed, had shifted into a state where anything was possible and nothing definite. She couldn't sense any particular feelings. Within her, a clear, still calm reigned.

She started with the least difficult part: the random piece of information that Cecilia seemed to have a bone to pick with Lucas Bell.

"Odd. I would have thought we'd have heard about that," Elis said, his chin on his knuckles. "If there was some kind of juicy drama, Dad would never have kept it to himself."

Elis had been told the story of Bell's novel countless times, too: the looming bankruptcy, their last wild roll of the dice, the success no one had dared to hope for. The depths of Bell's decay, the grimy flipside of decadence, and dissolving fame were exactly the kinds of themes their father liked to go on about at dinner parties.

"I can't recall any reason she'd have it in for him," Rakel said.

"Didn't he write a bad book afterwards?" Elis said.

Rakel burst out laughing, a snorting, unstoppable laugh that made her stomach and chest ache. Elis wanted to know what was so funny, and Rakel tried to explain that it was the thought of Cecilia, lofty and untouchable, coolly indifferent to people but reacting to literature with the full spectrum of human emotion.

"As though literature were real life, and everything else just some nonsense going on in the background. No human being can ever get through to her, but a *book* can."

"That sounds tragic," Elis said. "Wait, I don't get it. Is that why she doesn't like that Lucas bloke? Because he was good and then turned awful?"

"Of course not. Or… I don't think so. I honestly don't understand it either."

Her brother picked up the mobile phone that had lain forgotten for several minutes, the knee-jerk reaction of the younger generation to any kind of uncertainty. "Maybe she didn't like that he was a junkie?"

"I don't think she's moralistic like that."

"Why not?"

"Because she abandoned her children to live like an exiled nomad?" Rakel suggested. Her brain was feverish and exhausted. The nausea had not subsided.

"True." Elis held up his phone. "Still, he was pretty good-looking."

On the cover of *i-D* circa 1993, a slim young man in jeans posed bare-chested. His face was a good fit for Mills & Boon descriptions like "smouldering gaze" and "sculpted cheekbones". Dark hair fell in waves to his shoulders and his sinewy arms were tattooed: a row of flapping ravens along one, a Rimbaud quote on the other. *A thousand Dreams within me softly burn.* In his hand, a half-smoked cigarette.

"I know!" Elis snapped his fingers. "They had a thing, lots of drama, he dumped her, she could never forgive him."

Rakel laughed again. "Lucas Bell is gay, Elis."

"Damn. Other than that, a pretty solid theory, though, right?"

"Absolutely."

Something stirred in her memory, something Philip Franke had said, but he'd said so many things and it was all one big jumble. Elis babbled on and she lost her train of thought. Her brother had apparently only seen the film version of *A Season in Hell*, and now he was swiping through a series of PR pictures. Rakel for her part had muddled memories of a VHS tape in the stack of rentals from Videomix on Kaptensgatan (rainy evenings, chocolate cake, Lovisa, who wanted to watch *Children of the Corn*). In *A Season*, a rosy-cheeked Leonardo DiCaprio wandered the streets of London with a curtains haircut and an oversized leather jacket, while a voiceover did its best to render the plot intelligible. Winona Ryder played the girl who had a marginal part in the book but a significantly expanded presence in the Hollywood production. Her main function was to gaze at DiCaprio with doe eyes while he did various types of drugs, and to provide opportunities to zoom in on skinny legs in torn nylon stockings. Then, she died in a white hospital environment and it was supposed to be sad. A British indie band that had had one, and only one, hit played the title song.

"Lucas Bell isn't really all that important," she said, closing her eyes. "Philip told me other things, too." The heat was pressing on her head. She hadn't eaten anything since breakfast. At the thought of food, she had to swallow hard not to gag. Her stomach churned.

"Like what?" Elis put his phone face-down on the bench between them.

"I think I'm going to be sick," she mumbled.

"Right now?"

Rakel nodded. She'd thrown up in all kinds of public places in her life – various tram stops, behind a tree in Slottsskogen, at the intersection of Vasa and Viktoria after a truly terrific preparty – but that was years ago, under cover of darkness, and, not unimportantly, with drunkenness being the direct cause. Now, it was early afternoon outside a museum in central Paris. But there was nothing she could do to stop it from happening.

After parents of young children, teenagers were the group of people most used to handling the realities of vomit, and Elis immediately jumped to his feet. "Get up," he ordered. "There's a bathroom in the museum." He threw Rakel's tote bag over his shoulder, grabbed her firmly by the shoulders, guided her through an air-conditioned lobby and into the disabled bathroom, where he tactfully left her to her fate.

Rakel fell to her knees next to the toilet and retched.

Once her stomach had calmed down sufficiently, she pulled herself up to rinse out her mouth and splash some water on her face. The reflection greeting her was a sad sight: dishevelled damp hair, pale cheeks, dull eyes. Bile was burning in her throat. She turned the tap as cold as it would go and let the water stream over her wrists and hands, then bent down to drink.

Elis was in the gift shop, studying a model of an early flying machine.

"I'm considering buying this," he said. "What do you think?"

With closed eyes and her head against the metro carriage window, Rakel told Elis about Gustav and the woman who had to be Frederikke. From time to time, Elis asked her to repeat something and Rakel had to shout to make herself heard, because the top part of the window was open a crack and while it did let in some cool air, it also admitted the thunderous roar of the carriage hurtling through the underground. They got off at Gare du Nord.

Their hotel was a nineteenth-century building whose insides had been ripped out and replaced with a beehive structure of narrow hallways and tiny rooms with irregular floorplans. The floors were covered with a carpet that might be called beige. Their room contained two single beds, made up with immaculately white sheets and dappled bedspreads, a stiff armchair and a narrow desk at which probably nothing had ever been written.

Rakel collapsed on her bed. Elis paced back and forth between the door and the windows overlooking the train station and a heavily trafficked intersection. "So he's known all along? What a traitor."

"I'm sure there's an explanation..."

Elis snorted with derision. "That doesn't make it okay. Think about Dad." He claimed to need a cigarette and spent a good while trying to open the window.

Rakel's stomach was still bubbling. The noise from the street sliced sharply into her brain and the lamplight morphed into febrile flowers on the inside of her eyelids.

"What? Do you need to throw up again? Come on." Elis pulled her up and deposited her in the bathroom.

Rakel rolled up on the tiled floor. Unlike the bathroom at Arts et Métier, this one was meticulously clean. She could have spent forever in the foetal position on the cool floor, with the world happening at a safe remove. While she waited for the retching to start, she thought about past interactions with Gustav, everyday things that for unknown reasons had stuck in her memory and were now lifted out of history. Among those remembrances were his visits to Berlin.

During the year Rakel lived there to study German, which for the majority of the ex-pat Swedes was a euphemism for partying and letting loose, he would visit regularly. He claimed he was in town anyway – thanks to some exhibition or event he'd let himself "be dragged into" by his gallerist – but he often just seemed sick of Sweden. Rakel only had a few lectures a week and split the rest of her time between the Staatsbibliothek and the public pool. At the library, she read, memorised long vocab lists, and whispered verbs under her breath until her head was a tangled jumble of the simple past and present tense. At the pool, she got changed at a leisurely pace, surrounded by older German ladies who took no notice of her, and then she swam as many laps as she could before staggering into the sauna. Such were the days that surrounded Gustav's visits. He always called a few days in advance to check if she possibly had the time and inclination to see her old godfather, and every time she answered of course, and then rearranged any plans she might have. Their routine consisted of some kind of art activity, a stroll through the city, weather permitting, and dinner at one of Berlin's better restaurants. Rakel especially remembered an occasion at the start of her stay. They went to Borchardt. She'd put on her one decent dress, a black one with long lace sleeves she'd bought in a charity shop for five euros, and put her hair up so no one could tell she'd cut it herself with nail scissors while drunk. Gustav had looked unusually proper in a dress shirt and had insisted on a seven-course meal to celebrate selling a painting.

"I liked that painting an awful lot and didn't really want to part with it," he said. "It's of your mother, by the way. But it was a museum and they paid me a bloody ton of money. What's champagne in German? Or do they have some kind of German version that doesn't support the enemy nation of France?"

"I think that France thing is more or less in the past."

"Order a bottle, will you? Make it Dom Pérignon if they have it."

He pushed his caviar around his plate, offered her his scallops, rejected his halibut, topped Rakel up with the last of the champagne and waved to one of the silent waiters for more. Then he leaned back in his chair and wanted to know everything about Berlin.

Rakel straightened up and told him – fairly ramblingly, to her own mind – about her life.

"You're so hard-working," Gustav said, his face beaming. "Really disciplined. Just like Cecilia."

In his eyes, Rakel excelled at asceticism and virtue, a smaller version of the Pallas Athena figure that was her mother. But the truth was that she'd devised routines and rules as a means to handling life. She was broke and unhappy. Alexander was in love with someone else. It was impossible not to make a note of when he came and went, when he came home at all. It was better to simply not be in the flat and to keep very busy. If she was thinking about verb tenses, she didn't have to think about all the other things. If she swam herself to exhaustion, she had a moment's respite from the nagging worry in her chest. What Gustav viewed as hard work and discipline was in reality an attempt to stave off a complete collapse.

Rakel had never really studied properly – upper secondary had been a confused time of frenetic page flipping in the hallways and essay writing the day before the deadline – but now she'd discovered how well she could do if she actually applied herself. She was top of her class and her teachers felt she had a genuine knack for languages. Unfortunately, that was due not to any inherent genius, but rather the fact that she went to the library instead of Berghain. She didn't waste time on coming down from coke-fuelled party nights, didn't burn out her synapses like sparklers, and even though the hazy underwater world of drugs should, at least in theory, have seemed appealing, she had no desire to give up what little control she still had, which consisted primarily of learning flawless, fluent German.

Gustav studied her across the table. "Are you eating enough? You look a bit on the thin side."

"You sound like Dad."

"Well, we can't have you wasting away."

Rakel looked down at her plate and let slip: "Well, I guess things have been a bit tough lately." She instantly regretted it.

Gustav started fiddling with his napkin. "Life," he said. "What is there to say. A never-ending series of trials and disappointments. Here, have some more. Young people think it gets better with time, old people think it was better when they were young, since at least then they were young. Hey, this fish isn't bad, actually."

"Really."

"This is a great place, don't you think? Wildly bourgeois, of course, but I'm wondering if the bourgeoisie hasn't been undeservedly maligned all these years. After all, it's the bourgeoisie that carries the Fabergé egg of civilisation through the bleak trenches that constitute our beloved Europe – where is that from?"

"No idea."

"Could it be Céline? Or Hesse? Anyway…"

The loneliness grew vast and dark, spreading out like an impenetrable, oily moat between her and the world. At regular intervals, Gustav popped out to smoke. One time, he was gone for over twenty minutes. The waiter asked kindly if the Fräulein would like anything else, but the Fräulein shook her head and smiled, her lips pressed together. She was considering just getting up and leaving when Gustav finally returned, fiddling with his braces and pushing up his glasses, which had slipped down towards the tip of his nose, apologising a hundred times over for his rude absence and saying he simply had to have a slice of Black Forest cake.

Several months later, Rakel saw the painting he'd made after that same visit. It showed her on a street at dusk, with her coat wrapped around her and a big fox-fur hat on her head. It was an incisive and precise portrait of a sad, troubled young person, and for some reason it had made her feel even worse.

Now, with her cheek pressed against the bathroom floor at Hôtel du Nord, Rakel counted as well as her dazed brain would allow. That dinner must have taken place roughly at the same time Philip Franke was staring up at Cecilia's window. Gustav could easily have gone from meeting one of his Pallas Athenas to the other. They'd lived in Berlin at the same time. Walking through the university corridors with her head bowed, Rakel might have passed her mother on her way to her Greek course. As she crammed German vocab at the library, Cecilia might have been browsing the shelves just feet away. Gustav had known. Gustav could have told Cecilia exactly where her daughter was. And what had he done with that knowledge?

Rakel heaved herself up over the toilet bowl. Convulsions racked her body, her stomach lurched, she had no choice but to submit to the process, hugging the cool rim of the toilet, and hurling. It all had to come out.

Her throat burned.

Either he'd kept it to himself or he'd told her. If he had in fact told Cecilia, she must have decided not to make contact. Faced with the decision of being with her children or not, she had chosen not to. Once again, she'd turned her back and left.

And if Gustav simply hadn't said anything? Had known but kept it to himself?

She flushed the toilet and staggered to her feet. There was a knock on the bathroom door.

"Hello? How's it going in there? Do you need anything?" She opened the door and Elis shook his head. "You look like shit," he said.

Rakel collapsed onto her bed and must have passed out, because she woke up a while later with her brother's face hovering over her.

"Are you okay? I was thinking of going for a walk. Saint-Germain was where she and Dad lived, right?"

"Yes. By Rue de Rennes." Rakel took stock: the nausea seemed to have subsided. Now, she was just infinitely tired. "It's really far if you're walking. But you can take the metro over there. Give me the map, I'll show you."

Elis emptied the contents of his backpack onto his bed: a water bottle, the battered stack of papers that was the first part of her translation, a phone charger and their dad's map of Paris with a list of streets on the back. "Who needs Google Maps when you have an alphabetical list of streets?" he'd said, deaf to all protest. Now, as Elis unfolded it, something fell to the floor.

"Some kind of picture," he said indifferently, handing it to Rakel.

It was a Polaroid of a young Martin standing next to a cute brunette she didn't recognise. She had one arm around Martin and Martin had one hand on her thigh. They were laughing and she was leaning against him; her head fit under his chin, like puzzle pieces. The date was printed on the back: 03 Oct 86.

Elis's voice was distant and thin. "The purple line goes all the way to Saint-Sulpice. Are you sure you don't want anything from the pharmacy? My French teacher says they have properly strong over-the-counter drugs in France."

32

The freezing torrent of water knocked the breath out of Rakel. She counted to thirty and then to sixty. By the time she reached a hundred, her skin was covered with goosebumps but her head was clear, the meeting with Philip hazy like a fever dream and, for the first time, something akin to logic was coming to the fore.

Elis was still out.

Rakel left the hotel on wobbly legs. Her stomach was growling. It felt like she'd not eaten anything her entire life. In her bag were her translation notepad and *Ein Jahr*, whose ink-covered pages were beginning to fall out. But she only had a few chapters left to translate.

She walked down the street. It was early evening. Above the rooftops, the sky spread out in soft, blue pastels. The warmth of the day lingered, but the oppressive humidity was gone. The streets were full of people in summer clothing. When she came across a Vietnamese restaurant, Rakel stepped inside, blinking at the fluorescent light as she was led to a table covered by a garish wax tablecloth. She ordered a beer, spring rolls and noodle soup. The beer was cold, and she immediately knocked back half of it. When the spring rolls came, she devoured them. The greasy wrappers melted in her mouth.

Rakel wiped the grease from her fingers. She had a lot to think about, and she started with her mother. Think, think, Rakel Berg. Not too much, but not too little, either. Thinking without feeling trapped a person in her own head, and feeling without thinking had exactly the same result. It turned you inwards, towards your own world of experience. After all, a person could feel just about anything, and there was no guarantee those feelings were anchored in the real world. Something had driven Cecilia away from her children, from her husband, from her work, from her entire life, and it could hardly have been rationality. No, in this case, reason had failed the otherwise so sensible scholar Cecilia Berg. A complete breakdown of the ability to think rationally. Red flags waving wildly to anyone still in charge of their faculties. One rash decision after another.

First, there was her leaving, her disappearance, which drew a sharp line through her family's life as well as her own. Leaving like that was an action that could never be overlooked. It would always be there, like a wound in their history. There was no way of pretending her disappearance was no big deal, when in fact it was so outside the realm of normal behaviour. And there is only one thing to do when you've done something unspeakably stupid, Rakel mused, and that's to try to *speak about it*. But instead, years of silence had followed. Not a single sign of life. No attempt at reconciliation. Words could never erase what had happened, but they could have opened a path forward. But instead of speaking, this master of languages had stayed silent. The translator had had nothing to say.

Her soup came. Rakel slurped it down, spattering broth on her last clean shirt.

Then, it was Cecilia's flitting about on the outskirts of her old life. Regardless of what Gustav may have said or not said, his presence had been a means of contacting her family. *Is*, Rakel corrected herself. *Is* a means. She stared at her phone on the table. The screen was dark and silent.

Cecilia had left Martin, she'd left her children, she'd left Philip Franke. But she hadn't left Gustav. She had come back to him. She had chosen him and rejected them. Because that was undeniable: either way, you made a choice. Doing nothing is doing something. Life is constant forward motion through an infinite number of crossroads where you have to choose one way or another. You can't escape your life decisions by not making them. It just means your choices are made passively. For years, her children, Elis and her, had been a phone call away, but it was a phone call Cecilia had never made. On the other hand, that phone call was an ever-present possibility: she *could* call. She had placed herself in a Schrödinger situation where she could simultaneously come back and be gone forever. She could leave Gustav again – and maybe that was precisely why she had been able to come back to him. Because a person who comes back has to face the consequences of their leaving, and what did Gustav have to hold against Cecilia? He was an old friend who'd been abandoned, he could hold that against her. He could offer general ethical objections to her actions. But a friend armed with harsh reproaches, if Gustav was even capable of those – Rakel doubted it – was, after all, something entirely different from an abandoned family. And Cecilia wanted nothing to do with that family. She had no desire to play the role of mother. The empty space she'd left behind was apparently of no interest to her. She preferred to let there be a hole where she had once existed.

And accompanying the inescapable how-could-she-leave-her-children question always buzzing just within earshot during Rakel's childhood: why hadn't she come back? Every day that had passed since she walked out was also a day that she hadn't returned. As a child, Rakel had imagined a variety of comforting scenarios, all built on the premise that Cecilia was trying to get home but for various reasons couldn't.

Maybe she'd lost her memory like Geena Davis in *Long Kiss Goodnight*, which ten-year-old Rakel watched on TV late one night when Martin was busy with some important deadline and had forgotten that it was long past her bedtime. Maybe she'd been thrown in prison after being wrongfully convicted in a country without a functioning legal system. Maybe she'd been the only survivor of a shipwreck, crawling onto a desert island, where she was eating coconuts and struggling to make a fire with a magnifying glass and a piece of paper… In time, Rakel had come to realise those were childish notions, but she didn't want to consider the alternatives. The alternatives were worse. The alternatives were thoughts that bordered on unthinkable and that had to be shoved hard into the far back of her mind. And so, Rakel had ignored the alternatives, and every time she read or saw something about a person with amnesia, hope and expectation had flared deep inside her.

Remembering that now, fifteen years later, was like finding a box full of her old toys: the joy of the reunion interwoven with the realisation that their time was past. They were relics she would never have use for again. Their magic was gone, the veil of fairy tale had been lifted. What was left was reality and she had to find a way to live in it. And in reality, there existed a Cecilia Berg who had lived a few U-Bahn stops away from her daughter without making herself known. She had to try to comprehend that. Fantasies about desert islands were no help. Nor were recriminations, for that matter.

Rakel summoned the images Philip Franke's story had awakened inside her: mother and daughter at Humboldt University, one on her way to German class, the other to her Greek course. Cecilia Berg had always been frozen in time, forever thirty-three years old. To a child, thirty-three wasn't all that different from forty-three or fifty-three, but with every passing year, Rakel was pushed one notch closer to the number where their ages would converge. Wittgenstein's diaries had been published when Cecilia was twenty-eight, which meant she'd started work on them at twenty-five or twenty-six at the latest. Twenty-six was only two years older than Rakel was now. How had she even come up with the idea? Translating one of the great philosophers of the twentieth century was an undertaking in a completely different league to Rakel's dabbling with Franke's novel, which was a private project besides, intended only for her and Elis. But Cecilia had always pushed against the limits of the possible. Circling the last outpost of reason.

In hindsight, the course of events could easily be interpreted as inevitable, but once upon a time it had been as fluid and changeable as the present. *Now*, it was easy to wrap Cecilia in a narrative about genius and work ethic, but the question was if she could not just as easily have failed? The grand doctoral thesis, which had taken so many years to write, and had grown so expansive, could have foundered under its own weight. The Wittgenstein translation must have been far beyond her proven ability. Granted, her book of essays had been more reasonable in scope, but if Rakel wanted to come close to achieving something similar by her age, she would already have to be doing it full-time. How many hours had she spent on her little school assignment on Freud's death drive? And that was just *one* text. A fraction of the work that had gone into *Atlantic Flight*.

She was always so excessive, as Max had put it. Her world had different proportions.

Rakel spent a while fishing out the last of the noodles. By all appearances, Cecilia had continued along the same track after leaving. But this Ancient Greek thing really was a toe over the line. The Greek was a descent into Hades.

Unlike Philip – and Martin, too, for that matter – Rakel had some experience with the classical languages. After upper secondary, the university's course catalogue had thrown her into a spiral of anxiety, and through persistent emailing with her guidance counsellor, she'd managed to circumvent the cap for how many credits you were allowed take each term. Which meant she had room for something in addition to intellectual history and German. Should she go for theoretical philosophy? Religion? Because she was reading *The Secret History* during the application process, she went with Latin, which neither of her parents had studied, which was a relief because she didn't have to hear

"Ah – *Cecilia's* daughter", but also a problem because she had no one to guide her from the safe lookout point of experience.

The course was held in a lecture hall on Wednesdays between six and nine. The class consisted of a dozen disparate souls ranging in age from nineteen to seventy-two. The instructor was an ancient, owl-like man completely devoid of Julian Morrow qualities, who took forever to write verbs on the whiteboard with what then turned out to be a permanent marker. Rakel, who might have been the only member of the group with a fully functional prefrontal cortex, flipped to the end of the textbook and drew geometric figures in the margins of her notebook. Aside from a general sense of the linguistic structure and a handful of quotes she had with varying success thrown about in bars, her Latin studies had provided the foundation of a lesson she was only now wrapping her head around: there's not enough time for everything, so you have to choose. Learning Latin properly and then applying that knowledge in a productive way would take years. One term of part-time study was like lighting a match in a pitch-black cathedral and for a few flickering moments realising just how much was still hidden in the shadows. Granted, Rakel could have gone down the path of classical philology, but that would have meant closing other doors. Such were the basic realities of existence. There was no way to keep all doors open. Because a person's life is finite from the start, everything that happens does so at the expense of something else.

Martin sometimes said literature doesn't exist for its own sake. If a book is no longer being read, that might be a pity, sure, but it's also the inevitable march of history. The function of literature lay in its meeting with the reader, in the interaction that occurred when a text touched the hidden recesses of a human soul. A text without a reader was an artefact, a ceramic shard from a bygone era which was at best of interest to a small number of archaeologically minded individuals. At the end of the day, he said, the value of language and literature lay in their use. There was no point publishing books no one wanted to read. There was no point knowing a language unless you used it.

And this, Rakel thought, leaning back in her chair and looking around for the waitress, was the crux of the matter: her mother was too old to use her Greek for anything productive. If she dedicated all her time to learning the language, she could potentially master it enough to do something real with it within a few years, but that would require dropping all other potential projects. Which seemed unlikely. So what could Cecilia do with her Greek? She could read the *Odyssey* on sleepless nights, penetrate the dusty passages and forgotten tombs of Ancient Greek in exalted solitude, but *cui bono*? In her grand exit from the world, she'd rejected the opportunity to use her talent in the service of civilisation through teaching others. Since then, her life had consisted of a series of flights from one library activity to another, with herself as the only active participant. Endless aimless wanderings through the ruins for Cecilia Berg.

Rakel waved for the bill.

Outside, a balmy blue night was waiting, full of laughter and voices, a revving moped, windows being thrown open, snatches of music. Rakel stepped out into the street at the exact same moment the street lights turned on, a long string of milky-white lamps that with a faint humming lit up the boulevards.

*

The next morning, their train glided through the suburbs of Paris on its way to Copenhagen.

"I really hope we're on the right track with Frederikke," Rakel said. The idea that Frederikke might be involved hadn't occurred to her before. As it was, they had very little to go on other than Philip's description and the fact that the Danish woman had been the closest thing to a confidante their mother had had. It was perfectly plausible, but on the other hand, it was also possible Rakel was getting lost in a world of her own making, in which all information from the outside world was adjusted to fit her fantasies. How was she to tell the difference?

"We don't exactly have a lot of other leads." Elis peered out from under the British-style boating hat with which he'd covered his face. "Well, we could go to Berlin and hope to run into her on the street. Now that's a great plan. Anyway, I always thought Frederikke was a bit fishy." That last part was swallowed by a yawn.

He'd come back late from his Saint-Germain expedition and had launched straight into a thorough account of his evening. He'd tried to get into the building where their father had lived, but it had turned out to be locked. Foiled, he'd gone looking for Serge Gainsbourg's old house on 5 Rue de Verneuil instead, smoking a devotional cigarette outside it. Then he'd walked around, had a kebab, got lost and ended up by the Panthéon, where he'd been pretty sure Jacques Brel was buried, but that turned out not to be true. Then he'd had coffee at Café de Flore and the waiter had insisted on speaking English, which did not track with what everyone said about French waiters. Somewhere around that point, Rakel had dozed off, and she hadn't woken up again until her alarm yanked her out of oblivion, and they suddenly had to hurry to catch their train.

"I'm sure she doesn't know anything," Rakel said now, more to avoid tempting fate than because she believed it.

"I guess we'll find out, right?"

Their phones dinged in unison. First there was a picture of a bland-looking house set against an offensively blue sky. Then, in a series of individual messages:

Three weeks in July. What do you say?

It's by the sea. Walking distance to some kind of village

Elis: you could practise your French

Have talked to the renter. V confused person. Need reply ASAP

Google Cassis

Elis sighed. "A while ago, he wanted us to climb Machu Picchu together and was manically searching for a hotel."

"He didn't mention anything about that to me."

"That's because you say things like 'Why would I want to climb a giant phallic symbol?' He came really close to buying three plane tickets to Peru. I think he's under-stimulated. He should get a hobby."

"He's working on that Wallace biography, though, right?"

"If he ever finishes that, he's really going to go off the deep end."

Another ding.

Checking with Gustav, too. I'm sure he'll come.

Or something closer to Paris?

How's the continent btw?

Rakel closed the app. Overpasses and high-rises were swishing past outside. A few months ago, she would have been thrilled at the idea of a family getaway, but now it was impossible to imagine it as anything but a drawn-out chamber play. Her dad, going on and on about some house where William Wallace once spent two months. Gustav, drinking wine and reading the paper. Elis supplying involuntary comic relief. All while she herself walked around with a scream rolled up in her throat.

When the art history bloke at Ellen's party asked all the usual questions about Gustav – it felt like an eternity ago – Rakel had assumed she knew her godfather well, that she was able to answer any question but chose not to out of loyalty. Now, she wasn't so sure. Her entire life history had been shaken to its core, had slipped its moorings. Everything was in flux. Everything had to be re-evaluated. Her dad and Gustav had disqualified themselves from any claim to the truth through their stubborn silence, their shrugging and their winning smiles. In fact, at this moment she trusted Philip Franke, a man she'd met once, over the people she'd known her whole life. Philip's book was a eulogy to something lost. It was a confession and thus the opposite of wordlessness and silence. The masters of erasure Rakel had grown up with spent most of their time saying nothing at all.

She remembered one time in Berlin, an occasion that would probably have been forgotten were it not for the fact that the erasure had become glaringly explicit. The situation itself had not been particularly unusual. Gustav was exhibiting at his posh gallery and Rakel had gone to the vernissage. When she arrived, he'd exchanged a few words with her before flitting on to talk to someone else. Rakel had stood alone, surrounded by more grown-up, more confident people in expensive clothes. She'd wanted to leave immediately, but it would have seemed odd if she hadn't at least glanced at the paintings. She'd positioned herself at an appropriate distance from one of them, but the motif was blurred and diffuse. She'd blinked several times, her eyes burning.

"You must be Rakel?"

He'd introduced himself as Christopher Welton, a friend of Gustav's. Everything about him was pleasant: the handshake, the British accent, the deep tenor of his voice. He was somewhere between fifty and sixty, thinning grey hair, a relaxed posture under his blazer. She noted a camera dangling from a strap over his shoulder; he confessed he was a photographer.

"It's lovely to meet you," Welton said in English. He seemed to know quite a bit about her – how were her studies going? How did she like Berlin? – and his quiet, polite attention made her want to cry. When Gustav passed by, Welton had grabbed him and said: "I've had the immense pleasure of meeting your goddaughter."

Gustav had mumbled something. Welton's hand had stayed on his arm, resting heavily, as though to prevent him from leaving. Rakel had looked back and forth between the two of them and then begun to babble about how the paintings were terrific (she'd barely looked at them) but she had a party to go to (an outright lie).

The next evening, Gustav had taken her out for their usual dinner. He'd talked a lot about the exhibition, but hadn't so much as mentioned Christopher. He might as well not have existed. And the more time that passed without him being spoken of, the harder it became to ask the simplest of questions. At one point, Rakel had been about to say something completely innocent – that the Christopher Welton bloke had seemed nice, something like that – but it had felt almost physically impossible to get the words out, as though she'd suddenly gone mute.

"Well, I'm definitely not going on holiday with Gustav," Elis muttered under his straw hat. "But if Frederikke won't fess up, we can always hit him up next."

33

The room was as dark as a room gets on a Swedish summer night, the window was open a crack, the sheets were freshly laundered, but – and this was undeniably Martin's own fault, no two ways about it – the coffee he'd drunk at the office had probably ruined his already tentative ability to fall asleep. Thoughts were tumbling around his brain at high velocity, showing no sign of slowing down. The half-life of caffeine was supposedly six hours, or, put differently, the other side of midnight. To make matters worse, the rest of his evening had passed by in decadent depravity: instead of a proper dinner, he'd munched down a bag of crisps and had three beers while reading Lucas Bell's book *Notes from the Edge*, which had had a *Based on the True Story* slapped on under the title. The cover showed a picture of Bell in his prime. The joy of storytelling was there, you had to give him that. With a modicum of distance, an ounce more humour and extensive cuts, it could have been turned into a sharp-eyed account of the dark side of fame. Through myriad disparate scenes, the first-person narrator told the story of a past in which he'd been a celebrated author. First came his childhood in a grimy London suburb. One particularly long chapter took palpable delight in the description of a stepfather's depravity, another in that of an uncomprehending and rigid school where everyone was an idiot. Then, a grandmother-cum-fairy-godmother appeared, blessing our Author-To-Be with her faith in his potential, which no one else could sense at this point. His teachers, for instance, insisted on giving him mediocre grades, possibly to punish him for the fact that he was almost never there but outperformed his peers whenever he deigned to show up. "They couldn't tolerate," Bell wrote, "that I chose my own path instead of toeing the line of banal stupidity." After that, the author skipped ahead, straight to The Breakthrough. He'd always sensed he would one day achieve greatness, and at the age of eighteen, he began work on what would become his first novel. The writing of the book was covered in just a handful of pages; one day he had Decided and just like that, his book was published. That didn't quite tally with Martin's experience of how these things usually happened, but okay.

He flipped through a fragmented firework display of club nights, drugs and celebrities that were no longer quite so famous. Partying alternated with comedown and anxiety. After a while, the inescapable writer's block reared its ugly head. Bell's alter ego had spent the advance for his next book, and the advance after that, and the advance after *that*, and his publisher was becoming increasingly unwilling to fund his decadent lifestyle when they hadn't seen so much as a hint of a draft. (But then, they were a bunch of capitalists, with no sympathy for the torment of literary creation and the Author's endlessly fragile psyche.) The royalties from books sold also disappeared suspiciously quickly. (Though, granted, people were constantly hitting him up for money, and Bell would never say no, he was too kind-hearted, too kind-hearted for his own good. He lent people money left and right, but did anyone ever pay him back?) Other than on bars and clubs, he spent his money on a "Gothic castle" plus furnishings in the form of antiques, among other things, a stuffed peacock and a Victorian four-poster. In Martin's favourite paragraph, the narrator attended an auction while high, purchasing an inkhorn and a goose-feather quill that had supposedly belonged to French poet Arthur Rimbaud. For days, he worked on what he felt was an epic narrative – inkblots everywhere, he was having a hard time with the quill, being so wired – but when he sobered up a few days later, it all turned out to be gobbledygook. There were glimpses in that passage of Bell's eye for detail and black humour, like shimmering shards embedded in a pile of shit. After that, the story foundered into a narrative about a nervous but very talented artist whom the first-person narrator and his entourage picked up at a party that had gone off the rails, and who moved into the castle. The reader never found out what happened next, because Bell abruptly dropped the subject in favour of the filming of *A Season*, particularly his conflicts with the film's director, "an unmitigated imbecile and a malicious human being".

Martin rolled over onto his stomach and put the pillow over his head. Not publishing the book had been the right call, so why couldn't he just drop it? Why dwell on it like this? Why all this high-velocity activity in his brain? He should be exhausted. And soon enough, the birds would be singing, the trees in the park were full of them, all those birds with their tiny throats and vibrating tongues, singing like lunatics throughout the drawn-out dawn.

Lucas Bell had made him think about the nineties and thinking about the nineties meant taking the lid off an old, messy box. While Martin lay with his eyes closed, keeping his body as still as possible – Hemingway's method to combat sleeplessness, as he reminded himself – the chaotic period that had followed Cecilia's disappearance paraded through his head. He'd called Gustav the moment it was clear Cecilia was gone. And Gustav had with uncharacteristic initiative packed a bag and hopped on the first train to Gothenburg. He'd turned up at Djurgårdsgatan with a look on his face Martin didn't recognise: offended, slighted.

"What the fuck is she doing?" he snapped, dropping his seabag on the floor. "She just took off?"

Martin handed him the short letter she'd left. Gustav read it with raised eyebrows and shook his head.

They stayed up well into the night, sitting at the kitchen table with three bottles of good burgundy Martin had been saving for some more serious dinner party. At some point he must have dozed off, because when he woke up, Gustav was standing next to his bed with a breakfast tray.

"I didn't know if you wanted milk or not," he said, pulling up the blinds. Martin inspected the tray. Black coffee, cheese toast, the national and local morning papers. Among the mismatched tableware in their kitchen cabinets, Gustav had found a matching plate and cup. Gustav dug through his wardrobe and threw a pair of jeans and a sweater on the bed. "Get dressed." Then he closed the door behind him, and while Martin did his best to force down a slice of toast – he had absolutely zero appetite – he heard the muffled sounds of the usual morning conflicts. "You want a bottle, I assume. Okay: if you leave this teddy in my care for three minutes, I'll give you a bottle. How does that sound? Acceptable?"

The first week, Gustav slept on the sofa, then he moved into his studio in Masthugget. In the afternoons, he looked after the children, in a joint effort with Birgitta Berg. She'd taken the news of Cecilia's disappearance with her usual, sphinx-like calm.

"These things happen, I suppose," she'd said, at which point Martin had hurled a mug at the wall and shouted that these things don't fucking *happen*, people don't just take off, they might get divorced, and that was bad enough, surely if you married someone you had to consider it a fundamental agreement that you wouldn't just *fuck off*, if the marriage absolutely had to be dissolved, you had to do that the normal way, submit the relevant forms to the Tax Authority, you couldn't just leave, who the hell does that, it was insane, and in any event not something that just *happened*.

The mug broke into two pieces in a very unsatisfying manner. Birgitta picked them up and put them in the bin. She and Gustav exchanged significant looks. They finished each other's sentences. They went outside for a smoke when Martin banned them from smoking out of the kitchen window, with the unspoiled lungs of the children in mind. Birgitta took it upon herself to wash their clothes, even though Martin insisted he was doing fine on his own, and Gustav involved himself in all kinds of domestic tasks he'd never managed to perform properly for himself. Armed with a letter opener, he sat down to open and sort the post that had collected on the hallway dresser onto which Martin tossed all envelopes addressed to her face-down.

"All right," he said. "Let's see what we have here. No, Martin, don't leave. It might be something important. Let's have a little look, now…" The magazine *Divan* was offering a very significant discount on subscriptions at the moment. "No thanks," Gustav said. Cecilia's publisher announced that *Atlantic Flight* was back in print. "Who cares, as they say on the Continent." Max Schreiber had sent a photostat of a page from a German book, set in a Fraktur font, to which clung a Post-it note with a greeting in German. "*Trop tard, mon ami,*" Gustav sang. A notice from the head of department with information about construction on the third floor during the autumn term, which would affect a number of classrooms, but hopefully wouldn't cause too much disruption. And then there were some bills, which Martin mustn't forget to pay.

"That's it." He balled up the envelopes. "See, that wasn't so bad, was it? A hot tip is to open any manila envelopes, they're usually important."

It turned out Gustav also possessed a certain level of expertise when it came to what a person can eat when they can't eat. His meals consisted of a maximum of three ingredients, and usually just two – spaghetti and fishfingers, meatballs and macaroni, tinned pea soup which neither of the children liked but ate because it was Gustav serving it – while Martin was fed a special diet of tinned vegetable soup, a bowl of yoghurt, or, if the children weren't around, ice lollies. Gustav watched him eat. "Those last couple of bites, too," he urged. "You have to go to work tomorrow, you know."

You would have thought life would grant you some breathing room when your world unexpectedly fell apart, but, unfortunately, things carried on as usual. Martin had to pay rent and buy food and all sorts of other things, and in order to do that, he had to keep going to work, and in order to keep going to work, he had to get up in the morning, whether or not he'd slept that night. Sleeplessness, he discovered, came in two versions. One was that he simply didn't fall asleep, even though every fibre of his being was maximally wrung out. Sometimes he'd slip into a hazy slumber, but turning over or coughing was enough to make him resurface. The other version was when he woke up at half past three and couldn't get back to sleep. It was the witching hour, the time of day when all your misfortunes surround you like massive shadows, and the proportions of existence are twisted into unrecognisability. You just had to resign yourself to it. Martin counted the hours of sleep he'd managed to get. Anything above four was okay. You could absolutely go to work on four hours of sleep. He'd done it on two.

Even after Gustav moved up to Sjömansgatan, he came by every morning to wake Martin up.

"I've never got up this early in my life," he'd yawn, collapsing on the edge of the bed. "Half six. Jesus. It's brutal. We're being punished for our sins. Hey, no falling asleep now. Come on. *Au travail.*"

The face that greeted Martin in the bathroom mirror when he brushed his teeth looked like that of a man of at least forty. His hair stuck out above his ears in tufts. When was he supposed to find time to go have it cut? Unless the publishing company became more lucrative in the next two years, he was finding a new job. "You don't need to think about that now," Per said, putting a hand on his shoulder. "Just, you know – take things one step at a time." But no, Martin Berg was unable to take things one step at a time. He typed faster and faster on his computer. He made more and more phone calls. He shoved galley proofs into his backpack. He fell asleep surrounded by papers and woke up with a start when his alarm went off. He chivvied his children along in the hallway. He rode his bike without paying attention to the traffic. He went to the shops ten minutes before they closed. Trams rattled by on Karl Johansgatan. The horse chestnut trees unfurled their leaves, as though they were bestowing a blessing on the city's parks. The streets were swept clean of gravel. Bicycle bells rang. His children brought home weekly schedules from school. Post and papers that needed reading waited for him on his desk. Papers and more papers. He sorted them into piles. He went to the shops to buy pork chops. He told his daughter to put her book down at the table. He tumbled through time. Time was his only ally. He invested all his hope in time. Around him, people talked about how time heals all wounds, that it might sound like a cliché, but it's actually true. He nodded. Sure, he said. I guess so.

At night, he read manuscripts until the letters danced before his aching eyes.

When someone leaves, existence splits into a before and an after. This *after* seemed like it might be endless. The first few weeks, the mornings were not yet so bad, because every new day was the day she might return. Martin's heart raced every time footsteps echoed in the stairwell. When the phone rang or the post thudded onto the hallway floor, cruel hope slithered through him. Everyone seemed in complete agreement that she would be back any day now.

Cecilia's mother was convinced it was just "another one of her moods". Sooner or later, she'd come home. She'd always been selfish. She'd always been wilful. She'd never cared about the effect her actions had other people. Take, for example, her incomprehensible decision to give up painting. Would Cecilia have been able to give it up so lightly if she'd given even a moment's thought to how important it was to her father? If she had for one second considered how much it meant to someone who wasn't her? But Cecilia never thought about other people, Inger Wikner said over the phone. Only herself. She acted with no consideration for her loved ones. Take her "research", for instance, had she ever asked herself how it was impacting her family? Her children? She had preferred to bury her nose in books to spending time with her own children. She for her part, Inger said, had stayed home with all four of her children, Cecilia included, and they'd never had to go to nursery or been handed over to strangers. Granted, there had been nannies, but they could be viewed as complementary. She, Inger, had indisputably been their mother. She had cared for them, fed them, witnessed their first steps, dressed them and raised them. It hadn't always been easy, given that they were in Addis Ababa, far from any real civilisation, but she'd done her best and she'd done a good job. What Cecilia had never wanted to accept was that motherhood took time. It took everything you had. Not only during pregnancy, but for a number of years afterwards. You had to be prepared to give yourself over to the service of the child. How her daughter had grown into such a fickle and unpredictable person was a mystery. Possibly, Inger sighed, she had been too accommodating, too sensitive to her children's needs. Perhaps she had denied Cecilia some kind of necessary frustration. Perhaps her attentive care had laid the foundation for a worldview that revolved around Cecilia. It was possible. But she had only done what she'd felt was best, she'd followed her heart, because a mother's instinct could never lead you wrong, could it now? Could it? Anyway, she was sure Cecilia would reappear any moment now. How Martin could bear to live with someone like that was beyond Inger. Such a *betrayal*. Such a fundamental betrayal. She remembered one time, when—

Martin removed the receiver from his ear. Inger's voice buzzed, mosquito-like, from a distance.

She hadn't even given him a narrative to hold up to the world. Everyone understood "we're separated". But Cecilia had created an in-between state that evaded every satisfying label. She had "left". She had "disappeared". But had she "left him"? Empirically speaking, of course she had. It was an irrefutable fact that she had left her husband and children. She was no longer present in the flat. She never opened the door. Her typewriter could not be heard from the study. But *leaving* didn't preclude *returning*. A person who leaves can suddenly turn up again, teary-eyed and repentant, asking for forgiveness and to be taken back. On closer analysis of the simple verb *to leave*, what did it really mean? What was the actual meaning of the sentence "Cecilia Berg has left her family"? Should we assume from it that Cecilia Berg is never coming back? Is it a temporary absence? Is it a definitive and absolutely established fact, or something that could be negotiated in an as-of-yet-unknown future?

During one of his many sleepless nights, Martin flipped through *Tractatus logico-philosophicus* without being able to fully articulate why, other than that he was desperate for something to hold onto. (He could hear Cecilia's amused voice right next to his ear: "And you chose *Wittgenstein*?") Wittgenstein, Martin thought, had tried to bring order to the world through tightly controlled statements. In the middle of a world war, this utter misfit had lain in the trenches, formulating aphorisms which he then used to create short moments of clarity amid chaos, pockets of reason in a world that was falling apart.

There had been a time before Cecilia. There had been a time when she was just a gangly girl in a military parka. He remembered them sitting in a café. He was reading and commenting on her essay. He remembered her silence, her unwavering gaze, the way she squinted when she took a drag on her cigarette, her pale hand pushing a strand of hair behind her ear.

The book was full of underlining and marginal notes he couldn't remember writing. Now, he discovered a paragraph on a page whose untouched whiteness revealed that he'd paid it no attention the last time around:

> *The limits of my language mean the limits of my world.*
> *Logic fills the world: the limits of the world are also its limits.*
> *We cannot therefore say in logic: This and this there is the world, that there is not.*
> *For that would apparently presuppose that we exclude certain possibilities, and this cannot be the case since otherwise logic must get outside the limits of the world: that is, if it could consider these limits from the other side also. What we cannot think, that we cannot think: we cannot therefore say what we cannot think.*

Martin circled it in pencil and read on.

When two months had passed with no word from Cecilia, Gustav decided they needed to go away. He rented a cottage in Bokenäs he'd seen an ad for in the paper. They left the day after school ended.

The house was red with white trim, wavy window glass and creaking wooden floors, and located just a few hundred yards from the Gullmar fjord. Martin, who had spent his childhood sailing holidays below decks with comic books and seasickness, was completely unfamiliar with the area.

They returned the next few summers, but that first visit, that first summer without Cecilia, it was an undiscovered world. The morning after their arrival, Martin woke to early morning light trickling in through mosquito nets. He crept out of bed, pulled on a T-shirt, closed the door to the bedroom. While the coffee machine gurgled, he sat on the front steps. The grass glittered with dew. Over by the edge of the forest, tendrils of mist billowed just above ground level. It was still chilly, but he couldn't bring himself to go back inside for a jumper. With completely uncharacteristic foresight, Gustav had arranged for the morning papers to be forwarded, so Martin trudged over to the letterbox without any real hope of finding anything. But there they were, damp and fresh. An earwig fell out of *Dagens Nyheter*.

Timewise, every day seemed to stretch to breaking point, and Martin was never sure how long they actually spent there. Two weeks? Three? The delightfully monotonous passage of days was broken only by the occasional trip to Lysekil to stock up on provisions and rent a film to watch on the ancient TV Elis and Rakel had accepted, martyr-like, as the main source of entertainment. In the mornings, they went down to the sea, the children running ahead of them on the path. Martin had made sandwiches, and Gustav was talking about some kind of feud between two of his artist friends in Stockholm. Out on the cliffs, the world fell away, all that existed was the sun in his eyes and the wind snatching at his shirt, life shrank to include only the present; his one task was to stand on this cliff and watch his daughter's lutrine head bobbing among the miniature armada by the jetty. Gustav offered real-time critique of the children's swimming achievements like some sports commentator.

And so the days passed without any major drama. But Martin had left the phone number to the cottage on the answering machine at home, and every time the phone rang – thankfully not very often – he began to tremble all over. He was always the first to snatch up the receiver, because nipping hope in the bud was his best option. It was never her, of course. It was Per Andrén, his mum, an author who wanted his manuscript returned and, once, Gustav's gallerist. In order to manage a somewhat normal tone, Martin imagined being at work.

"Hi, KG, good, thanks… you?"

Gustav, seated at the kitchen table with a crossword puzzle, stiffened. "You talk to him," he hissed before slinking out of the room.

"I'm afraid Gustav's not here at the moment," Martin said.

KG cursed angrily. "I swear to god, he'd better be on a plane to New York," he said.

"Unfortunately, I don't think that's the case. Can I give him a message?"

The gallerist sighed. "Ask him to call me."

When Martin hung up, Gustav's face appeared around the door frame. "What was that about?"

"KG seems to be under the impression that you should be on your way to New York."

"Oh. Was that it? Yeah, his friend's gallery is having some sort of exhibition. They're nagging me about showing my face at the opening, but what's the point? They have my paintings, right? They have my *best* paintings, even. What do they need me for?" He laughed nervously. "I told him I wasn't going. I really did. Or, well, I'm pretty sure I did."

Over the next few days, Gustav combed the papers for any mention of the New York exhibition. When his search yielded no result, he threw the paper aside, muttering that art journalism in this country was a joke.

One night, they were sitting up late in the garden with beer and cold hot dogs. The sky shimmered opalescent and beyond the trees they could glimpse the silver shards of the sea. Their glowing cigarettes drew lines of light in the gloom. Somewhere in the distance, an owl hooted.

Gustav leaned back in his chair. His beautiful face was sketched with deep shadows. He took off his glasses and studied Martin. For a long moment, neither one of them looked away. A light was on above the porch and moths were fluttering around it, singeing their wings, veering aside only to immediately approach anew.

"I think you have to get used to the thought that it's over," Gustav said. "Even if she were to come back, it would be over. Even if she were sitting right next to you now, she would always be out of reach. And that's worse when you think about it. When someone is near and unreachable at the same time."

And around the porch light, the moths danced.

34

The linden trees on Vasagatan rustled, and Martin turned the page of
the manuscript. He'd neglected to print the cover letter, so he had no
idea what it was about or who the author was, and now the text itself
kept slipping away from him, too. It might be because he'd only slept
three hours the night before.

He deliberately refused to check his watch, because if he didn't
know how late Gustav was, he wouldn't be as annoyed when Mr
Renowned Artist eventually turned up. The soothing rustling of the
trees made him want to close his eyes.

He'd employed his usual strategy when faced with sleeplessness,
which was to get up and do something useful in the morning, even
though he'd barely slept a wink. At nine, he'd stepped through the
doors of Hagabadet, where he met Charlotte von Becker on her
way to a yoga session. He ran three miles on the treadmill and went
through his normal routine. Afterwards, he'd retired to Café Cigarren's
outdoor seating area. It was a cold, clear morning, and unlike the
night before, Järntorget Square was deserted. Seagulls were strutting
through the remnants of the previous night, snapping up dropped
chips. Life, Martin had thought, making sure to choose a table that
didn't belong to one of the regulars, wasn't so bad after all. He had
plans for the summer. He was meeting up with Gustav. Since his
body would need to recoup lost sleep, he would doubtless sleep like
a baby tonight. He had a fresh manuscript to read. His brain was
generating a raft of ideas related to the Austrian philosopher's book
of essays, and while his coffee cooled enough to be drinkable, he'd
written a long email to Max about those ideas and about contemporary philosophy in the wake of postmodernism more generally, then
changed his mind for some reason he couldn't put his finger on,
saved the email as a draft, changed his mind again, sent it. Within
minutes, there had been a reply from Max, at least as long. Martin
had decided to wait to give it a proper read until he was intellectually
intact again.

The rest of the day had passed in a sluggish fog. One by one, the hours were checked off as he waited for the moment he was going to leave for Valand. And now – Martin allowed himself to glance at his watch – Gustav was over thirty minutes late.

Martin would obviously have to sort out all the practical aspects of their holiday. Gustav probably didn't even have a valid passport. Fine, maybe he did have a valid passport since he'd been in England all spring. But tickets, reservations, travel insurance: all of that would fall to Martin. It wasn't the work he objected to (he could always delegate to Patricia, the intern) but rather this passivity-elevated-to-life-principle. Everything had a tendency to just work out around Gustav, but the question was if he realised that was because *someone else* made it work out. That it wasn't just the benevolent nature of the universe.

Martin shoved the sheaf of papers into his bag and took a walk around the hopeless intersection of Vasagatan and Avenyn, because after so many years away, Gustav might have forgotten that "see you at Valand" meant "see you at the corner shop by Valand".

Up by the art museum, the poster advertising Gustav's retrospective was everywhere. It was a remarkable painting, there was no denying it.

When Gustav still hadn't turned up after forty minutes, Martin called several times. No answer. He stood there with the phone in his hand. He could call Maria Malm and ask if she'd like to go for a glass of wine. This thought was followed by enormous weariness. He returned the phone to his inside pocket and started to walk westwards.

As long as he kept moving, it wasn't so bad. As long as he kept moving, he was on his way. It was when he stopped that the world began to spin. The facades of the buildings grew mute and heavy. Whole city blocks seemed drained of life. Emptiness spread out and gravity pulled him down, making it hard to lift his feet up properly, his body felt like concrete, and what was the point of walking anyway, it was just the same old streets, the same doorways, the same windows, the same people, the same restaurants serving greasy Thai food, the same cafés where bored young people drank expensive lattes, the same tourists pretending to be interested in Haga and eating bizarre cinnamon buns, the same cobblestones, the same books in the second-hand bookshops.

Linnégatan was deserted. The population seemed concentrated in the outdoor seating area outside the Haga Cinema. Maybe they could go for a pint there? Gustav had probably taken his phone off the hook and fallen asleep. Which was typical, by the way. Not that Martin would say anything. He would refrain from commenting. They were going to have a nice time and he was going to lay out his plan for a summer on the Riviera and Gustav's spirits would immediately rise, because he was no doubt morose and brooding in the wake of all his success. It would do him good to get away.

Without really knowing how it had happened, Martin found that he'd climbed the stairs at Oscar Fredrik and was now on Fjällgatan. He was flushed and out of breath. The sun stung his eyes. He fiddled with his Wayfarers and the world retreated into a muted shade of green. He walked up the hill. If he carried on straight, he would end up in Majorna. He was close to home, as a matter of fact. But instead he crossed the street, and there was the steep incline of Sjömansgatan. Gustav was unlikely to be home, of course. He'd probably got hammered and stayed the night at some old mate's house and was at this moment playing pool with no thought for Martin. He was going to call Maria and suggest a glass of wine somewhere, maybe around eight, that would give him time to go home and shower and relax for five minutes…

The door to the building was open. A young man was carrying in a floor lamp and an overflowing Ikea bag. New flooring had been put in in the lobby. He could hear music coming from one of the flats. Martin climbed up to the third floor.

Gustav's door looked exactly as it had thirty years ago. BECKER on the letterbox and a faded note that said NO CIRCULARS PLEASE!, written and taped up by Martin in a fit of annoyance at the piles of flyers that kept collecting on the hallway floor.

He rang the doorbell.

When nothing happened, he opened the mail slot. "Hello?" he called. "Gustav?" He hoped there were no neighbours watching him through their peepholes.

Martin tried the door, more because it was the kind of thing people did on film than because he had any hope of finding it unlocked.

It opened.

The blinds were down. The air was stuffy and smelled strongly of tobacco and something else, possibly the stale loneliness of a flat that was abandoned for most of the year. Stagnant time.

He turned on the hallway light and only later realised Gustav's shoes must have been sitting there, the same Converse he'd worn to the art opening and which Martin had taken as a sign of Gustav's unwillingness to accept the fact that he now belonged to the older generation. He must have registered the presence of the shoes subconsciously, because it was with an uneasy feeling in his stomach that he took the few steps through the hallway and into the only other room.

There, in the armchair.

Doubled over.

And then, everything blurred. Martin shouted something. Put his hands to Gustav's forehead and throat. Feeling for a pulse. Shook him, cursing. His hands were shaking so hard he almost dropped his phone, and after giving emergency services his name and Gustav's address, his stomach turned and he threw up.

35

It was the next morning, and Martin was in bed. He could move his arms. He could move his legs. He just couldn't get up. He just couldn't get himself to the bathroom and into the shower. Eating breakfast was an absurd idea. The phone rang. He didn't answer. It rang again. He still didn't answer. It rang one more time. The sound didn't really bother him. After a while, you got used to it. The shrill rings, the merciful silence in between. He stayed in the same position. Messages dinged. He stayed where he was. He wondered what time it was. He was floating in a timeless half-light. He couldn't tell if it was minutes or hours passing.

He woke up again. Dry mouth, heavy body. He stumbled out of bed, had to lean against the door frame. Every single object in the flat was in exactly the same place it had been when Martin Berg had left his home to meet a friend for dinner.

He drank some water. There were lines on his face from the creases on his pillow. Blots of colour danced before him. The clock in the kitchen said twenty past eleven. He was supposed to have attended a meeting at ten. The morning papers lay on the doormat. Gustav on the front page of *Göteborgs-Posten*, one of those really good black-and-white photographs. Photographer: Christopher Welton. Martin made a mental note to mention him to Amir. Sooner or later, you always needed a good photographer. Thinking about that, he forgot for a moment the fact the morning paper was shouting at him:

NATIVE SON GUSTAV BECKER DEAD. Internationally renowned painter Gustav Becker, born in 1962, was found dead in his flat in Gothenburg yesterday. The cause of death is not yet known. Becker's big breakthrough came with the…

The culture section of *Dagens Nyheter* had a full-page spread, too. The text blurred into a murky mass. Martin put the papers on the kitchen table, face-down.

He washed his face and brushed his teeth.

He needed his desk. He needed to answer "Martin Berg" when someone called looking to speak to Martin Berg. He needed the post he had to go through. He needed the stacks of manuscripts. The Post-it notes. He needed authors who came in to talk about their latest projects. He needed to talk to Per about what the accountant had said so he could busy himself with something as delightfully meaningless as numbers and figures.

He was about to put on the same clothes he'd worn the day before, but dropped them on the floor as though they'd burned him.

Under a steel-blue sky, heat stretched the air to breaking point. Martin got to the office around lunchtime. A hush fell the moment he stepped through the door. Per came over, white as a sheet. "I heard about Gustav…"

They tried to make him go home. Sanna grabbed him by the upper arms like a child. You're not working today, she said. Go home. Take it easy, pull yourself together. Be with your family.

Martin fled to his office and shut the door. His legs wouldn't carry him, so he sank to the floor. He dug his fingers into the fringe of the rug. There was a world of difference, Dr Wikner always claimed, between a genuine and a fake rug.

Go home and be with your family.

"We'll be there as soon as we can," Rakel had told him the day before. He'd still been in Gustav's flat. He'd called the people who had to be called. There weren't many of them. The children, the von Becker family. He'd found Charlotte's number in a small address book in Gustav's jacket pocket.

Rakel didn't say: We're on our way. We're getting on the first flight.

There had been no cracks in her voice, no gaps into which a question or even an insinuation could be wedged. It had been smooth like marble.

Per knocked on his door and Martin dragged himself up into his office chair so he could face Per's question about whether there was anything he could do with a measure of dignity. Did Martin need anything? Anything at all? Was there anyone he could call? Could he bring him some lunch?

"No, no, but thank you. I'm not staying long. I was just going to…" He gestured vaguely towards his desk, piled high with papers, always such a lot of papers. Papers, papers. The millions of words he'd read. What did he recall of them now? A few quotes he'd memorised back when he'd found quoting long paragraphs from memory amusing. If you made the words your own, if you could etch them into your flesh and the very structure of your soul, then they became something more than mere words. But that was unusual. You had to read a lot, and closely. It couldn't be achieved without effort.

He started to shuffle the manuscripts whose titles were sometimes better than the book itself and sometimes just juvenile and sometimes formulated according to the algorithms of crime fiction. The girl/boy/man/woman, preposition, place name.

Per nodded, his worried face disappeared, the door closed.

"When is the funeral?" Sanna asked. She didn't take her eyes off him for a second, fixing him as though he might collapse at any moment. He wanted to tell her he was fine, but her question about the funeral distracted him. He didn't know. In death, we belong to our blood kin. In death, you had to turn to the sisters von Becker, who knew how to keep up appearances. It was going to be a big affair with a sea of white lilies and a choir singing and broad-brimmed hats shading people's solemn faces. With black suits and impersonal speeches that revolved around Gustav being one of Sweden's Greats, a person taken from us far too soon.

He texted Charlotte von Becker.

She had sounded winded when he called her from Gustav's flat. Martin had asked where she was. On my way to the gym, she'd replied suspiciously. In Martin's memory, the woman on the phone was overlaid with the girls in leotards he'd once met in the von Beckers' hallway.

"I'm at Gustav's place," he'd said. "He's dead."

He heard a moan, then a long silence. "Oh my god," Charlotte had said at length.

"Yes," Martin said.

"Bloody hell," Charlotte said.

"Yes," Martin said.

"It's an awful thing to say, but I suppose it was just a matter of time," Charlotte had sighed.

This time she replied immediately. No date yet, she wrote. Will call as soon as I know. Take care of yourself. Then a series of hearts.

*

It was still early when Martin got home. His skin was crawling. The afternoon stretched out like an endless field of time. He packed his gym bag but then suddenly felt exhausted. He sat down on the sofa. After ten minutes, he turned on the TV, but the sounds were too sharp, hurt his ears, so he muted it and stared at the pictures flashing and flickering in the afternoon light.

After a while, he heaved himself up and rummaged through Elis's desk drawer. Score: a packet of Lucky Strikes. He found a box of matches, opened the kitchen window, and sucked the smoke into his lungs.

The phone rang again. Journalists whose names instantly trickled into oblivion. Did he want to comment on Gustav Becker's passing? One told him he intended to write a book about Gustav Becker, a biography, though not a straight-up biography, but also an account of the Swedish art scene in the eighties and nineties, centred on Becker's work. The voice grew more and more enthusiastic until the aspiring writer caught himself, coughed and continued in a more subdued tone. Would Martin be willing to be interviewed?

He hung up without responding.

An old friend who worked for *Göteborgs-Posten* got in touch to ask if he wanted to write an obituary. "I understand if you – but I thought, since you knew him better than anyone, well... but if you don't want to, it's not a problem, we can..."

Martin went straight to his computer. Deadline at 10 p.m. A deadline was a fixed point to cling to in the pointless chaos. Fix your eyes on the blinking cursor and you shall not be sucked into maelstroms and eddies in time.

He wrote one word. He wrote another word. Then a few more, in relatively quick succession. Read them. With a click, they were gone.

He started over. One word. Another word. He needed to write two thousand five hundred characters, including spaces.

He looked through the box of old photos. He'd always planned to frame it. It had to be in there somewhere.

His heart raced until he found it. A black-and-white photo of all three of them. From the year he and Gustav turned twenty-five. They were sitting on the ground, against a wall, Martin in the middle. His hair was too long, his face so clean and young. He was wearing a shirt with an abstract pattern. Cecilia was sitting on his right, with her legs out to one side. She was the only one not looking at the camera; it looked like she was talking, her hands were raised. Gustav was sitting on his left, his glasses askew, wearing a Helly Hansen jacket, and he was laughing.

Martin was unable to get back up. He leaned against the radiator and closed his eyes.

He had finished the obituary but went over it one more time anyway. When the phone rang, he gave such a violent start he spilled half of the glass of wine he'd told himself would send him straight off to sleep.

Cecilia. It took him a split second to slap down the thought and replace it with a more sensible alternative. His mother. No, they'd already spoken, she'd sounded genuinely shaken. He was such a lovely boy, she'd said. Rakel or Elis? But he didn't recognise the number on the screen and answered out of sheer reflex.

The voice was unfamiliar and authoritative. "I'm looking for Martin Berg."

"This is he." At least he sounded like himself.

A tidal wave of information that he had a hard time processing in the moment washed over him. The words *Gustav Becker's lawyer* hung in the air for so long he missed the sentences that followed them. Suddenly, there was silence on the other end.

"I'm sorry, I didn't quite catch…"

He must have sounded confused, because the voice spoke again, a bit slower this time.

"As I said, I'm the executor of Gustav Becker's estate. I'm calling to discuss his will."

"Okay…"

"You have been informed about this?"

"About what?"

There was a brief pause. "He didn't talk to you about his will?"

"Not a word."

The woman's almost imperceptible sigh seemed to say: Why can't people take care of their drama while they're still alive? Martin liked that sigh. It made it a bit easier to think.

"Mr Becker left the majority of the works in his possession," he heard the lawyer say, "to you and Cecilia Berg."

36

The fields of Zealand spread out in every direction, dichotomised by the silver streak of the motorway.

"Take the next exit." Elis squinted at his phone. "I'm pretty sure that's it."

"I don't recognise anything."

"How long has it been since we were here? Weren't you, like, seventeen? How are you supposed to recognise anything? But sure, Miss Perfect Sense of Direction, let's hear your suggestion."

Rakel glared at him and indicated right.

When they'd called that morning, Frederikke had just found out about Gustav's death. She assured them they were very welcome, sounding eager and upset in a way that made Rakel wonder if she should be more deeply affected. The seconds after Martin told her – the night before, while the train was making an hour-long stop somewhere in Germany – the world had warped around her, as though reality was folding in on itself, losing its moorings. Before long, however, she'd entered a crystalline state of mind, where the knowledge of what had happened was encapsulated and kept separate from anything that had to do with feelings. While her father launched into a disjointed monologue about everything from paramedics to the risk of death following a heart attack, Rakel had paced up and down the platform, inserting brief, sensible comments whenever she spotted an opportunity. Then she'd climbed aboard and gone to inform Elis. After the first shock ("What! Are you serious?") he wasn't particularly surprised, either, which was a relief since it indicated Rakel might not have an empathy disorder after all. At the end of the day, Gustav belonged to the generation before hers, and the generation before hers was predestined to die before she did. Dad and Frederikke seemed to think that it was somehow unfathomable that someone from their sphere had been snatched away, but perhaps they simply hadn't fully accepted their actual position in the trajectory of life.

"It's sick, this thing with Gustav," Rakel said now, as if to test out her emotional responses. Nothing much happened. The only thing that seemed to stir something inside her was recalling their last conversation at the museum.

"Well, he was old," Elis said.

Rakel laughed. "Fifty's hardly old, though, is it?"

"Well, he did drink like there was no tomorrow," Elis countered. "His body had to be at least eighty-five." In biology, he told her, they'd learned about the effects of alcohol on human cells and after that, no one in his class had wanted to party for weeks. "It's even worse than a sedentary lifestyle. Okay, so we're staying on this road for 1.4 miles, and then we're making a left."

Rakel had a strong feeling of having been here before. And she had, come to think of it. During the years that followed Cecilia's disappearance, their summers had been full of excursions like this one. They would drive to Denmark, visit Frederikke and go to Tivoli, which meant Dad and Gustav drank beer while Rakel shepherded her brother around various rides, stopping by the outdoor café area at pre-agreed times, so her increasingly jolly father could feel reassured they hadn't been kidnapped or injured and hand them colourful Monopoly notes that they spent on the chocolate roulette. And several years in a row, they'd rented a cottage in Bohuslän under the pretence that the children enjoyed being by the sea. But as far as Rakel remembered, neither she nor Elis had voiced much of an opinion, at least not until they were old enough to think any place without an internet connection was completely pointless. The cottage had been her dad's idea, and, if anything, its value lay in the fact that it was a place free of anything Wikner. She'd hear her dad's and Gustav's low voices and laughter from the garden when she woke up needing the bathroom, and she fell asleep safe in the knowledge that they were near and having a good time.

Now, all of that was over, Rakel thought, looking both ways several times before turning left. No more weekends in Copenhagen. No more summers by the sea. It might have felt worse if those trips hadn't actually ended years ago; at some point, they'd just stopped going. She couldn't remember when and didn't know why.

"We'll be there in just over half a mile," Elis said. "Is that the sea?"

Frederikke Larsen's house was set back from the road, surrounded by apple trees. A heavy, thunderous heat hit them the moment they climbed out of the air-conditioned rental car. After the cities and trains, the silence was deafening. Insects were susurrating in the motionless air and high above them, gulls screeched, but that was all.

Frederikke came to greet them wearing muddy jeans and a linen shirt. The look on her face was haunted and worried.

"It's so horrible," she said. "I can't believe he's gone." She dropped her gardening gloves and hugged them as though they were the victims of some terrible accident. Then she led them into the garden, talking non-stop in her cleaned-up version of Danish, in which the words had been washed clean of diphthongs and swallowed syllables. How were they feeling? When had they found out? She'd only heard the news this morning. How had the drive been? It was hard to take in. Would they like anything to eat, or drink? Coffee?

"Coffee would be great," Elis said in the polite voice he used with grown-ups he wasn't related to.

Frederikke sat them down at a table in the shade of tall lilac bushes but accepted Elis's insistent offer of help with the coffee. Rakel was left alone. Further off, she glimpsed a vegetable patch with a spade stuck into a pile of black soil, moist despite the heat. There was a heavy smell of rich plant life in the air.

The moment the others disappeared into the house, she emailed a link to an article in *Berliner Zeitung* to Philip Franke: *Der schwedische Künstler Gustav Becker wurde tot gefunden.*

Would it have changed anything if she hadn't confronted him at the art opening? She touched the thought as one might a loose tooth, with a matter-of-fact expectation of pain.

It was very hard to say, not knowing all the facts of the case, which no one did, except possibly Gustav, and the question was whether he would have been a reliable witness even before he died. Almost a week had passed between the opening and his death. There was no way of knowing if her question had set something in motion. Perhaps she'd prodded at his guilt, the way she was now prodding at her own. Ramming a finger straight into his secrets. But Gustav's journey towards death had begun a very long time ago. In his case, life had been the anomaly. He didn't participate, he observed. Of the two greatest things about human existence, work and love, he'd sought out the former as he fled the latter. His art, too – visually so close to reality – had been, perhaps, a way to conquer the world and shape it according to his own needs.

Elis and Frederikke came walking through the apple trees, carrying a tray laden with coffee and biscuits. Several snatched words reached her before there was a full sentence Rakel could latch onto: "…come the two of you are in Denmark?"

Elis shook a tablecloth out over the wooden table. "We decided to go Interrailing," he lied, "so we were in France, and last night, on the train, Dad called…"

"Well," Rakel said. "I guess it's actually a bit more complicated than that."

Her brother immediately veered straight into confession. "It's about Mum."

Frederikke squinted at them. "Cecilia?" Then, after a pause, she emitted a "Hmm!" – a curt, firm syllable – and leaned back in her chair. "And in what way is it about Cecilia?"

"We're looking for her," Rakel said. She couldn't think how to go on.

"Rakel read this book," Elis said and gave an incoherent account of the plot of *Ein Jahr*. His little speech ended with a dramatic: "And we think that's her."

"We went to see the author," Rakel added. "Just the other day."

Frederikke nodded, sighed and nodded again. Then she got up and went back into the house. For a moment, Rakel thought the conversation was over, but Frederikke soon returned with a hardback that she tossed onto the table. *Et År med Kærlighed.*

"It just came out a few days ago," she said. "Cecilia always claimed he was a good writer, and I suppose she's right. It's an accurate description of her less charming traits. As I'm sure you've figured out, I only met him very briefly once. I hardly had time to form an opinion of him."

"He's a fairly sensitive type," Rakel said. Her heart, she noted, was beating so hard the others had to be able to see it through her shirt.

Frederikke chuckled. "She should have known better than to get entangled with a sensitive writer. That's a sure-fire way to end up the subject of a novel or two. An author with a broken heart can be dangerous. You don't have to be a historian to know that."

"Has she read the book?" Rakel's palms were slippery with sweat, and she had to set her cup down or risk dropping it.

"I haven't talked to her in a long time, but when I did, she hadn't. She just mumbled something about how poets often turn out to be more spirited than they like to admit. 'They always find some under-handed way to profit from their misery,' she said."

"So you know where she is?"

"Unless she moved again, but I don't think she has. She's still in Berlin." Frederikke picked up matches and a cigarillo from the tray, lighting it with unhurried movements. "I'm sure you're wondering why

I never told you. The short version is that I didn't think it my place. But now you're here, looking for the truth, and I'm happy you are; I will do what I can to help you. I just wasn't in a position to force it on you. Over the years, I've thought a lot about what a person has a right to tell other people. As a therapist, it's simple: everything you're told is confidential. Outside the clinic, however, there are unfortunately no rules. There are those who believe the truth must come out at any cost, that the truth is always a force of good, and that in any given situation, you should insist on what you perceive as 'true'. But people construct their own narratives, for protection, to keep life in check. And if you disrupt a narrative, you have to be prepared for chaos to follow. If your narrative deviates too far from reality, if it's built on fundamental misconceptions and grave misinterpretations, then the narrative can be a problem in itself, of course. And yet, it may be that that particular construct is what makes life possible in that moment. Most of us reinterpret and censor things now and then. Human memory is deceptive that way. We're good at forgetting what's painful and hard. Instead, we pick out some little episode that we buff and polish and tinker with until it has become emblematic of our history. Does that make sense?"

"Sure," Elis said. He'd been silent for so long Rakel had almost forgotten he was there. "So what happened, then?"

"I think I'd better start from the beginning," Frederikke said.

37

The beginning turned out to be the early eighties. Frederikke had been dating an artist who lived in Gothenburg. Rakel had never heard his name, but Elis claimed it sounded familiar. Among the people hanging out in the artist's Haga flat was a considerably younger bloke who'd sit quietly in a corner, giggling at other people's jokes. He smoked French cigarettes and drank red wine other people gave him. One of the girls always looked after him when he got wasted. Frederikke had taken care of him once herself when he needed some fresh air and to sober up a little before heading home. She didn't know where he lived, but he said it was nearby. He was always polite, even when he was throwing up on a tree and his glasses fell off. "Would you mind helping me look – it would seem I've lost my… This is really very unfortunate." He wiped vomit from the corners of his mouth with his shirt sleeve. "Frederikke, I really do apologise…"

And she was surprised he knew her name, because he didn't seem to have noticed her at all until her boyfriend asked her to take him out for a little walk "so he doesn't throw up on the carpet". Like a dog, she'd thought to herself as they walked down the stairs, she with one arm around his slim shoulders.

Eventually, she got to know Martin, who spoke loudly and clearly, used words like "lugubrious" and "ambiguity" and defended Gustav no matter the situation. The two of them were inseparable. When Frederikke heard about Cecilia, she'd reacted with concern: that could only mean Martin was going to disappear into coupledom. When it was him and Gustav, there was no room for anyone else. Even though Martin had theoretically had a girlfriend before – Frederikke recalled a loud-mouthed girl with eyeliner and a leather jacket – she was, emotionally speaking, firmly in second place. But sooner or later, someone would outcompete Gustav, and Gustav needed someone in his life who made sure he got home when he was drunk, cheered him up when he was down, made him keep painting when he talked about quitting because, somehow, painting always seemed to keep him more or less on track. And so, it was with a degree of reservation that Frederikke first met Cecilia, in France, during the long summer of 1986.

As she was sure Elis and Rakel recalled, Frederikke said, Gustav's grandmother had owned a villa outside Antibes on the French Riviera. When she visited Sweden in the summers, she turned the house over to Gustav so he could "paint and enjoy himself". There were other grandchildren, the sisters von Becker, for example, who would have loved to borrow the house, too, but Nana was not to be swayed – the summers belonged to Gustav. Her favouritism had been felicitous for the history of art, because her talented nephew painted the Antibes Suite and a number of other works during his summers at the house. In one of the funny little postcards he used to send, he'd invited Frederikke to join them, and since she hadn't had anything better to do, she'd gone down there for a few weeks. She liked both Gustav and Martin, but they were very young, twenty-four or twenty-five to her thirty, and still wide-eyed about a world she'd already left behind. She had recently accepted her film-making was never going to generate any income and had started studying psychology with the express ambition of finding a well-paid job. It was a line of demarcation between her and the young men. Debasing themselves with a real job was not part of their agenda. Gustav intended to support himself through his painting and Martin was working on some kind of Bildungsroman. If it becomes unbearable, Frederikke had thought to herself, she could always shove off to Nice or Marseille.

But then, there was Cecilia. Martin's girlfriend, whose name Frederikke had only heard mentioned over the phone and in letters, was a tall, athletic girl with something wholesome and proper about her. She was beautiful, but her beauty was of the severe, solemn kind that would have fit better in a century full of starched collars and ermine. She dressed like a boy in button-downs and sailor trousers cut off halfway up the calf. She was lively and quick, laughed loudly, dived from cliffs and swam further out than anyone else. When they were introduced – Cecilia's handshake was firm and enthusiastic – Frederikke had trouble hiding her surprise.

When Frederikke arrived, the trio had already settled into the house. That Martin and Cecilia were a couple was barely noticeable; if anything, the three of them seemed an intertwined unit. They had their routines and habits. Everyone worked before lunch and in the afternoon they spent a few hours on the beach. Then they did another work shift. For a holiday, Frederikke thought, there was an awful lot of work going on. Gustav painted, Martin worked on his novel, and Cecilia was writing an ambitious essay, not because she had to but because she wanted to, and, as she put it, didn't quite know how and therefore had to learn.

Before Frederikke was integrated into their daily rhythm, there was a faint but palpable dissonance whose source was hard to pinpoint. She recalled an awkward exchange on the veranda. Cecilia was sitting under the sailcloth canopy that sifted the scorching sunshine into a clear, pure light. Frederikke had asked her something, in an effort to be polite, but had immediately realised she was interrupting the young woman's work on the typewriter. "I'm sorry, am I disturbing you?" she'd said.

"Yes," Cecilia said. "We can talk later."

The work was the frame around which their existence took shape, and it was, ultimately, maintained by Cecilia's immutability. Her straight-backed figure at the desk, the stacks of papers and books: all of it exuded a feeling of calm and contemplation that affected the atmosphere of the entire household. Without her, Martin and Gustav would probably have lazed about in the shade from time to time, playing cassette tapes on the battery-powered cassette player and drinking pastis, or made little excursions in the local area. Frederikke's arrival upset the balance or could have done if Cecilia had yielded so much as an inch.

Even though Frederikke had nothing on principle against drinking wine and letting the sun fry her halfway to a crisp, it all felt less tempting in the presence of the focused figure on the veranda. Luckily, she'd brought some emergency books, and now, twenty-five years later, her favourite copy of *On Dreams* was still the paperback with sand between its salt water-warped pages she'd read so thoroughly twice that summer.

Cecilia wasn't familiar with Freud – it turned out that, to her, the bar for being "familiar with" something was set at "having read the central works in the original" – and was very interested. In fact, Cecilia was interested in almost everything. "What, is that *true*?" was an oft-repeated exclamation. "Tell me *more*." In her eyes, everything was a puzzle piece that could be added to her knowledge of the world. Everything was potentially relevant. If she was wondering about something, she made sure to find out. Even though she wasn't a legal resident, she managed to circumvent the rigid bureaucracy that characterised French institutions and get herself a library card. She would cycle into town at regular intervals, returning dusty but happy, with a stack of books that might hopefully provide answers to the questions she was pondering. She'd sit down in a faded lounge chair in the shade under the lemon tree with a book on her lap and her legs crossed, revealing the sandy sole of one of her feet, and become unreachable until she felt it was time to go swimming.

The heat in Frederikke's garden was so dense and oppressive Rakel only had to close her eyes to image that first summer in Antibes: the polished steel disc of the sun, the sharp sparkle of the sea, the burning sand. The lemon grove and the sailcloth veranda roof she knew well from Gustav's paintings, but the figure in Frederikke's story didn't easily fit into the contours of the serious young woman he'd used as his model. No one, it suddenly occurred to her, had told her Cecilia was such a strong swimmer.

"From what I'm telling you," Frederikke went on, "it may sound odd that I felt somehow protective towards her. But I did. There was something premature about her, as though she'd been exactly that grown-up and capable since birth. Martin and Gustav thought of her as a link to reality and common sense, but she was only a very young person who had spent most of her youth reading and writing. It wasn't easy to tell what was going on inside her head."

In time, they became good friends – Cecilia wasn't unreasonable so long as you let her work in peace – and spent a lot of time just the two of them. One episode in particular stood out to Frederikke, and she had thought about it from time to time after Cecilia disappeared. It must have taken place that same summer, because it was before Rakel was born.

One afternoon, Cecilia had for whatever reason decided to skip writing and go into town instead, and she'd asked if Frederikke wanted to come with her. With her shirt flapping around her slender body, Cecilia pedalled quickly and effortlessly up a steep hill ahead of her. She waited at the top and Frederikke, who was beginning to accept the fact that she was never going to be anything more than an amateur film-maker, wished she'd brought her camera so she could have immortalised the bright figure outlined against the rust and ochre landscape.

Cecilia knew the town well and guided Frederikke down medieval alleys to a small city square. They sat down outside a restaurant, where Cecilia positively beamed at the waitress, ordering white wine and oysters and asking if she could possibly bother her for an ashtray. Frederikke went to the bathroom, and when she came back, a man had sat down at the table next to theirs and struck up a conversation with Cecilia.

A few days earlier, Frederikke had witnessed another exchange between her new friend and a man who was trying to talk to her on the beach. Then, Cecilia had simply said: Monsieur, I'm afraid I have to stop you there; I'm busy, and I can't talk to you any more. Monsieur asked what she was so busy with. *Ça ne vous regarde pas*, Cecilia announced and turned her attention back to her book. The man seemed unable to decide how to act. Possibly, he viewed a woman's no as encouragement to renew his efforts. But he hesitated for too long and it made him look ridiculous; he was standing there, arms dangling limply at his sides, ignored by the object of his courtship, and silently observed by her friend. Just then, Martin joined them, and the persistent conversationalist slunk away.

"Penelope's suitor is at it again, I see," Martin said, kissing Cecilia on the head. He rarely did things like that in public.

"I weave at my loom," she said, turning her face to him. He put a hand behind her head and kissed her on the mouth.

But this time, there was no Martin – he was bent over the manuscript he could never seem to finish, almost as though, like Penelope, he unravelled each night what he had achieved during the day. And the man at the next table said nothing about Cecilia being beautiful, blonde or Swedish, words she shied away from like a young mare from a fence judged too tall. He was, there was no denying it, pleasant and civilised in every way. He apologised for bothering them, explained that he was early for a meeting and had sought out the shade of the awning while he waited for an acquaintance. The polite phrases in easily understood French held out an offer to Cecilia: you can end our conversation or let me sit here. Both possibilities lay open before her and could be chosen without loss of dignity.

"By all means," Cecilia said. "You may wait with us."

It turned out he was a British archaeologist. He had noted that Cecilia was reading Aeschylus's tragedies. He specialised in Ancient Greece and had just spent three months at a dig at one of the temples outside Corinth, which explained his tan – he felt obligated to let them know, he said, so they wouldn't get the idea that he was some layabout idling his life away aboard one of the yachts in the bay. Sadly, he would be incapable of that kind of life, even if it were offered to him.

What temple was it, Cecilia asked, what kind of temple activity was performed in it?

He told them it was a temple dedicated to Pallas Athena. "You know the story of Athena?"

Do tell, Cecilia said.

Pallas Athena, he said, was one of the central figures of Greek mythology. She was a goddess of war and wisdom. She was born when Zeus, king of the gods, had a terrible headache one day; it was decided that his head be split open to find out what was wrong. Out came a fully grown Athena, dressed in armour.

Cecilia didn't take her eyes off him while he spoke. She took a cigarette from Frederikke's packet on the table and the man lit it for her. When he leaned forward, his hand brushed against hers, ever so lightly.

The thing was that, a few days earlier, Cecilia had talked about the Athena myth during dinner. Her recent library hauls had contained several works on the myths and history of the classical world, an interest awakened by Martin's struggle with Homer. Cecilia was intimately familiar with the story she'd asked the archaeologist to tell her, and Frederikke was pondering what to do with that fact when a confused man appeared on the other side of the square, bearing all the hallmarks of a tourist: slightly overweight in a rumpled linen suit, his face red from the sun, a camera around his neck, a map which he was studying with the expression of someone who is beginning to suspect that a terrible mistake has been made somewhere along the way.

"And here's Pendleton," the archaeologist sighed, checking his watch. "A man with a very casual relationship with time, unless it's counted in years BC. When it comes to *that*, he is horribly precise. He should not, however, be let out of Cambridge without a trusty squire by his side. *Mesdames*, I enjoyed our conversation. *Au revoir*."

They watched him cross the square and greet his colleague. Before disappearing into an alley, he turned around and smiled. Cecilia raised her hand in an archaic farewell gesture.

"You've never met him before?" Frederikke asked.

"Peter? Never."

"He liked you."

"Perhaps." Cecilia smiled at the table, turning her empty glass round and round. "Who knows?"

Only later did Frederikke realise the archaeologist had never said his name. She tried not to think about it. Maybe she'd just missed it. And yet, that little scene lodged itself in her memory, like a grain of sand that never quite stopped chafing.

38

The train was moving. Martin Berg stared at the cardboard box containing a plastic-wrapped breakfast roll, yoghurt and muesli. It made his stomach turn. The only seat left on the morning train to Stockholm had been in first class, but what did he get out of first class? Out of habit, he fetched a cup of black coffee and a copy of every newspaper, including *Dagens Industri*.

As they passed the Jewish cemetery, he looked for Rakel's window, but he wasn't sure if she lived on the third or fourth floor. He turned his attention back to the papers. His obituary was there in *Göteborgs-Posten*, accompanied by a large photograph of the unexpectedly departed PAINTER GUSTAV BECKER.

He realised he'd left his briefcase at home. He had no manuscripts to read. He had no laptop. He did have his phone, but he set it to silent and put it in his inside pocket. He had many hours to fill before he was due to meet Gustav's lawyer at his studio. Have you been to Gustav's studio before? he'd asked. No, she'd replied. Then this is your last chance, he'd said. Isn't it? Before everything's packed up and so on? Sure, she said. Why not. *Pourquoi pas*, Martin exclaimed. Then he'd cleared his throat and added in a normal voice: Great, great, all right, so I'll see you there at one.

First comes death, then comes the executor of the estate. I should write a will, too, Martin thought. Soon or later, something in the tangle of tiny vessels in his brain or the worn-out musculature of his heart would fail. Burst or snap. I leave all my billions of papers to my children, Rakel and Elis Berg, to be cherished and cared for. All my little notebooks. All my half-finished novels. My virtually completed master's dissertation in comparative literature. The entire stack of what could be a really good biography about the sadly overlooked author William Wallace. Here you go, kids. Here's your father's collected works.

The train shot past an unassuming little commuter-train station in the blink of an eye. Images from his solitary wake with Gustav lit up in Martin's brain now that there were no distractions to keep them out. He'd waited with Gustav for a long while, with the body that had once been Gustav's. The emergency services operator had asked if he had a pulse.

"How should *I* know?" Martin had replied. She instructed him to place two fingers on this throat. Martin reported that Gustav felt cold, that he couldn't find a pulse, but that he knew nothing about stuff like this, someone professional had to come and make a determination, right now, because what if he was alive and it was a matter of seconds...

"Of course, of course, I'm dispatching an ambulance," the woman had replied calmly.

One time, at the summer house, Martin had been stung by a wasp and suffered a serious allergic reaction, and an ambulance had materialised almost immediately. Since then, he'd assumed it took only moments from when you hung up the phone to when sirens could be heard and you were given over to the competent care of the Swedish healthcare system. But five minutes later, nothing had happened. He thought: I'll give it another five minutes, then I'll call back. Gustav can't just sit here in the gloom and reek. Gustav would have said: What difference does it make, I'm *dead*, aren't I? When you're dead, you're dead. Death is characterised by the fact that nothing makes any difference any more. Death is the great equaliser. It makes no difference if you've paid your debts. It makes no difference if your papers are in order. It makes no difference what you've said or not said to your loved ones, or whatever you want to call the poor sods who were forced to deal with you in life. When death enters, everything ceases to matter. Death is absolution. Death frees you from your life, from your inadequacy, from the sins you've committed, and the sins you refrained from but wish you'd had the courage to commit.

Somewhere, Martin had thought, there had to be a packet of cigarettes. He found one on the windowsill next to a white plastic lighter from 7-Eleven. He lit a Gauloise. He was standing in a studio flat on Sjömansgatan in Masthugget, Gothenburg. His heart was beating. In a month, he was turning fifty. He avoided looking at Gustav in the armchair. He had only seen one dead person before, his father, and in a double exposure of the dead, Martin relived standing next to his father's hospital bed, studying the distorted, smoothed-out face. So there lay Abbe Berg, a gifted man who had made nothing of himself. Not because the world was evil or fate adverse. If Abbe had wanted to be someone, he could have been, but he lacked the will to make it happen. What he really wanted to do was sail the seven seas. Instead, he'd had children, quit the shipping company, taken the first job he could find, ended up in the printers, and worked his way up to management, not because he had any interest in making decisions, but because he was reliable and competent. Things were comfortable enough for him to be content. His real life happened on the sea, a few weeks in the summer and during long weekends with fine weather.

The paramedics turned up twenty minutes later. It was two young men, with big muscles and shaved heads. Their uniforms were dark green with bright-yellow reflectors. They were carrying a stretcher and a red bag. They filled the flat with their presence and efficiency. They quickly established that Gustav was, indeed, dead and for a brief moment Martin felt deeply relieved he hadn't been wrong. They asked about Gustav's identity and Martin gave them his full name and personal identity number, including the last four digits.

While the paramedics unfolded the stretcher and spread a blanket over the dead man, Martin paced up and down the hallway. A radio crackled. They took down Martin's contact information. They were going to notify Gustav's relatives, but if he wanted to talk to them first, that was fine, of course. Martin assured them he would let the family know. And the police. Because shouldn't the police be looped in in a situation like this? He was going to call them, too. And should he go with them to the hospital? They shook their heads. Martin held the front door open for them. He heard the door to the street slam shut. The ambulance drove off without turning on its siren.

Martin locked the door. He lit another cigarette but felt nauseous. The flat suddenly felt very small. Next to the sink lay a plastic bag from the state-run liquor store in which Martin found a receipt, dated the day before. At 11.23 a.m., Gustav had purchased three bottles of vodka and six bottles of beer from the liquor store on Linnégatan. One of those bottles of vodka was now empty, placed in a tidy paper bag full of glass recycling. The second sat unopened in the fridge. The third lay half-empty under the armchair.

Over the back of a chair hung a tattered wool jacket. Martin went through its pockets and found four one-krona coins, a paper clip, a lighter, a packet of Gauloises, a bank note, a wallet that contained nothing but a credit card and an ID from 2004 in which Gustav looked like a criminal, and an old-fashioned pocket-sized address book with a black cover and red edges. You could still buy them in bookshops, but it had to be a product threatened with extinction, Martin thought to himself. It contained a dozen or so numbers, each written in large digits across a whole page and tagged with initials. The first one was Martin's own: MB. FL was probably Frederikke Larsen. CVB had to mean Charlotte von Becker.

And then there was a foreign number: CW.

39

A few hours and a confusing metro ride later, Martin Berg arrived at Gustav's address on Södermalm. He wasn't too late. A woman who had to be Sahar, the lawyer – wearing a suit, muttering into a headset – was waiting by the door. When Martin drew near, she ended the call and offered her condolences with professional detachment.

"He was very particular about his will," she said as they climbed the stairs. There was a bit of an echo. "We've gone over it several times since it was first drawn up. Most recently at the start of this year."

Keys jangled. For several long moments, the world seemed to be warping, and his legs threatened to give way, but Martin forced himself to stay upright. He heard his own voice inform Sahar that the studio was upstairs. He couldn't remember now why he'd insisted on meeting in Gustav's studio instead of a nice, impersonal office.

"For now, everything is covered by insurance," Sahar said. "But I would advise the two of you to look into that. After all, the objects are quite valuable."

The two of you. He cleared his throat.

"Well, speaking of Cecilia…"

"I know," she said, cutting him off. "I pointed out to him that, legally speaking, it would be easier to make you the sole heir. But he was very firm about it being both of you."

A newspaper lay open on the worktable next to a cup that still had coffee in it and a half-eaten cheese sandwich on a plate. The cheese had hardened into a sweaty disc. There was a canvas on the easel, primed for painting. It took oil paint weeks to dry. Gustav would turn on the radio, the news, on a low volume, fiddle with paintbrushes and tubes of paint, pour himself a drink, sit down in his armchair for a bit to study the painting from afar while he pondered how to proceed.

There were paintings leaning against the walls, some facing in, others out. A row of shelves held thick folders and stacks of rolled up canvases. Drawings and sketchbooks were kept in dressers with wide, slim drawers.

"Unfortunately, you won't be able to take anything with you today," the lawyer said as she began to pull folders out of her bag. "We need to catalogue everything first. It's going to take a few weeks. All right, so there are some documents we need to go over."

Without much success, Martin tried to read the papers he signed. In the end, he gave up and just scribbled his signature on the dotted line. Thankfully, at least that practised motion worked properly. There was nothing wrong with his signature. It looked the same as always.

"Would you like to have a look at the paintings?" he asked when they were all done and Sahar had returned the papers to their various folders. The lawyer seemed nonplussed but acquiesced. Martin heard himself tell her about Valand, the degree show, their year in Paris, the art market in the late eighties ("I suppose you were barely born then") and the breakthrough years that followed.

It was probably the only time he'd ever seen a sizeable collection of Gustav's paintings without…

They'd just turned over a canvas almost as tall as Martin and taken a few steps back. The painting was a full-body portrait of Cecilia Berg. She was sitting next to a window, dressed all in black with her running shoes on. Her posture was erect and her face proud, solemn, her chin raised slightly, her eyes fixed unwaveringly on them.

It wasn't so much that she looked older. It was the shoes. A new model. The kind people wore at his gym.

"This one isn't signed," Sahar said. She made a note, she had to look into this, she said, what the procedure was for unsigned works. She shot him a quick a smile, as if to say "nice painting", and moved on to the next one.

Not long after, Sahar disappeared into a taxi, leaving him alone on the streets of Stockholm. The sun was scorching. The city was full of tourists. He'd folded his jacket over his arm. He was a man on his way from a meeting. He didn't have a train ticket home and unfortunately didn't know how to get to the Central Station. Guided by the notion that he'd be able to orient himself better from a height, he walked up a hill lined by pastel-coloured buildings with plaster facades. Between the buildings, he did, in fact, catch a glimpse of water, this water that he could never learn what kind it was – a river or a bay, Lake Mälaren or the Baltic Sea – and he walked down towards it.

He needed to talk to someone who had known Gustav. His first thought was there was no one except Cecilia. Then he remembered Dolores. Dolores, Dolores. The sullen girl with the condescending manner and shiny black Sally Bowles bowler hat. She'd been hanging around since the early nineties.

Martin called but got no answer. He fired off a text and when his phone buzzed, he answered immediately. But instead of Dolores's hoarse, bored voice, he heard a soft, worried one. "Hi," it said, "it's Maria. I heard about Gustav. I just wanted to check on you, see how you're doing."

Maria? What bloody Maria? Martin closed his eyes and tried to connect the voice with an actual person before hitting on the idea of checking the screen. Maria Malm, the wondrous device informed him.

"It's really sweet of you to call, Maria." What had been intended as gratitude came off more like forced politeness. "I'm in Stockholm, dealing with some of Gustav's paperwork."

She talked about loss, grief, time that had to pass. When was he going to be back in town? Would he like to meet up when he was?

Using his work voice, Martin told her it wasn't a good time right now, he had his hands full, unfortunately, but maybe they could be in touch later, some other time.

He knew he didn't mean it. She should know it, too. But she replied: "Of course, absolutely," with such warmth there was a risk she was imagining that he was Beside Himself right now and Needed Some Time, and that there would be more opportunities if she was just patient. She would provide solace in his grief. They would be brought together by loss and the past. Intimacy and contact would suddenly be there. If the compassionate Maria Malm just waited, waited and waited, like a true sailor's wife, waited for all eternity, all would be well.

When the call ended, all strength drained out of Martin, and he collapsed on a park bench overlooking the water. A sightseeing boat passed by and the wind brought snatches of the guided tour. *And on your left, you can see Martin Berg, a liar and a coward, who despite his advanced age is still incapable of being honest with himself or others.* I'll never give you what you're looking for, he thought. You've used me for your own illusions about love, and reality would disappoint you. In time, you would blame me, criticise me, maybe hate me. You would slam doors. You would cry. You would want me to want something other than what I want. You would wonder why. You would blame yourself. You would think it's because of your own shortcomings. You would point to various offences. You would want restitution. You would want me to apologise and feel ashamed. But you should have known what I had to offer. You can't say you're done with love. You can't say it's a closed chapter, that all that remains for you is work and nothing but work. Admitting such a thing would be to open a cellar door to death. The future had to be there as potential and comfort. Our fantasies about the future are what saves us from the lead weight of the fact that this, what's happening right now, is what constitutes our lives on this earth.

*

When Dolores called back – Martin wasn't sure if it had been fifteen minutes or an hour, and what difference did it make? – she was composed and matter-of-fact, almost wary, as though he'd just been in a serious traffic accident and could be assumed to be unpredictable on account of the shock. What terrible news it was, she said. She would love to meet up. She was heading into a meeting now, but would five o'clock at Tranan work? Did he know how to get there? Karlbergsvägen, by Odenplan? Was that okay? Was he sure?

"Absolutely, absolutely, that's great, I'll see you there. Goodbye. Bye." He'd been to Tranan a hundred times. Granted, those had been raucous nights in another life, but still. The intellectually completely unaffected Martin Berg had no difficulty getting from this quayside on what had to be Södermalm to good old Tranan. Especially not – he squinted at a church clock – with an hour and a half to do it. *Pas de problème.* He just had to keep moving. The metro or a taxi would be too quick. Better to walk. First, he had to get across the water. The water was step one. In the distance, he could see a bridge. He gave himself a little talking to while he walked towards it. He had to focus on getting from point A to point B right now. He should put the painting of Cecilia out of his mind. There were any number of possible explanations for the new painting of Cecilia. Granted, he couldn't think of one off the top of his head, but everything would become clear in time. There was no hurry. All in good time. There was a time to ask himself why his wife had appeared in a painting in Gustav's studio, and there was a time to find his way to Tranan. One thing at a time.

He had to ask for directions several times, and several of the people he asked had no idea (bloody tourists), but in the end, he made it there. The outdoor seating area was full, but inside the dimly lit room was virtually deserted. The waitress seated him at a table next to the wall and decided he wanted a glass of wine. Martin engaged in the remarkably complicated task of buying a train ticket home that evening. If he drank two or three glasses, there was a good chance he might fall asleep, which would be preferable to almost everything else.

At five on the dot, Dolores appeared, holding a bike helmet. Martin wouldn't have recognised her if he'd run into her on the street. Her movements were quicker, as though the reptilian languor was something she'd shed with age.

"Bloody hell," she said, hugging him hard and slipping onto the chair across from him. "I was so bloody upset when I heard. You don't think things like that can happen but then they do. That sounds extremely trite, but it's true. Are you hungry? When was the last time you ate?"

When Martin took too long to answer, she said: "We'll both have the meatballs," to the waitress who had materialised at their table.

She was going to start to talk about Gustav any moment now. She was going to ask how it happened. He was going to have to tell her about Gustav in the armchair…

"It's been so long," he said. "What are you up to these days?"

She'd trained as a counsellor and was now middle management at Social Services. "Never mind that," she said, waving her hand dismissively when Martin asked about her work. "It's not interesting." She wanted to know about Gustav. She was really regretting not going down for the opening of his retrospective, she said. She'd planned to go, but then things had come up. In hindsight, it was easy to say that she should have prioritised it, but she had been to practically every gallery opening since 1988. And at some point, you have to ask yourself why you're doing something, right? You might have been at work all day, trying to shore up some project in a part of town where they torch cars and live twelve people in a one-bed flat, and then you get home from work, and it's six o'clock, and the only thing you want to do is have a glass of wine in the garden, since you're lucky enough to have a garden. My god, Dolores said, how she longed for something as simple as the absence of questions sometimes. For no one to call, expecting her to know about some obscure administrative detail. For there being no emails to answer while she rushed to the gym so they wouldn't suspend your membership over yet another missed group exercise session. She simply didn't have any desire to get dressed up and go to some gallery and mingle with distant acquaintances. *Now*, she obviously wished she'd gone down to see the exhibition. But that particular weekend had been bad because her husband had long-standing plans so she had to stay home with the children. And the exhibition was on until October. And unless she was mistaken it was coming to the Museum of Modern Art afterwards. No one could have known that—

Their food came: gigantic meatballs slathered with cream sauce, fluffy mashed potatoes, a dollop of lingonberry jam and pressed cucumbers. He had to do this.

"I remember the first time Gustav fell apart," Dolores said, tucking into her meal. He was still new in town and a rising star. This was before the art bubble burst; his paintings were selling like hotcakes. He'd bought that studio flat, which was empty for the longest time aside from a bed and a TV. "He was like a bullied kid who had finally been invited to the cool table," Dolores said. "But because the cool kids had bullied him, he didn't trust them one bit." It had taken her a long time to realise he hadn't been an outsider in Gothenburg, that, on the contrary, he'd had what she would today call a solid social network. "He talked about Gothenburg as though it were a city of mud and grime, saying it pulled you down, that it was all shit."

She'd been around twenty when they met and had been deeply wounded to discover that he had a secret life to which she had no access. She could tell from the pills in his bathroom cabinet, from the weeks that went by without her hearing from him. She would call and call but there'd be no answer. On one such occasion, she'd gone over to his house unannounced and just walked in. The flat had been in a right state. Empty bottles everywhere. The TV was on. Gustav had waved his arms at her as though she were some unpleasant but not particularly dangerous animal. "You can tell KG there won't be any more paintings," he'd said. "They can all fuck right off." Dolores had found several empty blister packs. She'd called a taxi and taken him to the psychiatric emergency ward at Sankt Göran Hospital. In the waiting room, he'd paced in circles, mumbling to himself and ripping a piece of paper into a thousand pieces. When they finally got to see a doctor, Gustav announced that he was a famous artist and that it was vital that he be allowed to go home and continue his work. The doctor immediately made a note in his file. Dolores cleared her throat and said Gustav was, in fact, an artist, maybe not super famous yet, but definitely on his way. The doctor looked from Gustav to Dolores and back. "He just had a solo exhibition at Hammarsten Gallery," Dolores added, and that seemed to impress the doctor. Gustav pulled on a loose thread on his sweater, unravelling part of the sleeve. He wanted a cigarette, he said, where were his cigarettes? Could the smoking ban really have spread to the godforsaken backwater where they currently found themselves? Might it be possible to acquire one little cigarette, or did he have to give up hope about even this fundamental human right? His eyes darted about incessantly, he kept patting his pockets, and one foot moved in tiny circles. The doctor gave him a cigarette and pushed a button. A nurse came to take him outside. She heard his loud voice die away in the hallway.

The doctor asked a series of questions and Dolores almost burst out crying because she had to answer so many with "I don't know". Was this the first time he'd behaved like this? She didn't know. Did he have any previous experience of mental illness? She didn't know. Was there bipolarism, schizophrenia or anything else in his family? She didn't know. Any suicide attempts? She shook her head even though she didn't know that either. What about his alcohol habits? At that point, she blew her nose and finally had something to say: he did drink quite a bit because they went out a lot, every Friday and Saturday and often other days, too, Wednesdays, Thursdays, but that was normal in their social circle, their regular bars were kind of like their living rooms, Prinsen and so on, it's how they hung out. You met up for a few pints. And how many pints would Gustav drink on a regular night at Prinsen, the doctor asked. Well, she said, counting on her fingers, it was quite a few sometimes, and when they went to his house he mostly drank spirits.

Later on, she visited him at Beckomberga Psychiatric Hospital, it was before they closed it down. Now, it's all flats, in fact, her brother-in-law had just moved into one of them – anyway. Dolores paused, chewing her food with a furrowed brow before continuing her story. She'd never been in that kind of environment before, she said. Long corridors with milky-white sphere lamps, gleaming linoleum floors, nurses in white with rubber-soled clogs, common rooms with a handful of patients sitting stock-still in front of a TV that was never turned off. The only thing that moved was the cigarette smoke. Gustav was lying on the bed in his room and barely reacted when she entered. A nurse escorted them out into a beautiful park.

Gustav was a more sluggish, slower version of himself, like when you play a record at half-speed. When Dolores handed over a carton of Gauloises and Gunnar Ekelöf's *Late Arrival on Earth* that she'd stolen from a second-hand bookshop, he brightened for a few seconds, but his enthusiasm was short-lived, like a sparkler. He was wearing elasticated trousers and slippers. Belts and shoelaces, he said, were banned, because apparently you could hang yourself with them. Some bloody idiot had tried the other week. Just before night rounds, too, so his chances of success had been minimal. If he'd just been patient, he would have had several hours to die undisturbed. How rude, actually. He made the rest of them look bad and sowed unnecessary suspicion. They barely let him have art supplies in his room. His metal-tipped marker had required special permission from the consultant.

But he thanked her for the cigarettes and the book. "I've learned enough about literary history from Martin to know that Ekelöf is an apt choice for someone in my situation." It wasn't the first time Dolores had heard Martin's name, but he was usually mentioned as "my mate Martin from Gothenburg" or some such. Now, Gustav talked about Martin as though he were a shared acquaintance. In fact, he talked more about Martin than about anything else. What would Martin say if he found out about this? Martin thinks this and that. Martin had probably called and was now wondering why he wasn't picking up. He had to go down to Gothenburg and see Martin. Time was short. She had to help him get out of there so he wouldn't miss his train. Enough about this Martin bloke already, Dolores thought to herself, and Gustav's talk about "getting out" worried her. And yet, he was sitting there calmly, his arms on the back of the bench, smoking, gazing up at the foliage. When she said he should probably talk to the doctor about being discharged, he accepted it without protest.

They never talked about his stint at Beckomberga afterwards. It was as though it had been excised from history and locked in a cupboard. Eventually, she forgot all about it, or thought about it as a strange dream.

Dolores paused to scrape up the last of her mashed potatoes and cucumber. "After that," she said when she had finished chewing, "things were pretty calm for several years." The next big collapse was London, obviously. He was in terrible shape then, but Martin already knew all about that. How Cecilia had gone to get him from that weird place, the throwing up in the taxi and all that. In the aftermath, Dolores had allied herself with Vendela, the widow, which was to say she'd sided with abstinence. Cecilia had called from time to time to check in. They'd had an unspoken agreement that neither one of them would tell Gustav they were talking.

Martin had conquered half his portion. That had to be considered a satisfactory effort. The meatballs were hard to swallow, but the mashed potatoes slipped right down. He put his cutlery down on his plate. "And what about now? How has he been doing?"

Dolores sighed. They'd drifted apart over the past ten, fifteen years. They had been stressful years – her husband was doing a degree, they had their first child, she started a new job, they moved from the one-bed on Söder to a two-bed in Midsommarkransen, had their second child, moved to the terraced house. A few years of renovations and parenting flew by. She stopped dying her hair, started wearing a bike helmet and no longer called herself a poet. She still called Gustav from time to time, and they met up in town sometimes. Had a few pints and it was nice, for the most part, though more often than not some of his new friends would join them, younger people from the art world who invariably made her feel old and boring even though she was actually pretty happy with her life. She still read almost all new poetry pub-lished. Now that the children were a bit older, she and her husband were able to go to films and concerts. In the summers, they visited her husband's family on Åland, where she'd discovered a knack for fishing. But they did meet up from time to time, absolutely, and she'd always considered Gustav one of her good friends.

Dolores walked him to the metro, repeating her instructions several times: T-Centralen, just three stops. He didn't have a bag or anything? Was he sure? He hadn't left anything in the restaurant? She was about to go back to ask, but he shook his head.

"I'll see you at the funeral," she told him and put on her helmet.

Standing on the platform, Martin took out Gustav's little address book. He found the number marked CW, held his breath, and dialled.

40

A breeze shook the apple trees, but the air felt as humid and heavy as before. A drowsy wasp was circling the ashtray. Rakel's palms were sticky with sweat. Frederikke poured glasses of water and urged them to drink.

"I hope I'm not boring you with all these details," she said.

"You're fine," replied Elis, as though they were doing her a favour and not the other way around. He devoured a jam biscuit in two bites. "But I don't quite get what this has to do with Berlin. Because she's in Berlin, right? Did she get with that archaeologist? What happened with him?"

Frederikke laughed. "I don't think they ever met again. But what do I know?"

"So then what happened?"

"What happened is that the years kept passing, as you will notice they are wont to do. Alarmingly quickly, too."

Frederikke and Cecilia wrote to each other. Cecilia's letters contained routine updates about her family but only rarely anything about her own feelings or thoughts. Sometimes she included a few lines about Gustav, usually about how she worried about him. Then, the letters from Sweden just stopped from one week to the next. It coincided with Frederikke starting a new job and separating from a man she'd been living with for several years, and like so many other things, writing to Cecilia became something she kicked down the road. Other than a brief phone call after Elis was born, there was silence until several months later, when Frederikke received a postcard, the kind you'd buy at a tourist spot, showing the Gradiva fragment in the Vatican Museum. *I'm not saying I'm being held captive*, Cecilia wrote, *but convalescence has me feeling like I'm trapped in the magic mountain.* She included the address of the summer house.

It was high summer when Frederikke arrived. She was taken aback at the sight of the woman who came to greet her: a thin, stooped figure with nervously darting eyes in a pallid, naked face. Her voice was raspy and so quiet Frederikke had to ask her to repeat herself more than once. When they walked through the garden, Cecilia moved slowly and cautiously, like a person in great pain. They stopped in a remote corner where a moss-covered pool opened up in the ground.

"I always thought this was a strange spot for a water feature," Cecilia said. "It would have made more sense to place it in the middle of the forecourt. That would have looked pretty swanky, too, which is usually the raison d'être of water features, no? But here, where no one can see it? What's the point of that?"

"How are you feeling?" Frederikke asked.

"Oh, you know." Cecilia's tone was light. "I am, as my mother puts it, overworked. I've been sleeping poorly and feeling nauseous. The birth was a bit rough. I've been told people usually forget suffering pretty quickly and only remember the good things – a small evolutionary twist of our human perception. Maybe that's not exactly how the midwife phrased it. She said: 'There, there, this will soon be forgotten, you'll see.' I'm still waiting for oblivion to set in. No one has ever waited more eagerly for oblivion than me. At night, I dream about them running with me on one of those rolling stretchers because I'm giving birth, and everyone seems to think my condition is very serious. I for my part am not worried at all, because I know there's been a misunderstanding: I'm not about to give birth. I try to reason with them, to make them see they're mistaken, but no one listens to me. It's frustrating that they're demanding I birth this child I'm not carrying – how is that supposed to work, I think to myself in my dream, how am I going to solve *this*? Then I discover that my stomach is gigantic, truly prodigious: I'm one hundred per cent about to give birth. Then I wake up." She chuckled. "And Elis has colic, to boot, which I take as a punishment for my sins. Thankfully, Martin is dealing really well with everything. He's really very competent in that area. Much more so than me."

"Both your children have biblical names," Frederikke said. It was, she suddenly thought, hardly what she would have said to any other friend who had just told her what Cecilia had.

"I never thought about it."

"The Old Testament. Elijah was a prophet in Israel and Rakel was Jacob's wife, the one who after long childlessness gave him two sons." They strolled down towards the lake and Frederikke quoted: "*Unto the woman he said, I will greatly multiply thy sorrow and thy conception, in sorrow thou shalt bring forth children and thy desire shall be to thy husband, and he shall rule over thee.* That's when Adam, Eve and the snake are chided after Eve ate the forbidden fruit that grants knowledge of good and evil, and persuaded Adam to do the same. God banishes them from the Garden of Eden and sets them to tilling the earth from which they came."

The jetty creaked beneath them. "If you could choose," Cecilia said, sitting down on the edge, "between eternal life in a Paradise of ignorance or knowledge at the price of a mortal life of hard toil on earth, which would you pick?" She lowered her feet into the water. Under the surface, her pale skin took on the colour of amber.

"Earthly toil," Frederikke said.

"Me too. Gustav would choose Paradise in a heartbeat. Martin... hard to know with Martin. He would stand with one foot in each camp and never manage to make up his mind." She paused. "It's a curse: being with child, giving birth, desiring one's husband. And all of it a punishment for wanting knowledge."

Without looking at Frederikke, she told her she'd taken up studying again, Ancient Greek. Surely learning Greek couldn't be that hard; in the olden days, Greek and Latin had been general knowledge, but now – she heaved a deep sigh – the whole education system had gone to the dogs.

They returned to the house to have coffee on the veranda.

Martin had grey hairs in his fringe and looked weary. He kept to the background and didn't say much. His eyes were usually on his wife. He asked if she was cold, placed a cushion on her chair, wrapped an arm around her slim shoulders while they talked. He handled Elis like a pro. At one point as they were sitting there, Elis, lying in his father's arms, fired off one of those tentative smiles infants sometimes produce more or less at random. Frederikke watched Martin's face undergo a complete transformation: his eyes were fixed on the child and a big, warm smile spread across his face, wrinkling his cheeks and bringing out his dimples.

"Here, I'll take him." Cecilia's mother had just emerged from the house with an overflowing plate of biscuits. Now, she held her hands out to Martin, as though to relieve him.

"It's okay, he can hang out," Martin said, not taking his eyes off the boy for a second. Elis gurgled.

Inger didn't retract her hands. "I think he needs a nappy change."

"We'll sort it out later."

"I don't mind."

Only then did Martin look up at her. "That's really nice of you, Inger, but we're good," he said in a tone Frederikke didn't recognise – warm but leaving absolutely no room for argument. "You relax for a change," he added, more softly. "Elis needs to practise mingling with the academic elite."

Once Inger had left, Martin handed the baby to Cecilia.

"He's just going to cry," she said.

"No, he's in the zone now. He's figured out how to smile. Look."

And as if on cue, Elis smiled at his mother. Cecilia undid her shirt and put the baby to her breast, hiding him in her kimono as if under a bird's wing.

At the time of Frederikke's visit, Inger and Emanuel Wikner were the only other people in the house, and for Cecilia's sake, Frederikke hoped they weren't representative of the rest of the family. Cecilia's youngest brother was coaxed out of his room with the promise of biscuits, and Frederikke was surprised when a tall young man appeared in the doorway. His long, tangled hair was in a ponytail, he smelled of sweat and shook hands with a clammy paw.

"Emanuel Wikner," he said, and then he informed Frederikke that his name was the one prophesied for the Messiah, that hers was the feminine form of Fredrik, which derived from the Germanic words for peace and ruler, and Cecilia came from the Roman word for blind and Martin traced its roots to the Latin name Martinus...

"...which means 'warlike' or 'martial'," Martin finished for him. He had evidently heard the list before.

The moment Emanuel sat down, he began to talk, and he went on for a long while without pause. It was mainly about the economic crisis and Berg & Andrén's impending bankruptcy.

"I think you're getting ahead of things," Martin said, even though he himself had told Frederikke something similar earlier. "Things aren't *that* bad."

"Let's keep our fingers crossed," Inger chirped.

Not so easily deterred, Emanuel launched into a long, tangled argument about banks, loans and interest rates, the ultimate inevitable consequence of which was the death of Martin's publishing company. In the end, Cecilia cut her brother off in the middle of a sentence.

"This is *Martin's business*," she said with equal stress on both words. "There's no need for you to worry. He knows what he's doing."

"But—" said Emanuel.

"There's no need for you to worry," Cecilia repeated. Her voice had regained some of its deep timbre.

"*You're* the ones who should be worried," Emanuel grumbled, then he left the veranda so abruptly he knocked his chair over.

Martin pulled an almost imperceptible face and Cecilia reached for his hand, pressing her fingers against the palm of his hand.

Inger Wikner next unleashed a barrage of questions, nodding incessantly in imitation of a person who actually listened to the answers. So

Frederikke was a psychologist? Where did she work? What university had she attended? Did she live in Copenhagen? Which part? Did she like it there? Copenhagen was a wonderful city, just wonderful, wouldn't she agree? Did she have a family? Children? It wasn't too late yet, absolutely not, Frederikke was still young, it would work itself out in time. At this point, she grabbed hold of Frederikke's arm with a slim, surprisingly strong hand, which closed around her skin like a talon. The gesture seemed intended to signal female intimacy, and Frederikke had a sudden urge to say something about her separation and the many miscarriages she'd suffered in the past few years just for the sadistic pleasure of watching Inger try to sweep that bloody mess under the rug.

Shortly afterwards, they said goodbye and Martin walked Frederikke to her car.

"It was nice of you to come," he said.

Without preamble and without her having asked, he told her the pregnancy had been very difficult. Cecilia had been in pain, unable to climb stairs for months. Her labour had lasted almost forty-eight hours and she'd been convinced she was going to die. She'd spent the past few months more or less bedbound. That she was up and about now was a big step forward.

"I hear she has taken up Ancient Greek," Frederikke said, thinking this was a promising sign, as well, but Martin just looked dejected, shaking his head.

"I see, so *that* she told you? She didn't say anything about being afraid she may never run again? About how she can only see her children in ten-minute increments? That Elis, bless his current relative silence, did nothing but scream a hole in her head during the first three months and that she was on the brink of actual insanity?"

"Well, in a way."

"'In a way?' Let me guess: she talked about some literary work whose contents provide an oblique parallel to her own situation."

And that was true – the Bible. "Though I think I started it," Frederikke admitted.

Martin sighed. "Sometimes it's the only path that's open with her. She's more intelligent than anyone I know, but she doesn't want to or can't deal with reality."

As she drove down the tree-lined road, Frederikke watched Martin in the rear-view mirror until she could no longer see him. A man standing alone in the driveway.

41

"I suppose you'd call it post-partum depression nowadays," Rakel said.

The wind from the sea had picked up, and the clouds lay heavy and slate-grey over the golden fields. In the Wikner family, though, she mused, people were never depressed. "Overworked" was okay, and Cecilia could probably have stayed "overworked" for the rest of her life if she'd wanted. Forever ensconced in her room upstairs, bedded down with freshly laundered sheets and with a breakfast tray next to her.

"Post-partum depression isn't *wrong*," Frederikke said, splitting the last of the coffee three ways between their cups. "She would probably have met the criteria for that diagnosis. But it doesn't capture the whole of the situation, does it? And besides, we end up using the vocabulary of psychiatry, which is always characterised by a certain level of illusory objectivity… Now I sound like Cecilia."

Rakel tried again. "How about this, then: her world had fallen apart. She was unable to take care of me and Elis, or even herself for that matter. She checked out of motherhood, dumped everything on Dad and Grandma and went to bed."

Until at some point she found her way out of the gentle, twilit existence of a patient freed of responsibilities and expectations. Perhaps she was even spurred on by hitting rock bottom; from what Rakel could remember, her mother had no time for people who only did what they were already good at. "They will amount to nothing," Cecilia would say about athletes who couldn't bear to lose or talented students who couldn't take criticism. "Leave them to muck about with their own egos or whatever it is that's holding them back. They're toast. People like them fizzle out as quickly as they flare up." Sooner or later, the marathon runner must have put on her shoes and faced the fact that she could barely run down the tree-lined road and back.

Frederikke smiled, a sad little smile. "I told her to talk to someone," she said. "But I doubt she did. Anyway, she slowly got better – whatever 'better' meant in her case. At least she went back to working. To reading and writing."

They resumed their correspondence and must have met up the next summer, unremarkable visits that had since faded from memory. Cecilia was consumed with her thesis. Frederikke had several other friends who did PhDs, but even though they all tore their hair as their deadlines approached, their projects seemed trivial compared to Cecilia's study of colonialism. It was as though she insisted on building a transatlantic steamship when everyone else had settled for a simple sailboat. During the latter half of 1996 and the first months of 1997, her letters consisted exclusively of handwritten, almost illegible reports on how her thesis was progressing. When it was time to defend the thing, Frederikke travelled up to Gothenburg. All the way there, a feeling that something was going to go wrong, that the whole project was going to be abandoned and turned into a monument to the megalomania of humankind gnawed at her. It was completely irrational, of course – no one was allowed to defend their thesis without their supervisor's approval – but there was no end to the catastrophic scenarios that played out in Frederikke's mind as the train carried her north. Her supervisor might have developed dementia. Cecilia might have fallen off her bike and suffered brain damage. Her opponent might have uncovered some fundamental error. To make matters worse, the auditorium was packed. Frederikke had to push her way to the front row, where Martin and Gustav had saved her a seat. Martin was beaming, Gustav looked shy but proud. Frederikke only had time for a brief greeting before the chair came out and the din died down. The grading board and the opponent, a lecturer from Lund, were introduced. Then the candidate entered through a side door, nodded to the audience, and took up position next to a lectern. She stood straight and still, looking externally calm and peaceful. As usual, she was dressed in light colours and Frederikke had to chuckle inwardly at the wry nod to the traditional sartorial style of the colonial overlord: the white suit.

Cecilia Berg dived into a presentation of her work. She was free the way a violin virtuoso is free with her instrument. She didn't so much as touch her script. After a while, she left the lectern, pacing to and fro along the blackboard that ran the length of the stage, talking, her voice clear and loud. Every once in a while, she drew a schematic or picture to illustrate a train of thought. Her answers to her opponent's questions were precise and to the point. If she needed time to think, she paused, sometimes for a long time, before speaking. When it was time for questions from the audience, she listened to everyone with the same solemnity and patience and then said things like: "That's a really good question you're asking, Max, and one I've given a lot of thought. Admittedly without much success… I will at least try to say something that may hopefully serve as a jumping-off point for further discussion."

Then, the board convened briefly. Cecilia Berg had passed her viva. Cecilia bowed her head at the applause.

Frederikke stopped. Her cigarillo had gone out and she borrowed Elis's lighter to light it again. The smoke and the oppressive heat were making Rakel dizzy.

"That was the second to last time I saw Cecilia," Frederikke said. "Just a few weeks later, she appeared at my door."

The day before, an angry and confused Martin had called, asking for his wife. He claimed she'd "just taken off" and ended the call the moment she confirmed Cecilia was not in Copenhagen. Consequently, Frederikke was prepared for something to be amiss, and she let Cecilia in with the feeling of luring a wild animal into a trap. It was, she supposed, a marital crisis of some kind. The Bergs seemed to have a very stable relationship, true, but the years and her profession had taught Frederikke not to be surprised at what she didn't know about people.

"I'm sorry to be coming here unannounced," Cecilia said. "Is this a bad time?"

With composed, minimal movements, she took off her shoes and set down her bags. She kept her camel hair coat on. She was very pale, the skin around her eyes grey. Her ash-blonde locks, streaked with platinum and silver in the summer, were pulled into a taut ponytail at the nape of her neck. She offered no explanation for her presence and replied evasively to Frederikke's questions about how she was doing.

"Would you like a cup of coffee?" Frederikke said finally, as though it were a completely normal Sunday-afternoon visit, and Cecilia said yes. Her feet made no sound as she followed Frederikke into the kitchen. True, she asked about Frederikke's work and life more generally, but with jaded politeness, and she paid no attention to the answers. She neither sat down nor removed her coat. Nor did she seem perturbed by the long silences between their lines. Frederikke was glad she had coffee and sandwich-making to busy herself with.

"Sit down and take off your coat," Frederikke said when she had finished. Cecilia obeyed, mechanically, like a marionette. Underneath the coat, she was dressed in black from top to toe. The high, narrow turtleneck brought to mind a nun's habit.

"Cecilia, sweetheart," Frederikke leaned forward. "Has something happened?"

A shadow of pain passed across Cecilia's face. She said nothing.

"Martin called yesterday. He was asking for you."

"I would be very grateful," Cecilia said, fixing her firmly for the first time, "if you didn't tell anyone I was here. Not even him. Can you promise me that?"

Frederikke considered that for a long moment, because she rarely made promises of any kind. "I promise," she said.

Cecilia shuddered as though a quantum of life had just trickled into her rigid body. "Nothing *happened*," she said. "I just…" She shook her head and opened her hands in a gesture that evoked depictions of Christ.

It was only a few weeks after her viva, but the contrast between the figure up on that stage in the auditorium and the woman sitting at her kitchen table was stark. Normally, Cecilia was a woman of words.

She spoke her thoughts as a way to reach deeper layers, as a means of anchoring herself to the foundation of existence so that from that point she could build a structure to contain the chaos of human existence. Now, she said nothing, just sipped her coffee, shaking her head again. Frederikke reached across the table and took her hand, and they sat like that until Cecilia's eyes welled up and she mumbled that she needed to use the bathroom. She was in there a long time. Frederikke didn't hear her return to the kitchen and the sudden sound of her voice made her jump.

"Thanks for the coffee. I have to go now."

"Are you sure? You're welcome to stay. Maybe you'd like to have a bit of a rest?"

"Don't look so *worried*," Cecilia said, smiling for the first time since she arrived. "I'm okay. I'll call you."

Afterwards, Frederikke stood by her window, watching as her friend walked down Matthæusgade, turned a corner, and disappeared. It was many years before she saw Cecilia again.

A gust of wind shook the trees, snatched at the tablecloth and set their cups rattling. Beyond the garden, the fields were billowing and over by the horizon the sea looked like a dark band.

"It never even occurred to me that she might not come back," Frederikke said. Had she known, she wouldn't have let Cecilia swear her to silence. For a long time, she, like everyone else, figured Cecilia would eventually return. She considered telling Martin about their strange meeting, but concluded that it would make no difference. There wasn't much to say about it. And how would Cecilia react if Frederikke broke her promise? She had no one else to confide in, and in the long run, it was probably more important to make sure their relationship remained undamaged.

"It would have been different if she'd told me where she was going. But she left me just as much as she left everyone else." Afterwards, Frederikke had thought about it in terms of the ship of an explorer, making landfall on the Azores before continuing west across the

Atlantic. Frederikke had been Cecilia's last port of call in the known world. Her journey was planned and the course set.

"Then what happened?" said Elis, who had no patience for metaphors.

"Well, ten years went by," Frederikke said. "I'd long since given up on ever hearing from her again. One day, I was visiting Gustav in Stockholm and popped up to his studio without asking. He was never private about his work; everyone was always welcome to have a look. On the easel was a portrait of Cecilia and I was surprised because he hadn't painted any portraits in a long time, and certainly not of her. He claimed to have used an old photograph, just for practice. I touched it and accidentally left a fingerprint, because the oil wasn't dry yet. He wasn't even annoyed about it. Normally, he would have had a hard time concealing his fury at me ruining his painting." On an impulse, she had then asked him straight out if there was something he hadn't told her. Nothing, he'd said. Don't lie to me, she'd pushed.

As ever when he was feeling guilty, Gustav was secretly keen to confess, and Frederikke only had to fix him with a level look to coax out the truth: a couple of years earlier, Cecilia had got in touch, and since then they'd been in contact. He didn't want to say anything else, and Frederikke was so shaken by the revelation that she didn't insist.

Not long after, Frederikke's phone rang in Copenhagen.

"Hi, long time no see," said a deep, slightly husky voice. "It's Cecilia Berg."

She could just as easily have said "It's me", the greeting she'd used with Martin and Gustav long before the invention of caller ID. With the receiver pressed against her shoulder, she'd throw out a *Yeah, it's me*, as though that statement couldn't possibly refer to anyone but her.

*

Frederikke made dinner and set them up for the night. With parentlike authority, she demanded their dirty clothes, considered the darkening sky, and concluded that they would have to hang them up in the basement instead of on the drying line outside; it was going to rain. She wrote down Cecilia's address on two notes and gave them each one, as though they were children who risked getting lost and might need a grown-up to help them find their way back home. Then she sent them off to bed wearing borrowed flannel pyjamas.

Thunder woke Rakel. It sounded like the sky was breaking. The alarm clock informed her it was half past three. She got up and went out into the garden. The dark-violet sky was a low dome over the fields. A bolt of lightning flashed underneath the clouds, followed immediately by several peals of thunder. Then it began to rain, scattered droplets at first, pattering against the roofs, stirring up the dust on the road, then heavier and heavier. The wind was blowing towards the sea; the storm was going to sweep across the sound, up along the Swedish coast. Another bolt of lightning zigzagged towards the horizon and a tremendous rumbling rolled across the world.

Back in her room, Rakel propped her pillows against the headboard and sat down with her computer and *Ein Jahr* on her lap. Rain was hammering against the window and the glare from the bedside light hurt her eyes. She only had a few pages left.

42

Martin's heart stood still while he listened to the ringback tone. Just as he was about to hang up, a man answered in a soft British accent. He thudded down on the nearest park bench, next to a teenage girl. The at once wary and bored look she shot him from under heavy lashes made him feel like some kind of rowdy drunk. This is *not* what I was expecting, he wanted to hiss at the girl, but that probably wouldn't have helped matters.

The whole debacle made him miss the lead-in, but it would seem the man knew who Martin was and had been expecting his call.

"I'm sorry, I didn't catch your name," Martin said. He felt very light-headed. He'd had water at Tranan, hadn't he? Or just wine? He could buy some water at Pressbyrån. Or there had to be a buffet car on the train, right? He could buy a bottle of water on board, drink it, try to catch some sleep.

"Oh, it's Christopher," the British man said in English. "Christopher Welton. Martin, I'm so very glad you called…"

Martin tried to explain that he'd found his number in Gustav's address book, but his English seemed to have short-circuited, he fumbled for the words in a dark void. For some inscrutable reason, only French came to him, clear and concise like in a textbook. *J'ai trouvé votre numéro dans le carnet d'adresse.* Christopher pretended his nonsense made total sense. *I see, I see*, he said. He told him he was coming to Sweden tomorrow, for the funeral. He wanted to spend a few days in Gothenburg since that was Gustav's hometown. He'd actually never been. Could they meet up, perhaps? It was about time, after all, even though the circumstances were terrible. Gustav had told him so much about Martin. He was going to be staying at Eggers, which was apparently centrally located…? "Good, it's decided then, I'll call you tomorrow and we can find a time that works."

The train pulled up to the platform. The doors opened with a hiss. Martin cast about for his briefcase, then remembered he hadn't brought it and set about his next big project in life, which was to locate his carriage and seat.

*

At least the sun had already risen when Martin woke up the next morning. The first thing he did was check his phone, but neither of his children had been in touch since Rakel's text late last night: Some kind of train madness here, will be back for the funeral.

The clock on the wall ticked while he drank some black coffee and ate half a piece of crispbread with butter. The newspapers were waiting for him on the doormat. Outside the windows gleamed a sky as blue as a thrush egg. It was going to be a hot day. Perfect for the beach, Martin Berg. Or for that charming fixer-upper in the country. Or he could really push the boat out and head into the office! But what was he supposed to do there? What could Publisher Berg possibly contribute any more? Sell the thing, sell it! Let it be absorbed into a large and robust publishing firm that knows how to handle the internet and audiobooks and Amazon establishing a presence on the Swedish market! Who wants to read quality fiction or incisive non-fiction these days anyway? Find a blogger to spew out a hundred and fifty thousand words about love, or whatever they choose to call the emptiness convulsing their bodies at night.

He wanted to call Gustav. For a split-second, he wanted to call Gustav before thinking: No, it's only seven, it's too early.

In the light of the newborn morning sun, Martin examined the contents of his drinks cabinet. Unexpected bottles were unexpectedly empty. Elis, the little house elf! He'd siphoned off his booze, thinking Martin wouldn't notice. Martin hoped he hadn't topped the bottles up with water to hide his crimes, a rookie error. The whisky bottle was reassuringly heavy and amber-coloured. When he was putting ice in his glass, several ice cubes skittered away across the floor. He wanted to ignore them, but they would leave ugly marks where they melted, and so, crawling on his hands and knees, he collected every last one.

The whisky was an abrasive little sun in his throat. How long would it take to become an alcoholic? If he really went for it? He had good genes on his father's side, Grandpa had died flying the flag of high blood-alcohol levels, after all, by not jumping out of the way of that iron girder down at the docks. In Gustav's family, on the other hand, the drinking had been passed down the maternal line. Martin remembered Marlene von Becker's bleary eyes and watered-down smile. And yet, she was now burying her son. Mummy Marlene standing next to the coffin, needing just one quick shot to fortify herself, and who could blame her? Defiant, with trembling fingers, she'd opened her bottle of vodka. And no one talked about her father any more, the less successful son of a prominent shipping family, who went out in his boat on a morning with no wind and drowned. Was he, Martin, going to be the only one who remembered all of this? Once Marlene's memories scattered permanently and only the two sisters remained? What would happen to Gustav once they were in charge of writing his history? Especially considering the stipulations of his will? It wasn't Martin's fault that he'd inherited paintings worth – best not to try to calculate it. Was the funeral going to be awkward? Should he consult a book on etiquette?

Martin topped up his glass even though he hadn't finished what was in it. Besides, there was always the awkward matter of his wife. *Cecilia Berg*. He'd never understood why she decided to give up her maiden name. She seemed like the kind of person who would have kept it, possibly with a new, cumbersome addition: Cecilia Wikner Berg, a name that evoked brisk walks across vast estates, snorting horses in a stable, summer afternoons with tennis and chilled drinks in highball glasses. Because what did the Berg family have to brag about? The archetype for the Swedish, twentieth-century class journey. That's what they were. From drunken dock workers in draughty flats to the education and financial stability the Swedish welfare system had made possible, in combination with sobriety and a Lutheran work ethic. On to a house, a car, children who grew up in the Technicolor sixties, the first in the family to attend university, to have children who considered higher education a given.

Standing by the bay window, Martin took small sips of his whisky. Djurgårdsgatan was waking up. A young mother cycled past with two young children in a trailer. All three were wearing helmets. A man was walking brisky in the opposite direction, his hands shoved deep into the pockets of his denim jacket. He looked like he might be on his way home after a long night of partying. Well done! It was nice to see that someone was still dedicated to decadence in this monument to middle-class moderation! You didn't get a lot of that these days. A girl in a post office uniform rolled by with white headphones in her ears. A man carrying a briefcase unlocked a shiny black Audi with a click of the key.

Who was he trying to fool? He wasn't the kind of person who drinks whisky at quarter past seven in the morning. Even though he was quite literally doing just that, he was, on a metaphysical plane, definitely not the kind of person who drinks whisky at quarter past seven in the morning. At most, he might overdo it with the wine sometimes. A glass here, a glass there. A practical little bag-in-box in the fridge. But spirits at odd times of day: *non*.

Martin put on his shoes. He walked down the stairs. He stepped out into the courtyard. He exited onto the street. Right or left? He dithered for a few moments before his body turned right. Long streets stretched out before him. He didn't need to think about where he was going. He continued up towards the petrol station. He reached the top of the hill on Ekedalsgatan and continued down towards Kungsladugård. He was a man out for a morning walk. Some fresh air before work. He should have worn his trainers, though. Not brogues. The brogues had been a mistake. The dress shirt, too. A man out for a morning walk wears trainers and a T-shirt. The sun was already high in the sky, sharp light reflexes bouncing off the tram tracks. At least he'd remembered his sunglasses. A win for our man at Mariaplan!

At the roundabout, he had to wait a long time for cyclists to pass.

The Western Cemetery was, as usual, endless. He had no idea where the grave might be. They didn't have a family tomb, that much he knew. Grandma and Grandpa Berg were buried elsewhere. He recalled a few vague uncles, but what had become of them was a mystery. But sailor-turned-printer Albert Berg's final resting place was here somewhere, just a few hundred yards from his home in Kungsladugård. Martin looked around. Everywhere he looked, long rows of headstones. Everywhere he looked, rhododendrons. Everywhere he looked, footpaths lined with linden trees or whatever they were. They'd stood near some trees at the interment, he remembered that. Tall trees with white trunks – birches, they'd been, birches like in Tolstoy. While the celebrant said whatever it is celebrants say, Martin had studied the dappled light among the birch leaves. Every individual leaf was periodically shaken by a frisky but not at all cold wind. When the leaves were at a certain angle relative to the sun, they flashed sharply golden for a second before their position changed again, for they were in constant motion, and they were once again green. It made him think of him and Gustav sleeping in the same bed in Paris, listening to Bowie a hundred or possibly a thousand years ago. *Ashes to ashes, funk to funky, we know Major Tom's a junkie.* He had glanced over at Gustav, but his friend didn't take his eyes off the coffin being lowered into the hole. His hands were folded in front of him. Gustav's own father had passed away just a few years earlier and his obituary had taught Martin things about him that he already knew, but that had been shaped by his teenage worldview and then never processed by a mature mind. Director von Becker had completed his engineering degree in the fifties and immediately gone to work for the shipping company his wife's family had founded. He'd succeeded one of the Strömbergs as CEO and had clung on through the shipbuilding crisis and the rapid modernisation of the past few decades. He'd spent his entire professional life perpetuating the institution he'd married into. And then he'd died at the age of seventy, before he could even retire.

Martin had written to Gustav's mother, who was now alone in the big flat on Olof Wijksgatan, a short letter of condolence. He remembered the harbour, the giant ships, the lowering horn signals, the chimneys, the forest of cranes, the half-finished Älvsborg Bridge, which always seemed on the brink of collapsing but somehow miraculously stayed up. He remembered his mum's warm hand. She would point out his dad's ship, heading out through the inlet. They would wave. Martin would imagine his dad in one of the round portholes. Waving back even though they couldn't see it.

The paved footpaths were endless. There had to be some kind of system, but the headstones gave him no clues. He turned right at random. Some people in this section had died in 1998, others in 2006. Where was the logic? Sweat trickled down his back. His throat felt like sandpaper. He set his course for the exit closest to his mother's house and on his way there, he found it: a simple granite stone, Albert Berg, and the dates. There were fresh flowers on the grave.

Birgitta Berg was knitting socks on the patio, listening to an audiobook a smidge too loudly. "Was I expecting you?" she said as he strode through the garden. For once, she sounded slightly surprised. "Oh Martin, are you okay?"

He fetched a glass of water and gulped it down. "What made you fall in love with him?" he said. "With Dad?"

She laughed. "What a question. How is a person to know something like that?"

43

The air stood still when Martin returned home. His trousers and shirt were damp with sweat. He threw open every window and took off his clothes. He felt faint. He lay down on the floor and closed his eyes. In six hours, he was supposed to go to a hotel and meet the British photographer. It was an unfathomable stretch of time. An awful lot of minutes if you were to count them one by one. The clock in his mother's kitchen had said 9.15 when he was standing by the sink, letting the tap run, waiting for it to get cold, not hearing what she was saying over the sound of the rushing water hitting stainless steel, but what was time anyway? Time was stretching out, treacle-like.

He stood back up and threw open the door to the boxroom. It must have been years since he last tidied in here. There was a stack of chairs, a suitcase, a vacuum cleaner. He could barely see the floor. He kicked the shoes out of the way in the hallway and set to taking everything out. Along one side of the room was a rack full of outerwear jammed in so tightly it was all he could do to pull anything out. He tugged out a tiny faux-leather jacket, a duffel coat Elis had bought at a flea market, a ski jacket he'd used three times at most, a herringbone coat with absurd shoulder pads, an anorak, and – at the very back – Cecilia's parka.

The sleeves were still rolled up. In one of the pockets, he found two desiccated chestnuts and a receipt whose text had faded away completely, in the other a pencil stump.

He didn't know where to put it. He didn't want to throw it in the pile with the other jackets. He walked around for a bit, then finally placed it on the sofa. Then he returned to the hallway. Now, he could glimpse the inside of the room: shelves laden with shoes, bike helmets, binders and boxes. *Et voilà*: stackable paper trays with very practical labels that would undoubtedly be of great help to future scholars. *Writing 1990. Writing 1991. Writing 1992.* Where the eighties were was a different question. Maybe in the attic? A box or two of old papers?

"We will obviously do our best to locate her," the lawyer had told him. The unfaltering observer that was Martin had noted that in the moment she said it, she'd looked away and touched her hair in an uncharacteristically nervous gesture. She'd rambled on about the inheritance being distributed, considerable sums, the appointing of trustees. He'd nodded his confidence-inspiring nod and said: "Yes... yes... absolutely... I understand... Is that right... okay..." Until she stopped talking.

Martin leaned in over the jumble on the floor and pulled with all his might on the paper trays. He swayed but kept his balance. He carried them into the living room. A good scholar gathered all his material before diving into his investigation. A project of this magnitude could easily become overwhelming and impossible to corral. It was important to get an overview.

*

It seemed appropriate to be at least presentable when going to meet a stranger who seemed to know who he was even though they'd never spoken, whose name he only vaguely recognised from the edge of newspaper photographs of the famous painter GUSTAV BECKER now DEAD, 1962–2012.

Martin had a shower and realised it was the first one he could remember having in quite some time. He shaved. He brushed his teeth. He put on a clean white shirt. He slipped Gustav's address book into his pocket. He stepped through the doors of Eggers at four on the dot. The hotel bar was dimly lit and cool, and at first he couldn't see anything, blinded as he was by the glaring sunlight outside.

"Martin?"

He noted a tall man, grey-haired, with a firm, dry handshake. They introduced themselves and exchanged pleasantries. Would he like something to drink, no thank you, he was fine; had his journey been okay, oh yes, very smooth. They were the only guests, aside from a man in shorts, socks and sandals, who was reading a guidebook with a furrowed brow.

The Englishman gestured towards two enormous leather armchairs. They sat down across from each other.

"How are things?" Christopher asked. "How are you feeling?"

"Good," Martin said, realising immediately that wasn't at all true, and that Christopher would know that, as well. Instead, he spread his hands and let them drop into his lap.

Christopher Welton nodded.

"And you?" Martin said.

"The same."

They sat in silence for a while, but it didn't feel awkward. As Martin's eyes adjusted to the gloom, the other man appeared more clearly. He was leaning back, his arms on the armrests and his legs crossed, which alerted Martin to his own forward-leaning posture, his hunched shoulders, his hands, which were folded so tightly the taut tendons of his forearms stood out like ridges under his skin. With some effort, he took a deep breath and imitated Christopher's position. He was older, but not by all that much. His facial features were nondescript and probably always had been, as thought they'd been drawn by someone who wasn't sure about the lines. His eyes were the exception: Christopher's gaze was level and searching, unyielding, and Martin felt at once seen and seen-through. There was no point trying to hide anything from this gaze, the very act of concealment would be enough to unmask him. What was left out was the thread that led to the whole tangled truth.

Christopher was the one who eventually broke the silence. "I hadn't really known him for very long," he said.

They'd met a few years earlier when Christopher had been hired to take pictures in the lead-up to an exhibition in London, the photographer told Martin. The theme was architecture, and several prominent artists were represented, but it was unknown Gustav Becker's exteriors that had made the greatest impression on Christopher: five gigantic canvases depicting buildings in various European cities, so realistically rendered they could have been mistaken for photographs from a distance. Even though there were no people in them, they were wondrously alive.

This quality was not, however, paralleled in their creator. Gustav was hungover. He'd run a hand through his poorly cut, thinning hair, which a vainer man would have shaved off a long time ago. "Let's get this over with, shall we?" he'd said, lighting a cigarette. His fingernails were stained yellow with nicotine. "Do you mind if I smoke?"

He was not easy to photograph. He glared suspiciously at the camera, twisted and turned as though he wanted to escape his own body, and was utterly unable to take instruction about standing this way or that without becoming stiff and tentative. Christopher suggested they pop down to the pub on the corner and grab a few pints. Gustav brightened significantly.

Because Christopher had only seen his exteriors, he'd assumed they were representative of the kind of paintings the Swede did, which Gustav for some reason took offence at.

"I'm a *portraitist*," he snapped, only to immediately apologise for his tone and try to make things right by repeating more or less the same thing more politely and indirectly. Buildings, he said, were what he painted when he couldn't bear people or when there were no people to be had, but they were primarily interesting as an expression of what people had left behind, not in and of themselves. A building was a building was a building. He wasn't doing some kind of bloody mausoleum crap. Did Christopher want another beer?

Then he insisted on showing him some of his "other paintings", possibly because Christopher was well known for his portraits and Gustav was well aware that Christopher was well known for his portraits. ("So you're the new Richard Avedon?" he'd said while the photographer set up his camera.) Out on the street, he flagged down a taxi and told the driver to drive them to Tate Modern. He was very proud, he said, to have a painting at the Tate. Might as well admit it. Dead pleased. He paid with a crumpled note and refused to listen to the driver's protests about keeping the change; maybe he thought Gustav was some clueless tourist who had no sense of the value of the pound, which was true in a way. Gustav was out of the car in a flash. There was nothing to do but follow.

As usual, the museum was packed, but Gustav made sure they were allowed to go straight in. He moved through the rooms as though they were in his own home, pointing out paintings and talking about why he liked or didn't like them, and then, finally, he stopped in front of a painting of a blonde woman with books in her arms. "*This* is what I do," he said. By then, he was fairly out of breath, because they'd moved at a brisk pace and he did smoke two packs a day.

"Sounds like *The Historian* from 1989," Martin commented.

"Precisely. And unless I'm mistaken, it's from his so-called 'commenting' period."

"Correct. With *The Historian*, he was doing Rembrandt, particularly that merchant couple."

"The technique was flawless," Christopher said. "The composition, the way he worked with light, the way he used the paint and the brush strokes to bring out such an intense presence in the motif. He wasn't even thirty when he painted it. Imagine – still virtually a boy and tackling that kind of portrait… That's balancing on the edge of madness."

While Christopher studied the painting, Gustav had paced back and forth with his hands in his pockets, feigning interest in the other paintings in the room, patting the breast pocket where he kept his cigarettes, and by all appearances trying hard not to say anything. Later on, Christopher would learn that *The Historian* was one of the artist's personal favourites, along with *The Wedding* and a few others. In other words, he'd cut right to the chase, showing this stranger whose opinion he for some reason cared about the very best of his production, and now he was awaiting judgment.

"Accepting criticism isn't exactly Gustav's forte," Martin said.

Christopher chuckled. "Indeed. Sometimes, people had the impression he was humble, since he was so liberal with his self-criticism. But he approached his craft in a way that required raw belief in his own abilities. If you don't have that, you don't tussle with that kind of painting."

In that room at the Tate, Christopher had found himself unexpectedly moved. Partly by the art, but also by the situation itself. He thought about how they'd both dedicated their professional lives to telling through the use of images something that went far beyond the images themselves. Seeing without judging, rendering without possessing, letting the world appear in all its simplicity and beauty: that was what they strived to do.

And that, or something like it, was what he said to Gustav, and he watched his restless body grow still and his wariness fade.

"And so it began," Christopher said now, and then he fell silent.

Martin recognised that the next move was his. So he began to tell his and Gustav's story, from the schoolyard at Hvitfeldtska in 1978 through the university years, about Cecilia, their Paris trip, his own work in publishing and Gustav's breakthrough after art school, about the distance created by family life and relocations, the golden summer months, time out of time in France, about Gustav's collapse in London and subsequently diminished production, which certainly wasn't helped by Cecilia leaving. He talked for a long time and the words came easily, until he reached the past few years. He didn't know what to say about them.

"I went to see the retrospective earlier today," Christopher said. It had been packed, which was usual after the sudden death of an artist. The atmosphere had been both hungry and reverent. The catalogues and the poster had all sold out. He'd seen an interview with the curator in the paper, and even though Christopher didn't understand the Swedish text, he'd recognised the process. He had, after all, had a disproportionate number of artistic friends, and a disproportionate number of them had died before their time, primarily from AIDS. Having survived them, Christopher had witnessed what the passage of time does to a work once death has made further creation impossible. He had experienced the extroverted grief and exaggerated praise that came first as well as the period of reflection that followed. Only time could tell what a work's place in history would be. Sometimes it sank into obscurity, sometimes it grew into a firm reference point for posterity. And now they were about to behold Gustav Becker's apotheosis. The human being, an in many ways broken and difficult person, someone they'd loved and whose life they'd shared in their different ways, would now go through the crucible of idealisation and myth-making.

"I've actually never seen so many of his paintings in one place," Christopher said. "It was – not a shock, but a reminder of how much of his life was unknown to me. And I would like to make an assertion, which I could never have made to *him* without the world ending, but I'm now free to make—"

"Now that he's dead," Martin cut in. It felt good to say it to someone who didn't seem scared of the word. It also felt good to say it in a language that wasn't his own. *Dead* didn't have the same sepulchral ring to it as the Swedish *död*. The Swedish word resonated on the same frequency as the German *Tod*, while the Romance languages' *mort, morte, muerte* had a lighter, more poetic feel that inspired notions of a life after this one. Martin silently mouthed these words for death until he realised he was probably coming off as deranged. With an effort, he turned his attention back to the man sitting across from him. "What was it you couldn't tell him?"

"That he was never as good after Cecilia disappeared."

Something that must have been a laugh escaped Martin, but it had nothing to do with mirth. "I don't know if she ever really disappeared," he said.

"It's not just about her. It's about *the three of you*, and that did disappear when she disappeared. His outstanding works are from those ten or twelve years. The portraits of Cecilia: magnificent. They were his *tour de force*."

Martin told him about the painting he'd seen in Gustav's studio. Any artistic assessment he could offer was, needless to say, clouded by

720

the shock of having discovered it, but if he were to take a step back and consider Gustav's works from the outside, he was prepared to cede Cristopher's point. Something was missing, but he couldn't put his finger on what.

"You, I would think," Christopher said, his face expressionless.

"*Me?*"

"I don't understand…" Martin said.

"That's my take on it," the photographer said. "We can never know for sure, of course. Resisting clear-cut answers is, after all, the nature of good art."

Martin cleared his throat. Something seemed stuck in it. "You're right about that," he said. At least this was firm ground, compared to the quagmire of the Cecilia portraits. "Ambiguity is an important part of what makes art art. Not knowing for sure forces you to think. To use your imagination. There's a literary scholar, I can't recall his name just now, but he says that—"

"What are *your* thoughts about the fact that Gustav portrayed Cecilia over and over again?" Christopher's voice was gentle and mild.

"I suppose she was a good model."

"A lot of people are."

"Maybe he liked the way the way she looked. Her appearance suited his aesthetics. What do I know?"

"I'm sure that's true, but that's a superficial explanation. You can do better than that."

"Accessibility? She was around, she was sitting there, writing, he might as well paint her as—"

Christopher leaned forward. "A lot of men would have felt less than comfortable with their wives spending hours and hours being painted by another man."

Martin burst out laughing. "Are you saying Gustav and Cecilia…? Surely, you're joking?"

"I'm not saying anything. I'm just pointing out a common reaction."

"My goodness. That's just too absurd." Laughter was still bubbling in his chest. He shook his head. "Maybe if it had been someone other than Gustav. But come on. *Gustav*. He's... he would never be interested in her in *that* way. That he painted her... I suppose he wanted to be included. Have a place with us."

Somewhere at the back of Martin's mind, the contours of comprehension were emerging. Of course Gustav loved Cecilia, the way he might have loved his sisters if they hadn't been – well, his sisters. But he'd painted her as unattainable. She was palpably present and unpretentious, but nevertheless out of reach. Always out of reach. As though there were a glass wall between the observer and the observed. Someone he had never really got through to even though she'd been so very close. A few words would have been enough.

"Or with me," he sighed.

They sat in silence.

At length, Christopher said: "There's this story," he said, "you hear a lot. I have no doubt that you, having dedicated your life to narratives, are familiar with it. It goes like this: a person lives a lonely, depressing life. Then he finds someone – a woman, a neighbour, a nephew, whatever. Love or friendship develops. The meeting is transformative. Our protagonist breaks out of the depressing rigidity that has been his life. He is liberated from his own history. He dares something he hasn't dared before. He succeeds at something he has never succeeded at before. In the meeting with the other person, he takes his first tentative steps down the road to happiness. A new dawn is breaking. The end."

"I'm familiar with it," Martin said.

"And have you ever experienced it yourself?"

Martin thought about that. "No."

"You think the other person will change," Christopher said. "That the power of your love will finally fix what was broken in his foundation and make everything right. You think to yourself: with *me*, things will be different. With *me*, he will be capable of what he wasn't capable of before. With *me*, his inclination and desire will turn down a different path. It may have been like this for forty-nine years, but I, and

I alone, will coax him out of his loneliness, his half-life, his mistrust." He spread his arms. "And we never learn."

"Hope is the last thing that dies in man," Martin said.

"Unfortunately. Gustav cared for me, and *he was tired.*" Christopher sometimes thought about Picasso's last wife, he said. Romantically inclined people with a superficial understanding of the nature of lust sometimes thought he'd found with her a perfect, pure love, which dissolved his need for constant sexual conquest and violent infatuation. But meeting 26-year-old Jacqueline Roque, whom he married and lived with until his death twelve years later, hadn't changed the 72-year-old Pablo Picasso one jot. He was an old man who had worked and loved with manic frenzy all his life, and now he was tired. It's not so hard for a tired man to be faithful. Gustav had been tired, too, though perhaps for different reasons. He let himself be swept up by the life that was Christopher's. They travelled. They played tennis. They went for walks on Hampstead Heath. They drank tea and read. They visited museums. Went to Italy in the winter. They drank fine wine, but when Gustav wanted to order another bottle, Christopher suggested going home instead, back to the beautiful villa on the hillside they'd borrowed from his friend the architect, and Gustav acquiesced, as he acquiesced to all of it. Christopher knew there was an undercurrent of rebellion in him, a need to break free, to destroy his gilded cage, and that if that impulse to be free was ever taken from Gustav – destructive as it may be – he would disappear. So he said nothing about his increasingly protracted sojourns in Stockholm. Better that he fall off the wagon sometimes than that he drink constantly. And so, he kept his reproaches to himself when Gustav appeared in his hallway after several months. And so, he didn't ask too much about things Gustav didn't want to tell him about, hoping everything important would eventually come out one way or another.

"Everyone wants to be seen," Christopher said. "Even a person who hides wants to be found."

"Did you meet Cecilia?"

"Never."

Martin took out the little address book. "You have the same initials. Before she got married. She signed her paintings CW."

"I didn't know she painted." The surprise in his voice was palpable.

"It was many years ago. Before we met her."

They parted ways outside the hotel. Christopher wanted to go for a walk, so Martin recommended Trädgårdsföreningen Park on the other side of the canal. "See you at the funeral," he said.

Christopher made no move to leave. "To him, they were moments of rest and grace," he said at length. "But I was not the love of his life."

"Rest and grace is not too shabby. It's more than some people can ever hope for."

"Indeed."

They shook hands and went their separate ways.

*

At Lejontrappan, Martin sat down and called Elis. His son answered after three rings. In the background, he could hear trains and PA announcements.

"I just wanted to check in," Martin said.

"We're good."

"What are you up to?"

"Nothing. We just ate."

Silence.

"I'm sorry about Gustav," Elis said. "How are you holding up?"

"I'm okay."

"We'll be back as soon as we can. For the funeral."

"No rush. Do your thing. Say hi to Rakel."

The canal was still. The gulls screeched. The light was very sharp. The sun pressed on his head with heavy hands. He needed to blow his nose but had no tissues. He sniffed and wiped his cheeks with his sleeve.

44

The Staatsbibliothek zu Berlin on Potsdamer Strasse opened at nine, and you had to be on time if you wanted a desk. On days when Rakel didn't need to go to the university, she would set her alarm, force her legs out over the edge of her bed, spend a little too long in the shower, rush to get her thermos ready and make some porridge, put on whatever clothes were at the top of the pile, close the front door ever so quietly so as not to wake Alexander, heave her bike out of the storage room, and pedal through Kreuzberg. The rhythm of the street was the same every day. People on their way to work. A steady stream of cars and cyclists. A beeping delivery van parked in the middle of the street. Tired pre-war buildings whose facades were covered with graffiti and posters at head height. A dry-cleaner, a pharmacy. A travel agency specialising in trips to Turkey whose roll shutters were perpetually pulled down halfway. A kebab place across from another kebab place. Coiffeur Ahmet not far from Coiffeur Metin. She normally arrived at the library at five to nine, joining the scattered regulars waiting outside. When they were let inside, everyone veered off towards their favourite spot, like a pack in which each member had a set task. She studied until lunch, which she ate in one of the nearby kebab places, and then returned for a few more hours of reading.

In the eyes of the world, spending all those hours in the library was unequivocally good. And since everyone agreed that she was dutiful and disciplined, she didn't need to form an opinion of her own about what she was really doing and why. The library was open seven days a week, and there was always room for her there. The world of humans was kept at a safe distance. When her father called, she told him about Gustav's latest visit, about the German literary scene, and other things he usually liked to hear about, until her watch told her they'd been on for half an hour. At that point, she pretended she had to go – a party, meeting friends – and went back inside the library.

Now, term had been over for weeks and the big building lay bright and deserted. Scattered visitors moved along the shelves in the quiet, cautious manner of library visitors everywhere. Everything was as it had always been, except Rakel herself.

The desk where she used to sit was free. She opened her laptop, placed her dictionary within easy reach and took out *Ein Jahr*. The book was in a sorry state – chunks of the text block were falling out, the covers were creased from being folded, and a coffee ring marred the front – but she only had one page left to translate.

She'd been using the Polaroid from her dad's map of Paris as a bookmark.

"How long is it going to take?" Elis leaned against the railing, gazing out at the lobby.

"An hour, maybe a bit more."

"Do I have time to go into town?"

"To do what?"

"I don't know. Look around. I've never been here before."

He sauntered off and she was alone. The text was unproblematic. By now, Philip Franke's voice was so familiar it seemed like part of herself, and the last few lines of the novel came to her as though brought forth by a force beyond Rakel's awareness. It was possible, granted, that she had simply replaced his voice with her own; she couldn't tell. A professional translator would need to look at the text and offer their comments. But all of that was a future problem. She had finished for now. At some point, you came up against the limits of your own ability, and it was better to finish something as best you could than to spend eternity fumbling for perfection. A person who spent their whole life on unfinished masterpieces had one foot in the world of the dead.

In her wallet, Rakel discovered an old print card that she topped up with fifty euros from a machine. The printer hummed to life and began to spit out pages. She sat down on the floor with her back to it.

When this was done, she was going to go see her mother. But what answers would Cecilia have to her many questions? She'd refused to talk to Martin, to Frederikke, to Philip Franke. *I have nothing to say.* And who really knew the truth about themselves anyway? Everyone had blind spots and undiscovered continents. At best, you had a hand-ful of shards to start with, things like times, dates and other fairly incontrovertible facts. The chronology, Cecilia Berg the scholar might have said, is central. When you organise events into an accurate time-line, something happens to the messy jumble of history. A pattern appears. Events and occurrences that were tumbling through timeless space are given structure and context. But Cecilia was not necessarily capable of turning on herself the clear-eyed view with which she stud-ied history. It was up to Rakel to fit the pieces together and identify the pivotal points.

She herself was such a pivotal point, of course. A child considers its own existence a given – the world didn't exist before it did – but from her current position in life, Rakel could sense the outline of a murkier context surrounding her conception. Her parents-to-be were young even by the standards of the eighties, neither one of them had finished university, and Martin had just come back from France where he'd got up to god knows what. Having a child must have felt like a stark demarcation in their life. Rakel's birth had divided it into a before and an after. *Before*, the world was free and open, obligations few and far between, they were tied only loosely to adulthood, everything was possible. And *after*… After, you were tied down by duty. The duty to provide. To care for. To stay.

The question was whether they'd understood that, Martin Berg and Cecilia Wikner, or whether that had only gradually become clear to them. Probably the latter. It was part of the unique folly of youth, she supposed, throwing yourself into a life project whose vastness you had no way of comprehending. Rakel chuckled: the idea of her being pregnant was bizarre, and not only for practical, biological reasons. (How would it have happened? Children weren't made in libraries.) It was psychological. She was too locked into being a daughter to be open to being anything else. After all, here she was, sitting among the book-shelves in Berlin, because she was looking for her mother. And now, everything was in flux. What would come of it, only time would tell.

But Cecilia had tumbled into adulthood reluctant and unprepared.

"People construct narratives they can live with," Frederikke had told Rakel and Elis when they'd said goodbye the previous day. "Cecilia thought it would just make things worse if she were to come back into your lives again. 'Martin is doing a fine job with them,' she told me when I questioned the fact that she was still keeping away. 'They're better off without me.'"

At least she was consistent, Rakel thought now. She never wavered. Her disappearance was a wound in their history, but it was a clean wound, the precise cut of a surgeon, and wounds of that kind heal more easily and leave smaller scars than more hesitant carving.

Cecilia's reasoning was flawed, true, but maybe not entirely unrealistic. In the Berg family, she'd been forced to be a parent, and in the end, she'd snapped. She could live in a world of work. German grammar and Greek vocab were fine. But all the other things, the things Martin had been doing all these years? All the hundreds of bags of shopping he'd lugged home from the supermarket, the parent–teacher conferences he'd attended, the summer holidays he'd planned, the dinners he'd made, the many hours he'd spent teaching them to drive and nagging them about homework, the decisions he'd made and stuck to despite their strident protests and threats of rebellion – all of that? Constantly putting others before yourself?

How it had got to that point was a story in itself. Full of parallel and intertwined causal relationships, as ever with stories. Wittgenstein had been wrong about one thing: it wasn't entirely true that *whereof one cannot speak, one must be silent*. Whereof one cannot speak can be expressed indirectly. There are countless ways of communicating what you can't bring yourself to say.

But there are also limits to what a daughter can know.

The printer hummed and clicked and spat out page after page of *Ett år av kärlek*. Rakel pushed herself up, studying the growing stack of papers. She'd been so focused on the answer, but maybe the question was more important? It was the question that had jolted her out of her library existence. It was the question that had forced her out of her closed little world. It was the question that had made the truth her guiding star. It was the question that had given birth to Rakel Berg, the translator. It was the question that had brought her here, to the end of childhood and the beginning of the rest of her life.

And the question was her inheritance from Cecilia.

"Neat," Elis said when he turned up at the agreed time. "But I still don't get why you had to sort that out right now."

Rakel purchased stamps and a padded envelope from a corner shop by the U-Bahn. It was the perfect size for her sheaf of papers. She wrote her father's name and address on it in large block letters. She considered putting the Polaroid picture in, too, but instead threw it in the bin next to the counter.

They found a postbox right next to the entrance to the station. Rakel pushed the envelope through the slot. It landed with a thud.

"All right, let's go," she said to her brother and led the way underground.

45

Martin moved the coffee table aside and began to empty the contents of folders and trays onto the rug. So many papers. Words and sentences hurled themselves at him. Papers, papers. Sooner or later, he'd have to do something with all these papers. Because one day, someone was going to have to call Rakel and Elis to say I'm so sorry, but your father... (Except who was going to make that call? Who was going to find him in an armchair? Who was it he thought was going to call the children?)

There will be a period of cleaning. The flat will be emptied of its history. Or, more accurately: some parts of its history will be incorporated into Rakel's and Elis's histories, and the rest will be lost. They have to go through his papers. So many papers! Elis wants to bin the lot, but Rakel insists on going through everything. So they sit at the kitchen table, turning page after page, reading, organising the papers into piles.

"Here's another novel," Rakel says.

"Mm," Elis replies. He's engrossed.

"What's that?"

"This is pretty good, actually. Here, this is chapter one."

Rakel reads. She tops up her coffee but doesn't drink. For a while, the only sound in the kitchen is the humming of the fridge and pages being turned.

"I wonder why he never said anything," Rakel says at length. "He must have been doing all of this in secret. Look, this addition is dated 2011."

"Do you have any more chapters over there?" Elis asks.

They call Per. "Maybe you should take a look at this…" Together, they edit the text and publish it. It becomes a bestseller and is soon translated into several languages. Imagine, people will say, that he never got to see it. All's well that ends well. Someone will make a film of it.

No, no. Martin Berg, publisher, knew there were no masterpieces in his desk drawers. He if anyone would have known. After all, it was his job to know.

He snatched up the Wallace notes, yanked open the desk drawers, piled his arms full of old letters and the *Night Sonnets* manuscript, depositing them among the other papers on the floor of the living room. Then he moved on to emptying the contents of the magazine holders on the floating shelves onto his bed. He needed to get an overview. A good general knows to seek out the highest point in an area before battle. There had to be more somewhere. The years with Cecilia. Back when it was still *the three of them*. When they'd all lived their lives and it hadn't been half bad.

Or – that couldn't be true. Martin stared at the stacks of paper. His brain felt febrile and clear at the same time. His thoughts were one big tangle. It couldn't be true, because in the middle of it was that thing Dolores had told him about, when Gustav was sectioned. And then there was London, when Cecilia had to bring him home. Cecilia, Cecilia. He pictured the portrait in Gustav's studio, the new one. She'd been there all along. Trying to keep him on the right track, like she always had. Making him work. That had always been her focus: work. Instead of demanding that he quit drinking, she'd helped him to keep painting. An alcoholic needed a reason to abstain. There had to be some form of love on the other side of the scale.

But when love itself is the problem…

Martin began to sort the stacks of paper.

He'd needed her, too. They'd both needed her. Not just separately, but together. When it was *the three of them* and not just *the two of them*, there had been balance, the machinery of life had functioned, things had kept moving along, more or less in the right direction. And when she disappeared, everything they'd had during those years collapsed. Not immediately, but over time. Gustav had his life, Martin his. With Cecilia, they had been able to live in close proximity, but without her…

An old exhibition catalogue had ended up mixed in with the manuscripts. Martin's hands were shaking when he picked it up – he'd had too much coffee again – and insight lit up his muddled thoughts like fireworks. *My possessions I leave to Martin and Cecilia Berg.* His possessions were art to the tune of millions of kronor. How long could an heiress to a fortune of that magnitude stay hidden? There had to be documents. Paragraphs. Signatures. Money to be distributed. Decisions to be made.

Gustav must have known that when he wrote his will. That his death would expose her, one way or another.

Martin staggered onto his feet and stared at his papers. There were undeniably a lot of gaps. He probably had to undertake an expedition to the attic storage space.

He rolled up his sleeves and got cracking.

46

These are the collected works of Martin Berg. Half-finished novels and short stories. Essays that foundered a few pages in. A pathetic attempt at a play. Countless notebooks. Piles of notes on which something was scribbled in the moment and then saved with the scholar's love of artefacts and fragments. He'd stored these papers in desk drawers, dresser drawers, all kinds of boxes, cupboards, shelves and any other space a person can put things in and then forget about them. Half-narratives. Unfinished stories. Attempts. To open one's mouth to speak but lack the words. At some point in the cottage by Gullmarsfjorden, Martin gets so drunk he can't walk straight. Gustav has to help him into the house, into bed.

"Don't go," Martin says, a firm grip around Gustav's wrist.

"You're drunk," Gustav says. He doesn't try to pull away.

"Elementary, my dear Watson." He rolls over to make room. "Stay with me."

"Drunk as a skunk," Gustav says and lies down.

If you speak, the gap can widen further. If you speak, you might lose what you have, whatever that is, that thing that resists being put into words. If you speak, the bubble that keeps reality out will burst.

The pattern of the wallpaper seems to be moving. He has to close his eyes to ward off the dizziness. The window is open to the night. Finally, sleep comes. Like a dark tidal wave it comes flooding in, freeing you from action and truth, from responsibility and words, and tomorrow the surface will be still once more.

47

Rakel and Elis Berg sat in silence on the westbound U-Bahn. When their stop was announced, Rakel's legs threatened to buckle, and the world went dark.

They were in an unfamiliar part of town. The streets were lined with long rows of trees. The address was not far from the station and their steps dragged more and more the closer they got, until the right building inevitably loomed up before them. Five storeys. Dark windows that revealed no secrets. A front door painted a shiny black.

Elis's cigarette was the only thing keeping them on the street, and when he had finished it, he ground it out with the toe of his shoe until there was barely anything left of it.

"Hey, let's just not," he said. "There's no point. Let's leave."

Rakel tried the door. It opened. They stepped into a dimly lit, cool lobby. When she pushed the light switch, light spread over the tiled floor. The stairs were wide and worn smooth, spiralling upwards like the inside of a seashell.

She began to climb. Inside, her stomach was plummeting. There were names on the doors. Maybe they wouldn't find hers. Maybe they would reach the top floor and breathe a sigh of relief, find a hotel, go over their leads, admit they'd done everything they could…

On the fourth floor, one of the doors said BERG.

She waited for Elis to catch up. She took his hand. Then she rang the doorbell.

And Rakel heard the silence on the other side shattering. She heard years being turned on end and mountains of time shifting. She heard the pause, the quick breath just before something begins.